John Leland

# A View of the Principal Deistical Writers

That Have Appeared in England in the Last and Present Century - Vol. 1

John Leland

**A View of the Principal Deistical Writers**
*That Have Appeared in England in the Last and Present Century - Vol. 1*

ISBN/EAN: 9783337143947

Printed in Europe, USA, Canada, Australia, Japan

Cover: Foto ©Andreas Hilbeck / pixelio.de

More available books at **www.hansebooks.com**

A

# VIEW

OF THE PRINCIPAL

## DEISTICAL WRITERS

THAT HAVE APPEARED IN ENGLAND IN THE LAST AND PRESENT
CENTURY.

WITH

## OBSERVATIONS UPON THEM,

AND

## SOME ACCOUNT OF THE ANSWERS

THAT HAVE BEEN PUBLISHED AGAINST THEM.

*IN SEVERAL LETTERS TO A FRIEND.*

THE FIFTH EDITION.

By JOHN LELAND, D.D.

TO WHICH IS ADDED,

## AN APPENDIX,

CONTAINING

## A VIEW OF THE PRESENT TIMES,

WITH REGARD TO RELIGION AND MORALS, AND OTHER IMPORTANT
SUBJECTS,

By W. L. BROWN, D.D.

PRINCIPAL OF MARISCHAL COLLEGE, PROFESSOR OF DIVINITY, AND
MINISTER OF GREYFRIARS CHURCH, ABERDEEN.

IN TWO VOLUMES.
VOL. I.

LONDON:
PRINTED FOR T. CADELL JUN. & W. DAVIES—W. CREECH, AND
BELL & BRADFUTE, EDINBURGH—AND A. BROWN, ABERDEEN.
MDCCXCVIII.

# PREFACE.

NO man that is not utterly unacquainted with the state of things among us can be ignorant, that in the laft, and efpecially in the prefent age, there have been many books publifhed, the manifeft defign of which was to fet afide revealed religion. Never in any country where Chriftianity is profeffed, were there fuch repeated attempts to fubvert its divine authority, carried on fometimes under various difguifes, and at other times without any difguife at all. The moft noted writers on that fide have been at liberty to produce their ftrongeft objections; thefe objections have been retailed by others; and many feem to take it for granted, that Chriftianity hath received very fenfible wounds by the feveral attacks that have been made upon it, and that they have greatly hurt its credit, and weakened its authority.

But whofoever will be at the pains impartially to examine thofe of the deiftical writers that have hitherto appeared among us, and to compare them with the anfwers which have been made to them, will find, that upon a nearer view they are far from being fo formidable as fome have been apt to apprehend. And fince there are few that have leifure or patience for a particular inquiry into the feveral writings which have appeared in this controverfy, fome judicious perfons, who wifh well to the intereft of our common Chriftianity, have been of opinion,

that

that it might be of real fervice to give a fummary view of the moft noted books that have been publifhed againft revealed religion for above a century paft, together with proper obfervations upon them. From fuch a view, the reader might be enabled to form fome notion of the feveral turns this controverfy hath taken, how often the enemies of revealed religion have thought proper to change their methods of attack, the different difguifes and appearances they have put on, and the feveral fchemes they have formed, all directed to one main end, viz. to fet afide revelation, and to fubftitute mere natural religion, or, which feems to have been the intention of fome of them, no religion at all, in its room.

Upon fuch a comparifon between thofe that have attacked Chriftianity, and thofe that have written in defence of it, it would appear, that if it be really true, that deifm and infidelity have made a great progrefs among us, it muft have been owing to fomething elfe than the force of reafon and argument; that the Chriftian religion is in no danger from a free and impartial inquiry; and that the moft plaufible objections which have been brought againft it, though advanced with great confidence, and frequently repeated, have been fairly and folidly confuted. Such a view would make it manifeft, that the enemies of Chriftianity have not generally behaved as became fair adverfaries, but have rather acted as if they judged any arts lawful by which they thought they might gain their caufe. And yet notwithftanding their utmoft efforts for above a century paft, they have really been able to fay but little againft the Chriftian religion, confidered in its

original

original purity, as delivered by Chrift and his apoftles, or to invalidate the folid evidences by which it is attefted and confirmed.

For thefe reafons it hath been judged, that a fhort and comprehenfive view of the deiftical writers of the laft and prefent age might be of great ufe. And as the courfe of my ftudies hath led me to be converfant in feveral of thofe writings which have been publifhed on both fides in this important controverfy, it was urged upon me, by fome perfons for whom I have a great regard, to undertake this work. There was one great objection, which hindered me for fome time from attempting it, and which ftill appeareth to me to be of no fmall weight, and that is, that as, according to the plan that was formed, it would be necefary to give an account of the anfwers publifhed to the books I fhould have occafion to mention, this would oblige me to take notice of fome of my own. I am fenfible how difficult it is for an author to fpeak of his own performances, in fuch a manner as not to intrench upon the rules of decency. If he give a favourable character of them, this will be interpreted as a proof of his vanity, any appearance of which is ufually turned to his difadvantage. And on the other hand, if he fhould make no mention of his own books at all, where the nature of the defign in which he is engaged makes it proper for him to mention them, this might perhaps be cenfured as a falfe and affected modefty. It is no eafy matter to keep clear of thefe extremes ; and, for this reafon, it would have been a particular pleafure to me to have feen this work undertaken by another hand ; but as this hath not been done,

done, I have chofen rather to attempt it myfelf, than that a work, which I cannot but think might be of real fervice, fhould be neglected. It cannot be expected, that a diftinct notice fhould be taken of all the writers that have appeared among us againft revealed religion for this century paft. This, if it could be executed, would take too large a compafs, and be of no great ufe. A view of the principal of them, or, at leaft, of thofe who have made the greateft noife, may be fufficient. And the defign is not to give an hiftorical account of the authors, or of their perfonal characters, but to give fome idea of their writings, which alone we have properly to do with.

The method propofed, and for the moft part purfued, is this: The feveral writers are mentioned in the order of time in which they appeared. Some account is given of their writings, and of the feveral fchemes they have advanced, as far as the caufe of revelation is concerned. And great care has been taken to make a fair reprefentation of them, according to the beft judgment I could form of their defign. Some obfervations are added, which may help to lead the reader into a juft notion of thofe writings, and to detect and obviate the ill tendency of them. There is alfo an account fubjoined of the anfwers that were publifhed; not all of them, but fome of the moft remarkable, or fuch as have come under the author's fpecial notice. And very probably fome have been omitted, which might well deferve to be particularly mentioned.

This may fuffice to give a general idea of the following work; at the end of which there are fome reflections fubjoined, which feem naturally to arife upon fuch a view as is here given. Obfervations are made on the conduct of the deifts in the management of the argument. And the whole concludes with a brief reprefentation of the evidences for the Chriftian religion, and its excellent nature and tendency.

. What has been now laid before the reader, is taken from the Preface to the firft edition : and it gives a juft account of the original nature and defign of this work, which was at firft intended only to make up one volume. But not long after the publication of it, I was put in mind of a confiderable omiffion I had been guilty of, in making no mention of Mr. Hume, who was looked upon to be one of the moft fubtile writers that had of late appeared againft Chriftianity. About the fame time was publifhed, a pompous edition of the works of the late Lord Vifcount Bolingbroke, in five volumes quarto, the three laft of which feemed to be principally intended againft revealed, and even againft fome important principles of what is ufually called natural religion. Some perfons, for whofe judgment and friendfhip I have a great regard, were of opinion, that, to complete the defign which was propofed in publifhing the *View of the Deiftical Writers*, it was neceffary to take a diftinct notice of the writings of Mr. Hume and Lord Bolingbroke : and that in that cafe it might be of ufe to make more large and particular obfervations upon them, than could properly be done where a number of writers came under confideration. This produced a fecond volume, which, though it had the fame title with the former, viz. *A View of the Deiftical Writers*, yet differed from it in this, that it did not contain ftrictures and obfervations upon a

variety

variety of authors, but a large and particular confideration of the only two there examined, viz. Mr. Hume and the late Lord Bolingbroke, efpecially the latter. And this was judged neceffary, confidering his Lordfhip's high reputation as a writer, and that there are fcarce any of the objections againft Chriftianity which he hath not repeated and urged in one part or other of his works, and that with a peculiar confidence, and with all the ftrength of reafon and vivacity of imagination he was mafter of. And as I then thought I had finished the defign, that volume ended with an *Addrefs to Deifts and profeffed Chriftians*, which appeared to me to be a proper conclufion of the whole.

But after the fecond volume was publifhed, fome letters were fent me, relating both to that and the former volume, which put me upon reconfidering fome things in them, and making farther additions and illuftrations, which I thought might be of advantage to the main defign. Thefe were thrown into a *Supplement*, which made up a third volume, and was publifhed feparately for the ufe of thofe who had purchafed the two former.

I am now called upon to publifh a new edition of the whole in a fmaller letter, which reduces the work to two volumes. The chief difference between this and the former edition in three volumes is this: that the *Supplement*, which before made a diftinct volume, is now taken into the body of the work: the feveral additions and illuftrations are inferted in the places to which they refpectively belong: and all that related to one author is laid together in a continued feries. To render that part of the work which relates to Lord Bolingbroke more complete, there

are

are subjoined to it, the *Reflections on the late Lord Boling-broke's Letters on the Study and Use of History*, which were republished in the Supplement, with considerable additions and improvements, though without the political part. The *General Reflections on the Deistical Writers*, together with the *Summary of the Evidences for Christianity*, were originally placed at the end of the first volume, then intended to be the only one. But now that the whole is published together in two volumes, it is judged they will come more naturally in the second volume of this edition; where also is placed, the *Address to the Deists and professed Christians*, which properly concludes the work; and the *Reflections on the present State of Things in these Nations* are added by way of *Appendix*. It gives me some concern, that this work is become so much larger than was at first intended, which I am afraid will prove a disadvantage to it, and disgust or discourage some readers. But I hope favourable allowances will be made, considering the extent of the design, and the variety of matters here treated of. I believe it will appear, that there are few objections which have been advanced in this controversy, but what are taken notice of in the following work, and either sufficiently obviated, or references are made to books where fuller answers are to be found.

May God in his holy providence follow what is now published with his blessing, that it may prove of real service to the important interests of religion among us, to promote which, as far as my ability reaches, I shall ever account the greatest happiness of my life. And it should be the matter of our earnest prayers to God, that all those
who

who value themselves upon the honourable name and privileges of Chriftians, may join in united efforts to fupport fo glorious a caufe, in which the prefervation and advancement of true religion and virtue, the peace and good order of fociety, and the prefent and eternal happinefs of individuals, are fo nearly concerned.

I have nothing farther to add, but that in this as well as the former editions, the whole is conducted in a feries of letters, which were written to my moft worthy and much efteemed friend, the reverend Dr. Thomas Wilfon, rector of Walbrook, and prebendary of Weftminfter, in the form in which they now appear.

# CONTENTS

## FIRST VOLUME.

———

# VIEW

OF THE

# DEISTICAL WRITERS, &c.

IN SEVERAL LETTERS TO A FRIEND.

---

## LETTER I.

*Some Account of those that first took upon them the Name of Deists.—Lord Herbert of Cherbury, one of the most eminent deistical Writers that appeared in England in the last Age— His Attempt to form Deism into a System—Observations upon his Scheme, and upon the five Principles in which he makes all Religion to consist—It is shewn that the Knowledge of them was very imperfect and defective in the heathen World; and that a Revelation from God for clearing and confirming those important Principles might be of great Advantage.*

DEAR SIR,

I NOW enter upon the task you have enjoined me, the giving some account of the principal deistical writers that have appeared among us for above a century past. The reasons given by you, and other judicious friends, have convinced me that such a work might be of use, if properly executed; we only differed as to the fitness of the person that was to execute it. My objections have been overruled; I must therefore set about it as well as I can: and if I were sure that others would look upon this attempt with the same favourable eye that your candour and friendship for me will incline you to do, I should be in no great pain about the success of it.

The name of Deists, as applied to those who are no friends to revealed religion, is said to have been first assumed about the middle of the sixteenth century, by some gentlemen in France

B and

and Italy, who were willing to cover their oppofition to the chriftian revelation by a more honourable name than that of atheifts. One of the firft authors, as far as I can find, that makes exprefs mention of them, is Viret, a divine of great eminence among the firft reformers, who in the epiftle dedicatory prefixed to the fecond tome of his *Inſtruction Chretienne*, which was publifhed in 1563, fpeaks of fome perfons in that time who called themfelves by a new name, that of deifts. Thefe, he tells us, profeffed to believe a God, but fhewed no regard to Jefus Chrift, and confidered the doctrine of the apoftles and evangelifts as fables and dreams. He adds, that they laughed at all religion, notwithftanding they conformed themfelves, with regard to the outward appearance, to the religion of thofe with whom they were obliged to live, cr whom they were defirous of pleafing, or whom they feared. Some of them, as he obferves, profeffed to believe the immortality of the foul ; others were of the *Epicurean* opinion in this point, as well as about the providence of God with refpect to mankind, as if he did not concern himfelf in the government of human affairs. He adds, that many among them fet up for learning and philofophy, and were looked upon to be perfons of an acute and fubtle genius ; and that, not content to perifh alone in their error, they took pains to fpread the poifon, and to infect and corrupt others, by their impious difcourfes and bad examples [*].

I leave it to you to judge, how far the account this learned author gives of the perfons that in his time called themfelves deifts is applicable to thofe among us who take upon them the fame title, and which they feem to prefer to that of chriftians, by which the difciples of Jefus have hitherto thought it their glory to be diftinguifhed. That which properly characterizes thefe deifts is, that they reject all revealed religion, and difcard all pretences to it, as owing to impofture or enthufiafm. In this they all agree, and in profeffing a regard for natural religion, though they are far from being agreed in their notions of it. They are claffed by fome of their own writers into two forts, mortal and immortal deifts [†]. The latter acknowledge a future ftate : the former deny it, or at leaft reprefent it as a very uncertain thing : and though thefe are, by fome among themfelves, reprefented under a very

---

[*] See Bayle's Dictionary, article Viret.
[†] Oracles of Reafon, p. 99.

difadvantageous character, and as little better than atheifts, they are, it is to be feared, the more numerous of the two. Indeed fome of their moft eminent modern writers feem to be very eafy about thefe differences. With them all are true deifts who oppofe revelation, whether they own future rewards and punifh-ments or not : and they fpeak with great regard of thofe dif-interefted deifts who profefs to purfue virtue for its own fake, without regard to future retributions *.

In giving an account of the deiftical writers that have appeared in thefe nations (for I fhall not meddle with thofe of a foreign growth), I fhall go back to the former part of the laft century : and the firft I fhall mention, and who deferves a particular no-tice, is that learned nobleman, Lord Edward Herbert, Baron of Cherbury. He may be juftly regarded as the moft eminent of the deiftical writers, and in feveral refpects fuperior to thofe that fuc-ceeded him. He may be alfo confidered as the firft remarkable deift in order of time, that appeared among us as a writer in the laft century; for the firft edition of his book *de Veritate* was in 1624, when it was firft publifhed at Paris. It was afterwards publifhed at London, as was alfo his book *de Caufis Errorum*, to which is fubjoined his treatife *de Religione Laici*. Some years after this, and when the author was dead, his celebrated work *de Religione Gentilium* was publifhed at Amfterdam, in 1663, in quarto; and it was afterwards re-printed there in 1700, octavo, which is the edition I make ufe of; and an Englifh tranflation of it was publifhed at London in 1705.

His Lordfhip feems to have been one of the firft that formed deifm into a fyftem, and afferted the fufficiency, univerfality, and abfolute perfection, of natural religion, with a view to difcard all extraordinary revelation as ufelefs and needlefs. He feems to affume to himfelf the glory of having accomplifhed it with great labour, and a diligent infpection into all religions, and applauds himfelf for it, as happier than any Archimedes †. This univerfal religion he reduceth to five articles, which he frequently men-tioneth in all his works. 1. That there is one fupreme God. 2. That he is chiefly to be worfhipped. 3. That piety and virtue are the principal part of his worfhip. 4. That we muft repent

---

* See Chriftianity as old as the Creation, p. 352, 333. ed. 8vo.
† De Relig. Gent. c. 15. init.

of

of our fins; and if we do fo, God will pardon them.  5. That there are rewards for good men, and punifhments for bad men, in a future ftate: or, as he fometimes expreffeth it, both here and hereafter.  Thefe he reprefents as common notices infcribed by God on the minds of all men, and undertakes to fhew that they were univerfally acknowledged in all nations, ages, and religions. This is particularly the defign of his book *de Religione Gentili-um;* though it is but comparatively a fmall part of that work which tendeth directly to prove that thefe articles univerfally obtained: the far greater part of it is taken up with an account of the hea-then religion and ceremonies, which he hath performed with an abundance of learning, and hath intermixed many foftening apo-logies for the pagan fuperftition and idolatry.

As he reprefents thefe five articles as abfolutely neceffary, the five pillars, as he calls them, on which all religion is built; fo he endeavours to fhew that they alone are fufficient, and that nothing can be added to them which can tend to render any man more virtuous, or a better man.   But then he fubjoins this limitation, " provided thefe articles be well explained in their full latitude *."  This univerfal religion which all men agree in, his Lordfhip re-prefents to be the only religion of which there can be any certainty, and he endeavours to fhew the great advantages that would arife from men's embracing this religion, and this only.   One of the reafons he offers to recommend it is this, that this catholic or univerfal religion anfwers the ultimate defign of the holy fcrip-tures.   " *Sacrarum literarum fini ultimo intentionique quadrat.*" He adds, that " all the doctrines there taught aim at the eftablifh-" ment of thefe five catholic articles, as we have often hinted; " there is no facrament, rite, or ceremony there enjoined, but " what aims, or feems to aim, at the eftablifhment of thefe five " articles."   See his reafons at the end of his *Religio Laici.*

One would be apt to think by what this noble writer here offers, that he muft have a very favourable opinion of Chrifti-anity as contained in the holy fcriptures; fince he reprefents it as the great defign of all its doctrines, and even of the rites and facraments there enjoined, to eftablifh thofe great principles in which he makes religion properly to confift.   Accordingly he ex-

---

* Appendix to Relig. Laici, qu. 3d.

prefsly declares in the above-mentioned treatife, that it was far from his intention to do harm to *the beſt religion*, as he there calls Chriſtianity, or the true faith, but rather to eſtabliſh both*.

But I am forry that I am obliged to fay, that, notwithſtanding thefe fair profeſſions, his Lordſhip on all occaſions inſinuateth prejudices againſt all revealed religion, as abſolutely uncertain, and of little or no ufe. He inveigheth promifcuoufly, as many others have done fince, againſt all pretences to revelation, without making a diſtinction between the falfe and the true. He often fpeaks to the difadvantage of *particular* religion, which is a name he beſtoweth on the Chriſtian religion, and any revelation that is not actually known and promulgated to the whole world: and he repreſenteth it as containing doctrines, which difguſt fome men againſt all religion, and therefore is for recommending what he calls the univerſal religion, as the beſt way to prevent men's having no religion at all. And particularly he inſinuates, that the Chriſtian religion granteth pardon on too eafy terms, and derogateth from the obligations to virtue†: a reflection which is manifeſtly owing to a mifapprehenſion or mifrepreſentation of the doctrine of Chriſtianity on this head. So he elfewhere fuppofeth, that the faith there required is no more than a bare aſſent to the doctrines there taught; though nothing is capable of a clearer proof, than that the faith on which fo great a ſtrefs is laid in the gofpel-covenant is to be underſtood of a vital operative principle, which purifieth the heart, and is productive of good works; and that the neceſſity of true holinefs and virtue is there ſtrongly inculcated. The charge he advanceth againſt Chriſtianity might be more juſtly retorted upon himfelf, who, though he mentions it to the praife of his univerſal religion, that it giveth no licence to fin, but bindeth men ſtrictly to the ſeverity of virtue, yet to ſhew what reafon finners have to hope for pardon, offereth feveral pleas and excufes that tend to extenuate the guilt of fin. Particularly he urgeth, that men's fins are not for the moſt part committed out of enmity againſt God, or to caſt diſhonour upon him, but with a view to their own particular advantage or pleafure, and are chofen by them under the appearance of fome

---

* Relig. Laici, p. 28.
† See the appendix to his Relig. Laici, qu. 6.

good.

good *. And in his book *de Veritate* he declares, that thofe are not lightly to be condemned, who are carried to fin by their particular bodily conftitution; and he inftances particularly in the rage of luft and anger; no more than a dropfical perfon is to be blamed for his immoderate thirft, or a lethargic perfon for his lazinefs and inactivity. He adds indeed, that he does not fet up as an apologift for wicked men, but yet that we ought to pafs a mild cenfure upon thofe who are carried to fin by a corporal and almoft neceffary propenfity to vice. *Neque tamen me hic confcelerati cujufvis patronum fifto; fed in id folummodo contendo, ut mitiori fententia de iis ftatuamus, qui corporea, brutali, & tantum non neceffaria propenfione in peccata prolabuntur.* This apology may be carried very far, fo as to open a wide door to licentioufnefs, and would foon introduce a very loofe morality.

But not to infift upon this, I would obferve that the principal defign of his treatife *de Religione Laici* feems to be to fhew, that the people can never attain to any fatisfaction as to the truth and certainty of any particular revelation, and therefore muft reft in the five articles agreed to by all religions. This particularly is the intention of his fourth and fifth queries in the appendix to that treatife. In his fourth query he fuppofes, that the things which are added to thofe common principles from the doctrines of faith are uncertain in their original; and that though God is true, the Laics can never be certain that what is pretended to be a revelation from God is indeed a true revelation from God. In his fifth query he urgeth, that fuppofing the originals to be true, yet they are uncertain in their explications. To this purpofe he takes notice of the multiplicity of fects among Chriftians; and that the Laics can never be fufficiently fure of the meaning of the revelation, concerning which there are fo many controverfies; that in order to arrive at any certainty in thefe matters, it would be neceffary either to *learn all languages, to read all the celebrated writers, and to confult all thofe learned men that have not written*, a method which is manifeftly abfurd and impracticable; or elfe to have recourfe to a *fupreme judge of controverfies* appointed by common confent.

It is an obfervation that will undoubtedly occur to you on this

---

* De Relig. Gentil. p. 268. Dr. Tindal talks in the fame ftrain. Chrift, as old as the Creat. p. 32. ed. 8vo.

occafion, that his Lordfhip here maketh ufe precifely of the fame way of talking, to fhew that the Laics can have no certainty about any revelation at all, which the writers of the Romifh Church have frequently urged to fhew the neceffity the people are under to rely entirely upon the authority of the Church or Pope, becaufe of the difficulties or the impoffibility of their coming to any certainty in the way of examination or private judgment.  But if the Laity cannot be certain of revealed religion, becaufe of the controverfies that have been raifed about the articles of it, for the fame reafon it may be faid, that they can arrive at no certainty with refpect to his Lordfhip's catholic univerfal religion: for though he reprefenteth men as univerfally agreed in the five articles in which he makes that religion to confift, it is undeniable that there have been great controverfies about them; and that the modern deifts, as well as ancient philofophers, are divided in their fentiments in relation to them, efpecially when explained, as he requireth they fhould be, in their full latitude. He ought not therefore to make a thing's being controverted to be a proof of its uncertainty, and that men can come to no fatisfaction about it: a principle which he and other deifts often infift upon, but which manifefly leads to univerfal fcepticifm.  But this is not the only inftance, in which arguments have been brought againft Chriftianity, that in their confequences tend to fubvert all religion, and all evidence and certainty of reafon.

From this general view of Lord Herbert's fcheme, it fufficiently appears that his defign was to overturn all revealed, or, as he calls it, particular religion, and to eftablifh that natural and univerfal religion, the clearnefs and perfection of which he fo much extols, in its room, as that which alone ought to be acknowledged and embraced as true and divine.

I fhall now freely lay before you fome obfervations that have occurred to me in confidering the fcheme of this noble author.

One is this, that he hath carried his account of natural religion much farther than fome others of the deifts have done.  It were to be wifhed, that all that glory in this character would agree with this noble Lord in a hearty reception of thofe articles which he reprefenteth as fo effentially neceffary, and of fuch vaft importance.  Thefe he would have to be explained in their full extent, and that except they be properly explained they are not

fufficient.

sufficient. Thus explained, they include the belief not only of
the existence, but the attributes of God; of some of which, in his
book *de Veritate*, he gives a good account, and of his providence
and moral government. He asserts, that God is to be worship-
ped, and that this worship includeth our offering up to him our
prayers and thankfgivings*; that piety and virtue are abfolutely
necessary to our acceptance with God: and he particularly urgeth
the necessity of obferving the ten commandments: that we are
obliged to repent of our fins in order to our obtaining forgivenefs,
and that this repentance includeth both a forrow for our fins, and
a turning from them to the right way. He alfo infifteth upon
the belief of the immortality of the foul, and a future ftate of rewards and punifhments, in which God will recompenfe men *according to their actions*, and even *according to their thoughts* †.
Thefe things he fuppofeth to be common notices, fo clear that he
can fcarce be accounted a reafonable creature who denieth them.
And yet I am afraid, if all thefe things are to be looked upon as
neceffary, many that call themfelves deifts will be as loth to admit
his Lordfhip's natural and catholic religion, as chriftianity itfelf.
There is reafon to apprehend, that fome of their ftrongeft prejudices againft chriftianity arife from its fetting thofe principles in
too clear a light, and enforcing them in too ftrong a manner. It
is true, that when they are for putting a fair glofs upon deifm,
and afferting the fufficiency and perfection of natural religion
abftracted from all revelation, they are willing to have it thought
that their religion includeth the belief of thofe important articles:
They are then obliged to have recourfe to his Lordfhip's fyftem,
and the arms he hath furnifhed them with; but at other times they
make it plainly appear that they are far from being fixed in thefe
principles. His Lordfhip declares, that it is neceffary thefe articles
fhould be well explained: but indeed they are expreffed in very
general and indefinite terms, and there is no great likelihood of
their agreeing in the explications of them. It is a thing well
known, that many who have made no fmall figure among our
modern deifts have denied fome of his Lordfhip's five articles, at
leaft taken in the extent in which he feems willing to underftand
them. God's moral government and particular providence; his
worfhip, efpecially as it includes prayer and praife; man's free

* De Veritate, p. 271, 272.          † De Relig. Gentil. p. 283.
                                          agency,

agency, the immortality of the foul, and a future ftate of retributions, have made no part of their creed. Some of them have been far from pleading for that ftrictnefs of virtue which his Lordfhip tells us natural religion obliges men to; and, inftead of urging the neceffity of repentance, have, after Spinofa, reprefented it as a mean, an unreafonable, and wretched thing\*.    And the rewards and punifhments of a future ftate have been exploded under the notion of bribes and terrors, a regard to which argueth a fordid and mercenary temper of foul, inconfiftent with a true and generous virtue.

Another reflection that it is proper to make on Lord Herbert's fcheme is this: that thefe five principles, in which he makes his univerfal religion to confift, were not fo very clear and well known to all mankind, as to make an external revelation needlefs or ufelefs.   His Lordfhip indeed fuppofeth them to be common notices, ·infcribed by a divine hand in the minds of men ; and accordingly he fets himfelf to prove, with a great fhew of learning, in his book *de Religione Gentilium*, that thefe principles were univerfally believed and acknowledged by the people in all ages, countries, and religions.   But any man that carefully examines his book will find, that all that he really proves is no more than this ; that there were fome imperfect veftiges of thefe important truths preferved among the Gentiles, and that the knowledge of them was never abfolutely and totally extinguifhed, which will be eafily allowed.   But he has not proved, that the people, or even all thofe that paffed for wife and learned, had a diftinct knowledge and affurance of thofe principles, efpecially if taken in their juft extent.   The teftimonies he hath produced by no means prove fuch an univerfal agreement : what he feemeth principally to rely upon is the reafonablenefs and evidence of the principles themfelves, which he fuppofeth to be fo plain, that no rational man can be ignorant of them.   Thus he declares, that he would fooner doubt whether the beams of the fun fhone upon thofe regions, than fuppofe that the knowledge of God, the evidences of whofe exiftence and perfections are fo obvious from his works, did not enlighten their minds †.   And he cannot be perfuaded, that any of them worfhipped the fun as the chief

---

\* Pœnitentia virtus non eft, five ex ratione non oritur : quem facti pœnitet bis mifer feu impotens eft.   Spin. Eth. Pt. 4. Prop. 54.

† De Relig. Gentil. p. 215.

deity,

deity, becaufe of the incredible abfurdity of fuch a practice, which he well expofes\*. ·But when we are inquiring what men do in fact believe and practife, we are not to judge of it from what we apprehend it is reafonable for them to believe and practife.

If this were a proper place to take a diftinct view of the proofs he hath offered in relation to his famous five articles, it would be no hard matter to fhew, that, according to his own reprefentation of the cafe, they were not fo univerfally acknowledged and clear-ly known among the Gentiles, as to make a farther revelation and enforcement of them to be of no ufe or advantage. This might be particularly fhewn with regard to the firft and fecond of thefe articles, .viz. That there is one fupreme God, and that this God is to be worfhipped ; which are principles of the greateft importance, and which lie at the foundation of all the reft. Nothwithftanding the pains he hath taken to excufe and palliate the pagan fuperftition and idolatry, and to prove that they worfhipped the one true God, the fame that we adore, under various names, and by various attributes ; yet he owns, that what were at firft only different names came, in procefs of time, as fuperftition increafed, to be regarded and worfhipped as different gods. It is plain, from exprefs and formal paffages, produced by him from ancient writers, that fome nations worfhipped no other deities but the fun, moon, and ftars. When in the third chapter of his book *de Relig. Gentil.* he mentions the names of the Deity which were in ufe among the Hebrews, and fhews that thofe names and titles were alfo ufed among the Gentiles ; he owneth that the Hebrews appropriated thefe names and titles to the one fupreme God, fuperior to the fun, but that the Gentiles underftood by them no other than the fun itfelf. He thinks it in-deed probable that the worfhip they rendered to the fun was fymbolical, and that they intended to worfhip God by the fun, as his moft glorious fenfible image ; and fometimes he is very pofi-tive that they did fo, and that they rendered no proper worfhip to any but the fupreme God ; but at other times he fpeaks very doubtfully about it, and pretends not pofitively to affert it, but leaves the reader to his own judgment in this matter †. And elfewhere he acknowledges, that the people perhaps did not fuf-

---

\* De Relig. Gentil. p. 27, 247.          † Ibid. p. 25. 310.

ficiently underſtand this ſymbolical worſhip.  *Symbolicum illum cultum haud ſatis forſan intellexit\*?*  It is indeed a little ſtrange, that if the notion and belief of one only ſupreme God univerſally obtained among the Gentiles, none but the Hebrews ſhould have made the acknowledgement of the One ſupreme God, the Maker and Lord of the univerſe, the fundamental article of their religion; and that in the laws of other ſtates, particularly among the learned and polite nations of Greece and Rome, polytheiſm was eſtabliſhed, and the public worſhip was directed to be offered to a multiplicity of deities.  Many of the heathens, by his own acknowledgement, thought that the God they were to worſhip ſhould be viſible, and looked upon it to be incongruous, that he who demanded worſhip from all ſhould hide himſelf from his worſhippers†.  And though it was a notion which generally obtained among them, that ſome kind of external worſhip was neceſſary to be rendered to their deities, yet as to the manner of their worſhip he doth not deny that ſome of the heathen rites were ridiculous, others abſurd and even impious.  To which it may be added, that ſome of their wiſeſt men acknowledged, that they were ignorant of the proper manner in which God is to be worſhipped, except he himſelf, or ſome perſon ſent by him, ſhould pleaſe to reveal it.  There is a remarkable paſſage in Plato's ſecond *Alcibiad,* which hath been often quoted.  Socrates, meeting Alcibiades, who was going to the temple to pray, proves to him that he knew not how to perform that duty aright, and that therefore it was not ſafe for him to do it; but that he ſhould wait for a divine inſtructor to teach him how to behave both towards the gods and men; and that it was neceſſary that God ſhould ſcatter the darkneſs which covered his ſoul, that he might be put in a condition to diſcern good and evil.  To the ſame purpoſe, Iamblichus, in *Vita Pythag.* c. 28. ſpeaking of the principles of divine worſhip, ſaith, " It is manifeſt that thoſe things are to be " done which are pleaſing to God; but what they are it is not " eaſy to know, except a man were taught them by God himſelf, " or by ſome perſon that had received them from God, or obtained the knowledge of them by ſome divine means."

The third article mentioned by his Lordſhip as univerſally

* De Relig. Gentil. p. 293.    † Ibid. p. 26.

agreed

agreed on is, that piety and virtue are the principal part of God's
worſhip.   But not to urge that the proof he brings of an univerſal agreement in this principle ſeems to be very defective, this
article would be of no great uſe, except men were alſo generally
agreed as to the nature and extent of true piety and virtue.   And
it can ſcarce be reaſonably denied, that a revelation from God,
pointing out our way to us, and containing a clear ſignification
of the divine will with regard to the particulars of the duty required of us, would be of great uſe.   Lord Herbert himſelf, after
having mentioned ſome virtues which were honoured among the
pagans, acknowledgeth, that beſides theſe there were many other
things looked upon to be neceſſary to true piety, eſpecially thoſe
things which ſhewed a devout or grateful temper towards the
gods, and the obſervance of the public rites and ceremonies of
religion \*; which is in other words to ſay, that the joining in
ſuperſtitious and idolatrous worſhip (for ſuch the eſtabliſhed public worſhip was) made up a neceſſary part of the heathen piety and
virtue, and was counted a principal ingredient in a good man's
character.

   As to the fourth article, that men muſt repent of their ſins,
and that if they do ſo God will pardon them, it might eaſily be
ſhewn that the Gentiles were far from being agreed what are to be
accounted ſins; ſince ſome ſins and vices of a very enormous
kind were not only practiſed and pleaded for by ſome of their
philoſophers, but permitted and countenanced by the public laws,
nor were they agreed what is included in a true repentance.—
His Lordſhip himſelf acknowlegeth, that the ancients ſeldom uſed
the word repentance in the ſenſe in which we take it †; and that
they did not look upon it to be an atonement for all crimes, but
for thoſe of a leſs heinous nature; and that they generally looked
upon other things to be alſo neceſſary, and laid the principal
ſtreſs upon luſtrations, and the rites of their religion, for purifying and abſolving them from guilt.   And any one who duly
conſiders, that the diſpenſing of pardon is an act of the divine
prerogative, the exerciſe of which depends upon what ſeemeth
moſt fit to his ſupreme governing wiſdom, cannot but be ſenſible
that it muſt needs be a great advantage to be aſſured, by an ex-

---

\* De Relig. Gentil. p. 250.              † Ibid. p. 268.

                                                      preſs

prefs revelation from God, upon what terms the pardon of fin is to be obtained, and how far it is to extend.

With regard to the fifth article about future rewards and punifh-ments, which he reprefenteth to be, as it really is, of vaft impor-tance, though he fometimes expreffeth himfelf as if the heathens were generally agreed, that good men would be rewarded with eternal life; at other times he intimates that they only agreed in this, that there would be rewards and punifhments in a future ftate; and fometimes, that they held this only, that there would be rewards for good men, and punifhments for bad men, either in this life or after it.   And he himfelf frequently owns in his book *de Veritate*, that what kind of rewards fhall be conferred, or punifhments inflicted, cannot be certainly known from the light of natural reafon *.

But we need not infift farther on thefe things.   His Lordfhip himfelf fairly granteth, that the knowledge the Gentiles had of the One fupreme God was lame and imperfect; which he attri-butes to the floth or cunning of the Priefts, who neglected to in-ftruct the people, or inftructed them wrong; and that from thence it came to pafs, that, the rays of the divine light being intercep-ted, a wonderful darknefs overfpread the minds of the vulgar. " *Unde etiam factum, ut radiis divini luminis interceptis, mira* " *caligo vulgi animis obducta effet* †."   And he obferves, that by what was added by the priefts, poets, and philofophers, the whole fabric of truth was in danger of falling to the ground.   *Tota in-clinata in cafumque prona nutavit veritatis fabrica* ‡.   And at the clofe of this book *de Relig. Gentil.* he owns, that at length the purer parts of divine worfhip being neglected, the whole of religion funk by degrees into fuperftition: and that thofe five ar-ticles were almoft overwhelmed with a heavy load of errors, fo as to be perceived only by the wifer fort of men, *a perfpicaci-oribus viris*, i. e. by thofe who had a penetration above the vulgar §.

Now this being a true reprefentation of the cafe as it ftood in fact, whatever it was owing to, it can fcarce be reafonably de-nied, that if God fhould, in compaffion to the corrupt and igno-

---

* De Veritate, p. 57, & alibi.
† De Relig. Gent. p. 225.     ‡ Ibid. p. 283.     § Ibid. p. 330.

rant ſtate of mankind, grant an exprefs revelation of his will, to clear and reſtore thofe great principles which had been ſo much obfcured and perverted, to recover men to the right knowledge and worſhip of God, and to explain and enforce the main important parts of their duty, this would be of ſignal benefit to the world, and a remarkable proof and effect of his great goodnefs. His Lordſhip indeed, in ſeveral parts of his works, throws out hints and ſufpicions as if either ſuch a revelation from God could not be given, or at leaſt that there can be no way of knowing, or being affured, that ſuch a revelation has been really given; but he no where offers any proof of it. The general invectives he ſo frequently makes againſt prieſts, oracles, impoſtures, prove nothing; except it be allowed to be a reafonable principle, that becaufe there have been falfe pretenders to revelation, therefore there never was, nor can be a true one: a way of talking and reafoning this, that might pafs among the inferior tribe of deiſtical writers, but which is abfolutely unworthy of his Lordſhip's fenfe and learning. Whereas it may rather be gathered from it, that mankind in all ages have been generally perfuaded, that it was both poffible for God to grant an extraordinary revelation of his will, and that, if he did, it would be of great advantage. Impoſtors have built upon this principle; but this doth not ſhew the principle itſelf to be falfe, which hath as good a title to pafs for a common notion, as fome of the five articles which he reprefenteth to be fo clear and univerfally acknowledged. The only reafonable conclufion that can be drawn from the many impoſtures and falfe revelations which have been put upon mankind is, not that all pretences to revelation are falfe and vain, but that we ought to be very careful to diſtinguiſh the falfe from the true, and impartially to confider and examine the proofs that are brought, and not to receive any revelation without fufficient credentials of its divine authority. But it would be a moſt unreafonable limitation of the divine power and wifdom to affirm, either that God cannot make extraordinary difcoveries of his will to particular perfons, in ſuch a manner that the perfons to whom they are immediately communicated may be certain that they came from God; or that he cannot commiffion and enable ſuch perfons to communicate to others what they have received from him, or cannot furniſh them with ſuch credentials

dentials of their divine miffion, as may be fufficient to convince the world that they were fent of God, and to make it reafonable for others to receive the doctrines and laws which fuch perfons deliver in his name. And it hath been proved, with great ftrength and evidence, that this hath actually been the cafe with regard to the chriftian revelation.

There are other reflections that might be made on Lord Herbert's fyftem. But I am willing to give you and myfelf a little refpite, and fhall therefore referve them to be the fubject of another letter.

# LETTER II.

*Farther Observations on Lord Herbert's Scheme—The Philoso-
phers not qualified to recover Mankind from the Darkness and
Corruption into which they were fallen.—The Usefulness of the
Christian Revelation to that Purpose.—Its not having been
universally promulgated in all Nations and Ages, no just Prejudice against it—Other Objections of Lord Herbert considered
—Writers that have appeared against him.*

SIR,

IN my former letter an account was given of Lord Herbert's
scheme; and it was shewn, that, taking the state of mankind
and of the Gentile world as it really was, according to his own
representation of the case, an express revelation from God, confirmed by his divine authority, for clearing and enforcing those
articles which his Lordship supposeth to be necessary, would be
of great use.    I now add, that in fact the christian revelation hath
been of signal advantage to the world, for giving men a clearer
knowledge and fuller certainty of those important truths than
they had before.    Our noble author indeed speaks with admiration of the ancient philosophers, as capable of instructing men in
a proper manner, if they would have attended to their instruc-
tions: but then he owns, that the people had little regard to the
purer doctrine of the philosophers*.    And indeed I do not see
how it could be expected, that they should place any dependance
upon their dictates, which were for the most part regarded only
as the tenets of their several schools, in which the people had
little concern.    They were not the ministers of religion, nor
could pretend to any authority that should make them be regarded as the guides and instructors of mankind, or cause their opinions to pass for laws.    The most eminent among them were contradicted by others of great name: many of them laboured to make
all things appear doubtful and uncertain; and those of them that
had the noblest notions frequently affected to conceal them, or

* De Relig. Gentil. p. 310.

were

were afraid to divulge them.　What Alcinous hath obferved concerning Plato, with refpect to the inquiry concerning the chief
good, might be applied to fome other matters of great importance.　"That which is worthy of all honour, fuch as the fu-
"preme Good, he conceived not eafy to be found, and, if found,
"not fafe to be declared *."　His Lordfhip affureth us, that
the philofophers were always difpleafed with the fuperftitious
worfhip of the people.　But, if this was the cafe, they feem
to have been very improper perfons to reclaim them from it,
fince it was an univerfal maxim among them, and particularly
recommended by one of the beft of them, Epictetus, that every
man ought to worfhip according to the laws or cuftoms of his
country †: And it is well known that their eftablifhed worfhip
was polytheifm and idolatry.　Varro, in a paffage quoted by his
Lordfhip, divides the heathen theology into three kinds: the
*fabulous*, which belonged to the poets; the *phyfical*, which was
that of the philofophers; and the *civil*.　He fpeaks with difre-
gard of the two former, and reprefents the laft as that in which
the people were concerned, and which alone could be of real ufe
to them : and this he explaineth to be that which was eftablifhed
by the laws, and adminiftered by the priefts, and which fhewed
what gods they were publicly to worfhip, what rites they were to
obferve, and what facrifices it was proper for any man to offer ‡.

If a reformation of the world by the philofophers was not to
be expected, for the reafons now given, his Lordfhip will own it
was not to be hoped for from the priefts, againft whom he bitterly
inveighs, as the authors of all fuperftition, and of the great corruption of religion in the heathen world.　And as little was it to
be expected from the lawgivers and great men of the ftate, who
generally patronized the eftablifhed fuperftition, of which they
themfelves had been in a great meafure the authors or promoters,
and were ready to punifh any that oppofed it.　And if there
were any of them who were for reforming and correcting fome
abufes in the public fuperftitions, and exploding fome of the grof-
fer fables that were received among the people, as his Lordfhip

---

* See Alcinous's Doctrine of Plato, c. 27. in Stanley's Lives of the Philofophers.

† Epict. Enchirid. c. 38.

‡ De Relig. Gent. p. 306, 307.

　　　　　　　obferves

obferves Mutius Scævola the chief pontiff, and Varro, were for doing, he owns that the attempts were vain and ineffectual, becaufe the errors and fuperftitions were become inveterate\*. This being the true ftate of the cafe, it is hard to fee what other method could be taken, that would prove fo effectual to recover mankind from their fuperftition and idolatry, as the giving an extraordinary revelation, attended with fufficient credentials, to inftruct men in the name of God, concerning the nature of true religion, to affure them of the certainty of its great principles, and to enforce the practice of its important duties by the ftrongeft and moft prevailing motives.

And accordingly, when Chriftianity appeared with the moft illuftrious atteftations of a divine miffion and revelation from heaven, it effected what no precepts or doctrines of the philofophers had been able to do. The pagan polytheifm and fuperftition fell before it: and it hath actually produced this great advantage, that the principles upon which our author layeth fo much ftrefs have been better known and underftood, and more univerfally acknowledged, than they were before. It is inconteftable, that Chriftians are more generally agreed in thofe great principles, than ever men were in the pagan world. They are fet in a clearer light, and men come to a greater certainty about them. That they are fo far preferved among the Mahometans, was alfo originally owing to the light of the Jewifh and Chriftian revelation. And it is very probable that his Lordfhip himfelf is very much obliged to Chriftianity, though he doth not acknowledge it, for the full perfuafion he every where expreffeth as to thefe important articles; feveral of which were denied by fome, and doubted by others of the ancient philofophers.

Though therefore it is not to be wondered at, that thofe among the deifts who have an averfion to thefe principles, when taken in their juft extent, fhould be againft Chriftianity, yet Lord Herbert, who afferteth them to be of fuch vaft confequence, ought, one fhould think, to have been very thankful to God for having enforced them by an exprefs and well-attefted revelation, and given them a divine fanction. And if he were fincere in the acknowledgment he fometimes makes, that the explaining and en

* De Relig. Gen. p. 311.

forcing

forcing thofe great principles is the ultimate defign of the holy
fcripture, to which all its doctrines, and even its rites and facraments tend, he ought certainly to have entertained very favourable thoughts of Chriftianity, of its doctrines as well as precepts,
and even of its rites and pofitive inftitutions.

But that which feemeth principally to have prejudiced his
Lordfhip againft Chriftianity is, that it is what he calleth a *particular religion:* whereas the true religion muft be univerfal, and
promulgated to all mankind. He frequently urgeth, that nothing
lefs than fuch an univerfal religion as he pleadeth for can fupport the honour of God's univerfal providence, and the care he
exercifeth towards the whole human race; which no particular
religion can do; and that otherwife the Gentiles muft be fuppofed
to be univerfally loft and damned, which it were cruel and injurious to God to imagine. This is what hath been often urged
and repeated by the deifts fince.

To this it may be juftly anfwered, that thofe who maintain the
Chriftian revelation may think as honourably as any others confiftently can, of the univerfal care and providence of God towards
mankind. No where is this more clearly afferted than in the facred
writings, which declare God's univerfal goodnefs and benignity
towards the human race in ftrong terms; and that he hath been
continually doing them good, and hath never left himfelf without
witnefs among them. We muft not indeed carry this fo far as to
affert, that all men have an actual knowledge of the great principles of religion, and of their duty, becaufe we may imagine that
the univerfal care of providence towards mankind requireth that
it fhould be fo; which feems to be the courfe of his Lordfhip's
reafoning; for this is contrary to evident and undeniable fact and
experience. But we acknowledge that God hath given to all men
the principle of reafon, together with a natural fenfe of right and
wrong, which would be of great ufe to affift them in the knowledge
of religion, and to direct them in the practice of their duty, if
duly cultivated and improved to the utmoft that it is naturally
capable of. But befides this, Chriftians generally maintain, and
the holy fcriptures lead us to think, that God hath from time to
time made extraordinary difcoveries of his will to mankind; that
fome fuch difcoveries were made to the firft anceftors of the human race, who were bound by all obligations to tranfmit them to

their

their pofterity;. that therefore there was an original univerfal religion, embraced by the firft parents of mankind, and tranfmitted
from them to their defcendants; that accordingly fome of the moft
eminent ancient philofophers afcribed the knowledge and belief
of fome of the great principles infifted upon by this noble author,
to a tradition derived from the moft early ages, though his Lordfhip never maketh the leaft mention of tradition, as one fource of
that knowledge and belief of thefe things, which obtaineth among
the nations; that this religion, which was both originally derived
from revelation, and agreeable to nature and reafon, was gradually obfcured, and became greatly corrupted, though ftill fome
remarkable traces and veftiges of it remained among the Gentiles;
that God was pleafed, in his wife and good providence, to interpofe by various methods, and by raifing up excellent perfons
from time to time, to keep thofe remains of the ancient religion
from being totally extinguifhed; that at laft he was gracioufly
pleafed to fend his Son into the world, a perfon of divine dignity
and glory, to recover men to his true knowledge and pure worfhip, to direct and affift them in the practice of their duty, to fhew
them the true means of their reconciliation and acceptance with
God, and to bring life and immortality into the moft clear and
open light; that this revelation was attended with the moft illuftrious atteftations, and made a wonderful progrefs through a confiderable part of the known world, and would have fpread ftill
further, if it had met with fuch a reception as the excellency and
importance of it well deferved; and finally, that as to thofe
to whom it was actually communicated, God will deal with
them in a juft, a wife, and equitable way, and will make all proper allowances for any want of the advantages which others enjoy.
The afferters of the Chriftian revelation are under no obligations
to limit God's univerfal benevolence. They leave thofe that are
deftitute of this revelation to God's infinite mercy; and can think
more favourably of their cafe, than thofe confiftently can do, who
will not allow that they were under any great darknefs, and fuppofe them to have acted in manifeft oppofition to the moft clear
univerfal light.

The objection arifing againft the Chriftian revelation, for want
of its being univerfally known and promulgated, hath been often
confidered and obviated, nor is this a proper place to enter upon

a large

a large and particular difcuffion of it. At prefent it may be fufficient to obferve, that the objeftion proceeds upon a wrong foundation, *viz.* that the univerfal goodnefs and benignity of the common Parent of the univerfe require that he fhould communicate his benefits to all his creatures alike, and in equal degrees. It is evident, in faft, that in the diftribution of his benefits God afteth as a free and fovereign benefaftor, difpenfing them in very various degrees, always undoubtedly for wife reafons, but thofe reafons often not known to us. It cannot reafonably be denied, that he hath made fome whole claffes of beings vaftly fuperior to others in valuable gifts and endowments, and capacities for happinefs: and fome individuals of the fame clafs of beings are favoured with much greater advantages than others. And, if we look particularly into God's dealings with the human race, we may obferve a very remarkable variety. Some are from the beginning endued with much greater natural abilities and more excellent difpofitions, and are placed in a more favourable fituation and happier circumftances. Some whole nations are eminently diftinguifhed from others, not only with refpeft to many other advantages of human life, but with refpeft to the means of moral improvement, and are furnifhed with more excellent helps for making a progrefs in wifdom and virtue, and confequently in true happinefs. All thefe differences between perfons and nations are under the direftion of divine providence, as all muft own that acknowledge a providence, as his Lordfhip profeffeth to do. And thofe that are diftinguifhed from others by fuperior advantages ought to be thankful to God for thofe advantages, and to afcribe them to his goodnefs, and not deny that God hath given them thofe advantages, becaufe there are others that have them not, or not in an equal degree. Since therefore the diftinguifhing fome perfons and nations with valuable advantages above others is not inconfiftent with the univerfal benignity of the great Parent of mankind (for if it were, he would not do it), it can never be proved, that he may not grant a revelation to any part of mankind, except at the fame time it be granted equally to the whole world. Indeed, if all men every where were required aftually to believe that revelation, and were to be condemned for not believing it, it would be neceffary to have it univerfally promulgated: but fince the aftual belief of it is required of thofe only

to whom it is actually publifhed, and they to whom it is not made
known are not put into a worfe condition than if there had been
no fuch revelation granted at all, no argument can be brought to
fhew that it is inconfiftent with the divine wifdom or goodnefs,
to grant fuch a revelation to fome part of mankind, though it be
not actually promulgated to the whole human race: efpecially
if, in its own nature and original intention, it was fitted and defigned to be of univerfal extent: which is the cafe of the Chriftian revelation. Thofe therefore who are fo circumftanced as
to have an opportunity of knowing it, ought to be very thankful
to God on that account, and not refufe or reject their own advantages and privileges, becaufe all others are not partakers of
them as well as they. This would be a moft abfurd and irrational
conduct.

I fhall only further obferve, that this author feems frequently
to make it a great objection againft what he calls *particular religion*, that it infifteth upon other things as neceffary, befides the
religion of nature, as contained in thefe five articles. Religion,
according to him, is *notitiarum communium fymbolum**, a creed
containing common notions or truths: and thefe common notices
he reduceth to the five above-mentioned. But will any man undertake to prove, that God cannot reveal any truths to mankind,
but precifely thefe five articles, or that all ufeful religious knowledge is wholly abforpt in them? May there not be truths
which, though not precifely the fame with thofe articles, may be
of great ufe for clearing and confirming them, for inftructing
men in the fuller knowledge of God, and of his will, and of the
methods of his grace towards us, or for directing us in our duty,
and animating us to the practice of it? And muft all thefe be
difcarded at once, as of no ufe in religion, becaufe they are diftinct from the articles fo often referred to? Or muft a well-
attefted revelation be rejected, becaufe it containeth fome things
of this kind? Our noble author himfelf, though he fuppofes
thefe articles to be abfolutely neceffary, feems not to be quite fure
that they are fufficient: for he obferves, that God's judgments
and proceedings are not fully known to any man: and therefore he will not take upon him pofitively to pronounce, that

---

* De Verit. p. 55. 221.

thefe

thefe articles are fufficient. *Quam ob caufam neque eos fufficere protinus dixerim* *. But if they fhould be fuppofed to comprehend all that is required from the heathens, who never had the light of the Chriftian revelation, it doth not follow that they are alfo alone fufficient for thofe to whom this revelation is made known: for fuppofing God to give an extraordinary revelation of his will for reftoring religion when greatly corrupted, and clearly directing men in the way of falvation, and helping forward their improvement in divine knowledge, and in a holy and virtuous practice, as it would be a fignal advantage to thofe to whom fuch a revelation is given, fo it muft neceffarily lay them under additional obligations. Some things would, in confequence of it, be neceffary to be believed and done, by thofe to whom this revelation is made known, which they were not fo exprefsly obliged to believe and practife before: and it would be a ftrange thing to complain againft that revelation on this account, or accufe it of falfehood, and to choofe rather to be without the fignal advantage of fuch a revelation, and its glorious benefits, privileges, and hopes, than to be obliged to receive the difcoveries it brings, and to practife the duties which refult from them.

One of the firft Englifh writers that publifhed animadverfions on Lord Herbert's fcheme (for I fhall not take notice of what fome learned foreigners have done this way) was Mr. Richard Baxter, in a book publifhed in 1671, which he calls, *More Reafons for the Chriftian Religion, and no Reafon againft it:* and which he defigned as an appendix to his excellent treatife of the reafons of the Chriftian religion. One part of this book contains, " Animadverfions on a Tractate *de Veritate*, written by the noble " and learned Lord Edward Herbert, Baron of Cherbury." This writer makes judicious reflections on feveral paffages in that book, but takes no notice of his Tract *de Religione Laici*, nor of that learned work *de Religione Gentilium*, which probably he had not feen. The celebrated Mr. Locke, in his *Effay on Human Underftanding*, hath fome obfervations on Lord Herbert's five articles, to fhew, that, however reafonable they may appear to be, they cannot be juftly accounted common notices in the fenfe in which that Lord reprefents them; *viz.* as clearly infcribed by the

* De Relig. Gentil. p. 293.

hand

hand of God in the minds of all men *. And in his *Reasonableness of Christianity as delivered in the Scriptures*, he hath, without
formally mentioning Lord Herbert, furnished a proper antidote
against his scheme, by shewing, with great clearness and force, the
usefulness of divine revelation, for setting the great principles of
the law of nature, and the important duties of religion and morality
in a strong and convincing light, and enforcing them with the most
powerful motives; and that the mere natural unassisted light of
reason was, as things were circumstanced, insufficient and ineffectual for that purpose†. This matter is also fully and distinctly
treated in Dr. Whitby's learned work, intituled, *The Necessity
and Usefulness of the Christian Revelation, by Reason of the Corruptions of the Principles of natural Religion among Jews and
Heathens.* London, 8vo, 1705.

The only author among us, that I know, who hath formally
considered the whole of Lord Herbert's scheme, and undertaken a
direct answer to his writings, is the reverend Mr. Halyburton,
professor of divinity in the university of St. Andrews, in a book
which was published after the author's death, at Edinburgh, in
1714, 4to, intituled, *Natural Religion insufficient, and Revealed
necessary to Man's Happiness* —— " in which, particularly,
" the writings of the learned Lord Herbert, the great patron of
" deism; to wit, his books *de Veritate, de Religione Gentilium,*
" and his *Religio Laici*, in so far as they assert nature's light able
" to conduct us to future blessedness, are considered, and fully
" answered." In this elaborate performance he sets himself
largely and distinctly to shew that the light of nature is greatly
defective, even with respect to the discoveries of a Deity, and
the worship that is to be rendered to him; with respect to the inquiry concerning man's true happiness; with respect to the rule
of duty, and the motives for enforcing obedience: that it is unable certainly to discover the means of obtaining pardon of sin;
or to eradicate inclinations to sin, and subdue its power. And,
lastly, he argues its insufficiency, from a general view of the experience of the world. He afterwards proceeds distinctly to consider the five articles to which the Lord Herbert reduces his

---

* Essay on Human Understanding, book i. c. 3, s. 15, 16, 17, 18, 19.
† See his works, vol. ii. p. 574, & seq. 4th edit.

catholic

catholic religion.  He anfwers the proofs his Lordfhip has brought
to fhew that thefe articles did univerfally obtain; and, on the
contrary, offers feveral proofs to fhew that they did not fo obtain.
And he endeavours diftinctly to anfwer the principal arguments
and pleas urged by Lord Herbert; and, after him, by Mr. Blount,
for the fufficiency of natural religion.  Whofoever carefully
examines what this learned and pious author has offered on thefe
feveral heads will find many excellent things; though the narrownefs of his notions in fome points hath prejudiced fome perfons againft his work, and hindered them from regarding and
confidering it fo much as it deferves.

I fhall here conclude my account of Lord Herbert, in which I
have been the more particular, becaufe as he was one of the firft,
fo he was confeffedly one of the greateft writers that have appeared among us in the deiftical caufe.

---

## POSTSCRIPT.

*A remarkable Incident relating to Lord Herbert confidered.*

SIR,

AFTER I had finifhed the two foregoing letters, I faw a large
anonymous letter, which was fent to you, and by you communicated to me, relating to Lord Herbert of Cherbury.  This letter deferves particular notice; and what I have to obferve upon
it may be properly inferted here, immediately after the obfervations which have been made upon that noble writer in the preceding letters.  I readily agree with this gentleman in acknowledging, what, as he obferves, Mr. Baxter owns in his animadverfions on Lord Herbert's tract *de Veritate*, that there are excellent things in that book, and that many of the rules there propofed may be of great ufe.  But I had no occafion to take
particular notice of them, as I propofed only to make fome general obfervations on his Lordfhip's fcheme, as far as the caufe
of Chriftianity is concerned.  I hope the writer of that letter,
who appears to be a man of fenfe, and a friend to Chriftianity,
as well as a great admirer of Lord Herbert, will find, on perufing
the foregoing reflections, that I have done his Lordfhip juftice,
and not pufhed the charge againft him farther than there is juft
ground

ground for it.   What I have there faid is perfectly agreeable to
what this ingenious gentleman has obferved in this letter; where,
after having faid that Lord Herbert is commonly reputed to have
been the firft ftarter of deifm in the laft century, he adds, " Sup-
" pofing the charge to be true, as I greatly fufpect it is, yet I am
" convinced upon feveral good reafons, that he was neverthelefs
" a deift of more honour, and of greater candour and decency,
" as he was of far greater parts and learning, than many that have
" appeared under that denomination fince." He fubjoins, " Had
" he lived in thefe days, wherein the fubject, then new, has been
" thoroughly canvaffed, and no ftone left unturned to find out
" the truth, and bring it into fair light, I own I have charity
" enough to fuppofe, and almoft to believe, that Lord Herbert
" would either have been an advocate for revelation, or at leaft
" have forborne oppofing it."

This gentleman takes notice of a manufcript which he had
lately feen, containing the life of the Lord Herbert of Cherbury,
drawn up from memorials penned by himfelf, and which is now
in the poffeffion of a gentleman of diftinction whom he does not
name.   He mentions that Lord's good conduct when he was
ambaffador at Paris, and fome other things that do not come
within the compafs of my defign, which is not to give an account of the lives and characters of the authors I mention, but
only to confider their writings, and thefe no farther than they
relate to the controverfy between the Chriftians and the deifts.
But there is one thing in that manufcript life of Lord Herbert,
which the writer of the anonymous letter calls a *furprifing inci-*
*dent*, and which is indeed of fuch a nature, that I cannot pafs it
by without a particular notice.

After having obferved that Lord Herbert's tract *de Veritate*
was his favourite work, he produceth a large extract relating to
it, in that Lord's own words, fignifying, that though it had been
approved by fome very learned men to whom he had fhewn it,
among whom he mentions Grotius, yet as the frame of his whole
book was fo different from what had been written heretofore on
this fubject, and he apprehended he fhould meet with much oppofition, he did confider, whether it were not better for him for
a while to fupprefs it.   And then his Lordfhip proceeds thus:

" Being thus doubtful, in my chamber, one fair day in the
" fummer, my cafement being open towards the fouth, the fun
                                                              " fhining

" shining clear, and no wind stirring, I took my book *de Veritate*
" in my hands, and, kneeling on my knees, devoutly said these
" words. *O thou eternal God, author of this light which now*
" *shines upon me, and giver of all inward illuminations: I do*
" *beseech thee, of thine infinite goodness, to pardon a greater re-*
" *quest than a sinner ought to make: I am not satisfied enough,*
" *whether I shall publish this book: if it be for thy glory, I be-*
" *seech thee give me some sign from heaven: if not, I shall suppress*
" *it.* I had no sooner spoken these words, but a loud, though
" yet gentle noise, came forth from the heavens (for it was like
" nothing on earth); which did so cheer and comfort me, that I
" took my petition as granted, and that I had the sign I demanded;
" whereupon also I resolved to print my book. This, how
" strange soever it may seem, I protest before the eternal God,
" is true: neither am I any way superstitiously deceived herein;
" since I did not only clearly hear the noise, but in the serenest
" sky that ever I saw, being without all cloud, did, to my think-
" king, see the place from whence it came."

The ingenious writer of the letter says, he will make no remarks
on this incident, but sends it as he finds it; but he makes no
doubt, that some observations upon this and other things in that
life would be acceptable to the friends of religion.

I shall mention some reflections that have occurred to me upon
this occasion.

I have no doubt of his Lordship's sincerity in this account.
The serious air with which he relates it, and the solemn protesta-
tion he makes, as in the presence of the eternal God, will not
suffer us to question the truth of what he relates; *viz.* that he
both made that address to God which he mentions, and that, in
consequence of this, he was persuaded that he heard the noise he
takes notice of, and which he took to come from heaven, and
regarded as a mark of God's approbation of the request he had
made: and accordingly this great man was determined by it to
publish this book. He seems to have considered it as a kind of
imprimatur given to it from heaven, and as signifying the divine
approbation of the book itself, and of what was contained in it.

I cannot help thinking, that if any writer, zealous for Christianity, had given such an account of himself, as praying for and
expecting a sign from heaven to determine his doubt, whether

he

he should publish a book he had composed in favour of the chriftian cause; and upon hearing a noise, which he took to be from heaven, had looked upon it as a mark of the divine approbation, and as a call to publish that book; it would have passed for a high fit of enthusiasm, and would no doubt have subjected the author to much ridicule among the gentlemen that oppose revealed religion. What judgment they will pass upon it in Lord Herbert's cafe I do not know: but considering the great partiality they have often shewn in their own favour and against chriftianity, it is not improbable, that some of them may be apt to interpret this incident as giving a divine fanction to a book, which contains indeed several important truths, but withal hath some principles which are unfavourable to the chriftian religion; or at leaft, they may be willing to have it believed that this is as much to be depended upon as the figns and atteftations faid to be given from heaven to the firft preachers and publifhers of the gofpel revelation.

There are fome things obfervable in Lord Herbert's folemn addrefs to God which, I think, are highly commendable, and would incline one to think very favourably of his Lordfhip's intentions. He difcovereth in it a great veneration for the Deity, and a deep fenfe of his dependence upon him as the *author of light, and the giver of all inward illuminations*. This is agreeable to the fentiments of the beft and wifeft men in all ages; but yet I think it may be juftly doubted, whether an addrefs of fuch a particular kind as that made by his Lordfhip was proper or regular. It does not feem to me, that we are well founded to apply for or to expect an extraordinary fign from heaven, for determining doubts concerning the expediency of publifhing a book. Methinks, if a man hath ufed his beft endeavours to find out truth, and (which certainly ought not to be neglected) hath humbly applied to God to affift and direct him in his inquiries; if he hath the teftimony of his own confcience to the uprightnefs of his own intentions, and that he is not actuated by pride and vain glory, by an affectation of fingularity, or any worldly finifter ends and views; and if he is fatisfied, upon the moft diligent and impartial examination, that what he hath advanced is both true and of great importance to mankind, and is only afraid of the oppofition it may meet with; I think, in fuch a cafe, efpecially

if

if he hath alfo the advice of good and judicious friends concerning it, he hath fufficient grounds to proceed upon, and doth not need a particular fign from heaven to determine him. This feems to be a putting it on a wrong foot, fince God hath not in his word given us any ground to expeçt that he will anfwer fuch a requeſt; nor is there any reaſon to expeçt it from the nature of the thing. His Lordſhip himfelf feems to have fufpeçted that fuch an addrefs and expeçtation was not regular, when he begs of God to *pardon* it, as being a *greater requeſt than a finner ought to make.* I believe it will be acknowledged, that fudden impreſſions, or fuppoſed figns from heaven, like that upon which Lord Herbert feemeth to lay fo great a ſtrefs, are very equivocal, and not much to be depended upon for information in truth, or direçtion in duty: They may lay perfons open to miſtake and delufion. It cannot be denied, that, in fuch cafes, men are in danger of being impoſed upon by the warmth of their own imaginations, efpecially if they be wrought up to a ſtrong defire and expeçtation of an extraordinary fign from heaven, in favour of a defign which they heartily wiſh ſhould fucceed.

I think it is evident, from his own account of it, that this was Lord Herbert's cafe. His mind was full of his book, highly prepoffeffed in favour of its truth and ufefulnefs. He feems not to have been diffident of the truth and goodnefs of the book itſelf, but only to have been in doubt about the expediency of its publication; and he took a very extraordinary way to obtain direction concerning it. Nothing lefs would fatisfy him than a fign from heaven; and it is plain that he was big with expeçtation. His imagination was warmed with the hope of a fign that ſhould be a mark of the divine approbation. It is not to be wondered at, that a mind thus prepared ſhould be difpoſed to interpret any incident that ſhould happen, in favour of its own prepoffeffions, and as countenancing the purpofe he had entertained in his own breaſt. Taking it in this view, nothing happened, but what may reafonably enough be accounted for, without fuppoſing any thing fupernatural in the cafe. He doth not mention any articulate voice, or words fpoken to him as from heaven, direçting him what to do, or fignifying an approbation of his defign: he only maketh mention of a noife that feemed to him to come from heaven. He giveth no particular account what kind of noife it was, but only that

that it was *loud and yet gentle*, and that *it came from heaven, for it was like nothing on earth;* that it was in *a serene sky*, and that, *to his thinking, he saw the place from whence it came.* In this situation of his mind, any noise that happened at that precise juncture, and which had something unusual in it (and it is easy to suppose several things of this kind), might be apt to make an impression on his imagination. I shall only put one supposition, and it is this; that at that time it might happen to thunder at a distance, which might well be in summer-time, though in that part of the sky which was within his view there was no cloud to be seen, and all seemed perfectly serene; and the " noise of thunder heard remote" (to use Milton's phrase) coming at that instant when the soul was filled with expectation of something extraordinary, would undoubtedly greatly affect him, and might be regarded as a sign of approbation from heaven, which was what he sought for: and then no wonder that it comforted and cheered him, as his Lordship observes it did.

It is, I must confess, a great satisfaction to me to reflect, that the evidence of the Christian religion doth not depend upon such equivocal signs as this. The attestations given to the first preachers and publishers of the gospel were of such a kind, that, supposing them to have really happened, they could not reasonably, or with the least appearance of probability, be ascribed to any thing but a divine interposition; and therefore might justly be regarded as marks of the divine approbation of the Christian scheme.

Upon this occasion, I cannot help drawing some kind of parallel in my own mind, between this incident that happened to this noble Lord, and that extraordinary appearance from heaven which St. Paul gives an account of; and which, with what followed upon it, had such an effect upon him, as to conquer his obstinate prejudices, and to engage him to profess and preach that faith in Christ which he himself had zealously persecuted before. I believe the warmest advocates for Christianity would be ready to own, that if that great apostle had had no better account to give of the reasons and motives of his conversion, than such a sign from heaven as Lord Herbert mentions, this would have been a very slender foundation either for himself or others to go upon, in receiving the Christian doctrine as of divine original. But the

slightest

flighteft comparifon of the cafes may let us fee that there is a wide and amazing difference between them.  Lord Herbert's mind was prepoffeffed with the expectation of a fign from heaven: he fought it, he applied to God for it, he had an hope that fomething of this kind would happen: and when the thing came which he took for a fign, it was in favour of what he no doubt ftrongly wifhed and defired before: yet, prepoffeffed as his imagination was, he heard no voice of words, nor articulate language, fignifying to him the divine will.  But St. Paul was the fartheft in the world from defiring or expecting a fign from heaven in favour of the religion of Jefus: on the contrary, his mind was at that very inftant wholly poffeffed with the ftrongeft prejudices againft it.  He was then going to Damafcus, with a commiffion from the high-prieft to feize the difciples of Jefus, and bring them to Jerufalem to be punifhed; and he was perfuaded in his own confcience that he was right in doing fo.  He *breathed out threatnings and flaughter* againft them, as the facred writer expreffeth it: and he himfelf tells us, that *he verily thought with himfelf, that he ought to do many things contrary to the name of Jefus of Nazareth.*  In this circumftance of things, if we fhould fuppofe him feized with a fudden pang of enthufiafm, though this is by no means likely to have happened to him, as he was travelling along the road at noon-day, with feveral others in his company; but if we fhould fuppofe that fomething of this kind happened to him, and that he faw an extraordinary light from heaven, which he took to be a fign that heaven approved the work in which he was then engaged; or if he had thought he alfo heard a voice from above fpeaking to him, and animating him to go on, and courageoufly to execute the commiffion he had received from the high-prieft, and promifing him fuccefs in it; there might poffibly be fome pretence for afcribing it to the working of an over-heated imagination, filled with the defign he was upon, which engaged all his thoughts and refolutions.  But it is plain that, in the temper he was then in, he could not have the leaft expectation of Jefus of Nazareth's appearing to him with a celeftial fplendour and glory, calling to him with a majeftic voice from heaven, and, in words which he diftinctly heard, reproving him for his enmity to him, and perfecuting rage againft his difciples, appointing him his minifter and apoftle, and commiffion-

ing

ing him to preach the gofpel to the Gentiles, and to invite them to a participation of the benefits and privileges of his kingdom; which were things the moft remote from his apprehenfion that could poffibly be conceived.

I need not here particularly repeat all the circumftances of a ftory fo well known as that of the divine appearance which oc-cafioned St. Paul's converfion: but taking in the whole, as he himfelf relateth it, it is abfolutely impoffible that it fhould have been the effect of his own enthufiaftic imagination, confidering how his mind was at that time difpofed: To which may be added the confequent effects which fhewed the reality of it. Struck blind with the glory of the appearance, he was obliged to be led to Damafcus; and it was only by the laying on of Ananias' hands in the name of Jefus, that he had his fight reftored. There was immediately a wonderful change in his difpofitions, notions, and inclinations. He became enlightened at once, without human inftruction, in a perfect knowledge of the religion of Jefus, than which nothing could be more contrary in many points to the pharifaical principles and prejudices he had fo deeply imbibed. He was endued with the moft extraordinary gifts of the Holy Ghoft, and had a power of communicating thofe gifts to others, by the laying on of his hands in the name of a crucified and rifen Jefus; and in the fame facred name was enabled to perform the moft illuftrious miracles. Thefe were matters of fact in which he could not be deceived himfelf, and of which there were num-bers of witneffes: and accordingly he went through the nations preaching Jefus Chrift, and him crucified, as the Saviour and Lord; which he did with fuch evidence, and had fuch extraor-dinary atteftations from heaven accompanying him, that vaft num-bers were brought over by his miniftry to embrace a religion which was abfolutely contrary to their moft rooted prejudices, inclinations, and interefts.

There might poffibly be fome fufpicions with regard to the re-lation of a fact fo circumftanced as was that of Lord Herbert. It might be thought poffible, that an author might feign an appro-bation from heaven in favour of fome peculiar notions he had entertained, and of a book of which he was very fond, and upon which he feems to have valued himfelf: not that I think there is any reafonable ground of fufpicion, that this noble writer feigned

what

what he relates concerning this incident; but yet fome may fuppofe, that an author might poffibly be under fome temptation to
deviate from the rules of truth in fuch a cafe.   But no fuch fufpicion can be entertained in St. Paul's cafe, that he fhould have
feigned a heavenly appearance in favour of a religion which he
was well known to have hated, perfecuted, and defpifed, and
which was abfolutely contrary to the prejudices to which he had
been fo obftinately addicted, and to all his worldly expectations,
connections, and interefts: to which it may be added, that he gave
the higheft poffible proof of his own fincere belief of the fact as
he has related it, by his inviolable adherence to that religion to
which he was by this extraordinary means converted; that he expofed himfelf by it to the different perfecutions, and to the greateft and moft various labours and fufferings that any one man ever
endured; and which he bore with an invincible conftancy, and
even with a divine exultation and joy, fupported by the teftimony
of a good confcience, and the hope of a glorious reward in the
heavenly world.

Upon the whole, let us put the fuppofition, that Lord Herbert,
in the account he hath given of what happened to him, has had
the ftricteft regard to truth (which, for my part, I have no doubt
of), and that the account St. Paul hath given of the extraordinary
appearance to him from heaven is alfo true, there is this vaft difference between the cafes: that, granting all that happened to
Lord Herbert to have been as he relates it, there is nothing in it
but what may be accounted for in fome fuch manner as that mentioned above, without fuppofing any thing fupernatural in the
cafe; but, granting the truth of the relation which St. Paul gives
of the divine appearance to him, with the effects that followed
upon it, there is no poffibility of accounting for it in a natural
way, or indeed in any other manner than by owning an extraordinary and fupernatural interpofition.   Though therefore the former, granting it to be true, can by no means be depended upon
as a certain mark of the approbation of heaven given to Lord
Herbert's book; yet the latter, fuppofing it in like manner true,
affordeth a convincing proof of an extraordinary atteftation given
from heaven to the divine miffion and glory of a crucified Jefus,
and to the truth and divine original of the Chriftian revelation.

I may perhaps be thought to have expatiated too much in my

reflections on this occasion; but I hope I shall be excused when
it is considered, that the incident is of so uncommon a nature;
that it relateth to a person of Lord Herbert's character and eminence; and that the account of it is extracted from memorials
written by himself.

I shall make no farther remarks on the anonymous letter, than
to observe, that the writer of it makes mention of the answers to
Lord Herbert, published by Mr. Baxter and Mr. Halyburton.
He also takes notice of the Weekly Miscellany, as having lately
appeared against him. The two former I have taken notice of
above; the latter I have not seen, and therefore know not how
far some of the observations there made may have coincided with
mine.

# LETTER III.

*Obſervations on Mr. Hobbes's Writings—He ſometimes profeſſeth a Regard to the Scripture as the Word and Law of God: at other times ridicules Inſpiration or Revelation—He attempts to invalidate the ſacred Canon, and makes Religion and the Authority of Scripture to depend entirely on the Authority of the Magiſtrate—His ſtrange Maxims in Morality and Politics—His Scheme tends to ſubvert Natural Religion as well as Revealed—Confuted by ſeveral learned Authors.*

SIR,

IN my two former letters ſome obſervations were made on the writings of that eminent deiſt, Lord Herbert of Cherbury. The next writer I ſhall mention was in ſeveral reſpects of a different character from that noble Lord, though alſo very famous in his time, the noted Mr Thomas Hobbes of Malmſbury. There have been few perſons whoſe writings have had a more pernicious influence in ſpreading irreligion and infidelity than his ; yet as none of his treatiſes are directly levelled againſt revealed religion, I ſhall content myſelf with ſome brief general reflections upon them. He ſometimes affects to ſpeak with veneration of the ſacred writings. He expreſsly declareth, that though the laws of nature are not laws as they proceed from nature, yet, " as " they are given by God in holy ſcripture, they are properly call- " ed laws ; for the holy ſcripture is the voice of God, ruling all " things by the greateſt right\*." But though he ſeems here to make the laws of ſcripture to be the laws of God, and to derive their force from his ſupreme authority, yet in many other paſſages, ſome of which I ſhall have occaſion to mention, he ſuppoſeth them to have no authority but what they derive from the prince or civil power. He ſometimes ſeems to acknowledge inſpiration to be a ſupernatural gift, and the immediate hand of God ; at other times he treats the pretence to it as a ſign of madneſs ; and, by a jingle upon the words, repreſents God's ſpeaking

---

\* De Cive, cap. iii. ſect. 33.

to the ancient prophets in a dream or vision, to be no more than
their dreaming that he spoke to them, or *dreaming between sleep-
ing and waking* \*. To weaken the authority of the sacred Canon,
he endeavours to shew, that the books of Moses, and the histori-
cal writings of the Old Teſtament, were not written by thoſe
whoſe names they bear, and that they are derived to us from no
other authority but that of Eſdras, who reſtored them when they
were loſt †: a ſuppoſition in which he hath been ſince followed
by others on the ſame ſide, and very lately by a noble Lord;
though the abſurdity of it is manifeſt, and hath been fully expoſed ‡. As to the writings of the New Teſtament, he acknowledgeth, that they are as ancient as the times of the apoſtles, and
that they were written by perſons who lived in thoſe times, ſome
of whom ſaw the things which they relate; which is what many
of our modern deiſts ſeem unwilling to own. And though he
inſinuates that the copies of the ſcriptures were but few, and only
in the hands of the Eccleſiaſtics, yet he adds, that he ſees no
reaſon to doubt, but that the books of the New Teſtament, as we
have them, are the true regiſters of thoſe things which were
done and ſaid by the prophets and apoſtles §. But then he moſt
abſurdly pretends, that they were not received as of divine
authority in the Chriſtian church, till they were declared to be ſo
by the council of Laodicea, in the year after Chriſt 364: though
nothing is capable of a clearer proof, than that their authority
was acknowledged among Chriſtians from the apoſtolic times.

He expreſsly aſſerts, that we have no aſſurance of the certainty
of ſcripture, but the *authority of the church*, and this he reſolveth
into the *authority of the commonwealth:* and declares, that till
the ſovereign ruler had preſcribed them, " the precepts of ſcrip-
" ture were not obligatory laws, but only counſel and advice,
" which he that was counſelled might without injuſtice refuſe to
" obſerve, and being contrary to the laws could not without in-
" juſtice obſerve;" that the word of the interpreter of ſcripture is
the word of God, and the ſovereign magiſtrate is the interpreter
of ſcripture, and of all doctrines, to whoſe authority we muſt

---

\* Leviath. p. 196.                    † Ibid. p. 200, 201, 203.
‡ Reflections on Lord Bolingbroke's Letters, p. 51, &c.
§ Leviath. p. 204.

stand\*.    Yea, he carrieth it so far as to pronounce, that Christians are bound in conscience to obey the laws of an infidel king
in matters of religion; that " thought is free; but when it comes
" to confession of faith, the private reason must submit to the
" public, that is to say, to God's lieutenant."    And accordingly,
he alloweth the subject, being commanded by the sovereign, to
deny Christ in words, holding firmly in his heart the faith of
Christ: and that in that case, " it is not he that denieth Christ
" before men, but his governor and the laws of his country †."
And he expresly declareth, that idolatry to which a man is compelled by the terror of death is not idolatry.    And this being the
case, it is not to be wondered at, that he speaks with contempt
of the ancient martyrs.    In this the succeeding deists have not
failed to imitate him.    They have reproached those excellent
persons as having *died as a fool dieth* ‡; as if it were a ridiculous
and senseless thing to endure hardships and sufferings, for the
sake of truth and conscience: and yet those have been always
justly admired, who have exposed themselves to the greatest dangers in a noble cause, and who would not do a base thing to save
their lives.

Mr. Hobbes acknowledgeth the existence of God, and that we
must of necessity arise from the effects which we behold, to the
eternal Power of all powers, and Cause of all causes; and he
blames those as absurd who call the world, or the soul of the
world, God: but he denies that we know any more of him than
that he exists, and seems plainly to make him corporeal; for he
affirms, that that which is not body is nothing at all §: and though
he sometimes seems to acknowledge religion and its obligations,
and that there is an honour and worship due to God, prayer,
thankfgivings, oblations, &c. yet he advanceth principles which
evidently tend to subvert all religion.    The account he gives of
it is this, " that from the fear of power invisible, feigned by the
" mind, or imagined from tales publicly allowed, ariseth religion,
" not allowed superstition."    And he elsewhere resolveth religion into things which he himself derides; *viz.* " opinions of

---

\* See Quest. concerning Liberty, p. 136.    De Cive, c. 17.    Leviath,
p. 169. 283, 284.
† Ibid. p. 238. 271.
‡ See Christ. not founded on Argument, p. 32, 33.
§ Leviath. p. 214. 371.

" ghosts,

" ghofts, ignorance of fecond caufes, devotion to what men fear,
" and taking of things cafual for prognoftics\*." He takes pains
in many of his works to prove man to be a neceffary agent, and
exprefsly afferts the materiality and mortality of the human foul;
and he reprefents the doctrine concerning the diftinction between
foul and body in man to be an error contracted by the contagion of
the demonology of the Greeks. We may obferve by the way the
great difference there is in this refpect between Mr. Hobbes and
Lord Herbert. This noble writer has reckoned the notion and
belief of a future ftate among the common notices naturally obvious to the minds of all men: but the account Mr. Hobbes is
pleafed to give of it is this, that the belief of a future ftate after
death " is a belief grounded upon other men's faying, that they
" knew it fupernaturally, or that they knew thofe, that knew
" them, that knew others, that knew it fupernaturally †."

That we may have the better notion of this extraordinary writer, it may not be amifs to mention fome other of his maxims.
He afferts, that by the law of nature every man hath a right to
all things, and over all perfons, and that the natural condition
of man is a ftate of war, a war of all men againft all men: that
there is no way fo reafonable for any man as to anticipate, that is,
by force and wiles to mafter all the perfons of others that he can,
fo long till he fees no other power great enough to endanger him:
that the civil laws are the only rules of good and evil, juft and
unjuft, honeft and difhoneft; and that antecedently to fuch laws
every action is in its own nature indifferent: that there is nothing
good or evil in itfelf, nor any common laws conftituting what is
naturally juft and unjuft; that all things are meafured by what
every man judgeth fit, where there is no civil government, and
by the laws of fociety where there is one ‡. That the power of
the fovereign is abfolute, and that he is not bound by any com-
pacts with his fubjects: that nothing the fovereign can do to the
fubject can properly be called injurious or wrong; and that the
king's word is fufficient to take any thing from any fubject, if
there be need, and the king is judge of that need §.

---

\* Leviath. p. 54.                                     † Ibid. p. 74.
‡ De Cive, c. vi. f. 18. c. x. f. 1. c. 12. f. i. Leviath. p. 24, 25. 60, 61,
62, 63. 72.
§ Leviath. p. 90. 106.

In

In Mr. Hobbes we have a remarkable inftance what ftrange extravagancies men of wit and genius may fall into, who, whilft they value themfelves upon their fuperior penetration, and laugh at popular errors and fuperftition, often give into notions fo wild and ridiculous, as none of the people that govern themfelves by plain common fenfe could be guilty of. It will hardly be thought too fevere a cenfure to fay, that Mr. Hobbes's fcheme ftrikes at the foundation of all religion, both natural and revealed: that it tendeth not only to fubvert the authority of the fcripture, but to deftroy God's moral adminiftration: that it confoundeth the na-tural differences of good and evil, virtue and vice, and taketh away the diftinction between foul and body, and the liberty of human actions: that it deftroyeth the beft principles of the human nature, and, inftead of that innate benevolence and focial dif-pofition which fhould unite men together, fuppofeth all men to be naturally in a ftate of war with one another: that it erecteth an abfolute tyranny in the ftate and church, which it confounds, and maketh the will of the prince or governing power the fole ftandard of right and wrong; and that it deftroyeth all the rights of private confcience, and indeed leaveth no room for con-fcience at all.

But notwithftanding the ill tendency of many of Mr. Hobbes's principles, yet the agreeablenefs of his ftile, of which he was a great mafter, joined to his dogmatical way of pronouncing with a very decifive air, and the very oddnefs and apparent novelty of his notions, gave them a great run for a time, and did no fmall mifchief. He himfelf boafteth of the good reception his *Levia-than* met with among many of our gentry: but the manifold ab-furdities and inconfiftencies of his fcheme, and the pernicious confequences of it to religion, morality, and the civil govern-ment, have been fo well expofed, and fet in fo clear a light, that there are not many of our modern deifts that would be thought openly to efpoufe his fyftem in its full extent: though indeed it cannot be denied, that there are not a few things in their writ-ings borrowed from his, and that fome of them have chofen rather to follow him than Lord Herbert in feveral of his principles, and particularly in afferting the materiality and mortality of the human foul, and denying man's free agency.

Mr. Hobbes met with many learned adverfaries, among whom

we

we may particularly reckon Dr. Seth Ward, afterwards bifhop of Sahfbury, and archbifhop Bramhal. The latter argued with great acutenefs againft that part of his fcheme which relates to liberty and neceffity, and afterwards attacked the whole of his fyftem, in a piece called the *Catching of the Leviathan*, publifhed at London in 1658; in which he undertakes to demonftrate, out of Mr. Hobbes's own works, that no man who is thoroughly an *Hobbift* can be " a good Chriftian, or a good commonwealth's " man, or reconcile himfelf to himfelf." The reverend Mr. Tenifon, afterwards archbifhop of Canterbury, gave a fummary view of Mr. Hobbes's principles, with a judicious confutation of them, in a book called *The Creed of Mr. Hobbes examined*, publifhed in 1670. To thefe may be added, the famous Earl of Clarendon, who wrote *A brief View and Survey of the dangerous and pernicious Errors to the Church and State in Mr. Hobbes's Book, entitled " Leviathan."* This was publifhed in 1676. Bifhop Parker, Mr. Tyrrel, but, above all, Bifhop Cumberland, in his juftly celebrated work *de Legibus Naturæ*, did alfo diftinguifh themfelves in this controverfy. It is to be obferved, that the learned writers who oppofed Mr. Hobbes did not fo much apply themfelves to vindicate revealed religion, or the Chriftian fyftem, as to eftablifh the great principles of all religion and morality, which his fcheme tended to fubvert: and to fhew, that they had a real foundation in reafon and nature. In this they certainly did good fervice to religion: yet fome of the enemies of revelation endeavoured to take advantage of it, as if this fhewed that there is no other religion but the law of nature, and that any extraordinary revelation is needlefs and ufelefs. Thus, on every fuppofition, thefe gentlemen feem refolved to carry their caufe againft Chriftianity. If there be no law of nature, no real difference, in the nature of things, between moral good and evil, virtue and vice, there is no fuch thing as religion at all, and confequently no Chriftian religion. On the other hand, if it be proved that there is fuch a thing as the religion and law of nature, which is founded in the very nature and relations of things, and agreeable to right reafon, then it is concluded, that this alone is fufficient, and that it is clear and obvious to all mankind, and therefore they need no revelation to inftruct them in it, or affure them of it. A very wrong conclufion this! fince it is manifeft

that

that a well-attested revelation from God would be of very great use, both farther to clear and confirm some of the important principles of natural religion, which, though in themselves reasonable, were in fact greatly obscured and perverted in the corrupt state of mankind; and also to instruct men in things which, however highly useful to be known, they could not have clearly discovered or been fully assured of, by the mere unassisted light of nature, without a divine revelation.

This might lead one into a train of reflections on the connection there is between natural and revealed religion: but I must content myself with giving short hints of things: to enlarge farther upon them would not suit my present design. You will probably hear from me again soon; and in the mean time, I am, &c.

# LETTER IV.

*Mr. Charles Blount's Notes on the Life of Apollonius Tyanæus, designed to expose Christianity—His* Religio Laici *copied, for the most Part, from Lord Herbert—He had a chief Hand in the Oracles of Reason—He attacks the Doctrine of a Mediator, as unworthy of God—His remarkable Concession, that it is not safe to trust to Deism alone, without Christianity joined with it.——Mr. Toland, another deistical Writer; very fond of asserting Paradoxes—The Design of his Amyntor to render the Canon of the New Testament uncertain—He gives a large Catalogue of spurious Gospels, and attempts to shew that they were equally received and acknowledged in the primitive Times, with the Gospels which are now looked upon as authentic—The contrary fully proved in the Answers that were made to him.*

SIR,

AMONG those who openly avowed the cause of deism, and seemed zealous to promote it, may be reckoned Charles Blount, Esq. In 1680 he published a translation of the two first books of Philostratus's Life of Apollonius Tyanæus, with large notes, which are manifestly intended to strike at revealed religion. Apollonius, you know, was a Pythagorean philosopher that lived in the first century, whose character and miracles were opposed by the pagans to those of our Lord Jesus Christ. Hierocles wrote a book to this purpose, which was answered by Eusebius, who hath plainly proved, that Philostratus was a vain and fabulous writer, and that his accounts are full of romantic stories and ridiculous fables: and whoever impartially considers Philostratus's book, which is still extant, must be convinced that Eusebius's censure upon it is just. Nothing can be supposed more different than Philostratus's manner of writing, stuffed with rhetorical flourishes and vain ostentations of learning, is from the plain, sober, artless narration of the evangelists, which hath all the characters of genuine unaffected simplicity, and a sincere regard to truth: To which it may be added, that Apollonius's philosophy, and the wonders he is said to have wrought, all tended to uphold the

reigning

reigning eſtabliſhed ſuperſtition and idolatry, which at the ſame time had all worldly advantages on its ſide, and yet was not able to oppoſe the progreſs of Chriſtianity, which triumphed over it, though deſtitute of all thoſe advantages, and though it had all the powers of the world againſt it:—a manifeſt proof this, how vaſtly ſuperior the evidence of our Saviour's divine character and miracles was to any thing that could be produced in oppoſition to it! And yet many of our modern deiſts have been fond of running the parallel between Apollonius and Jeſus Chriſt. Mr. Blount, in his notes, has thrown out ſeveral inſinuations againſt the miracles of our Saviour, in which he has been followed and even exceeded by ſome ſucceeding writers, of whom I may afterwards give ſome account. This gentleman has on ſeveral occaſions diſcovered a ſtrong prejudice againſt the ſcriptures, and ſhewn how willing he is to lay hold on whatſoever he thinks may expoſe them: it could be only owing to this, that he finds fault with that manner of expreſſion, *he opened his mouth; and ſaid* [*]: a cenſure which may be thought to proceed from an extraordinary nicety, rather than a true juſtneſs of taſte. But though this, and other oriental idioms and forms of ſpeech, may differ from what is uſual among us, the language of ſcripture has been always admired by the beſt judges.

In 1683 the ſame gentleman publiſhed a ſmall book intitled *Religio Laici*, which is little more than a tranſlation of Lord Herbert's treatiſe of the ſame name. The additions and improvements he has made are ſo few, and of ſuch ſmall moment, as not to deſerve a diſtinct conſideration, and therefore I ſhall refer to the reflections already made on Lord Herbert's ſcheme.

Some years after, in 1693, there was another book publiſhed, in which Mr. Blount had a principal concern, and which was plainly intended to propagate infidelity. It had a pompous title, *The Oracles of Reaſon*, and was publiſhed after Mr. Blount's unhappy end, by his friend Mr. Charles Gildon, who uſhered it into the world by a preface in defence of ſelf-murder, which that gentleman had been guilty of, to get rid of the uneaſineſs of a paſſion which proved too violent for him. The title of the book ſeemed to promiſe demonſtration, as if it were intended to ſerve

---

[*] Blount's Notes on Philoſtratus, p. 69.

as an infallible guide in matters of religion: but there is little order or method in it, or regularity of defign. It is a collection of different pieces, confifting for the moft part of letters between Mr. Blount and his friends, intermixed with fragments and tranflations from fome Greek and Latin authors, done with no great exactnefs.

That part of the book which relates to natural religion and its fufficiency, proceeds chiefly upon Lord Herbert's plan. There are two of the tracts particularly remarkable this way: the one is *A Summary Account of the Deift's Religion*, by Mr. Blount: the other is a letter from A. W. to Mr. Blount, concerning natural religion, as oppofed to divine revelation. In the former of thefe, Mr Blount, having fet himfelf to fhew that God is not to be worfhipped by an image or by facrifices, next endeavoureth to prove that he is not to be worfhipped by a mediator. He pretends that the worfhip of God by a mediator derogateth from his infinite mercy, equally as an image doth from his fpirituality and infinity.

But his argument is founded upon a mifapprehenfion or mifreprefentation of the gofpel fcheme. Far from derogating from the mercy or goodnefs of God, the appointment of fuch a mediator as the gofpel propofeth is one of the moft fignal inftances of his grace and goodnefs towards mankind: It is a wife and gracious provifion for exercifing his mercy towards guilty creatures, in fuch a way as is moft becoming his own glorious government and perfections, and moft conducive to their peace and comfort, and moft proper to remove their guilty jealoufies and fears.

But he farther urgeth, that if God appointed the mediator, this fhews that he was really reconciled to the world before, and confequently that there was no need of a mediator. It fheweth indeed that God had kind thoughts of mercy, and gracious intentions towards the human race; but this doth not prove that therefore the appointment of a mediator was needlefs. On the contrary, his wifdom determined him to take this method as the propereft way of exercifing his mercy, and difpenfing the effects of his goodnefs; of which he is certainly the fitteft judge: And whofoever duly confiders the fublime idea given us in the gofpel of the mediator, the work upon which he was fent, and the offices he was invefted with, may obferve fuch characters of the divine wifdom and goodnefs in it, fuch a regard to the honour of

God,

God, and to the comfort and benefit and happinefs of mankind, as ought greatly to recommend the gofpel fcheme. But the diftinct confideration of thefe things would take up more room than the prefent defign will allow.

To this tract is prefixed a letter from Mr. Blount to Dr. Sydenham, in which there is this remarkable paffage: that " un-" doubtedly, in our travels to the other world, the common " road is the fafeft; and though deifm is a good manuring of a " man's confcience, yet certainly, if fowed with Chriftianity, it " will produce the moft plentiful crop." Here he feems plainly to own, that it is not fafe to truft to deifm alone, if Chriftianity be not joined with it *.

As to the other tract I mentioned, the letter written by A. W. to Mr. Blount, concerning natural religion as oppofed to divine revelation, the chief heads of natural religion are there reduced to feven articles. 1. That there is an infinite and eternal God, creator of all things. 2. That he governs the world by his providence. 3. That it is our duty to worfhip and obey him as our creator and governor. 4. That our worfhip confifts in prayer to him, and praife of him. 5. That our obedience confifts in the rules of right reafon, the practice of which is moral virtue. 6. That we are to expect rewards and punifhments hereafter according to our actions in this life, which includes the foul's immortality, and is proved by our admitting providence. 7. That when we err from the rules of our duty, we ought to repent, and truft in God's mercy for pardon †. Here Lord Herbert's five articles, which were all that he accounted neceffary, are enlarged to feven, which indeed may be regarded as farther explications of the former: and with other explications they might be enlarged to a ftill greater number. . What was obferved concerning Lord Herbert's articles may be applied to thefe. It will be acknowledged, that they are agreeable to right reafon; but this is no proof that therefore an exprefs divine revelation would not be needful, in the prefent ftate of mankind, to fet them in a ftronger light, and give them additional force. Several of the deifts would be far from agreeing with this writer in fome of the articles he mentions. The firft article runs thus, that *there is*

---

* Oracles of Reafon, p. 87. 91.          † Ibid. p. 197.

*one eternal self-exiftent* God, *creator of all things:* where it is plainly fuppofed, that the world was created; and yet in another part of that book, Mr. Blount has taken the pains to tranflate a large fragment of Ocellus Lucanus, which is defigned to prove the eternity of the world *: and it appears that he himfelf does not difapprove it. In another part of thefe pretended *Oracles*, in a letter from Mr. Gildon to Mr. Blount, the opinion of the origin of good and evil, from two different eternal principles, the one good, the other evil, is reprefented as not unreafonable †. In another of the above-mentioned feven articles it is declared, that the *worſhip we owe to God confifts in prayer to Him, and praiſe of Him:* and yet it is well known, that this has been contefted and denied by fome of the ancient philofophers and modern deifts; and Mr. Blount himfelf, in his notes upon the Life of Apollonius Tyanæus, having obferved that fome of the heathens ufed no prayers at all, infinuates, in their names, objections againft that duty ‡. With regard to the fifth article, that *our obedience confifts in the rules of right reaſon, the practice whereof is moral virtue,* this is eafily faid in general; but there is no great likelihood, that, if they were to come to a particular explication, they would agree what is to be looked upon as included in the rules of right reafon, and in the practice of moral virtue. Some of them would probably think it reafonable to indulge the appetites and paffions in inftances which others would not think reafonable or proper: even in a point of fuch confequence as felf-murder, fome of the ancient philofophers and modern deifts have pleaded for it, whilft others have condemned it; and it is openly juftified (as was before obferved) in the preface to thefe *Oracles of Reaſon.* One fhould therefore think no reafonable man could deny, that exprefs precepts, determining by a divine authority the particulars of moral duty, would be of great advantage. As to the article of future rewards and punifhments, and the foul's immortality, this is reprefented by Mr. Blount, in a letter *to the right honourable the* moft *ingenious* Strephon, and by A. W. in his letter to Mr. Blount, as a neceffary part of natural religion; and yet he obferves, that the ancient heathens dif-

---

* Oracles of Reafon, p. 212—228.     † Ibid. p. 194.
‡ Notes on Philoftratus, p. 38.

agreed

agreed about it *. In another part of thefe *Oracles*, it is declared
to be probable, that the foul of man is not of an entirely diftinct
nature from the body, but only a purer material compofition †.
Now the foul's materiality is not very confiftent with the doctrine of its immortality: and from this we may judge of A. W's
argument againft Chriftianity, that " if the reafons of the Chrif-
" tian religion were evident, there would be no longer any con-
" tention or difference about it: and if all do not agree in it,
" thofe marks of truth in it are not vifible, which are neceffary
" to draw our affent ‡." This argument, if it were good for any
thing, would prove that there are no vifible marks of truth in natural religion, no more than in revealed; fince it cannot be denied that men differ about the one as well as the other: but the
truth is, the argument doth not conclude in either cafe.

There are feveral things in the *Oracles of Reafon* which are
particularly defigned againft the holy fcriptures, and which have
been repeated by others fince: but the facred writings have been
fully vindicated againft thofe exceptions. Mr. Blount has particularly attacked the writings of Mofes, and the moft confiderable part of what he has offered to this purpofe is borrowed either
from the learned author of the *Archæologiæ-Philofophicæ*, who,
though he differed in fome things from what is generally looked
upon as the true interpretation of Mofes's fenfe, was far from
intending to fubvert the authority of the Mofaic writings; or
from the author of the hypothefis of the *Pre-Adamites*, who afterwards retracted his own book. From this writer Mr. Blount
hath given us a literal tranflation for feveral pages together, in
different parts of this book, without making the leaft acknowledgment of it, or taking any notice of the anfwers that had been
returned. In like manner he hath thought proper to repeat the
objections which have been frequently urged againft the Mofaic
writings, from the irreconcilablenefs of the accounts there given
with the antiquities pretended to by the moft learned heathen nations, particularly the Chaldeans and Egyptians. Our great
Stillingfleet had, in the firft book of his *Origines Sacræ*, very
amply confidered that matter, and clearly fhewn the vanity of
thofe pretences; yet they are here again advanced with as much

---

* Oracles of Reafon, p. 201.　　† Ibid. p. 154. 187.　　‡ Ibid. p. 201. 206.

confidence as if they had never been refuted. The fame obfervation may be made with regard to the arguments of Ocellus
Lucanus about the eternity of the world, which are tranflated and
produced with great pomp by Mr. Blount, though they had been
unanfwerably expofed in the laft-mentioned learned treatife *.

The *Oracles of Reafon* were animadverted upon by Mr. John
Bradley, in a book publifhed at London in 1699, in 12mo. intitled, *An Impartial View of the Truth of Chriftianity, with the
Hiftory of the Lfe and Miracles of Apollonius Tyanæus: To
which are added, fome Reflections on a Book called " Oracles of
Reafon."* This book I have not feen. Dr. Nichols's *Conference
with a Theift* was alfo particularly defigned by the learned and
ingenious author in oppofition to the *Oracles of Reafon;* and he
hath not left any material part of that book unanfwered. The
firft part of this *Conference* was publifhed at London in 12mo. in
1696, and the other three parts in the following years. But what
deferveth our fpecial notice, Mr. Gildon, the publifher of the
*Oracles of Reafon,* and who had recommended them to the world
with a pompous eulogium, was afterwards, upon mature confideration, convinced of his error; of which he gave a remarkable
proof, in a good book which he publifhed fome years after, in
1705, intitled *The Deift's Manual.* It is obfervable, that the
greateft part of this book is taken up in vindicating the doctrines
of the exiftence and attributes of God, his providence and government of the world, the immortality of the foul, and a future
ftate : and his reafon for it was, as he himfelf intimates, becaufe
many of the deifts, with whom he was well acquainted, did really
deny thofe great principles which lie at the foundation of all religion, or at leaft reprefented them as doubtful and uncertain ;
and their not admitting natural religion in its juft extent formed
fome of their principal prejudices againft the chriftian revelation.

The next writer of whom I fhall give fome account is Mr.
Toland, who, though he called himfelf a chriftian, made it very
much the bufinefs of his life to ferve the caufe of infidelity, and
to unfettle men's minds with regard to religion. There are many
things in his writings which fhew, that he was very fond of afferting things that had an appearance of novelty, however deftitute

---

* Origines Sacræ, book iii. c. 2. f. 4, 5, 6, 7.

of reafon or probability; a remarkable inftance of which he has given, in his ftrange attempt to prove that motion is effential to matter. See his letters to *Serena*, Letter III.*.  In another book, which he calls *Pantheifticon*, publifhed in 1720, he has fhewn himfelf a favourer and admirer of the *Pantheiftic* philofophy, *i. e.* that of Spinofa, which acknowledgeth no other God but the univerfe. The firft thing that made Mr. Toland taken notice of, was his *Chriftianity not myfterious; or, a Difcourfe fhewing, that there is Nothing in the Gofpel contrary to Reafon, nor above it, and that no Chriftian Doctrine can be properly called a myftery.* This was publifhed in 1696, and was animadverted upon by feveral writers of learning and reputation, as Mr. Becconfal, Mr. Beverly, Mr. John Norris, Dr. Payne, Mr. Synge, afterwards archbifhop of Tuam, and Mr. Brown, afterwards bifhop of Cork. In 1709 he publifhed at the Hague two Latin differtations. The firft is intitled, *Adeifidæmon, five Titus Livius a fuperftitione vindicatus. In qua differtatione probatur Livium hiftoricum in facris, prodigiis, et oftentis enarrandis, haudquaquam fuiffe credulum aut fuperftitiofum: ipfamque fuperftitionem non minus Reipublicæ (fi non magis) exitiofam effe, quam purum putum atheifmum.* The fecond differtation bears the title of *Origines Judaicæ, five Strabonis de Mofe et religione Judaica hiftoria breviter illuftrata.* In this differtation he feems to prefer the account of this pagan author concerning Mofes and the Jewifh religion, before that which is given by the Jews themfelves. Thefe two differtations were anfwered by Mr. la Faye, minifter at Utrecht, in a book printed in 1709, and intitled, *Defenfio religionis, nec non Mofis et gentis Judaicæ, contra duas differtationes Joannis Tolandi;* and by Mr. Benoit, minifter at Delft, in his *Mélange de remarques critiques, hiftoriques, philofophiques, théologiques, fur les deux differtations de Mr. Toland, intitulées, l'un l'Homme fans fuperftition, et l'autre les origines Judaïques,* printed at Delft in 1712. But what I fhall here particularly take notice of, and by which he hath chiefly diftinguifhed himfelf, is the pains he hath taken to invalidate the authority of the facred Canon of the New Teftament, and to render it uncertain and precarious. This feems to have been the defign of

---

* This is confuted in Dr. Clarke's Demonftration, &c. p. 14. Edit. 7th.

the book he calls *Amyntor*, which he publifhed in 1698, and in which he hath given a catalogue of books, attributed in the primitive times to Jefus Chrift, his apoftles, and other eminent perfons, " together with remarks and obfervations relating to the Canon of Scripture." He hath there raked together whatever he could find relating to the fpurious gofpels, and pretended facred books, which appeared in the early ages of the Chriftian church. Thefe he hath produced with great pomp, to the number of eighty and upwards ; and though they were moft of them evidently falfe and ridiculous, and carried the plaineft marks of forgery and impofture, of which, no doubt, he was very fenfible, yet he has done what he could to reprefent them as of equal authority with the four gofpels, and other facred books of the New Teftament, now received among Chriftians. To this end he has taken advantage of the unwary and ill-grounded hypothefes of fome learned men, and has endeavoured to prove, that the books of the prefent Canon lay concealed in the coffers of private perfons till the latter times of Trajan or Adrian, and were not known to the clergy or churches of thofe times, nor diftinguifhed from the fpurious works of heretics ; and that the fcriptures which we now receive as canonical, and others which we now reject, were indifferently and promifcuoufly cited and appealed to by the moft ancient Chriftian writers. His defign in all this manifeftly is to fhew, that the gofpels, and other facred writings of the New Teftament, now acknowledged as canonical, really deferve no greater credit, and are no more to be depended upon, than thofe books which are rejected and exploded as forgeries : and yet he had the confidence to pretend, in a book he afterwards publifhed, that his intention in his *Amyntor* was not to invalidate, but to illuftrate and confirm, the Canon of the New Teftament *. This may ferve as one inftance, among the many that might be produced, of the writer's fincerity.

* See Toland's preface to his *Nazarenus*, p. 9. This very odd book was well anfwered by Mr. (afterwards) Dr. Mangey, in his *Remarks upon Nazarenus*; on which Mr. Toland made fome reflections, in a Tract he called *Mangoneutes*. Mr. Paterfon alfo publifhed his *Anti-Nazarenus*, in anfwer to Mr. Toland's book. And Dr. Thomas Brett took fome notice of it, in the Preface to his *Tradition neceffary to explain and interpret the Holy Scriptures.*

Several

Several good anfwers were returned to Toland's *Amyntor.*
Mr. (afterwards) Dr. Samuel Clarke publifhed a fmall traƈt in
1699, intitled, *Some Reflections on that Part of the Book called
" Amyntor," which relates to the Writings of the primitive Fathers, and the Canon of the New Teftament.*   In this he gave an
early fpecimen of thofe talents, which he afterwards employed
to fo great advantage in the defence of Chriftianity.   The fame
book was afterwards anfwered by the ingenious Mr. Stephen
Nye, in his *Hiftorical Account and Defence of the Canon of the
New Teftament, in Anfwer to " Amyntor";* and by Mr. Rich-
ardfon, in his *Canon of the New Teftament Vindicated,* whofe
work hath been juftly and generally efteemed, as executed with
great learning and judgment.   To thefe may be added, Mr. Jones,
who hath confidered this matter diftinƈtly, and at large, in his
*New and full Method of fettling the Canonical Authority of the
New Teftament,* which was publifhed at London in 1726, in two
volumes 8vo.; to which a third fmall one was afterwards added,
publifhed in 1727, but left unfinifhed by reafon of the author's
death.

Thefe learned writers have plainly fhewn Mr. Toland's great
unfairnefs and difingenuity in his whole management of the argument: That he has frequently impofed upon his readers by
falfe quotations, or by grofsly mifreprefenting the authors he
cites : That he has been guilty of great blunders and ridiculous
miftakes: That feveral of the writings he produces, as having
been written in the apoftolic age, were forged fo late as the third
or fourth century : That by far the greateft part of thofe writings, of which he hath given fo pompous a catalogue, and which
he would put upon the world as moft ancient and apoftolical, are
exprefsly rejeƈted by the authors whom he himfelf refers to, as
fpurious and apocryphal, or even as abfurd and impious forgeries : That as to thofe few of them which are not exprefsly rejeƈted and condemned by the writers who have mentioned them,
it doth not appear by any one teftimony, that they were ever
generally received and acknowledged in the Chriftian church, or
equalled with the books of the facred Canon : and that even thofe
authors who have been thought to quote fome of them with approbation, yet exprefsly declare, that none but the four gofpels
were received in the Chriftian church, as of divine authority:

That

That though some of the false gospels, that they might the better pass upon the people, were compiled out of the genuine gospels, with such additions, omissions, and interpolations, as might
best answer the design of the compilers, this did not hinder their
being generally rejected; whereas the four gospels, the same
which we now receive, were generally acknowledged from the
beginning: That these and other sacred books of the New Testament were, even in the earliest ages, spread into distant countries, and were in the possession of great numbers of persons,
and read in the churches as divine: And finally, that several of
the genuine writers of the three first centuries have left us catalogues of the sacred books of the New Testament, but in none of
these catalogues do any of the apocryphal books appear.

To set this whole matter in a clearer light, Mr. Jones has
given us a complete enumeration of all the apocryphal books of
the New Testament, and made a critical inquiry into each of
these books, with an English version of those of them which are
now extant, and a particular proof that none of them were ever
admitted into the Canon: and he hath distinctly produced and
considered every testimony relating to them that is to be found
in any Christian writer or writers of the first four centuries after
Christ.

Upon all that hath been written on this subject, it is a just
and natural reflection, that as the number of spurious gospels
which were rejected by the primitive Christians shews, how scru-
pulous they were not to admit any books as canonical, but those
of whose truth and authenticity they had sufficient proofs; so
their admitting, and receiving with so general a consent, the four
gospels which are now in our hands, affordeth a strong argument,
that they had undoubted evidence of the genuine truth and certainty of the evangelical records, which fully satisfied them who
lived nearest those times, and who had the best opportunities of
knowing; and that to this it was owing, that these, and no others,
were generally received and acknowledged as of divine authority.

On this occasion it is proper to mention Dr. Lardner's excellent work of the *Credibility of the Gospel-History;* in the second
part of which, consisting of several volumes, he hath made a full
and accurate collection of the passages which are to be found in
the writers of the first ages of the Christian church, relating to
                                                              the

the four gofpels, and other facred books of the New Teftament. This he hath executed with fo much fidelity and diligence, and with fuch exactnefs of judgment, that the Englifh reader, who hath not opportunity to confult the originals, will be able to judge for himfelf, upon confidering the paffages of the original authors, which are very faithfully tranflated.    This affordeth fo clear and continued a proof of their having been generally received in the earlieft ages of the Chriftian church, that one would hope it fhould put an end to this part of the controverfy.

# LETTER V.

*The Earl of Shaftesbury, a fine and much admired Writer—Not very confiſtent in the Account he gives of Chriſtianity—He caſteth Reflections on the Doctrine of future Rewards and Puniſhments, as if it were of Diſſervice to the Intereſts of Virtue—The contrary ſhewn from his own Acknowledgments—His Lordſhip reſolves the Credit of holy Writ wholly into the Authority and Appointment of the State—He frequently takes Occaſion to expoſe the Scriptures, and repreſents them as uncertain, and not to be depended upon—What he ſaith concerning Ridicule, as the Teſt and Criterion of Truth, examined—It is ſhewn, that a turn to Ridicule is not the propereſt Diſpoſition for finding out Truth: and that there is great Danger of its being miſapplied—His Lordſhip's own Writings furniſh Inſtances of ſuch a wrong Application—Authors mentioned that have written againſt him.*

SIR,

IT gives me a real concern, that, among the writers who have appeared againſt revealed religion, I am obliged to take notice of the noble author of the *Characteriſtics.* Some indeed are not willing to allow, that he is to be reckoned in this number. Paſſages are produced out of ſome of his writings, in which he expreſſeth very favourable ſentiments of Chriſtianity. This he doth particularly in a preface, which, and I believe juſtly, is aſcribed to his Lordſhip as the author, prefixed to a volume of ſelect ſermons of Dr. Benjamin Whichcot, publiſhed in 1698. In that preface he finds fault with thoſe in this profane age that repreſent not only the inſtitution of preaching, but even the goſpel itſelf, and our holy religion, to be a fraud. He expreſſeth his hope, that from ſome things in theſe ſermons, even they that are prejudiced againſt Chriſtianity may be induced to like it the better; and that the vein of goodneſs which appears throughout theſe diſcourſes will make ſuch as are already Chriſtians prize Chriſtianity the more; and the fairneſs, ingenuity, and impartiality,

tiality, which they learn from hence, will be a fecurity to them against the contrary temper of thofe other irreconcilable enemies to our holy faith. In 1716 fome of his letters were publifhed at London, under the title of *Several Letters written by a noble Lord to a young Man in the Univerfity*, 8vo. In thefe letters, which were written a few years before the Earl of Shaftefbury's death, in the years 1707, 1708, 1709, there are excellent fentiments and advices, and fome which feem to difcover a real regard for the Chriftian religion.

It were greatly to be wifhed, on many accounts, that his Lordfhip had always expreffed himfelf in an uniform manner on this fubject. No impartial man will deny him the praife of a fine genius. The quality of the writer, his lively and beautiful imagination, the delicacy of tafte he hath fhown in many inftances, and the graces and embellifhments of his ftyle, though perhaps fometimes too affected, have procured him many admirers. To which may be added, his refined fentiments on the beauty and excellence of virtue, and that he hath often fpoken honourably of a wife and good providence, which minifters and governs the whole in the beft manner; and hath ftrongly afferted, in oppofition to Mr. Hobbes, the natural differences between good and evil; and that man was originally formed for fociety, and the exercife of mutual kindnefs and benevolence; and not only fo, but for religion and piety too[*]. Thefe things have very much prejudiced many perfons in his favour, and prepared them for receiving, almoft implicitly, whatever he hath advanced. And yet it cannot be denied, that there are many things in his books, which feem to be evidently calculated to caft contempt upon Chriftianity and the holy Scriptures.

It is in the *Characteriftics* that we are properly to look for an account of his Lordfhip's fentiments. They were firft publifhed in three volumes 8vo, in 1711; and the laft part of his life was employed in revifing them, and preparing for a new and moft correct edition of them, which accordingly was publifhed immediately after his death. In them he completed the whole of his works which he intended fhould be made public : and thefe books are fo generally read, and by many fo much admired, that

[*] Characteriftics, vol. iii. p. 224.

it is neceffary to take notice of thofe things in them which feem
to have a bad afpect on religion, and to be of a dangerous influence and tendency.

Of this kind are the frequent reflections he hath caft on the
doctrine of future rewards and punifhments. This, as I obferved
in a former letter, is reprefented by Lord Herbert as a fundamental article of natural religion: and though he carries it too
far, in making it an innate principle, in which all mankind are,
and have been always agreed; yet it cannot be denied, that there
were fome notices and traces of it generally fpread among the nations, though mixed with much obfcurity, and which probably
had a great effect in preferving the remains of religion and virtue
among the people, though contradicted by feveral fects of their
philofophers. It is the great advantage and glory of Chriftianity,
that it hath cleared and confirmed this important principle, and
hath brought life and immortality into an open light. But the
author of the *Characteriftics* frequently expreffeth himfelf in a
manner, which tendeth to raife a prejudice againft this great principle of natural and revealed religion, as if it were of little ufe
in morals, yea, and in many cafes of a bad tendency. Thus,
after having made an elegant reprefentation of the happy ftate of
things in the heathen world, and the liberty and harmony which
then prevailed, he proceeds to fhew the different ftate of things
among Chriftians, which he feems chiefly to attribute to the notion and belief of a future ftate. " A new fort of policy (faith
" he) which extends itfelf to another world, and confiders the
" future lives and happinefs of men rather than the prefent, has
" made us leap beyond the bounds of natural humanity, and, out
" of a fupernatural charity, has taught us the way of plaguing one
" another moft heartily. It has raifed an antipathy which no
" temporal intereft could ever do, and intailed upon us a mutual
" hatred to all eternity. The *faving of fouls* is now the heroic
" paffion of exalted fpirits\*." This is not the only place where
his Lordfhip fpeaks with ridicule of the *faving of fouls*, and of
thofe *who act for their fouls' fakes*, and *make a careful provifion
for hereafter* †. And he elfewhere tells us, fpeaking of the expectation of God's difpenfing rewards and punifhments in a fu-

---

\* Characteriftics, vol. i. p. 18, 19. edit. 5th.　　† Ibid. vol. iii. p. 302.

ture life, that " an expectation and dependency so miraculous
" and extraordinary as this is, must naturally take off from other
" inferior dependencies and encouragements.   Where infinite
" rewards are thus enforced, and the imagination strongly turned
" towards them, the other common and natural motives to good-
" ness are apt to be neglected, and lose much by disuse.   Other
" interests are hardly so much as computed, whilst the mind is
" thus transported in the pursuit of a high advantage, and self-
" interest, so narrowly confined within ourselves.   On this ac-
" count, all other affections to our friends, relations, or mankind,
" are often slightly regarded, as being worldly, and of little mo-
" ment in respect of the interest of our souls*."   To the same
purpose he represents it, as if the Christian were so urged to have
his *conversation in heaven*, as not to be obliged to *enter into any
engagements with this lower world*, or to concern himself either
with the businesses of life, or with the offices of *private friendship*,
or the service of the public: and that these are to be regarded as
*embarrassments to him in working out his own salvation†*.   It
seems to be a natural inference from all this, that, according to his
representation of the matter, it were better for mankind not to
believe, or have any regard to a future state at all; for if the
belief be weak, he tells us it will be of the worst consequence.
" There can (says he) in some respects be nothing more fatal to
" virtue than the weak and uncertain belief of future rewards and
" punishments: for the stress being wholly laid on this founda-
" tion, if this foundation seem to fail, there is no farther prop
" or security to men's virtue‡."   And, on the other hand, if the
belief be strong, and deeply impressed on the mind, it will cause
men to neglect the interests and duties of this present life, the
duties they owe to their friends, their neighbours, and their country.   This is the account his Lordship gives of it; but it is grossly
misrepresented: for since that virtue and goodness which is to
be rewarded hereafter includes, according to the scripture account of it, the doing good here on earth as far as we have an
opportunity, and even a diligence in the business of our several
callings, and the exercise of social duties, it is evidently wrong

---

* Characteristics, vol. ii. p. 68.      † Ibid. vol. i. p. 99, 100.
‡ Ibid. vol. ii. p. 69.

to fay, that a regard to the recompences of a future ftate muft carry us off from thofe duties, when, on the contrary, it bindeth us more ftrongly to the performance of them. Our having our con-verfation in heaven is not defigned to caufe us to neglect the duties incumbent upon us here on earth; for thefe are moft ex-prefsly enjoined in the gofpel-law, as being comprehended in that righteoufnefs which intitleth us to that future glory; but that we fhould not take up with the inferior things of this prefent world as our proper ultimate portion and happinefs, but raife our views to a nobler ftate, where we hope to arrive to the true felicity and perfection of our natures. And this certainly is an admirable leffon, highly to the honour of Chriftianity; fince it is a too great affection and efteem for worldly enjoyments that puts men upon wrong purfuits, and is the principal fource of the greateft diforders of human life.

Several other paffages might be produced, in which his Lord-fhip feems to reprefent the belief and expectation of a future ftate as of pernicious influence. Thus he obferves, "that the prin- "ciple of felf-love, which is naturally fo prevailing in us, is "improved and made ftronger every day by the exercife of the "paffions on a fubject of more extended intereft;" (by which he refers to the expectation of eternal happinefs in a future ftate) "and that there may be reafon to apprehend, that a temper of "this kind will extend itfelf through all the parts of life. And "this has a tendency to create a ftricter attention to felf-good "and private intereft, and muft infenfibly diminifh the affection "towards public good, or the intereft of fociety, and introduce "a certain narrownefs of fpirit, which is obfervable in devout "perfons of almoft all religions and perfuafions*." Here he lays a heavy charge on the hope of future happinefs; as if it had a bad tendency, to fpread an inordinate criminal felfifhnefs through the whole of human life, to diminifh the public-good affections, and introduce a narrownefs of fpirit. A moft unjuft charge this! Since it might eafily be fhewn, that the belief and hope of fuch an happinefs as the gofpel fets before us, and which is there reprefented as a ftate of perfect goodnefs and the moft extended benevolence, and for which that *charity* which *feeketh*

* Characteriftics, vol. ii. p. 58.

*not*

*not her own* is one of the best preparatives, has a tendency, if rightly understood, to enlarge the heart, to purify and ennoble the soul, and raise it above the little narrow interests of the fleshly self, and to fill it with the highest idea of God, and his immense goodnefs.

But his Lordfhip urges, that " thofe who talk of the rewards " of virtue make it fo very mercenary a thing, and have talked fo " much of its rewards, that one can hardly tell what there is in it " after all that is worth rewarding\*." He obferves that the moft *heroic virtue, private friendſhip,* and *zeal for the public* †, have little notice taken of them in our *holy religion,* nor have any reward promifed them: though if they be comprehended in the things that are *lovely* and *virtuous* and *praife-worthy*, they are both commanded there, and fhall according to the gofpel fcheme be rewarded; but his Lordfhip who fuppofes the contrary, mentions it as an advantage, that no premium or penalty being inforced in thefe cafes, it leaves *more room for difintereftednefs.*

---

\* Characteriftics, vol. i. p. 97.

† It has been noted by the deiftical writers, that zeal for the public, or love to a man's country, which was fo much inculcated by fome of the ancient philofophers and moralifts, is paffed over in the Gofpel; and this is mentioned as a defect in the Chriftian morality. But if the matter be rightly confidered, there is no juft foundation for this objection. To have recommended as by a divine authority, what the Romans generally underftood by love to their country, a ftrong paffion for the glory of it, and which often carried them to do great injuftice to thofe of other nations, would not have been fuited to the nature of a revelation, which was defigned for the general good of mankind, and to promote univerfal benevolence. And if our Saviour had exhorted the Jews in the name of God to a zeal for their country and its liberties, this, in the difpofition they were then in, could have been looked upon in no other light, than as ftirring them up to tumults and infurrections. But of love to our country, as it fignifies a true and affectionate concern for the public good, he gave an admirable example; and his example hath the force of a precept, according to the Chriftian fyftem. This will be evident to any one that impartially confiders the affection he fhewed to the Jewifh nation, from whom he fprung according to the flefh; the amiable concern he expreffed for the miferies he forefaw were coming upon them, and the endeavours he ufed to prevent thofe evils, by checking the tumultuous fpirit which was then working among them, and engaging them to a peaceable fubjection to the Roman government. The fame obfervation may be made with regard to the apoftles and firft publifhers of Chriftianity after our Saviour's refurrection. If they had in the name of God urged

*nefs*, the virtue is a *free choice*, and *the magnanimity is left entire**. And does not this infinuate, that if no reward had been promifed at all, to any part of our duty, it would have been the better for us, and our virtues would have been the more excellent? In like manner he reprefents that refignation to God, which depends upon the hope of infinite retributions or rewards, to be a *falfe refignation*, which *difcovers no worth nor virtue*; fince it is only a man's refigning his prefent life and pleafure conditionally, for that which he himfelf owns to be beyond an equivalent†.

And yet this right honourable author himfelf acknowledgeth, that if by the hope of reward be underftood the hope and defire of virtuous enjoyments, or of the very practice and exercife of virtue in another life, it is far from being derogatory to virtue, but is rather an evidence of our loving it‡. And nothing is more evident to any one that is acquainted with the holy fcriptures, than that though the future happinefs is there fometimes metaphorically defcribed under fplendid fenfible images, which his Lordfhip is pleafed to reflect upon as trifling and childifh §,

it upon the Jews and Gentiles, among whom they preached the gofpel, to be zealous for their country, and had promifed divine rewards to fo heroic a virtue, this would undoubtedly have been regarded as an attempt to raife difturbances in the ftate. It could not, as things were circumftanced, have produced any good effects, and might probably have had very bad ones. But if by zeal for the public be meant a hearty defire and endeavour to promote the public good, and the real welfare of the community, nothing can be better fitted to anfwer that end than the Chriftian law. It hath a manifeft tendency, wherever it is fincerely believed and embraced, to make good magiftrates, and faithful and peaceable fubjects, and to render men truly ufeful to the public, by engaging them to a diligent difcharge of the duties of their feveral ftations and relations, and to the practice of univerfal righteoufnefs. Chriftianity, which requires us to exert fo noble a fpirit of difinterefted benevolence, as to be ready to lay down our lives for the brethren, 1 John iii. 16. would certainly engage and animate us, if properly called to it, even to lay down our lives for the good of the community. A virtuous regard to the public happinefs, and a contributing as far as in us lies to promote it in our feveral ftations, make a part of that excellent and praife-worthy conduct, which it is the great defign of the Chriftian religion to promote, and which, according to the divine promifes there given us, fhall be crowned with a glorious reward.

* Characterift. p. 98, 99, 100, 101.        † Ibid. vol. ii. p. 59.
‡ Ibid. vol. ii. p. 55, 56.        § Ibid. vol. i. p. 282.

yet

yet the idea there given us of it is the nobleſt, the ſublimeſt, that can be conceived.    It is repreſented as a ſtate of conſummate holineſs, goodneſs, and purity, where we ſhall arrive to the true perfeƈtion of our natures; a ſtate into which *nothing ſhall enter that defileth;* where the ſpirits of the juſt ſhall be *made perfeƈt,* and even their bodies ſhall be refined to a wonderful degree; where they ſhall be aſſociated to the glorious general aſſembly of holy and happy ſouls, and to the moſt excellent part of God's creation, with whom they ſhall cultivate an eternal friendſhip and harmony; and, which is chiefly to be conſidered, where they ſhall be admitted to the immediate viſion of the Deity, and ſhall be transformed, as far as they are capable of it, into the divine likeneſs.    Such is the happineſs the goſpel ſetteth before us, and which certainly furniſheth a motive fitted to work upon the worthieſt minds.    And the being animated by the hope of ſuch a reward hath nothing mean or mercenary in it, but rather is an argument of a great and noble ſoul.

And even as to the fear of puniſhment, this alſo may be of ſignal uſe to reſtrain the exorbitancies of the paſſions, to check the career of vice, and to awaken men to ſerious thoughts, and thereby put them in the way of better impreſſions.    His Lord-ſhip himſelf aſſerteth the uſefulneſs of puniſhments, as well as rewards, in all well-regulated governments.    And with reſpeƈt to future puniſhments he acknowledgeth, that " though this ſer-" vice of fear be allowed ever ſo low and baſe, yet religion being " ſtill a diſcipline and progreſs of the ſoul towards perfeƈtion, the " motive of reward and puniſhment is primary, and of the higheſt " moment with us, till being capable of more ſublime inſtruƈtions, " we are led from this ſervile ſtate to the generous ſervice of " affeƈtion and love[*]."    And he elſewhere expreſsly declareth, that " the hope of future rewards, and fear of future puniſhments, " how mercenary or ſervile ſoever it may be accounted, is yet " in many inſtances a great advantage, ſecurity, and ſupport to " virtue;" and he offereth ſeveral conſiderations to prove that it is ſo[†].    I cannot therefore help thinking that this admired writer has done very wrong in throwing out ſo many inſinuations againſt the doƈtrine of future retributions, and againſt the holy ſcrip-

---

[*] Charaƈteriſt. vol. ii. p. 63. 273.    [†] Ibid. vol. ii. p. 60. & ſeq.

tures and Chriftian divines for infifting fo much upon it, as though
it were of ill influence to morals. I am perfuaded, that any one
who duly confiders the ftate of mankind, and what a mighty influence
our hopes and fears have upon us by the very frame of
our nature, muft be fenfible, that if the fcripture had only contained
fine and elegant difcourfes on the beauty of virtue, and
the deformity of vice, inftead of propofing the fanctions of eternal
rewards and punifhments, it would neither have been fo becoming
the majefty and dignity of the fupreme legiflator, nor fo well
fitted to anfwer the end of a revelation defigned for common ufe.
The fcripture indeed doth every where fuppofe, and frequently
reprefenteth the excellence of holinefs and virtue, and the turpitude
and deformity of vice and fin, and the good effects of the
one, and bad effects of the other, even in this prefent ftate. But
it is the great advantage of the Chriftian revelation, that it carrieth
our views beyond this narrow tranfitory fcene to a future eternal
ftate, and deriveth its moft important motives from thence, which
he himfelf acknowledgeth to be of infinitely greater force; and,
which is very odd, he feemeth to make the very force of thofe
motives an objection againft infifting upon them, as if they would
render all other motives and confiderations ufelefs.

The prejudices his Lordfhip hath conceived againft Chriftianity
fufficiently appear from feveral of thofe paffages that have been
mentioned; to which many others might be added. He is pleafed
indeed more than once to declare himfelf a very orthodox believer.
He hath affured us, in his ironical way, of his *fteady
orthodoxy*, and *entire fubmiffion to the truly Chriftian and Catholic
doctrines of our holy church, as by law eftablifhed:* and
that he faithfully embraces the *holy myfteries of our religion even
in the minuteft particulars, notwithftanding their amazing depth*\*.
For which he gives this reafon, that " when the fupreme powers
" have given their fanction to a religious record or pious writ,
" it becomes immoral and profane in any one to deny or difpute
" the divine authority of the leaft line or fyllable contained in
" it †." To the fame purpofe he elfewhere declares, that the
myfteries of religion are to be *determined* by thofe to whom the
ftate has *affigned* the *guardianfhip* and *promulgation of the di-*

---

\* Characteriftics, vol. iii. p. 315, 316.      † Ibid. p. 231.

vine

*vine oracles;* and that the *authority and direction of the law* is the *only security against heterodoxy and error*, and the only warrant for the authority of *our sacred symbols* [*]. So that according to him, Christianity has no other foundation than what will serve a false religion as well as the true. And elsewhere, in the person of the sceptic, he talks of our *visible sovereign's answering for us in matters of religion* [†]. In this his Lordship exactly agrees with Mr. Hobbes: he is indeed far from asserting with that writer, that there is nothing good or evil in its own nature, and that virtue and vice depend wholly on human authority and laws; this he on all occasions strenuously argueth against. But he comes into another part of his scheme, the making the magistrate or supreme civil power the sole judge of religious truth and orthodoxy, and resolving all doctrines and opinions in religion, and the authority of what shall be accounted holy writ, into the appointment of the state; a scheme which absolutely destroyeth the rights of private judgment and conscience, and which evidently condemneth the conduct and judgment of Christ and his apostles, and the primitive Christians at the first plantation of Christianity, and of those excellent men that stood up for the reformation of it since.

But notwithstanding our noble author's pretended veneration and submission to the holy writ *by public authority established*, he hath taken occasion to expose the scripture, as far as in him lay, to ridicule and contempt, of which many instances might be produced. Not to mention the insinuations he has thrown out relating to particular passages both in the Old Testament and the New, he hath endeavoured to expose the spirit of prophecy, and made a ludicrous representation of it, and compared it with the extravagancies of the maddest enthusiasts [‡]. Miracles he will not allow to be any proofs, though ever so certain [§]; or that there is any ground to believe their having been done, but the authority of our governors, and of those whom the *state* hath appointed the *guardians of holy writ* [||]. He speaks with ridicule, as other deistical writers have often done, of what he calls the

\* Characteristics, p. 71. vol. i. p. 360.     † Ibid. vol. ii. p. 353.
‡ Ibid. vol. i. p. 45. vol. iii. p. 67.          § Ibid. vol. ii. p. 331, 332.
|| Ibid. vol. iii. p. 71, 72, 73.

*specious*

*specious pretence of moral certainty*, and *matter of fact* \*, and infinuates, that the facts recorded in the gospels are absolutely uncertain, and that he that relies upon those accounts must be a
*sceptical Christian* †. He represents St. Paul as speaking *scep-
tically*, and as *no way certain or positive as to the revelation made
to him*, though the contrary is manifest from the apostle's own
most express declarations ‡. The very encomiums he sometimes
pretends to bestow upon the scriptures are of such a kind, as
tend rather to give a low and mean idea of them. Thus he commends the *poetical parts of scripture*, Job, Psalms, Proverbs,
*and other entire volumes of the sacred collection, as full of hu-
mourous discourses, and jocular wit;* and faith, that the sacred
writers " had recourse to humour and diversion, as a proper
" means to promote religion, and strengthen the established faith."
In like manner he tells us, that our Saviour's discourses were
*sharp, witty, and humourous;* and that his miracles were done
with a *certain air of festivity; and so that it is impossible not to
be moved in a pleasant manner at their recital;* i. e. it is impos-
fible not to laugh at them §. But though he seemeth here to
commend his *good humour*, as he calls it, and elsewhere represents Christianity as, *in the main, a witty good-natured religion*,
he infinuateth that this may be all an artful pretence to cover deep
designs, and schemes laid for worldly ambition and power. Having observed, that the affection and love which procures a true
adherence to the *new religious foundation*, must depend either
on *a real or counterfeit goodness in the religious founder*, whom
he had called before the *divinely-authorized instructor, and
spiritual chief;* he adds, that, " whatever ambitious spirit may
" inspire him, whatever savage zeal or persecuting principle may
" be in reserve, ready to disclose itself, when authority and
" power is once obtained, the first scene of doctrine however
" fails not to present us with the agreeable views of joy, love,
" meekness, gentleness, and moderation ||." I believe few that
confider how this is introduced, will doubt its being designed as
an infinuation against the character of the holy Jesus; an infinuation for which there is not the least foundation in his whole

---

\* Characteristics, vol. i. p. 44.      † Ibid. vol. iii. p. 72.
‡ Ibid. p. 74, 75.    § Ibid. vol. iii. p. 118. 122, 123.    || Ibid. p. 114, 115.

conduct, or in the scheme of religion he hath taught, and which therefore is as malicious as it is groundless.

Agreeably to this he elsewhere intimates, that the gospel was only a scheme of the clergy for aggrandizing their own power. He represents it as a *natural suspicion* of those who are called sceptical: " that the holy records themselves were no other than " the pure invention and artificial compliment of an interested " party, in behalf of the richest corporation, and most profitable " monopoly, which could be erected in the world\*." But any one that impartially considers the idea of religion set before us in the New Testament, in its primitive simplicity, will be apt to look upon that which his Lordship representeth as a *natural suspicion* to be the most unreasonable supposition in the world. If an ambitious and self-interested clergy, and particularly the favourers of the papal hierarchy, had been to forge a gospel or sacred records to countenance their own claims, or if they had had it in their power to have corrupted and new-modelled them in their favour, the Christian religion and worship would in many instances have been very different from what it now appeareth to be in the sacred writings of the New Testament. Mr. Hobbes himself was so sensible of this, even where he inveighs against the clergy, as endeavouring to put their own laws upon the Christian people for the laws of God, and pretends that the books of the New Testament were in the first ages in the hands only of the Ecclesiastics, that he adds, " he is persuaded " they did not falsify the scripture; because, if they had had an " intention so to do, they would surely have made them more " favourable to their power over Christian princes, and civil " sovereignty, than they are†."

His Lordship on many occasions insinuates, that the original records of Christianity are not at all to be depended upon. He frequently repeats the charge of corruptions and interpolations; and particularly concludes the last Miscellany of his third volume with a heap of objections against the scriptures, drawn from the great number of copies, various readings, different glosses and interpretations, apocryphal and canonical books, frauds of those through whose hands they have been transmitted to us, &c.‡

---

\* Characterist. p. 336.        † Hobbes's Leviath. p. 203, 204.
‡ Characterist. vol. iii. p. 317—344.

These objections are put into the mouth of a gentleman, whom he makes go off the stage with an air of triumph, as if they were unanswerable: and yet they are no other than what have been frequently considered and obviated by the learned defenders of the Christian cause. Dr. Tindal hath since urged all these objections, and more of the same kind, more largely and with greater force than his Lordship had done; and a full answer hath been returned to them, sufficient to satisfy an impartial enquirer *.

I have already dwelt longer on this right honourable author than I at first intended; but you will undoubtedly expect that, before I leave him, I should take some notice of that part of his scheme, where he seems to set up ridicule as the best and surest criterion of truth: This deserves the rather to be considered, because there is not perhaps any part of his writings, of which a worse use hath been made. I am sensible that some ingenious writers have been of opinion, that in this his Lordship has been greatly misunderstood or misrepresented: that his opinion, if fairly examined, amounts only to this, that ridicule may be of excellent use, either against ridicule itself, when false and misapplied, or against grave, specious, and delusive impostures: that he distinguishes between true and false ridicule, and between *genteel wit*, and *scurrilous buffoonry*, which, without decency or distinction, raises a laugh from every thing. This he condemneth, as justly offensive, and unworthy of a gentleman and a man of sense. He would have religion treated with *good manners*, and is for subjecting ridicule to the judgment of reason; and he declares, that as he is in *earnest in defending raillery*, so he can be *sober in the use of it*. Several passages are produced to this purpose †. But whatever apology may be made for this noble writer, I think it cannot be denied, that he has frequently expressed himself very incautiously on this head, and in a manner that may lead persons into a very wrong method of inquiring and judging concerning truth. He not only expressly calls ridicule a *test*, and a *criterion of truth*, but declares for applying it to every thing, and in all cases. He would have us carry the *rule* of ridicule constantly with us, *i. e.* that we must be always in a disposition to apply

* See particularly Answer to Christianity as old as the Creation, vol. ii. chap. 5. 7, 8.

† Characterist. vol. i. p. 11. 63. 83, 84, 85. 128.

ridicule

ridicule to whatever offers, to fee whether it will bear\*.  He
obferves, that " truth may bear all lights; and one of thofe prin-
" cipal lights or natural mediums, by which things are to be
" viewed in order to a thorough recognition, is ridicule itfelf, or
" that manner of proof (for fo he calls it) by which we difcern
" whatever is liable to juft raillery on any fubject † :" and though
he doth not approve the feeking to *raife a laugh for every thing,*
yet he thinks it right to *feek in every thing what juftly may be
laughed at ‡.*  He declares that " he hardly cares fo much as to
" think on the fubject of religion, much lefs to write on it,
" without endeavouring to put himfelf in as good a humour as
" poffible § :" *i. e.* treating it, as he himfelf expreffeth it, in a
way of *wit* and *raillery, pleafantry* and *mirth.*  And indeed what
kind of ridicule his Lordfhip is for, and how he is for applying it in matters of religion, plainly appears from many fpecimens
he has given us of it in feveral parts of his works; efpecially in
his third volume, which is defigned as a kind of review and defence of all his other treatifes.

The beft and wifeft men in all ages have always recommended a calm attention and fobriety of mind, a cool and impartial
examination and enquiry, as the propereft difpofition for finding
out truth, and judging concerning it.  But according to his Lordfhip's reprefentation of the cafe, thofe that apply themfelves to
the fearching out truth, or judging what is really true, ferious,
and excellent, muft endeavour to put themfelves in a merry humour, to raife up a gaiety of fpirit, and feek whether in the object they are examining they cannot find out *fomething that may
be juftly laughed at.* And it is great odds, that a man who is thus
difpofed will find out fomething fit, as he imagines, to excite his
mirth, in the moft ferious and important fubject in the world.
Such a temper is fo far from being an help to a fair and unpreju-
diced enquiry, that it is one of the greateft hindrances to it.  A
ftrong turn to ridicule hath a tendency to difqualify a man for
cool and fedate reflection, and to render him impatient of the
pains that are neceffary to a rational and deliberate fearch.  A
calm difpaffionate love of truth, with a difpofition to examine

* Characterift. p. 11, 12.          † Ibid. vol. i. p. 61.
‡ Ibid. p. 128.                     § Ibid. p. 128.

carefully

carefully and judge impartially, and a prevailing inclination to
jeſt and raillery, ſeldom meet together in the ſame mind.   This
diſcovereth rather an odd turn and vivacity of imagination, than
ſtrong reaſon and ſound judgment; and it would be a ſtrange
attempt to ſet up wit and imagination, inſtead of reaſon and
judgment, for a judge and umpire in matters of the greateſt
conſequence.

Our noble author indeed frequently obſerves, that truth cannot be hurt by ridicule, ſince, when the ridicule is wrong placed,
it will not hold.   " Nothing is ridiculous, but what is deformed,
" nor is any thing proof againſt raillery, but what is handſome
" and juſt: this weapon therefore can never bear an edge againſt
" virtue and honeſty, and bears againſt every thing contrary to
" it\*."   It will be readily allowed, that truth and honeſty cannot be the ſubjeƈt of *juſt* ridicule; but then this ſuppoſeth, that
ridicule itſelf muſt be brought to the teſt of cool reaſon: and
accordingly his Lordſhip acknowledges, that it is *in reality a ſerious ſtudy to temper and regulate that humour*†.   And thus
after all, we are to return to gravity and ſerious reaſon as the
ultimate teſt and criterion of ridicule, and of every thing elſe.
But though the moſt excellent things cannot be juſtly ridiculed,
and ridicule, when thus applied, will, in the judgment of wiſe
and thinking men, render him that uſeth it ridiculous; yet there
are many perſons on whom it will have a very different effeƈt.
The ridicule will be apt to create prejudices in their minds, and
to inſpire them with a contempt, or at leaſt a diſregard of things,
which, when repreſented in a proper light, appear to be of the
greateſt worth and importance.   *The face of truth* indeed, as his
Lordſhip obſerves, *is not leſs fair and beautiful for all the counterfeit vizards that have been put upon it;* yet theſe vizards may
ſo conceal and diſguiſe its beauty, as to make it look a quite different thing from what it really is.   It cannot be denied, that
truth, piety, and virtue, have often been the ſubjeƈts of ridicule;
and bad, but witty, men have met with too much ſucceſs in expoſing them to the deriſion and contempt, inſtead of recommending them to the eſteem and veneration, of mankind.   It is our
author's own obſervation, that *falſe earneſt is ridiculed, but the*

* Characteriſt. vol. i. p. 11. 128, 129.          † Ibid. p. 128.

*falſe*

*falſe jeſt paſſes ſecure.* And though he ſays, he cannot conceive how any man ſhould be *laughed out of his wits*, as ſome have been *frightened out of them*, yet there have been and are too many inſtances of perſons that have been laughed out of their religion, honeſty, and virtue. Weak and unſtable minds have been driven into atheiſm, profaneneſs, and vice, by the force of ridicule, and have been made aſhamed of that which they ought to eſteem their glory.

His Lordſhip is pleaſed to repreſent ridicule as the fitteſt way of dealing with *enthuſiaſts*, and *venders of miracles and prophecy;* and having mentioned the reveries of the French prophets, and recommended *Bartlemy-Fair drollery*, as proper to be uſed on ſuch occaſions, he gives a broad hint, that if this method had been taken againſt the reformation, or againſt Chriſtianity at its firſt riſe, it would have been effectual to deſtroy it, without having recourſe to perſecution*. He has here plainly let us know in what light he regardeth our holy religion. On other occaſions, he declares only for genteel raillery : but here it ſeems what he calls the *Bartlemy-Fair method*, which I believe will hardly paſs for very genteel raillery, is ſuppoſed to be ſufficient, not only againſt that ſet of *enthuſiaſts* who were called the French prophets, but againſt Chriſtianity itſelf. But he ſeems not to have conſidered, that the great author and firſt publiſhers of the Chriſtian religion were ſcoffed and derided, as well as expoſed to grievous ſufferings and torments, and that they had *trial of cruel mockings*, as well as of *bonds* and *impriſonments*. It appears from what remains of the works of Celſus, as well as from what Cæcilius ſaith in Minucius Felix, that no ſarcaſm or ridicule was ſpared among the heathens, by which they thought they could expoſe Chriſtianity; though when they found this ineffectual to ſuppreſs it, they from time to time had recourſe to more violent and ſanguinary methods : and indeed thoſe that have been moſt prone to ſcoff at religion and truth have often been moſt prone to perſecute it too. A ſcornful and contemptuous ſpirit, which is an uſual attendant on ridicule, is apt to proceed to farther extremes; nor am I ſure, that they, who on all occaſions throw out the bittereſt ſarcaſms againſt religion and its miniſters, would not, if it were in their power, give more ſub-

* Characteriſt. vol. i. p. 28, 29.

ſtantial

ftantial proofs of their averfion. His Lordfhip indeed honoureth
that rail'ery and ridicule which he recommends, with the name
of *good-humour;* and by fhuffling one of thefe for the other, and
playing u- on the words, maketh himfelf merry with his reader.
But *good-humour* taken in the beft fenfe, for what he calls the
*fweeteft, kindeft difpofition,* is a different thing from that fneering
faculty, which difpofes men to caft contempt upon perfons and
things, and which is often managed in a manner little confiftent
with a true benevolence.

The proper ufe of ridicule is to expofe fuch follies and abfurdities as fcarce deferve or admit a very ferious confideration:
but to recommend raillery and ridicule as fit to be employed on
all occafions, and upon the moft weighty and important fubjeĉts,
and as the propereft means for difcerning truth, appears to be an
inverting the juft order of things. It is, even when innocently
ufed, for the moft part a trifling employment; and a man of great
genius cannot addiĉt himfelf much to it, without defcending beneath his charaĉter. Indeed there needs no more to give one a
difguft at this pretended teft of truth, than to confider the ufe his
Lordfhip has made of it. When he is in any degree ferious, he
fhews how capable he is to inform and pleafe his reader; but
when he gives a loofe to gaiety and ridicule, he often writes in
a manner unworthy of himfelf. And I am apt to think, that if
nothing of his had been publifhed, but the two firft treatifes of
his firft volume, and the third volume, in which he chiefly in-
dulges himfelf in thofe liberties, he would have generally paffed
in the world for a fprightly and ingenious, but very trifling writer. He often throws out his fneers and flirts againft every thing
that comes in his way; and with a mixture of low and folemn
phrafe, and grave ridicule, he fometimes manages it fo, that it
is not very eafy to difcern his true fentiments; and what it is that
he really aims at. This is not very confiftent with the rule he
himfelf has laid down more than once; viz. That " it is a mean,
" impotent, and dull fort of wit, which leaves fenfible perfons
" in a doubt, and at a lofs to underftand what one's real mind
" is." And again he cenfures " fuch a feigned gravity, as immoral
" and illiberal, foreign to the charaĉter of a good writer, a gentle-
" man, and a man of fenfe\*." There feems to be no other way

---

\* Charaĉterift. vol. i. p. 63, vol. iii. p. 225.

of fcreening him from his own cenfure, but by fuppofing, that he
imagined his true intention with regard to Chriftianity and the
holy Scriptures might be perceived by any fenfible perfon,
through his concealed ridicule.   And it muft be acknowledged
that, for the moft part, it is fo; though, in fome particular places,
it is hard to know whether he be in jeft or earneft.   By this
covered way of ridicule he fometimes fteals upon the reader before he is aware, and, under the guife of a friend, gives a more
dangerous blow, than if he had acted the part of an open and
avowed enemy.

Upon the whole it may be juftly faid, that in this noble and
ingenious author we have a remarkable inftance of the wrong
application of that talent of ridicule, of which he was fo great a
mafter.   And if it has fucceeded ill in his hands, how much more
may it be expected to do fo in thofe who, for want of his genius,
are not able to rife above low buffoonry, nor capable of diftinguifhing grofs and fcurrilous raillery and fcandal from wit and
delicate ridicule!   His Lordfhip hath fince had many awkward
imitators, and probably will have more, who will be apt to apply
his teft of ridicule, not only, as he himfelf hath given them an example, againft revealed religion, but againft all religion, even that
which is called natural, and againft that virtue, of which, in his
ferious moods, he hath profeffed himfelf fo great an admirer.

I fhall conclude my account of this celebrated author with
obferving, that the *Characteriftics* have been attacked, or at leaft
fome particular paffages in them have been occafionally animadverted upon, by feveral learned writers, by bifhop Berkley, Dr.
Wotton, Dr. Warburton, and others.   That part of his Lordfhip's fcheme which reprefents a regard to future rewards, as derogating from the dignity and excellence of virtue, hath been
particularly confidered by Mr. Balguy, in a fhort but judicious
tract, written, like his other tracts, in a very polite and mafterly
manner. It is intitled, *A Letter to a Deift, concerning the Beauty
and Excellency of Moral Virtue, and the Support and Improvement which it receives from the Chriftian Revelation*, 8vo. 1729.
But I know of none that has undertaken to anfwer the whole,
but Mr. (now) Dr. John Brown, in a treatife intitled, *Effays on
the Characteriftics*, publifhed in 1750. This work is divided into
three effays: the firft is on ridicule, confidered as a teft of truth:

F 4                                              the

the fecond is on the obligations of men to virtue, and the neceffity of religious principles: the third is on revealed religion and
Chriftianity.   Under thefe feveral heads, he hath confidered
whatever appeared to be moft obnoxious in the writings of our
noble author.

The length of this letter may feem to need an apology.   But
you, I know, will agree with me, that as it was proper, in pur-
fuance of the defign in which I am engaged, to take notice of this
admired writer, fo it was neceffary to make fuch obfervations as
might help to obviate the prejudices fo many are apt to entertain
in his favour, to the difadvantage even of Chriftianity itfelf.

## LETTER VI.

*The Account given of the Earl of Shaftefbury's Writings in the foregoing Letter, vindicated againſt the Exceptions that had been made againſt it—The being influenced by the Hope of the Reward promiſed in the Goſpel hath nothing in it diſingenuous and ſlaviſh—It is not inconſiſtent with loving Virtue for its own ſake, but tends rather to heighten our Eſteem for its Worth and Amiableneſs—The Earl of Shaftefbury ſeems, in his* Inquiry concerning Virtue, *to erect ſuch a Scheme of Virtue as is independent of Religion, and may ſubſiſt without it—The Apology he makes for doing ſo—The cloſe Connection there is between Religion and Virtue ſhewn from his own Principles and Acknowledgments—Virtue not wholly confined to good Actions towards Mankind, but takes in proper Affections towards the Deity as an eſſential Part of it—He acknowledges that Man is born to Religion.—A remarkable Paſſage of Lord Bolingbroke's to the ſame Purpoſe.*

SIR,

WHEN I firſt publiſhed the *View of the Deiſtical Writers,* the foregoing letter contained the whole of what I then intended with regard to the obſervations on the Earl of Shaftefbury. But not long after the publication of it, ſome perſons, who profeſs to be real friends to Chriſtianity, and I doubt not are ſo, let me know that they wiſhed I had not put his Lordſhip into the liſt of deiſtical writers: and they thought the charge againſt him had in ſome inſtances been carried too far. This put me upon reviſing what I had written relating to that matter, with great care: and if I had found juſt cauſe to think, that in this inſtance I had been miſtaken in the judgment I had formed, I ſhould have thought myſelf obliged publicly to acknowledge it. For when I formed the deſign of taking a view of the deiſtical writers, I fixed it as a rule to myſelf, to make a fair repreſentation, as far as I was able, of the ſentiments of thoſe writers, and not to puſh the charge againſt them farther than there appeared to me to be juſt ground for. And it would have

given

given me a real pleasure to have reason to rank so fine a writer as the Earl of Shaftesbury among the friends of the Christian cause. But upon the most impartial enquiry I was able to make, I have not seen reason to retract any thing I had offered with regard to that noble Lord. I thought it necessary therefore, in the *Supplement to the View of the Deistical Writers*, to publish a letter on that subject, which I shall here subjoin to the preceding one, that the reader may have all before him which relates to that noble writer in one view.

It can scarce, I think, be denied by any impartial person who hath read the *Characteristics* without prejudice, which are the only works he avowed, and which had his last hand, that there are several passages in them, which seem plainly intended to expose Christianity and the holy scriptures. And there is great reason to apprehend, that not a few have been unwarily led to entertain unhappy prejudices against revealed religion, and the authority of the scriptures, through too great an admiration of his Lordship's writings. Some instances of this kind have come under my own particular observation: and therefore it appeareth to me, upon the most mature consideration, that I could not, in consistency with the design I had in view, omit the making some observations upon that admired author, as far as the cause of Christianity is concerned.

That part of my observations on Lord Shaftesbury's works which I find hath been particularly excepted against, is the account given of his sentiments with regard to future rewards and punishments. It hath been urged, that his design in what he has written on this subject was, not to insinuate that we ought not to be influenced by a regard to future rewards and punishments, the usefulness of which he plainly acknowledgeth; but only to shew, that it is wrong to be actuated merely by a view to the reward, or by a fear of the punishment, without any real inward love to virtue, or any real hatred and abhorrence of vice. To this purpose his Lordship observes, that " to be bribed only, " or terrified into an honest practice, bespeaks little of real " honesty or worth; and that if virtue be not really estimable " in itself, he can see nothing estimable in following it for " the sake of a bargain*." He asks, " how shall we deny that

* Characterist. vol. i. p. 97.

" to ferve God by compulfion, or for intereft merely, is fervile
" and mercenary *?" And he puts the cafe of a perfon's being
" incited by the hope of reward to do the good he hates, and
" reftrained by the fear of punifhment from doing the ill to
" which he is not otherwife in the leaft degree averfe;" and obferves, that " there is in this cafe no virtue whatfoever †." If his
Lordfhip had faid no more than this, he would have faid no more
than every real friend to Chriftianity will allow; though in this
cafe there would ftill be great reafon to complain, of his Lordfhip's having made a very unfair reprefentation of the fenfe of
thofe divines, who think it neceffary to urge the motives drawn
from future rewards and punifhments. It is true, that if the
belief of future retributions fhould have no other effect than the
putting fome reftraint upon men's outward evil actions, and regulating their external behaviour, even this would be of great
advantage to the community: but this is far from being the only
or principal thing intended. Thofe certainly muft know little
of the nature and tendency of the Chriftian religion, who fhould
endeavour to perfuade themfelves or others, that though a man
had a real love of vice in his heart, and only abftained from fome
outward vicious practices for fear of punifhment; and though he
had an inward averfion to true goodnefs and virtue, and only
performed fome outward acts that had a fair appearance; this
alone would denominate him a good man, and intitle him to the
future reward: for this were to fuppofe, that though he were
really a vicious and bad man, without that purity and fincerity
of heart on which the fcriptures lay fo great a ftrefs, yet the
practifing fome external acts of obedience, deftitute of all true
goodnefs, and of virtuous affections, would intitle him to the
favour of God, and to that eternal happinefs which is promifed
in the gofpel. If any perfons fhould teach this, I would readily
join with his Lordfhip in condemning them. But he hath not
contented himfelf with ftriking at the fuppofed wrong fentiments of divines, whom he loves on all occafions to expofe.
There are feveral paffages in his Lordfhip's writings, which appear to be directly intended to reprefent the infifting, fo much
as is done in the gofpel, upon the eternal rewards and punifhments

---

* Characterift. vol. ii. p. 272.        † Ibid. p. 55.

of

of a future ftate, as having a bad influence on the moral temper, and particularly as tending to ftrengthen an inordinate felfifh-nefs, and to diminifh the affections towards public good, and to make men neglect what they owe to their friends, and to their country. He plainly intimates the difadvantages accruing to virtue from the having *infinite rewards* in view, and that in that cafe the *common and natural motives to goodnefs are apt to be neglected, and lofe much by difufe\**. He reprefents the being in-fluenced by a regard to future rewards and punifhments as at the beft *difingenuous, fervile, and of the flavifh kind;* and to this he oppofes a *liberal fervice,* and the *principle of love,* and the *loving God and virtue for God and virtue's fake†:* and according-ly he determines, that thofe duties, to which men are carried without any view to fuch rewards, are for that reafon more noble and excellent, and argue a higher degree of virtue. If the cafe really were as his Lordfhip is pleafed to reprefent it, it muft certainly give a very difadvantageous idea of Chriftianity; as if the infifting upon thofe moft important motives, drawn from a future eternal world, which our Saviour came to fet in the ftrongeft light, tended to introduce and cherifh a wrong temper of mind, narrow and felfifh, difingenuous and fervile, to weaken our benevolent affections both public and private, and to take us off from the duties and offices of the civil and focial life. At that rate, it could not be faid that the gofpel is a friend to fociety and to mankind; and inftead of promoting the practice of true virtue, it would rather derogate from it, and degrade it from its proper dignity and excellence. It was therefore neceffary to fhew, as I endeavoured to do in my obfervations on Lord Shaftefbury's writings, that this is far from being a juft reprefentation of the nature and tendency of the Chriftian doctrine of future rewards and punifhments. The moft noble and extenfive benevolence, exerting itfelf in all proper effects and inftances, in oppofition to a narrow felfifh difpofition, is what Chriftianity every where recommendeth and enforceth in the moft engaging manner; and it is its peculiar advantage, that it carrieth our views to a better

---

\* Several paffages to this purpofe were produced out of the Characler-iftics in the preceding Letter, which I need not here repeat.

† See Characterifics, vol. ii. p. 271, 272, 273.

ſtate, where the benevolence which is now begun ſhall be completed, and ſhall be exerciſed in a more enlarged ſphere, and extend to a nobler ſociety.    And can the hope of this poſſibly tend to
diminiſh our benevolence, or muſt it not rather heighten and improve it ?   When a man hath a firm and ſteady perſuaſion, that the
Supreme Being will reward his perſevering conſtancy in a virtuous
courſe with everlaſting felicity, this, inſtead of weakening his inward affeſtion to virtue, and his moral ſenſe of its worth and excellency, muſt in the  nature of things greatly confirm and eſtabliſh
it.   There is therefore  an entire conſiſtency between the loving
virtue for its own ſake, *i. e.* as his Lordſhip explains it, *becauſe
it is amiable in itſelf* \*, and the being animated to the purſuit
and practice of it by ſuch rewards as the goſpel propoſeth:  for
it never appears more excellent and lovely, than when it is conſidered as recommending us to the favour and approbation of Him,
who is the ſupreme original Goodneſs and Excellence, and as
preparing us for a complete happineſs in a future ſtate, where it
ſhall be raiſed to the higheſt degree of beauty and perfection.   In
like manner it muſt mightily ſtrengthen our abhorrence of vice,
and our ſenſe of its turpitude and malignity, to conſider it as not
only at preſent injurious and diſgraceful to our nature, but as
an oppoſition to the will and law of the moſt wiſe and righteous
Governor of the world,  who will in a future ſtate of retribution
inflict awful puniſhments upon thoſe who now obſtinately perſiſt
in a preſumptuous courſe of vice and wickedneſs.

Our noble author himſelf, when he propoſeth to ſhew *what
obligation there is to virtue, or what reaſon to embrace it,* which
is the ſubject of the ſecond book of his *Inquiry,* reſolveth it into
this: that *moral rectitude or virtue muſt be the advantage, and
vice the miſery and diſadvantage of every creature;* and that *it
is the creature's intereſt to be wholly good and virtuous* †.   To
prove this ſeems to be the entire deſign of that book, which he
concludes with obſerving, that *virtue is the good, and vice the
ill of every one.*  He ſeems indeed, in diſplaying the advantages
of the one and diſadvantages of the other, to confine himſelf
wholly to this preſent life, and to abſtract from all conſideration
of a future ſtate.  But if the repreſenting virtue be to our intereſt

---

\* Characteriſt. vol. ii. p. 67.          † Ibid. p. 81. 98.

here on earth, and conducive to our prefent happinefs, be a juft ground of *obligation to virtue*, and a proper *reafon to embrace it*, which his fecond book is defigned to' fhew, then furely, if it can be proved, that it tendeth not only to our happinefs here, but to procure us a perfect happinefs in a future ftate of exiftence, this muft mightily heighten the obligation to virtue, and ftrengthen the reafon for embracing it. If having regard to the prefent advantages of virtue be confiftent in his fcheme with loving virtue for its own fake, and as amiable in itfelf, and doth not render the embracing it a mercenary or flavifh fervice, why fhould it be inconfiftent with a liberal fervice to be affured that it fhall make us happy for ever? Or why fhould they be accounted greater friends or admirers of virtue, who confider its excellency only with regard to the narrow limits of this tranfitory life, than they who regard it as extending its beneficial influence to a nobler ftate of exiftence, and who believe that it fhall flourifh in unfading beauty and glory to eternity? That an affection in itfelf worthy and excellent fhould grow lefs fo, by confidering it as fo pleafing to the Supreme Being, that he will reward it with everlafting happinefs, and raife it to the higheft perfection it is capable of in a future ftate, would be a ftrange way of reafoning.    •

It was obferved in the account given of the Earl of Shaftefbury's writings, in the preceding letter, that there are feveral paffages in which he acknowledgeth, that the hope of future rewards, and fear of future punifhments, is a great advantage, fecurity, and fupport to virtue. If thefe paffages had been concealed or difguifed, there might have been juft ground of complaint. But they were fairly laid before the reader, as well as thofe that feemed to be of a contrary import, that he might be able to form a judgment of his Lordfhip's fentiments, how far he is confiftent with himfelf, and whether the cenfures be well founded, which he paffeth upon thofe who infift upon the rewards promifed in the gofpel as powerful motives to virtue. He chargeth them as " reducing " religion to fuch a philofophy, as to leave no room for the prin- " ciple of love—and as building a future ftate on the ruins of vir- " tue, and thereby betraying religion and the caufe of God\*." He reprefenteth them as if they were againft a *liberal fervice, flow-*

---

\* Characterift. vol. ii. p. 272, 279.

*ing*

*ing from an esteem and love of God*, or a *sense of duty and gratitude*, and a *love of the dutiful and grateful part, as good and amiable in itself*\*. And he expresly declareth, that " the hope of
" future reward, and fear of future punishment, cannot consist in
" reality with virtue or goodness, if it either stands as essential to
" any moral performance, or as a *considerable motive* to any act,
" of which some better affection ought alone to be a sufficient
" cause †." Here he seems not willing to allow, that the regard
to future retributions ought to be so much as a *considerable motive* to well-doing; and asserteth, that to be influenced by it as
such a motive cannot consist in reality with virtue or goodness.
This is in effect to say, that we ought not to be influenced by a
regard to future rewards and punishments at all: for if they be
believed and regarded at all, they must be a considerable motive;
since, as he himself observes, where infinite rewards are firmly
believed, they must needs have a mighty influence, and will overbalance other motives ‡. If therefore it be inconsistent with true
virtue or goodness, to be influenced by them as a considerable
motive, it is wrong to propose them to mankind: for why should
they be proposed, or to what purpose believed, if it be inconsistent with true goodness to be influenced by them in proportion to
their worth or importance? His Lordship elsewhere observes,
" that, by making rewards and punishments" (*i. e.* the rewards
and punishments proposed in the gospel; for to these he evidently
refers) " the principal motives to duty, the Christian religion in
" particular is overthrown, and the greatest principle, that of
" love, rejected §." When he here brings so heavy a charge
against those who make the rewards of the gospel their *principal
motives*, his meaning seems to be this: That they make the hope
of future eternal happiness a more powerful motive than the present satisfaction and advantages virtue hath a tendency to produce, which are the motives he so largely insists upon, and which
he calls *the common and natural motives to goodness*. And is
the being more animated by the consideration of that eternal
happiness which is the promised reward of virtue, than by any
of the advantages it yields in this present state (though these also

---

\* Characterist. vol. ii. p. 270.     † Ibid. p. 58.
‡ Ibid. p. 68.     § Ibid. p. 279.

are allowed to have their proper weight and influence) fo great a
fault, as to deferve to be reprefented as a fubverting of all religion, and particularly the Chriftian? If the eternal life promifed
in the gofpel be rightly underftood, the hope of it includeth a
due regard to the glory of God, to our own higheft happinefs,
and to the excellence of virtue and true holinefs; all which are
here united, and are the worthieft motives that can be propofed
to the human mind.    There is a perfect harmony between this
hope, and what his Lordfhip fo much extols, the principle of divine love, *fuch as feparates from every thing worldly, fenfual,*
*and meanly interefted:* nor can it be juftly faid, concerning this
hope of the gofpel reward, what he faith of *a violent affection*
*towards private good,* that the more there is of it, *the lefs room*
*there is for an affection towards goodnefs itfelf,* or any good
*and deferving object,* worthy of *love and admiration for its own*
*fake, fuch as God is univerfally acknowledged to be*\*. The very
reward itfelf includeth the perfection of love and goodnefs; and
the happinefs promifed principally confifteth in a conformity to
God, and in the fruition of him; and therefore the being power-
fully animated with the hope of it is perfectly confiftent with *the*
*higheft love and admiration of the Deity, on account of his own*
*infinite excellency.*

It appeareth to me, upon confidering and comparing what hath
been produced out of Lord Shaftefbury's writings, that though
his Lordfhip's good fenfe would not allow him abfolutely to deny
the ufefulnefs of believing future retributions, yet he hath in
effect endeavoured on feveral occafions to caft a flur upon Chriftianity, for propofing and infifting upon what he calls *infinite re-*
*wards:* and thus he hath attempted to turn that to its difadvantage
which is its greateft glory, *viz.* its fetting the important retributions of a future ftate in the cleareft and ftrongeft light, and
teaching us to raife our affections and views to things invifible
and eternal.    His Lordfhip hath, upon the moft careful and diligent revifal of his works, fuffered thofe obnoxious paffages ftill
to continue there.    Nor will any man wonder at this, who confidereth the defign and tendency of many other paffages in his
writings : That he hath taken occafion to ridicule the fpirit of

---

\* Characteriftics, vol. ii. p. 58, 59.

prophecy,

prophecy, and to burlefque feveral paffages of holy writ: That he hath reprefented the fcriptures as abfolutely uncertain, and the important facts by which Chriftianity is attefted, as not to be depended upon: That he hath infinuated injurious reflections upon the character and intentions of the bleffed Founder of our holy religion: That he hath reprefented our faith in the gofpel as having no other foundation than the authority of the ftate; and hath hinted, that it could hardly have ftood the teft of ridicule, and even of *Bartholomew-Fair drollery*, had it been applied to it at its firft appearance *.

As I have been engaged fo far in an examination of Lord Shaftefbury's writings, I fhall take this occafion to make fome farther obfervations on his celebrated *Inquiry concerning Virtue*.

He fets out with obferving, that " religion and virtue appear " to be fo nearly related, that they are generally prefumed infe- " parable companions: but that the practice of the world does " not feem in this refpect to be anfwerable to our fpeculations:" That " many who have had the appearance of great zeal in reli- " gion, have yet wanted the common affections of *humanity* †. " Others again, who have been confidered as mere atheifts, have " yet been obferved to practife the rules of morality, and act in " many cafes with fuch good meaning and affection towards " mankind, as might feem to force an acknowledgment of their " being virtuous ‡." His Lordfhip therefore propofeth to inquire, " What honefty or virtue is, confidered by itfelf, and in what " manner it is influenced by religion: how far religion neceffarily " implies virtue: and whether it be a true faying, that it is im- " poffible for an atheift to be virtuous, or fhare any real degree " of honefty and merit §."

In that part of the *Inquiry*, in which he propofeth to fhew what virtue is, he feems to make it properly confift in good affections towards mankind, or in a man's having " his difpofition of mind " and temper fuitable and agreeing to the good of his kind, or of

---

* See all this clearly fhewn, p. 63, & feq.

† It will readily be acknowledged, that the appearance of religion is often feparated from true virtue: but real practical religion neceffarily comprehendeth virtue; and as far as we are deficient in the practice of virtue, we are deficient in what religion indifpenfibly requireth of us.

‡ Characterift. vol. ii. p. 5, 6.      § Ibid. p. 7.

" the

" the fystem in which he is included, and of which he constituteth
" a part \*." And he had before declared, that some who have
been considered as mere atheists have acted with such good affection towards mankind, as might seem to force an acknowledgment that they are virtuous.

And as this is the notion his Lordship gives of the nature of
virtue; so when he treats of the obligation to virtue, and the reason there is to embrace it, which is the subject of the second
book of the *Inquiry*, he seems to place it in its tendency to promote our happiness in this present life, without taking any notice
of a future state.

Accordingly, many have looked upon the *Inquiry* as designed
to set up such a notion of virtue and its obligations, as is independent on religion, and may subsist without it. And in the progress of that *Inquiry*, his Lordship takes occasion to compare
atheism with superstition or false religion, and plainly gives the
former the preference; and seems sometimes to speak tenderly of
it. Having observed, that nothing can possibly, in a rational
creature, exclude a principle of virtue, or render it ineffectual,
except what either, " 1. Takes away the natural and just sense
" of right and wrong: 2. Or creates a wrong sense of it: 3. Or
" causes the right sense of it to be opposed by contrary affec-
" tions †:" As to the first case, the taking away the natural
sense of right and wrong, he will not allow that atheism, or any
speculative opinion, persuasion, or belief, is capable immediately
or directly to exclude or destroy it; and that it can do it no other
way than *indirectly* by the intervention of opposite affections,
*casually* excited by such belief ‡. As to the second case, the
*wrong sense*, or *false imagination of right and wrong*, he
says, that, " however atheism may be indirectly an occasion
" of men's losing a good and sufficient sense of right and wrong,
" it will not, as atheism merely, be the occasion of setting up a
" false species of it; which only false religion, or fantastical
" opinion, derived immediately from superstition and credulity,
" is able to effect §." As to the third case, which renders a principle of virtue ineffectual, *viz.* its being opposed by contrary

---

\* See Characterist. vol. ii. p. 31. 77, 78. 86, 87, & passim.
† Ibid. p. 40.        ‡ Ibid. p. 44, 45.        § Ibid. p. 46. 51, 52.

affections,

affections, he fays, that " atheifm, though it be plainly deficient,
" and without remedy, in the cafe of ill judgment on the happi-
" nefs of virtue, yet it is not indeed of neceffity the caufe of fuch
" ill judgment : for without an abfolute affent to any hypothefis
" of theifm, the advantages of virtue may poffibly be feen and
" owned, and a high opinion of it eftablifhed in the mind\*."

Our noble author was fenfible of the offence he had given, by
feeming to fpeak favourably of atheifts, and by erecting a fyftem
of virtue independent of religion, or the belief of a Deity ; and
in a treatife he publifhed fome years after the *Inquiry,* intituled,
*The Moralifts, a Philofophical Rhapfody,* makes an apology for it :
That " he has endeavoured to keep the faireft meafures he could
" with men of this fort," (*viz.* atheiftical perfons, and men of no
religion) " alluring them all he was able, and arguing with a
" perfect indifferency even on the fubject of a Deity ; having
" this one chief aim and intention, how in the firft place to re-
" concile thofe perfons to the principles of virtue ; that by this
" means a way might be laid open to religion, by removing
" thofe greateft, if not only obftacles to it, which arife from the
" vices and paffions of men : That it is upon this account chiefly
" he endeavours to eftablifh virtue upon principles by which he
" is able to argue with thofe, who are not yet inclined to own a
" God, or future ftate.—He owns, he has made virtue his chief
" fubject, and in fome meafure independent on religion ; yet he
" fancies he may poffibly appear at laft as high a divine as he is a
" moralift :"—And fays, " He will venture to affirm, that who-
" foever fincerely defends virtue, and is a realift in morality,
" muft of neceffity in a manner, by the fame fcheme of reafon-
" ing, prove as very a realift in divinity†." And elfewhere he
fays, that " we may juftly as well as charitably conclude, that
" it was his defign, in applying himfelf to the men of loofer prin-
" ciples, to lead them into fuch an apprehenfion of the conftitu-
" tion of mankind, and of human affairs, as might form in them
" a notion of order in things, and draw hence an acknowledg-
" ment of the wifdom, goodnefs, and beauty, which is Supreme ;
" that being thus far become profelytes, they might be prepared
" for that divine love which our religion would teach them,

---

\* Characterift. vol. ii. p. 69.　　　† Ibid. p. 266, 267, 268.

" when

" when once they fhould embrace it, and form themfelves to its
" facred character *."

This muft be owned to be a handfome apology: fo that if we
take his Lordfhip's own account of his intention in his *Inquiry*,
it was not to favour atheifm, but rather to reclaim men from it;
to reconcile atheifts to the principles of virtue, and thereby bring
them to a good opinion of religion. It may no doubt be of real
fervice to the interefts of virtue, to endeavour to make men fenfible of its great excellence in itfelf, and its prefent natural advantages, which his Lordfhip fets forth at large, and in a very elegant
manner: and this is no more than hath been often reprefented
by thofe divines, who yet think it neceffary to infift on the rewards and punifhments of a future ftate. There are indeed
many that have faid, what no man who knows the world and
the hiftory of mankind can deny, that in the prefent fituation
of human affairs, a fteady adherence to virtue often fubjects a
man to fevere trials and fufferings; and that it frequently hap-
peneth, that bad and vicious men are in very profperous outward
circumftances; but I fcarce know any that have maintained
what his Lordfhip calls that *unfortunate opinion*, viz. that
" virtue is *naturally* an enemy to happinefs in life;" or who
fuppofe, that " virtue is the *natural ill*, and vice the *natural*
" *good* of any creature †." Nor would any friend to Chriftianity
have found fault with his Lordfhip's endeavouring to fhew, that
by the very frame of the human conftitution, virtue has a friendly
influence to promote our fatisfaction and happinefs, even in this
prefent life; and that vice has naturally a contrary tendency.
But certainly it was no way neceffary to his defign, fuppofing
it to have been, as he profeffes, to ferve the caufe of virtue in the
world, to throw out fo many infinuations as he has done againft
the being influenced by a regard to future rewards and punifhments; as if it argued a higher degree of virtue to have no regard to them at all. And though in feveral paffages he fhews the
advantage which arifes to virtue from religion and the belief of a
deity, yet whilft he feems to allow that virtue may fubfift, and
even be carried to a confiderable degree without it, I am afraid
it will give encouragement to thofe he calls *the men of loofer*

---

* Characteriftics, p. 279.        * Ibid. p. 71, 72.

*principles;*

*principles;* and that inſtead of reclaiming them from atheiſm, it will tend to make them eaſy in it, by leading them to think they may be good and virtuous men without any religion at all.

His Lordſhip ſeems, from a deſire of *keeping the faireſt meaſures,* as he expreſſes it, *with men of this ſort,* to have carried his complaiſance too far, when he aſſerts, that atheiſm has no direct tendency either to take away and deſtroy *the natural and juſt ſenſe of right and wrong,* or to the ſetting up *a falſe ſpecies of it.* This is not a proper place to enter into a diſtinct conſideration of this ſubject. I ſhall content myſelf with producing ſome paſſages from the moſt applauded doctor of modern atheiſm, Spinoſa, and who hath taken the moſt pains to form it into a ſyſtem. He propoſeth, in the fifteenth chapter of his *Tractatus Theologico-politicus,* to treat of *the natural and civil right of every man. De jure uniuſcujuſque naturali & civili.* And the ſum of his doctrine is this; that every man has a natural right to do whatever he has power to do, and his inclination prompts him to; and that the right extends as far as the force. By *natural right, or law, jus et inſtitutum naturæ,* " he underſtands nothing elſe " but the rules of the nature of each individual; according to " which it is determined to exiſt and act after a certain manner *."

And

* Per jus & inſtitutum naturæ nihil aliud intelligo, quam regulas naturæ uniuſcujuſque individui, ſecundum quas unumquodque naturaliter determinatum concipimus ad certo modo exiſtendum & operandum. Ex. gr. piſces a natura determinati ſunt ad natandum, magni ad minores comedendum, adeoque piſces ſummo naturali jure aqua potiuntur, & magni minores comedunt —" Sequitur unumquodque individuum jus ſunimum habere ad omnia quæ poteſt.—Nec hic ullam agnoſcimus differentiam inter homines & reliqua naturæ individua, neque inter homines ratione præditos, & inter alios qui veram rationem ignorant, neque inter fatuos, delirantes, & ſanos." Quare inter homines quamdiu ſub imperio ſolius naturæ vivere conſiderantur, tam ille qui rationem nondum novit, vel qui virtutis habitum nondum habet, ex ſolis legibus appetitus ſummo jure vivit, quam ille qui ex legibus rationis vitam ſuam dirigit. Hoc eſt, ſicuti ſapiens jus ſummum habet ad omnia quæ ratio dictitat, ſive ex legibus rationis vivendi; ſic etiam ignarus et animi impotens ſummum jus habet ad omnia quæ appetitus ſuadet, ſive ex legibus appetitus vivendi. Jus itaque naturale uniuſcujuſque hominis, non ſana ratione, ſed cupiditate et potentia determinatur—Quicquid itaque unuſquiſque qui ſub ſolo naturæ imperio conſideratur, ſibi utile vel ductu ſanæ rationis, vel ex affectuum impetu judicat, id ſummo naturæ jure appetere, et quacun-

que

And after having obferved, that " the large fifhes are determined
" by nature to devour the fmaller, and that therefore they have a
" natural right to do fo," and that " every individual has the
" *higheſt right* to do all things which it has power to do;" he
declares, that " in this cafe he acknowledges no difference be-
" tween men and other individuals of nature, nor between men
" that make a right ufe of their reafon and thofe that do not fo ;
" nor between wife men and fools: That he who does not yet
" know reafon, or has not attained to a habit of virtue, hath as
" much the higheſt natural right to live according to the fole laws
" of appetite, and to do what that inclines him to, as he that di-
" rects his life by the rules of reafon hath to live according to rea-
" fon." Accordingly, he directly afferts, " that the natural
" right of every man is determined not by found reafon, but by
" inclination, or appetite and power : That therefore whatever
" any man, confidered as under the fole government of nature,
" judges to be ufeful for himfelf, whether led by found reafon, or
" prompted by his paffions, he has the higheſt natural right to
" endeavour to procure it for himfelf any way he can, whether
" by force or fraud ; and confequently to hold him for an enemy,
" who would hinder him from gratifying his inclination ; and
" that from hence it follows, that the right and law of nature,
" under which all are born, and for the moſt part live, only
" prohibits that which a man does not defire, or which is out of
" his power ; nor is it averfe to contentions, hatred, wrath, de-

que ratione, five vi, five dolo, five precibus, five quocunque demum modo
facilius poterit, ipfe capere licet, et confequenter pro hoſte habere eum, qui
impedire vult, quo minus animum expleat fuum. Ex quibus fequitur jus et
inſtitutum naturæ fub quo omnes nafcuntur, et maxima ex parte vivunt, nihil
nifi quod nemo cupit, et nemo poteſt, prohibere ; non contentiones, non
odia, non iram, non dolos, nec abfolute aliquid quod appetitus fuadet, aver-
fari. Nec mirum, nam natura non legibus humane rationis, quæ non nifi
verum utile et converfationem intendunt, fed infinitis aliis, quæ totius naturæ, cujus homo particula eſt, æternum ordinem refpiciunt : ex cujus fola
neceſſitate, omnia individua certo modo determinantur ad exiſtendum et
operandum.—Oſtendimus jus naturale fola potentia cujufque determinari.—
Nemo, nifi promiſſo aliud accedat, de fide alterius poteſt effe certus, quan-
doquidem unufquifque naturæ jure dolo agere poteſt ; nec pactis ſtare tene-
tur, nifi fpe majoris boni, vel metu majoris mali.—Tract. Theolog. Polit.
cap. xvi.

" ccit,

" ceit, or to any thing that the appetite puts him upon. And no
" wonder; for nature is not confined within the laws of human
" reason, which only intend the true benefit of mankind, but
" depends upon infinite other things which respect the eternal
" order of universal nature, of which man is only a minute part;
" from the necessity of which alone all individuals are determined
" to exist and operate after a certain manner." He often repeats
it in that chapter, that " natural right is only determined by the
" power of every individual." And he expressly asserts, that
" no man can be sure of another man's fidelity, except he think
" it his interest to keep his promise; since every man has a na-
" tural right to act by fraud or deceit, nor is obliged to stand to
" his engagements, but from the hope of greater good, or fear
" of greater ill."

I think it must be owned, that these principles have not merely
an *indirect* and *casual,* but a plain and direct tendency, to take
away or pervert the natural sense of *right* and *wrong,* or to introduce a false species of it, if the substituting power and inclination instead of reason and justice can be accounted so. This
is to argue consequentially from atheism, when all things are resolved into nature and eternal necessity, by which are understood
the necessary effects of matter and motion. Spinosa indeed owns,
that it is more profitable to live according to the dictates of reason, or the prescriptions of the civil laws, than merely according
to appetite or natural right. But whilst men think they have the
highest natural right to do whatever they have power to do, and
inclination prompts them to, civil laws will be but feeble ties,
and bind a man no farther than when he has not power, or thinks
it not for his interest to break them. Virtue and vice, fidelity
and fraud, are on a level: the one equally founded in natural
right as the other: and how any man can be truly virtuous upon
this scheme I cannot see.

It appears to me therefore, that, instead of endeavouring to
shew that virtue may subsist without religion, or the belief of
a God and a future state, one of the most important services that
can be done to mankind is to shew the close connection there is
between religion and virtue or good order, and that the latter
cannot be maintained without the former. And this indeed
plainly follows from some of the principles laid down by our
noble author in his *Inquiry.*

       Although

Although he feems to have intended to fhew, that an atheift may be really virtuous; and obferves, in a paffage cited above, that, without the belief of a Deity, " the advantages of virtue " may poffibly be feen and owned, and a high opinion of it ef- " tablifhed in the mind," he there adds, " however it muft be " confeffed, that the natural tendency of atheifm is very differ- " ent*:" Where he feems plainly to allow, that atheifm is *naturally* an enemy to virtue, and that the direct tendency of it is to hinder the mind from entertaining a right opinion of virtue, or from having a due fenfe of its advantages. And elfewhere, fpeaking of the atheiftical belief, he obferves, that it " tends to " the weaning the affections from every thing amiable and felf- " worthy: for how little difpofed muft a perfon be to love or " admire any thing as orderly in the univerfe, who thinks the " univerfe itfelf a pattern of diforder †!" To this may be added another remarkable paffage, in which his Lordfhip declares, that " he who only doubts of a God may poffibly lament his own un- " happinefs, and wifh to be convinced: but that he who denies " a Deity is daringly prefumptuous, and fets up an opinion againft " the fentiments of mankind, and being of fociety:" Where he feems plainly to pronounce, that atheifm is fubverfive of all virtue, which in his fcheme hath an effential relation to fociety, and the good of the public. And accordingly he adds, " that it is eafily " feen, that one of thefe" (*viz.* he that only doubts) " may " bear a due refpect to the magiftrates and laws, but not the other," (*viz.* he that denies a Deity), " who being obnoxious to them is " juftly punifhable ‡."

Several paffages might be produced, in which his Lordfhip re-prefents the tendency religion hath to promote virtue. He ob-ferves, that " nothing can more highly contribute to the fixing of " right apprehenfions, and a found judgment or fenfe of right and " wrong, than to believe a God, who is reprefented fuch, as to " be a true model or example of the moft exact juftice, and higheft " goodnefs and worth §!" And again, that " this belief muft " undoubtedly ferve to raife and increafe the affection towards " virtue, and help to fubmit and fubdue all other affections to " this alone.—And that, when this theiftical belief is intire and

* Characterift. vol. ii, p. 69.      † Ibid. p. 70.
‡ Ibid. p. 260.      § Ibid. p. 51.

" perfect,

" perfect, there muſt be a ſteady opinion of the ſuperintendency
" of a Supreme Being, a witneſs and ſpectator of human life, and
" conſcious of whatſoever is felt or acted in the univerſe; ſo that
" in the perfecteſt receſs, or deepeſt ſolitude, there muſt be one
" ſtill preſumed remaining with us, whoſe preſence ſingly muſt
" be of more moment than that of the moſt auguſt aſſembly upon
" earth: and that in ſuch a preſence, as the *ſhame* of guilty ac-
" tions muſt be the greateſt of any, ſo muſt the honour be of
" well-doing, even under the unjuſt cenſures of a world.    And
" in this caſe it is very apparent, how conducing a perfect theiſm
" muſt be to virtue, and how great a deficiency there is in athe-
" iſm\*."      He ſhews, that " where by the violence of rage,
" luſt, or any other counter-working paſſions, the good affection
" may frequently be controuled and overcome—if religion inter-
" poſing creates a belief, that the ill paſſions of this kind, no leſs
" than their conſequent actions, are the objects of a Deity's ani-
" madverſion; it is certain, that ſuch a belief muſt prove a ſea-
" ſonable remedy againſt vice, and be in a particular manner
" advantageous to virtue†.    And he concludes the firſt book of
the *Inquiry concerning Virtue* with obſerving, that " we may
" hence determine juſtly the relation which virtue has to piety:
" the firſt not being complete but in the latter.   And thus," ſaith
he, " the perfection and height of virtue muſt be owing to the
" belief of a God‡.

From theſe paſſages it ſufficiently appears, that thoſe who
would ſeparate virtue from religion cannot properly plead Lord
Shafteſbury's authority for it.    And indeed not only is religion
a friend to virtue, and of the higheſt advantage to it, but as it
ſignifies proper affections and diſpoſitions towards the Supreme
Being, is itſelf the nobleſt virtue.    It is true, that his Lordſhip
ſeems frequently to place virtue wholly in good affections towards
mankind.    But this appears to be too narrow a notion of it.    He
himſelf makes *virtue* and *moral rectitude* to be equivalent terms§;
and moral rectitude ſeems as evidently and neceſſarily to include
right affections towards God, as towards thoſe of our own ſpecies.
He that is deficient in this, muſt certainly be deficient in an eſ-

* Characteriſt. vol. ii. p. 57.          † Ibid. p. 60, 61.
‡ Ibid. p. 76.                           § Ibid. p. 77. 81.

fential branch of good affection, or moral rectitude. If a human
creature could not be faid to be rightly difpofed, that was deftitute
of affections towards its natural parents, can he be faid to be
rightly difpofed, who hath not a due affection towards the *Common Parent*, as Lord Shaftefbury calls him, of all intellectual
beings? This noble writer defcribes virtue to be that which is
beautiful, fair, and amiable in difpofition and action. And he
afks, " Whether there is on earth a fairer matter of fpeculation,
" a goodlier view or contemplation, than that of a *beautiful, pro-
" portioned*, and *becoming* action \* ?" And is there any thing
more beautiful, more juftly proportioned, and more becoming,
than the acting fuitably to the relation we bear to the Supreme
Being, and the ferving, adoring, and honouring him, as far as
we are capable of doing fo? Is there fuch a beauty and harmony
in good affections towards thofe of our own fpecies, and muft
there not be ftill more beauty and excellency in having our minds
formed to proper affections and difpofitions towards our Maker,
Preferver, and Benefactor, the *fource and principle*, to ufe our
author's expreffions, *of all being and perfection, the fupreme and
fovereign beauty, the original of all which is good and amiable?*
His Lordfhip fpeaks in the higheft terms of the pleafing confcioufnefs which is the effect of love or kind affections towards mankind. But certainly there is nothing that can yield more of a
divine fatisfaction, than that which arifeth from a confcioufnefs
of a man's having approved himfelf to the beft of beings, and endeavoured to promote his glory in the world, and to fulfil the
work he hath given us to do. And it will be readily acknowledged, that a neceffary part of this work is the doing good to our
fellow creatures.

The very notion he fo frequently gives of virtue, as having an
effential relation to a fyftem, feems, if underftood in its proper
extent, to include religion, and cannot fubfift without it. His
Lordfhip indeed frequently explains this as relating to the fyftem
of the human fpecies, to which we are particularly related, and
of which we conftitute a part. But he alfo reprefents the human
fyftem as only a part of the univerfal one, and obferves, that
" as man muft be confidered as having a relation abroad to the

---

\* Characterift. vol. ii. p. 105.

" fyftem

" fyftem of his kind; fo even the fyftem of his kind to the animal
" fyftem: this to the world (our earth), and this again to the big-
" ger world, the univerfe\*." And that " having recognize i
" this uniform confiftent fabric, and owned the univerfal fyftem,
" we muft of confequence acknowledge an univerfal mind †."
He afferts, that " good affection, in order to its being of the right
" kind, muft be *intire:*" and that " a partial affection, or focial
" love in part, without regard to a complete fociety or whole, is
" in itfelf an inconfiftency, and implies an abfolute contradic-
" tion ‡." But how can that affection to the fyftem be faid to be
intire, or of the right kind, which hath no regard to the author
of it, on whom the whole fyftem, the order, and even the very
being of it, abfolutely depends? and without whom indeed there
could be properly no fyftem at all, nothing but diforder and confufion? On this occafion it will be proper to produce a remarkable paffage in his third volume; where he obferves, that " if
" what he had advanced in his *Inquiry,* and in his following
" *Philofophic Dialogue,* be real, it will follow, that fince man is fo
" conftituted by means of his rational part, as to be confcious of
" this his more immediate relation to the univerfal fyftem, and
" principle of order and intelligence, he is not only by nature
" *fociable* within the limits of his own fpecies or kind, but in a
" yet more generous and extenfive manner. He is not only born
" to virtue, friendfhip, honefty, and faith, but to piety, adoration,
" and a generous furrender of his mind to whatever happens
" from the *Supreme Caufe* or order of things, which he acknow-
" ledges intirely juft and perfect §."

I have infifted the more largely upon this, becaufe many there
are among us that talk highly of virtue, who yet feem to look
upon religion to be a thing in which they have little or no concern. They allow that men are formed and defigned to be ufeful
to one another; but as to what is ufually called piety towards
God, or thofe acts of religion of which God is the immediate
object, this does not enter at all into their notion of virtue or
morality. They flight it as a matter of no confequence; and
think they may be good and virtuous without it. But not to

---

\* Characterift. vol. ii. p. 286.     † Ibid. p. 290.
‡ Ibid. p. 110. 113, 114.     § Ibid. vol. iii. p. 224.

urge, that religion or a true regard to the deity is the best security for the right performance of every other part of our duty,
and furnisheth the strongest motives and engagements to it (which
certainly ought greatly to recommend it to every lover of virtue),
there is nothing which seems to be capable of a clearer demonstration, from the frame of the human nature, and the powers and
faculties with which man is endued, than that he alone, of all the
species of beings in this lower world, is formed with a capacity
for religion; and that consequently this was one principal design of his creation, and without which he cannot properly answer the end of his being. To what hath been produced from
the Earl of Shaftesbury, I shall add the testimony of another
writer, whom no man will suspect of being prejudiced in favour
of religion, the late Lord Viscount Bolingbroke: who, though
he sometimes seems to make man only a higher kind of brute,
and blames those who suppose that the soul of man was made to
*contemplate God*, yet at other times finds himself obliged to acknowledge, that man was principally designed and formed for religion. Thus, in the specimen he gives of a meditation or soliloquy of a devout theist, he talks of feeling the superiority of
his species; and adds, " I should rouse in myself a grateful
" sense of these advantages above all others, that I am a creature
" capable of knowing, of adoring, and worshipping my Creator,
" capable of discovering his will in the law of my nature, and
" capable of promoting my happiness by obeying it *." And
in another passage, after inveighing, as is usual with him, against
the pride and vanity of philosophers and divines, in exalting
man and flattering the pride of the human heart, he thinks fit to
acknowledge, that " man is a *religious* as well as *social* crea-
" ture, made to know and adore his Creator, to discover and to
" obey his will: That greater powers of reason, and means of im-
" provement, have been measured out to us than to other ani-
" mals, that we might be able to fulfil the *superior* purposes of
" our *destination, whereof religion is undoubtedly the chief:*
" And that in these the elevation and pre-eminence of our spe-
" cies over the inferior animals consist †." I think it plainly

---

* Lord Bolingbroke's Works, vol. v. p. 390, 391. See also to the same
purpose, ibid. p. 340.　　　　　　　† Ibid. p. 470.

followeth

followeth, from what Lord Bolingbroke hath here obferved, and which feems to be perfectly juft and reafonable, that they who live in an habitual neglect of religion, are chargeable with neglecting the chief purpofe of their being, and that in which the true glory and pre-eminence of the human nature doth principally confift: and that confequently they are guilty of a very criminal conduct, and which they can by no means approve to the great author of their exiftence, who gave them their noble powers, and to whom, as the wife and righteous Governor of the world, they muft be accountable for their conduct.

I have been carried farther in my obfervations on this fubject than I intended; but if this may be looked upon as a digreffion, I hope it will not be thought unfuitable to the main defign I have in view.

I am, Sir, &c.

# LETTER VII.

*Mr. Collins's Difcourfe of Free-thinking—He gives a long Cata-*
*logue of Divifions among the Clergy, with a View to fhew the*
*Uncertainty of the Chriftian Religion—His Attempt to prove*
*that there was a general Corruption of the Gofpels in the fixth*
*Century—The Abfurdity of this manifefted—His Pretence that*
*Friendfhip is not required in the Gofpel, though ftrongly re-*
*commended by Epicurus, fhewn to be vain and groundlefs—An*
*Account of his Book, intitled,* The Grounds and Reafons of
the Chriftian Religion—*The pernicious Defign and Tendency*
*of that Book fhewn—He allows Chriftianity no Foundation but*
*the allegorical, i. e. as he underftands it, the falfe Senfe of the*
*Old Teftament Prophecies—His Method unfair and difingenu-*
*ous—Some Account of the principal Anfwers publifhed againft*
*that Book, and againft the* Scheme of Literal Prophecy confidered, *which was defigned to be a Defence of it.*

SIR,

IN the year 1713 came out a remarkable treatife, which it will
be neceffary to take fome notice of, intitled, *A Difcourfe of*
*Free-thinking, occafioned by the Rife and Growth of a Sect called*
*Free-thinkers.* It was written by Anthony Collins, Efq. though
publifhed, as his other writings are, without his name. The
fame gentleman had in 1707 publifhed an *Effay concerning the*
*Ufe of Reafon in Propofitions, the Evidence whereof depends upon*
*human Teftimony:* in which there are fome good obfervations,
mixed with others of a fufpicious nature and tendency. In this
effay there are animadverfions upon fome paffages in a tract
written by Dr. Francis Gaftrel, afterwards Lord Bifhop of Chef-
ter, intitled, *Some Confiderations concerning the Trinity, and the*
*Way of managing that Controverfy,* publifhed in 1702. To the
third edition of which, publifhed in 1707, that learned and judicious divine fubjoined a vindication of it, in anfwer to Mr. Collins's effay. This gentleman alfo diftinguifhed himfelf by writing againft the immateriality and immortality of the human foul,

as

as he afterwards did againſt human liberty and free agency; and
with regard to both theſe, was anſwered by Dr. Samuel Clarke,
with that clearneſs and ſtrength for which that author was ſo remarkable. The *Diſcourſe of Free-thinking* is profeſſedly intended
to demonſtrate the neceſſity and uſefulneſs of free-thinking, from
reaſon, and from the examples of the beſt and wiſeſt men in all
ages. But there is great reaſon to complain of a very unfair and
diſingenuous procedure throughout the whole book. He all
along inſinuates, that thoſe who ſtand up for revealed religion
are enemies to a juſt liberty of thought, and to a free examination and inquiry. His deſign is certainly levelled againſt Chriſtianity, and yet he ſometimes affects to ſpeak of it with reſpect.
He nowhere argues directly againſt it, but takes every occaſion
to throw out ſneers and inſinuations, which tend to raiſe prejudices in the minds of his readers. No ſmall part of this book
is taken up in invectives againſt the clergy, and in giving an
account of the diviſions that have been among them about the
articles of the Chriſtian faith. If there hath been any thing unwarily advanced by any of them, if they have vented any odd or
abſurd opinions, or have in the heat of diſpute caſt raſh and angry
cenſures upon one another, theſe things are here turned to the
diſadvantage of Chriſtianity itſelf: as if this excellent religion
were to be anſwerable for all the paſſions, follies, and exorbitancies of thoſe that make profeſſion of it: or, as if the differences which have been among Chriſtians were a proof, that there
is nothing in the Chriſtian religion that can be ſafely depended
upon. This indeed has been a ſtanding topic for declamation in
all the deiſtical writings, though it is founded upon a principle
which is manifeſtly falſe, *viz.* that whatever has been at any time
controverted is doubtful and uncertain: a principle which, as I
had occaſion to obſerve before, would ſet aſide the moſt important truths of natural religion as well as revealed. But theſe
gentlemen too often act, as if they were not very ſolicitous about
the former, provided they could deſtroy the latter with it.

A great noiſe is raiſed in this *Diſcourſe of Free-thinking*, about
the pious frauds of ancient fathers and modern clergy, and their
forging, corrupting, and mangling of authors; and it is inſinu-
ated, that they have altered and corrupted the Scriptures, as beſt
ſerved their own purpoſes and intereſts. Lord Shafteſbury had
                                                     inſinuated

infinuated the fame thing before; and thefe clamours are continually renewed and repeated, though it hath been often fhewn
with the utmoft evidence, that a general alteration and corruption
of the holy Scriptures was, as the cafe was circumftanced, an
impoffible thing.    And we have the plaineft proof in fact, that
even in the darkeft and moft corrupt ages of the Chriftian church,
the Scriptures were not altered in favour of the corruptions and
abufes which were then introduced; fince no traces of thofe corruptions are to be found there: on the contrary, they furnifh the
moft convincing arguments for detecting and expofing thofe corruptions.

But what he feems to lay the greateft ftrefs upon, is a paffage
from Victor of Tmuis, in which it is faid, that at the command
of the emperor Anaftafius, the holy gofpels were corrected and
amended.    This our author calls *an account of a general alteration of the four gofpels in the fixth century:* and he fays, it
was difcovered by Dr. Mills, and was very little known before\*.
But then he fhould have taken notice of what Dr. Mills has added, *viz.* that it is certain as any thing can be, that no fuch
altered gofpels were ever publifhed; and that if the fact had been
thus, it would have been mentioned with deteftation by all the
hiftorians, and not be found only in one blind paffage of a puny
chronicle.    Indeed there cannot be a plainer inftance of the power
of that prejudice and bigotry againft Chriftianity, which has poffeffed the minds of the gentlemen that glory in the name of *Free-
thinkers,* than their laying hold on fuch a ftory as this to prove a
general corruption of the gofpels, contrary to all reafon and common fenfe.    Let us fuppofe the emperor Anaftafius to have had an
intention to alter the copies of the gofpels (which yet it is highly
improbable he fhould attempt), he could only have got fome of the
copies into his hands: there would ftill have been vaft numbers
of copies fpread through different parts of the empire, which he
could not lay hold of, efpecially confidering how much he was
hated and oppofed: or if we fhould make the abfurd and impoffible
fuppofition of his being able to get all the copies throughout the
eaft into his hands; yet as there were ftill innumerable copies in
the weft, where he had little or no power, they would have im-

\* Difcourfe of Free-thinking, p. 89, 90.

mediately

mediately detected the alteration and corruption, if there had been any. Loud complaints would have been made of the attempt; but no such complaints were ever made: and in fact it is evident, that there have been no greater differences since that time between the eastern and western copies than there were before. And it is undeniably manifest, from great numbers of authors, who lived in the preceding ages, and whose works are come down to us, that the scriptures, a great part of which is transcribed into their writings, were the same before that pretended alteration, that they have been since.

With a view of shewing the uncertainty of the sacred text of the New Testament, this author takes notice of the various readings collected by Dr. Mills, which he says amount to thirty thousand. This objection has been so fully exposed, and this whole matter set in so clear a light by the famous Dr. Bentley, under the character of *Phileleutherus Lipsiensis*, that one should think it would have been for ever silenced. And yet it has been frequently repeated since by the writers on that side, and particularly by Dr. Tindal, in his *Christianity as old as the Creation*, without taking the least notice of the clear and satisfactory answer that had been returned to it.

The ancient prophets have been the constant objects of the sneers and reproaches of these gentlemen: and accordingly this writer has told us, that, *to obtain the prophetic spirit, they played upon music, and drank wine*[*]. That they might very lawfully and properly drink wine, in a country where there was great plenty of it, may well be allowed, without any diminution of their character; and that they employed music, particularly in singing praises to God, may be concluded from several passages in the sacred writings. But certainly, if they had the prophetic spirit at all, neither wine nor music gave it them, or could enable them to foretel things to come. But then he does them the honour to say, *they were great free-thinkers*, and that " they writ with " as great liberty against the established religion of the Jews " (which the people looked on as the institution of God himself), " as if they looked upon it all to be imposture." That the prophets freely declared against the Jewish corruptions, against their

---

[*] Discourse of Free-thinking, p. 153.

idolatries and immoralities, and againſt their laying the chief
ſtreſs on ritual obſervances, whilſt they neglefted the weightier
matters of the law, is very true.　And this is here, by an unpardonable
diſingenuity, repreſented as an inveighing againſt the
Moſaic diſpenſation, as if they did not believe it to have been
originally of divine inſtitution: whereas it is to the laſt degree
evident, that they all along ſuppoſe the law of Moſes to have been
inſtituted by God himſelf, and reprove the people and prieſts, not
for their adherence to that law, but for their deviations from it,
and neglef of the moſt important duties there enjoined.

This gentleman has given us a long liſt of *free-thinkers;* but
there is none of them all of whom he ſeems to ſpeak with greater
complacency than Epicurus, though he owns that his ſyſtem
was a *Syſtem of Atheiſm*\*.　And after having obſerved, that Epicurus
was eminent for that *moſt divine of all virtues, friendſhip,*
he ſays, *that we Chriſtians ought to have a high veneration of
him* on this account, *becauſe even our holy religion itſelf does
not any where particularly require of us this virtue.*　The noble
author of the *Charaƈteriſtics* had made the ſame obſervation before
him: and both the one and the other cite a paſſage from biſhop
Taylor, to ſhew that there is no word properly ſignifying *friendſhip*
in the New Teſtament.　Thus they have happily hit upon
an inſtance in which the morality of the goſpel is defeftive, and
exceeded by that of Epicurus.　But it ought to be conſidered,
that friendſhip, when underſtood of a particular affeftion between
two or more perſons, is not always a virtue.　It may in ſome caſes
incroach upon a nobler and more extenſive benevolence, and
may cauſe perſons, and hath often done ſo, to ſacrifice the moſt
important duties to private affeftions.　Or, where this is not the
caſe, yet where friendſhip ariſeth from a particular conformity
of natural tempers and inclinations between ſome men and others,
or, as Lord Shafteſbury expreſſes it, that peculiar relation which
is formed by a conſent and harmony of minds, it does not properly
come under the preſcription of a law, nor can be the matter
of a general precept.　But if it be underſtood of that benevolence
which uniteth virtuous minds in the ſacred bands of a
ſpecial cordial affeftion, never was this more ſtrongly recom-

\* Diſcourſe of Free-thinking, p. 90. 129.

mended

mended and enforced than in the gospel of Jesus. It requireth us to love and do good to all mankind, in which sense bishop Taylor rightly observes, in the very passage referred to, that *Christian charity is friendship to all the world.* And the last-mentioned noble writer asketh, *Can any friendship be so heroical as love to mankind\*?* And, besides this general affection towards all men, the gospel requireth us to cultivate a still nearer, stronger, and more intimate affection towards good men, whom it representeth as obliged to *love one another with a pure heart fervently.* Lord Shaftesbury is pleased to mention St. Paul's saying, that *perhaps for a good man one would even dare to die,* and observes, that the *apostle is so far from founding any precept upon it, that he ushers it in with a very dubious peradventure†.* But it is to be supposed, his Lordship had not considered that noble passage of St. John, *Hereby perceive we the love of God, because he, our Lord Jesus Christ, laid down his life for us, and we ought to lay down our lives for the brethren,* 1 John iii. 16. Can friendship be carried to a nobler height, or be enforced by more engaging motives, or a more powerful example? Can it be pretended, that the *most divine of all virtues, friendship,* is not *required* of us in our *holy religion,* when we are there required, if properly called to it, to give so glorious a proof of our friendship to our Christian brethren, whom we are taught to regard as united to us by the most sacred ties?

We shall dismiss this *Discourse of Free-thinking* with observing, that as the author of it hath put Solomon into his list of freethinkers, for asserting, as he pretends he did, the mortality of the soul, and denying a future state, though the contrary is manifest from what Solomon himself saith, Eccles. xii. 7. 14. so he takes that occasion to inform his reader, that the immortality of the soul was *first taught by the Egyptians,* and was an *invention of theirs‡.* Mr Toland had said the same thing before in his letters to Serena§; and this may help us to judge how far some of our boasted free-thinkers are from being friends to natural religion taken in its just extent.

Soon after this *Discourse of Free-thinking* appeared, the re-

---

* Characterist. vol. ii. p. 229.          † Ibid. vol. i. p. 102.
‡ Discourse of Free-thinking, p. 152.          § Letter 2d.

verend Mr. Hoadley, now lord bishop of Winchester, published some very sensible *Queries addressed to the Authors of a late* " *Discourse of Free-thinking;*" in which the dishonest insinuations, false reasonings, and pernicious tendency of that treatise are laid open in a short and concise, but clear and convincing manner. There were several other ingenious pamphlets published to the same purpose: but none of them was so generally admired and applauded as the *Remarks on a late* " *Discourse of Free-thinking,*" *by Philcleutherus Lipsiensis, i. e.* Dr. Bentley. This learned writer hath so fully and effectually detected and exposed the great and inexcusable mistakes committed by the author of that discourse, his blunders and absurdities, his frequent wrong translations, and misunderstanding of the authors he quotes, or wilful perversions and misrepresentations of their sense, that it might, one should think, have discouraged him from appearing any more as a writer in this cause\*.

But such was this gentleman's zeal against Christianity, that, some years after, he thought fit to attack it in another way, which was more subtil and more dangerous.  He published a *Discourse on the Grounds and Reasons of the Christian Religion*, London, 1724, 8vo. as if his design had been to do real service to Christianity, by establishing it upon a sure and solid foundation.  The scheme he lays down is this: that our Saviour and his apostles put the whole proof of Christianity solely and entirely upon the prophecies of the Old Testament: that if these proofs are valid,

Chris-

---

\* There was a French translation of the " Discourse of Free-thinking," carried on under Mr. Collins's own eye, and printed at the Hague in 1714, though it bears London on the title page.  In this translation several material alterations are made, and a different turn is given to several passages from what was in Mr. Collins's original English.  This is plainly done with a view to evade the charges which had been brought against him by Dr. Bentley, under the character of " Philcleutherus Lipsiensis," some of which charges that bore very properly against Mr. Collins's book, as it was first published, will appear impertinent to those that judge only by this translation.  But care is taken not to give the least notice of these alterations to the reader, upon whom it is made to pass for a faithful version of the original.  All this is clearly shewn by the author of the French translation of " Dr. Bentley's Remarks on the Discourse of Free-thinking," which was printed at Amsterdam in 1738, under the title of " Friponerie Laique des pretendus Esprits forts d'Angleterre: The Lay-craft of the pretended Free-thinkers of England."

Chriſtianity is eſtabliſhed upon its true foundation; but if they are invalid, and the arguments brought from thence be not concluſive, and the prophecies cited from thence be not fulfilled, *Chriſtianity has no juſt foundation, and is therefore falſe.* Accordingly he ſets himſelf to ſhew, that the prophecies cited in the New Teſtament from the Old, in proof of Chriſtianity, four or five of which he particularly conſiders, are only typical and allegorical proofs; and that allegorical proofs are no proofs, according to *ſcholaſtic rules,* i. e. as he plainly intends it, according to the rules of ſound reaſon and common ſenſe. He aſſerts, that the expeÄtation of the Meſſiah did not obtain among the Jews, till a little before the time of our Saviour's appearing, when they were under the oppreſſion of the Romans; and that the apoſtles put a new interpretation on the Jewiſh books, which was not agreeable to the obvious and literal meaning of thoſe books, and was contrary to the ſenſe of the Jewiſh nation: That Chriſtianity deriveth all its authority from the Old Teſtament, and is wholly revealed there, not literally, but myſtically and allegorically; and that therefore Chriſtianity is the allegorical ſenſe of the Old Teſtament, and is not improperly called *Myſtical Judaiſm;* and that conſequently the Old Teſtament is, properly ſpeaking, the *ſole true Canon of Chriſtians:* That the allegorical reaſoning is ſet up by St. Paul, and the other apoſtles, as the true and only reaſoning proper to bring all men to the faith of

land." This gentleman, Mr. de la Chapelle, has made it appear, that Mr. Collins, and his Tranſlator, who aÄted under his direÄtion, have been guilty of palpable falſifications and frauds; which ill became one who had in that very book raiſed a loud outcry againſt the clergy for " corrupting and mangling of authors, and for pious frauds in the tranſlation or publiſhing of books." And I cannot but obſerve on this occaſion, what muſt have occurred to every one that has been much converſant in the deiſtical writers, that it would be hard to produce any perſons whatſoever who are chargeable with more unfair and fraudulent management in their quotations, in curtailing, adding to, or altering, the paſſages they cite, or taking them out of their connexion, and making them ſpeak direÄtly contrary to the ſentiments of the authors. It is well known that they affeÄt frequently to quote Chriſtian divines; but they ſeldom do it fairly, and often wilfully miſrepreſent and pervert their meaning. Many glaring inſtances of this ſort might be produced out of the writings of the moſt eminent deiſtical authors, if any man ſhould think it worth his while to make a collection to this purpoſe.

Chriſt,

Chrift; and all other methods of reafoning are wholly difcarded. Thus it appeareth, that the evident defign of this auther's book is to fhew, that the only foundation on which Chriftianity is built is falfe: that the firft publifhers of the gofpel laid the whole fupport and credit of Chrift's divine miffion, and of the religion he taught, upon pretended Jewifh prophecies, applied in a fenfe which had no foundation in the prophecies themfelves, and contrary to the plain original meaning and intention of thofe prophecies; which the Jews had never underftood nor applied in that fenfe, and which had nothing to fupport it but allegory; *i. e.* the mere fancy of him that fo applies it. If we needed any farther proof of our author's intentions towards Chriftianity, it might be obferved, that he reprefents Jefus and his apoftles as having founded their religion on *prophecy*, in like manner as the feveral fects among the heathens did theirs on *divination*. And thefe prophets, he tells us, manifefted their divine infpiration by the *difcovery of loft goods, and telling of fortunes*\*. So that he makes Jefus and his apoftles found their religion on the predictions of fortune-tellers and diviners, and thofe mifapplied too; which plainly fhews what a defpicable idea this writer intended to convey of the Chriftian religion, and the bleffed author of it.

Few books have made a greater noife than this did at its firft publication. The turn given to the controverfy had fomething in it that feemed new, and was managed with great art; and yet, when clofely examined, it appears to be weak and trifling. The very fundamental principle of the author's whole fyftem, viz. That the prophecies of the Old Teftament are the fole foundation of Chriftianity, and the only proofs and evidences infifted upon by our Saviour and his apoftles in confirmation of it, is abfolutely falfe; as any one may know that can read the New Teftament: for it is undeniable, that our bleffed Lord often appealeth to his wonderful works, as manifeft proofs that the Father had fent him; and the apoftles in like manner frequently appealed to his miracles and refurrection, and to the miracles wrought, and the extraordinary gifts of the Holy Ghoft poured forth in his name, as uncontefted proofs of the divine authority of that fcheme of religion which they publifhed to the world.

---

\* Difcourfe on the Grounds, &c. of the Chriftian Religion, chap. vi.

With

With regard to the prophecies, the courfe of his reafoning really amounts to this: that becaufe there are difficulties and obfcurities attending fome very few paffages cited out of the Old Teftament in the New, as having a reference to the times of the gofpel; and we cannot well, at this diftance, fee the propriety of the application; therefore the whole of the New Teftament is falfe; and the accounts given of our Saviour, his excellent difcourfes, the miracles he performed, and the illuftrious atteftations given to him from heaven, are of no force at all; and all the arguments drawn from thence are ineffectual and vain. It is in the fame ftrain of reafoning that he concludes, that becaufe four or five prophecies (for he produces no more) cited in the New Teftament from the Old, feem not to relate to the gofpel times in a literal, but in a fecondary and typical, *i. e.* as he explains it, an allegorical fenfe, therefore none of the Old Teftament prophecies can be applied directly and literally at all, or have any relation to our Saviour and the gofpel difpenfation. And becaufe the modern Jews conteft the application of fome prophecies to the Meffiah, which are applied to our Saviour in the New Teftament, therefore the ancient Jews allowed none of thofe prophecies to be applied to the Meffiah, which in the New Teftament are applied to him: and yet the contrary is invincibly evident from their writings ftill extant, by which it appeareth, that moft of the prophecies applied to our Saviour in the New Teftament, and many others not there mentioned, were underftood of the Meffiah by the ancient Jews, as many of them ftill are by the moft celebrated of the modern Jews themfelves. And it was certainly a ftrange attempt in this author, to endeavour to prove, that the Jews had no notion or expectation of the Meffiah, till a little before the times of our Saviour, when all their writers, with one confent, ancient and modern, who are the proper judges . in fuch a cafe, agree, that there had been all along among them an hope and expectation of the Meffiah, founded, as they univerfally believed, on the facred writings. It may further let us fee this writer's ingenuity, that becaufe St. Paul makes ufe of an allegory in his epiftle to the Galatians, though he there manifeftly introduces it by way of illuftration, and exprefsly declares to thofe to whom he writes, that thefe things are *allegorized*, therefore he layeth the whole ftrefs of his arguments upon allegory as

H 4                                              the

the principal and only proof; and that he and the other apoftles abfolutely rejeft all other reafoning but the allegorical, which is no reafoning at all.    And yet any one that ever read St. Paul's epiftles muft know, that he often makes ufe of reafoning and argument, and very clofe reafoning too.    The laft inftance I fhall produce of this author's extraordinary way of arguing is, that becaufe the apoftles and facred writers of the New Teftament acknowledge the authority of the Old, and draw proofs from thence, therefore the New Teftament is of no authority at all, and the Old Teftament is the fole Canon of Chriftians, *i. e.* becaufe there is an harmony between the Old Teftament and New, and becaufe the former had foretold a glorious perfon who was to introduce a new and more perfeft difpenfation; therefore that new and more perfeft difpenfation is no new difpenfation at all, but is abfolutely and in all refpefts the fame with that old and more imperfeft one in which it was prefigured and foretold, and which was defigned to prepare the way for it.

Having made thefe general obfervations, it will be proper to take notice of fome of the anfwers that were made to this book; and here that which was written by Dr. Chandler, the lord bifhop of Coventry and Litchfield, deferves fpecial notice.    It was publifhed in 1725, and is intitled *A Defence of Chriftianity, from the Prophecies of the Old Teftament.*    This is a very learned and elaborate performance, and executed with great judgment.    In it the bifhop firft fets himfelf to fhew, that there was a general expeftation of the Meffiah at the time when our Saviour appeared; and he traces this expeftation from that time to the very age of the prophets themfelves.    He then proceeds to fhew, that to fupport this expeftation there were exprefs literal prophecies, that truly concern the Meffiah, of which he produces twelve, which he particularly confiders; and he proves with great evidence, that they were applied by the ancient Jews to the Meffiah, and that it appeareth from the prophecies themfelves, that they could not be applied to any other.    He then goes on to fhew, that, befides thefe, there were typical prophecies to the fame effect, and which were intended to be applied to the Meffiah.    The author of the *Grounds,* &c. had every where reprefented typical prophecies, as fignifying no more than that they were afterwards applied in an allegorical fenfe, and had afferted

that

that there appear not the least traces of a typical intention in the writers of the Old Testament, or any other Jews of those times. In opposition to which, the bishop plainly proves, from the writings of the prophets themselves, that they were wont to prophesy by types, and to speak of themselves or others as types of other persons and people, on purpose to foretel what should be done by or to single persons or nations hereafter; of which he gives several instances: That therefore typical actions and typical discourses made part of the prophetic language, and were understood by the people to carry a reference to something future. And consequently, if the prophets speak of the Messiah in their own persons, or of other persons as types of him, there is nothing in this but what is agreeable to the known prophetic language. He makes it appear, that the prophets themselves understood some of those prophecies as typical of the Messiah, and, at the time of delivering those prophecies, gave intimations that they were thus to be referred: That accordingly the Jews acknowledge, that there were types in the Old Testament, and particularly that there were types of the Messiah; and that both the ancient and modern Jews understand many texts of the Messiah as the Christians do, which are plainly typical; and he shews, that there were good reasons for covering some of the events relating to the Messiah under the veil of types, which were not to be fully explained till the age in which they were fulfilled.

He next proceeds to give a distinct account of the texts pretended by the author of the *Grounds* to be misapplied. He justly observes, that if the principal characters of the Messiah be evidently found in the Jewish scriptures, to the same intent for which they are cited by Christ and his apostles, it is unreasonable to quit a certain truth, because every individual circumstance is not equally clear; and it doth not plainly appear at this time how two or three authorities are to be applied to the Messiah. And that the expression *that it might be fulfilled*, on which the author layeth so great a stress, was sometimes designed by the Jews to mean no more than that something answered alike in both cases, or that there was a suitableness in the cause or circumstance of one event to the other: and he shews, that the same way of speaking continueth among the Jews to this day.

With regard to the allegorical way, he observes, that it was chiefly

chiefly in condefcenfion to the Jewifh Chriftians that St. Paul at all ufed it; but that nothing can be more falfe and difingenuous, than to pretend that he never ufed any other way of reafoning than this. Finally, he thinks it may be allowed, that, confider-ing the illuftrious atteftations given to our Saviour, which plainly fhewed that he was a teacher fent from God, his interpretation of the prophecies ought to be acquiefced in; fince he wrought his miracles by the fame fpirit by which thofe prophecies were delivered; and he inftances in feveral prophecies, the interpre-tation of which given by our Lord, though different from that of the Jews, was actually fulfilled and verified by the event.

There was another learned author of the fame name with the bifhop, Mr. (now Dr.) Samuel Chandler, who alfo diftinguifhed himfelf on this occafion, in a book intitled, *A Vindication of the Chriftian Religion*, publifhed in 1725, 8vo. In the former part of that work, he hath a difcourfe on the nature and ufe of mi-racles; in which, after having ftated the true notion of a miracle, and given the characters that diftinguifh true miracles from falfe, he clearly vindicates the miracles of our Saviour, and fhews, that as they were circumftanced, they were convincing proofs of his divine miffion. The fecond part of the fame book is particularly defigned as an anfwer to the author of the *Grounds and Reafons of the Chriftian Religion*. After having fhewn, that the prophe-cies of the Old Teftament are not the only proofs of Chriftianity, and that it is very abfurd to pretend, as that author had done, that the Old Teftament is the fole canon of Chriftians, he clearly evinceth, that many of thofe prophecies had a farther reference than to the times when they were firft delivered; and particu-larly, that they contain a defcription of a great and good perfon, to proceed from David, who, notwithftanding his fufferings, fhould be highly exalted, and under whom true religion and righteoufnefs fhould be more extenfive than before; that thefe prophecies relate principally to a fpiritual falvation and deliver-ance; and that the Jews in our Saviour's time, as appeareth from their moft ancient writings, applied many of thofe prophecies to the Meffiah. He next treats of the double fenfe of prophecies, which the author of the *Grounds* had ridiculed, and fhews that there is no abfurdity in fuppofing, that as fome prophecies relate wholly to the Meffiah, fo others may relate partly to his time, and

and partly to the times when they were firſt delivered: and that
this double ſenſe of the prophecies was originally intended, and
was ſo underſtood by the Jews. He accounts for the particular
places excepted againſt by the author of the *Grounds*, and obſerves, as the biſhop had done, that the apoſtles ſometimes quote
paſſages from the Old Teſtament, not in a way of direct proof,
but to illuſtrate the argument they are upon ; and ſometimes by
way of accommodation, to ſignify a correſpondence of events,
and to deſcribe things that happened in their own times, by expreſſions derived from the ancient prophetic writings. That as
arguments *ad hominem* have been always allowed, ſo if there were
ſome particular paſſages in the ancient prophets, which were applied by the Jews to the Meſſiah, the reference of which was not
ſo natural and clear, the apoſtles were fully juſtifiable in applying them to Jeſus Chriſt, in their reaſonings with the Jews, as
far as they did agree with his perſon and character ; but that there
are few inſtances of this kind ; nor did the apoſtles make uſe of
this way of argument, except to the Jews or Jewiſh proſelytes ;
and even to them they did not put the chief ſtreſs on theſe things,
but laid before them other ſolid and ſubſtantial proofs of Chriſtianity. Finally, if the difficulties which attend the quotations
out of the Old Teſtament were much greater than they really
are, yet this would not affect the credit or truth of the Chriſtian
religion, which hath many ſo evidences to ſupport it.

There were ſeveral other good anſwers publiſhed to the
*Grounds,* &c. and which were ſo well executed, as to deſerve
that a particular account ſhould be given of them, if my preſcribed limits would allow. Among others, Dr. Bullock's ſermons were very juſtly and highly eſteemed, in which " the rea-
" ſoning of Chriſt and his apoſtles in their defence of Chriſtianity
" is conſidered. To which is prefixed, a preface, taking notice
" of the falſe repreſentations of Chriſtianity, and of the apoſtles'
" reaſoning in defence of it, in a book intitled *A Diſcourſe of the*
" *Grounds and Reaſons of the Chriſtian Religion,*" London, 8vo.
1725. Dr. Sykes alſo publiſhed an *Eſſay upon the Truth of the
Chriſtian Religion, wherein its real Foundation in the Old Teſtament is ſhewn, occaſioned by the* " *Diſcourſe of the Grounds,*"
London, 8vo. 1725. In this book it is both clearly proved, that
there are ſome direct prophecies relating to the Meſſiah in the

Old

Old Testament, especially in the book of Daniel; and there are many good observations to shew, that the New Testament writers often quote passages by way of accommodation and allusion only; and that most of the texts produced as prophecies by the author of the *Grounds* are of this kind. To these may be added, an ingenious treatise, intitled, *The true Grounds and Reasons of the Christian Religion, in Opposition to the false ones set forth in a late Book, intitled " The Grounds, &c."* London, 8vo, 1725. *Letters to the Author of the " Discourse of the Grounds," shewing, that Christianity is supported by Facts well attested; that the Words of Isaiah, Chap.* vii. 14. *in their literal Sense are a Prophecy of the Birth and Conception of the Messias; and that the Gospel-Application of several other Passages in the Old Testament is just,* by John Greene, 8vo, London, 1726. Mr. Whiston also published, *The literal Accomplishment of Scripture-Prophecies, being a full Answer to a late " Discourse of the Grounds, &c."* London, 8vo, 1724: and he afterwards published *A Supplement to the literal Accomplishment of the Scripture-Prophecies,* London, 8vo. 1725. It may be proper also to mention a book, which was occasioned by the *Grounds*, &c. though not directly in answer to it, intitled, *The Use and Intent of Prophecy in the several Ages of the Church,* by Dr. Thomas Sherlock, bishop of London. This is an excellent performance, in which a regular series of prophecy is deduced through the several ages from the beginning, and its great usefulness shewn. The various degrees of light are distinctly marked out, which were successively communicated in such a manner as to answer the great ends of religion, and the designs of Providence, till those great events to which they were intended to be subservient should receive their accomplishment. There was another valuable book, which, though not published till some years after, may be considered as peculiarly designed against the *Grounds*, &c. viz. *The Argument from Prophecy, in Proof that Jesus is the Messiah, vindicated, in some Considerations on the Prophecies of the Old Testament, as the Grounds and Reasons of the Christian Religion,* by Moses Lowman, London, 8vo, 1733. The last book I shall here take notice of, as published on this occasion, was *A Review of the Controversy between the Author of the " Discourse of the Grounds and Reasons of the Christian Religion" and his Adversaries, faries, in a Letter to the Author*, 8vo, 1726, by Mr. Thomas Jeffrey. This is drawn up in a clear and judicious manner, and was deservedly well esteemed.

The author of the *Grounds*, &c. thought fit, in 1727, to publish a second book, which was to pass for a defence of his first, in answer to his several adversaries, and particularly to the bishop of *Litchfield*. It was intitled, *The Scheme of Literal Prophecy considered*. In this book he very slightly passeth over the chief things he ought to have proved, and on which in his former book he had laid the greatest stress. Instead of confirming what he had so positively asserted before, that the prophecies of the Old Testament were the only proof on which Christianity is founded, he only shews that they are part of the proof insisted on by our Saviour and his apostles, and most disingenuously supposes, that his adversaries would not allow them to be any proofs at all. He had affirmed with great confidence, that none of the ancient Jews ever understood any of those prophecies of the Messiah, which are applied to Christ in the New Testament: but the utmost that he now attempts to shew is, that some of those prophecies were not understood by the ancient Jews of the Messiah; and even for this he can give no other reason than that some of the modern Jews do not so apply them. He has nothing now to prove, that the Old Testament is the only canon of Christians, or that the allegorical sense is the only sense of prophecies intended by our Saviour and his apostles. And whereas his answerers had urged, that though most of the prophecies applied in the New Testament to our Lord Jesus Christ were literally fulfilled in him, yet some particular passages might be used only in a way of illustration and accommodation, and not as direct proofs; he sets himself, as his manner is, with a mighty pomp of quotations, to shew the absurdity of supposing, that the apostles' method of citing prophecies was nothing but a mere accommodation of phrases, as if his adversaries had held, that all the passages cited in the New Testament from the Old were applied only by way of accommodation, which not one of them ever asserted. He puts on an appearance of answering what the bishop had alledged concerning the general and constant tradition, which had obtained among the Jews with regard to the Messiah; and he considers the twelve prophecies that learned writer had produced

duced, as literally fulfilled in the Meffiah. But any one that will take the pains to compare what he hath here offered with the book he pretends to anfwer, will find how little he has been able to fay, that is really to the purpofe, and how far he has been from invalidating the proofs which had been brought. He often flips over the moft material things that had been urged, and, as the bifhop afterwards complained, takes no more notice of them than if he had not read them. If he can but find a fingle paffage in any Jewifh or Chriftian writer, though but a modern one, and contrary to the general confent of interpreters, this is laid hold on to fet afide the bifhop's interpretation, and to fhew that the Jews did not generally underftand a prophecy of the Meffiah, or apply it to him, though clear evidence had been produced that they fo applied it.

But there is no part of the *Literal Scheme, &c.* which the author has fo much laboured, as that where he hath collected together all that he could meet with againft the antiquity and authority of the book of Daniel, and the prophecies contained there. This occafioned a fecond anfwer from the learned bifhop, intitled, *A Vindication of the Defence of Chriftianity from the Prophecies of the Old Teftament*, publifhed in 1728, in which he hath largely and very folidly vindicated the antiquity and authority of the book of Daniel, and the application of the prophecies there contained to the Meffiah, againft the author's objections: and hath alfo fully obviated whatfoever he had farther advanced againft the antiquity and univerfality of the tradition and expectation among the Jews concerning the Meffiah. The learned Dr. Rogers had before this publifhed his very valuable fermons, on the *Neceffity of divine Revelation, and the Truth of the Chriftian Religion.* " To " which is prefixed a preface, with fome remarks on a late book, " intitled, *The Scheme of Literal Prophecy confidered*," London, 1727, 8vo. Soon after which, there came out an ingenious pamphlet, intitled, *The true Grounds of the Expectation of the Meffiah*, in two letters by *Philalethes*, London, 1727, faid to be written by Dr. Sykes. Dr. Bullock alfo appeared again to great advantage in this controverfy, in a treatife intitled, *The Reafoning of Chrift and his Apoftles vindicated*, in two parts. 1. *A Defence of the Argument from Miracles, proving the Argument from Prophecy not neceffary to a rational Defence of our Religion.*

*gion.* 2. *A Defence of the Argument from Prophecy, proving the Chriſtian Scheme to have a rational Foundation upon the Prophecies of the Old Teſtament*, in anſwer to a book intitled *The Scheme of Literal Prophecy conſidered*, London, 1728, 8vo. In this book, Dr. Bullock finds great fault with our author's way of managing the argument: he obſerves, that he has not only " raked together the unguarded expreſſions of ingenious men, " but by altering, adding to, and curtailing paſſages referred to, " and by other diſingenuous methods unbecoming a man of hon- " our and ſincerity, wreſteth them to purpoſes apparently contrary " to their true import." And yet no man had raiſed a louder outcry againſt the clergy, for abuſing, corrupting, and mangling of authors to ſerve their own purpoſes, than this gentleman had done in his *Diſcourſe of Free-thinking.* The biſhop, in his *Vin-dication*, makes the ſame complaint againſt him; ſo does Dr. Sa-muel Chandler, who publiſhed, on this occaſion, a judicious *Vin-dication of the Antiquity and Authority of Daniel's Prophecies, and their Application to Jeſus Chriſt:* in anſwer to the objec-tions of the author of the *Scheme of Literal Prophecy conſidered*, London, 1728, 8vo. About the ſame time was publiſhed, *Chriſt-anity the Perfection of all Religion, natural and revealed; where-in ſome of the principal Prophecies relating to the Meſſiah in the Old Teſtament are ſhewn to belong to him in the literal Senſe, in Oppoſition to the Attempts of the Literal Scheme,* &c. by Thomas Jeffreys, London, 1728. I ſhall conclude this letter with obſer-ving, that this attack againſt Chriſtianity, though carried on with great art as well as malice, produced this advantage, that it gave occaſion to a full and accurate examination into the nature, de-ſign, and extent of many of the Old Teſtament prophecies, and to the placing ſome difficult paſſages in a clearer light.

# LETTER   VIII.

*Mr. Woolſton's Diſcourſes on the Miracles of our Saviour—*
*Under pretence of ſtanding up for the allegorical Senſe of*
*Scripture, he endeavours abſolutely to deſtroy the Truth of the*
*Facts recorded in the Goſpels—His diſingenuous Repreſentation*
*of the Senſe of the Fathers on this Head, and his falſe Quota-*
*tions—He charges the Accounts given of Chriſt's Miracles as*
*abſurd, falſe, and incredible—His groſs and profane Buf-*
*foonry, and baſe Reflections on the Character of our Saviour;*
*and yet he pretends a Zeal for his Honour and Meſſiahſhip—A*
*Specimen of his way of Reaſoning with regard to ſeveral of*
*Chriſt's Miracles, and his Reſurrection—Many good Anſwers*
*publiſhed againſt him.*

SIR,

I HAVE already taken notice of ſeveral attempts, which were
manifeſtly intended to ſubvert the truth and divine authority
of our holy religion.   The laſt that was mentioned was, that of
the author of the *Diſcourſe of the Grounds and Reaſons of the*
*Chriſtian Religion,* who, under pretence of ſetting Chriſtianity
on a ſure and ſolid foundation, had endeavoured to ſhew that it
hath no foundation at all; that it is founded wholly on the Old
Teſtament prophecies, taken not in a literal, but merely in an allegorical, *i. e.* as he plainly deſigned it, in a falſe ſenſe, contrary to
the original intention of the prophecies themſelves.   In oppoſition to him it was clearly ſhewn, that many of the Old Teſtament
prophecies are juſtly applied to our Saviour in their proper and
literal ſenſe.   Beſides which it was urged, that there were other
ſolid proofs of Chriſtianity, particularly that of our Saviour's
miracles, and his reſurrection from the dead; and the illuſtrious atteſtations given to him from heaven were evident proofs of his
divine miſſion.   And now, under pretence of acting the part of
a moderator in this controverſy, a new antagoniſt aroſe, Mr.
Woolſton, who endeavoured to allegorize away the miracles of
our Saviour, as Mr. Collins had done the prophecies.   This he
firſt attempted in a pamphlet, intitled, *A Moderator between an*
*Infidel*

*Infidel and an Apoftate;* and in two *Supplements* to it: and afterwards more largely in fix Difcourfes on the miracles of our Saviour, which were fucceffively publifhed at different times, in the years 1727, 1728, and 1729: the defign of all which is to fhew, that the accounts of the great facts recorded in the gofpels are to be underftood wholly in a myftical and allegorical fenfe; and that, taken in the literal and hiftorical fenfe, they are falfe, abfurd, and fictitious.  This attempt he hath carried on with greater rudenefs and infolence than any of thofe that appeared before him.  The Earl of Shaftefbury, even where he unhappily fets up ridicule as the teft and criterion of truth, expreffeth his difapprobation of *fcurrilous buffoonry, grofs raillery,* and *an illiberal kind of wit.*  And if there ever was any performance to which thefe characters might be juftly applied, it is this of Mr. Woolfton.  The fame noble writer obferves, that to *manage a debate fo as to offend the public ear, is to be wanting in that refpect that is due to the fociety —— and that what is contrary to good breeding is, in this refpect, as contrary to liberty.*  If we are to judge of Mr. Woolfton's writings by this rule, they are as inconfiftent with a juft liberty, as they certainly are with good breeding and decency.

There are two ways by which he endeavours to anfwer the defign he hath in view.  The one is, by fhewing that the literal fenfe of our Saviour's miracles is denied by the moft ancient and venerable writers of the Chriftian church; the other is, by fhewing the abfurdity of the accounts given in the gofpels, taken in the literal fenfe.  With regard to the firft of thefe, he hath with great pomp produced many teftimonies of the fathers, for whom he profeffeth the profoundeft veneration; and, by a ftrange difingenuity, endeavoureth to reprefent them as abfolutely denying the facts themfelves related in the gofpel; becaufe, according to a cuftom which then obtained, they added to the literal, a fpiritual and allegorical fenfe, and took occafion from thence to make pious allufions.  He pretendeth, that if we will adhere to the fathers, *the gofpel is in no fort a literal ftory;* and that *the hiftory of Jefus's life is only an emblematical reprefentation of his fpiritual life in the fouls of men.*  But it is certain, and was evidently proved by his learned anfwerers, that in giving the allegorical and myftical fenfe, the fathers firft fuppofed the literal fenfe, and the hiftorical truth of the facts, and upon them built their allegorical interpretations.  It is acknowledged, that in thefe they often exceeded juft bounds, and too much indulged the vagaries of a pious fancy : but to pretend, that they intended to deny that the facts recorded by the evangelifts were really done, is one of the moft confident impofitions that were ever put upon mankind ; and it is not to be doubted, but the author himfelf was fenfible of this.    Many glaring inftances of unfairnefs and dif-ingenuity in his quotations from the fathers were plainly proved upon him.    It was fhewn, that he hath quoted  books generally allowed to be fpurious, as the genuine works of the fathers ; and hath, by falfe tranflations and injurious interpolations, and foifting in of words, done all that was in his power to pervert the true fenfe of the authors he quotes; and that fometimes he interprets them in a manner directly contrary to their own declared fenfe, in the very paffages he appeals to, as would have appeared, if he had fairly produced the whole paffage.

It is not to·be wondered at, that an author who was capable of fuch a conduct fhould ftick at no methods to expofe and mif-reprefent the accounts given by the evangelifts of our Saviour's miracles.  Under pretence of fhewing the abfurdity of the literal and hiftorical fenfe of the facts recorded in the gofpels, he hath given himfelf an unreftrained licence in invective and abufe.  The books of the evangelifts, and the facts there related, he hath treated in a ftrain of low and coarfe buffoonry, and with an in-folence and fcurrility that is hardly to be paralleled.    He afferts, that they are full of *improbabilities, incredibilities,* and *grofs abfurdities:* that they are like *Gulliverian tales of perfons and things, that out of the romance never had a being: that neither the fathers, nor the apoftles, nor Jefus himfelf, meant that his miracles fhould be taken in the literal, but in the myftical and pa-rabolical fenfe.* And he exprefsly declares, that *if Jefus's miracles, literally taken, will not abide the teft of fenfe and reafon, they muft be rejected, and Jefus's authority along with them* \*.  He cafteth feveral reflections on our bleffed Lord, fo bafe and fcur-rilous, that they cannot but be extremely offenfive to a Chriftian ear; and which even fober heathens, many of whom regarded

---

\* Difcourfe IV. p. 16.

him

him as a perſon of great wiſdom and virtue, would have been aſhamed of; and yet this author charges the biſhop of London with *ignorance* or *malice*, in repreſenting him as a *writer in favour of infidelity*. He declares, that he is the *fartheſt of any man from being engaged in the cauſe of infidels or deiſts:* and that he *writes not for the ſervice of infidelity, which has no place in his heart, but for the honour of the holy Jeſus, and in defence of Chriſtianity*. The like declarations he frequently repeateth. He ends his fourth diſcourſe on our Saviour's miracles with avowing, that his deſign in theſe his diſcourſes is *the advancement of the truth and of the Meſſiahſhip of the holy Jeſus, to whom be glory for ever, Amen*. He concludes his ſixth diſcourſe in the ſame manner; and expreſſes himſelf in his firſt and ſecond Defence to the like purpoſe. Any one that compares theſe declarations with the whole ſtrain of his diſcourſes, will be apt to entertain the worſt opinion imaginable of the writer's ſincerity; and the moſt extenſive charity will ſcarce be able to acquit him from the moſt groſs and ſhocking prevarication.

But not to inſiſt farther on this, one would have expected, that, after all the clamours he hath raiſed againſt the evangelical accounts of our Saviour's miracles, he ſhould have had ſome formidable objections to produce; and yet, when ſtripped of the ridiculous turn he hath given them, they are, except ſome few difficulties, which are far from being new, and have been ſolidly anſwered, contemptibly vain and trifling. It is an objection he frequently repeats againſt what we are told concerning our Saviour's curing the diſeaſed, the blind, the lame, &c. that the evangeliſts have not given us an exact account of the nature and ſymptoms of their diſtempers, as phyſicians and ſurgeons would have done, that we might know whether the cure was ſupernatural. And if they had done this, it would, no doubt, have been improved as a ſtrong preſumption of art and contrivance in the relaters, and as no way conſiſtent with that honeſt, artleſs ſimplicity of narration, for which the evangeliſts are ſo remarkable. With regard to the cure of the man that was born blind, he finds fault that our Saviour did not cure him with a word ſpeaking, which he ſays would have been a great and real miracle; and if he had done ſo, as he did in ſeveral other caſes, this writer would have been as far from believing it as before. He will

have

have it, that, under pretence of anointing the blind man's eyes with clay and fpittle, Jefus made ufe of a fovereign balfam which wrought the cure; and fuppofes, in direct contradiction to the whole ftory, that his blindnefs was only a flight diforder of the eyes, which was wearing away with age, and that therefore the reftoring him to his fight was no miracle at all, though the man himfelf, his parents, and friends that had known him all along, and the chief priefts and pharifees, who made a ftrict inquiry into the cafe, could not help acknowledging that it was a very great one.    Our Saviour's difcovering to the Samaritan woman the fecrets of her paft life, which convinced her of his being a prophet, and from whence he took occafion to give her the moft excellent inftructions concerning the nature of true religion, paffes with this writer for the trick of a *fortune-teller*. And whereas it appeareth from the account given by the evangelift, that the Samaritans looked for the Meffiah under the idea of a divine teacher, and the *Saviour of the world*, he reprefents it as if they expected the Meffiah, not as a *prince* or a *prophet*, but a *conjurer* only.    Several other inftances might be produced, in which he addeth or varieth circumftances, and altereth the ftory as recorded by the evangelifts, that he may take occafion to place it in a ridiculous light.

It is a remarkable conceffion which is made by him in the beginning of his fifth Difcourfe, that " it will be granted on all " hands, that the reftoring a perfon indifputably dead to life is a " ftupendous miracle; and that two or three fuch miracles, well- " attefted and credibly reported, are enough to conciliate the be- " lief, that the author of them was a divine agent, and vefted " with the power of God\*."    Three miracles of this kind are recorded in the gofpel to have been wrought by Jefus; *viz.* his raifing Jairus's daughter, the widow's fon at Naim, and Lazarus. And what has our author to object againft thefe accounts?    He objects in general againft them all, that the perfons raifed ought to have been magiftrates or perfons of eminence.    But the raifing fuch perfons would not have been fo agreeable to the reft of our Saviour's conduct and character, who fhunned what might have the appearance of oftentation, or be looked upon as an attempt to make an intereft with the great.    He farther objects, that the

* Difcourfe V. p. 3.

perfons

perfons that were raifed fhould have told what they had feen and done in the feparate ftate.   And if the evangelifts had been romantic writers that wanted to amufe their readers with ftrange ftories, they might probably have inferted fome things of this kind into their accounts: but they confined themfelves to the plain facts, as far as they knew them, which they have related with the greateft fimplicity.   He objects particularly againft the ftory of raifing Jairus's daughter, becaufe fhe was but *a girl of twelve years old;* as if the raifing one of that age was not as great a miracle as if fhe had been twenty.   He next pretends that fhe was only *in a fit;* though all the perfons about her, and her neareft relations, were fatisfied that fhe was dead, and were making the ufual preparations for her funeral.   It is enough with him, to difcredit the ftory of raifing the widow's fon at Naim from the dead, that he was not a perfon of importance, but a youth, and the fon of a poor woman: and he has with great fagacity difcovered, that Jefus's accidental meeting the corpfe, and touching the bier, is a plain proof that it was all a contrivance between him and the young man.   To mention fuch objections is to confute them. But perhaps he hath ftronger ones to produce againft the ftory of the refurrection of Lazarus, which he pronounceth to be fuch *a contexture of folly and fraud, as is not to be equalled in all romantic hiftory:* and yet the principal objection he hath to offer is no more than this, that three of the evangelifts have not mentioned it.   But no argument can be drawn againft the truth of the fact from their filence; fince it is evident that they never defigned or pretended to record all the remarkable miracles which our Saviour wrought; and St. John, who was an eye-witnefs, and who chiefly taketh notice of the things which the others had omitted, hath given us a very diftinct and particular account of it.   Among the circumftances which Mr. Woolfton looks upon to be fufficient to fet afide that ftory, one is, that we are told, *Jefus wept.* This was a fign of his great humanity, and the goodnefs of his temper; but our author thinks *a ftoical apathy* would have become him better.   Another is, that Jefus called to Lazarus with *a loud voice* to *come forth;* which was certainly very proper, that all who were prefent might attend and obferve.   And what is very odd, he makes Lazarus's being *bound in grave cloaths,* and having his *head bound about with a napkin,* to be a very fufpicious

I 3                                                    fign

fign that he had not been really dead; and very wifely has found out, that Lazarus by a concert with Jefus, who was at a confiderable diftance when it happened, contrived to be buried, and lie in the grave four days, that Jefus might have the honour of feeming to raife him up from the dead. And becaufe the Jews took counfel to kill Jefus, and he withdrew for a while from their rage, this is produced as a proof, that the Jews knew he was guilty of a fraud, and that he himfelf was confcious of it; whereas it appears from the whole account, that their taking counfel to put him to death was owing to their being fenfible of the greatnefs of the miracle, and that it was too evident to be denied, and was likely to draw the people after him.

The objections which he makes in the perfon of a Jewifh rabbi, againft the evangelical ftory of our Lord's refurrection, which he declareth to be a *complication of abfurdities, incoherences, and contradictions*, are equally frivolous. He infinuates, that the guards fet by the Roman governor, at the defire of the chief priefts, to watch the body of Jefus, fuffered themfelves to be bribed or intoxicated by the difciples; in which he is more quick-fighted than the chief priefts and pharifees, whom it more nearly concerned, who, it is plain, fufpected no fuch thing; in which cafe, inftead of excufing, they would have endeavoured to get them feverely punifhed. But what he feems to lay the principal ftrefs upon is, a fuppofed covenant between the chief priefts and Jefus's difciples, that the feal with which the ftone of the door of the fepulchre was fealed fhould not be broken, till the three days were entirely paft: and that therefore the rolling away the ftone from the fepulchre, and breaking the feal before the three days were ended, was a breach of that covenant, and a proof of an impofture. A moft extraordinary conceit this! as if the rulers of the Jews would have troubled themfelves to enter into a concert with Jefus's difciples, whom they hated and defpifed, and who at that time had hid themfelves for fear of them, and were fled; or as if fuch a covenant could bind our Lord from rifing when he judged fitteft. As to that part of the objection which fuppofes, that he ought to have lain in the grave, according to his own prediction, three whole days and nights, it proceeds from a real or affected ignorance of the Jewifh phrafeology. This is a modern objection. The ancient enemies of Chriftianity did

not

not pretend that Jesus rose before the time prefixed: for they very well knew that, according to a way of speaking usual among the Jews and other nations, his rising again on any part of the third day was sufficient to answer the prediction. This matter was set in a clear light in *The Trial of the Witnesses:* yet the objection was again repeated by the author of the *Resurrection of Jesus considered;* and was so fully exposed by the learned answerers, that one would hope we shall hear no more of it[*].

Mr. Woolston makes it also a great objection against the truth of Jesus's resurrection, that he did not shew himself after his death to the chief-priests and rulers of the Jews. And indeed there is no objection with which the deistical writers have made a greater noise than this. It is urged particularly by the author of the *Resurrection of Jesus considered*; but, above all, Mr. Chubb has insisted upon it at large, and with great confidence, in his posthumous works, vol. i. p. 337, *& seq.* And yet good reasons may be assigned, why it was not proper that it should be so. Considering the cruel and inveterate malice they had shewn against Jesus, and the power of their prejudices, there is no likelihood of their submitting to the evidence. They had attributed his miracles to the power of the devil; and his raising Lazarus from the dead, of which they had full information, only put them upon attempting to destroy him. Instead of being wrought upon by the testimony of the soldiers, they endeavoured to stifle it. And if Jesus had shewn himself to them after his passion, and they had pretended it was a spectre or a delusion, and had still refused to acknowledge him after this, it would have been insisted upon as a strong presumption against the reality of his resurrection. But let us suppose that Jesus had not only appeared to them after his resurrection, but that they themselves had acknowledged the truth of his resurrection and ascension, and had owned him for their Messiah, and brought the body of the Jewish nation into it; can it be imagined that they who now make that objection would have been satisfied? It may rather be supposed, that those great men's coming into it would have been represented as a proof that all was artifice and imposture; and that the

---

[*] See the Evidence of the Resurrection cleared, p. 64, &c. and Mr. Chandler's Witnesses of the Resurrection re-examined, p. 14—19.

defign was to 'fpirit up the people againft the Roman government, and carry on fome political fcheme, under pretence of reftoring the kingdom to Ifrael.  The whole would have been treated as a national Jewifh affair, a thing concerted between the chief
priefts and the difciples; and there would have been a greater
clamour raifed againft it, than there is now: I am perfuaded that
the evidence which was actually given of Chrift's refurrection by
the apoftles and difciples of Chrift, in oppofition to their own
prejudices, and to the authority and power of the Jewifh chief
priefts and rulers, and notwithftanding the perfecutions to which
their teftimony to it expofed them, was much more convincing
and lefs exceptionable than it would have been, if they had had
the favour and countenance of the chiefs of the Jewifh nation, or
of thofe perfons who were of the greateft intereft and authority
among them.

What has been mentioned may ferve for a fpecimen of this
writer's objections againft the accounts of our Saviour's miracles
recorded in the evangelifts: and he might by the fame way of
management, by arbitary fuppofitions, and adding or altering
circumftances as he judged proper, have proved the moft authentic accounts in the Greek or Roman hiftory to be falfe and incredible.  He might at the fame rate of arguing have undertaken to
prove, that there was no fuch perfon as Jefus Chrift, or his
apoftles, or that they were only allegorical perfons, and that
Chriftianity was never planted or propagated in the world at all.

This extraordinary writer thought fit to begin his fecond Difcourfe on our Saviour's miracles, with boafting, that none of the
clergy had publifhed their exceptions againft what he had offered
in his firft; and that this fhewed that his caufe was juft, and his
arguments and authorities unanfwerable.  But he did not continue long unanfwered: many learned adverfaries foon appeared
againft him: but they were far from imitating him in his low and
fcurrilous way of treating the fubject.  They fhewed themfelves
as much fuperior in the temper, calmnefs, and folid and ferious
manner of treating the argument, as in the goodnefs of their
caufe.  They confidered even his moft trifling objections; and
whatever things he had urged, that had any real or feeming difficulty in them (and fome fuch things muft be expected in ancient writings, which relate to times and cuftoms different from

ours,

ours, and especially with regard to facts of an extraordinary nature), were coolly examined, and fully obviated.

The late worthy bishop of London, Dr. Gibson, published on this occasion an excellent pastoral letter, written, as all his are, with great clearness and strength. The learned and ingenious Dr. Zachary Pearce, now Lord Bishop of Rochester, published *The Miracles of Jesus Vindicated,* in four parts, which came out at different times in the year 1729, and were deservedly much esteemed. But the largest answer was that by Dr. Smallbrook, Lord Bishop of St. David's, in two volumes, 8vo. This learned work is intitled, *A Vindication of our Saviour's Miracles; in which Mr. Woolston's Discourses on them are particularly examined; his pretended Authority of the Fathers against the Truth of the literal Sense are set in a just Light; and his Objections, in point of Reason, answered*—London, 1729. There were other good answers published, which also took in the whole of Mr. Woolston's Discourses: such were Mr. Ray's *Vindication of our Saviour's Miracles,* in two parts, the first published in 1727, the second in 1729; and Mr. Stevenson's *Conference on the Miracles of our Saviour,* published in 1730, an ingenious and solid performance. Besides which there were several excellent pamphlets, that were designed to vindicate some particular miracles against Mr. Woolston's exceptions. Such were Mr. Atkinson's *Vindication of the literal Sense of three Miracles of Christ—his turning Water into Wine—his whipping the Buyers and Sellers out of the Temple—and his exorcising the Devils out of two Men—against Mr. Woolston's Objections, in his first and second Discourses on the Miracles of our Saviour; in three Letters to a Friend,* London, 8vo, 1729. Dr. Harris's two sermons on the *Reasonableness of believing in Christ, and the Unreasonableness of Infidelity: with an Appendix, containing brief Remarks upon the case of Lazarus; relating to Mr. Woolston's fifth Discourse of Miracles,* London, 8vo, 1729. That discourse of Mr. Woolston was also animadverted upon by Mr. Simon Brown, in a treatise written with great smartness and spirit, intitled, *A fit Rebuke to a ludicrous Infidel, in some Remarks on Mr. Woolston's fifth Discourse on the Miracles of our Saviour: with a Preface concerning the Prosecution of such Writers by the Civil Power,*

London,

London, 8vo. 1732. The following tracts also deserve special notice, as being written with great clearness and judgment. *A Vindication of three of our blessed Saviour's Miracles, in Answer to the Objections of Mr. Woolston's fifth Discourse on the Miracles of our Saviour,* by Nathaniel Lardner, now Dr. Lardner, London, 1729. *A Defence of the Scripture History, as far as it concerns the Resurrection of Jairus's Daughter, the Widow's Son at Naim, and Lazarus; in Answer to Mr. Woolston's fifth Discourse,* London, 1729. This is said to have been written by Dr. Henry, who afterwards published *A Discourse on our Saviour's miraculous Power of Healing; in which the six Cases excepted against by Mr. Woolston are considered; being a Continuation of the Defence of Scripture History,* London, 1730. And as Mr. Woolston had bent his efforts with a particular virulence against the resurrection of our blessed Lord, this was fully and distinctly considered, especially in a pamphlet written by Dr. Sherlock, Lord Bishop of London, intitled, *The Trial of the Witnesses of the Resurrection of Jesus,* London, 1729, which has been very justly admired for the polite and uncommon turn, as well as the judicious way of treating the subject. There were also published on the same occasion, *An Answer to the Jewish Rabbi's two Letters against Christ's Resurrection, and his raising Lazarus from the dead; with some Observations on Mr. Woolston's own Reflections on our Saviour's conduct,* London, 1729. *An impartial Examination and full Confutation of the Arguments brought by Mr. Woolston's pretended Rabbi against the Truth of our Saviour's Resurrection,* London, 8vo, 1730. And two Discourses by Dr. Wade: the first, *An Appeal to the Miracles of Jesus Christ for his Messiahship:* the second, *A Demonstration of the Truth and Certainty of his Resurrection from the dead,* London, 8vo, 1729. Among the writers that appeared against Mr. Woolston, Mr. Joseph Hallet ought not to be forgotten, on the account of his judicious *Discourse of the Reality, Kinds, and Numbers of our Saviour's Miracles, occasioned by Mr. Woolston's six Discourses:* this was published in the second volume of his notes and discourses, 8vo, 1732. The last I shall mention is Mr. Stackhouse, who published *A fair State of the Controversy between Mr. Woolston and his Adversaries,* London,

8vo,

8vo. 1730: in which he hath given a very clear account of Mr. Woolston's objections, and the answers that were returned by those who had written against him.

Mr. Woolston published what he called, *A Defence of his Dif- courses on the Miracles of our Saviour, against the Bishop of London and St. David's, and his other Adversaries,* in two pamphlets: the first was published, London, 1729; the second in 1730. These are very trifling performances, in which there is a continued strain of low drollery, but little that has a shew of reason and argument, in answer to what had been strongly urged against him. He has scarce attempted to take notice of the in- stances which had been brought to shew his great dishonesty in his quotations, and his gross falsifications of the fathers and an- cient writers. This seems to have given him very little distur- bance, though if he had any regard to his own reputation, it highly concerned him to clear himself, if he had been able to do it, from so heavy a charge.

But I believe you will be of opinion, that I have dwelt long enough upon such an author, though he himself boasts of *cutting out such a piece of work for our Boylean lectures, as shall hold them tug* (as he politely expresseth it),.*so long as the ministry of the letter, and a hireling priesthood last* *.

* See his fifth Discourse on Miracles, p. 65, 66.

# LETTER IX.

*The present Age a happy Time of Liberty, but that Liberty greatly
abused—An Account of Dr. Tindal's Christianity as old as
the Creation—He pretends a great Regard for the Christian
Religion, yet uses his utmost Efforts to discard all Revelation,
in general, as entirely useless and needless; and particularly
sets himself to expose the Revelation contained in the holy Scriptures of the Old and New Testament—The high Encomiums he
bestows on the Religion of a Deist, and on his own Performance
—Observations upon his Scheme—It is shewn to be absurd and
inconsistent—What he offers concerning the absolute universal
Clearness of the Law of Nature to all Mankind, contrary to
plain undeniable Fact and Experience—His Scheme really
less favourable to the Heathens than that of the Christian Divines—An Account of the Answers published against him.*

I BELIEVE, Sir, you will agree with me, that never had any
nation a fuller enjoyment of liberty than we have had since the
Revolution. What Tacitus celebrates as the felicity of the times
of Trajan, " that men might think as they pleased, and speak
as they thought," may be more justly applied to our own. *Rara
temporum felicitate, ubi sentire quæ velis, et quæ sentias dicere
licet* *. The noble author of the *Characteristics* is pleased to
mention it to the honour of the heathen world in ancient Greece
and Rome, that " visionaries and enthusiasts were tolerated; and
" on the other side, philosophy had as free a course, and was
" permitted as a balance against superstition. Thus matters were
" happily balanced: reason had fair play; learning and science
" flourished†." It would be no hard matter to shew that this representation is not altogether just: for, not to mention the case of
Socrates and others, it is capable of a clear proof, that though
they might bear with the disputes among the several sects of philosophers in their schools, yet they would not suffer the established
religion of the state to be called in question, and were ready to

* Tacit. Hist. l. i. in prœm. † Characterist. vol. i. p. 18.

punish

punifh thofe that oppofed it, of which they gave the moft fangui-
nary proofs when Chriftianity appeared.　But what his Lordfhip
has faid of thofe heathen times, the felicity of which he fo much
extols, is undoubtedly true of ours.　Vifionaries and enthufiafts
are not perfecuted, but tolerated: philofophy has a free courfe:
reafon has fair play: learning and fcience have greatly flourifhed.
Nor can any age or country be mentioned, in which men have
had a greater freedom of openly declaring their fentiments, either
with regard to civil or religious matters.　This is our privilege
and our glory; but the greateft advantages are capable of being
perverted through the corruption of mankind.　Liberty, which,
rightly improved, is the beft friend to truth and to pure and
undefiled religion, is often abufed to a boundlefs licentioufnefs.
Of this we have had many inftances: but in nothing has it more
remarkably appeared, than in the open repeated attempts that have
been made againft all revealed religion.　It cannot be pretended,
that the adverfaries of Chriftianity have not been at liberty to
produce their ftrongeft objections againft it.　They have not only
offered whatfoever they were able in a way of reafon and argument, but they have in many inftances given a loofe to the moft
offenfive ridicule and reproach: and if they have frequently
thought fit to cover their attempts with a pretended regard for
Chriftianity, we may fafely affirm, that it has not been fo much
out of fear of punifhment, as that under that difguife they might
the better anfwer the end they had in view, and give religion a
more deadly wound as pretended friends, than they could as
avowed adverfaries.　This advantage however hath arifen from
it, that it hath given occafion to many noble defences of Chriftianity, and to the clearing various difficulties, and placing the
excellence and evidences of our holy religion in the ftrongeft and
moft convincing light.

The attacks againft Chriftianity, of which I have taken notice
in my former letters, feemed for fome time to have been carried
on almoft without intermiffion.　Animated with a ftrange kind
of zeal, the enemies of revelation were unwearied in their endeavours to fubvert it.　When repelled in one attempt, they were
not difcouraged, but renewed it in another form.　Of this we
now are going to have a frefh inftance.　Woolfton's attempt was

fo

fo conducted as to raife a kind of horror and juft indignation in all that had not utterly extinguifhed all remaining regard to the religion in which they were baptized. Such outrageous abufe, fuch undifguifed reproach caft upon our bleffed Saviour and his holy gofpel, fuch coarfe ridicule and contempt, though it did a great deal of mifchief among men of empty and vicious minds, with whom fcurrilous jeft and grofs buffoonry, efpecially when levelled againft things facred, paffeth for wit and argument; yet was apt rather to create difguft in perfons of any degree of tafte or refinement. It was therefore judged neceffary, that Chriftianity fhould be attacked in a more plaufible way, which had a greater appearance of reafoning, and might be better fitted to take with perfons of a more rational and philofophic turn. This feems to have been the defign of Dr. Tindal's laboured performance, intitled, *Chriftianity as old as the Creation; or, the Gofpel a Republication of the Law of Nature;* which was firft publifhed in 4to, London, 1730, and afterwards in 8vo. One would have been apt to expect from the title of this book, that he fhould have fet himfelf to prove, that the gofpel is perfectly agreeable to the law of nature; that it hath fet the great principles of natural religion in the cleareft light; and that it was defigned to publifh and confirm it anew, after it had been very much obfcured and defaced through the corruption of mankind. And if fo, this author, who every-where profeffeth fuch a high efteem for the genuine law and religion of nature, ought to have done all in his power to recommend the gofpel-revelation to the efteem and veneration of mankind, and to have reprefented it as a great advantage to thofe that enjoy it, and a fignal inftance of the divine goodnefs: And what would induce one farther to think that this was his view, he exprefsly declareth, that Chriftianity is the *external,* as natural religion is the *internal revelation of the fame unchangeable will of God,* and that they differ only in the manner of their being communicated: and he propofeth greatly to *advance the honour of external revelation,* by fhewing *the perfect agreement there is between that and internal revelation.* He profeffeth to agree with bifhop Chandler, that " Chriftianity " itfelf, ftripped of the additions that policy, miftake, and the " circumftances of time have made to it, is a moft holy religion;
" and

" and that all its doctrines plainly speak themselves to be the will
" of an infinitely wise and good God\*." Accordingly he honoureth himself and his friends with the title of *Christian Deists*.

But whosoever closely and impartially examineth his book
will find, that all this plausible appearance and pretended regard
to Christianity is only intended as a cover to his real design,
which was to set aside all revealed religion, and entirely to destroy
the authority of the scriptures. Others have attacked particular parts of the Christian scheme, or of its proofs. But this
writer has endeavoured to subvert the very foundations of it, by
shewing, that there neither is nor can be any external revelation
at all, distinct from what he calls *the internal revelation of the
law of nature in the hearts of all mankind:* that such external
revelation is absolutely needless and useless; that the original law
and religion of nature is so perfect, that nothing can possibly be
added to it by any subsequent external revelation whatsoever;
nor can God himself lay any new commands upon us, or institute
any positive precepts, additional to the immutable eternal law
of nature, without the imputation of erecting an unreasonable
tyranny over his creatures. And as the religion and law of nature is absolutely perfect, so it always was and is clear and obvious to all mankind, even to those of the meanest capacity: so
clear that it is impossible to be rendered more plain to any man
by any external revelation, than it is to all men without it; that
therefore all pretences to such revelation are only owing to enthusiasm or imposture; that reason and external revelation are inconsistent; and to be governed by the authority of such revelation is really to renounce our reason, and to give up our understandings to implicit faith: that this hath been the source of all
the superstitions and corruptions which have prevailed among
mankind: and that therefore the best thing that can be done for
them is to engage them to throw off all regard to revelation, and
to *adhere to the pure simple dictates of the light of nature.*

And as he thus endeavoureth to set aside all external supernatural revelation as needless and useless, and all pretences to it
as vain and groundless; so he particularly setteth himself to expose the revelation contained in the holy scriptures of the Old

---

\* Christianity as old as the Creation, p. 382. edit. 8vo.

and New Teſtament. He attempteth to invalidate the original
proofs on which the authority of that revelation is founded, and
particularly that which is drawn from the miracles that atteſted
it: and he alſo taketh pains to prove, that we cannot poſſibly have any aſſurance, that this revelation is tranſmitted to us
in a manner which may be ſafely depended upon. He examineth the revelation itſelf, and endeavoureth to ſhew, that it is
uncertain and obſcure; that its precepts are delivered in a looſe,
general, undetermined manner, ſo as to be incapable of giving
clear directions to the bulk of mankind; that the *keys of ſolution*
neceſſary for underſtanding the ſcriptures, are what the people are
wholly unacquainted with; that, far from being of uſe as a rule
to direct men in faith and practice, the ſcriptures are only fit to
perplex and miſinform them; that they tend to give them very
wrong and unworthy apprehenſions of the Deity, and the duty
they owe him; and that there are many things either commanded
or approved there, which are apt to lead men aſtray in relation to
the duties they owe to one another. He farther endeavoureth
to ſhew, that there is a contraſt and oppoſition between the parts
of this revelation, particularly between the Old Teſtament and
the New. And it may be ſaid upon the whole, that he hath
ſpared no pains to rake together whatſoever he thought might be
capable of expoſing the ſcriptures, or the Chriſtian religion.
He concludes his book with arguing againſt the Chriſtian revelation, from its having not been univerſal in all times and places,
and from the corruptions of Chriſtians.

Whilſt he thus uſeth his utmoſt endeavours to expoſe Chriſtianity as a falſely-pretended revelation, and as not only needleſs
and uſeleſs, but of pernicious influence to mankind; he hath
taken care to make the moſt advantageous repreſentation of that
ſcheme of natural religion he would recommend, and to ſhew the
great advantage the religion of the deiſts hath above that of the
Chriſtians. He ſometimes ſpeaks as if he thought the deiſts were
infallibly guided, in making uſe of the reaſon God hath *given
them, to diſtinguiſh religion from ſuperſtition,* ſo that they *are ſure
not to run into any errors of moment*\*. On the other hand, he
honours all thoſe that are for poſitive precepts in religion with

---

\* Chriſtianity as old as the Creation, p. 336. edit. 8vo.

the

the character of Demonifts: and he reprefents divines in all ages, as, *for the moft part, mortal enemies to the exercife of reafon,* and even *below brutes.*

He ends his book as he had begun it, with a high panegyric upon his own performance: That by this attempt of his, " as " nothing but rubbifh is removed, fo every thing is advanced " which tends to promote the honour of God, and the happinefs " of human focieties: That there is none who wifh well to " mankind, but muft alfo wifh his hypothefis to be true; and that " there cannot be a greater proof of its truth, than that it is in all " its parts fo exactly calculated for the good of mankind, that " either to add to it, or take from it, will be to their manifeft " prejudice: That it is a religion, as he hopes he has fully " proved, founded upon fuch demonftrable principles, as are " obvious to the meaneft capacity, and moft effectually prevents " the growth both of fcepticifm and enthufiafm."

This may fuffice to give a general idea of this boafted performance; but, if carefully examined, it will appear, that it is far from deferving the magnificent encomiums which he himfelf, and others who are favourers of the fame caufe, have fo liberally beftowed upon it.

The fcheme which this writer hath advanced, in order to fhew that there is no place or need for extraordinary revelation, dependeth chiefly upon two principles. The one is, that the law or religion of nature, obligatory upon all mankind, was from the beginning abfolutely perfect and immutable, fo that nothing could ever be added to it by any fubfequent revelation. The other is, that this original law or religion of nature, comprehending all that men were from the beginning obliged to know, believe, profefs, and practife, always was and ftill is fo abfolutely clear to all mankind, that it cannot be made clearer to any man by any external revelation, than it is to all men without it.

As to the firft, he argues, that becaufe God is unchangeable and abfolutely perfect, therefore the religion he gave to man from the beginning muft have been unchangeable and abfolutely perfect; fince nothing can proceed from a God of infinite perfection but what is perfect; and that to fuppofe any fubfequent addition to it, or alteration in it, is to fuppofe a change in God. But this will not anfwer the author's end, except he can prove that man is unchangeable too; and that the ſtate of mankind muſt neceſſarily in all ages and ſeaſons continue preciſely the ſame that it was at the beginning of the world:   For if there ſhould be a change in the ſtate and circumſtances of mankind, *e. g.* from pure religion to ſuperſtition, or from a righteous and innocent to a guilty and corrupt ſtate, God may ſee fit for excellent ends to lay new injunctions upon men, or make ſome farther diſcoveries of his will, ſuited to that alteration of circumſtances. Nor would this ſhew that he was changeable, but that he was moſt wiſe and good: and it would be a ſtrange thing to affirm, that there could not poſſibly be any farther ſignifications or diſcoveries of the divine will ever made by God himſelf, or any other thing required by him of men, or any additional help or advantages ever offered to them, in any ſuppoſable ſtate or circumſtances of mankind, but what were afforded and made from the beginning of the creation.   This is a moſt abſurd ſcheme; and if ſuch a one had been advanced by the advocates for revelation, plentiful ridicule would have been beſtowed upon it.

And it is equally abſurd to pretend, as this writer doth, that God cannot at any time, or in any circumſtance of things, injoin poſitive precepts.   If there be any external worſhip to be rendered to God at all (and this gentleman hath not thought fit openly to deny this), it would be the moſt unreaſonable thing in the world to pretend, that he cannot inſtitute or appoint what are the propereſt outward rites, or manner of performing that worſhip; eſpecially ſince our author allows, that men themſelves may appoint them: and to deny God the power which he alloweth to human magiſtrates in ſuch a caſe, is abhorrent to the common ſenſe of mankind; eſpecially, conſidering that there is nothing in which men have more groſsly erred, or as to which they ſtood in greater need of being properly directed, than in what relateth to religious worſhip.   I would only farther obſerve, that this writer, in the whole diſpute about poſitive precepts, always ſuppoſes *poſitive* and *arbitrary* precepts to be terms of the ſame ſignification: and by *arbitrary* he means things for which there is no reaſon at all.   But this is a very unfair ſtate of the caſe; for when we ſay God hath inſtituted poſitive precepts, though the matter of them be antecedently of an indifferent nature, it is ſtill ſuppoſed there were wiſe reaſons for injoining them, and that,

when

when injoined, they are defigned to be fubfervient to things of a moral nature, and to help forward the great ends of all religion. And that the pofitive precepts required in the Chriftian religion are fuch, and of an excellent tendency, hath been often clearly fhewn.

The other main principle of the author's fcheme is, that that law or religion of nature, which he fuppofes to be abfolutely perfect, always was and is fo clear and obvious to all men, that there is not the leaft need or ufe of external revelation. This is what he hath greatly laboured; and if ftrong and confident affertions, frequently repeated, may pafs for proofs, he hath fully proved it. This part of his fcheme coincides with that of Lord Herbert of Cherbury, who had reprefented the five great principles, in which he makes religion to confift, to be common notices, infcribed by a divine hand in the minds of all men, and univerfally acknowledged in all ages and nations. In like manner the author of *Chriftianity as old as the Creation* afferteth, that that religion, the perfection of which he fo much extols, is *apparent to the whole world, to thofe of the meaneft as well as higheft capacity*, and who are *unable to read their mother tongue*. He exprefsly declareth, that God could *not more fully make known his will to all intelligent creatures than* he hath done this way; no, *not if he fhould miraculoufly convey the fame ideas to all men*[\*]. He frequently fpeaks, as if the principles and obligations of natural religion were fo clear, that men could not poffibly miftake them; that all men fee them at firft view; and that the actual knowledge of the law of nature is naturally neceffary, and infeparable from rational nature; fo that it is as impoffible for any reafonable creature to be ignorant of it, as it is for animals to live without the pulfe of the heart and arteries.

This fcheme, though it has been mightily applauded, is contrary to evident fact and experience: It fuppofeth the law or religion of nature, in its important principles and obligations, to be neceffarily known to all mankind, and to be fo clear that they cannot miftake it; when nothing is more certain and undeniable, than that they have miftaken it in very important inftances, and that fome of its main principles have been very much per-

---

[\*] Chriftianity as old as the Creation, p. 22. edit. 8vo.

      verted

verted and obfcured. I fhall not here repeat what was offered
to this purpofe in a former letter in my remarks on Lord Herbert's fcheme, in which it is plainly proved, that men have
fallen into a grofs darknefs with refpect to fome of thofe great
principles in which that noble writer makes the true religion to
confift; and that after all his efforts to the contrary, he hath
found himfelf under a neceffity of acknowledging it. The like
acknowledgments the author of *Chriftianity as old as the Creation* hath been obliged to make. He himfelf in feveral parts of
his book, though in plain contradiction to his own fcheme, reprefenteth almoft all mankind in all ages, excepting the *Free-
thinking few* *, as having had very unworthy apprehenfions of
God, and wrong notions of the religion and law of nature. And
no fmall part of his book is employed in inveighing againft that
fuperftition which he fuppofeth to have generally prevailed
among mankind at all times, and which in his opinion is worfe
than Atheifm; and confequently it muft be acknowledged, even
according to his own reprefentation of the cafe, that men had
fallen from the right knowledge of the religion of nature into
great darknefs and corruption. Cicero was fo fenfible of this,
that, fpeaking of *fome fmall fparks of virtue implanted in us,* he
complaineth, that they are *foon extinguifhed by corrupt cuftoms
and opinions, fo that the light of nature no-where appears* †.
From whence he infers the great neceffity and ufefulnefs of
philofophy to direct and affift us; and certainly this will conclude much more ftrongly for the neceffity and ufefulnefs of a
divine revelation, which would be much more advantageous,
and more to be depended on.

The argument therefore which Dr. Tindal urgeth from the fuppofed univerfal clearnefs of the law of nature, 'to fhew that there
is no need or ufe for external revelation, falls to the ground. And
indeed his way of arguing, if it proves any thing, equally proves,
that all the writings of philofophers and moralifts, all the inftructions that have been ever given to mankind in matters of
religion and morality, have been perfectly needlefs and of no
ufe; and that confequently, all books which have been written

---

* Chriftianity as old as the Creation, p. 149.
† Tufcul. Quæft. lib. iii. in prœm.

on thefe fubjects, the nobleft in the world, and the beft worth
writing upon, muft be difcarded, as well as the fcriptures: fince
all mankind have fuch a perfect knowledge of their duty, that
they ftand in no need of inftruction or information. Yea, he
fometimes reprefents it, as if inftructing them by words tended
only to miflead them from the knowledge of things. Thus, according to this goodly fcheme, all men are to be left to what he
calls the fimple dictates of the light of nature, without any inftruction at all: the certain confequence of which would be
univerfal ignorance and barbarifm. He often expreffeth himfelf,
as if he thought that all men have an equal knowledge of the law
of nature; and indeed I do not fee but that upon his fcheme it
muft be fo: yet at other times he fuppofeth the knowledge men
have of it to be more or lefs clear according to the circumftances
they are in: for he fays, it is not neceffary that all men *fhould
have equal knowledge of it, but that all fhould have fufficient
for the circumftances they are in*＊; and talks of a man's *doing
his beft, according as his circumftances permit, to difcover the
will of God; and of men's being accepted, if they live up to their
different degrees of light.* But though others may charitably
make ufe of this way of fpeaking, it is hard to fee how this writer can do it in confiftency with his fcheme; or how he can fuppofe any allowances to be made for involuntary errors: fince according to his reprefentation of the cafe, all errors in matters of
religion or morals muft be voluntary, in oppofition to the cleareft
univerfal light. Though therefore he fets up for a mighty advocate for the heathen world, and blames the Chriftian divines
for paffing too fevere a cenfure upon them, he himfelf muft, if
he be confiftent, judge much more harfhly of them than they:
fince his hypothefis quite deftroys the plea with regard to the
heathens, drawn from the great darknefs and difficulties they
laboured under; for he pofitively afferteth, that the law of
nature is fo clear, that *no well-meaning Gentile could be ignorant
of it* †. He muft therefore fuppofe all of them, who were involved
in the general fuperftition and idolatry, which he himfelf acknowledgeth to be contrary to the law of nature, to have been deftitute of that fincerity, which he maketh to be the only title to
happinefs, and to the favour of God.

---

＊ Chriftianity as old as the Creation, p. 4. edit. 8vo.　　　† Ibid. p. 36.

It may not be improper to obferve farther, that though he often fpeaks of the law of nature, as if it were a fyftem of principles and rules fixed and unalterable, to which nothing could ever be added, and in which nothing could ever be altered (which rules and principles he fuppofes to be neceffarily known to all mankind), yet at other times he expreffes himfelf, as if he thought there were no fixed unchangeable principles and rules of morality at all. The goodnefs of actions is, according to him, to be wholly meafured by their tendency; and this is to be judged by the circumftances a man is under, which circumftances he reprefents as *continually changing**. It appears from feveral paffages, that, after all his magnificent talk of the perfection and immutability of the law of nature, all that he would have to be underftood by it is only this, that it is the will of God that every man fhould act, according as the circumftances he is under point out his duty. This is the fole univerfal rule or ftanding law given to all mankind for their conduct, and by which they may know their duty in all cafes whatfoever; as if it were fufficient to tell men, even the moft illiterate, that they muft act as the circumftances they are placed in do require, without any other or farther direction. But furely any one that knows the world and mankind muft be fenfible, that if every man were to be left to himfelf, to find out what is good and fit for him to do, merely by what he apprehendeth to be moft for his own benefit in the circumftances he is under, and to gratify his appetites and paffions, as far as he himfelf thinketh to be moft for his own advantage and happinefs, without any other direction or law to reftrain or govern him, it would foon introduce a very loofe morality. I cannot help looking upon it to be a ftrange way of thinking, to imagine that it would be better for every man to be left thus to form a fcheme of religion and morals for himfelf, than to have his duty urged and enforced upon him, by plain and exprefs precepts, in a revelation confirmed by the authority of God himfelf.

As this book made a great noife, many good anfwers were returned to it. A fecond *paftoral Letter* was publifhed on this occafion by the late bifhop of London, which, like his former, comprifed a great deal in a fmall compafs, and was very well

* Chriftianity as old as the Creation, p. 16. 317, 318.

fitted

fitted to anfwer the end it was intended for, to be an antidote againſt the ſpreading infection of infidelity.   Several other valuable treatiſes might be mentioned, ſuch as, *The Argument ſet forth in a late Book intitled, " Chriſtianity as old as the Creation," reviewed and confuted in ſeveral Conferences,* by Dr. Thomas Burnet.   Dr. Waterland's *Scripture Vindicated;* which was particularly deſigned to vindicate the holy Scripture, which this author had taken great pains to vilify and expoſe: A good account is here given of a great number of paſſages in the ſacred writings, and his objections againſt them are fully obviated.   Mr. Law's *Caſe of Reaſon, or Natural Religion, fairly and fully ſtated, in Anſwer to a Book, intitled, " Chriſtianity as old as the Creation."*   Mr. Jackſon's *Remarks on a Book, intitled, " Chriſtianity as old as the Creation."*   Dr. Stebbing's *Diſcourſe, concerning the Uſe and Advantage of the Goſpel-Revelation, in which are obviated the principal Objections contained in a Book, intitled, " Chriſtianity as old as the Creation,"* London, 8vo. 1731.   The ſame learned and judicious writer publiſhed another excellent tract againſt Dr. Tindal, intitled, *A Defence of Dr. Clarke's Evidences of Natural and Revealed Religion, in Anſwer to the fourteenth Chapter of a Book, intitled, " Chriſtianity as old as the Creation,"* London, 8vo. 1731.   Mr. Balguy, the worthy author of a *Letter to a Deiſt,* of which ſome notice was taken before in the account of the Earl of Shaftcſbury's writings, publiſhed on this occaſion *A ſecond Letter to a Deiſt, concerning a late Book, intitled, " Chriſtianity as old as the Creation;" more particularly that Chapter which relates to Dr. Clarke,* London, 8vo. 1731.   And, ſeveral years after, he publiſhed a very valuable tract, which was particularly intended to defend the mediatorial ſcheme, againſt the objections which Dr. Tindal had advanced, intitled, *An Eſſay on Redemption, being the ſecond Part of Divine Rectitude,* London, 8vo. 1741.   To theſe ought to be added, a piece which has been deſervedly much eſteemed, written by the ingenious Mr. Anthony Atkey, though without his name, intitled, *The main Argument of a late Book, intitled, " Chriſtianity as old as the Creation," fairly ſtated and examined; or, a ſhort View of the whole Controverſy,* London, 8vo. 1733.   Beſides theſe and other tracts that were publiſhed on this occaſion, there were ſome large

anſwers

anfwers made to this book, of which I fhall give a more particular account.

The firft of them that I fhall mention is intitled, *The Ufeful-neſs, Truth, and Excellency of the Chriſtian Revelation, defended againſt the ObjeEtions contained in a late Book, intitled, " Chriſ-tianity as old as the Creation,"* by James Foſter, afterwards Dr. Foſter, London, 8vo. 1731. This is generally and juſtly acknowledged to be an ingenious performance, and written with great clearneſs of thought and expreſſion. It is divided into five chapters. The firſt is deſigned to ſhew the advantages of revela-tion in general, and particularly of the Chriſtian: it is plainly proved, that whatever the power of reaſon may be ſuppoſed to be, if duly exerciſed and improved to the utmoſt, yet when the light of nature is darkened, and ignorance, idolatry, and ſuper-ſtition have overſpread the world, which was undoubtedly the caſe when our Saviour appeared, an extraordinary revelation would be highly uſeful, and of great benefit to mankind. He then proceeds to conſider what is the proper evidence of the truth and divinity of any particular revelation; and how thoſe to whom it is given may be ſatisfied that it really came from God: and here it is ſhewn, that miracles, when conſidered in conjunEtion with the good tendency and excellence of the doEtrines, furniſh a proper and ſufficient evidence. In the ſecond chapter, he vindicates the conduEt of God's providence in not making the Chriſtian religion univerſally known to all nations, and in all times and ages; and proves, that this is analogous to the general courſe of providence both in the natural and moral world, and that it is conſiſtent with the divine perfeEtions, and conſequently with the notion of its being a divine revelation. In the third chapter, which is the largeſt in the whole book, it is ſhewn, that we have a ſufficient probability, even at this diſtance, of the au-thenticity, credibility, and purity of the books of the New Teſta-ment; and that the common people are able to judge of the truth and uncorruptedneſs of a traditional religion: and a good anſwer is returned to the arguments drawn from the change of languages, the different uſe of words, and the ſtyle and phraſe of ſcripture, to prove it an obſcure, perplexed, and uncertain rule. The fourth chapter contains a general defence of poſitive commands, which Dr. Tindal had urged as alone " ſufficient to make all
                                                          " things

" things elfe, that can be faid in fupport of any revelation, totally
" ineffeftual." It is proved, that they are not repugnant to reafon, nor fubverfive of moral obligation, nor inconfiftent with
the wifdom, juftice, and goodnefs of God: and that inflituted
religion is not fuperftition, and, if rightly underftood, has no more
a tendency to fuperftition, than natural religion itfelf. And the
fifth contains a particular vindication of the peculiar pofitive inftitutions of Chriftianity; in which it is fhewn, that they are of
excellent ufe for begetting and ftrengthening good moral habits,
and for exciting and engaging men to a more diligent practice of
moral duties.

Another anfwer, which particularly engaged the attention of
the public, was that publifhed by Dr. John Conybeare, rector
of Exeter College, Oxford, late lord bifhop of Briftol, viz. *A
Defence of Revealed Religion, againft the Exceptions of a late
Writer, in his Book intitled " Chriftianity as old as the Creation,"* London, 1732. This book is divided into nine chapters. The firft is defigned by the acute and learned author to fhew,
what we are to underftand by the law or religion of nature, from
what the obligation of it arifes, and how far it extends. He
fhews, that the religion or law of nature does not take in every
thing that is founded in the nature or reafon of things, which
feems to be the fenfe the author of *Chriftianity as old as the Creation* takes it in throughout his whole book, but only fuch a collection of doctrines and precepts, as is difcernable to us in the
ufe of our natural faculties: and this, though founded in nature, becomes then only properly a law to us, when it is regarded as the
will of God, the fupreme legiflator; and our obligation to it,
ftrictly fpeaking, is founded on the divine fanction of rewards
and punifhments. In the fecond chapter it is fhewn, that the
law or religion of nature, in the fenfe already explained, is not
abfolutely perfect. Since the law of nature is only what men are
capable of difcerning, in the ufe of their natural faculties, it can
be no more perfect than human reafon. If the law of nature were
abfolutely perfect, it muft have fuch a clearnefs as to the meaning and authority of it, as can admit of nothing more in any
poffible circumftance; it muft have fuch a ftrength of inforce-
ment, that it cannot be heightened in any way whatfoever; and
fuch an extent of matter, as to comprehend every thing that
may

may be fit and proper to be known or done, and not to admit of
any poffible article to be added to it. And he plainly proves,
that the law or religion of nature is not abfolutely perfect in any
of thefe refpects. Chapter third is intended to fhew, that the
law of nature is not immutable, in fuch a fenfe efpecially as to
be incapable of admitting any additional precepts. And here
the queftion concerning pofitive precepts is accurately ftated,
and it is proved that God may appoint them; and an anfwer is
returned to the author's objections to the contrary. In chapter
fourth he inquires, whether natural and revealed religion be
neceffarily the fame; and if not, wherein the proper diftinction
between them both doth confift. In the former chapter he had
fhewn, that pofitive precepts might be given; here he carries it
farther, and proves that fome pofitive inftitutions might reafonably be expected, if ever God fhould reveal his will at all; both
as tokens of his authority and our fubmiffion, and for the better
order and decency of his worfhip, and the outward part of religion, and for the increafe and advancement of inward piety.
The fame thing is urged from the concurrent fenfe of mankind in
all ages, and under all religions. It is further fhewn, there are
other things of higher importance in which natural and revealed
religion differ, though they are not properly oppofed to each
other, *e. g.* with regard to principles and doctrines not difcoverable by nature's light, or as to precepts which, though founded
in the nature of things, yet are not certainly knowable in the
ufe of our own reafon. They alfo differ in point of clearnefs, and
in efficacy. He inftances particularly in the affurance given us
of the pardon of fin, divine affiftances, and the eternal retributions of a future ftate. Chapter fifth is defigned to fhew, that a
proper rule of life is not perfectly and eafily difcoverable by
every man, even by thofe of the meaneft capacity: and here it
is evinced, that the author's own fcheme of natural religion,
which he pretends is fo obvious to all mankind, is perplexed,
obfcure, and defective. In chapter fixth he inquires, whether a
proper rule of life be more eafily and perfectly difcoverable by
us in the ufe of our own reafon, than the proof or meaning of
a revelation can be. He fhews the poffibility of immediate revelation or infpiration, and that this gives the higheft evidence: and
that as to traditional revelation, though the evidence be not ftrictly

demonftrative,

demonſtrative, it may be ſuch as is ſufficient to determine the
aſſent of a ſober thinking man: and he anſwers what the author
had brought to prove, that the ſenſe and meaning of ſuch a revelation cannot be fixed and aſcertained.　Chapter ſeventh is deſigned
to ſhew, that a revelation is expedient, in order to a more eaſy,
more perfeɛt, and more general knowledge of the rule of life.
This is diſtinɛtly evinced, both with regard to the wiſer and better
part of men, particularly the philoſophers, and with reſpeɛt to
perſons of a lower rank and meaner abilities: and a good anſwer
is made to what the author had urged, concerning the ſuppoſed
inconſiſtency between our being governed by reaſon and revelation.　In chapter eighth it is ſhewn, that a revelation is expedient
in order to inforce the general praɛtice of the rule of life: that
the mere pleaſure of doing well, or a moral taſte or ſenſe, is not
alone a ſufficient balance for all the inconveniences of doing
otherwiſe, amidſt all the embarraſſments of paſſion and temptation; nor if to this be added the civil ſanɛtions of human authority, are theſe alone ſufficient: for theſe are deſigned not ſo much
to reward virtues, ſeveral of which do not come under the cog-
nizance of human courts, as to puniſh crimes, and thoſe only
ſuch as tend to the hurt'of the ſociety.　Virtue can only be
ſufficiently inforced by ſanɛtions eſtabliſhed by God himſelf;
and a revelation is expedient for that purpoſe.　He concludes
this chapter with giving a clear anſwer to two objeɛtions urged
by the author: the one is, that if a revelation be expedient to be
made to any, it muſt be equally expedient to be made to all, and
at all times: the other is, that the revelation hath not in faɛt anſwered that purpoſe for which we affirm it to be expedient.　The
ninth, and laſt, chapter is intended to evince, that there is ſufficient evidence of the reality of a revelation, eſpecially of the
Chriſtian.　He obſerves, that what is uſually called the internal
evidence of a revelation is not ſtriɛtly and properly an evidence,
but only a neceſſary condition or qualification of a true revelation: that external proof is the only direɛt evidence of a divine
revelation; and this conſiſteth in miracles, as including prophecies,
which may be conſidered as one ſort of miracles.　He ſhews what
reaſon we have to believe, that the miracles recorded to have
been done in favour of the Chriſtian religion were really wrought;

and

and that, fuppofing them to have been wrought, they were real
and fatisfactory proofs of a divine original.

There was another anfwer to Dr. Tindal's book, which I
fhould not have chofen to take notice of, if the method I am in
did not make it proper for me to do fo, as I am fenfible how
hard it is for an author to fpeak of his own work, without offending his own modefty, or the delicacy of the reader. It was
publifhed at Dublin in two volumes, 8vo. in 1733, under the
title of *An Anfwer to a late Book, intitled " Chriftianity as old as
the Creation;"* and was afterwards reprinted at London in 1740.
It is much larger, and takes a wider compafs than the other anfwers; and therefore the account here given of it will be alfo
larger. It is divided into two parts: In the firft part, which takes
up the firft volume, the author's account of the law of nature
is confidered, and his fcheme is fhewn to be inconfiftent with
reafon, and with itfelf, and of ill confequence to the interefts of
virtue, and to the good of mankind. This volume confifteth of
e'even chapters, befides a large introduction, containing obfervations upon the author's fpirit and defign, and the way of reafoning made ufe of by him, and others of our modern deifts. In
the firft chapter there is a general account of that writer's fcheme,
which lies fcattered in his book with little order or method, but
is here brought together in one view, and the various and inconfiftent fenfes, in which he takes the law of nature, examined.
The fecond chapter relates to the vaft extent he gives to the law
of nature, as taking in whatfoever is founded in the nature of
things. This is fhewn to be a ftrange hypothefis, when he is
fpeaking of that law which he fuppofes to be known to all
men, as if the whole reafon and nature of things were open
to every man; whereas, taken in this comprehenfive view, it is
only perfectly known to God himfelf. In the third and fourth
chapters, what he hath offered to prove, that the religion or law
of nature given to mankind at the beginning was fo abfolutely
perfect that nothing could ever be afterwards added to it, and
particularly that God could never inftitute any pofitive precepts,
is diftinctly confidered: and it is proved, that God may both give
men new laws fuited to new circumftances of things, and may, if
he feeth fit, inftitute pofitive precepts; and that thefe may anfwer

fwer very valuable ends; and particularly, that there were wife
reafons for the pofitive inftitutions both of the Jewifh and Chriftian religion. The fifth and fixth chapters relate to what our
author had advanced concerning the univerfal clearnefs of the
law of nature. It is fhewn at large, that it is not fo obvious to
all mankind, as to render an extraordinary revelation needlefs:
that even as to thofe principles and duties which, abfolutely
fpeaking, are difcoverable by human reafon, revelation may be
of great ufe to give a clearer and more certain knowledge of
them, than the bulk of mankind, or even the wifeft, could have
without it. Befides which, there are feveral things of great importance to us to know, of which we could not have a certain
affurance by the mere light of natural reafon without revelation,
and with regard to which, therefore, an exprefs revelation from
God would be of fignal advantage, and ought to be received
with great thankfulnefs : as particularly, with relation to the methods of our reconciliation with God when we have offended
him, the terms and extent of forgivenefs, and the nature, greatnefs, and duration of that reward, which it fhall pleafe God to
confer on imperfect obedience. In the 7th and 8th chapters it
is evinced, that this writer's fcheme of natural religion is very
defective; and that he giveth a wrong account of fome of the
main principles and duties of the law of nature: that he in effect
depriveth it of its ftrongeft fanctions ; and that his fcheme tendeth to take away the fear of God, and to make men eafy in their
fins. The ninth is defigned to fhew, that his fcheme is not fitted
to anfwer the end he propofes by it, the delivering mankind
from fuperftition and prieftcraft ; and that a ftrict adherence to
the Chriftian revelation in its original purity would have a happier influence this way. The tenth chapter relates to thofe paffages, in which he pretends to defcribe the religion of deifts, and
to draw a parallel between that and Chriftianity; and it is fhewn,
that the advantages he would appropriate to deifm do much more
properly belong to the Chriftian religion, as laid down in the
holy Scriptures. In the eleventh chapter, his pretence of introducing a new and glorious ftate of things is examined; and
the whole concludes with a brief reprefentation of the pernicious tendency and manifold inconfiftencies of the author's
fcheme.

In

In the second part, the authority and usefulness of the revelation contained in the sacred writings of the Old and New Testament, is asserted and vindicated against the objections and misrepresentations of this writer. This part is divided into sixteen chapters. The first contains some considerations concerning divine revelation in general, and what are the proper characters and evidences by which it may be known that such a revelation is really given; and that our being governed by the authority of such a revelation is not inconsistent with our being governed by reason, as this author has attempted to prove. The second chapter examines his objections against the characters of the first publishers and witnesses of the Jewish and Christian revelation; and it is shewn, that we have all the assurance that we can reasonably desire, that they were neither imposed upon themselves, nor had a design to impose upon others; nor indeed, as things were circumstanced, had it in their power to do so, if they had designed it. In the third chapter his objections against the proof from miracles are considered. It is shewn, that they are neither needless nor uncertain proofs: that there are certain marks and characters by which true divine miracles may be distinguished from those pretended to be wrought by imposture, or the agency of evil spirits; and that these characters are to be found in the miracles wrought in favour of the Jewish and Christian revelation. The design of the fourth chapter is to prove, that we have all the evidence that can be reasonably desired: that the revelation contained in the holy Scriptures, with an account of the facts and attestations by which that revelation was originally confirmed and established, is transmitted to us with such a degree of purity and certainty, as may be safely depended upon: and this is particularly shewn with regard to the writings of the Old Testament, especially the law of Moses. In the fifth chapter, the authority and integrity of the sacred records of the New Testament are asserted and vindicated against the author's exceptions: and that we have both sufficient external proofs of their being safely transmitted to us, and that they carry in them the greatest internal evidences of genuine truth and uncorruptedness, that can be found in any writings whatsoever. The sixth chapter shews, that the wonderful success the gospel met with, and its speedy and general propagation, furnish a strong proof, as the case

was

was circumftanced, of the truth of the facts on which it is founded. The following chapters are defigned to confider his objections againft Scripture, drawn from the nature and manner of
the revelation there contained. And firft, his attempt to prove,
that it is uncertain and obfcure, is obviated. What he urgeth to
this purpofe, concerning the ambiguity and uncertainty of words,
concerning the fcriptures being written in dead languages, and
that the tranflations are not to be depended on, is in the feventh
chapter diftinctly examined. The eighth relates to the keys
of folution neceffary for underftanding the Scripture, which
he pretends the people are wholly unacquainted with; and what
he offers concerning the figurative language of Scripture, and
the parables and proverbial expreffions made ufe of by our Saviour, is confidered. The ninth chapter makes it appear, that
many of thofe paffages, which this writer cenfures as obfcure
and apt to miflead the people, are fo noble and of fuch excellent
ufe, that a candid critic would have judged them worthy of admiration. In the tenth, an anfwer is given to his objections
againft the gofpel precepts, drawn from their being delivered in
a loofe, general, and undetermined manner; and his argument
for the obfcurity of fcripture, from the divifions among Chriftians
about the fenfe of it, and his pretence that this would infer the
neceffity of an infallible guide, is fhewn to be vain and inconclufive. The eleventh and twelfth chapters contain a diftinct
and particular examination of all thofe paffages, whereby he
pretends to prove, that the fcriptures tend to lead the people
into wrong apprehenfions of God, and into a wrong practice
with relation to the duties they owe to one another. Chapter
thirteenth confiders what he has offered to fhew, that there is a
contraft between the fpirit of the Old and New Teftament. In
the fourteenth and fifteenth chapters, the Mofaic account of
man's original dignity and the fall, and the Chriftian doctrine of
a Mediator, are vindicated againft this writer's exceptions. The laft
chapter contains an anfwer to two objections againft Chriftianity,
which have been often urged, and with which the author concludes his book: the one drawn from its not having been given
and made known to all mankind in all ages and places from the
beginning; the other drawn from the corruptions of Chriftians.
                                                              And

And it is fhewn, that no argument will juftly hold from either of thefe againft the ufefulnefs and divine authority of the Chriftian revelation.

There was alfo a folid and excellent anfwer to *Chriftianity as old as the Creation*, drawn up by the reverend Mr. Simon Brown, and which well deferves a particular nótice. But I fear I may be thought to have been too tedious and particular already in the account that has been given of the anfwers to this book, though the opinion many have entertained of it, as if it were a very formidable attack upon Chriftianity, will I hope in fome degree plead my excufe.

# LETTER X.

*Another Attempt against Christianity in Dr. Morgan's Book, call-*
*ed,* The Moral Philosopher—*He seems to acknowledge the*
*great Usefulness of Revelation, but leaves no Way of knowing*
*when a Revelation is really given—He discards all Authority,*
*even a divine one, in Matters of Religion, and all Proof from*
*Miracles and Prophecy—His Invectives against the Law of*
*Moses and the Prophets—Though he professeth himself a Chris-*
*tian on the Foot of the New Testament, he insinuates several*
*Reflections on the Character of our Saviour, and endeavours*
*to invalidate the Attestation given to Christianity by the extra-*
*ordinary Gifts and Powers of the Holy Ghost—He pretends,*
*that the Apostles preached different Gospels, and that the New*
*Testament is a Jumble of inconsistent Religions—His Book*
*fully confuted in the Answers that were published against him—*
*Some Account of those Answers, as also of the second and third*
*Volumes of the* Moral Philosopher.

SIR,

AS you still insist upon my continuing the correspondence
on the subject of my former letters, I shall now take notice
of a fresh attempt against Christianity, in a book that appeared
with a pompous title, *The Moral Philosopher, in a Dialogue be-*
*tween Philalethes, a Christian Deist, and Theophanes, a Christian*
*Jew*—" In which the grounds and reasons of religion in general,
" and particularly of Christianity as distinguished from the re-
" ligion of nature; the different methods of conveying and pro-
" posing moral truth to the mind; and the necessary marks or
" criteria on which they must all equally depend; the nature of
" positive laws, &c. with many other matters of the utmost con-
" sequence to religion, are fairly considered and debated, and the
" arguments on both sides impartially represented." London, 8vo.
1737. The author of this book, Dr. Morgan, seems at first view
to go much farther in his concession, than other his fellow-la-
bourers in the same cause. If we were to judge by some parts
of his book, we should be ready to look upon him as having
very friendly dispositions towards the Christian religion: since

L                                                              he he feems exprefsly to acknowledge the great ufefulnefs of divine revelation in general, and of the Chriftian revelation in particular. He fpeaks of man's natural weaknefs and inability; and reprefents thofe as conceited of themfelves, who in the prefent ftate of mankind talk of the *ftrength of human reafon in matters of religion.* He obferves, that at the time of Chrift's appearing, " mankind in general were in a ftate of grofs ignorance and " darknefs, with refpect to the true knowledge of God, and of " themfelves, and of all thofe moral relations and obligations we " ftand in to the Supreme Being, and to one another: That they " were under great uncertainty concerning a future ftate, and " the concern of divine providence in the government of the " world, and at the fame time were filled with a proud and " vain conceit of their own natural abilities and felf-fufficiency: " That our Saviour's doctrines on thefe heads, though they ap- " peared to be the true and genuine principles of nature and rea- " fon, when he had fet them in a proper light, yet were fuch as " the people had never heard or thought of before, and never " would have known, without fuch an inftructor, fuch means " and opportunities of knowledge: That they who would judge " uprightly of the ftrength of human reafon in matters of morality " and religion, under the prefent corrupt and degenerate ftate of " mankind, ought to take their eftimate from thofe parts of the " world which never had the benefit of revelation ; and this per- " haps might make them lefs conceited of themfelves, and more " thankful to God for the light of the gofpel." He afks, " if the " religion of nature, under the prefent pravity and corruption of " mankind, were written with fufficient ftrength and clearnefs " upon every man's heart ; why might not a Chinefe, or an In- " dian, draw up as good a fyftem of natural religion as a Chrif- " tian, and why have we never met with any fuch?" He adds, that " let us take Confucius, Zoroafter, Plato, Socrates, or the " greateft moralift that ever lived without the light of revelation, " and it will appear, that their beft fyftems of morality were in- " termixed and blended with fo much fuperftition, and fo many " grofs abfurdities, as quite eluded and defeated the main defign " of them *". This author could fcarce have declared more ex- prefsly than he hath here done againft Tindal's darling fcheme,

* Moral Philofopher, vol. i. p. 144, 145.

concerning

concerning fuch an abfolute univerfal clearnefs and fufficiency
of the light of nature in the prefent ftate of mankind, as renders
revelation entirely needlefs and ufelefs.　To which it may be
added, that he fpeaks in many paffages very honourably of Jefus
Chrift, and the religion he hath introduced, as having brought
clearer difcoveries of our duty, and enforced it by ftronger motives, and provided more effectual aids, than ever was done before.　And accordingly he exprefsly declareth himfelf to be a
*Chriftian on the foot of the New Teftament.*

If we were to form our judgment of him merely from fuch
paffages as thefe, it might be thought to be doing wrong to our
moral philofopher, to rank him in the lift of the deiftical writers:
but by a prevarication and a difingenuity which is not eafily
paralleled, except among fome of thofe that have appeared on
the fame fide, under all thefe fair pretences and difguifes, he hath
covered as determined a malice againft the honour and authority
of the Chriftian revelation, as any of thofe that have written
before him.

It is not eafy to form a diftinct notion of what he underftand-
eth by that revelation, the ufefulnefs of which he would be
thought to acknowledge.　He granteth, " that God may, if he
thinks fit, communicate his will by *immediate infpiration,* or *fupernatural illumination;* yea, and that what he thus communi-
cates may come with evidence equal to a mathematical demon-
ftration\*".　Yet he plainly intimates, that it can never be proved,
that God had ever thus communicated his will; and treats fuch
infpiration as the invention of our *fpiritual fcholaftics* or *fyfte-
matical divines.*　By feveral paffages of his book, efpecially if
compared with what he faith in his fecond volume, which he
publifhed in defence of it, it appeareth, that by *revelation* he un-
derftandeth any difcovery of truth, in *what way foever a man
comes by it,* even *though it be by the ftrength and fuperiority of
his own natural faculties†:* So that all that have difcovered rational or moral truth by their own ftudy and application, in the
ufe of their natural faculties, may be faid, according to this
account of it, to have had the light of revelation: and if fo, it
is not eafy to fee how he could confiftently reprefent whole na-

---

\* Moral Philofopher, vol. i. p. 83, 84.
† Ibid. p. 345. vol. ii. p. 12, 13. 25, 26. 44.

　　　　　　　　　　　tions,

tions, among whom he reckoneth the Indians and Chinefe, as *having never had the benefit of revelation;* or how he could fay, that the moft eminent philofophers and moralifts, fuch as Confucius, Zoroafter, Plato, Socrates, *lived without the light of revelation.* For will he fay, that none of them had any difcovery or manifeftation of rational moral truth made to them in any way whatfoever, no, not fo much as in the exercife of their own natural faculties?

The great principle he hath laid down, and which runs through his whole book, is, that there is but one certain and infallible mark or criterion of divine truth, or of any doctrine or law as coming from God, and that is, the moral truth, reafon or fitnefs of the thing itfelf, when it comes to be fairly propofed to, and confidered by the mind or underftanding. He frequently declareth, that we are not to receive any thing as true in religion upon any authority whatfoever *, or upon any other foundation than its own intrinfic evidence, or moral fitnefs: and this he explaineth to be its conduciblenefs to our happinefs, as appearing to our reafon, independently of all authority: So that after all his fair pretences about the benefit of revelation, we are not to receive any thing upon the authority of revelation at all. Suppofing any perfons to have been extraordinarily fent of God, to make a difcovery of his will concerning truth or duty, whatever credentials they produce to prove their divine miffion, we are not to receive any thing upon that authority, no more than if they were not thus extraordinarily fent of God. The doctrines and laws they deliver as from God, in what way foever they are attefted and confirmed, are really and entirely on the fame footing with the opinion of philofophers or moralifts, who do not pretend to be extraordinarily fent of God at all; *i. e.* we are to believe the doctrines they teach, if upon examining them we find them to be true, by reafons drawn from the nature of things; and we are to fubmit to their precepts and directions, if upon confidering them we are fatisfied that they tend to our own advantage and happinefs; but their authority, abftractly from the reafon of the thing, muft have no weight to determine us. Thus the proper ufe and advantage of revelation, which is to affure us by a di-

---

* Moral Philofopher, vol. ii. p. 6. 21, &c.

vine teſtimony of the truth of things, which either we could not have known at all, or not ſo certainly or clearly, by our own unaſſiſted reaſon; and with regard to our practice, to direct us to our duty, and bind it upon us by expreſs precepts, confirmed by a divine authority, is entirely ſet aſide by this author. Accordingly he will not allow either miracles or prophecy to be any proof of divine revelation, or any reaſon at all for our believing any doctrines, or ſubmitting to any laws, which have this atteſtation given to them. This being the true ſtate of the caſe, according to him—that nothing is to be received upon the authority of revelation—it is to no great purpoſe to inquire how this revelation is communicated to us. Yet he makes a great noiſe about the uncertainty of the manner of conveying a revelation to us. He frequently ſeems to make a mighty difference between *immediate* and *traditional revelation;* and ſometimes puts on an appearance of granting, that inſpiration or extraordinary revelation from God is a ſufficient ground of aſſurance to the perſon or perſons to whom this revelation is originally and immediately communicated. But upon a cloſe examination, and by comparing ſeveral paſſages in his book, it will be found, that he does not, and indeed cannot in conſiſtency with his ſcheme, allow, that thoſe perſons to whom this revelation is immediately made, have any way of being ſure of the truth of what is thus communicated, but by the reaſon of the thing, by its own intrinſic evidence, or apparent tendency to our benefit. And thoſe to whom this revelation is traditionally communicated, may have the ſame kind of aſſurance; *i. e.* they may believe it, if upon examining they find it to be true, by arguments drawn from the nature and reaſon of the thing. So that, upon his ſcheme, immediate revelation makes no difference, though he often talks as if there were a very great one.

It appeareth upon this view, that though he ſometimes ſeems abſolutely to contradict and ſubvert the ſcheme of the author of *Chriſtianity as old as the Creation;* yet at the bottom, his own ſcheme cometh pretty much to the ſame thing. He, as well as that author, is for diſcarding all authority, even a divine one, in matters of religion; and repreſents the receiving any thing purely upon ſuch authority, as a renouncing our reaſon. According to him, the only way any man, even of the meaneſt capacity, can

have

have to be fully affured of the truth of any doctrine in religion, is by the reafon of the thing, or its own intrinfic evidence, independent of all authority or teftimony: and in like manner, with regard to practice, the only way any man hath of knowing any thing to be his duty, is its conduciblenefs to his own happinefs in the circumftances he is in; of which every man is to be the judge for himfelf. To put all duty and obedience upon this foot, would go a great way to diffolve all bands of government, human and divine: fince upon this fcheme, it is in effect left to men themfelves, whether and how far they fhall obey; *i. e.* fo far only as they apprehend the thing required to tend to their own happinefs. And certainly it cannot be denied, that confidering the prefent darknefs and corruption of mankind, and how much they are influenced by their appetites and paffions, they would be in great danger, if left to themfelves, of forming wrong judgments concerning their own happinefs, and what is conducible to it, or connected with it. Such a fcheme might be confiftently advanced by Dr. Tindal, who fuppofed, though contrary to evident fact and experience, that the whole law of nature and fitnefs of things is obvious to all mankind, even to thofe that cannot read their mother tongue. But it feems not fo eafily reconcileable to the conceffions made by the *Moral Philofopher*, who acknowledgeth the prefent *weaknefs* and *inability* of reafon, and that the law of nature is not written *with fufficient ftrength and clearnefs in every man's heart*, in the *prefent corrupt and degenerate ftate of mankind.*

We have feen the regard this writer hath to revelation in general. As to the revelation contained in the holy Scriptures, he exprefsly and avowedly rejecteth the Old Teftament, and openly declareth that he will have nothing to do with it in his religion. He reprefenteth the law of Mofes, as " having neither truth nor " goodnefs in it, and as a wretched fcheme of fuperftition, blind- " nefs, and flavery, contrary to all reafon and common fenfe, " fet up under the fpecious popular pretence of a divine inftruc- " tion and revelation from God." And he endeavours to prove, that this was the fentiment of St. Paul. Among other heavy charges which he hath advanced againft that law, one is, that it encouraged human facrifices, as the higheft act of religion and devotion, when offered not to idols, but to God; and he takes
occafion

occasion to confider the cafe of Abraham's being commanded to
offer up Ifaac, which he reprefents as abfolutely unhinging and
diffolving the whole law of nature. He then goes on to confider
the fpirit of prophecy. He reprefenteth the Urim and Thummim
as a prieftly cheat, and afterwards proceedeth to make a very
odious, though inconfiftent, reprefentation of the character and
conduct of the ancient prophets; againft whom he exclaimeth as
the great difturbers of their country, the authors of all the civil
wars and revolutions in the kingdoms of Ifrael and Judah, and
the caufe of the final ruin of both; though the contrary is evident from the very hiftorical accounts to which he pretendeth to
appeal. And he praifeth Ahab and Jezebel, and other idolatrous
princes, for having endeavoured to deftroy them.

As to the New Teftament, though he frequently affecteth to
fpeak with great veneration of Jefus Chrift, yet he infinuateth
very bafe and unworthy reflections upon his perfon and character:
That he pretended to be the Meffiah foretold by the prophets,
though he very well knew that thofe prophets had only fpoken
of a temporal Jewifh prince, who was to arife and reign in Judea;
and that accordingly he fuffered himfelf to be carried about by
the mob as their Meffiah for a twelvemonth together; and did
not renounce that character till his death, when he abfolutely
difclaimed his being the Meffiah foretold in the prophetical writings, and died upon that renunciation. As to the apoftles, the
firft authorized teachers and publifhers of the religion of Jefus,
he affirms, that they themfelves never fo much as pretended to be
under the unerring guidance and infpiration of the Holy Ghoft:
that they differed among themfelves about the moft concerning
parts of revelation; and preached different, and even contrary,
gofpels: and that all the apoftles, except St. Paul, preached what
he calls the Jewifh gofpel, viz. *falvation by Jefus Chrift as the
Jewifh Meffiah, i. e.* the national prince and deliverer of the
Jews. This, which he all along explodes as falfe and abfurd, he
reprefents as the only proper effential article of the Chriftian
faith. As to the atteftations given to our Saviour's divine miffion, and to the doctrines taught by the apoftles, by miracles,
prophecy, and the extraordinary gifts of the Holy Ghoft, he
abfolutely denieth them to be any proofs at all. Finally, though
he profeffeth himfelf to be a *Chriftian on the foot of the New*

*Teftament,*

*Teſtament,* yet he repreſenteth it as leaning ſtrongly towards Judaiſm, which is, in his opinion, a ſyſtem of ſuperſtition and *tyranny.* He pretends, that Chriſt's own diſciples repreſented things
according to their Jewiſh prejudices, and therefore *are not to be
depended upon for a juſt account either of doctrines or facts:* and
that the New Teſtament was corrected, reviſed, and publiſhed by
the Jews, who altered it according to their own prejudices and
falſe opinions; ſo that, as it now ſtands, it is a ſyſtem of Judaiſm,
a *jumble of inconſiſtent religions.*

   You will allow me here to obſerve, that a writer muſt have an
uncommon degree of confidence, to repreſent the New Teſtament
as corrupted and altered by the Jews according to their own prejudices and falſe opinions, when not one of their peculiar and
moſt darling notions and prejudices is to be found in this book,
but much to the contrary; whereas, if they corrupted it at all,
it muſt be ſuppoſed that they would have corrupted it in favour
of thoſe notions and prejudices. No-where is the obſervance
of the Moſaic law preſcribed to Chriſtians, or inſiſted upon as
neceſſary to the favour of God under the goſpel. The Meſſiah
there ſpoken of is the author of a ſpiritual ſalvation, and the Saviour of the world, not the national deliverer of the Jews only.
And the Gentiles are repreſented as incorporated into his church
and kingdom, and as ſharers in his benefits, equally with the converted Jews. The New Teſtament is ſo far from being a jumble
of inconſiſtent religions, that it is evidently one and the ſame
ſcheme of religion that is carried on in the writings of the Evangeliſts, the Acts of the Apoſtles, and the Apoſtolical Epiſtles.
The ſame doctrines are every-where taught, relating to God, to
our Lord Jeſus Chriſt, the great and only mediator between God
and man, and the methods of our redemption and ſalvation
through him; relating to the terms of our acceptance with God,
to the reſurrection of the dead, the general judgment, and the
eternal retributions of a future ſtate. The ſame excellent laws
and precepts are every-where inculcated, the ſame duties injoined
towards God and man, the ſame purity of heart and life indiſ-
penſably required, the ſame noble motives are every-where propoſed to animate our obedience, the ſame diſcoveries and diſplays
of the divine grace and mercy, the ſame encouragements given
to the truly penitent, the ſame gracious aſſiſtances promiſed and
                                                        provided

provided for the upright and fincére, the fame awful threatnings denounced againſt thofe that go on in a courſe of preſumptuous fin and difobedience. Thus one beautiful and harmonious ſcheme of religion appears throughout, uniform and conſiſtent in all its parts, which ſhews that thofe ſacred writings have not undergone any material corruption. Some have found fault, that ſome of thofe writings feem to have been written occaſionally, and that the Chriſtian religion is not delivered there in a ſyſtematical way: but it has been much more wifely ordered. If it had been delivered once for all in a formal fyſtem, it might have been more eaſily altered and corrupted, or at leaſt there would have been greater ground of fuſpicion that it was ſo: whereas, as the cafe now ſtands, the doctrines and laws of it, and the moſt important facts relating to it, are repeated and inculcated in fo many places, and on fo many different occaſions, that without a total alteration and corruption of thofe original writings, which could not be effected, the religion muſt ſtill be maintained and preferved,

But to return to our *Moral Philofopher*, he honoureth himſelf, and thofe of his ſentiments, with the title of *Chriſtian Deiſts*, as the author of *Chriſtianity as old as the Creation* had done before him, as if they only were the true Chriſtians; and brandeth all others, *i. e.* thofe that acknowledge the divine authority of the Chriſtian religion, as taught in the New Teſtament, with the character of *Chriſtian Jews.* He frequently inveighs againſt all *hiſtorical faith,* and *books of hiſtorical religion,* as he calls the holy Scriptures, as of no ufe or importance at all; as if the belief of the important facts recorded in the goſpel, relating to our Lord Jeſus Chriſt, had nothing to do with the faith of a Chriſtian. All the religion he is pleafed to allow to thofe whom he characterizeth as Chriſtian Jews, is only an *hiſtorical, political, clerical, mechanical faith and religion;* whilſt he appropriateth *real religion,* and *moral truth and righteoufnefs,* to himſelf, and thofe of his own faction.

One of the firſt tracts which appeared againſt the *Moral Philofopher* was an ingenious piece, written by Mr. Joſeph Hallet, viz. *The Immorality of the Moral Philofopher, being an Anſwer to a Book lately publiſhed, intitled, " The Moral Philofopher,"* 8vo. 1737. He afterwards publiſhed *A Vindication* of it *in a Letter to the Moral Philofopher,* whò had anſwered it. Some

time

time after, there were two large anfwers publifhed to that book, of both which I fhall give a diftinct account. The firft I fhall mention is intitled, *Eufebius, or the true Chriftian's Defence, againft a late Book, intitled,* "*The Moral Philofopher,* Cambridge, 8vo. 1739, by John Chapman, M. A. now Dr. Chapman. In this learned and accurate work, the author doth not examine the whole of the *Moral Philofopher's* book, nor concern himfelf with the particular objections he had brought againft the Jewifh and Chriftian revelation, but applies himfelf to confider the main principles of his fcheme, and on which the whole ftructure depends.

He begins with his fundamental principle, viz. " that moral truth, reafon, and the fitnefs of things, are the fole certain mark or criterion of any doctrine as coming from God." He fhews the ambiguity of the phrafe, and the various fenfes it is capable of, and that in no fenfe can it be underftood to be a proper mark or criterion of any doctrine or law, as having come from God in a way of extraordinary revelation, concerning which alone the queftion lieth: That therefore we muft have fome other mark or criterion, which may evidence an extraordinary interpofition of God, and his teftimony to the truth of what is delivered in his name. And particularly he fetteth himfelf to prove, that miracles and prophecy are evidences of an extraordinary divine interpofition and teftimony. He treats the queftion about miracles, largely and diftinctly; and, after having ftated the true notion of a miracle, fhews, that miracles may be of fuch a nature, and fo circumftanced, as in fome cafes to prove the divine miffion of the perfons by whom they are wrought, and the truth and divine authority of the doctrines which are attefted by them, independently of all confideration of the doctrines themfelves; but that when they are all confidered in conjunction with the good tendency of the doctrines and laws that are thus attefted, they inconteftably demonftrate the divine original of thofe doctrines and laws. He hath good obfervations on the great ufe of miracles, as the plaineft and moft popular, the moft fhort and compendious way of proving a divine revelation, and judicioufly obviates the objections made againft the proof from miracles, both by the *Moral Philofopher,* and by others that have written on the fame argument before him. He alfo vindicates the argument from prophecy againft this writer's exceptions.

Having

Having fhewn what are the true proofs of original revelation, he proceeds to confider *traditional revelation*, concerning which the *Moral Philofopher*, after many others, had raifed a great clamour, under pretence that there can be no fuch thing as divine faith upon fallible human teftimony. This, Dr. Chapman hath examined very fully, and hath clearly fhewn, that the original revelation itfelf, together with the accounts of the proofs or extraordinary facts whereby it was at firft attefted, may be tranfmitted to after-ages, with fuch a degree of evidence, as may make it reafonable for thofe to whom it is thus tranfmitted to receive it as divine, or as having originally come from God, and confequently may lay a juft foundation for their receiving it with a divine faith. He afterwards applieth what he had faid concerning the original proofs of revelation, and concerning that revelation's being fafely tranfmitted to after-ages, to the revelation which was publifhed by our Lord Jefus Chrift, and his apoftles. He fheweth at large, that the miracles which were wrought were of fuch a kind, as were fufficient alone to prove to eye-witneffes his and their divine miffion, and, when farther confidered in conjunction with the doctrines taught by him and them, amounted to a full demonftration of it. He then proceeds to fhew, that thefe miracles, together with particular accounts of our Lord's doctrines, and thofe of his apoftles, were faithfully recorded, and committed to writing by thofe who were witneffes to them; and that thefe writings have been tranfmitted with unqueftionable evidence of their being genuine and uncorrupted in all material points: and that therefore we cannot refufe to receive them, but upon principles which would abfolutely deftroy the credit of all paft facts whatfoever.

He next proceeds to confider and explain the nature of the Chriftian religion as diftinguifhed-from deifm, which the *Moral Philofopher* and others would confound. He anfwers the objections thofe writers had urged from the pretended ambiguity and obfcurity of fcripture, and the differences among Chriftians about the interpretation of the Chriftian doctrines; and concludes with a vindication of that great article of the Chriftian faith, which this writer had endeavoured to pervert and expofe, concerning our Lord Jefus Chrift, as the true Meffiah foretold by the prophets. The prophecies relating to the Meffiah are confidered;

confidered; and from thence it is evinced, that he was not to be
merely a national Prince, and deliverer of the Jews, but the Saviour of the world; and was not merely to erect a temporal dominion, but a fpiritual kingdom of truth and righteoufnefs.

There was another anfwer publifhed about the fame time, *viz.*
*The divine Authority of the Old and New Teftament afferted,* &c.
*againft the unjuft Afperfions and falfe Reafonings of a Book, in-
titled " The Moral Philofopher,"* London, 8vo. 1739. After
what was faid on a like occafion in my laft letter, I fhall make
no apology for giving fome account of this anfwer; which is the
rather neceffary, becaufe the *Moral Philofopher,* in the fecond
volume he publifhed, and of which fome notice muft be taken
afterwards, bent his force principally againft it. The defign of
this anfwer was to take a diftinct view of what Dr. Morgan had
offered both againft revelation in general, and againft the holy
Scriptures in particular: and it coft fome pains to range the objections of that writer in fome order, which are fcattered with a
ftrange confufion through his book. This anfwer begins with
ftating the queftion concerning revelation in general, the ufefulnefs of which the *Moral Philofopher* makes a fhew of acknowledging, and yet in effect leaveth no way of knowing when fuch
a revelation is really given. His pretended fole criterion of moral truth and fitnefs is examined; and it is fhewn, that miracles
may be fo circumftanced for number, nature, and continuance,
as to yield a fufficient atteftation to the divine miffion of the perfons by whom, and to the divine authority of the doctrines and
laws in confirmation of which they are wrought: and that the account of thefe extraordinary miraculous facts, as well as the laws
and doctrines attefted and confirmed by them, may be tranfmitted to us in fuch a manner, that it would be perfectly unreafonable to deny or doubt of them.

From the queftion concerning revelation in general, the author
of this anfwer proceeds to what is the principal defign of his
book, *viz.* to vindicate the revelation contained in the holy
Scriptures of the Old and New Teftament. And firft, the law
of Mofes is vindicated at large againft the objections of the *Moral
Philofopher;* and the excellent defign, nature, and tendency of
it is diftinctly fhewn. Particularly, that law is cleared from the
charge of countenancing and encouraging human facrifices: and

as

as the cafe of Abraham's offering up Ifaac has been often infifted upon, and particularly is reprefented by this writer, as abfolutely fubverfive of the whole law of nature, and a command which it was impoffible for God to give, or for us to have any proof that it was given, care is taken to fet this whole matter in a proper light, and to anfwer the objections that have been made againft it. The fame is done with regard to the war againft the Benjamites in the affair of Gibeah, of which our author had made a moft odious reprefentation, with a view to caft a reflection on the oracle of Urim and Thummim. The prophet Samuel and David are cleared from the unjuft afperfions he had caft upon them: and the fcandalous reprefentation he had made of the latter's dancing naked before the ark; as alfo what Lord Shaftefbury had offered on the fame fubject, and concerning the *naked faltant fpirit of prophecy*, are confidered, and the injuftice and abfurdity of it fhewn. The characters of the ancient prophets are vindicated; and the author's grofs falfifications, and ftrange perverfions of the Scripture-hiftory expofed. With regard to the objections brought by the *Moral Philofopher* againft the New Teftament, particular notice is taken of his bafe infinuations againft the character of our bleffed Saviour, and efpecially of his pretence, that Jefus at his death renounced his being the Meffiah foretold by the prophets. It is fhewn, that he claimed to be the Meffiah, and that he was really fo in the true fenfe of their prophetical writings. As to the apoftles, it is proved, in oppofition to what he had confidently afferted to the contrary, both that they themfelves profeffed to be under the guidance of the Holy Spirit, and that they gave fufficient proofs to convince the world of their divine miffion. The atteftation given to them by the extraordinary gifts of the Holy Ghoft is particularly confidered; and the author's pretence, that the falfe teachers, as well as the true, had thofe extraordinary gifts and powers, and made ufe of them in confirmation of their falfe doctrines, is examined, and fhewn to be vain and groundlefs. The account he giveth of the Jewifh Gofpel, which he pretends was preached by all the apoftles but St. Paul, is fhewn to be entirely his own fiction; and the harmony between St. Paul and the other apoftles, and the wifdom and confiftency of their conduct, are manifefted. The attempt he maketh againft the whole canon of the New Teftament,

as

as if it were corrupted and interpolated by the Jews, is confidered. And whereas, under pretence of rectifying the errors of Chriftianity with regard to fome particular doctrines of Chriftianity, he had feverely inveighed againft the doctrine of Chrift's fatiffaction; this is vindicated againft his exceptions. Finally, the argument he would draw from the differences among Chriftians, to prove that none of the doctrines of revealed religion are of any certainty or ufe to mankind, is fhewn to be vain and inconclufive.

The author of the *Moral Philofopher*, who was a writer of great vivacity, did not continue long filent. He publifhed a defence of his former book, in what he called *The fecond volume of the Moral Philofopher; or, a farther Vindication of Moral, Truth and Reafon.* This was chiefly defigned againft the author of the anfwer laft mentioned, except a long letter addreffed to Eufebius, *i. e.* Dr. Chapman. In this book, he talks with the fame confufion that he did before, concerning moral truth and reafon, as being the fole criterion of divine truth, or truth as coming from God; without adding any new proof, or diftinctly explaining what he means by it. He reprefents his adverfaries, and all the advocates for revelation, as *renouncing all evidence from nature and reafon in matters of religion;* and that, in their fcheme, natural and revealed religion are two *effentially different and oppofite religions.* This is a very unfair reprefentation: fince he could not but know, that they maintain, that there is a harmony and connection between reafon and revelation; and that revelation leaves all the proofs of religion drawn from reafon in their full force, and adds to them the atteftation of a divine authority or teftimony. And this muft certainly be of great weight. It gives a farther degree of certainty and evidence, even with regard to thofe things, of which we might have fome difcovery by our reafon before, as well as furnifheth a fufficient ground of affent with regard to things, which we could not have known by mere unaffifted reafon.

As to the proofs of revelation, he ftill infifteth upon it, that miracles are no proofs: but he takes very little notice of what his anfwerers, and particularly Dr. Chapman, who had treated this queftion largely and diftinctly, had offered to prove that they are fo. He lays down feveral obfervations tending to fhew the

great

great difficulty there is in knowing which are true miracles. To
this purpose he obferves, that men may eafily be miftaken, and
think thofe things to be miracles which are not fo; or they may
be impofed upon by artifice, or the ftrength of their own imaginations, fo as to take thofe things to have been done, which really
were not done: That perfons are much more liable to be deceived,
and often have been fo, in judging of things fuppofed to be fupernatural, than in things that come in the common courfe: and
that if even thofe before whom they are fuppofed to have been
originally wrought may be thus deceived, much more thofe to
whom they come only by report. All that follows from thefe,
and other obfervations to the fame purpofe, amounts really to no
more than this, that great and particular care and caution is neceffary to guard againft deception in things of fo extraordinary a
nature. But it is far from proving, either that it is impoffible that
any true miracles fhould ever be done, or that we fhould have
any fatisfactory evidence or certainty concerning them. Notwithftanding all that this writer hath offered, it is ftill true, that
miracles may be fo circumftanced with regard to their number,
nature, and continuance, that perfons may be as certain of their
having been really done, as they can be of any facts whatfoever
for which they have the teftimony of all their fenfes; and may
be alfo certain, that they are things abfolutely exceeding all human power. They may alfo be of fuch a nature and tendency,
and fo manifeftly defigned to promote the caufe of righteoufnefs
and virtue, that we may be fure they were not done by any evil
being fuperior to man; and muft therefore have been done either
by the immediate power of God himfelf, or by fuperior good
beings acting under his direction. It hath been often fhewn,
that fuch were the miracles wrought at the firft eftablifhment of
the Jewifh and Chriftian difpenfation. They were done in fo
open a manner, and produced fuch effects, that thofe before
whom they were wrought had as full an affurance of the reality
of them, as they could have of any facts whatfoever; and at the
fame time could not be but fenfible that they exceeded all the
power of man. And they were alfo of fuch a nature, that they
could not without the higheft abfurdity be fuppofed to have been
wrought by any evil being or beings; and therefore ought to
be regarded as the teftimony of God to the divine miffion of
the

the perfons by whom, and to the truth and divine original and authority of the doctrines and laws in confirmation of which they were wrought.

Our author indeed hath in this book made an extraordinary attempt, with regard to the miracles of Mofes, to prove, that though that vaft affembly of people were made to believe that thofe things were done before their eyes, and that they them-felves faw them done, yet they were never really done at all; and in order to account for this, he makes fome of the wildeft fuppofitions that ever entered into the head of any man that was not abfolutely out of his fenfes. But left this fhould not take, his next attempt is to prove, that thofe miracles, if wrought at at all, were done by an evil power: as if any evil being, even fuppofing, what is abfurd to imagine, that he were capable of exerting fuch amazing acts of divine power as were exhibited at the eftablifhment of the Mofaic difpenfation, would do it, to confirm a fyftem of laws, which prefcribed the adoration of the one living and true God, in oppofition to the then fpreading idolatry, and ftrongly obliged men to the practice of virtue and righteoufnefs. The chief proof he bringeth for fo ftrange an affertion is, the command relating to the deftruction of the Ca-naanites, on account not only of their impure and cruel idolatries, but of the moft abominable crimes and vices, which then uni-verfally prevailed among them; as if it were impoffible for God, in any circumftances of things, ever to give fuch a command. This, which hath been frequently urged by the writers on that fide, particularly Dr. Tindal, was confidered in the *Anfwer to Chriftianity as old as the Creation*, vol. ii. p. 352—358, 2d edit. And upon its being here repeated by the *Moral Philofopher*, was again examined and obviated in the 2d volume of *The Divine Authority of the Old and New Teftament afferted*, p. 97, &c. It is alfo fet in a proper light by Mr. Lowman, in his *Differtation on the Civil Government of the Hebrews*, p. 220, &c.

As to our Saviour's miracles, this writer pretendeth, contrary to Chrift's own moft exprefs declarations, that he did not appeal to them as proofs of his divine miffion. He alfo repeateth the ftale objection, which hath been often anfwered and expofed, that the miraculous cures which Jefus wrought were owing to the ftrength of fancy and imagination in the patient, and not to

power

power in the agent. But, whatever we fuppofe the force of imagination in fome cafes to be, there are many of our Lord's miracles of fuch a kind, that there cannot poffibly be the leaft room
or pretence for fuch a fuppofition.

With regard to the conveyance of divine revelation, it had
been fhewn, that doctrines and laws which were originally received by revelation from God, together with an account of the
extraordinary facts or proofs whereby that revelation was attefted,
may be tranfmitted to after-ages in a manner that may be fafely
depended upon; and that the doctrines and facts of the Chriftian revelation have been fo tranfmitted.  He hath little to oppofe to the clear and diftinct proofs that were brought for this,
but fome general clamours, which he repeateth on all occafions,
about the uncertainty of tradition and fallibility of human teftimony; though it be inconteftably evident, that laws and facts
may be, and often have been, tranfmitted in this way, with fuch
a degree of evidence and certainty, that it would be perfectly unreafonable, and contrary to common fenfe, to deny or doubt of
them: and yet all along throughout his whole book, he argues
as if it were fufficient to deftroy the authority of the fcripture-
revelation, that its doctrines and laws, and the account of its important facts, have been tranfmitted through the hands of weak
and fallible men.  This he reprefenteth as a placing the moft
important divine truth on the foot of fallible human teftimony.
But however fpecious this may appear, and fitted to impofe upon
fuperficial inquirers, there is nothing in it of real weight: for if
a revelation or law had any original divine authority, and, that
it might be of ufe to fucceeding ages, was committed to writing,
which is the fureft method of conveyance; and if we have fufficient evidence to give us reafonable affurance, that this written
revelation has been fafely tranfmitted to us, without any material
corruption or alteration, as hath been often plainly fhewn with
regard to the Chriftian revelation; then it is as really of divine
authority now as it was at firft, and we are obliged to receive
and fubmit to it as fuch.  For it doth not lofe its authority by
being committed to writing; nor doth its authority depend on
the intermediate conveyers, any more than the authority of a law
formerly enacted by the legiflature can be faid to depend upon

the perfons by whom it has been tranfcribed or printed, but upon its having been originally enacted by the legiflature*.

As to the objections this writer had urged in his former book againft the revelation contained in the holy fcriptures of the Old and New Teftament, and which had been particularly confidered, he repeats them again in this book with greater confidence than before, and often without taking the leaft notice of what was offered to the contrary; or if he makes a fhew of anfwering, very lightly paffeth over what was of principal importance in the argument. He gives himfelf little trouble about the grofs mifreprefentations and falfifications of the facred hiftory which had been plainly proved upon him, but ftill perfifteth in the charges he had advanced, and addeth farther invectives; at the fame time affuring his reader, that his anfwerer *had not faid one word to the purpofe,* and that what he had offered was *one continued rant.* And fometimes, as in the cafe of the Meffiah's being, according to the prophetical writings, a mere temporal prince of the Jews only, our author, inftead of anfwering the proofs which had been brought to the contrary, declares it to be a point fo evident, that he *fcorns to difpute with any man that will deny it,* *i. e.* he fcorns to difpute with any man that 'will not give him up the very point in queftion.

Thefe are arts of controverfy which none would envy him the honour of. And he frequently expreffeth himfelf in a manner that fhews little regard to common decency: as when he faith of David, *Away with him to the devil from whence he came!* And fpeaking of the Jews, he avers, that this *miraculoufly ftupid people was always infpired and poffeffed with the fpirit of the devil.* And the Chriftians come in for their fhare of the compliment; for he adds, that *they, i. e.* the Jews, have *transfufed their fpirit and faith into Chriftians.*

It would not be worth while to mention thefe things, if it were not to give fome idea of the temper and genius of this writer. He has gone fo far as boldly to pronounce, that the God of Ifrael, to whom the priefthood was *inftituted,* and *facrifices* were *offered,* was a *cheat* and an *idol,* as much fo as any of the Pagan

---

* See concerning this, " Divine Authority of the Old and New Teftament afferted," vol. ii. p. 24, 25.

deities,

deities, and that he was only confidered as a local tutelar deity;
though one would think it fcarce poffible for any man ferioufly
to read the Old Teftament, and not be fenfible that the God
there every-where recommended to our adoration and obedience,
and whom the people of Ifrael were obliged by their law to worfhip, exclufively of all idol deities, is reprefented as the maker of
heaven and earth, the fovereign Lord of the univerfe. In his
former book, he had fometimes fpoken with great feeming refpect
of Chriftianity; but here he throws off all difguife, and does what
he can to expofe it to the derifion and contempt of mankind.
Nothing can be more fcandalous than the reprefentation he makes
of the effufion of the Holy Ghoft on the day of Pentecoft. He
avers, that thofe who had the gift of tongues could not fpeak thofe
languages with any fenfe, coherence, or confiftency; that they
only uttered a ftrange kind of gibberifh, which neither they themfelves nor any body elfe could underftand. And yet it appears
from the account that is given us, that the people of many different countries, which were come from all parts to Jerufalem
at the feaft of Pentecoft, underftood the apoftles, as fpeaking to
them in their feveral languages the *great things of God*, and
were filled with fuch admiration on this account as produced the
converfion of great numbers of them to the Chriftian faith. He
pronounces, that they who feemed to have thefe gifts *were out
of their wits for the time,* and exprefsly calls them *frantic fits;*
and what is very extraordinary, pretends to prove all this from
the authority of St. Paul himfelf, who, according to his reprefentation, muft have been one of the maddeft enthufiafts that ever
lived; though at other times he thinks fit to extol him as *the bold
and brave defender of religion and liberty.*

He concludes his book with a frefh invective againft the law
of Mofes, as if it were defigned to indulge men in perfonal in-
temperance, and were wholly calculated for the intereft of his
own family; though no lawgiver ever gave greater proofs of his
difintereftednefs than Mofes did; as he made no provifion for
raifing his own children to honours and dignities in the ftate,
but left them to continue in the rank of common Levites. The
laft thing he mentions is the law about the trial of jealoufy, of
which he gives a ftrange account. But this, as was clearly proved
againft him, dependeth wholly upon his own falfe and arbitary

fuppofitions,

suppofitions, which betray either great ignorance or wilful mif-reprefentation*.

It could not be a very agreeable employment to carry on a controverfy with fuch a writer. There is however a fecond volume publifhed of the *Divine Authority of the Old and New Teftament afferted*, by the author of the firft, which was defigned as an anfwer to the fecond volume of the *Moral Philofopher*, London, 8vo, 1740. In this reply, every thing in his book is confidered that had any appearance of reafon and argument; and his unfair reprefentations, his unjuft afperfions, and confident attempts to impofe falfehoods upon his reader, are detected and expofed. And whereas there is no part of his book that feems to have been more laboured, than where he undertakes to prove, that the tribe of Levi had above twenty fhillings in the pound upon all the lands of Ifrael, the extravagance of his computations is plainly fhewn. But no man hath fet this matter in a clearer light, than Mr. Lowman, in his learned and judicious *Differtation on the Civil Government of the Hebrews; in which the Juftice, Wifdom, and Goodnefs of the Mofaical Conftitution are vindicated; in particular from fome late unfair and falfe Reprefentations of them in the* " *Moral Philofopher,*" London, 8vo, 1740.

But this author was not to be convinced or filenced. He foon after publifhed what he called the *Third Volume of the Moral Philofopher; or, Superftition and Tyranny inconfiftent with Theocracy,* London, 8vo, 1740. In the body of this book, which is particularly defigned as an anfwer to the fecond volume of the *Divine Authority of the Old and New Teftament afferted,* there is fcarce any thing new attempted. The fame things are repeated over again, in a ftrain of confidence peculiar to this writer; and at this rate it is eafy to write books and carry on controverfies without end. But there fcarce needs any other confutation of what he hath here offered, than to defire the reader carefully to compare it with the book to which it is pretended to be an anfwer. The only farther obfervation I would make upon it is, that our author, contrary to his ufual cuftom, has in one inftance condefcended to acknowledge a miftake he had been guilty of in

---

* See " Divine Authority of the Old and New Teftament afferted," vol. ii. p. 362, & feq.

his former volume. It is in his computation of the Levitical
revenues, in which he had made an overcharge in one single article of no lefs than one million two hundred thoufand pounds a
year. Yet fo fond is he of what he had advanced concerning the
Levites having, by the Mofaical conftitution, the whole wealth
and power of the nation in their hands, that he ftill endeavours
to fupport it by fome very extraordinary calculations; the falfity and abfurdity of which was foon after clearly and fully expofed by Mr. Lowman, in an appendix to his *Differtation on the
Civil Government of the Hebrews*, London, 1741. But the moft remarkable thing in the third volume of the *Moral Philofopher*, and
that part of it which may be moft properly called new, is a long
introduction, of above an hundred pages, in which he pretends to
give an account of the ancient patriarchal religion, and an hiftorical relation of the defcent of the Hebrew fhepherds into Egypt;
the rife and foundation of the Mofaic theocracy; the inconfiftencies and felf-contradictions of the Hebrew hiftorians, &c. In
this part of his work he hath, if poffible, exceeded himfelf in
mifreprefentation and abufe: but I fhall take no farther notice of it
than to obferve, that there were folid and ingenious remarks made
upon it, by a gentleman that ftiles himfelf " Theophanes Canta-
brigienfis," in a pamphlet intitled, *The ancient Hiftory of the Hebrews vindicated*, Cambridge, 8vo, 1741. And afterwards by Dr.
Samuel Chandler, in his *Vindication of the Hiftory of the Old
Teftament, in anfwer to the Mifreprefentations and Calumnies of
Thomas Morgan, M. D. and Moral Philofopher:* the firft part
of which was publifhed, London, 1741, and a fecond part came out
in 1743, and after Dr. Morgan's death. It is here plainly proved,
that this writer hath been guilty of manifeft falfehoods, and of the
moft grofs perverfions of the fcripture-hiftory, even in thofe very
inftances in which he affureth his reader, he hath kept clofe to
the accounts given by the Hebrew hiftorians. The author of the
*Refurrection of Jefus confidered*, who wrote foon after, thought
fit to make a very contemptuous reprefentation of Dr. Chandler's
performance. He is pleafed to reprefent him, as having levelled all his artillery of wit, learning, and fpleen againft the *Moral
Philofopher*, Dr. Morgan, inftead of anfwering; and as having
fired off twenty fheets to fhoot one of his, and miffed the mark.*

* Refurrection of Jefus confidered, p. 71, 72. edit. 3d.
M 3                                This

This no doubt muſt paſs for a full confutation of Dr. Chandler's work.   But all that can be gathered from it is, that, with theſe gentlemen, the proving of any of them guilty of the moſt groſs falſifications of ſcripture, which had been fully proved upon Dr. Morgan, is to paſs for a thing of no conſequence; as if falſehood and miſrepreſentation were to be looked upon as very allowable, when put in practice for ſo good an end as the expoſing Chriſtianity and the holy ſcripture.   It is proper here to obſerve, that the ingenious Mr. Hallet, who, as was mentioned before, had early appeared againſt the firſt volume of the *Moral Philoſopher*, publiſhed alſo *A Rebuke to the Moral Philoſopher for the Errors and Immoralities contained in his third Volume, 8vo*, 1740.

I ſhall conclude this account of the *Moral Philoſopher* with obſerving, that ſoon after his third volume appeared, Dr. Chapman publiſhed a ſecond volume of his *Euſebius, or the true Chriſtian's farther Defence againſt the Principles and Reaſonings of the Moral Philoſopher*, London, 8vo, 1741.   In this he conſiders at large all that this writer had offered concerning what he calls the Jewiſh goſpel, which he confidently affirms was preached by all the apoſtles but St. Paul, and of which he pretends the temporal kingdom of Chriſt in the Jewiſh ſenſe was the principal article.   He ſhews, with the cleareſt evidence, that this was not preached by any of the apoſtles, and that there was a perfect harmony between them and St. Paul, as to what concerned the authority and obligation of the Jewiſh law under the goſpel.   He alſo judiciouſly explains and vindicates the ſcripture-doctrine of redemption, and the ſatisfaction of Chriſt, againſt that author's objections and groſs miſrepreſentations.

The following this extraordinary writer through his ſeveral books, and the anſwers that were made to him, has engaged me in a detail which I am afraid has not proved very agreeable to you, any more than it has been ſo to myſelf. But it may be of ſome uſe to ſhew, that, notwithſtanding his boaſted pretences, there have been few writers who have been more effectually confuted and expoſed, than he that was pleaſed to honour himſelf with the title of the *Moral Philoſopher*.

## LETTER XI.

*Observations upon the pernicious Tendency of the Pamphlet in-*
*titled* Christianity not founded on Argument—*The Design of*
*it is to shew, that the Christian Faith has nothing to support it*
*but a senseless Enthusiasm—The Author's great Disingenuity*
*and Misrepresentations of Scripture detected—He strikes at*
*natural Religion, as well as revealed, destroys all Certainty of*
*Reason, and declares against Education, and the instructing*
*Children in any Principles at all—The principal Arguments*
*he hath offered in Support of his Scheme considered—Chris-*
*tianity no Enemy to Examination and Inquiry—Men's being*
*commanded to believe, no Presumption that Faith is not a rea-*
*sonable Assent—The Faith required in the Gospel is properly*
*a Virtue, and the Unbelief there condemned is really a Vice—*
*His Pretence, that the People are not capable of discerning the*
*Force of the Proofs brought for Christianity, and therefore*
*cannot be obliged to believe it, examined—Account of the An-*
*swers published against him.*

SIR,

THE controversy with the *Moral Philosopher* was scarce at
an end, when a new and very remarkable pamphlet appeared,
intitled, *Christianity not founded on Argument*, London, 1742.
The author of this carried on his design against the Christian religion, in a way somewhat different from what others had done
before him. Under specious appearances of zeal for religion,
and under the cover of devout expressions, he hath endeavoured
to shew, that the Christian faith hath no foundation in reason,
nor hath any thing to support it but a wild and senseless enthusiasm, destitute of all proof and evidence. And if this could be
made out, it would no doubt answer the intention he too plainly
appears to have had in view, the exposing the Christian religion
to the derision and contempt of mankind. With great gravity
and seeming seriousness he sets himself to shew, that a rational
faith, *i. e.* as he explains it, " an assent to revealed truth founded
" upon the conviction of the understanding, is a false and un-
M 4                              " warrantable

" warrantable notion\*." That " that perſon beſt enjoys faith
" who never aſked himſelf one ſingle queſtion about it, and never
" dealt at all in the evidence of reaſon †." That God never intended that we ſhould make uſe of our reaſon, or intellectual
faculty at all in believing, or that our faith ſhould be founded
upon any evidence which might convince the judgment, or make
it reaſonable for us to believe. This he undertakes formally to
prove, firſt by ſeveral arguments drawn from the nature of reaſon
and religion; and afterwards he endeavoureth to prove the ſame
thing from the account given us in ſcripture.

Having thus, as he pretends, removed the falſe grounds of
faith and religion, and ſhewn that it hath nothing to do with reaſon or argument, he next proceeds to declare what is the true
principle of faith; and this he reſolves wholly into a *conſtant
particular revelation, imparted ſeparately and ſupernaturally to
every individual* ‡: That " the Holy Ghoſt irradiates the ſouls
" of believers at once with an irreſiſtible light from heaven, that
" flaſhes conviction in a moment; ſo that this faith is completed
" in an inſtant, and the moſt perfect and finiſhed creed produced
" at once, without any tedious progreſs in deductions of our
" own §." He repreſents this great dictator and infallible guide,
as having promiſed " to abide with us to the end of the world,
" that we might not be left liable one moment to a poſſibility of
" error and impoſture ‖; and as ſpeaking the ſame thing to all,
" and bringing them to think all alike \*\*. Nothing can be more
abſurd in itſelf, nothing more contrary to plain undeniable fact,
than this immediate infallible inſpiration of every particular perſon, which cauſes *men to think all alike*, and does not leave them
liable one moment to a *poſſibility of error and impoſture;* and
yet this he makes to be the ſole foundation of the Chriſtian faith.
He repreſents it to be of ſuch a nature as to render all outward
inſtruction, and even the ſcriptures themſelves, entirely needleſs;
and that thoſe who are thus inſtructed by the ſpirit, " need not
" concern themſelves about the credit of ancient miracles, or
" the genuineneſs of diſtant records:" as if the Chriſtian faith
had nothing to do with the facts recorded in the goſpels. This

---

\* Chriſtianity not founded on Argument, p. 7.      † Ibid. p. 29.
‡ Ibid. p. 112.      § Ibid. p. 89.      ‖ Ibid. p. 60.      \*\* Ibid. p. 89.

he calls the *revealed and scriptural account of the matter* \*; and pretends, that " this account depends not upon the strength of " any single quotation whatever, but on the joint tendency and " tenor of the whole †."

This pamphlet was received by the enemies of Christianity with great applause; and yet, upon a close examination, there are such apparent marks of great disingenuity in it, as should tend, with fair and candid minds, to give very disadvantageous impressions both of the author, and of a cause that needs such base arts to support it.

The whole turn of the pamphlet is in a religious strain: he formally pretends to offer up his most ardent prayers in behalf of his friend at the throne of grace, " that God would be pleased " himself to illuminate and irradiate his mind with a perfect and " thorough conviction of the truth of his holy gospel; that the " same Holy Spirit that first dictated the divine law would power- " fully set on his seal, and attest its authority in his heart ‡." Such a strain of ridicule as this, for whosoever impartially con- siders this treatise can regard it in no other view, is one of the most solemn mockeries that were ever offered to the Supreme Being.   In many other passages, under pretence of exalting the influence of the Holy Spirit, the scriptures are depreciated, as of no use: They are called, by way of contempt, *manuscript au- thorities*, and *paper revelations;* as if the being committed to writing could destroy the authority of a divine law; when the man would be thought out of his senses that should, under the same pretence, attempt to invalidate the authority of human laws. It is observable, that the most highflown enthusiasts have always spoken with disregard of the holy scripture, and represented it as a *dead letter;* which by the way is no great sign of its being of an enthusiastic nature and tendency: and this writer hath endeavoured to take advantage of their madness for exposing the authority of the sacred writings.   Thus the deists can upon occasion run into the wilds of enthusiasm, and join with the men they most heartily despise, in order to answer their design of ex- posing Christianity.   Such hath been the fate of holy writ, to be

---

\* Christianity not founded on Argument, p. 68.
† Ibid. p. 105. •            ‡ Ibid. p. 111.

under-

undervalued by thofe that had no religion at all, and by thofe that have carried religion up to madnefs and phrenzy.

But what greatly ſtrengthens the charge of diſingenuity againſt this writer is, that he is guilty of the moſt groſs miſrepreſentations of ſcripture, and the matters of faƈt therein contained: ſome of which are of ſuch a kind as to be ſcarce reconcileable to any degree of honeſty and candour. He pretends to prove, from the plain narrative part of the New Teſtament hiſtory, that Chriſt and his apoſtles, in planting the goſpel, never propoſed arguments or evidences of any kind to engage men to believe: whereas it is manifeſt, from the accounts given in the *goſpels*, the *aƈts*, and the *epiſtles*, that the method Chriſt and his apoſtles took to make converts was, by aſſiduous inſtruƈtion, by teaching and preaching, and by laying before them evidences of the moſt convincing kind, and which made it reaſonable for them to believe.

There can ſcarce be a more glaring inſtance of diſingenuity than to aſſert, as this writer does, contrary to Chriſt's own moſt expreſs declarations (concerning which, ſee John v. 36. x. 25. 38. xiv. 11. Matth. xi. 3, 4, 5, 6.), that he himſelf never deſigned, that his miracles ſhould be regarded as proofs and evidences of his divine miſſion; that he was *always remarkably upon the reſerve when he happened among unbelieving company:* and that he took particular care that his miracles ſhould not come to public notice, and *See thou tell no man* was generally the charge: though it is manifeſt from the whole goſpel, that he generally wrought his miracles in the moſt public way, before great numbers of people, and in the preſence even of his moſt malicious adverſaries; and there were only a very few inſtances in which he ſeemed to be upon the reſerve, for which no doubt there were good reaſons, ſome of which may be gathered from the circumſtances of the caſes mentioned. But ſuch is the manner of this writer; if he can find a particular inſtance or two that°ſeems favourable to his intention, he lays hold of this, contrary to the whole tenor of the goſpel-hiſtory, and would put it upon his reader, as if what was done for ſpecial reaſons in a very few inſtances, were conſtantly and always the caſe in every inſtance. Thus he poſitively aſſerts, that our Saviour " conſtantly ſtipu" lated before-hand, for a certain degree, and no ordinary one, " of confidence and perſuaſion in the perſons on whom he wrought

" his

" his miracles\*." This he feems to lay a particular ftrefs upon; and yet it is fo far from being true that this was *conftantly* the cafe, that there are comparatively but a very few inftances in which he previoufly required perfons to profefs their belief in him. In one of the anfwers to this pamphlet, there are near fifty inftances produced of miracles wrought by our Saviour where no fuch thing was required †. And in the few inftances where it was infifted upon, it was not a commanding thofe to believe in an inftant who did not believe before: it was only a requiring them to profefs the faith they already had, and a declaring his approbation of their faith, and was defigned as a means to ftrengthen it more and more. And the propriety of his taking this method in fome inftances is manifeft, as it tended to direct men's views to that which was the principal ufe and end of his miracles, and which our author hath thought fit to deny, *viz.* to confirm their faith in his divine miffion.

With the fame unfairnefs he confidently avers, that, according to the fcripture accounts, the apoftles always expected to make their converts by a word's fpeaking; that they never allowed any time for deliberation, but denounced damnation againft thofe that hefitated in the leaft; and that they difcouraged all examination and inquiry: when on the contrary it appeareth, that they often ftaid a confiderable time together in a place, reafoning in the fynagogues, repeating their excellent inftructions, and performing the moft illuftrious miracles, as proofs of their divine miffion. Thus St. Paul abode for a long time at Iconium, for a year and fix months at Corinth, and for above two years at Ephefus. It is alfo evident that they encouraged men to examination and inquiry, and commended them when they did fo: a remarkable inftance of which we have in the encomium beftowed upon the Bereans, who examined the apoftles' doctrine, and *fearched the fcriptures daily, whether thefe things were fo,* as they had taught them: and the confequence of this their diligent examination was, that *many of them believed,* Acts xvii. 10, 11, 12.

The reprefentation this author makes of the influence of the Holy Spirit imparted to all believers is alfo highly difingenuous,

---

\* Chriftianity not founded on Argument, p. 49.
† Benfon's Reafonablenefs of the Chrift. Relig. &c. p. 181—188.

though in it he pretends to keep clofe to the fcripture accounts. He reprefents it as abfolutely excluding all outward teaching, and all ufe of our own endeavours: and yet nothing can be more evident than it is from the whole gofpel, that we are required to be diligent in the ufe of our own endeavours; and the great ufefulnefs of outward teaching is conftantly fuppofed, and provifion is made for its continuance in the Chriftian church. With the like candour he pretendeth, that, according to the fcripture account, faith is perfected in an inftant, and admitteth of no degrees; and that the Spirit caufeth all believers to *think all alike*, and raifeth them above all *poffibility of error:* whereas it is evident, that faith is there reprefented as not ordinarily completed at once, but capable of continual growth and improvement, and as admitting of various degrees. And it is everywhere fuppofed, that believers may in many things be of different fentiments, and are to bear with one another in their differences.

Thefe, and other things of the like kind, are fo palpably mifreprefented, that it can hardly be fuppofed that this writer himfelf, who is quick-fighted enough when he pleafes, fhould not have been fenfible that they were fo.

Another thing that may give us no very advantageous notion of the author's defign is, that he hath advanced feveral things which feem to have a bad afpect on natural religion as well as revealed, and reprefenteth the former as not founded on reafon and argument any more than the latter. He pretends, that all attempts to prove the principles of natural religion by reafon hath done more harm than good; and that " even upon the plaineft " queftion in nature, the exiftence of a Deity, the laboured pro- " ductions of Dr. Clarke himfelf have rather contributed to make " for the other fide of the queftion, and raifed a thoufand new " doubts in the reader's mind *. Accordingly he takes a great deal of pains to deftroy all certainty of reafon. He reprefents it as perpetually fluctuating, and never capable of coming to a certainty about any thing; and as if truth and falfehood may be equally proved by it. The bulk of mankind are, according to him, under a natural incapacity of acting at all: and as to *the ableft and beft of men*, " they are equally difqualified for fair reafoning

---

* Chriftianity not founded on Argument, p. 81.

" by

" by their natural prejudices; which, being ever earlier than the
" firſt efforts of reaſon, is as abſolute a diſqualification for ſuch
" a trial, as the greateſt natural incapacity*."

But ſurely all who have any regard to religion, or who think
that reaſon is an advantage or privilege, and that men are to be
regarded as rational thinking beings, moral agents, muſt look
upon this way of repreſenting things as abſolutely ſubverſive of
all religion and morality. It tendeth to debaſe and vilify human
nature, and to caſt diſhonour upon God's government and providence; as if he had taken no care of mankind at all, but gave
them up entirely to their paſſions, without any principle of reaſon
to guide or govern them; or at leaſt had placed them in ſuch
circumſtances, that, as this writer declares, reaſon always *comes
too late with its aſſiſtance*, and not till we *are loſt in the power of
evil habits beyond recovery*.

To all this it may be added, that there are ſeveral paſſages in
his book, in which he abſolutely declares againſt inſtructing children in religious or moral principles, as a wicked attempt to pre-
poſſeſs their tender minds, and as barring all farther improvement.
No care is to be taken to cultivate the minds of young perſons,
under pretence that this would only tend to fill them with prejudices. Thus there is no advantage at all in being born in an
enlightened or civilized age or nation; and a child in Great
Britain muſt be left as much without inſtruction, as if he were
born in the wilds of America. To make this ſcheme of a piece,
and perfectly conſiſtent, it ſhould be ſo contrived, that children
ſhould not be trained up to any language at all, and that they
ſhould be kept from all converſe with others, for fear of their
being prepoſſeſſed; and that they ſhould be left wholly to nature, without inſtruction of any kind. And what a hopeful
ſtate of things this would introduce, is eaſy to ſee. Thus, to
avoid Chriſtianity, theſe gentlemen ſeem willing to ſink us into
the loweſt degree of barbariſm and brutality.

Having made theſe general obſervations on the ſpirit and deſign of this applauded performance, and the pernicious tendency
of it to ſubvert all certainty of reaſon, and natural religion as
well as revealed, I ſhall now take ſome notice of the principal

---

* Chriſtianity not founded on Argument, p. 17, 18. 23. 26.

things

things he hath offered in fupport of his fcheme, and to fhew that Chriftianity hath no foundation in reafon.

One of his arguments bears a near affinity to what has been juft mentioned concerning education : for he produceth it as a proof, that the chriftian religion is not a rational one, becaufe we are baptized into it, and obliged to train up children in the knowledge and belief of it. A ftrange argument this ! fince common fenfe tells us, that the more rational and excellent any religion is, the more requifite it would be to inftruct children in the principles of it, and to fet its doctrines and evidences in a proper light before them, as far as they are capable of receiving them : for this would be the beft prefervative againft the pernicious influence of corrupt principles, and the power of wrong affections and evil habits, which otherwife, by the author's own acknowledgment, would be apt to get the ftart of them, and give a wrong bias to the mind.

He feems to lay a great ftrefs on the fudden converfions we fometimes read of in the New Teftament : but they are far from being proofs of what he brings them to prove, that thofe perfons were converted without reafon and evidence. All that can be fairly concluded from thofe inftances is, that the evidence that was offered was fo ftrong, and came with fuch light and force, as did more to produce conviction in a fhort time, than a long courfe of abftracted reafonings would have done. If there were fome thoufands, as he obferves, converted at one lecture *, thefe inftances only relate to the converfions that were wrought at Jerufalem foon after our Lord's refurrection and afcenfion, of which the people had fuch convincing evidences by the extraordinary effufion of the Holy Ghoft on the day of Pentecoft, and the fignal and undeniable miracles wrought by the difciples in the name of a rifen Jefus, as, joined with what they had known before of our Saviour's admirable difcourfes and illuftrious miracles, as well as the extraordinary events that had happened at his crucifixion, to which they themfelves had been witnefles, rendered the evidence fo ftrong and ftriking, that it was perfectly rational to fubmit to it, and receive it.

The paffage of the apoftle, 2 Cor. x. 4, 5. *The weapons of our*

* Chriftianity not founded on Argument, p. 39.

*warfare*

*warfare are not carnal, but mighty through God to the pulling down of strong holds, casting down imaginations, or reasonings, and every high thing that exalteth itself against the knowledge of God, and bringing into captivity every thought to the obedience of Christ,* is produced by this writer to shew that the gospel is not only without all evidence, but contrary to reason. And yet the manifest design of it is to shew, not that the gospel had no evidence to support it, but that the evidences accompanying it were so strong and convincing, as were vastly superior to any arguments or reasonings that could be brought against it. But there is no injunction there laid upon Christians, as the author pretends, " to lay reason under the most absolute restraint and " prohibition, and not to permit it the least opportunity or " freedom to exert itself, or interpose upon any occasion what- " soever *."

Another argument with which he makes a mighty parade is to this purpose, that no religion can be rational that is not founded on a free and impartial examination †. And such examination supposes a perfect neutrality to the principles which are examined, and even a temporal disbelief of them, which is what the gospel condemneth. But this proceeds upon a wrong account of the nature of free examination and inquiry. It is not necessary to a just inquiry into doctrines or facts, that a man should be absolutely indifferent to them before he begins that inquiry, much less that he should actually disbelieve them; as if he must necessarily commence atheist, before he can fairly examine into the proofs of the existence of God. It is sufficient to a candid examination, that a man applieth himself to it with a mind open to conviction, and a disposition to embrace truth on which side soever it shall appear, and to receive the evidence that shall arise in the course of the trial. And if the inquiry relateth to principles in which we have been instructed, then, supposing those principles to be in themselves rational and well founded, it may well happen, that, in inquiring into the grounds of them, a fair examination may be carried on without seeing cause to disbelieve, or doubt of them through the whole course of the enquiry; which in that case will end in a fuller conviction of them than before.

---

\* Christianity not founded on Argument, p. 84.　　† Ibid. p. 5.

But there is no argument on which he seems to place a greater
stress, to shew that Christianity is not founded on reason and evidence, than this, that we are there authoritatively commanded to
believe, and penalties are denounced against us if we do not believe: whereas it is plain, that " no proposition can be tendered
" to our reason with penalties annexed, or under the restraint
" of threats and authority:*" since assent or dissent is an
" independent event, under no influence of ours." Men are
constantly determined to believe according to the evidence that
appeareth to them, and the will hath nothing to do with it: and
therefore there can be no virtue in believing truth, or fault in rejecting it. And he expresly affirms, " that a determination
" either right or wrong in matters which are not self-evident,
" and in which there is any thing of induction or inference, is
" equally meritorious†." This is a very convenient plea for
infidelity, and so it is for atheism itself: since it proceeds upon
this foundation, that men can never be obliged to believe any
principles at all in which there is any thing of induction or inference, nor consequently those relating to the existence of God
and a providence. And if there be no fault in disbelieving those
principles, there can be no fault in refusing to obey, or worship
him, which necessarily dependeth upon the belief of his existence.
But the foundation this goes upon is manifestly false; as if men
were always, and in all cases, determined by mere evidence, and
that assent and dissent were therefore necessary acts, and absolutely out of their power. Nothing is more undeniable from
common observation and experience, than that the will and affections have a great influence on the judgment; and that we have
a great deal of freedom in the right or wrong use of our reasoning faculties, and consequently are liable to praise or blame on
that account. Let the proofs that are offered be ever so plain,
we may choose whether we will attend to them; or we may turn
our eyes from the evidence; or, if we profess to examine, may,
through prepossession and wrong dispositions of mind, institute
a slight, a partial, and defective examination. Men may be, and
often are, so biassed by the influence of affections and interests,
as to cause things to appear to them in a quite different light than

---

* Christianity not founded on Argument. p. 8.          † Ibid. 17, 18.

otherwise

otherwife they would do. All the world owns, that a candour and fimplicity of heart, the love of truth, and a readinefs to embrace it when fairly propofed, is a very commendable difpofition of mind; and that refufing to receive it through the influence of corrupt affections and paffions is really culpable. But this efpecially holdeth in truths of a religious and moral nature. Our believing or difbelieving them is very much influenced by the good or bad difpofitions of our minds, and muft have a great effect upon the practice : and therefore in thefe cafes to receive and embrace thefe truths may be an important duty, and to difbelieve or reject them may be highly criminal : and God may very juftly interpofe his authority to require the one, and warn men againft the other.

The author all along fuppofeth, that the faith required in the gofpel is no more than a bare affent of the underftanding, and the unbelief there condemned is a mere fpeculative diffent. But this is a wrong reprefentation : nothing is more evident than that the faith required in the gofpel of thofe to whom it is made known, that faith to which the promifes are made, is a complex thing : it includeth a love of truth, and a difpofition to embrace and profefs it, which, in the circumftances in which Chriftianity firft appeared, argued a great deal both of candour and fortitude : and it is always reprefented to be of a vital operative nature, a principle of holy obedience, and which purifieth the heart, and leadeth men to do the will of God, and obey his commands. And fuch a faith is certainly a virtue, and very properly the fubject of a divine command : and the unbelief there condemned is fuppofed to proceed from men's being under the influence of corrupt affections and prejudices, and from their unwillingnefs to receive the truth, becaufe their deeds are evil. It is expreffed by their *fhutting* their eyes, and *hardening* their hearts, left they fhould *fee with their eyes*, and *underftand with their hearts*, and be *converted* and *healed*. And this certainly argueth a bad and vicious difpofition of foul, and leadeth to difobedience; and is therefore very properly forbidden in the divine law.

With regard to human laws, when they are once fufficiently promulgated, it would fcarce be accepted as a plea for men's neglecting or breaking thofe laws, that they are not fatisfied that they are the king's laws; and that no man can be juftly obliged, under the reſtraint of authority and penalties, to aſſent to this propoſition, that theſe are the king's laws; ſince aſſent is not in our own power. It is very probable, that a way would ſoon be found to over-rule this plea, and convince them that authority could interpoſe in this matter. In like manner, it ſeems to be obvious to the com-mon ſenſe and reaſon of mankind, that if God hath given a re-velation or diſcovery of his will, concerning doctrines and laws of importance to our duty and happineſs, and hath cauſed them to be promulgated with ſuch evidence as he knoweth to be ſufficient to convince reaſonable and well-diſpoſed minds, that will care-fully attend to it, he hath an undoubted right to require thoſe to whom this revelation is publiſhed to receive and to obey it. And if, through the influence of corrupt affections and luſts, thoſe to whom this revelation is made known refuſe to receive it, he can juſtly puniſh them for their culpable neglect, obſtinacy, and diſobedience. Our author himſelf, ſpeaking of the ſpirit's working faith in all men, ſaith, though in evident contradiction to his own ſcheme, that " the tender of this conviction, however potent in " its influence, may yet depend greatly upon the proper diſ-" poſitions of our minds to give it a reception for its efficacy ; " and ſo far will give place, and afford ample matter of trial and " probation, and become indeed a teſt of our obedience. And " that in this caſe diſbelief and guilt have a meaning when put " together ; ſince the compliance required is, not a compliance " out of our power, nor any longer that of the underſtanding, " but of the will, in its nature free, and therefore accountable ; " and though we are not by any means chargeable for the effects " of our apprehenſion, yet there is no reaſon but that we may " be with all juſtice called to the ſtricteſt account for our ob-" ſtinacy, impiety, and perverſeneſs [*]."

I ſhall only take notice of one thing more, and which is indeed the moſt plauſible thing in his whole book, and that is, that the generality of mankind, even of thoſe among whom Chriſtianity is publiſhed, cannot be obliged to believe it, becauſe they have not a capacity to diſcern and judge of the proofs and arguments which are brought for it. But though it ſhould be allowed, that they could not of themſelves trace thoſe proofs and evidences;

[*] Chriſtianity not founded on Argument, p. 64.

yet

yet there are few but may be made fenfible of the force of thofe proofs and evidences, when fet before them by others. And this is fufficient. It is evident to any one that knows mankind, that we are fo conftituted, as to ftand in need of mutual affiftance and information, in matters of great confequence to our duty and happinefs. Moft of the principles of fcience of every kind are things that muft be taught; and there are few that reafon out thofe principles for themfelves, but proceed upon them as demonftrated by others, and apply themfelves to practife the rules that are founded on thofe principles. In like manner religion muft be taught, or the moft of mankind will know but little of it. And if it requireth care and application to underftand its doctrines and precepts, and the evidences whereby it is confirmed, this is no argument at all, either againft its reafonablenefs or excellence: for nothing that is truly excellent in knowledge or practice is to be attained to without care and diligence. It is every man's duty in this cafe to take in what helps and informations he can get: and if we can come to perceive the evidence by the affiftance of others, this will anfwer the purpofes of religion as well as if we could do it merely by the force of our own reafon without any affiftance at all.

It would undoubtedly be a thing above the capacity of the generality of mankind, and what the moft learned would not be well fitted for, to trace out all the parts of religion and morality, by a regular deduction from the firft principles in a way of abftracted reafoning: and therefore it is a great advantage, that God hath given a clear revelation of his will, containing, in plain and exprefs propofitions, the principles and doctrines which are of greateft importance to be known, and the duties which are moft neceffary to be practifed. Such a revelation is fet before us in the gofpel: and the evident marks of difinterestednefs that appear in it, without the leaft traces of a worldly fpirit or defign, the purity and excellence of its doctrines and precepts, and the uniform tendency of the whole for promoting the glory of God, and the good of mankind, and the caufe of virtue and righteoufnefs in the world, furnifh arguments obvious to common capacities, that this religion owed not its rife to human policy, to the arts of impoftors, or to evil beings, but was of a godlike and heavenly original. And as to hiftorical evidence, perfons of common

mon

mon found underflanding may be made fenfible, by the help of
the learned, that we have all the evidence of the truth of the
extraordinary facts, whereby the divine authority of the Chriftian
religion was attefted, which can be reafonably defired :  That
moft of thofe facts were of a public nature, which might have
been eafily detected and expofed if they had been falfe; in which
cafe that religion, which had nothing elfe to fupport it, and was
deftitute of all worldly advantages, muft have fallen at once.
But that this was fo far from being the cafe, that the greateft enemies of Chriftianity are not able to deny, that, upon the credit of
thofe facts, this religion, though directly oppofite to the prejudices which then univerfally obtained, and though it had the moft
unfurmountable difficulties to encounter with, and had all the
powers of the world engaged againft it, foon made a wonderful
progrefs both among Jews and Gentiles; which, as things were
circumftanced, cannot otherwife be accounted for, than by admitting the truth of thofe extraordinary facts : That the original
revelation itfelf, together with an account of thofe facts, was
committed to writing in the very age in which that revelation was
firft given, and thofe facts were done; which is a fure method of
conveyance, though oral tradition is a very uncertain one : And
that thefe accounts, which were written by perfons who were
perfectly acquainted with the things they relate, and which have
all the characters of purity, artlefs undifguifed fimplicity, and an
impartial regard to truth, that any writings can poffibly have,
were in that very age received with great veneration, as of facred
authority.  The copies of them were foon fpread abroad into
many different countries : they were read in the public affemblies,
tranflated into various languages, and they have been ever fince
fo conftantly cited and appealed to in every age by perfons of
different fects and parties, many of whom have tranfcribed large
portions of them into their writings, that it may be juftly faid,
they have been tranfmitted with a continued evidence, far
greater than can be produced for any other books in the world;
and that a general corruption of them, if any had attempted it,
would have been an impoffible thing.  There is nothing in all
this, but what perfons of common found fenfe, who are defirous
of information, may be fufficiently affured of by the affiftance of
the learned : and when, befides this, they feel the power and

influence

influence of the doctrines and motives proposed in those sacred writings upon their own hearts, comforting them in all the viciffitudes of mortal life, and animating them to all virtue and goodnefs, this completeth their fatisfaction and affurance; efpecially when it is farther confidered, that we are taught in fcripture to hope, that God's gracious affiftances will not be wanting to thofe that with honeft hearts and upright intentions endeavour to know and do the will of God. *For if any man will do his will,* faith our Saviour, *he fhall know of the doctrine, whether it be of God, or whether I fpeak of myfelf,* John vii. 17.

Our author, in order to fhew that the generality of mankind are incapable of judging of the evidence for Chriftianity, hath taken upon him to pronounce, that there are few that are capable of reafoning at all, *if there is the leaft of induction or inference in the cafe*.* And this, if it proveth that they are under no obligation to believe Chriftianity, equally proveth, that they are under no obligation to believe natural religion, not even the exiftence of a God, or a providence; fince here there is certainly room for induction and inference. But the truth is, this is a very falfe and bafe reprefentation of human nature: it would follow from it, that the generality of men are incapable of moral agency, of virtue and vice, or of being governed by laws: for this fuppofeth them capable of underftanding what thofe laws are, and what is the duty required of them, and of making inferences and deductions. And with regard to religion, and its proofs and evidences, it can fcarce be doubted, that if men applied themfelves to it with the fame care and diligence that they generally do in matters of much lefs confequence, they would attain to fuch a fenfe of religion and its evidences, as would both make it reafonable for them to believe it, and to govern their practice by it.

There were feveral good anfwers publifhed to *Chriftianity not founded on Argument.* One of the firft that appeared was that written by Dr. Doddridge, which I remember to have read with pleafure, but as I have not had an opportunity of feeing it for fome years, cannot give a particular account of it. I fhall confine myfelf to thofe anfwers which I have now by me.

* Chriftianity not founded on Argument, p. 17, 18.

The

The firſt I ſhall mention is intitled, *The Reaſonableneſs of the Chriſtian Religion, as delivered in the Scriptures, being an Anſwer to a late Treatiſe, intitled, " Chriſtianity not founded on Argument,"* by George Benſon, afterwards Dr. Benſon, London, 8vo. 1743. This may be regarded not merely as an anſwer to that pamphlet, but as a good defence of Chriſtianity in general, and ſo the learned author deſigned it. It conſiſteth of three parts. In the firſt part, after having ſettled the meaning of the word *faith*, and ſhewn what that faith is, which the goſpel requireth of thoſe to whom it is made known, and to which rewards are there annexed, and that it is really a virtue; and what that un-belief is which is there forbidden and condemned, and that it is really a vice; he goes on to produce ſome of the principal argu-ments which prove the truth of the Chriſtian religion. He firſt conſiders what are uſually called the internal evidences of Chriſtia-nity, the reaſonableneſs of its doctrines, of its moral precepts, of its poſitive inſtitutions, and of the ſanctions by which it is en-forced; and then conſiders the external evidences ariſing from prophecy and miracles, particularly from the reſurrection of Chriſt, and the extraordinary gifts of the Holy Ghoſt poured forth upon the apoſtles and firſt Chriſtians. Theſe things are here ſet in a fair and agreeable light; and it is alſo ſhewn, that the accounts given of theſe things in the New Teſtament may be depended on, and that we have ſufficient evidence of the truth and authenticity of the goſpel records. In the ſecond part a ſolid anſwer is given to the ſeveral objections and difficulties propoſed by the author, with a view to ſhew that religion cannot be a ra-tional thing. The third part contains a diſtinct explication of thoſe texts of ſcripture which he had perverted and miſapplied. And there is ſcarce any one text cited or referred to in his whole book which is not here particularly conſidered.

Not long after this, there was another valuable anſwer publiſhed, intitled, *The Chriſtian's Faith a rational Aſſent, in Anſwer to a Pamphlet, intitled, " Chriſtianity not founded on Argument,"* by Thomas Randolph, D. D. London, 1744. It was publiſhed in two parts, and divided into ſix chapters. In the firſt, the queſtion in diſpute is clearly ſtated, which is reduced to this: whether the Chriſtian faith be founded on argument, and is ordinarily attainable in a rational way, or is to be acquired only

by

by a *particular revelation imparted supernaturally to every individual?* And he undertakes, in opposition to the author of that pamphlet, to shew, that the Christian's faith ought to be founded upon the conviction of the understanding, and that it is a rational assent, by which he means, that just and satisfactory reasons may be given for the hope and faith we profess. He considers the nature of assent, and shews, that we are not wholly passive in believing or disbelieving, but have a great compass of liberty in the use of those faculties on which assent depends; and that therefore faith may be a virtue, and argue a good disposition of mind, and unbelief be vicious and criminal. In his second chapter, he fairly examines and clearly confutes the author's arguments drawn from the nature of reason and religion: and in the third, the arguments from scripture, by which he pretends to prove, that we are not to use our understandings in matters of religion. In his fourth chapter, he inquires into the author's own scheme, and the principle of gospel evidence which he has thought fit to assign, which he wholly resolveth into an immediate, infallible, supernatural revelation, darted with an irresistible light into the mind of every particular person: the absurdity of this Dr. Randolph exposes, and answers the pretended proofs brought from scripture in support of it. The fifth chapter contains a good account of the proofs of the Christian religion, with a particular consideration of the objections of this writer against miracles and traditional testimony. Lastly, he takes notice of the reflections thrown out by the author of that pamphlet against the Church of England in particular.

You will probably expect, that I should take some notice of another answer, which appeared about the same time, and which also met with a favourable reception from the public, viz. *Remarks on a late Pamphlet, intitled, "Christianity not founded on Argument."* These remarks, which were drawn up by me at your own desire, were contained in two letters that were published separately, London, 1744. The design of this answer, which was much shorter than either of the former, was not to enter upon a distinct and particular account of the evidences which are usually produced in proof of the Christian religion, which the author of these letters had considered largely on some former occasions, but to represent in a clear and concise manner

the

the abfurdity and ill tendency, as well as manifold inconfiftencies, of this writer's fcheme; to give a plain confutation of the
principal arguments from fcripture and reafon, by which he has
pretended to fupport it, and to detect and expofe his fallacies and
mifreprefentations.

But it is time to take leave of this writer, whom I have taken
the more particular notice of, becaufe fome of his objections are
managed with great art, and have a fpecious appearance.

# LETTER XII.

*The Refurrection of Chrift an Article that lies at the Foundation of the Chriftian Faith—Attacked with great Confidence in a Pamphlet, intitled,* The Refurrection of Jefus confidered— *What this Writer offers to prove, that Chrift did not foretel his own Refurrection, and that the Story of the Chief Priefts fetting a Watch at the Sepulchre is a Forgery and Fiction, examined and confuted—Obfervations on the extraordinary Way he takes to fix Contradictions on the Evangelifts—The Rules by which he would judge of their Accounts would not be endured, if applied to any other Writings—He infifts on farther Evidence of Chrift's Refurrection; and yet plainly intimates, that no Evidence that could be given would fatisfy him— Extravagant Demands of the Deiftical Writers on this Head confidered—The Evidence that was actually given, the propereft that could be given—The feeming Variations among the Evangelifts, if rightly confidered, furnifh a Proof of the Truth and Genuinenefs of the Gofpel Records—An Account of the Anfwers publifhed to this Author, efpecially of Mr. Weft's* Obfervations on the Hiftory and Refurrection of Jefus Chrift —*Sir George Littleton's* Obfervations on the Converfion and Apoftlefhip of St. Paul *commended.*

SIR,

THE refurrection of Chrift is an article of vaft importance, which lieth at the foundation of Chriftianity: if this faileth, the Chriftian religion cannot be maintained, or may be proved to be falfe. *If Chrift be not rifen* (faith St. Paul), *then is our preaching vain, your faith is alfo vain,* 1 Cor. xv. 14. On the other hand, if this holdeth good, the divine miffion and authority of the bleffed Founder of our holy religion is eftablifhed. This is what he himfelf appealed to, as the great and ultimate proof, which was to convince mankind that he was what he profeffed himfelf to be, the Son of God, the Saviour of the world. If he had been an artful impoftor, it can fcarce be fuppofed that he would have appealed to fuch a proof as this, which would have

been

been the moſt effectual way he could have taken to detect and expoſe the vanity of his own pretences, and overturn the whole ſcheme of his religion: or, if he had been an enthuſiaſt, and was impoſed upon by the warmth of his own imagination, to believe that God would indeed raiſe him from the dead, the event would have effectually ſhewn the folly and madneſs of his expectations. And, therefore, ſince he put the proof of his divine miſſion upon a thing of ſo extraordinary a nature, which manifeſtly exceeded all human power, and was actually enabled to accompliſh it, this ſhews, both that he certainly knew that he was ſent of God, and that he really was ſo.   And indeed it cannot be conceived how a more illuſtrious atteſtation could poſſibly have been given to him from heaven, than his reſurrection from the dead, in accompliſhment of his own prediction, and what followed upon it, his aſcenſion into heaven, and the extraordinary effuſion of the Holy Ghoſt upon his diſciples, as he himſelf had promiſed.   This the enemies of our holy religion are ſenſible of; and therefore, though they have ſometimes affected to argue, that, ſuppoſing Chriſt to have really riſen from the dead, this would not be a valid proof of the truth of the Chriſtian revelation *, they have in all ages bent their utmoſt efforts againſt it.   Celſus employed all his wit and malice to ridicule it: ſo have others done ſince: of late Mr. Woolſton had diſtinguiſhed himſelf this way; and no part of his diſcourſes on the miracles of our Saviour was ſo much laboured, as that wherein he endeavoured to ſhew, that the account given by the evangeliſts of Chriſt's reſurrection is a falſe and incredible ſtory.   But the weakneſs of his objections was clearly ſhewn in the anſwers that were made to him; among which *The Trial of the Witneſſes,* &c. was eſpecially remarkable, both for the ſtrength of the reaſoning, and the ingenious and polite manner of treating the argument.   Mr. Woolſton himſelf never attempted to vindicate that part of his Diſcourſes againſt the anſwers that had been given to it.   But after ſeveral years had paſſed, a bold adventurer appears in a pamphlet, intitled, *The Reſurrection of Jeſus conſidered, in Anſwer to the Trial of the Witneſſes, by a Moral Phi-*

---

* See a Letter, ſaid to be written by Mr. Collins, to the author of the "Diſcourſe on the Grounds, &c." in anſwer to Mr. Green's Letters, publiſhed in 1726.

*loſopher,*

*lofopher*, London, 1744; fo this gentleman thinks proper to ftile himfelf, as Dr. Morgan had done before him. Like that writer, he appears to be of great vivacity, and no fmall degree of confidence, and to have a high opinion of his own abilities and performances; and, like him, feems refolved to put all the arts of controverfy in practice, by which he thinks he might carry his point, without being very folicitous whether they are properly reconcileable to truth or candour. He has with great diligence raked together all that a lively imagination, animated with the moft determined malice, could invent or fuggeft, for mifreprefenting and expofing the gofpel-hiftory: nor does he, as fome others had done, any-where pretend a regard to the religion of Jefus, but all along openly declares againft it; in which he is fo far to be commended, if he had but acted the part of a fair, as he doth of a profeffed adverfary.

The principal things obfervable in this treatife, with relation to the declared defign of it, the overthrowing the accounts that are given us of the refurrection of Jefus, may be reduced to thefe three heads: 1. He undertakes to prove, that Chrift did not foretel his death and refurrection at all, neither to the Jewifh priefts and Pharifees, nor to his own difciples: and that all that the evangelifts fay on this head is mere fiction and forgery. 2. That the whole ftory of the Jewifh priefts and rulers fetting a watch at the fepulchre, and fealing the ftone, is falfe, and a moft abfurd and incredible fiction. 3. That the accounts given by the evangelifts of Chrift's refurrection are in every part inconfiftent and felf-contradictory, and carry plain marks of fraud and impofture. I fhall make fome obfervations on each of thefe; and that I may not return to this fubject again, fhall take notice, as I go along, of fome things advanced by Mr. Chubb, in his pofthumous works, to enforce the objections of this writer.

It is of great importance to our author's caufe to prove, if he was able to do it, that Jefus did not foretel his own death and refurrection: for if he did foretel it, and it was known that he did fo, this makes the precautions taken by the chief priefts to prevent an impofition in this matter abfolutely neceffary; and the whole ftory is perfectly confiftent. Befides that, as hath been already hinted, his foretelling a thing of fuch a nature, which, if he had been an impoftor, he muft have known it would

be

be abfolutely out of his power to accomplifh, and which yet was actually fulfilled, affords the moft convincing proof, that he was really that extraordinary and divine perfon he profeffed himfelf to be.   Our author faw this, and therefore has made an attempt to fhew, that Jefus did not foretel his death and refurrection, neither to the Jewifh priefts and Pharifees, nor to his own difciples. With regard to the former, it appeareth from the teftimony of the evangelifts, St. Matthew and St. Luke, that when the Scribes and Pharifees defired Jefus to fhew them a *fign from heaven*, he told them, that *no fign fhould be given, but the fign of the prophet Jonas*.   And St Matthew farther informs us, that he then openly declared to them, that *as Jonas was three days and three nights in the whale's belly,* fo fhould the *Son of man be three days and three nights in the heart of the earth*, Matth. xii. 38, 39, 40. Which plainly fuppofed, that, in that fpace of time, he fhould, after lying in the earth or grave, rife out of it, as Jonas came alive out of the belly of the fifh.   From this prediction therefore, which was uttered more than once in the hearing of the Scribes and Pharifees, they might gather that he intended to fignify that he fhould rife again from the dead.   What this writer hath offered against this is very trifling.   Becaufe St. Luke, in mentioning what our Saviour faid concerning the fign of the prophet Jonas, doth not exprefsly take notice of his declaring, that the Son of man fhould lie three days and nights in the heart of the earth, he pretends that this is a proof that St. Matthew forged it.   Whereas all that it proves is, that St. Matthew hath given a fuller relation of what our Saviour faid on that occafion, than St. Luke hath done; though what the latter relateth concerning Chrift's mentioning the fign of the prophet Jonas, plainly implieth it.   He alfo repeats what Mr. Woolfton had urged, that Chrift did not lie three days and nights in the grave; of which I took fome notice before in my remarks on Mr. Woolfton's difcourfes.   He farther hints at what Mr. Chubb, who wrote after our author, and endeavours to reinforce his objections, has enlarged upon for feveral pages together *, that Jefus could not have made fuch a declaration as this, that *no fign fhould be given to that wicked and adulterous generation, but the fign of the prophet Jonas;*

* Chubb's pofthumous works, vol. i. p. 342—347.

both

both becaufe their being a wicked generation was rather a reafon for giving them a fign, fince in that cafe they needed it moft, and the defign of his coming was to call finners to repentance; and becaufe in fact Chrift did work figns and wonders among them after this.   But to take off the force of this, it is fufficient to obferve, that by comparing Matth. xvi. 1. Luke xi. 16. Mark viii. 11. it appeareth, that the fign they demanded was a *fign from hea-ven*, by which they probably meant fome glorious appearance in the heavens.   They had a little before attributed his miracles to Beelzebub: and now they infifted that he fhould give them a par-ticular kind of fign; and it was perfectly confiftent with his charac-ter to refufe to humour them in this demand, which he well knew proceeded from a cavilling temper, and not from minds honeftly willing to fubmit to evidence.   But though he refufed to give them at that time precifely fuch a fign as they demanded, he yet both continued to work miracles among them, and referred them to his refurrection, which, taking in the circumftances that at-tended it, and followed upon it, was, in the fulleft and propereft fenfe, *a fign from heaven*, and was fufficient to convince them, if they were difpofed to receive conviction.   To this it may be added, what St. John informs us of, that in a difcourfe addreffed to a great number of the Jews, among whom were feveral of his malicious enemies, he plainly fpoke of his *laying down his life*, and *taking it again*, and declared that *this commandment he had received of his father,* John x. 17, 18, 19, 20.

As to his own difciples, under which character others befides the twelve apoftles are often comprehended, the author himfelf acknowledgeth, that the evangelifts reprefent him as having de-clared to them in plain and exprefs terms, on five different occa-fions, that he fhould fuffer and die, and rife again on the third day.   But becaufe they tell us, that the difciples *did not under-ftand this faying*, and that it was *hid from them*, and that they queftioned among themfelves, *what this rifing from the dead fhould mean*, he would have the whole pafs for forgery and fic-tion.   He thinks it incredible, that twelve men could hear fuch plain expreffions, fo clearly foretelling his dying and rifing again, and yet not be able to underftand them.   But this is eafily ac-counted for, confidering that the difciples were at that time un-der the power of thofe prejudices, which then generally prevailed

among

among the Jews, relating to the Meſſiah. They could not conceive how the Meſſiah, who, according to their notions of things,
was *to abide for ever*, and not die at all*, could be ſubjeſt to
ſufferings and death: nor conſequently how he ſhould riſe again
from the dead. When therefore they heard Jeſus, whom they
looked upon to be the Meſſiah, talk of his dying and riſing again
on the third day, they thought it muſt be underſtood in ſome
myſtical or figurative ſenſe, and that ſome meaning which they
did not at preſent comprehend lay hid under thoſe expreſſions,
however plain they might appear: ſo that this only ſhews the dul-
neſs of their apprehenſions, and the force of their prejudices,
and at the ſame time the impartiality of the evangelical hiſtorians
who have recorded it. But though the diſciples could not conceive how Chriſt ſhould die and riſe again on the third day, yet
as he ſo often repeated it on different occaſions, without ever
giving the leaſt injunſtion to them to conceal it, it may juſtly
be ſuppoſed that the ſaying got abroad, and was known to many.
And this coming to the ears of the Jewiſh chief-prieſts and Phariſees, who alſo knew what he had ſaid to ſome of the Phariſees
and Scribes concerning the ſign of the prophet Jonas, was a
ſufficient foundation to them to ſay to Pilate, *We remember that
that deceiver ſaid* (not that he *ſaid to us*, as this gentleman thinks
iit to quote it, but that *he ſaid*), *while he was yet alive, after three
days I will riſe again.* There needed no more to put them upon
all proper precautions to prevent an impoſture in this matter.

This leads me to take ſome notice of the ſecond main thing
this writer inſiſteth upon, which is, that the ſtory St. Matthew
tells of the chief-prieſts ſetting a watch at the ſepulchre, and
ſealing the ſtone, is a falſe and abſurd fiſtion. Mr. Woolſton
had allowed the truth of the ſtory, and built one of his principal
arguments againſt the reſurreſtion of Jeſus upon the circumſtance
of ſealing the ſtone. And this argument was mightily cried up
for a while. But our author had the ſagacity to diſcern, that if
this was admitted, it would afford a ſtrong preſumption of the
truth and reality of Chriſt's reſurreſtion; and therefore thinks
it more for the intereſt of his cauſe to deny it. The chief thing
he urgeth againſt the ſtory proceeds upon the ſuppoſition, that

* See John, xii. 34.

Jeſus

Jefus did not foretel his refurrection at all, nor had the Jewifh priefts and Pharifees heard that he had foretold it; and therefore it is abfurd to think they would give themfelves concern about it. But the falfehood of this fuppofition hath been already fhewn; nor is there any thing in the whole ftory, as related by St. Matthew, that is not perfectly confiftent, and highly probable. It is very natural to fuppofe, confidering their characters and difpofitions, and the circumftances of the cafe, that they would take the fitteft precautions, that the difciples of Jefus might not have it in their power to pretend he was rifen from the dead, as it was reported he had foretold: and there could not be a more probable method fixed upon for this purpofe, than the fetting a watch to guard the fepulchre, and fealing the ftone that was rolled to the mouth of it. And though we fhould allow them to have known, as this writer affirms they did, that Nicodemus and Jofeph of Arimathea had wound up the body in linen and fpices, which fhewed they did not expect his refurrection, yet they knew he had other difciples; and befides might fufpect, that all this preparation for embalming the body, was only the better to cover their defign of carrying it away. What he farther urgeth concerning their believing him to have been, what they called him to Pilate, a deceiver, inftead of being an argument, as he would have it to be, againft their ufing this precaution, would furnifh a ftrong reafon for it: fince in that cafe they might be apt to fufpect that his difciples would act the part of deceivers too, and endeavour to carry on the impofture, which therefore they were refolved to prevent. And they might think this one of the moft effectual methods they could take to convince the people, many of whom they knew had a high veneration for Jefus, that he was a falfe prophet, by fhewing the falfehood of his prediction, concerning his rifing again the third day, which would juftify their own conduct in putting him to death.

This author thinks it incredible, that the Jews fhould bribe the foldiers to be filent, when they themfelves muft upon their report have been convinced of the truth of the fact. But their conduct on this occafion was no other than might be expected from perfons of their character. Whofoever confiders their determined malice and envy againft Jefus, who had unmafked their hypocrify, and oppofed their traditions; how deeply their reputation
tation

putation was engaged, and their authority with the people, as well as that of the Sanhedrim, who claimed to themfelves a power of trying prophets, and had condemned him as a falfe prophet and blafphemer, muft be fenfible how unwilling they would be to have it thought, that they had wrongfully procured a moft excellent perfon to be crucified, and that they would take all poffible methods, by ftifling the evidence, to throw off the odium from themfelves. To which may be added the power of their prejudices, which would not fuffer them to imagine, that a perfon who had been crucified could poffibly be their Meffiah, which was abfolutely fubverfive of all their maxims. They who, when they could not deny his miracles, afcribed them to a diabolical power, fhewed what they were capable of. And indeed the force of obftinate prejudice, hatred, envy, pride, and a defire of maintaining their own authority, all which concurred in this cafe, is amazing, and hath often caufed perfons to ftand out againft the cleareft evidence.

The laft thing he hath to offer is, that St. Matthew is the only evangelift who relateth the ftory of fealing the ftone, and placing the watch; but this is of fmall moment: St. Matthew's relation of it is fufficient. He wrote his gofpel, by the confent of all antiquity, the firft of the evangelifts, in a few years after our Lord's afcenfion, and defigned it efpecially for the ufe of the Jewifh converts: and his relating this ftory in a gofpel publifhed among the Jews, and fo early in that very age when the ftory muft have been frefh in remembrance, and when, if falfe, it might have been eafily contradicted, fhews that it was a thing well known, and that he was fully affured of the truth of it, and in no fear of being detected in a falfehood. And what farther confirmeth this, is his referring to a report as current among the Jews at the time when he wrote, concerning the difciples having ftolen the body, whilft the foldiers that were fet to watch the fepulchre flept. The ftory indeed was not very confiftent; but yet, as the cafe is circumftanced, it was the beft thing they had to fay. The body was gone out of the fepulchre; either therefore it muft be acknowledged that he rofe again from the dead, or that his difciples had taken it away: and this, if done at all, muft have been done either with the connivance of the guards that were fet to watch it, or when they were afleep: the guards,

'if

if charged with having connived at it, and with having been
bribed by the difciples, would have been obliged to juftify themfelves againft that charge, and would have told the faft as it really
happened: there was nothing therefore left but to pretend that
it was done whilft they were afleep.   And yet the rulers never
pretended to convict the difciples of having ftolen the body, nor
inftituted any procefs againft them on that account; but contented themfelves with threatening to punifh them if they preached
the refurrection of Jefus, which yet they boldly avowed to their
faces.   As to the author's infinuation, how came St. Matthew
to know of the angel's appearing to the foldiers with fuch circumftances of terror, if they were hired to conceal it; this is
eafily accounted for: it is only faid that *fome of the watch* went
and told the chief priefts, Matth. xxviii. 11.   It may therefore
be reafonably fuppofed, that others of them might, immediately
after the thing happened, tell it to fome other perfons: yea, it
might probably happen, that fome of thofe who were then hired
and bribed might difcover it afterwards, when all was over; or
that fome of the priefts, many of whom were afterwards converted
to the Chriftian faith, as we learn from Acts vi. 7. might have
known and divulged it.

Thus it appeareth, that this writer's principal objections againft
this ftory, and which he infifteth upon as manifeft proofs of the
abfolute falfehood and forgery of the gofpel-hiftory, are of no
force.   And yet he taketh upon him to pronounce, that *it is in
all views abfurd* to fuppofe, *that the Priefts and Pharifees fhould
guard againft a refurrection, fraudulent or real.*

He next proceeds to inquire how the witneffes agree in their
evidence, and endeavoureth to prove, that the accounts the evangelifts give of the refurrection of Jefus are in every part inconfiftent and felf-contradictory, and carry plain marks of fraud and
impofture.   And here I fhall not enter into a diftinct examination
of the feveral more minute particulars he infifteth upon, which
are all confidered and difcuffed in the anfwers that were made to
him, but fhall content myfelf with fome general obfervations
upon his management of the fubject: and firft I would obferve,
that he has thought fit to confider the accounts of the three evangelifts, Matthew, Mark, and Luke, feparately from St. John;
whereas they ought all to be taken together, fince they all relate

to the fame fact of Chrift's refurrection: he pofitively afferteth, that the three evangelifts mention in general but three appearances of Jefus; whereas there are plainly feven appearances of Jefus after his refurrection referred to by them, befides two others peculiarly mentioned by St. John: 1. His appearing to Mary Magdalen alone, Mark xvi. 9. John xx. 14, 15, 16, 17. 2. His appearing to the women, Matth. xxviii. 9. 3. His appearing to the two difciples going to Emmaus, Mark xvi. 12. Luke xxiv. 13—32. 4. His appearing to Simon Peter, Luke xxiv. 34. 1 Cor. xv. 5. 5. His appearing to the eleven as they fat at meat on the evening of the day on which he rofe, Luke xxiv. 36—43. John xx. 19—23. 6. His appearing to his difciples on a mountain in Galilee, Matth. xxviii. 16, 17. 7. His appearing to his difciples on the day of his afcenfion, Mark xvi. 19, 20. Luke xxiv. 50, 51, 52. Acts i. 6—11. Befides thefe, there are two other appearances of Jefus recorded by St. John, which are not taken notice of by the other evangelifts: one is, that to the eleven, when St. Thomas was with them, eight days after the firft, John xx. 26—29. The other is, that at the fea of Tiberias, to feven of the difciples, John xxi. 1—14. Here are nine diftinct appearances pointed out by the evangelifts, which were at different times, and are plainly marked out by diftinct characters. But this author, in order to have a pretence for charging thefe writers with contradictions, thinks fit to confound thefe different appearances: and the different circumftances and variations, which fhew that they belong to different appearances, are reprefented by him as fo many inconfiftencies in the relation of the fame appearance. But by this way of management, inftead of proving contradictions upon the evangelifts, he only proves his own unfairnefs and abfurdity. Thus, *e. g.* St. Luke relates an appearance of Jefus to his difciples at Jerufalem, on the very evening of the refurrection day ; St. Matthew tells of an appearance of his to his difciples at a mountain in Galilee, which muft have been fome time after. The time and place of thefe appearances are manifeftly different; which fhould lead every perfon of candour to regard them as different appearances; but our author is pleafed to fuppofe them to relate to the fame appearance, and then chargeth thefe different circumftances as to time and place, as fo many contradictions and inconfiftencies. This muft be owned

to

to be a very extraordinary way of proceeding; and at this rate it will be eafy to expofe the moſt authentic hiſtory that ever was written.

There is another rule frequently made ufe of by this writer, and upon which his charge of contradictions againſt the evangeliſts principally dependeth, and that is, that if any one of them takes notice of any circumſtance or event not mentioned by the reſt, this is to pafs for a proof of fiction and forgery. According to this new rule of criticifm, where feveral hiſtorians give an account of the fame facts, if fome of them relate thofe facts with more, and fome with fewer circumſtances, this fhall be fufficient abfolutely to deſtroy the credit of the whole; and they that omit a circumſtance, or fay nothing at all about it, muſt be looked upon as contradicting thofe that mention it. Upon this principle, St. Mark and St. Luke are made to contradict one another; becaufe the latter mentions Bethany or mount Olivet as the place from whence Jefus afcended, and the former, in mentioning Chriſt's afcenſion, takes no notice of the place from whence he afcended.    In like manner it is pretended, that St. Matthew and St. John, in contradiction to the two other evangeliſts, fay, that Jefus never afcended at all, becaufe they give no diſtinct account of his afcenſion, though they evidently fuppofe it; and there are more references to it in St. John's gofpel, than in any one of the evangeliſts: fee John vi. 62. vii. 39. xiv. 2. 28. xvi. 7. 16. 28. xvii. 5. 11. xx. 17.    So becaufe the laſt mentioned evangeliſt is the only one of them that mentions the piercing the fide of Jefus with a fpear, of which he himfelf was an eye-witnefs, and gives an account of fome appearances of Jefus to his difciples not mentioned by the other evangeliſts, this fhews, according to our author, that he forged thofe accounts, and that *his evidence deſtroys theirs, or they his;* though one defign of his writing his gofpel was to take notice of things which they had omitted: nor do any of them give the leaſt hint that they propofed diſtinctly to recount all Chriſt's appearances.

In order to fix the charge of contradictions and inconfiſtencies upon the evangeliſts, he pretendeth, that, according to St. Luke, our Lord afcended the very evening of the day of his refurrection. The only proof he bringeth for fo ſtrange an aſſertion is, that St.

Luke,

Luke, immediately after having given an account of our Lord's
appearing to the eleven difciples, and others with them, Luke
xxiv. 36. and which, by comparing ver. 29 and 33, was pretty
late in the evening of the day on which he rofe, tells us, that he
led them out as far as Bethany, where *he was parted from them,
and carried up into heaven,* ver. 50, 51. And this he might
juftly fay, though there was an interval of feveral days between
the one and the other; and it is manifeft from other accounts
there was, and particularly from what St. Luke himfelf faith in
the beginning of the Acts of the Apoftles. It is plain that he intends here only to give a fummary narration; and therefore, after
having taken notice of his firft appearance to the eleven, the account of which ends at ver. 43, he paffeth over the other appearances without a diftinct mention; only giving the fubftance of
what Jefus faid on fome of thofe occafions, and which he introduces thus, εἶπε δὲ αὐτοῖς, which may be thus underftood, *he faid
befides,* or *moreover, unto them:* and then he proceeds to give a
fhort account of Chrift's afcenfion, and of what followed upon it,
which he more diftinctly relateth in the book of the Acts.

St. Luke obferves, that the women, when they went to the
fepulchre, *found not the body of Jefus,* Luke xxiv. 3. This our
candid author reprefents as if he had faid, that they never faw
Jefus at all after his refurrection, dead or alive; and then would
have this, which is a manifeft perverfion of St. Luke's meaning,
pafs for a contradiction to the other evangelifts, who tell that
Jefus was feen of the women after he rofe again from the dead.
To prove that the other evangelifts contradict St. John, he reprefents St. Matthew, Mark, and Luke, as exprefsly declaring, that
Jefus appeared to the eleven difciples *but once* after his refurrection; and yet certain it is, that not one of them fays any fuch
thing. Nor do the evangelifts any where fay, as he affirms they
do, that Jefus appeared *but to a very few* after he rofe from the
dead, which he thinks contradicts the ftory of the hundred and
twenty, and five hundred, mentioned by the author of the Acts
and St. Paul. He might as well have pretended, as Mr. Chubb
did afterwards, though without offering the leaft proof to fupport
it, that the word *hundred* in that paffage, Acts i. 15. is an inter-
polation, and that inftead of *an hundred and twenty,* it fhould be
                                                          read

read *twenty\**. Such wretched fhifts only difcover a fixed refolution not to believe any accounts that fhould be given.

Our author endeavours to take great advantage, in which he
is followed by the laft-mentioned writer, of what is told us concerning Chrift's appearing to the two difciples going to Emmaus.
Becaufe they did not for fome time know Jefus, it is argued, that
he had not a true body, and that they could not be afterwards
fure that it was he: fince, if their fenfes were deceived at firft,
they might be fo afterwards too; and the like may be fuppofed,
as to all Chrift's other appearances to his difciples. That the two
difciples did not at firft know Jefus, is plain from the ftory: and
this may be accounted for in a natural way, if we fuppofe, that
befides fome change which there might be in his countenance,
occafioned by his fufferings and death, he might on purpofe alter
the tone of his voice, or have fomething in his garb, his air and
manner, different from what had been ufual with him before, or
in fome other way difguife himfelf; which feems to be fignified,
when St. Mark, referring to this, faith, he *appeared in another
form*, Mark xvi. 12. And this might hinder them from knowing
him, confidering how little at that time they expected to fee him.
Or, if we fhould fuppofe, that he employed a miraculous power
to prevent their at firft knowing him, which was done for a valuable end, that he might have the better opportunity of inftructing them in a familiar way in the true meaning of the fcriptures
relating to the Meffiah, his fufferings and glory, and thereby the
better prepare them for the difcovery he intended afterwards to
make of himfelf; it by no means follows, that, becaufe they were
withheld from knowing him for a while, therefore when he fully
difcovered himfelf to them, they could not be certain that it was
he. It is plain, that they had afterwards fuch convincing proofs
that it was Jefus, as left no room for doubt in their minds. And
that very evening he fhewed himfelf again to them, and to the
eleven apoftles, and others with them; and the more effectually
to convince them, fhewed them his hands and his feet, and ate
and drank before them; and by the proofs which were given
them, both on that and other occafions, they had as full evidence
of the reality of his rifen body, as they could have of any thing

---

\* Chubb's pofthumous Works, vol. i. p. 378.

O 3                                                     that

that came to them confirmed by the teſtimony of their ſenſes. And to ſuppoſe an extraordinary miraculous power employed all along to deceive them and overrule all their ſenſes, would be to ſuppoſe as great a power employed to make them believe a falſe-hood, *i. e.* to make them believe that Jeſus was riſen when he was not ſo, as would have ſufficed for the truth of the reſurrec-tion; ſince it would have been as eaſy for the divine power to have raiſed his body really from the dead, as to give all thoſe proofs and evidences that were given of a true body without the reality. As to his appearing among them when the *doors were ſhut,* which is alſo urged againſt the truth of his riſen body, all that can be fairly concluded from it is, that when the doors were ſhut, which the evangeliſt tells us was for fear of the Jews, Jeſus came ſuddenly among them, opening the doors at once by his miraculous power; not that his body paſſed through the doors by a penetration of dimenſions, which is the conſtruction the author puts upon it; for this would have entirely deſtroyed our Lord's own argument, which he uſed at that very time to convince them that he had a real body. *Behold* (ſaith he), my *hands,* and *feet, that it is I myſelf. Handle me, and ſee, for a ſpirit hath not fleſh and bones, as you ſee me have.* See Luke xxiv. 36. 39. com-pared with John xx, 19, 20.

It is obſervable that this writer, in his great eagerneſs to ex-poſe the evangelical accounts, ſeems not to conſider that ſome of the arguments he hath produced may be turned againſt him, and prove the contrary to what he produced them for. He frequent-ly lays a mighty ſtreſs on thoſe paſſages which relate to the diſci-ples not having underſtood our Saviour, when he foretold his reſurrection before his death, and to their doubting of his reſur-rection after it. And yet it is this very thing that gives the greateſt force to their teſtimony. If they had been prepoſſeſſed beforehand with a ſtrong belief that he would riſe again, or if they had immediately believed that he was riſen from the dead upon the firſt meſſage that was brought to them, it would un-doubtedly have been aſcribed to the warmth of their imagination, and to a too forward credulity; but as the caſe is circumſtanced, there is no room for this pretence. It is plain, that nothing but the irreſiſtible evidence of their ſenſes brought them to believe at all; and their believing it ſo firmly at laſt, ſo as to be ready to feal their teftimony to it with their blood, fhews, that they were conftrained to believe by an evidence which they could not withftand, and which abfolutely removed their doubts, and overcame all their prejudices.

The account given by the evangelifts of Chrift's refurrection is farther confirmed by the teftimony of St. Paul, who mentions his having been feen by Peter, by James, and by the twelve apoftles; concerning which he had many opportunities of inform-ing himfelf from the perfons themfelves. He alfo maketh men-tion of his having been feen of above five hundred brethren at once, and exprefsly affirms, as a thing he was well affured of, that the greater part of them were alive at the time when he wrote this; and it is not to be doubted, that he had feen and known many of them, to whofe living teftimonies he could then appeal. Thefe things he refers the Corinthians to in his epiftle, as things known to be certainly true, and which could not be contefted, and concerning which he himfelf had fpoken to them more at large when he was with them, 1 Cor. xv. 1, 2, 3, &c. And in a difpute which he there maintaineth againft fome who denied the future refurrection of the dead, he principally argueth from the refurrection of Chrift, as a fact fo fully proved, that they could not deny it. Yet our author is pleafed to reject all this at once, becaufe St. Paul *writes by hearfay, i. e.* becaufe he was not himfelf prefent at thofe appearances, though he had the ac-count from thofe who were fo: and fo fond is he of this thought, that he repeats it, as his manner is, in three or four different parts of his book. According to this rule, an hiftorian is not to be credited in any fact of which he himfelf was not an eye-witnefs, though he might have undoubted affurance of it; a maxim which would deftroy the credit of the beft hiftorians now in the world. But one fhould think this writer would at leaft allow, that St. Paul ought to be credited, when, after mentioning Chrift's hav-ing appeared to others, he affirms, that he himfelf had feen Jefus, 1 Cor. xv. 8. ix. 1. But it feems this alfo is to be rejected, under pretence that he only faw him in a vifion; though it was at noon-day, as he was travelling with feveral others in his com-pany, and which was attended with fuch remarkable circum-ftances, and produced fuch real effects, that if he could not be fure of this, no man can be certain of any thing that he hears or fees. Mr Chubb indeed, who faithfully treads in our author's fteps,

takes

takes upon him to affirm, that St. Paul's teftimony weakens, inftead of ftrengthening, the evidence of Chrift's refurrection: for
which he gives this reafon, that though St. Paul had known
Jefus before his refurrection, which it doth not appear he did,
yet as that glorified body muft have been different from what it
had appeared to be whilft he was on earth, he could not be a proper judge of the identity of that body with that body which had
been crucified\*.    But it is to be confidered, that what St. Paul
was to be convinced of, and of which he himfelf was afterwards
to be a witnefs, was, that Jefus was raifed again, and invefted
with a divine dominion and glory.    And of this the appearing
of Jefus to him in the manner he did, as he was going to Damafcus, and affuring him by a voice from heaven, that it was Jefus
whom he had perfecuted who then fpoke to him, attended with
fuch amazing difplays of a divine glory and fplendor, together
with the remarkable confequences which then followed upon it,
efpecially the extraordinary miraculous gifts and powers with
which he himfelf was endued, and which he was enabled to confer upon others in the name of a rifen Jefus, exhibited the moft
illuftrious and convincing proof and evidence that could poffibly
be defired, and which abfolutely overcame all the ftrong and obftinate prejudices with which his mind was at that very time
poffeffed.    So that all things confidered, there never was a teftimony which deferved greater regard than that of St. Paul, and
accordingly it has juftly had the greateft weight in all ages.

I pafs by other inftances that might be mentioned of our author's great unfairnefs and difingenuity, particularly his grofs
perverfions of feveral paffages of fcripture, and putting a meaning
upon them contrary to the plain intention of the writers, with
many other things which are fully detected and expofed by his
learned anfwerers.    But what is wanting in reafoning, is made
up in confidence.    He boldly pronounceth, that " the witneffes
" do not all agree in one circumftance, but palpably contradict
" one another in every particular; and that fuch inconfiftencies,
" improbabilities, abfurdities, and contradictions, would deftroy
" the credit of other hiftories;" but he fneeringly adds, " that
" the faith of this is founded on a rock†."    And I believe it

---

\* Chubb's pofthumous Works, vol. 1.
† Refurrection of Jefus confidered, p. 56, 57, 58.

will hardly be thought too fevere a cenfure to fay, that any man who would treat any other hiftorians as this writer hath treated the evangelifts, and who would advance fuch rules of judging concerning any other books whatfoever, as he feems to think fair with regard to theirs, would, inftead of paffing for a candid and judicious critic, be generally exploded as a malicious and impertinent caviller, that had betrayed a great defect of fenfe, manners, or honefty.

In my remarks on Mr. Woolfton's difcourfes in the feventh letter, notice was taken of that grand objection, that our Lord ought to have appeared publicly to the chief priefts and rulers of the Jews after his refurrection. I fhall not repeat what is there offered in anfwer to it; but fhall only obferve, that our author has endeavoured to ftrengthen that objection by pretending, that Jefus had actually engaged to do fo: and that " not to appear " to the Jews when he had promifed it, and put the truth of his " miffion upon it, was a denying the truth of his miffion, and a " falfifying his word\*." Thus he reprefents it, as if the evangelifts had faid, that Chrift promifed to appear publicly to the Jews, and particularly to their chief priefts and rulers after his refurrection. But this is entirely his own fiction: our Lord made no fuch promife. He declared indeed, that a fign, like that of the prophet Jonas, fhould be given to *that evil and adulterous generation, i. e.* that fufficient evidence fhould be given to convince them of the truth of his refurrection. And fuch evidence there was given, if their minds had been open to conviction: and vaft numbers of the Jews were actually convinced by it. But this writer carrieth it ftill farther: he thinks Jefus fhould have fhewn himfelf to the Jews as their deliverer from the Roman yoke, and as their temporal king, that he might prove that he was the Meffiah, and fulfil the prophecies.

A reflection occurs to me on this occafion, which you will allow me to mention: It relates to the feveral demands that have been made by thefe gentlemen with regard to the evidence, which they pretend ought to have been given to the Jews of our Saviour's refurrection. The author of *Chriftianity not founded on Argument* thinks, that Jefus ought to have taken one turn in

---

\* *Refurrection of Jefus confidered*, p. 59. 61.

the market place in the prefence of all the people, and that " this
" might have fpared both the painful labours and lives of fo
" many holy vouchers*." Mr. Chubb infifts upon it, that when
Chrift was rifen, " he fhould have repaired to the houfe of fome
" friend, and made it the place of his refidence the time he ftaid
" upon earth, that fo the reft of his friends, and all others, might
" know where to fee him, and have accefs to him †." And if
he had done fo, and been publicly vifited, and the people had
gathered together in crowds, as might in that cafe have been expected, this muft have awakened the jealoufy both of the Jewifh
chief priefts and rulers, and of the Roman government, and might,
in the temper the Jews were then in, have probably produced
tumults and infurrections, which would have brought a great
flur upon Chriftianity at its firft appearance. And fo undoubtedly thefe gentlemen would have had it: for, according to our
author, if Jefus had appeared publicly to the Jews after his refurrection, this would not have been fufficient, if he did not alfo
head their armies. And then to be fure this would have been infifted upon as a manifeft proof, that the whole fcheme of his
religion was falfe, and a mere piece of carnal policy.

I cannot help thinking upon the whole, that after all the clamour that hath been raifed againft it, the evidence which was
actually given of our Lord's refurrection was the propereft that
could be given. His making a public perfonal appearance to the
people of the Jews would have been on many accounts improper, and might probably have had bad confequences. But befides the evidence arifing from the teftimony of the foldiers, who
had been fet to watch the fepulchre, which was well known to
the chief priefts, and, notwithftanding all their precautions, had
come to the knowledge of others too; befides this, his appearing,
in the manner he did, to a confiderable number of perfons, who
had been immediately acquainted with him, to whom he frequently fhewed himfelf alive after his paffion by many infallible
proofs during the courfe of forty days; his afcending afterwards
into heaven in their fight, and the effufion of the Holy Ghoft in
his extraordinary miraculous gifts and powers, as he himfelf had

* Chriftianity not founded on Argument, p. 68.
† Chubb's pofthumous Works, vol. 4.

promifed,

promifed, upon his difciples, the authorized witneffes of his refurrection, which was done in the moft public manner poffible,
before many thoufands of perfons of all nations, which were then
affembled at Jerufalem; all this, with the following divine atteftations that were given them, to confirm their teftimony where-
ever they went, preaching the gofpel for many years together,
to which teftimony they unalterably adhered, in oppofition to
the greateft fufferings and perfecutions to which it expofed them;
all this taken together furnifhed the moft proper and convincing
evidence, not only of Chrift's refurrection, but of his exaltation to
glory. And accordingly we find in fact, that his refurrection
was accompanied with fuch proof and evidence, as convinced
many myriads (for fo it fhould be rendered) of the Jewifh nation,
and among them *great numbers of the priefts*, Acts vi. 7. xxi. 20.
and brought them over, contrary to all their prejudices, to acknowledge one that had been crucified by the heads of their own nation for their Meffiah, their Saviour, and their Lord; and afterwards convinced vaft numbers of the Gentiles, and gained them
over to a religion the moft oppofite that could be imagined, not
only to their prejudices and fuperftitions, but to their vices, and
which expofed its profeffors to the moft grievous reproaches, perfecutions, and fufferings.

But to return to our author :—Whofoever carefully confiders
and compares what he hath offered may eafily perceive, that,
whatever pretences he may make of demanding other and farther
evidence of Chrift's refurrection than was given, no evidence
that could have been given of it would have fatisfied him. If
Jefus had fhewn himfelf alive, not only to the Jewifh rulers, but
to every fingle perfon of the Jewifh nation, he would have been
as far from believing it as he is now: for he intimates, that it
would be neceffary that Chrift fhould appear again in every
age, and every country, and to every particular perfon; and
that all the miracles fhould be wrought over again *: And even
this, upon his principles, would not be fufficient; for he lets
us know more than once, that in thefe cafes we are not to truft
our own eyefight. He roundly afferteth, that " every miracle
" is an abfurdity to common fenfe and underftanding, and con-

* Refurrection of Jefus confidered, p. 62.

" trary

" trary to all the attributes of God *." And that " pretended facts,
" which are contrary to nature, can have no natural evidence;
" and that these facts cannot be admitted on any evidence, be-
" caufe they in their own nature exclude all evidence, and allow
" of no poffible proof †. This point he hath laboured for feveral pages together, where he ftrongly afferteth (for I do not find
that he bringeth any thing that can be properly called a proof),
that miracles are impoffible. And he had better have ftuck entirely to this, fince if he could but have proved it, he might have
faved himfelf the trouble of writing the reft of his book.

There is another extraordinary paffage in this writer, which
deferves to have a particular notice taken of it. After having
treated the account given by St. John of the piercing of Chrift's
fide with a fpear, and of which he himfelf was any eye-witnefs,
as a fiction, for no other reafon but becaufe the other evangelifts
do not mention it; he infinuates, that if his fide was not thus
pierced, he might not *be really dead when he was put into the
fepulchre;* and then no wonder that *he rofe again ‡.* Thus it
comes out, that he doubteth even of the death of Jefus, which
neither Jews nor heathens ever doubted of. Was there ever a
more obftinate or unreafonable incredulity? He might as well
doubt, whether there ever was fuch a perfon as Jefus, or his
apoftles, or whether ever the Chriftian religion was propagated
in the world at all. And indeed if, as he affirms, the refurrection of Chrift was *the moft incredible ftory that could be told,*
and the evidence that was given for it was the *worft evidence that
could be given §,* he might have argued more plaufibly than he
hath done in moft other cafes, that it was impoffible, as the cafe
was circumftanced, that fuch a filly ftory fhould ever make its
way into the world, either among Jews or Gentiles, confidering
the religion that was founded upon it was abfolutely contrary to
their moft prevailing prejudices, and had no worldly advantages
on its fide, but all the powers of the world engaged againft it:
that therefore it is abfurd to fuppofe that Chriftianity made
any progrefs at all in the firft ages, though there is no fact of
which we have fuller evidence. And then he would only have

---

* Refurrection of Jefus confidered, p. 51, 52.          † Ibid. p. 73, 74.
‡ Ibid. p. 50.                    § Ibid. p. 67.

one

one ftep to advance farther, and which is indeed the natural confequence of this, and that is, to doubt whether there is any fuch thing as the religion of Jefus, or any perfons in the world that now profefs it.

I fhall conclude my remarks upon this writer with obferving, that the very variations among the evangelifts, which he produceth as fo many contradictions, do really confirm the truth of the main facts. What he feemeth to infift upon is, that every one of them fhould tell all the fame facts, in the fame order and manner, and with the fame circumftances, neither more nor lefs; and that no one of them fhould mention any thing which is not related by all the reft. And if they had done fo, then no doubt this would have been improved as a plain argument, that the whole was a concerted fiction; and that to derive a credit to it, it was pretended to have been written and publifhed by four different perfons at different times, whereas thefe four pretended hiftorians were really but one hiftorian, or, if they were different, they only tranfcribed one 'another. But as the cafe now ftands with the evangelifts, there is a harmony in the main facts, and in the fubftance of Chrift's difcourfes: and yet at the fame time there is a confiderable variety in the order and manner of their narration: fuch a variety as plainly fheweth thefe accounts to have been written by different hiftorians, not copied from one another; and that they did not write by concert, in which cafe they would have been more careful to fhun all appearance of contradiction. They write with an unaffected fimplicity, and with a confidence of truth, as becometh thofe that were fully affured of what they relate: each writeth what he knew beft, or what he thought propereft to take notice of: and yet notwithftanding the feeming variations in the order of their narration, and that fome facts, or circumftances of facts, are taken notice of by fome of them which are not mentioned by others, it will be found, if narrowly examined, that there is no contradiction between them, and that their accounts may be fairly reconciled. And it is to be hoped, that this author's attempt to expofe their authority, however ill intended, will only tend to ftrengthen it; fince though his malice and prejudice are very apparent, and though it is plain that he came to examine their accounts, not with a calm, impartial, and difpaffionate temper of mind, but with a refolution,

if

if poſſible, to find out abſurdities and contradictions in them; yet he has not been able to make good the charge. It turns out, that they are perfectly conſiſtent, and that their ſeeming contra- dictions admit of a juſt reconciliation.

I have been carried farther than I at firſt intended in making obſervations upon this pamphlet, which gives a true ſample of the deiſtical ſpirit, and may be regarded as one of the boldeſt and openeſt attacks that was ever made upon that grand article of the Chriſtian faith, the reſurrection of our Lord Jeſus Chriſt. And I have been the larger and more particular in my remarks upon it, both becauſe of the importance of the ſubject, which concerneth the very foundation of our holy religion, and becauſe I thought it might be of uſe to take this occaſion to obviate ſome of the moſt plauſible objections that have been urged againſt it. And what hath been here offered may equally ſerve to take off the force of that part of Mr. Chubb's poſthumous works which relates to the ſame point, and which he hath very much laboured.

But though this letter may ſeem already to have exceeded its due bounds, it will be neceſſary, according to the method I have hitherto purſued, to take notice of the anſwers that were made to this book. Dr. Samuel Chandler, who had on ſome former occaſions appeared to great advantage in the defence of Chriſti- anity, publiſhed on this occaſion a valuable treatiſe, intitled, *The Witneſſes of the Reſurrection of Jeſus re-examined, and their Teſtimony proved entirely conſiſtent*, London, 1744. It is divided into eight chapters. In the firſt, it is ſhewn, that the ſufferings and glory of Chriſt were foretold by the ancient prophets. In the ſecond, that Chriſt plainly foretold his own ſufferings and death, and reſurrection to his own diſciples. In the third, that he declared his death and reſurrection publicly to the Jews. In the fourth, it is proved, that the Jewiſh rulers and Phariſees pro- cured a guard to be ſet on the ſepulchre of Jeſus; and a ſolid anſwer is returned to the author's objections againſt it. The fifth chapter relateth to the appearance of the angels to the ſoldiers; the propriety of which is vindicated againſt his exceptions. The ſixth chapter is concerning the appearances of the angels to the women after the reſurrection. The ſeventh treats of the ſeveral appearances of Chriſt to the women and to his diſciples; and this author's charge of inconſiſtencies in the evangelic accounts is

distinctly

diftinctly confidered. In the eighth chapter, Dr. Chandler concludes with fumming up the evidence for the refurrection of Jefus, which he hath done with great clearnefs and judgment.

About the fame time there was another anfwer publifhed by a learned and ingenious but anonymous author, which is intitled, *The Evidence of the Refurrection cleared, in Anfwer to " The Refurrection of Jefus confidered."* He follows the author of that pamphlet clofely, and fhews, that he grofsly mifreprefents the arguments in the *Trial of the Witneffes,* which he undertakes to anfwer, and that he ufes the evangelifts ftill worfe. The things which we have mentioned, as taken notice of by Dr. Chandler, are alfo confidered by this writer: particularly it is clearly proved, that Chrift foretold his death and refurrection, both to his own difciples and to the Jews: and the author's reafoning and exceptions againft the ftory of fetting the guard, and fealing the ftone, are fhown to be vain and groundlefs. The accounts given by the evangelifts of the appearances of the angels to the women, and of Chrift to them and to the difciples, are diftinctly confidered; and the feeming variations, which the author pretends to be fo many contradictions, are accounted for, though in a way fomewhat different from Dr. Chandler. The folutions of thefe difficulties propofed by each of thefe learned writers, are very ingenious, and may fuffice to obviate the charge of contradictions the author hath brought againft the evangelifts; but fome of them are judged not to be quite fo clear and natural, as thofe afterwards given by Mr. Weft. This anonymous writer concludes with a diftinct examination of what the author of *The Refurrection of Jefus confidered* had offered againft miracles in general. He hath clearly and judicioufly expofed the weaknefs and fallacy of thofe reafonings, whereby that author pretendeth to prove, that miracles are impoffible both in a phyfical and moral fenfe ; that they are contrary to God's immutability ; that they are perfectly needlefs, and anfwer no valuable end at all ; and that if they were once neceffary, they would be always neceffary. Befides the two anfwers above-mentioned, there was another then publifhed, which I have not feen, and of which therefore I cannot give a particular account, though from the character I have heard of it, as well as from the known abilities of the author, I make no doubt of its being well executed: it is intitled, *An Addrefs to Deifts,*

*being*

*being a Proof of Revealed Religion from Miracles and Prophe-cies, in Answer to a Book intitled, " The Resurrection of Jesus considered,* by John Jackson, Rector of Rossington, London, 8vo, 1744.

Some time after, there was another book published, which was also occasioned by *The Resurrection of Jesus considered,* and which particularly engaged the attention of the public, both by its own excellence, and because the author of it was a lay-man: it is intitled, *Observations on the History and Resurrection of Jesus Christ,* by Gilbert West, Esquire, London, 1747. He very justly commends the two learned and ingenious answers above-mentioned, as containing a solid confutation of many objections against Christianity advanced by the author of *The Resurrection of Jesus considered;* but declares himself not to have been so fully satisfied with the manner of their clearing the sacred writers from the contradictions charged upon them. This put him upon examining the scriptures themselves, and comparing the several accounts of the evangelists with each other, which he hath done with great exactness: and the result of his inquiries was, that by carefully distinguishing the different appearances and events recorded by the evangelists, several of which had been hitherto confounded, he hath happily removed the difficulties and inconsistencies charged upon them, and hath taken away the very foundation of the principal objections that have been so often repeated almost from the beginning of Christianity to this day. I shall not enter upon the particulars of his scheme, which may be seen with great advantage in his book. I shall only ob-serve, that he hath not made use of strained and arbitrary sup-positions, but such as seem clearly to arise from the accounts of the evangelists, carefully considered and compared.

By comparing the several parts of the history together, he hath made it to appear, that the women came at different times to the sepulchre, and in different companies, and not all at once, as many have supposed; that there were several distinct appear-ances of angels, of which he reckons three, besides that to the Roman soldiers, *viz.* to the other Mary and Salome, to Mary Magdalene, to Joanna and others with her; that these several facts were reported to the apostles at different times, and by different persons; that there were two distinct appearances of Christ to the
women;

women; one of which was to Mary Magdalene alone, the other to the other Mary and Salome; that St. Peter was twice at the fepulchre, once with St. John, after the firſt report by Mary Magdalene, concerning the body's not being found in the fepulchre; the fecond time after the report made by Joanna, and the women with her, of the appearing of the angels to them. He obſerves, that Chriſtian writers, dazzled by fome few points of refemblance, have confounded thefe different facts, and thereby given great advantage to the infidel: whereas, the facts being rightly diſtinguiſhed, all the objections againſt this part of the goſpel hiſtory, as contradictory and inconfiftent, entirely vaniſh; and it appeareth, that the evangeliſts, inſtead of claſhing and difagreeing, mutually confirm, illuſtrate, and ſupport each other's evidence.

This learned gentleman hath made excellent and judicious reflections upon the feveral incidents in the hiſtory of the refurrection, and upon the order in which they happened, and in which the feveral proofs of the refurrection were laid before the apoſtles. He ſhews, that the difcovery of it which was made to them was wifely ordered to be gradual; and that as they were to be the chofen witneſſes of the refurrection of Jefus, there was a great propriety in the feveral ſteps that were taken to give them the higheſt conviction of it.   There is a train of witneſſes, a fucceſſion of miraculous events, mutually ſtrengthening and illuſtrating each other, equally and jointly concurring to prove one and the fame fact.   And whereas their doubting and unbelief, ſpoken of by the evangeliſts, feem principally to have confiſted in this, that though they might believe that Chriſt had appeared to thofe who declared they had feen him, yet they did not believe that he had appeared to them with a real body, therefore, in condefcenfion to their infirmity, he gave them the fulleſt evidence of the reality of his bodily appearance.

The proofs of Chriſt's refurrection laid before the apoſtles are digeſted by Mr. Weſt under four heads.   1. The teſtimony of thofe that had feen him after he was rifen.   2. The evidence of their own fenfes.   3. The accompliſhment of the words he had ſpoken to them, while he was yet with them.   4. The fulfilling of the things which were written in the law of Mofes, and in the Prophets, and in the Pfalms, concerning him; of which Mr. Weſt hath given a judicious fummary.

Upon recapitulating the feveral particulars which conftitute the evidence of the refurrection, he concludes, that never was there any fact more fully proved than the refurrection of Jefus Chrift; and that thofe who were appointed to be the witneffes of it had every kind of proof that in the like circumftances the moft fcrupulous could demand, or the moft incredulous imagine.

Having confidered the proofs of the refurrection of Jefus Chrift, as they were laid before the apoftles, he proceeds to confider fome of the arguments that may induce us, at this diftance of time, to believe that Chrift rofe from the dead; and thefe he reduceth to two principal heads: The teftimony of the chofen witneffes of the refurrection recorded in the fcriptures: and the exiftence of the Chriftian religion.

With regard to the former, he fheweth, that the apoftles and evangelifts had the two qualities neceffary to eftablifh the credit of a witnefs, a perfect knowlege of the facts he gives teftimony to, and a fair unblemifhed character; and that their teftimony is tranfmitted down in writings either penned by themfelves, or authorized by their infpection and approbation. He offereth feveral confiderations to fhew the genuinenefs of thofe writings, and takes notice both of the internal marks of the veracity of the facred writers, obfervable in the fcriptures, and of the external proofs of their veracity and infpiration; efpecially the exact accomplifhment of the prophecies recorded in thofe writings. He inftances in thofe relating to the different ftates of Jews and Gentiles, different not only from each other, but from that in which both were at the time when thofe prophecies were written. He obferves, that there are feveral particulars relating to the condition of the Jewifh nation, which were moft exprefsly foretold; as the deftruction of the city and temple of Jerufalem, and the figns preceding that deftruction; the miferies of the Jews before, at, and after the famous fiege of that city; the general difperfion of that people, the duration of their calamity, and their wonderful prefervation under it; and finally, their reftoration. And fince the other parts of thefe predictions have been exactly accomplifhed, there is great reafon to think, the laft will be fo too in the proper feafon.

He concludes the whole with the argument drawn from the prefent exiftence of the Chriftian religion; and fheweth, that, without fuppofing the truth of Chrift's refurrection, there is no accounting

accounting for the propagation and prefent exiftence of Chriftianity in fo many regions of the world.   To fet this in a proper
light, he reprefenteth, in an elegant and ftriking manner, the
great difficulties this religion had to ftruggle with at its firft appearance, and the inabilities of its firft preachers, humanly fpeaking, to oppofe and overcome thofe obftacles.  They had the fuperftition and prejudices of the Jews to encounter with; and at the
fame time, religion, cuftom, law, policy, pride, intereft, vice,
and even philofophy, united the heathen world againft Chriftianity.   Its oppofers were poffeffed of all the wifdom, power,
and authority of the world: the preachers of it were weak and
contemptible; yet it triumphed over all oppofition.   And this,
as the cafe was circumftanced, affordeth a manifeft proof of a
divine interpofition, and of the truth of the extraordinary facts
by which it was fupported; the principal of which is the refurrection of Jefus Chrift.

Thus have I endeavoured to give fome idea of this excellent
performance, and have been the more particular in my account
of it, becaufe a work of this kind, done by a lay-man, is apt to
be more taken notice of and received with lefs prejudice: and
for the fame reafon, though it does not come fo directly within
my prefent defign, I hope you will indulge me in giving fome
account of a fhort, but juftly admired, treatife which appeared
foon after, and was alfo written by a learned lay-man, Sir George
Littleton.  It is intitled, *Obfervations on the Converfion and
Apoftlefhip of St. Paul, in a Letter to Gilbert Weft, Efquire*, London, 1747.   The great advantage of this performance is, that the
evidence for Chriftianity is here drawn to one point of view, for
the ufe of thofe who will not attend to a long feries of argument.
The defign is to fhew, that the converfion and apoftlefhip of St.
Paul, alone confidered, is of itfelf a demonftration fufficient to
prove Chriftianity to be a divine revelation.  This defign is very
happily executed.   He firft confidereth the account St. Paul himfelf hath given of the miraculous manner of his converfion; and
thence argueth, that it muft of neceffity be, that the perfon attefting thefe things of himfelf either was an impoftor, who faid
what he knew to be falfe, with an intent to deceive; or he was
an enthufiaft, who by the force of an over-heated imagination
impofed on himfelf; or he was deceived by the fraud of others;

or laſtly, what he declared to be the cauſe of his converſion, and
to have happened in conſequence of it, did all really happen;
and therefore the Chriſtian religion is a divine revelation.    That
he was not an impoſtor, he proves, by ſhewing, with admirable
clearneſs and ſtrength, that he could have no rational motive to
undertake ſuch an impoſture; nor could poſſibly have carried it
on with any ſucceſs by the means we know he employed.    With
equal evidence he ſheweth that St. Paul was not an enthuſiaſt;
that he had not thoſe diſpoſitions which are eſſential ingredients
in that character; and that he could not poſſibly have impoſed
on himſelf by any power of enthuſiaſm, either with regard to
the miracle that cauſed his converſion, or to the conſequential effects of it, or to ſome other circumſtances which he bears teſtimony to in his Epiſtles; eſpecially the miracles wrought by
him, and the extraordinary gifts conferred upon him, and upon
the Chriſtian converts to whom he wrote.    To ſuppoſe all this
to have been only owing to the ſtrength of his own imagination,
when there was in reality no ſuch thing at all, is to ſuppoſe him
to have been all this time quite out of his ſenſes: and then it is
abſolutely impoſſible to account, how ſuch a diſtempered enthuſiaſt and madman could make ſuch a progreſs, as we know he
did, in converting the Gentile world.    He next proceeds to ſhew,
that St. Paul was not deceived by the fraud of others; if the
diſciples of Chriſt could have conceived ſo ſtrange a thought as
that of turning his perſecutor into his apoſtle, they could not
poſſibly have effected it in the manner in which it was effected,
with the extraordinary conſequences that followed upon it.    It
is evident then, that what he ſaid of himſelf could not be imputed
to the deceit of others, no more than to wilful impoſture, or enthuſiaſm: and then it followeth, that what he relateth to have
been the cauſe of his converſion, and to have happened in conſequence of it, did all really happen, and therefore the Chriſtian
religion is a divine revelation.    He concludeth with ſome good
obſervations to ſhew, that the myſteries of the Chriſtian religion
do not furniſh any juſt reaſon for rejecting the ſtrong and convincing evidence with which it is attended: that there are ſeveral
incomprehenſible difficulties in deiſm itſelf; ſuch as thoſe relating to the origin of moral evil, the reconciling the preſcience of
God with the free-will of man, which Mr. Locke owns he could

not

not do, though he acknowledged both, the creation of the world in time, or the eternal production of it.    And yet no wife man, becaufe of thefe difficulties, would deny the being, the attributes, or the providence of God.

But it is time to conclude this long epiftle; and here I intend- ed, as you know, to have clofed my accounts of the deiftical writers.    But as you infift upon it, that, in order to complete this defign, it will be neceffary to take a more particular notice than I have done of Mr. Chubb's *Pofthumous Works*, this will engage me to continue my correfpondence on this head for fome time longer.

## LETTER XIII.

*An Account of Mr. Chubb's Posthumous Works; his specious Pro*
*fessions, and the advantageous Character he gives of his own*
*Writings—He doth not allow a particular Providence, or that*
*Prayer to God is a Duty—His Uncertainty and Inconsistency*
*with Respect to a future State of Existence, and a future Judg-*
*ment—He absolutely rejects the Jewish Revelation—His Ob-*
*jections against it briefly obviated—He expresses a good Opinion*
*of Mahometanism, and will not allow that it was propagated*
*by the Sword—He seems to acknowledge Christ's divine Mission,*
*and sometimes gives a favourable Account of Christianity;*
*but it is shewn, that he hath done all he can to weaken and ex-*
*pose it, and to subvert its Credit and divine Authority.*

SIR,

AMONG the deistical writers of this present age, Mr. Chubb
made no inconsiderable figure. He was, though not a
man of learning, regarded by many as a person of strong natural
parts and acuteness, and who had a clear manner of expression.
He was the author of a great number of tracts, in some of which
he put on the appearance of a friend to Christianity; though it
was no difficult matter to discern that his true intention was to
betray it. One of the most remarkable of these tracts was his
*True Gospel of Jesus Christ asserted;* in which, under pretence
of asserting the gospel of Christ in its genuine simplicity, he
really endeavoured to subvert and expose it. This was answered
by Mr. Joseph Hallet, in a valuable tract, intitled, *The consistent*
*Christian: being a Confutation of the Errors advanced in Mr.*
*Chubb's Book, intitled, " The true Gospel of Jesus Christ asserted,*
*relating to the Necessity of Faith, the Nature of the Gospel, the*
*Inspiration of the Apostles, &c." with Remarks on his Disserta-*
*tion on Providence:* 8vo. 1738. Another noted tract of Mr.
Chubb's was, his *Discourse on Miracles,* in which he proposed
to give a representation of the various reasonings that relate to
the subject of miracles. But it is manifest, that his intention was
not to clear but to perplex the subject; and to shew, that the
proof

proof from miracles is not at all to be depended upon. To this there was a folid and full anfwer returned by Mr. Abraham Le Moine, which was publifhed at London, 8vo, 1747. Several of Mr. Chubb's tracts were alfo anfwered by Mr. Caleb Fleming; but his anfwers I have not feen. What I propofe to confider are thofe that are called his *Pofthumous Works*, fome of which were printed in his own life-time, and the reft carefully corrected and prepared by himfelf for the prefs, and publifhed after his death, in two volumes, 8vo, London, 1748. The firft volume begins with a fhort tract, intitled, *Remarks on the Scriptures.* But the far greater part of this volume, and the entire fecond volume, is taken up with what is called " *The Author's Farewell to his* " *Readers*, comprehending a variety of Tracts on the moft im- " portant fubjects of religion." It is divided into eleven large fections ; and the principal defign he appears to have had in view is, to deftroy, as far as in him lay, the credit and authority of the Chriftian revelation. I know of no anfwer that has been publifhed to this book, and therefore fhall be more particular in my remarks upon it, to obviate in fome meafure the mifchief it is fitted to produce.

It is plain from feveral hints which he hath given us, that he looked upon himfelf to be a writer of no fmall importance. He declares, that he hath treated the feveral fubjects he has difcuffed with *plainnefs and freedom*, and *of courfe muft have miniftered to the pleafure of the intelligent part of mankind*, whether they ap- *proved his fentiments, or not*[*]. He begins the firft fection of what he calls his *Farewell to his Readers*, with expreffing his hope, that his " correfpondence with them by writing for many " years paft, has been not altogether ufelefs nor unacceptable to " them †." And in the laft fection of his *Farewell*, which he calls his *Conclufion*, he expreffeth himfelf as one that in thefe his laft writings was leaving a very valuable legacy to the world. I know few authors, who have taken leave of their readers with a greater air of folemnity than he has done. He calls God to wit- nefs to the goodnefs of his intentions ; and declares, that in what he has offered to the world, he has " appealed to the underftand- " ing, and not to the paffions of men ‡": That " with fincerity

---

* Chubb's pofthumous Works, vol. i. p. 64, 65.   ● † Ibid. p. 97. ‡ Ibid. vol. ii. p. 354, 355.

" and

" and truth he can fay, he has had a real concern and regard to
" the prefent well-being of his fellow-creatures, as well as to their
" future happinefs:" And that as he was " in the decline of
" life, and perhaps not far from the conclufion of it, and being
" in the full exercife of his intellectual faculties, which are not
" in the leaft clouded or impaired, he chofe to take his leave of
" the world as a writer, hoping, that what he has offered to public
" confideration has had, and may have, fome good effect upon
" the minds and lives of his readers *." And he concludes the
whole with again affuring his readers, that he has laid before
them, in the *plainest manner* he was able, both in this difcourfe,
and in what he had before publifhed to the world, *thofe truths*
which he thought to be of *the higheft importance.* And fo, faith
he, " I bid you fa ewell, hoping to be a fharer with you of the
" divine favour, in that peace'u and happy ftate, which God
" hath prepared for the virtuous and faithful, in fome other fu-
" ture world."

Who that confiders thefe folemn profeffions, would be apt to
fufpect, that this very author, in thefe his farewell difcourfes, has
not only ufed his utmoft efforts to expofe Chriftianity and the
holy Scriptures, but has endeavoured to weaken fome of the moft
important principles of natural religion?

He had, in one of his tracts formerly publifhed, fhewn himfelf to be no friend to the doctrine of a particular providence;
and there are feveral paffages in his *Pofthumous Works*, which
look that way. He plainly intimates, that he looks upon God
as having nothing now to do with the good or evil that is done
among mankind †; and that men's natural abilities or endowments of body or mind, their fortunes, fituation in the world,
and other circumftances or advantages by which one man is diftinguifhed from another, are things that entirely depend upon fecond caufes, and in which providence does not interpofe at all ‡.
And when he endeavours to fhew, that no proof can be brought
for a future ftate from the prefent unequal diftribution of things,
his argument amounteth in effect to this, that providence hath
nothing to do with thefe prefent inequalities, nor concerneth itfelf with fome men's being in a profperous condition or circum-

---

* Chubb's pofthumous Works, vol. ii. p. 357. 359. 361.
† Ibid. vol. i. p. 127.      ‡ Ibid. p. 225.

ſtances, and others in a calamitous or ſuffering ſtate*. He evidently ſuppoſeth all along, that God doth not interpoſe in any thing where ſecond cauſes are concerned †: So that all agency of divine providence in diſpoſing, governing, and overruling ſecond cauſes, in which ſo much of the wiſdom of God's providential adminiſtrations doth conſiſt, is upon his ſcheme abſolutely excluded.

Agreeably to this, he diſcardeth all hope or expectation of divine aſſiſtance in the practice of that which is good; though he owns, that ſomething of this kind hath been generally believed in all religions. This is the deſign of a conſiderable part of the firſt ſection of his *Farewell to his Readers* ‡; which would deſerve to be particularly examined, if this were a proper place for it. I ſhall only obſerve, that what he ſeems to lay a principal ſtreſs upon, to ſet aſide the notion of divine influences or aſſiſtances, is, that we have no way of certainly diſtinguiſhing them from the operations of our own minds; whereas, ſuppoſing this to be the caſe, all that it would prove is, not that there are no gracious aſſiſtances or influences communicated at all, but that they are ordinarily communicated in a way perfectly agreeable to the juſt order of our faculties, and without putting any unnatural conſtraint upon them.

And as he allows no particular interpoſition of divine providence in human affairs, it is not to be wondered at, that he has done what he can to ſhew, that prayer to God is no part of natural religion §. He ſuppoſes it as a thing certain, that God doth not fulfil our requeſts by granting what we pray for, ſince things will go on in their natural courſe, whether we pray to God or not. He owns indeed, that prayer, conſidered as a *poſitive inſtitution*, may be of uſe, by *introducing proper reflections, and thereby proper affections and actions;* and provided it be made uſe of only for this purpoſe, without expecting to obtain any thing from God in conſequence of it, he thinks it cannot be ſaid to be a *mocking of God:* but yet he apprehends that even in this

---

* Chubb's poſthumous Works, vol. i. p. 394, 395.

† See concerning a particular providence, Woolaſton's Religion of Nature delineated, p. 98, & ſeq.

‡ Chubb's poſthumous Works, vol. i. p. 114, & ſeq.   § Ibid. p. 287, &c.

cafe, there is still an impropriety in it, and puts the question, whether such an impropriety should be *a bar to prayer*, or whether it be *difpleafing to God;* and he plainly intimates, that in his opinion it is fo\*.    I need not take particular notice of the objections he hath urged against the duty of prayer, which have been often fufficiently obviated†; but I think it is evident, that there is little room left, upon this author's fcheme, for what hath been hitherto looked upon by the wifeft and beft of men to be a principal part of true piety, or of the duty we owe to God, *viz.* a conftant religious dependence upon his wife and good providence, a thankful fenfe of his goodnefs, and gratitude to him for the benefits we receive, a patient fubmiffion and refignation to his will under afflictions, an ingenuous truft and affiance in him, and a looking up to him for his gracious affiftances to help our fincere endeavours.

The doctrines concerning the immortality of the foul, and a future ftate of retributions, are juftly regarded as important parts of natural religion, and have been acknowledged to be fo by fome of the deifts themfelves.    Mr. Blount, in a letter to the right honourable and moft ingenious Strephon, in the *Oracles of Reafon*, fays, " There are many arguments from reafon and phi- " lofophy to prove the immortality of the foul, together with its " rewards and punifhments; but that there is no argument of " greater weight with him, than the abfolute neceffity and con- " venience that it fhould be fo, as well to complete the juftice " of God, as to perfect the happinefs of man, not only in this " world, but in that which is to come."    Another deiftical wri- ter obferves, that " to fay, man's foul dies with the body is a " defperate conclufion, which faps the foundation of human " happinefs‡."    And one would think, by fome paffages in Mr. Chubb's book, that he was of the fame opinion.    He begins the firft fection of his *Farewell* with affuring his readers, that what he hath *principally aimed at in all his writings*, has been both to *evince*, and *to imprefs deeply upon their minds*, a juft fenfe of thofe truths, which are of the higheft concern to them: and one

---

\* Chubb's pofthumous Works, p. 283, 284.

† See particularly Religion of Nature delineated, p. 125, 126. and efpecially Benfon's ingenious tract On the End and Defign of Prayer.

‡ Letter to the Deifts, p. 25. cited by Halyburton.

of

of thofe truths which he there exprefsly mentions is this, " that
" God will reward or punifh men in another world, according
" as they have by their good or bad behaviour, rendered them-
" felves the proper objects of either in this *." He repeats this
again in very ftrong expreffions at the end of his tenth fection,
where he propofes to fet before the reader, the *fum total*, as he
expreffeth it, of his principles † : and again, in what he calls his
conclufion, he fpeaks of God's calling our fpecies to an account
for their practice and behaviour, " at which tribunal," faith he,
" he will moft certainly deal with me, and the reft of mankind,
" in juftice and equity, according to the truth and reality of our
" refpective cafes." And in the very laft words of his *Farewell
to his Readers*, which I cited before, he declares his hope " to
" be a fharer with them of the divine favour in that peaceful and
" happy ftate, which God had prepared for the virtuous and
" faithful, in fome other future world ‡."

And yet, notwithstanding thefe exprefs and repeated declarations concerning a future ftate of exiftence, and a future judgment and retribution, he hath taken pains to unfettle the minds
of men in thefe important points.

In his fourth fection, in which he profeffedly inquireth concerning a future ftate of exiftence to men, he reprefenteth it as
abfolutely doubtful, whether the foul be material or immaterial; whether it be diftinct from the body; and, if it be, whether
it is equally perifhable as the body, and fhall die with it, or fhall
fubfift after the diffolution of the body. Thefe are points which,
he fays, he cannot poffibly determine, becaufe he has nothing to
ground fuch determination upon; and at the fame time he declareth, that " if the foul be perifhable with the body, there can
" furely be no place for argument with regard to a future ftate
" of exiftence to men, or a future retribution, becaufe when the
" human frame is once diffolved by death, then man ceafes to
" be, and is no more §." In what follows, he declares himfelf
quite unfatisfied with the arguments which are brought to prove,
that the foul is not material, or that matter is not capable of in-

* Chubb's pofthumous Works, vol. i. p. 97. 99.
† Ibid. vol. ii. p. 348, 349.          ‡ Ibid. p. 355.
§ Ibid. vol. i. p. 312, 313.

telligence;

telligence; and though he doth not take upon him exprefsly to determine that point, it is eafy to fee that he inclineth moft to the materialifts*: and after having declared, that the philofophical arguments and reafonings on this head are too abftract and fubtle for him to underftand, and that therefore he cannot form any judgment about them, nor draw any conclufion from them, he adds, that divine revelation does not afford a proper ground of certainty with refpect to man's future exiftence, becaufe we cannot come to any certainty with regard to the divine original of any external revelation†.    He finds fault with St. Paul for faying, that *life and immortality are brought to light by the gofpel,* and will not allow that the refurrection of Chrift, fuppofing it true, though he takes a great deal of pains to fhew that it is not fo, proves either the poffibility or certainty of a refurrection and a future ftate‡.    Thus it appears, that, in this fection, where he profeffedly treateth of a future ftate of exiftence to men, he does all he can to render it abfolutely uncertain, and to fhew that no proof can be given of it, either from reafon or revelation: and yet, that he may make a fhew of faying fomething, he concludes this fection with obferving, that from man's being an accountable creature, there arifes a probability, that there will be a future ftate of exiftence to men: the farther confideration of which he referves for the following fection, which is concerning a future judgment and retribution.

In this therefore, which is his fifth fection, the reader might perhaps expect fome determination of this point; and yet, though this is a pretty long fection, the proper fubject of which is the future judgment, it is managed in fuch a manner, as to leave the reader at an uncertainty about it, and as much at a lofs as before.    He begins indeed with obferving, that " man, by his fa-" culties and endowments, is an accountable creature, account-" able for his behaviour to all whom it may concern, namely, to " the intelligent world, and alfo to the Deity, who is the moft " perfect intelligence§."    But he abfolutely difcards the proof that is drawn from the prefent unequal diftributions of divine providence.    This argument he ftates very unfairly, and endea-

---

* Chubb's pofthumous Works, vol. i. p. 317, 318. 324. 326.

† Ibid. p. 327, 328.        ‡ Ibid. p. 333, & feq.        § Ibid. p. 387.

vours to place it in a ridiculous light. He compares men's different conditions here on earth to that of horfes, fome of whom meet with bad mafters, and others happen to have good ones; and pretends, the argument would equally conclude for a future retribution with regard to all other animals, as it does for the fpecies of mankind[*]: but, admitting there will be a future retribution, he thinks it may be doubted, whether it fhall be univerfally extended to all our fpecies. He plainly intimates, that, in his opinion, thofe who die in their youth will not be called into judgment, nor thofe who act a very low part in life; and he feems to think, that thofe only fhall be called to an account whofe lives have been of much greater confequence to the world, and who have been greatly fubfervient to the public good, or hurt of mankind[†]: So that, according to his reprefentation of the cafe, fuppofing there were to be a future judgment and retribution, it is what the generality of mankind would have little concern in. And as, upon his fcheme, there are but few who fhall be called to an account, fo it is but for fome particular actions that they fhall be accountable. He obferves, that no man ever intended to do difhonour to God, or to be injurious to him, however foolifhly they may have ufed the names or terms by which the Deity is characterized; and that therefore there will be no inquiry at the laft judgment about fuch offences as thefe; *i. e.* about blafphemies againft God. The only offence man can be guilty of againft God is, he thinks, the want of a juft fenfe of his kindnefs and beneficence, and the not making a public profeffion of gratitude to him: but whether this will make a part of the grand inqueft, he declares himfelf certainly unable to judge; and he plainly infinuates, that in his opinion it will not; fince " among men it has been looked upon to be a mark of greatnefs " of foul, rather to defpife and overlook fuch ingratitude, than " to fhew any refentment of it[‡]." The only thing, therefore, for which he fuppofes men fhall be accountable, is for the injuries or benefits they do to one another: and even as to thefe, he feems not to allow, that the good or evil particular perfons do to one another, will come into judgment, but only " the good or

---

[*] Chubb's pofthumous Works, vol. i. p. 395.　　　　[†] Ibid. p. 400.
[‡] Ibid. p. 391, 392.

" bad part men act, by voluntarily contributing to the good or hurt
" of the commonweal\*." He afterwards fetteth himfelf to fhew,
that things would be as well ordered in the world without the
fuppofition and expectation of a future judgment, as with it; that
men's duties and obligations would ftill be the fame, and fo would
the motives to adhere to virtue, and to avoid vice: nor is the
belief of it of any great advantage to fociety †: To all which it
may be added, that here again, in treating concerning a future
judgment, he takes care to repeat what he had faid in the foregoing fection, *viz.* that if the foul be perifhable, and is diffolved
with the body, then this world feems to be *man's all*, and that
on fuch a fuppofition, a *refurrection* or *reftoration*, and a *future
retribution*, feem to be excluded: and at the fame time he declareth, that whether the foul perifheth with the body or not, is
a thing which admitteth of no proof ‡. So that, upon the whole,
he really leaveth it as a matter quite uncertain, whether there
fhall be a future judgment or not: and yet, when he has a mind
to make a boaft of the good tendency of his principles, he is for
making a merit of it, that it is one of thofe important truths,
which he has taken pains to inculcate on the minds of men.

I have infifted the longer upon thefe things, that I may un-
mafk the fair pretences of this author, who fets up for an uncommon degree of opennefs and candour. His admirers may
hence fee how confiftent he is, and how far his profeffions are
to be depended on.

I fhall now confider what he hath offered in this his folemn
*Farewell to his Readers*, with regard to revealed religion.

As to revelation in general, he feems to make a very fair
conceffion. " When men (faith he) are funk into grofs igno-
" rance and error, and are greatly vitiated in their affections and
" actions, then God may, for any reafon I can fee to the con-
" trary, kindly interpofe, by a fpecial application of his power
" and providence, and reveal to men fuch ufeful truths as other-
" wife they might be ignorant of, or might not attend to; and alfo
" lay before them fuch rules of life as they ought to walk by;
" and likewife prefs their obedience with proper motives, and

---

* Chubb's pofthumous Works, vol. i. p. 395. 397.        † Ibid. p. 401. 410.
‡ Ibid. p. 399.                                          § Ibid. p. 292, 293.

" thereby

" thereby lead them to repentance and reformation\*." But, as if he was afraid that in this he had made too large a conceffion, he adds, " but then that it is fo, and when it is fo, will in the " nature of the thing be matter of doubt and difputation." And in his fixth feftion, where he treateth exprefsly of revelation, he afferteth, that, in what way foever God communicateth knowledge to men, " it muft be a matter of uncertainty, whether the reve- " lation be divine or not, becaufe we have no rule to judge, or " from which we can with certainty diftinguifh divine revelation " from delufion :" and that if this be the cafe with thofe who receive the revelation at firft hand, then furely it muft be un- certain to thofe who receive it from them,†. Thus, though he feems to grant, that God may on fome occafions *kindly interpofe, by a fpecial application of his power and providence*, to reveal to men ufeful truths, and to direft and excite them to their duty; yet he will not allow that he can communicate the knowledge of his will in fuch a way, as to give them a fufficient fatisfying af- furance that it is a divine revelation, and came from him. This is a moft prefumptuous and unreafonable limitation of the divine power and wifdom, and is in effect the fame thing as to fay, that he cannot communicate any revelation of his will to mankind at all; even though his goodnefs fhould difpofe him to do fo, and their circumftances fhould require it.. Dr. Tindal had in effect faid the fame thing with our author; and what he offered to this purpofe was fully confidered and obviated in the anfwers that were made to him ‡.

From the queftion concerning revelation in general, Mr. Chubb proceeds, in his fixth feftion, to make fome obfervations on the Jewifh, Mahometan, and Chriftian revelation in particular.

The firft of thefe he abfolutely rejefteth. He pretends, that God's moral charafter is fullied by it: that St. Peter and St. Paul condemn it as unworthy of the Deity; that it had a vaft multi- plicity of rites and ceremonies, which he fuppofes to be perfeftly arbitrary, and inftituted without any reafon at all: that it repre- fents God as afting partially, in choofing the Jewifh nation to be

---

\* Chubb's pofthumous Works, vol. i. p. 292, 293.    † Ibid. vol. ii. p. 5.
‡ See Conybeare's Defence of Revealed Religion, chap. vii. Anfwer to Chriftianity as old as the Creation, vol. ii. chap. 1.

a peculiar

a peculiar people: and that, in that conſtitution, a twelfth part of the people lived idly on the labour of the reſt: that the appearances of God to the patriarchs, to Moſes, &c. could only belong to a local circumſcribed deity: and that the God of Iſrael was not the ſupreme Being, but only ſome tutelar ſubordinate god, conſonant to the pagan idolatry: and that his conduct in ordering the Iſraelites to extirpate the Canaanites was inconſiſtent with the moral character of the Deity. This is the ſum of what he urges, for ſeveral pages together in his ſixth ſection, with regard to the Jewiſh revelation*. And he had inſiſted upon the ſame things before at greater length in his ſecond ſection †, where he alſo condemns the puniſhing idolatry with death under the Jewiſh conſtitution as unjuſt, and as tending to juſtify perſecution for conſcience ſake. Theſe, and other objections to the ſame purpoſe, had been urged with great vivacity by Dr. Morgan, in his *Moral Philoſopher*, and were fully conſidered and obviated in the firſt and ſecond volumes of *The divine Authority of the Old and New Teſtament aſſerted*. Mr. Chubb has thought fit to repeat the objections, without giving any new ſtrength to them that I can find, or taking off the force of the anſwers which had been returned.

Referring therefore to what I have more largely inſiſted upon in the books now mentioned, I ſhall at preſent only obſerve in brief, that the idea given of God in the Jewiſh ſcriptures, of his greatneſs and majeſty, of his power and wiſdom, of his juſtice, goodneſs, and purity, and of his univerſal preſence and dominion, is the nobleſt that can be conceived by the human mind, and the moſt fitted to produce holy affections and diſpoſitions towards him: That nothing can be more evident, than that the God propoſed to the Jews, as the proper object of their worſhip, is the one living and true God, the ſovereign Lord of the univerſe, who created all things by his power, who preſerveth and governeth all things by his providence: That as to the divine appearances mentioned in the Old Teſtament, no argument can be brought to prove, that the ſovereign Lord of the univerſe may not ſee fit on ſome occaſions to exhibit himſelf by a viſible ex-

---

* Chubb's poſthumous Works, vol. ii. p. 19—29.
† Ibid. vol. i. p. 189—231.

ternal

ternal glory and fplendour, in order to ftrike men with a more ftrong and lively fenfe of his immediate prefence; or that he may not in that cafe make ufe of a glorious fubordinate being or beings of an order fuperior to man; and fome fuch beings have been acknowledged by the beft and wifeft men in all ages, in delivering meffages in his name: That it is no way inconfiftent with God's univerfal care and providence towards mankind, to make extraordinary difcoveries of his will to particular perfons, or to a people, or to give them wife and excellent laws, and eftablifh a conftitution among them, the fundamental principle of which is the acknowledgment and adoration of the one living and true God, in oppofition to all idolatry. Nor is there the leaft fhadow of reafon to prove, that he could not in fuch a cafe make the obfervance of this the principal condition on which the national privileges and benefits he thought fit to confer upon that people fhould be fufpended; in which cafe, whofoever was guilty of idolatry under that peculiar conftitution, was juftly obnoxious to the penalties inflicted upon the enemies and fubverters of the community. That as to God's choofing the people of Ifrael, they not only proceeded from anceftors, eminent for piety and virtue, and pure adorers of the Deity, but may be juftly fuppofed, at the time of God's erecting that facred polity among them, to have been, notwithftanding all their faults, freer from idolatry and other vices than any of the neighbouring nations. They feem to have been much better than the people of Egypt, from whence they were delivered; or than the Canaanites, whofe land was given them, and who appear to have been a moft wicked and abandoned race of men, univerfally guilty, not only of the groffeft idolatries, but of the moft monftrous vices and abominations of all kinds. And if God faw fit on that occafion to order them to be extirpated, as a monument to all ages of his juft deteftation of fuch crimes and vices, this cannot be proved to be inconfiftent with the character of the wife and righteous governor of the world: though our author reprefents this as a millftone that hangs at the neck of the Mofaic difpenfation. With refpect to the laws that were given to the people of Ifrael, thofe of a moral nature, of which there is a comprehenfive fummary in the Ten Commandments, are unqueftionably holy and excellent; the judicial laws are wife and equitable; and the pofitive precepts, though

many and various, wifely fuited to the ftate and circumftances
of that time and people. The reafons of feveral of them may be
affigned even at this diftance; and that there were very proper
reafons for the reft may be juftly fuppofed.    And St. Peter and
St. Paul, even when they reprefent them as burdenfome, plainly
fhew, that they look upon them to have been originally inftituted
for wife ends, though no longer to be obferved, when a more
perfect difpenfation was introduced, to which they were defigned to be fubfervient.    The appointing the Priefts and Levites, and diftributing them among the other tribes, is fo far from
being a juft objection againft that conftitution, that it may be
juftly regarded as a wife and excellent inftitution, well fitted for
preferving and fpreading the knowledge of religion, and the law
among the people, and inftructing them in their duty; and the
provifion made for them was juftly due, both as a reward for their
fervice, and as an equivalent for their not having had a diftinct
portion and fhare of the land affigned them with the other tribes.
Finally, the Mofaic conftitution was attended at its firft eftablifhment with the moft glorious and amazing demonftrations of
a divine power and majefty, and which plainly fhewed an extraordinary divine interpofition: and thefe facts were done not in
fecret, but in the moft open public manner, of which the whole
nation were witneffes; and the memory of them conftantly preferved, both by folemn public memorials, and in authentic records, which have all the characters of genuine antiquity, fimplicity, and a fincere regard to truth, and have been always regarded by the whole nation with the profoundeft veneration.    Nor
is there any juft foundation for the author's pretence, that the
facred hiftory was entirely in the hands of the priefts, or that from
Solomon's time to the Babylonifh captivity none had accefs to it
but the high-prieft, and that in that captivity their law was entirely deftroyed and loft * : a fuppofition that has been frequently repeated by the deiftical writers, though the abfurdity of it has
been fully expofed.

Though Mr. Chubb hath abfolutely rejected the Jewifh revelation, he fpeaks very favourably of that of Mahomet †.    Among
other inftances of his regard to it, he takes upon him to pronounce,

* Chubb's pofthumous Works, vol. ii. p. 26, 27.    † Ibid. p. 30, &c.

that

that " it cannot furely be true, that the great prevalence of Ma-
" hometanifm was owing to its being propagated by the fword;
" becaufe it muft have prevailed to a very great degree before
" the fword could have been drawn in its favour." And yet it is
a thing capable of the cleareft proof, that Mahometanifm from
its firft appearance was propagated by the fword. This was what
Mahomet himfelf moft exprefsly required and recommended,
and he accordingly fpread his religion confiderably by force of
arms in his life-time; and immediately after his death, the chief
apoftles of Mahometanifm were captains and mighty generals,
who fpread their conquefts far and wide. Our author concludes
his account of Mahometanifm with faying, " whether the Ma-
" hometan revelation be of a divine original, or not, there feems
" to be a plaufible pretence, arifing from the circumftances of
" things, for ftamping a divine character upon it[*].

As to the Chriftian revelation, it is evident he has done all in
his power to expofe it; and yet he feems plainly to acknowledge
Chrift's divine miffion. " That there was fuch a perfon as Jefus
" Chrift, and that he, in the main, did and taught as is recorded
" of him, appears (faith he) to be probable, becaufe it is impro-
" bable that Chriftianity fhould take place in the way and to the
" degree it did, or at leaft that we are told it did, fuppofing the
" hiftory of Chrift's life and miniftry to be a fiction." He adds,
that " if fuch power attended Jefus Chrift in the exercife of his
" miniftry, as the hiftory fets forth, then feeing his miniftry and
" the power that attended it feems, at leaft in general, to have
" terminated in the public good, it is more likely that God was
" the primary agent in the exercife of that power, than any other
" invifible being. And then it is probable, that Jefus Chrift,
" upon whofe will the immediate exercife of that power de-
" pended, would not ufe that power to impofe upon and miflead
" mankind to their hurt, feeing that power appears to have been
" well directed and applied in other refpects, and feeing he was
" accountable to his principal for the abufe of it." He adds—
" from thefe premifes, or from this general view of the cafe, I
" think this conclufion follows, *viz.* it is probable Chrift's mif-
" fion was divine; at leaft it appears fo to me from the light or

* Chubb's pofthumous Works, vol. ii. p. 40.

" inform-

" information I have received concerning it *." And as he seems here to acknowledge Chrift's miffion to be divine, fo he undertakes to give an account what was the fubjeƈt of his miffion, or what it was that he was fent to publifh to the world. This he reduceth to three main principles, for which he referreth to a traƈt he had formerly publifhed, intitled, *The true Gofpel of Chrift,* viz. 1. That nothing but a conformity of mind and life to the eternal rule of righteoufnefs will render men acceptable to God. 2. That when men have deviated from that rule, nothing but a thorough repentance and reformation will render them the proper objeƈts of God's mercy. And laftly, that God will judge the world in righteoufnefs, and will render to every man according as his works fhall be. He adds, that thefe propofitions feem to him to contain the fum and fubftance of Chrift's miniftry : and as they are altogether worthy of the Deity, fo, he thinks, they may with propriety and truth be called, *the Gofpel of Jefus Chrift.* This is what he declares in his fecond volume, p. 82, 83.; and he had faid the fame thing before, vol. i. p. 98, 99, where he obferves, that " thefe things contain the fubftance of what Chrift " was in a fpecial manner fent of God to acquaint the world with." And again he declares, that by Chriftianity he means, " that re- " velation of God's will which Chrift was in a fpecial and particu- " lar manner fent to acquaint the world with; and as far as the " writings of the apoftles are confonant with it, they come un- " der the denomination of Chriftianity † :" where he feems fair- ly to own, that Chrift was fent in a *particular and fpecial man- ner to acquaint the world* with a *revelation of God's will.* He alfo acknowledges, that " the writings of the apoftles contain ex- " cellent cautions, advices, and inftruƈtions, which ferve for the " right conduƈting our affeƈtions and actions : That the Chrif- " tian revelation, one would hope, was kindly intended to guide " men's underftandings into the knowledge of thofe truths, in " which their higheft intereft is concerned, and to engage them " to be juftly affeƈted therewith, and aƈt accordingly ; and that " it naturally tends to reform the vices, and rightly to direƈt the " affeƈtions and behaviour of men." And finally, " that it may

---

* Chubb's pofthumous Works, vol. ii. 41, 42, 43. compared with p. 394, 395, 396.

† Ibid. p. 346.

" perhaps

" perhaps be a piece of juſtice due to Chriſtianity (could it be
" certainly determined what it is, and could it be ſeparated
" from every thing that hath been blended with it), to acknow-
" ledge that it yields a much clearer light, and is a more ſafe
" guide to mankind, than any other traditionary religion, as be-
" ing better adapted to improve and perfect human nature\*."

Theſe things would naturally lead us to think, that he had a
friendly deſign towards Chriſtianity and the holy Scriptures.
But, notwithſtanding all theſe ſpecious profeſſions, whoſoever
reads what he calls his *Farewell to his Readers*, with ever ſo little
attention, muſt be convinced, that the principal deſign of it was
to ſubvert the credit and divine authority of the Chriſtian revelation.

Though he declares, that he looks upon it to be probable that
Chriſt's miſſion was divine, yet he has taken great pains to ſhew,
that the proofs which are brought for it are not at all to be depended upon. Having obſerved, that the two principal arguments
or evidences uſually inſiſted on to prove the divine original of
the Chriſtian revelation are prophecy and miracles, he uſes his
utmoſt efforts to invalidate both theſe: two long ſections of his
*Farewell to his Readers* are employed this way, *viz.* the ſeventh
and eighth: and as to the reſurrection of Chriſt, he labours
for near fifty pages together to repreſent it as an abſurd and incredible thing †.

In his ninth ſection, in which he propoſes to treat of the perſonal character of Jeſus Chriſt, he does all he can to expoſe the
account given of his being born of a virgin, as a fiction ‡.   And
whereas Chriſt is repreſented as having been perfect, and without
ſin, he will have it to be underſtood, not that he was abſolutely
ſinleſs, but that no public or groſs miſcarriages could be charged
upon him §.   The higheſt character he ſeems willing to allow
him is, that he was the " founder of the Chriſtian ſect ‖," or, as
he elſewhere expreſſeth it, that he " collected a body of diſciples,
" and laid a foundation for a new ſect among the Jews \*\*: for he
ſuppoſes, that, according to Jeſus's original intention, Chriſtianity

---

\* Chubb's poſthumous Works, vol. ii. p. 297. 344. 347. 370.
† Ibid. vol. i. p. 333, &c.        ‡ Ibid. vol. ii. p. 268—285.
§ Ibid. vol. ii. p. 269.            ‖ Ibid. vol. i. p. 50.
\*\* Ibid. vol. ii. p. 375.

was only defigned to be a *supplement* to Judaifm, and that the Mofaical conftitution was to continue always in full force, and that his gofpel was to be preached only to the Jews in all nations, and not to the Gentiles at all, though the apoftles afterwards deviated from his plan \*. He owns indeed, that he advanced fome proper precepts of his own, in which he feemed to correct the conftitutions of Mofes; but he endeavours to fhew, that in thefe he made alterations for the worfe, and that thofe precepts by which he is thought to have been moft diftinguifhed, inftead of being more excellent than thofe of other teachers and law-givers, are really lefs excellent, and lefs perfect; and, if taken in their proper and natural fenfe, are contrary to the reafon of things, and inconfiftent with the welfare and happinefs of mankind. This is the principal defign he appears to have had in view, in what he calls *Remarks on the Scriptures;* which is the firft tract in his *Pofthumous Works.*

In fome of the paffages above cited, he feems to give a favourable account of Chriftianity, and proceeds fo far as to fpecify what the true gofpel of Chrift is, and what that meffage is, which he allows Chrift was fent of God to deliver to the world; yet in plain contradiction to himfelf, he afferts in feveral parts of his book, that it is utterly uncertain what meffage Chrift was fent to publifh to the world, or wherein true Chriftianity doth confift. This is what he particularly endeavoureth to fhew in his fixth fection †. And in that very paffage before cited, where he pretends that it is a *piece of juftice due to Chriftianity,* to acknowledge, that it *yields a much clearer light,* and is a *more fafe guide than* any other *traditionary religion,* he at the fame time infinuates, that it *cannot be defined or determined what Chriftianity is* ‡. He afferts, that " it has been fo loofely and indeter-" minately delivered to the world, that nothing but contention " and confufion has attended it from its firft promulgation to this " time: and that the books of the New Teftament have been fo " far from being a remedy to this evil, that they have contri-" buted to it §." Accordingly, he exprefsly calls the New Teftament, that *fountain of confufion and contradiction* ||. And

---

\* Chubb's pofthumous Works, vol. ii. p. 85, 86. 168.    † Ibid. p. 72—122.
‡ Ibid. p. 270.           § Ibid. p. 57. 315.           || Ibid. p. 246, 247.

whereas

whereas Mr. Chillingworth had faid, that *the Bible is the reli-gion of Protestants*, Mr. Chubb thinks, that " unlefs it be fo
" interpreted as to be made conformable to the great rule of
" right and wrong, which, he fays, in fome inftances cannot
" be done without force and violence, it muft be an unfafe guide
" to mankind\*;" and that to appeal to Scripture " would be
" a certain way to perplexity and diffatisfaction, but not to find
" out the truth †." And before this he had faid, that " the Bible
" has been the grand fource of herefies and fchifms; and that it
" exhibits doctrines feemingly the moft oppofite, fome of which
" are greatly difhonourable to God, others the moft injurious to
" men ‡." I think it is not eafy to give a worfe idea of the
fcriptures than this author has done. If his account of them be
a juft one, it muft be very dangerous to read them; and it would
be a kindnefs to keep them out of the hands of the people: for
he feems directly to charge all this upon the fcriptures themfelves,
and not upon the fault of thofe that pervert and abufe them. And
yet this very confiftent writer declares againft *locking up the
Bible from the people*, and that " this is moft unfafe, as it has
" put the people fo far under the power of the clergy, as to in-
" volve them in the moft grofs ignorance and fuperftition, and
" the moft abfolute flavery both in civil and religious matters §."
Is not this plainly to acknowledge, that the being well acquainted with the holy fcriptures is one of the beft prefervatives
againft ignorance, prieftcraft, and fuperftition, and a great advantage and fecurity to truth and liberty? And what then muft
we think of the attempt made by him and other deiftical writers
to expofe and vilify the holy Scriptures, and deftroy all veneration for them in the minds of men, which, if believed, muft induce an abfolute negleét, and even contempt, of thofe facred
writings? Ought not this, by his own acknowledgment, to be
regarded as an attempt to bring us back into the *moft grofs ignorance, fuperftition, and flavery?*

As a farther proof of the author's good-will towards Chriftianity, it may be obferved, that he reprefents it as favouring of enthufiafm; and he explains enthufiafm to be " a groundlefs per-

---

\* Chubb's pofthumous Works, vol. ii. p. 326.      † Ibid. p. 335.
‡ Ibid. vol. i. p. 6. 57.                          § Ibid. vol. ii. p. 327. 345.

                                                  " fuafion,

" fuafion, that the Deity dictates and impreffes upon the mind of
" the promulger the fubject matter of his miniftry, and therefore
" fuch miniftry is fuppofed to be not of or from men, but of and
" from God*." And as he here fuppofes Chriftianity to be the
product of enthufiafm, fo he elfewhere charges the apoftles and
firft publifhers of Chriftianity with impofture. He reprefents
them as capable of giving a *falfe teftimony* to ferve the Chriftian
caufe, and that they acted upon this principle, "that truth in fome
cafes may and ought to be difpenfed with, and made to give
way to falfehood and diffimulation;" and upon this he afks,
" How then will the miracles wrought by Jefus Chrift and his
" apoftles be proved to be other than impoftures? fuppofing
" them to be much better attefted than at prefent they appear
" to be†."

These and other things that might be mentioned may let us
into the true fpirit and defign of this writer, and may help us to
judge of the proteftations he has made with great folemnity in
the conclufion of his *Farewell to his Readers.* " If any fay, that
" what I have written is out of difrefpect to the perfon and mi-
" niftry of Jefus Chrift, the accufation is falfe." And he adds,
" as upon the Chriftian fcheme, Jefus Chrift will be the judge of
" quick and dead, fo I affure my readers, that in this view, and
" upon this confideration, I have no difagreeable apprehenfion
" on account of any thing that I have publifhed to the world‡."

Having given this general idea of our author's work, I fhall
in my next letter offer fome remarks upon thofe parts of his book
which may feem to require a more particular confideration.

---

* Chubb's pofthumous Works, vol. ii. p. 49. 53.
† Ibid. p. 92, 93. 130, 131. 230, 231.          ‡ Ibid. p. 533.

# LETTER XIV.

*Some farther Remarks on Mr. Chubb's* Poſthumous Works—
*The unfair Repreſentation he makes of our Saviour's Precepts
in his Sermon on the Mount—His groſs Perverſions of Scripture—His Charge againſt it, as uncertain, and as having been
greatly depraved and corrupted by the Church of Rome, conſidered—Obſervations upon the Attempt he makes to invalidate
the Proof from Prophecy and Miracles—The Parallel he draws
between the Propagation of Chriſtianity and the Progreſs of
Methodiſm examined—The Falſehood of his Pretence, that the
Apoſtles quite changed the original Plan of Chriſtianity, and
that they laid a Scheme for worldly Wealth and Power—His
Invectives againſt St. Paul malicious and unjuſt—He repreſents all Religions to be alike with regard to the Favour of
God, and pretends to direct Men to an infallible Guide.*

SIR,

IN my laſt, I gave a general account of Mr. Chubb's poſthumous treatiſes.  I ſhall now add ſome farther obſervations
relating to ſome parts of thoſe tracts which may ſeem to deſerve
to be more particularly conſidered.

Of this kind is the attempt he hath made to expoſe our Saviour's precepts in his admirable ſermon on the mount, which
is deſigned to teach the moſt pure and excellent morality.  In
ſeveral of theſe precepts,  our Lord evidently maketh uſe of a
proverbial way of ſpeaking,  ſhort and comprehenſive aphoriſms,
delivered in phraſes, ſome of which  may perhaps appear not ſo
uſual among us, but  which were familiar to thoſe to whom they
were at firſt delivered.  Every one knows, that, in ſuch caſes,
every expreſſion is not to be taken in the utmoſt ſtrictneſs, but
the general intention is to be regarded, which is plain enough to
an honeſt and attentive mind.   But this writer ſeems reſolved to
take them in the moſt abſurd ſenſe he can poſſibly put upon
them.   Thus, he interprets the precept againſt reſiſting evil,
which is manifeſtly intended to check and ſuppreſs private
revenge, and to teach us that wiſe leſſon, " that it is better in
*many*

many cafes, patiently to bear injuries, efpecially in fmaller inftances, than to give way to a keen and forward refentment and
retaliation of them," as if it were defigned abfolutely, and in
all cafes, to forbid us to fhun or guard againft the evils and injuries offered to us, and required us rather to expofe ourfelves to
thofe evils.   But this certainly could not be the intention of
that excellent teacher, who exhorteth his difciples to be *wife as
ferpents* in avoiding evil, as well as *innocent as doves;* and di-
rećteth them, inftead of needlefsly expofing themfelves, when
*perfecuted in one city, to flee unto another.*   The precept about
loving our enemies is defigned to reftrain and heal that bitter and
malevolent fpirit which men are fo apt to indulge, and to carry
benevolence to the nobleft height.   It teacheth us, that no private enmities or difgufts fhould caufe us to forget the common
ties of humanity: that with regard to our enemies themfelves,
we fhould be earneftly defirous of their amendment and true
happinefs, and fhould be ready, when a proper opportunity offers,
to do them good offices, and to overcome their enmity with kindnefs, which is the nobleft victory.   But our candid author would
have it to be underftood to fignify, that we fhould put no difference in our affection and efteem between good and bad men, but
fhould have an equal complacency in perfons of the vileft characters as in thofe of the beft*.   And becaufe our Saviour fpeaks
of God's doing good, in the methods of his common providence,
even to the unthankful and the evil, he pretends, that, according
to his reprefentation, the perfection of the Supreme Being confifteth in his being affected towards all intelligent beings alike,
and fhewing equal love and favour to the righteous and to the
wicked; than which nothing can be more contrary to Chrift's
manifeft intention, and to the whole tenor of his teaching and
miniftry.   Our Lord's excellent difcourfe againft anxious cares,
and a diftracting or diftruftful thoughtfulnefs for to-morrow, he
interprets as defigned to recommend *thoughtleffnefs and indolence,*
and abfolutely to forbid that *thoughtfulnefs and induftry, which
man's prefent indigent condition, and the prefent conftitution of
things, make neceffary* †.   And the precept by which we are directed *not to lay up* for ourfelves *treafures on earth,* but to lay

---

* Chubb's pofthumous Works, vol. i. p. 18, 19.    † Ibid. p. 22, 23.

up

up for ourfelves *treafures in heaven*, which is plainly intended to check a too eager purfuit of worldly riches, and a placing our chief happinefs in thefe things, he reprefents as if it were defigned abfolutely to condemn all worldly acquifitions, however lawfully obtained, and well ufed and employed. In like manner, he interprets what our Saviour fays in a parabolical way, Luke xvi. 12, 13. concerning inviting the poor, the blind, and the lame; and which, as may be gathered from the context by comparing ver. 7, &c. was defigned to rebuke the vanity of expenfive and oftentatious entertainments, whilft the poor and indigent were neglected; as if it were his intention, that all Chriftians fhould deny themfelves the pleafure of ever entertaining, or being entertained by friends, relations, and thofe of their own rank, and were to confine themfelves wholly to the company, converfation, and friendfhip of the *poor*, the *maimed*, the *lame*, and the *blind\**: though it is very evident from his own practice, that our Lord Jefus was far from difcouraging an agreeable intercourfe and converfation among friends, and the offices and entertainments of the focial life; and I dare fay, not one either of the Jews, or of his own difciples, ever underftood him in this fenfe.

But Mr. Chubb takes upon him to pronounce, that thefe and the like precepts are all to be underftood in the moft ftrict literal fenfe, and do not admit of *any limitation*, or any palliating interpretation to be put upon them; and he reprefents them as the proper precepts of Chriftianity, *peculiar*, as he expreffeth it, to the *Chriftian fect*, and *in which their founder's honour is peculiarly concerned*; and pretends, that the obfervance of thefe alone, in the abfurd fenfe he puts upon them, is what conftitutes a true Chriftian. And as thefe are the precepts that are acknowledged to be peculiarly Chriftian, he thinks that from thence a judgment may be formed, whether there be any juft ground for boafting, that Chriftian morals are much more excellent and perfect, than any other fyftem of morals that hath been exhibited to men\*.

Nothing can poffibly be more unfair and difingenuous, than this conduct of our author. No man of candour, who confiders the deep wifdom and good fenfe which appeareth in our Saviour's difcourfes, can reafonably fuppofe, that it was his intention to

---

\* Chubb's pofthumous Works, vol. i. p. 25, 26.

† Ibid. p. 27, 20. 31. 39, 40.

recommend fuch abfurd inftructions and advices as they muſt have been, according to this writer's reprefentation of them. Our Lord's defign, in his excellent fermon on the mount, was not, as he himſelf declares, to deſtroy the law and the prophets; it was to vindicate them from the narrow and corrupt gloſſes of the Jewiſh doctors. And what could be more worthy of a teacher ſent from God, the great Saviour and lover of mankind, than to forbid the being angry without a cauſe, all injurious and reproach-ful expreſſions, all adultery and impurity, even in heart and thought; and to recommend purity, charity, meekneſs, bene-volence, the forgiveneſs of injuries, and even a rendering good for evil, and overcoming evil with good? to warn men againſt an exceſſive love of worldly riches, which hath in all ages been the fource of numberleſs evils and diforders among mankind, and engage them to raiſe their affections and views to things of a far higher and nobler nature, things celeſtial and eternal? to direct men to a calm contentment and dependence on divine pro-vidence, in every condition, as the beſt preſervative againſt thoſe anxious diſtracting cares and folicitudes, which, when they prevail, deſtroy the reliſh of life? What our Saviour hath deliver-ed on theſe, and on other heads of great importance to the happi-neſs of mankind, is comprehended in ſhort maxims, ſtrongly and cloſely expreſſed, which makes them more apt to ſtrike, and more eaſily remembered; but without defcending to particular exceptions and limitations, which, for the moſt part, common fenſe, and the nature of the thing, eaſily direct to. He, who was perfectly acquainted with human nature, very well knew, that there was no great danger of men's taking them in too ſtrict a fenſe, and that they would be forward enough to find out limitations for themſelves. And any one that impartially confiders the variety of matters treated of, in that excellent fermon on the mount, fuch a vaſt extent of pure and noble morals comprized in fo ſmall a compaſs, and delivered with the moſt comprehenſive brevity, will be apt to admire the wifdom of this heavenly teacher, and to have a juſt diſlike of a writer that could turn thoſe admirable lef-fons to the difadvantage of the holy Jefus and the Chriſtian re-ligion. And I am perfuaded, that any man who ſhould treat the maxims and wife fayings of the philofophers or great men of an-tiquity, as this author has done thoſe of our Saviour, would be

regarded

regarded by all rational and thinking men among the deifts themfelves, as a rude and impertinent caviller. What renders Mr.
Chubb more inexcufable is, that he himfelf feems to have been
very fenfible, that thofe precepts were not intended in the fenfe
he has thought fit to put upon them: for though, in what he calls
*Remarks on the Scriptures*, he contends, as hath been fhewn,
that no other interpretation ought to be admitted, yet in another
part of his *Pofthumous Works*, viz. in the ninth fection of his
*Farewell*, where he profeffes to treat concerning the perfonal
character of Jefus Chrift, he produces thefe very precepts as inftances of Chrift's figurative way of fpeaking, and plainly owns,
that they ought not to be taken, nor were originally intended, in
the ftrict literal fenfe he had put upon them. To this purpofe
he particularly mentions the precepts of not refifting evil, of loving our enemies, and giving to every one that afketh*; and
from thence concludes, that we muft ufe our reafon in judging
of the fenfe of fcripture, and of our Saviour's precepts; which
will be readily allowed. The fcripture undoubtedly fuppofeth
us to be reafonable creatures, and our Saviour addreffeth himfelf
to us as fuch: but it by no means follows, as he infinuates, that
becaufe we are to ufe our underftandings in judging of the fenfe
of fcripture, and all laws, that therefore our own reafon could
guide us as well without them, and that thefe precepts are of no
ufe, and that it is of no advantage to have them enforced by a divine authority.

It may not be improper on this occafion to take notice of fome
other of his grofs perverfions of fcripture. A fignal inftance of
this kind we have in the fame tract, in which he makes fo ftrange
a reprefentation of feveral of our Saviour's precepts. Speaking
of that noted paffage, 1 John ii. 1, 2. *My little children, thefe
things write I unto you, that ye fin not; and if any man fin, we
have an advocate with the Father, Jefus Chrift the righteous:
and he is the propitiation for our fins, and not for ours only,
but alfo for the fins of the whole world.* He obferves, that " this
" paffage may be fuppofed to befpeak comfort and fafety to a
" wicked Chriftian, *i. e.* to a wicked man who is a believer in
" Jefus Chrift, and profeffes difciplefhip to him; and that it

* Chubb's pofthumous Works, vol. ii. p. 289. 293, 294, &c.

" is

" is but for a man to apply thefe words of John to himfelf, and
" the practice of vice is made eafy to him *." That this could
not poffibly be St. John's meaning in this paffage, is evident
from the whole tenour of his epiftle, and particularly from the
words immediately following, in which he declares, *hereby we
do know* that we know him, *i. e.* Jefus Chrift, *if we keep his commandments. He that faith, I know him, and keepeth not his
commandments, is a liar, and the truth is not in him,* ver. 3. 4.
Our author himfelf is fenfible, that the interpretation he hath
given of this paffage is not confiftent with what St. John hath
faid in other parts of his epiftle. But that gives him no concern;
it will only fhew that St. John contradicts himfelf; which is
what he would have him thought to do: and therefore with an
unparalleled affurance he infifteth upon it, that the account he
hath given of St. John's meaning, is the true one, " whatever
" St. John, or any other writer of the New Teftament, in op-
" pofition to this, may have elfewhere faid to the contrary."
His manner of expreffing himfelf plainly fhews, that he is refolved this fhall be St. John's fenfe, contrary to his own moft
exprefs declarations, and to the entire ftrain of the New Teftament; becaufe he thinks it tends to expofe Chriftianity, though
in reality by fuch a procedure he has only expofed himfelf. But
he urgeth, that " if Chrift be the propitiation for all fins, then
" the moft wicked Chriftian muft needs be in a fafe and com-
" fortable ftate; and even wicked pagans and infidels, as well as
" Chriftians, penitent and impenitent, becaufe God would not
" be fo unreafonable and unjuft, as to take double fatisfaction
" for the fame offences." And in fome other parts of his book,
he inveighs againft the doctrine of Chrift's being the propitiation
for fins, as contrary to truth, and the eternal reafon of things †.
But in all that he has faid on this head, he either difcovers a grofs
ignorance of the fcripture-doctrine of Chrift's being the propitiation for our fins, or makes a wilful mifreprefentation of it; fince
nothing can be more evident than it is from the whole New
Teftament, that Chrift's dying for our fins was not defigned to
free men from an obligation to holinefs and obedience, but rather
to lay them under ftronger engagements to it; and that acccord-

* Chubb's pofthumous Works, vol. i. p. 37, 38.
† Ibid. p. 250, and vol. ii. p. 111, 113, 304.

ing

ing to the gofpel covenant, none can expect an intereſt in the
benefits ariſing from Chriſt's ſufferings and ſacrifice, or from
his mediation and interceſſion, but thoſe that turn from their
ſins by a ſincere repentance, and who ſubmit to be governed by
his holy and moſt excellent laws. The doctrine of Chriſt's ſatisfaction, rightly underſtood, is ſo far from giving the leaſt encouragement to ſin, that it tendeth to impreſs men's hearts with
the deepeſt ſenſe of the heinous evil and malignity of ſin, and of
God's juſt diſpleaſure againſt it. Not only do thoſe who teach
that doctrine as delivered in the ſcriptures, inſiſt as ſtrongly as
any others upon the neceſſity of repentance and perſonal holineſs,
in order to their acceptance with God, but they maintain, that
at the ſame time that God promiſeth pardon to the truly penitent,
he taketh care to diſpenſe that pardon in ſuch a way, as to make
an awful declaration of his hatred againſt ſin, and to vindicate
the authority of his government and laws. What can have a
greater tendency to prevent our abuſing his pardoning mercy,
and to excite in us a holy fear of offending him, than to conſider
that he would not receive even penitent ſinners to his grace and
favour, without a ſacrifice of infinite virtue offered up on their
behalf, conſiſting in the perfect obedience and ſufferings of the
great Mediator? And that it was upon the merit of his obedience
and ſufferings, that that covenant was founded and eſtabliſhed,
in which God hath graciouſly engaged to accept of our repentance, and to reward our ſincere though imperfect obedience
with eternal life?

Many other inſtances might be mentioned of Mr. Chubb's
ſtrange gloſſes upon ſcripture. He ſeems particularly to take
pleaſure in miſrepreſenting and expoſing the writings of St.
Paul. Thus, becauſe that great apoſtle, in arguing againſt the
falſe Jewiſh teachers, who inſiſted upon the obſervance of the
Moſaic law and ceremonies, as abſolutely neceſſary to ſalvation
under the gofpel, urgeth, that, if they were *juſtified by the law,*
they were *fallen from grace, i. e.* from the grace of the gofpel,
and the way of juſtification there propoſed, Gal. v. 4. he charges
him with maintaining in the height of his zeal, that *obedience to
the law of Moſes was incompatible with ſalvation;* and that let
men otherwiſe be ever ſo good and excellent perſons, this error
concerning the obligation of the Moſaic law would exclude them

from

from the favour of God, and from eternal salvation. *And in this,* saith he, *the Apostle must surely have greatly erred\**. But it ought to be considered, that those Jewish teachers, whom St. Paul there opposes, are represented as men of corrupt minds, who acted from worldly and sinister ends and views, and who were not strict in keeping the law themselves, though they were for binding it upon others, Gal. vi. 12, 13. And the apostle there expressly declareth, that in Christ Jesus, or under the gospel dispensation, *neither circumcision availeth any thing, nor uncircumcision, i. e.* neither the observance nor non-observance of these outward rites, *but faith which worketh by love,* or, as he elsewhere expresseth it, the *new creature, i. e.* a real sanctifying change of heart and life. See Gal. v. 6. vi. 15. 1 Cor: vii. 19. Again, he pretends, that St. Paul represents the calling of the Gentiles as not originally designed by God, or as an effect of his goodness towards the Gentiles, but as springing only from his having *taken up a pique or resentment against the Jews,* which, he says, " is a spring of action much too low, and altogether un- " worthy of the supreme Deity †." But nothing is more evident than that this apostle frequently ascribes the calling of the Gentiles to the free grace and gratuitous favour of God, and speaks of it in noble terms, as having been designed in the councils of the divine wisdom and love before the foundation of the world, Eph. i. 3, 4, 5, 6. iii. 8, 9. Farther to expose that excellent apostle, he represents it, as if in saying, that *if in this life only we have hope in Christ, we are of all men the most miserable,* 1 Cor. xv. 19. he intended to signify, that the practice of piety and virtue is not in its own nature so eligible, or so conducive to the real satisfaction of this present life, as that of vice and sin. Nor will he allow that St. Paul in this part of the argument has any reference to the case of persecution; and yet certain it is, that he most expressly refers to it, ver. 29, 30, 31, 32.; and his evident design is to signify the unhappy condition Christians would be reduced to, under the grievous persecutions to which they were then exposed, if it were not for their future hopes. But he especially finds great fault with St. Paul for his doctrine concerning subjection to the higher powers, Rom. xiii. 1. 6. as

---

\* Chubb's posthumous Works, vol. ii. p. 96, 97.　　† Ibid. p. 88.

if

if it were calculated for promoting tyranny and flavery. This he infifts upon for feveral pages together, in two different parts of his *Pofthumous Works;* and yet the apoftle's doctrine, rightly confidered, is admirable.  He fhews, that obedience to the civil powers is a duty which Chriftianity enjoins; that it was not defigned to exempt men from fubjection to their lawful governors, though heathens, or to relax the bands of civil duty and allegiance. He doth not meddle with the queftions concerning the rights of Senates, or particular forms of polity, but fpeaks of the duty of private perfons, and therefore prefles their obedience and fubjection, without reftrictions and limitations; and to have mentioned fuch reftrictions would certainly have been of bad confequence; efpecially confidering the feditious difpofitions of the Jews, and how they were then affected.  But our author is not willing to allow, that religion has any thing to do with obedience to our civil governors; and, in exprefs oppofition to St. Paul, declares, that government cannot be faid to be the ordinance, or by the appointment, of God.  He maintains, that the proper argument for obliging men to fubjection and obedience is, not government's being the ordinance of God, but its being neceffary to the well-being of mankind.  And does not the apoftle manifeftly urge this?  He both raifeth our views to the original of government in the authority and appointment of God himfelf, and pointeth out to us the proper ends of government, and its great ufefulnefs to mankind, and excellently argueth from both thefe.  So that he is far from what this writer here thinks fit to charge him with, a *fallacious and injurious way of reafoning.*

He takes particular notice of the allegory * St. Paul makes ufe of, Gal. iv. 21, &c. and ufes his utmoft endeavours to place it in a moft ridiculous light.  Nothing can be more unfair and difingenuous than the account he is pleafed to give of it, in which he entirely mifreprefents the defign and ftrain of the apoftle's difcourfe.  But a particular examination of what he offers, with regard to this and feveral other paffages of Scripture, would carry me too far.  It is fufficient to obferve, that a careful and un-

---

* Mr. Collins had endeavoured to expofe that allegory; and the defign and confiftency of it was fully cleared in the anfwers that were made to that writer.  Nor has Mr. Chubb offered any thing upon it that can be called new.

prejudiced confideration of the context, and a comparing one part of Scripture with another, might eafily have fet him right as to the fenfe of moft of the paffages he mentions; or he might have found his difficulties cleared by able and judicious commentators, if he had been as willing to have his objections fatisfied, as he was to raife them, or as a fincere inquirer after truth ought to be. Candid critics, if they meet with a paffage in Homer, Plato, Ariftotle, Tully, or any other celebrated profane author of antiquity, which at firft view has fomething in it that they cannot well explain or account for, are very unwilling to charge the original author with nonfenfe and abfurdity, and think themfelves obliged to ufe their utmoft endeavours to find out a convenient or favourable fenfe of the paffage in queftion. But with this writer, and many others of the fame clafs, it feems to be a rule to interpret every paffage of Scripture in the moft abfurd fenfe that can poffibly be put upon it.

Several paffages were produced in my former letter, to which many others might be added, in which Mr. Chubb exclaims againft the fcripture as the fource of endlefs contentions and divifions, as if it were to be charged with all the abfurd and contradictory opinions, that have at any time been grafted upon it. This he reprefents, as owing to its being " expreffed in a loofe " indeterminate way, which would be a defect in a human com- " pofition, but is fcarce fuppofable in the cafe of divine revela- " tion *." But it is no argument, that a thing is loofely and indeterminately expreffed, becaufe men differ or contend about the fenfe of it. This is owing to other caufes. Suppofing a divine revelation given to mankind, ever fo clear and determinate, it could fcarce be avoided, without a conftant miraculous interpofition, irrefiftibly impreffing and overruling the minds of all men, but that there would be a difference of fentiments and opinions among mankind, about many things in it: and yet this would not hinder but that fuch a revelation would be of fignal ufe for inftructing men in things of great importance. The fallacy of fuch a way of arguing, as if men's differing about any thing were a proof of its uncertainty, has been often expofed, as what would banifh all religion, truth, reafon, and evidence, out

* Chubb's pofthumous Works, vol. ii. p. 246, 247.

of the world: yet this is a common-place with the deiftical writers, to which they have recourfe on all occafions. Many made ufe of it before our author: and fince the publifhing of his works, a late right honourable writer hath been pleafed to renew the charge. I fhall not here repeat what I have elfewhere offered in anfwer to his Lordfhip, and which will equally ferve to obviate all that Mr. Chubb hath advanced on this head[*].

The fame obfervation may be made with regard to his attempts againft the facred canon. He pretends, as others had done before him, that there is no proof that the books of the New Teftament were written in the firft age of the Chriftian church; that there were many fpurious gofpels in the primitive times, and that the Chriftians had no way of diftinguifhing the genuine from the falfe. Thefe, and other things to the fame purpofe, he very frequently repeats in feveral parts of his *Farewell to his Readers,* as if he thought the frequent repetition of them would perfuade his readers of their truth. But I fhall not need to take any particular notice of them here, but refer to what was faid on this fubject in the fourth letter, where fome account is given of the anfwers that were made to Toland's *Amyntor:* to which may be added, what hath been lately offered in anfwer to the fame objections, when urged by the noble writer laft-mentioned[†].

Mr. Chubb hath alfo raifed a great clamour about the corruption of Scripture. He layeth it down as a principle, that if God gave a revelation for the ufe of mankind, he would take care that it fhould be tranfmitted fafe and uncorrupted to all fucceeding generations, and would, by a particular and conftant application of his power and providence, have defended it from all injury, wherever it was promulged, and whatever language it was rendered into. He intimates, that God ought to have punifhed with a fudden death, as in the cafe of Ananias and Sapphira, every man that had committed any error, either in tranfcribing or tranflating it. And if this had been the cafe, the confequence would have been, that no man would have ventured to tranfcribe or tranflate it at all: and this, no doubt, is what thefe gentlemen would wifh. But there is no neceffity for having recourfe to fuch

* See Reflections on Lord Bolingbroke's Letters, p. 125, &c.
† Ibid. p. 98, &c.

extraordinary

extraordinary methods; we have fufficient evidence to fatisfy
any reafonable perfon, that this revelation is tranfmitted to us,
without any fuch corruptions or alterations as can deftroy the
ufefulnefs of that revelation, or defeat the important ends for
which it was originally given.    This hath been often clearly
fhewn.    Our author indeed pronounces with great confidence,
that " it is a thing abundantly evident, that the Chriftian revela-
" tion hath been greatly depraved and corrupted; that its pre-
" tended guardians have extracted the myftery of iniquity from
" it: and that we have received the books referred to from that
" grand fountain of corruption the church of Rome, who muft
" have been naturally, and almoft unavoidably led to corrupt them
" in thofe times of ignorance, to juftify herfelf in all other cor-
" ruptions and abufes."  This he frequently repeats, as his manner
is, in feveral parts of his book, and it hath been often urged by
the deiftical writers*; and it muft be acknowledged, that if a
general corruption of the Scriptures could have been poffibly
effected, none had fo good an opportunity, or a ftronger temptation to attempt it, than the church of Rome: and yet it is evident
in fact, that they have not corrupted the Scriptures in thofe inftances in which it was moft their intereft, and we might imagine
alfo moft in their inclination, to have corrupted them.    There
might be fome pretence for fuch a charge, if there had been any
exprefs and formal paffages inferted in the New Teftament, in
favour of the papal fupremacy, of St. Peter's having been bifhop
of Rome, the worfhip of images, the invocation of faints and
angels, purgatory, the communion in one kind, againft priefts'
marriage, and in favour of the monaftic vows, &c.; but our author hath not attempted to produce any paffages of this kind; and
he himfelf has obferved, that " the New Teftament was not fuf-
" ficient to fupport the weight of the conftitution of the church
" of Rome, and therefore its builders prudently annexed tradi-
" tion to it †."    He alfo finds fault with their locking up the
Bible from the laity, as what hath put them fo far under the
power of the clergy, as to involve them in grofs ignorance, fuperftition, and flavery.    Thus, this very confident writer, with

---

* Chubb's pofthumous Works, vol. ii. p. 65, 66. 118. 121, 122.
† Ibid. vol. ii. p. 58.

a view

a view to expofe the New Teftament, would perfuade us, that
popery is taught and founded there, and yet would have the
Bible kept in the hands of the people as a proper prefervative
againft it,

The arguments in favour of the Jewifh and Chriftian revelation from prophecy and miracles have always been looked upon
as of great weight; and Mr. Chubb hath taken great pains to invalidate both thefe.   With regard to prophecy, which is the entire fubject of the feventh fection of his *Farewell to his Rea-
ders\**, he pretends not to deny, that there may be true prophecy;
that God may certainly foreknow future events, and may enable
perfons to foretel them: but he denies, that the prediction of
future events can be admitted as an evidence of divine revelation, becaufe a prophecy can never be known to be a true prophecy till it be fulfilled; and therefore can never be a proof or
evidence at the time of its delivery, becaufe it muft appear as
yet uncertain.   His argument here proceeds upon a wrong fuppofition, as if the advocates for revelation maintained, that the
mere prediction of a future event, even before the completion of
it, were alone a fufficient proof to thofe who heard the prediction, of the divine miffion of the perfons who delivered it,  This
was far from being the only proof that was given either of the
Mofaic or Chriftian revelation.   They were both of them at
their firft promulgation attefted and eftablifhed by an amazing
fucceffion of the moft wonderful works, and which plainly argued an extraordinary divine interpofition: befides which, both
Mofes and the prophets under the Old Teftament, and our Lord
Jefus Chrift and his apoftles under the New, were enabled to
give many exprefs predictions of future events; fome of which
related to things which were to happen in their own time, and
received a fpeedy accomplifhment; others related to events that
were not to happen till fome ages after the prediction, and thefe
alfo received their accomplifhment in the proper feafon.   And
this, added to the other evidences, exhibited a farther illuftrious
proof of a divine interpofition in favour of the Jewifh and Chriftian revelation, and fhews, that the firft publifhers of it were extraordinarily infpired by God, who, by the author's own acknow-

---

\* Chubb's pofthumous Works, vol. ii. p. 139—174.

R 3                                        ledgment,

ledgment, can alone forefee and foretel future contingent events. It was wifely ordered, that miracles and prophecy fhould go together; whereby not only the moft ftriking evidence was given to the truth and divinity of the revelation, at the time when it was firft promulgated, but provifion was made that there fhould be a growing evidence, which might acquire new force and ftrength by the fucceffive accomplifhment of the prophecies in the feveral different periods to which they refer.   Indeed, if it were only a fingle prediction or two, the fulfilling of them might be looked upon to be accidental, and to amount to no more than a lucky conjecture: but a feries of prophecies, fuch as is fet before us in the facred writings, many of them relating to things of a moft contingent nature, removed at the diftance of feveral ages, and which depended upon things that no human fagacity could forefee, muft be afcribed to an extraordinary divine affiftance; and it cannot reafonably be fuppofed, that God would impart his prefcience to give credit to impoftors, who falfely pretended to be infpired by him to deliver doctrines and laws to mankind.

As to that part of the evidence of Chrift's divine miffion, which refulteth from the prophecies of the Old Teftament, this had been fully confidered in the controverfy between Mr. Collins and his adverfaries, of which fome account was given in the fixth letter.   What Mr. Chubb has offered on this head is very inconfiderable: but he has one reflection that may deferve fome notice: it is this: That, " fuppofing thofe prophecies to have " been fulfilled in Jefus Chrift, they are not fo much to be re- " garded as an evidence of the divine authority of the Chriftian " revelation, as of the divine character of its primary promulger, " who, being a free being, muft have been at liberty whether he " would have faithfully delivered thofe truths to the world, that " had been delivered to him by his principal.   And this," faith he, " muft of neceffity be the cafe of all divine revelation*." But, fuppofing there was a feries of prophecy, relating to a wonderful perfon, who was to appear, at a time prefixed, as a divine teacher and Lord, and who was to erect a difpenfation of truth and righteoufnefs, and that his coming, perfon, offices, miracles,

* Chubb's pofthumous Works, p. 152, 153.

fufferings,

fufferings, and the glories that fhould follow, were defcribed and pointed out by many remarkable predictions, delivered at fundry times and in divers manners, all which were fulfilled in Jefus Chrift, and in him only; this certainly muft be looked upon as an illuftrious atteftation, not only to the divinity of his miffion, but to the truth of the revelation he brought in the name of God: for it were moft abfurd to fuppofe, that God would have infpired fo many perfons, in different ages, to foretel his coming and character as a divine teacher of truth and righteoufnefs, if he had not perfectly foreknown that he would certainly fulfil that character, and fulfil the great truft repofed in him. And the preparing mankind for his coming by fuch a fucceffion of prophecies, and pointing him out by the moft glorious and peculiar characters, fo many ages before his actual appearing, tended to give him an atteftation of a peculiar kind, and which was never equalled in any other cafe.

With regard to the prophecies of Daniel, this author thinks it is impoffible, " that God fhould deliver a prophecy fo darkly, " as that one man only, and he a prodigy, amidft the millions " of men that have taken place fince that prophecy was deliver- " ed, fhould be able to difcover the true fenfe and meaning of " it *;" where he goes upon a fuppofition which is manifeftly falfe, *viz.* that no man before Sir Ifaac Newton was ever able to difcover the meaning and intent of Daniel's prophecies. Many there have been who have laboured happily this way, both formerly and of late: and though there are feveral things in thofe prophecies that are attended with great difficulty, there are others of the predictions contained in that book, which are fo clear, that the application of them is comparatively eafy. And they have been wonderfully verified, in a manner which fhews they could only have proceeded from that all-feeing mind which prefides over contingencies, and clearly fees through the fucceffion of ages. And the predictions there given relating to the Meffiah, the defign and end of his coming, and the defolation of the Jewifh city and temple that fhould be connected with it, are of fuch a nature, as to give a moft remarkable atteftation to our Lord Jefus Chrift, as the true promifed Meffiah. And it may

---

* Chubb's pofthumous Works, p. 147, 148.

be

be obferved by the way, that this ſhews the vanity and falſe-hood of another of our author's ſuppoſitions, who pretends, that the Jewiſh expectation of the Meſſiah was ſolely owing to the notion they had of their being God's peculiar people, from whence it was natural for them to believe, that God would raiſe them up a glorious deliverer, who ſhould exalt their nation to the higheſt degree of proſperity and grandeur; and that the pro-phets humoured them in this their notion and expectation: For if this had been the caſe, the prophets would not have ſpoken of a ſuffering Meſſiah; nor would they have foretold, as they have done, his being rejected by the Jews, and the judgments which ſhould be then executed upon that nation, and that the Gentiles ſhould be partakers of the benefits of his kingdom.

This writer, who ſeems to value himſelf upon thinking out of the common way, can ſee nothing extraordinary in the predic-tions relating to the calamities and diſperſions of the Jews, and their wonderful preſervation, under all their diſperſions and cala-mities, for a long ſucceſſion of ages: and yet certain it is, that their being ſo generally diſperſed among all nations over the whole earth, and being ſtill preſerved as a diſtinct people, not-withſtanding the unexampled diſcouragements, reproaches, and ſufferings, to which they have been expoſed, is one of the moſt wonderful things, taken in all its circumſtances, that is to be found in the whole hiſtory of mankind: and as it hath no paral-lel, its being ſo plainly foretold above three thouſand years ago (for ſo long it is ſince the time of Moſes, who firſt propheſied of it) is a moſt ſignal inſtance of a true prophetic ſpirit, and could only be owing to the inſpiration of that omniſcient Being, who *declareth the end from the beginning, and from ancient times the things which are not yet done.*

I ſhall only take notice of one obſervation more, which our author hath made with regard to the proof from prophecy, *viz.* that it appears from St. Paul's account, that the gift of prophecy was a diſtinct gift from that of knowledge, 1 Cor. xii. 8, 9, 10. and " that they had no connection or dependence upon one ano-" ther:" and he thinks therefore, " that a perſon's foretelling " things to come, does not prove a ſuperiority of knowledge, " and that the prophet's knowledge extends farther than the pro-" phecies he delivers." But if we examine that paſſage of St.

Paul

Paul which he refers to, we fhall find it is far from anfwering the end he propofes by it, *viz.* to invalidate the proof from prophecy in favour of the Chriftian revelation. The apoftle is there fpeaking of the feveral gifts of the Holy Ghoft, which were poured forth on many of the Chriftian converts in that firft age, in various proportions and degrees according to his will. One of thefe was, that of prophecy. It is not certain, that by *prophecy*, in that particular paffage, is to be underftood the foretelling things to come; for the word prophecy is fometimes taken in that epiftle in another fenfe: but allowing it to be fo, fince it appears from other paffages that fuch a gift there was in the firft age of the Chriftian church (and it was what our Saviour had promifed, John xvi. 13.), in that cafe it muft be faid, that fuch a gift, if really conferred, could only proceed from God, or his Holy Spirit: and as thofe extraordinary gifts, of which this was one, were communicated by the laying on of the hands of the apoftles in the name of a crucified and rifen Jefus, the conferring thefe gifts on any of the Chriftian converts may be juftly regarded as a moft illuftrious proof of a divine interpofition in favour of Chriftianity, and of the divine miffion of the apoftles, the firft authorized publifhers of it.

Having confidered the principal things this writer has urged on the head of prophecy, I fhall take fome notice of what he hath offered concerning the proof from miracles: This is the fubject of his eighth fection*. He will not allow, that miracles can be any proof of the divine miffion of perfons or truth of doctrines. What he chiefly infifteth upon to this purpofe is, that the power of working miracles may be equally annexed to falfehood and truth: and whereas it might be objected, that God will not fuffer miraculous power to be mifapplied, becaufe, were that the cafe, mankind would be greatly expofed to impofition, he anfwers, " that when a miracle is once wrought, it muft and will " be in the option of the operator to apply that power as he " pleafes, either well or ill, nor could God prevent it, otherwife " than by deftroying his being or his agency." But fuppofing, which is the prefent fuppofition, a real power of working miracles communicated from God, with a view to give atteftation to

---

* Chubb's pofthumous Works, vol. ii. p. 177—249.

the divine miffion of perfons fent to inftruct the world in important truths, it is abfurd to fuppofe, that he would continue that
power to them, if they applied it to the confirming of falfehood;
or that he would have given them that power for attefting truth,
if he forefaw they would ufe it in favour of falfehood; and in that
cafe he muft have forefeen it.  With regard to the power of
working miracles in the firft age of the Chriftian church, it was
not at the option of the perfons who had that power to ufe it
when or to what purpofe they pleafed.  They could only
work thofe miracles, when and upon what occafion it feemed fit
to the Holy Ghoft that they fhould do them; in which cafe
they had an extraordinary impulfe, which is ufually called *the
faith of miracles,* which was a kind of direction to them, when
to work thofe miracles, and whereby they knew and were perfuaded that God would enable them to do them.  The proper ufe
and defign of thofe miracles was, to confirm the teftimony given
by the apoftles to our Saviour and his refurrection, and the truth
of the doctrines they taught as received from him: nor can any
one proof be brought, though he takes it for granted, that any
falfe teachers in that age did, by virtue of any extraordinary gift
or powers of the Holy Ghoft communicated to them, work
miracles to confirm the falfe doctrines they preached.  On the
contrary, St. Paul appeals to the Galatians themfelves, as in a
matter of fact which could not be contefted, that miracles were
only wrought, and the extraordinary gifts of the fpirit communicated, in atteftation to that true doctrine of the gofpel which he
had preached, and not to that *other gofpel,* as he calleth it, which
the falfe teachers would have impofed upon them, Gal. iii. 2. 5.
But I have elfewhere confidered this matter at large, and fhall
not here repeat what was there offered*.

But what our author chiefly bends himfelf to prove is, that the
accounts given us of the miracles recorded in the New Teftament
are falfe or uncertain, and not at all to be depended on.  To this
purpofe he mentions feveral of our Saviour's miracles, and repeats the fame objections againft them that had been urged by
Mr. Woolfton before, and to which folid anfwers had been re-

---

* See Divine Authority of the Old and New Teftament afferted, vol. i.
p. 380—387.

turned. Every thing in the evangelical accounts that appears to him strange or extraordinary, he rejects at once. I cannot here enter into a distinct consideration of the several particulars he allegeth. I shall only mention one, on which he seems to lay a greater stress than any of the rest, and which he insists upon more than once, as alone sufficient to destroy the credit of the evangelical historians. It relates to the account given of our Saviour's temptations in the wilderness. It will be readily owned, that the fact referred to is of a very extraordinary nature. But a thing may be very strange and wonderful, and yet very true, and is to be received as such, if it comes to us vouched by a sufficient authority: and in this case the authority is sufficient; for I think it cannot reasonably be doubted, that the account came originally from our Lord himself, since no other could be supposed to know it, and that it was well known to the apostles and disciples to have come from him. It is distinctly related by two of the evangelists, St. Matthew and St. Luke, and referred to by a third, St. Mark. St. John, according to the method he pursues, of insisting chiefly upon things not mentioned by the rest, had no occasion to take notice of it. There is not the least reason to suppose, that the evangelists would have inserted such an account as this, if they had not been assured that the information came from Christ himself; and his authority is a sufficient warrant for believing it; nor is our author able to prove, that there is any thing here ascribed to Satan, which he might not be able, or might not be permitted to perform. In what manner he pretended to shew to our Saviour, *all the kingdoms of the world, and all the glory of them*, we are not told; nor is there any necessity here of taking the word *all* in the strictest sense. But in what way soever this was done, concerning which we cannot pretend certainly to judge, this writer doth not know enough of the case to pronounce it impossible. Supposing there are evil spirits, can any man take upon him positively to determine how far their power and ability may extend? And that there are both good and evil spirits superior to man, hath been the general belief of mankind in all nations and ages, and even of the best and wisest of men; nor can a shadow of reason be brought to prove the existence of such spirits to be either impossible or improbable, though our author, in his great wisdom, has all along rejected all

accounts

accounts where there is any mention made of angels or devils, with as much confidence, as if he could clearly demonstrate that there cannot possibly be any such thing.

He frequently speaks of the weakness and credulity of the sacred historians, and represents the accounts given in the gospels, and in the Acts of the Apostles, as mere fictions, *more like Jewish fables, or popish legends, than real facts* *. He expressly declares, " that some of the popish miracles, though generally re-" jected by Protestants as fraud and imposture, are better attested " than any of the miracles which were wrought, or supposed to be " wrought, in the first century: and that had the like strict scru-" tiny been made in former times that is at present, those ancient " miracles would have been rejected †." But every thinking person will easily see a mighty difference in the case between miracles wrought before persons highly prejudiced in their favour, and in proof of the reigning religion, where power and interest is on their side, and where there is not a full liberty allowed to make a strict inquiry in the view of enemies themselves, and where the public prejudices lie on the other side, and power, interest, and authority are engaged against them. There will always be ground of suspicion in the former case, not equally so in the latter. The miracles said to be wrought by the Romish church are done in countries where popery is the established religion, and have power and the prejudices of the people, and an evident worldly interest, on their side: and they are not performed openly in the view of Protestants and for their conviction, in places where there is a full liberty of examining into all the circumstances relating to them: whereas the miracles whereby Christianity was established were done openly, and in the view of enemies, able and willing to have detected the imposture, if there had been any; they were done to establish a scheme of religion, the most opposite that could be imagined to the prevailing prejudices both of Jews and Gentiles, and even to the prejudices that had possessed the minds of the very persons by whom these miracles were wrought; and when all the power and authority of the world, as well as the influence and artifices of the priesthood, and every worldly advantage, lay wholly on the other side: and yet vast numbers were

* Chubb, ubi supra. p. 192, 193.   † Ibid. p. 226, 227.

brought

brought over to receive a crucified Jesus as their Saviour and their Lord, in that very age, by the evidence of those miracles and extraordinary facts, concerning which they had the best opportunity of being informed, in opposition to all their worldly interests, and their most inveterate prejudices. In vain then it is to inveigh, as this writer does, against the historians, and to pretend, that " they were weak enough to give credit to any re-" lations they might pick up, and had courage enough to put upon " the world whatever might be put upon them†:" for the things related by them are of such a public nature, that if they had been false, it would have been the easiest thing in the world for their enemies, of whom there were many, to have detected them ; which would have crushed this religion in its infancy. Our author himself is sensible how difficult it would have been to impose facts of so extraordinary and so public a nature, as those recorded in the gospels, and in the Acts of the Apostles, in the very age in which the facts were said to be done ; and therefore, without so much as attempting to offer the least proof, takes upon him to affirm, that the accounts of these facts were not published till a long time after, when there was nobody alive that could contradict them ; and he declares as positively as if he could prove it to be so, that they were not made public till the second century, which he represents as an age of fiction and forgery. This is what he particularly affirms concerning the accounts given in the Acts of the Apostles; though it is evident from the book itself, that it was written in the apostolical age, and before the second imprisonment or the death of St. Paul. In the second century, Christianity had already made a wonderful progress through the nations, of which there are unquestionable proofs : and by a strange absurdity he supposes, that the extraordinary facts whereby the Christian religion was attested and confirmed, were not published till that time, *i. e.* that they were not heard of or made public, till long after the founding of the Christian church, though it was wholly upon the credit of those facts that the Christian church was founded. He pretends farther, that the accounts of these things " were kept as a treasure in the hands of believers, " not known to unbelievers, who therefore had it not in their

* Chubb's posthumous Works, p. 194.

" power

" power to confute them, or detect the fraud\* :" and yet certain it is, that the apostles went every-where preaching the religion of Jesus to an unbelieving world. All those to whom the first publishers of Christianity preached the gospel, and published the accounts of the important facts on which it was founded, were at first unbelievers: and it was upon the convincing assurance they had of the truth of these facts, that they were brought over to embrace it, and of unbelieving Jews or heathens became Christians, or believers in Jesus Christ. And whereas he adds, that " those facts were not published at or near the place of the " performance, but in Greece, Italy, &c. where the people " could not contradict them;" he seems not to have considered, that all these things were first published in Judea, where the first Christian churches were founded; and that great numbers of Jews were converted in the places where all the facts were done. It was not till after they had been published some years in Judea, that they were made known to the Gentiles. And in all those countries where the gospel was preached, there were vast numbers of Jews, who had a continual correspondence with those in Judea, and went frequently to Jerusalem to the public feasts, and could therefore easily procure information whether those facts were as they had been represented.

I shall not need to make any observations upon what Mr. Chubb hath offered against the accounts given by the evangelists of our Lord's resurrection: for, as he has only enlarged on some of the same objections which had been advanced by the author of *The Resurrection of Jesus considered*, it may be sufficient to refer to what has been said on this subject in the twelfth letter.

Having considered the attempts made by Mr. Chubb to invalidate the argument in behalf of divine revelation from prophecy and miracles, it will not be improper to take some notice of what hath been offered to take off the force of the argument, which he hath frequently urged, from the wonderful propagation of Christianity, in behalf of its divine original. He acknowledgeth, that " it is improbable that Christianity should take place, " and prevail in the world, and to the degree it did, or at least " that we are told it did, supposing the history of Christ's life

---

\* Chubb's posthumous Works, vol. ii. p. 203, 204, 205.

" and

" and miniftry to be a fiction *:" but then, as if he had granted
too much, he obferves, that " the prefent run of Methodifm,
" without any miraculous power attending it, or any external
" evidence to back it, takes off from the weight and force of the
" argument †." He often returns to this, and in feveral parts
of his book feems willing to run a parallel between the progrefs
of Chriftianity and that of Methodifm. But this only fhews
the ftrong prejudices of thofe who glory in the character of free-
thinkers, and how forward they are to catch at the flighteft pretences for fetting afide the evidences brought in favour of Chriftianity: for in reality there can be no reafonable parallel drawn
between the one and the other. There is no great wonder in it,
that profeffed Chriftians, pretending to a high degree of purity
and piety, and to teach true fcriptural Chriftianity, fhould make
fome progrefs (not in pagan and mahometan, or even in popifh
countries; for I do not find our Methodifts take upon them to
make many converfions there, but) in a country where fcriptural
Chriftianity is profeffed, and a full toleration allowed. There
is nothing in this but what may be eafily accounted for, without
fuppofing any thing fupernatural in the cafe. They do not pretend to new extraordinary revelations, nor appeal to any miraculous facts, as the French prophets did; in which cafe the
failure of thofe facts might eafily fubject them to a detection:
but they build upon the religion already received among us, and
only pretend to explain and enforce the doctrines there taught.
But the cafe was entirely different with regard to the apoftles
and firft publifhers of Chriftianity. The religion they preached,
and efpecially the great fundamental article of it, the receiving
a crucified Jefus for their Saviour and Lord, was contrary to the
moft rooted prejudices both of Jews and Gentiles: it tended entirely to fubvert the whole fyftem of the pagan fuperftition and
idolatry, and alfo the pleafing hopes the Jews had entertained
concerning a temporal Meffiah, who fhould raife their nation to
the height of fecular dominion and grandeur: it was holy and
felf-denying in its nature and tendency, and was defigned not to
flatter, but to fubdue and mortify, the corrupt lufts and paffions

---

* Chubb's pofthumous Works, vol. ii. p. 40, 41.
† Ibid. marginal note.

of men: it appealed to facts of the moſt extraordinary and public nature, and which could not fail being detected, if they had been falſe: the firſt publiſhers of it were not only deſtitute of every worldly advantage, but had the moſt inſurmountable difficulties to encounter with: they were expoſed to the moſt grievous perſecutions, reproaches, and ſufferings, and had all the powers of the world engaged againſt them; that therefore they ſhould be able in ſuch circumſtances to bring over vaſt numbers both of Jews and Gentiles to the faith of the crucified Jeſus, and that the religion they taught ſhould in ſpite of all oppoſition prevail, and at length overturn the whole eſtabliſhed ſuperſtition, which had every worldly advantage to ſupport it; this cannot be reaſonably accounted for, without ſuppoſing the interpoſition of a divine power, and the truth of the extraordinary facts on which it was founded.

Mr. Chubb ſeems to lay a particular ſtreſs *on the great change which,* he pretends, *took place in Chriſtianity, whilſt in its moſt primitive ſtate.* He affirms, that " the apoſtles ſet out upon two " principles, which may be conſidered as the foundation or cor- " ner ſtone of the Chriſtian building. 1. That Chriſtianity is a " ſupplement to Judaiſm, and therefore was to be grafted upon " it; and that the law of Moſes was not to be aboliſhed, but ſtili " continued. 2. That the Goſpel was a favour to be vouch- " ſafed to the Jews only, and that to them only it was to be " preached." And he pretends, that " the apoſtles were una- " voidably led into theſe principles by their maſter himſelf:" but that " in a little time they quite changed the original ſcheme or " plan of Chriſtianity, and dug up and deſtroyed the foundations " they themſelves had laid:" and then he aſks, " How do we know " in what inſtances they may be depended upon? and if they " acted wrong in this, how does it appear that they ever act " right\*?" This he returns to on ſeveral occaſions. But this whole matter is entirely miſrepreſented: it is plain from ſeveral hints given by our Lord himſelf during his perſonal miniſtry, that it was really his intention, and the deſign upon which he was ſent, to erect a new and more perfect diſpenſation than the Moſaical was, though it was not as yet a proper ſeaſon to make

* Chubb's poſthumous Works, vol. ii. p. 84, & ſeq.

a public

a public declaration of it: That his gofpel was to be preached not to the Jews only, but alfo to the Gentiles; and that the latter were to be taken into his church, and to be made partakers of his benefits, and of the great falvation he came to procure. Any one will be convinced of this, who impartially confiders the following paffages, Matth. viii. 10, 11, 12. xv. 10, 11. xxi. 43. John iv. 21, 23. x. 16. The utmoft that our author's pretence can be made to amount to, is really no more than this: that the apoftles, for fome time after our Lord's afcenfion, were not entirely freed from their Jewifh prejudices. And fuppofing, which was really the cafe, that the Jewifh difpenfation was originally from God, and was defigned to give way to the more perfect difpenfation of the gofpel, for which it was preparatory, there was a great propriety in it that the change fhould not be brought about all at once, which might have been too great a fhock even to honeft and well-difpofed minds. The gradual method of unfolding the Chriftian fcheme, and difpelling the apoftles' prejudices, inftead of being a juft objection, fhews that the whole was conducted with a divine wifdom and goodnefs: and their having continued for fome time under thefe prejudices, giveth a mighty force to their teftimony, and furnifheth a manifeft proof that the Chriftian difpenfation was not of their own invention, nor was owing to a fudden pang of enthufiafm; fince it was with fuch difficulty that they themfelves were brought to difcern and embrace it, confidered in its proper harmony. And it was only owing to the ftrength of the overpowering light and evidence, that all their prejudices were at length overcome and difpelled.

Befides the two principles mentioned above, Mr. Chubb has thought fit to take notice of a third, which he alfo pretends was a fundamental principle of Chriftianity, as laid down by the apoftles, *viz.* " That the difciples of Chrift were to have one " common ftock or property, of which the clergy were confti- " tuted the truftees and directors:" and he thinks, that " from " this it appears, how groundlefs that pretence muft be, that the " apoftles and minifters of Jefus Chrift could have no worldly " advantage in view, when they went forth to preach the gofpel: " whereas nothing can be more evident, than that they had a fair " profpect of, and a very plaufible pretence for, gathering great " riches into their hands, as keepers and managers of the church's " property or treafure." This he is fo fond of, that he infifteth

upon it for feveral pages together\*. And the author of the *Refurrection of Jefus confidered* had hinted at the fame thing before
him, to fhew, that the apoftles were interefted witneffes, and that
therefore their teftimony to Chrift's refurrection is not to be depended on†. But all this is built on a falfe foundation ; for there
was no divine or apoftolical conftitution obliging Chriftians to
put their whole worldly fubftance into the common flock, and to
commit it to the apoftles as the directors. It appeareth plainly
from St. Peter's words to Ananias, that it was a matter which
depended entirely on the free choice of the Chriftian converts,
and was the effect of their voluntary zeal and charity; and it
was an illuftrious proof of the ftrong conviction and perfuafion
they had of the truth of the gofpel, and of thofe great and extraordinary facts by which Chriftianity was fupported. This was
the more remarkable, as it was at Jerufalem that this was done,
foon after our Lord's refurrection and afcenfion, and the extraordinary effufion of the Holy Ghoft on the day of Pentecoft, and
where they had the beft opportunity of knowing the evidences
of thofe facts. But whatever was done this way, in the extraordinary circumftances in which the firft Chriftians were placed,
it is manifeft from fome paffages in the New Teftament, and particularly from St. Paul's directions to the Corinthians, that this
was not defigned to be generally obligatory upon all Chriftians.
See 1 Cor. xvi. 1, 2. 2 Cor. viii. 9. And indeed it feems to
have been peculiar to thofe at Jerufalem; for which undoubtedly there were particular reafons: and even there, fo far were
the apoftles from claiming to themfelves the direction of the public flock, that they exprefsly refufed to have any thing to do with
the management of it, that they might apply themfelves to their
proper work, the miniftry of the word: and it was given into
the hands of perfons of unexceptionable characters, chofen by
the Chriftian fociety for that purpofe, that they might impartially
diftribute out of the common flock to thofe that needed it, Acts
vi. 1, 2, 3. If the apoftles had been actuated by worldly views,
they would certainly have chofen a fcheme of religion, more
cunningly accommodated to the prevailing humours and prejudices of mankind; for what profpect could they have of per-
fuading people to give up their treafures and worldly fubftance

\* Chubb's pofthumous Works, p. 102—110.
† Refurrection of Jefus confidered, p. 68.

                                                                into

into their hands, by preaching up to the Jews a perfon that had
been condemned and crucified by the chief priefts and rulers of
their own nation for their Meffiah, and preaching up to the Gentiles a crucified Jew for their Lord and Saviour?   Our author
himfelf is fenfible of this, and therefore at the fame time that he
talks of the fair worldly profpeƈt they had, he owns that thefe
profpeƈts muft have depended upon their expeƈting fuccefs in
their miniftry, and upon their being perfuaded that they had God
and his promifes on their fide, and that Chrift would be with
them, as he had foretold, to the *end of the world* \*: fo that, according to his own way of ftating the cafe, and indeed according to the reafon of the thing, their profpeƈt of fuccefs was
founded in the firm belief they had of the truth and divinity of
Chrift's miffion, and of his refurreƈtion and exaltation to glory.
So inconfiftent is this writer's hypothefis, that, in order to make
good his charge of worldly interefted views againft the apoftles,
he is forced to go upon a fuppofition of the truth of the illuftrious
atteftations that were given to the Chriftian religion, and which
he elfewhere endeavours to invalidate.   And yet, fuppofing the
apoftles to have believed what their Lord had told them, they
could have no worldly advantage to expeƈt; fince he had affured
them, that they fhould be expofed to all manner of reproaches,
perfecutions, and fufferings, both from Jews and Gentiles, and
fhould be *hated of all men for* his *name's fake.*   And this was
aƈtually the cafe: what the apoftles got by preaching up the religion of Jefus is in a very affeƈting manner reprefented by St.
Paul, who was one of them: from whence it is manifeft, that
never were there any perfons expofed to a greater variety of
hardfhips and fufferings, 1 Cor. iv. 9. 11, 12, 13. xv. 19. 32.
2 Cor. iv. 8, 9, 10, 11. xi. 23—28.

It is particularly evident, that this laft mentioned great apoftle
could have no worldly advantage in view in embracing Chriftianity.   His interefts, reputation, and prejudices, lay wholly the
other way, and tended ftrongly to bias him againft it.   Nothing
but conviƈtion, and the power of evidence, could overcome his
obftinacy; after which he became the moft eminently inftrumental to propagate the Chriftian religion in the world, of which he

\* Chubb's pofthumous Works, vol. ii. p. 108, 109.

had

had been a moſt zealous perſecutor before. And this ſeems to be the cauſe of that peculiar rancour and prejudice which this writer every-where diſcovers againſt him. The beſt judges have admired the ſtrength and cloſeneſs of St. Paul's reaſoning; this particularly was the judgment of one of the beſt reaſoners of the age, Mr. Locke, who ſtudied his writings with great application. But our author has thought fit to repreſent him as a *looſe unguarded writer*, who did *not attend to his own argument, or to the ſubject.* He frequently charges him with drawing wrong concluſions from his premiſes; and that his epiſtles were crude, indigeſted performances, which were *probably ſent as they were firſt wrote, without being reviſed by him;* and that this ſometimes *involved him in confuſion.* He endeavours to give the moſt abſurd and ridiculous turn poſſible to ſeveral paſſages in his writings: ſome inſtances of which were taken notice of above, to which many others might be added. Not content with this, he repreſents this excellent perſon, who was no leſs remarkable for his humility than for his many other virtues, as a vain-glorious boaſter, and treats the account which, with a remarkable modeſty, and as it were by conſtraint, he gives of his labours and ſufferings, as *a bravado, and paſt all belief\**. He accuſes him and St. James as guilty of the *moſt groſs and notorious diſſimulation and hypocriſy,* and repreſents him as the great author of *pious frauds* in religion: and that he acted upon this principle, " that truth in ſome caſes may and ought to be diſpenſed with;" and that therefore he and the other apoſtles were capable of giving a *falſe teſtimony to ſerve the Chriſtian cauſe†.* But this certainly was not St. Paul's principle; he has condemned in the ſtrongeſt terms thoſe who maintained, that it is lawful to lie for the glory of God, and *to do evil that good may come of it;* which is the great principle upon which pious frauds are built, Rom. iii. 5, 6. All that Mr. Chubb has advanced, to prove the heavy charge he has brought againſt this great apoſtle, is reducible to two facts. The one is, his ſaying before the council, that *of the hope and reſurrection of the dead he was called in queſtion,* Acts xxiii. 6.; upon which our author obſerves, that in this " he acted a deceitful " part, and coined a lie to ſave himſelf, ſince he was not called

---

\* Chubb's poſthumous Works, vol. ii. p. 364, 365.

† Ibid. p. 92, &c. 235, &c.

" in

" in queſtion about the reſurrection, nor was this any part of
" the charge againſt him\*." But that the preaching through
Jeſus Chriſt the reſurrection of the dead, was one reaſon of the
perſecution which was raiſed againſt Chriſt's diſciples; and that
this was what particularly excited the rage of the Sadducees againſt
them, of which party the high prieſt, or at leaſt many of thoſe
about him, and who were men of power and intereſt, appear to
have been, is plain from the account given in the Acts of the Apoſtles, chap. iv. 1, 2, 3, v. 17. And it was very allowable for the
apoſtle to take advantage of this, for creating a diviſion among
his adverſaries, who were not themſelves agreed what charge to
bring againſt him. This is a proof of his prudence and addreſs,
and that he did not run upon his ſufferings with a blind enthuſiaſtic
heat; but it is no proof of his diſhoneſty. The other inſtance
upon which the charge of hypocriſy and lying againſt St. Paul
is founded, is taken from what he did at Jeruſalem, by St.
James's advice, in purifying *himſelf in the temple*, Acts xxi. 20—
26†. But if this had been fairly repreſented, it would have appeared, that there was nothing in his conduct on this occaſion inconſiſtent with honeſty and integrity. What the Jewiſh Chriſtians
had been informed of concerning St. Paul was, that he had *taught*
*the Jews which were among the Gentiles to forſake Moſes, ſaying*
*that they ought not to circumciſe their children, neither to walk*
*after the cuſtoms*, ver. 21. They repreſented him as having
taught, that it was abſolutely unlawful for the Jews to circumciſe their children, or to obſerve the Jewiſh rites. This accu-
ſation was falſe: St. Paul had not taught this; he only had argued againſt the neceſſity of obſerving that law, and had urged
Jews and Gentiles to a mutual forbearance with one another in
this matter. And what he did purſuant to the advice of St.
James, ſhewed that he did not look upon it to be then unlawful
to obſerve the Jewiſh rites; and that he judged it both lawful
and expedient in ſome caſes to obſerve them, for avoiding ſcan-
dal: and upon this principle he proceeded in circumciſing Timothy. This whole matter had been ſet in a clear light, and
the wiſdom and conſiſtency of the conduct of St. Paul and the
other apoſtles fully juſtified, in the anſwers that were made to

---

\* Chubb's poſthumous Works, vol. i. p. 330, 331. vol. ii. p. 258.
† Ibid. vol. i. p. 92, 93, 98.

the

the *Moral Philofopher.* But Mr. Chubb repeats the charge, without troubling himfelf to take off the force of what had been offered for clearing it.

After what hath been obferved, it will be no furprize to find, that this writer reprefents the being converted to Chriftianity as of no importance at all, and that he frequently lets us know, that he looks upon all religions to be alike, with regard to the favour of God. " The turning from Mahometanifm to Chrif- tianity," fays he, " or from Chriftianity to Mahometanifm, is " only a laying afide one external form of religion, and making " ufe of another, which is of no more real benefit, than a man's " changing the colour of his cloaths, by putting off a red coat, " and putting on a blue one in its ftead\*." He elfewhere re- prefents it as an indifferent matter, " whether a man adopts Ju- " daifm, or Paganifm, or Mahometanifm, or Chriftianity;" and what is more extraordinary, he would put this upon us, as St. Peter's fentiment as well as his own; and endeavours, after his manner, to prove it from that noted paffage, Acts x. 34, 35. *Of a truth I perceive that God is no refpecter of perfons; but in every nation, he that feareth him, and worketh righteoufnefs, is accepted with him.* He pretends, that St. Peter here teacheth, " that faith in any religious leader, or his miniftry, is altogether " fupernumerary, and that he hath excluded both faith and infi- " delity out of the cafe†:" as if the apoftle there defigned to tell Cornelius, that it was of no manner of importance whether he believed in Jefus Chrift or not; which is to make him fpeak in direct contradiction to the very defign of his being fent to Cornelius, and of all his fubfequent difcourfe to him. St. Peter fignifieth indeed, in the words cited by this author, that whofo- ever in any nation, like Cornelius, truly feared and worfhipped God, and practifed righteoufnefs, fhould be accepted of him, though not belonging to the Jewifh nation, or initiated into the Mofaic polity: but he certainly never intended to fignify, that the embracing Chriftianity was a matter of mere indifference. Cornelius's piety and good difpofitions would have rendered him acceptable to God, though he had not heard of Chrift; but when he had an opportunity of being informed, that very piety and fear of God led him to receive thofe fignifications of the divine

---

\* Chubb's pofthumous Works, vol. ii. p. 33, 34. † Ibid. vol. i. p. 295—302.

will,

will, and to believe in Jesus Christ, whom he had sent   The
great importance and advantage of faith in Christ, in such a case,
is evidently supposed in St. Peter's whole discourse, who was
extraordinarily sent on purpose to instruct him in it.   This writer thinks proper to find fault with the author of the Acts of the
Apostles, for laying so great a stress on the conversion of Jews
or heathens to Christianity, which, in his opinion, is " of little
" consequence as to the favour of God, or their future safety,
" because, if they were virtuous and good men, they were secure
" without such conversion, and if they were bad vicious men,
" they were not secured by it*."   But if they were good men
before, and were thereby put in the way of greater improvements in goodness, more fully instructed in religion, raised to
more glorious hopes, and furnished with more excellent helps,
and more powerful animating encouragements to all virtue and
universal righteousness ; or if they were bad men, involved in
gross ignorance and idolatry, superstition and vice, which was
the general character of the heathens when the gospel appeared,
and by turning to Christianity were brought to the knowledge
and pure adoration of the only true God, and engaged to forsake
their evil ways, and to live soberly, righteously, and godly in this
present world; and no other were accounted true Christian converts; this, by the author's own acknowledgment, must have
been a signal advantage.   He himself had said a little before, " if
" the revelation referred to could furnish me with useful know-
" ledge, or with a better rule of life, or with more powerful ex-
" citements to the practice of virtue and true religion, than at
" present I am in possession of, and thereby I should be made
" a wiser and a better man, then I acknowledge, that such con-
" viction would be beneficial to me in proportion to such im-
" provement †."   This is evidently the case of the Christian revelation, wherever it is sincerely believed and embraced, and
men give themselves up to its divine conduct ; and therefore
those to whom this revelation is offered, and who yet despise and
reject it, are justly chargeable with great guilt: for it cannot be
a slight guilt to reject the valuable means and helps which God
hath, in his infinite wisdom and goodness, provided, for promoting our spiritual improvement, and engaging and enabling us to

* Chubb's posthumous Works, vol. ii. p. 33.      † Ibid. p. 32.

work

work out our own salvation: nor can any thing be more unreafonable than to pretend, as the enemies of revelation have often
done, that becaufe virtue and righteoufnefs are what God ap-
proves, therefore faith is unneceffary, and of no confequence at
all.  The very contrary follows from it: for, if moral improvement and true holinefs be of fuch vaft importance, then certainly
the beft and propereft means for attaining to it are very needful, and to be highly valued; and fuch are the means and helps
which the religion of Jefus affordeth, as laid down in the Holy
Scriptures: and to reject thofe means and affiftances, under pretence of obtaining the end without them, is a moft abfurd and
criminal conduct, juftly difpleafing in the fight of God, and a
moft unworthy return to his infinite goodnefs.

I fhall conclude my remarks on Mr. Chubb's *Pofthumous
Works*, with taking notice of a remarkable paffage at the end of
the eighth fection of his *Farewell to his Readers*.  After having
done all he could to expofe the Scriptures, and fhew that it is
not fafe to appeal to them, he draws this conclufion from the
whole: that " this fhews the great propriety of our returning
" back to that prior rule of action, which is the ground and foun-
" dation of moral truth, and confequently of moral certainty;
" *viz.* that eternal and invariable rule of right and wrong, as to
" an infallible guide, and as the folid ground of our peace and
" fafety, which rule we are too eafily diverted from *."  He
feems to fpeak here, as if Chriftians, and thofe that were for ad-
hering to Scripture as their rule, had no regard to the rule of
right and wrong, or to the nature and reafon of things, which is
a grofs mifreprefentation; and as if the deifts were under the conduct of an infallible guide.  Particularly it is to be fuppofed, that
he would have it to be underftood that he himfelf hath taken care
to follow the infallible guide he recommends: but if we are to
judge by the effect it has had upon himfelf, we have no great
encouragement to entertain a very favourable opinion of the advantage we fhall obtain by forfaking the Scripture, under pretence
of following fuch a guide.  For what is it, that his infallible
guide has directed him to?  It has inclined him to deny a particular providence, or that God now interpofeth in ordering or governing the affairs of men, and the events relating to them,

---

* Chubb's pofthumous Works, vol. ii. p. 249.

whether with regard to nations or particular perfons, and confequently has directed him not to make a dependence on providence, a truft in God, or refignation to his will, any part of his
religion: it hath taught him not to expect any gracious affiftances
from God, or to apply to him for them: it leaveth him at a lofs
whether it be proper to pray to God at all, and inclineth him to
think that it is the fafeft way to let it alone: nor doth this guide
inform him, whether mens fouls are material or immaterial, or
whether they fhall fubfift after death, or fhall die and perifh with
the body, or whether there fhall be a future ftate in which God
will call men to an account for their actions: or, if there fhall be
a future judgment, his guide leadeth him to apprehend that it
fhall extend but to a fmall part of the human race, and but to a few
of the actions they perform; that they fhall not be called to an account for the blafphemies they may have uttered againft God, or
for any neglect of duties that more immediately relate to the Deity,
or for private injuries they do to one another, or for any actions
at all but thofe which concern the public; and how far thefe are
to extend, he hath not thought fit to inform us. I cannot fee
therefore but that it is much better to follow the light the Scripture affordeth us, which giveth us clear inftructions in thefe and
other things of great importance, concerning which our author's
infallible guide, according to his account of the matter, hath
given him no directions at all, or hath given him wrong ones.

I have now finifhed my obfervations on Mr. Chubb's *Pofthumous Works*, which I have perhaps enlarged upon more than
they really deferve. But I have chofen to do it, both becaufe
they feem to be of a dangerous tendency, and well fitted to do
mifchief, and have by fome perfons been very much extolled,
and becaufe there has been no anfwer, that I know of, given to
thofe books. I do not love to make reflections that feem to bear
hard upon any man's integrity: but I think it cannot be denied,
that, notwithftanding his great pretences to plainnefs and candour,
and an impartial love of truth and liberty, there are very apparent
marks of great difingenuity in his writings. The nature of this
work would not admit of my entering into a more minute examination; but there are few things of confequence in his two
volumes which are not here taken notice of.

L E T.

# LETTER XV.

*Observations upon a Pamphlet, intitled,* Deism fairly Stated, and *fully Vindicated—The Author's pompous Account of Deism, and his Way of stating the Question between Christians and Deists, considered—Concerning the Differences among Christians about the Way of knowing the Scriptures to be the Word of God—The Charge he brings against the Christian Religion, as consisting only of unintelligible Doctrines and useless Institutions, and his Pretence, that the Moral Precepts do not belong to Christianity at all, but are the Property of Deists. shewn to be vain and groundless—The Corruptions of Christians no just Argument against true Christianity—A brief Account of Lord Bolingbroke's Attempt against the Scriptures in his Letters on the Study and Use of History.*

SIR,

HAVING confidered pretty largely Mr. Chubb's *Posthumous Works,* I shall now send you some observations upon a pamphlet, which, though originally written by another hand, is said to have been revised by Mr. Chubb, and to have undergone confiderable alterations and amendments: it is intitled *Deism fairly Stated, and fully Vindicated,* and was published in 1746. And as it hath been much boasted of, I shall distinctly confider both the account the author of it gives of deism, and the attempt he hath made to expose the Christian revelation.

In his account of deism he treads in the steps of Dr. Tindal, and it might be sufficient to refer to the remarks that have been made upon that writer's scheme, of which some account was given in the tenth Letter. But let us examine our author's pretensions more distinctly.

He tells us, that " deism is no other than the religion effential " to man, the true original religion of nature and reafon\*." And because Christian divines have afferted, that the gofpel contains the true religion of reafon and nature, he reprefents them, and

\* Deifm fairly Stated, &c. p. 5.

particularly

particularly the prefent bifhop of London, and Mr. (now Dr.)
Samuel Chandler, as acknowledging, that " deifm is the alone ex-
" cellence and true glory of Chriftianity," and pretends that
what he has cited from them proves, that " deifm is all in the
" Chriftian inftitution that can poffibly approve itfelf to the true
" genuine reafon of man *." And accordingly he declares, that
" every thing that is enjoined in the gofpel to be believed as a
" rational doctrine, or practifed as a natural duty, relating to
" God, our neighbours, and ourfelves, is an eftablifhed part of
" deifm †." And through his whole book he fuppofes deifm to
comprehend every doctrine and precept which is founded in reafon and nature, or, as he fometimes expreffeth it, in *truth* and
*reafon*, *i. e.* it comprehendeth every doctrine and precept that is
true and juft and reafonable.

That we may judge of the fairnefs of this writer in ftating the
point, it is proper to obferve, that the thing he would be thought
to vindicate is the religion of thofe that call themfelves deifts,
and who reject revelation, and oppofe Chriftianity. This is the
only deifm in queftion, and which it concerneth him to ftate and
vindicate. But he has thought fit all along to reprefent deifm
and natural religion as terms of the fame fignification; whereas
deifm, as we are now confidering it, is to be underftood, not precifely of natural religion, as comprehending thofe truths which
have a real foundation in reafon and nature, and which is fo far
from being oppofite to Chriftianity, that it is one great defign of
the gofpel to clear and enforce it; but of that religion which every
man is to find out for himfelf by the mere force of natural reafon, independent of all revelation, and exclufive of it. It is
concerning this that the inquiry properly proceeds. Dr. Tindal
was fenfible of it; and therefore is for fending every man to the
oracle in his own breaft as the only guide to duty and happinefs,
which alone he is to confult, without having any regard to revelation: and accordingly he frequently reprefents the religion
of nature as fo clearly known to all men, even to *thofe that cannot read in their mother tongue*, as to render any farther revelation perfectly needlefs and ufelefs. But if the queftion be concerning natural religion in this fenfe, it is far from deferving all

* Deifm fairly Stated, &c. p. 6.          † Ibid. p. 7.

the

the fine encomiums which this writer, after Dr. Tindal, fo liberally beftows upon: he reprefents it as fo perfect, that nothing can be
added to it; and therefore will not allow, that Chriftianity can be
faid to be " grounded on natural religion, or to be an improve-
" ment of it:" for he declares, that he " cannot poffibly con-
" ceive how an entire and perfect ftructure (which is the cafe of
" natural religion) can be only a foundation of a perfect ftructure,
" or how a perfect religion can be improved*." Here he fecurely affumes the very thing in queftion, *viz.* that the religion which every man knoweth of himfelf by his own unaffifted
reafon is fo perfect, as to be incapable of receiving any addition
or improvement, even from divine revelation: which is in other
words to fay, that every man by his own reafon, exclufively of
all revelation, takes in the whole of religious truth and duty,
which is founded in the nature of things, and knows as much of
it already as God can teach him: and that a divine revelation can
give him no farther light or ftronger affurance, relating to any
thing that it is proper for him to believe or practife in religion,
than what his bare reafon informs him of without it.

Among the encomiums which our author beftows upon deifm,
one is, that it is " no other than the religion effential to man †;"
a phrafe that he and others of the deiftical writers feem fond of.
But will thefe fagacious gentlemen undertake to inform the world
what kind or degree of religion is effential to the human nature?
Or, if they could oblige the world with that difcovery, is nothing
valuable in religion but what is effential to man? If revelation
difcovereth to us fome things of importance which we could not
attain to the knowledge of by bare unaffifted reafon; or giveth
us farther affurances concerning fome things, as to which we
were doubtful before, and fetteth them in a clearer light; or
exhibiteth a more complete fyftem of duty; or furnifheth more
powerful motives to animate us to the practice of it; muft all
thefe difcoveries be rejected, under pretence that what we thus
receive by revelation is not effential to man? Might not all improvements of every kind be difcarded for the fame reafon? And
fo man muft be left in his pure effentials. And then what a fine
figure would the human nature make!

* Deifm fairly Stated, &c. p. 13.        † Ibid. p. 513.

Befides

. Besides this general account of deism, our author takes upon him to exhibit some fundamental *credenda* of a deist; and he might easily find a plausible scheme of natural religion formed ready to his hand by Christian writers, and then put it upon the world for pure genuine deism. Among these fundamental articles of the religion of a deist, he reckons the belief of a future state of rewards and punishments. But is this a point in which the deists are agreed? Lord Bolingbroke every-where sets up for a deist of the first rank, and glories in that character, and yet he does all he can to weaken or subvert that which is here put upon us as a fundamental article of the deistical creed: and Mr. Chubb, who no doubt would pass with our author for a true deist, though sometimes, like this writer, he makes a great shew of believing not only the truth but the importance of that doctrine, yet in several passages of his *Farewell to his Readers*, and especially in his fourth and fifth sections, where he treats professedly of this subject, setteth himself to shew that it is altogether uncertain, and incapable of being proved, and that the probability lies against it\*. Thus it is that these gentlemen are sometimes willing to make a fair appearance with their principles, till persons are drawn in, and fully initiated in the mysteries of deism.

This author gives us twelve propositions with great pomp, most of which have nothing to do with the debate between Christians and deists, and others of them are very ambiguous†. In his seventh proposition he layeth it down as a principle, that " to govern our conduct by our reason is our duty, and all that " God requireth of us." If the meaning be, that God requireth nothing from us but what we know by our bare unassisted reason to be our duty, and that if any thing farther be revealed to be our duty, we are not obliged to perform it, because we did not know it to be so by our own natural reason independently of that revelation, it is false and absurd: for when God requireth us to be governed by our reason, it must be supposed to be his intention, that we should take in all proper helps and assistances. And if he is pleased in his great goodness to give us additional discoveries of his will and our duty for enlightening and assisting our reason, then certainly we are obliged, and it is what reason itself and

---

\* See before, p. 220, & seq.     † Deism fairly Stated, &c. p. 37—40.

the religion of nature requireth of us, to pay a regard to those discoveries; so as to believe the truths which he has been pleased to reveal, and to practise those duties which he has seen fit to enjoin: and not to do so would be highly criminal.

The four last of his twelve propositions are designed to shew, that reason and nature sufficiently instruct us without revelation, as to the methods of reconciliation with the Deity, when we have offended him by our sins, and give us a certain assurance that God will reinstate us in his favour upon our repentance and reformation. I have elsewhere considered this subject at large in answer to Tindal, who had particularly insisted upon it *. At present I shall only observe, that though nature and reason seem to direct us to repentance and reformation in case of our being conscious of having offended God and transgressed his holy laws, yet reason and nature could not give us certain information, how far repentance shall be available to avert the punishment we had incurred, or what shall be the extent of the divine forgiveness, or how far an obedience like ours, mixed with many failures and defects, and which falleth short in many instances of what the divine law requires, shall be rewarded. We do not know enough of God, of the reasons and ends of the divine government, and of what may be necessary for vindicating the authority of his laws, to be able to pronounce with certainty, by the mere light of our own unassisted reason, what measures his governing wisdom and righteousness may think fit to take with regard to guilty creatures that have sinned against him. Will any reasonable man pretend, that God himself cannot discover any thing to us, which it may be proper for us to know, relating to the methods of his dealings towards us, the terms of our acceptance with him, or the retributions of a future state, but what we ourselves knew as well before? Or, if he should condescend to make discoveries to us of this sort, and give us assurances relating to matters of such great importance, ought we not to be thankful for such discoveries? especially since it is certain in fact, that men in all ages and nations have been under great anxieties and uncertainties about the proper means of propitiating an offended Deity.

* The Answer to Christianity as old as the Creation, vol. i. c. 6.

Our

Our author mentions it to the praise of deifm, that " it is that
" religion of nature and reafon, which was believed and prac-
" tifed by Socrates, and thofe of old," whom he reprefents as
having been *ornaments* to human nature\*.  Thus he feems to
think it a greater honour to be a difciple of Socrates than of Jefus Chrift.  But why are we to be turned back to the religion
of Socrates, who have a light fo vaftly fuperior to that which
he enjoyed?  However he may be juftly commended for having
attained fo far, confidering the circumftances he was under
(though in many things he fell in with the eftablifhed fuperftition of his age and country), is this a reafon why we fhould be
fent to that philofopher to learn a right fcheme of religion, when
we have a far more excellent one in our hands, and recommended by a much higher authority?  He was himfelf fenfible of his
need of farther affiftances, and a divine inftructor; and fhall we
who have that ineftimable advantage, defpife the light given us
from heaven, and be defirous to return to that ftate of darknefs
and uncertainty of which he complained, and from which he
wanted to be delivered?

The remarks that have been made will help us to judge of
thofe paffages in which he pretendeth to give the true ftate of the
queftion between deifts and Chriftians.  " The fingle queftion,"
faith he, " between Chriftians and deifts is, whether the belief
" of rational doctrines, and the practice of natural duties, are all
" that are ftrictly neceffary with regard to the divine approba-
" tion, and confequently human happinefs†?"  And again, when
he profeffes to come to the point, he fays, " The grand founda-
" tion of the difference between the deifts and the religious of
" all other perfuafions is, whether any doctrine or precept that
" has not its foundation *apparently* in reafon or nature, can be
" of the effence of religion, and with propriety be faid to be a
" religious doctrine or precept‡."  Here he fuppofes, and it
runs through his whole book, that nothing can be properly faid
to belong to religion, but what plainly appeareth to the underftanding of every man, without any affiftance from divine revelation, to be founded in nature and reafon.  The queftion then,

---

\* Deifm fairly Stated, p. 5.     † Ibid. p. 7. See alfo p. 8, 9, 10.
‡ Ibid. p. 14.

though

though not clearly stated by this writer, is this: whether God can make any additional difcoveries in relation to doctrines to be believed, or duties to be practifed, concerning which we had no certain information by the bare light of unaffifted nature and reafon? And if God hath made fuch difcoveries, whether it would not in that cafe be neceffary, that thofe to whom thefe difcoveries are made fhould believe thofe doctrines, and practife thofe duties? Whether, becaufe our own natural reafon did not inform us of them without revelation, therefore when they are revealed to us, we may fafely and innocently reject them as ufelefs and unneceffary, and as not belonging to religion at all? Or, whether reafon and nature do not require it of us as an indifpenfable duty, to pay a juft fubmiffion and regard to the fignifications and difcoveries of the divine will concerning truth or duty, in whatever way they are made known to us? Thefe are queftions, which one fhould think would admit of an eafy decifion; fince nothing could be more abfurd, than to lay it down as a principle, that God can make no farther difcoveries of truth and duty to be believed and practifed by us, but what all men know of themfelves by their own unaffifted reafon; or that, if he fhould, we are not obliged to receive or regard thefe difcoveries.

It is very ufual with the deiftical writers, and this author among the reft, to put the queftion, whether reafon or revelation be the beft guide, as if there were an oppofition or inconfiftency between them: but the proper queftion is, whether reafon left merely to itfelf, and with the many frailties, corruptions, and defects to which it is now fubject, or reafon with the affiftance of divine revelation, be the beft guide to duty and happinefs? Revelation indeed would be of little ufe, if we were to take his account of it. He tells us, that by " pure revelation muft be meant, that " which is of fuch a nature as to be quite out of reafon's province " to form any judgment about it: That matters fupernatural are " incapable of an examination by natural reafon, or of being " approved as reafonable: And that furely no man can be ration-" ally convinced of what lies quite out of the reach of his rea-" foning faculties to form any judgment at all about \*." This

---

* De'fm fairly Stated, p. 2. 24.

he

he frequently repeats, and seems to value himself upon this way
of putting the case. But it is grossly misrepresented. None of
the friends of revelation understand by it, that about which we
are not capable of forming any judgment at all: on the contrary,
they generally agree that we must make use of our reason, both
in judging of the evidences of divine revelation, whereby it is
proved to be from God, and of the sense and meaning of its
doctrines and precepts. But our author thinks fit to play upon
the word *supernatural,* as if by it were meant that which is absolutely unintelligible and absurd: whereas a thing may be so far
supernatural, that we could not have discovered it merely by our
own reason without a divine revelation, and yet, when discovered
to us, we may be able to form a judgment concerning it, and
may see it to be worthy of God, and of an excellent tendency,
and as such our reason may approve it.

Having considered that part of the pamphlet in which the author pretends to give a fair state and vindication of deism as opposed to revelation, I shall now take some notice of what he hath
advanced with regard to the Christian revelation in particular.

He says, " the material question between rational Christians
" and deists depends upon the proof that is made by Christians,
" that the Scriptures are a divine revelation, and the very word
" of God: for if this point be proved, the controversy is at an
" end." But here he complains of the want of unanimity among
Christians, in a point of such importance. " The Roman Catho-
" lics say, We know the Scriptures to be the word of God only
" by the testimony of the church: and among protestants, some
" say, They are known to be the word of God by *themselves,* to
" those only whose eyes the spirit of God is pleased to open, to
" perceive the characters of divine truth impressed on them:
" others maintain, that they will manifestly appear to be the
" word of God by themselves, upon an honest investigation of
" mere natural reason, to any man who shall impartially exercise
" it about them\*." But if the matter be rightly considered,
there is not so great a difference among Christian writers about
the way of knowing the Scriptures to be the word of God, as is
pretended. Christians in general are agreed, that the extraordi-

---

\* Deism fairly Stated, p. 16—24.

nary facts recorded in the gofpel are true, and that thofe facts prove the divine miffion of our Lord Jefus Chrift, and the truth and divinity of that fcheme of religion which was publifhed to the world in his name.    They agree, that the Scriptures contain a faithful and authentic account of the doctrines and laws delivered by Chrift and his apoftles, and of the illuftrious atteftations whereby they were confirmed: That they were committed to writing by the apoftles themfelves, who were eye and ear witneffes of what they relate, or by their moft intimate companions, and were publifhed in the firft age of the Chriftian church, the age in which thofe doctrines and laws were delivered, and the facts were done: That thefe writings have remarkable internal characters of truth and divinity in the goodnefs and excellence of the doctrines, the purity of the precepts, the force and power of the motives, that unaffected fimplicity and impartial regard to truth which every-where appears, and in the admirable tendency of the whole to promote the glory of God, and the good of mankind, without any traces or views of worldly policy, ambition, avarice, or fenfuality.    And though fome talk of thefe characters as difcernible by the aid of the Holy Spirit, and others by the inveftigation of human reafon, yet neither do the former intend to exclude human reafon from having any concern in that inquiry, nor do the latter defign to exclude the affiftance of the Holy Spirit; fince it is generally acknowledged among Chriftians, and is highly agreeable to reafon itfelf, that it is proper to apply to God, *the author of light, and giver of all inward illumination*, as Lord Herbert calls him, to affift us in our inquiries, and, by purifying our fouls from vicious affections and corrupt prejudices, to prepare our minds for a due reception of religious and moral truth.    I add, that though fome have talked of corruptions in the facred writings, yet Chriftians are generally agreed, that the Scriptures are tranfmitted to us without any fuch general corruption as to make any alteration in the doctrines and facts, and that they are delivered down to us by a credible uninterrupted tradition, greater than can be produced for any other books in the world; by the teftimony not merely of the church in one age, but in every age, from the time in which they were written; and not merely by any one party of Chriftians, but by thofe of different fects and parties, by friends and enemies.    Any

one

one that confidereth the feveral things now mentioned, and which have been often urged by Chriftians of all denominations, by the beft of the Popifh as well as Proteftant writers, who have appeared in defence of Chriftianity, will fee that there is a more general agreement among them, in what concerneth the proofs of the divine original and authority of the facred writings, than our author feems willing to allow.

With regard to *prophecy* and *miracles*, which are infifted on by all Chriftian writers as proofs of the divinity of the Chriftian religion, he will not allow them to be any proofs of it at all: becaufe they do not prove, that " the collection of tracts com-
" monly called the Bible were written by the perfons refpectively
" whofe names they bear: that the Deity immediately dictated
" to each writer the fubject matter contained therein: and that
" thefe books have been faithfully tranfmitted down to us with-
" out any corruption, alteration, addition, or diminution*." Mr. Chubb has the fame thought, and feems very fond of it, for he has it over and over again in his *Farewell to his Readers*. But if prophecies and miracles exhibited fufficient credentials to the divine miffion of our Lord Jefus Chrift and of his apoftles, who publifhed to the world the doctrines and laws of the Chriftian religion; and if the Scriptures contain a juft and faithful ac-count of thofe prophecies and miracles, and of the doctrines and laws fo attefted and confirmed, and delivered by thofe divinely-authorifed teachers; doth not this lay a juft foundation for re-ceiving thofe doctrines and laws as of divine authority? As to their being written by the perfons whofe names they bear, and their being fafely tranfmitted to us, without any material cor-ruption or alteration, this needeth no miracles to prove it: it muft be proved by other mediums, fuch as by the acknowledg-ment of all mankind are fufficient to prove things of that kind. If thefe writings can be traced up, as they certainly may, from our own times, by unqueftionable evidence, to the very age in which they were written; and if they have been all along ac-knowledged to have been written by thofe to whom they are afcribed, and even the enemies who lived neareft thofe times never contefted it; and if it can be demonftrated, that, as the

* Deifm fairly Stated, p. 22. 26.

cafe

cafe was circumſtanced, a general corruption of thoſe writings in the doctrines and facts, if any had attempted it, would have been an impoſſible thing; this ought to ſatisfy an impartial inquirer: and this is capable of as clear a proof as the nature of the thing can admit, and which, as hath been already hinted, is ſuperior to what can be produced for any other book in the world. And the man that would doubt of ſuch evidence in any other caſe, would be looked upon as ridiculouſly ſcrupulous, and be thought to carry his ſcepticiſm to an unreaſonable height.

As to the ſubject matter of the Chriſtian revelation, this writer is for ſtripping it of every doctrine that is founded in nature and reaſon; though there are ſeveral important doctrines of that kind, *e. g.* thoſe relating to the attributes and providence of God, and a ſtate of future retributions, which Chriſtianity was manifeſtly intended to confirm and eſtabliſh, and ſet in a clearer light. If we are to take his account of it, it conſiſteth wholly of *ſpeculative, metaphyſical, unintelligible* doctrines, which lie out of the reach of reaſon to determine whether they be true or falſe, or to paſs any judgment at all about them; and of poſitive inſtitutions, which he pretends by the confeſſion of Chriſtian divines are no *conſtituent parts of religion* \*. By ſaying they are no conſtituent parts of religion, he evidently intends, that they have nothing to do with religion, and are of no uſe or ſignificancy at all: whereas the divines he refers to agree, that the poſitive inſtitutions of Chriſtianity do belong to religion as valuable inſtrumental duties, which have a tendency to ſubſerve and promote the great ends of all religion, and are, when rightly improved, of ſignal uſe and benefit.

After having obſerved, that many parts of Scripture are *myſterious* and *unintelligible,* he ſaith, that to ſuppoſe that God *gives forth unintelligible inſtructions and propoſitions to his creatures, is to prove him in fact a mere trifler* †. And he urges, that " as " certain as a being of perfect rectitude has given a revelation, " ſo certain it is, that not any thing in that revelation can be found " on a ſtrict inquiry unrevealed, *i. e.* not underſtood by men of " learning, penetration, diligence, and induſtry \*." The deſign

---

\* Deiſm fairly Stated, p. 2. 6. 15. 24. 58.    † Ibid. p. 26. 34.    ‡ Ibid. p. 83.

of

of this is to infinuate, that if there be any one thing in the bible, even in the prophetical parts of it, which is not underftood by men of learning and diligence, the whole is falfe: or if there be any circumftance in the revelation obfcure, it cannot be a true divine revelation.  But may it not reafonably be fuppofed, that in a revelation defigned not merely for any one particular age, but for the ufe of mankind in every fucceeding age, as there are many things, and thofe of the greateft importance, fufficiently clear and intelligible at all times, fo there may be fome things not well underftood at one time, which afterwards are cleared up by farther inquiry, or a more diligent fearch, or by comparing predictions with events?  Or, may not things which are revealed to us as far as it is neceffary they fhould be fo, yet have fome things attending them, the manner of which we are not able clearly to explain and underftand?  Is not this the cafe of many important points of what is called natural religion, relating to the providence and attributes of God, the divine eternity, immenfity, omnifcience, the creation of the world, &c.?  And muft we reject what we do underftand, and the great ufefulnefs of which we clearly apprehend, becaufe there is fomething relating to it which we cannot diftinctly conceive?

As to the objections he makes againft fome particular doctrines of Chriftianity, as unintelligible and abfurd, or at leaft as abfolutely ufelefs, this entirely depends upon the ftrange and unfair reprefentation he has been pleafed to make of them.  Thus he fuppofes Chriftians to maintain it as a doctrine of Scripture, that " an original, uncompounded, immaterial, and pure fpirit, fhould, " like one of the derived, compounded, material, human fpecies, " have a Son‡:"  As if Chriftians underftood God's having a Son, in the fame grofs, literal, and carnal fenfe, in which one man begets another.

He pronounces, that " the fuppofed fatisfaction for fin by " Chrift's death, is a doctrine entirely repugnant to reafon, and " as fuch ought to be rejected with fcorn*."  Mr. Chubb has paffed the fame cenfure upon it, which is owing to the abfurd light in which he has thought fit to reprefent it, concerning which fee before, p. 238.  But the doctrine of our redemption

---

* Deifm fairly Stated, p. 66.                † Ibid. p. 41.

and

and reconciliation through the obedience and fufferings of our Lord Jefus Chrift, confidered as taught in the holy Scriptures, hath nothing in it but what is worthy of God, and of an excellent tendency.

He mentions another doctrine, which he owns to be intelligible enough, but reprefents it as good for nothing, and as of no more confequence to the world in general, than there being a burning mountain in the kingdom of Naples, is an advantage to the people of England. And he thinks " it is greatly improbable, " that God fhould efpecially interpofe to acquaint the world with " what mankind would do altogether as well without *." The doctrine he here refers to is that of God's judging the world by Jefus Chrift. But this, rightly confidered, is a noble part of the gofpel fcheme, and capable of being improved to the moft excellent purpofes. It renders the whole harmonious and confiftent, in that the fame glorious and divine Perfon by whom God made the world, and by whom as the great inftrument he carried on his gracious defigns for recovering mankind from their ruinous and loft eftate, is appointed to be the judge of all men, and difpenfer of future retributions. And what farther fhews the propriety of appointing Chrift to be the judge is, that this is the laft perfective act of the kingdom and dominion committed to him as Mediator, and that it is to be regarded as a reward of his amazing humiliation and felf-abafement, and of his unparalleled obedience and fufferings in our nature, in compliance with his heavenly father's will. To which it may be added, that nothing can be fuller of comfort to good men, than that the benevolent Saviour of mankind will judge the world in the father's name; fince it yields a fatisfactory proof, that it is the will of God, that the judgment fhould be conducted, not with the utmoft rigour of unallayed juftice, but with great equity, fo as to make all proper allowances for human weaknefs and infirmity, as far as is confiftent with unbiaffed truth and righteoufnefs. And at the fame time it hath a manifeft tendency to ftrike an awe into the impenitent rejecters of the divine grace and goodnefs, to confider that they muft be accountable to that Lord and Saviour whom they rejected and defpifed. What a mighty enforcement muft it give

* Deifm fairly Stated, p. 35.

to his authority and laws, that he himself shall call us to an account as to our obedience or disobedience to those laws, and will have it in his power to fulfil his own glorious promises to them that believe and obey him, and to execute his awful threatnings against the finally impenitent and disobedient!

There are several other things he repeats which are urged by almost every deistical writer, and which I have had occasion frequently to mention, such as the contradictory interpretations put on several passages of Scripture, different translations, errors of transcribers, &c.  But that which he seems to lay a particular stress upon is the corruption of Christians.  He speaks of the *abominable wickedness that has rode triumphant* in the Christian world: and that " the Americans have too much reason to con-" sider the coming of Christians and Christianity among them as " the greatest evil and curse that ever befel them\*."  But if professed Christians have made religion a cover for their ambition, avarice, and cruelty, Christianity is not accountable for this. And whosoever considers the best accounts of the Americans before Christianity came among them; their gross ignorance and barbarity, their human sacrifices, and the abominable vices and customs which prevailed among them†, must be sensible, that if the pure religion of Jesus, as taught in the gospel by Christ and his apostles, had been published and received among them in its genuine purity and simplicity, it would have been the happiest thing that could have befallen them: and the greatest fault is, that little care has been taken to instruct them and the other heathen nations, in the true Christian religion as delivered in the holy Scriptures.  Notwithstanding the corruptions so complained of in the Christian world, it is undeniable, that what there is of knowledge and true religion among men, is principally where Christianity is professed.  But if all were true that is pretended concerning the depravity of those that call themselves Christians, it would only prove, that they are very much fallen from the religion they profess, but not that Christianity itself is false, or was not originally from God.  Whilst it can be shewn, as it may be with the utmost evidence, that considered in itself, and as contained in the Scriptures, it is of the most excellent tendency, and

---

\* Deism fairly Stated, p. 47, 48.
† See Bayle's Dictionary, under the article Leon [Peter Cuccade].

that

that the uniform defign of its doctrines, precepts, promifes and threatnings, is to promote the caufe of virtue and righteoufnefs in the world, and to reclaim men from vice and wickednefs; it is certainly very unreafonable and unfair to make Chriftianity anfwerable for the abufes and corruptions it condemneth. If every thing muft be rejected which hath been abufed, government and civil polity, knowledge and literature, religion, liberty, and reafon itfelf muft be difcarded.

One of the moft remarkable things in the tract we are now confidering is, that the author will not allow that the moral precepts of Chriftianity properly belong to it at all, or make any part of the Chriftian religion. He pretends, that Chriftian divines, in order to render Chriftianity amiable, have decked her with the graceful ornaments of moral precepts; whereas in Chriftianity the moral precepts are but borrowed ware, the property of the deifts, and as much diftinguifhed from Chriftianity, as Chriftianity is from Mahometanifm. Thus he hath found out an admirable expedient to ftrip Chriftianity of what hath been hitherto efteemed one of its principal glories. The holy and excellent precepts which the great Author of our religion taught and enjoined in the name of God, and to enforce which by the moft weighty and important motives was one great defign of his and his apoftles' miniftry, do not, it feems, belong to Chriftianity at all. Moral precepts, according to this writer, make no part of divine revelation, and of the fcheme of religion delivered in the Gofpel; though to clear and fhew them in their juft extent, and enforce them by a divine authority, and by the moft prevailing motives, feems to be one of the nobleft ends for which a divine revelation could be given to mankind. Suppofing, which was really the cafe, that the world was funk into an amazing darknefs and corruption, there was nothing that was more wanted than to have a pure fyftem of morals, containing the whole of our duty with refpect to God, our neighbours, and ourfelves, delivered not as the opinions of wife men and philofophers, but as the laws of God himfelf, and enforced by all the fanctions of a divine authority, and by all the charms of the divine grace and goodnefs. This is what hath been done by the Chriftian revelation; and its great ufefulnefs to this purpofe, and the need the world ftood in of it, is excellently reprefented by Mr. Locke,

Locke, in his *Reafonablenefs of Chriftianity*\*, quoted at large by Dr. Benfon in his remarks on this pamphlet, who very juftly obferves, that this great man had fully obviated before-hand all that the author of *Deifm fairly Stated* hath advanced on this fubject.

The laft argument he urgeth againft the Chriftian revelation is drawn from its not having been univerfally fpread in all ages and nations. I fhall not fay any thing here to this objection, which hath been often repeated and anfwered. It had been particularly infifted upon by Dr. Tindal, and was fully confidered in the anfwers that were made to him. Some notice was taken of it in the obfervations on Lord Herbert's fcheme†. And it may be obferved, as Mr. Chubb himfelf feems to think, that no great ftrefs fhould be laid upon it; and he will not take upon him to affirm, that the non-univerfality of a revelation is a juft objection againft its divinity‡.

Soon after *Deifm fairly Stated*, &c. appeared, Dr. Benfon publifhed animadverfions upon it, in the fecond edition of the *Reafonablenefs of Chriftianity as delivered in the Scriptures*, London, 1746: To which there is added an appendix, in which he folidly vindicates the arguments he had offered in his *Reafonablenefs of Chriftianity*, &c. againft the exceptions of this writer, and charges him not only with falfe reafonings, but with grofs mifreprefentations. The fame charge is urged againft him in a tract publifhed by the reverend Mr. Capel Berrow, though without his name, intitled, *Deifm not confiftent with the Religion of Nature and Reafon:*—" wherein are obviated the moft popu-" lar objections brought againft Chriftianity, thofe efpecially " which are urged by a moral philofopher, in a late extraordinary " pamphlet, ftyled *Deifm fairly Stated, and fully Vindicated*, in " a letter to a friend—London, 1751." There were other anfwers to *Deifm fairly Stated*, which I have not feen. I fhall conclude my reflections upon it with obferving, that this pamphlet furnifhes remarkable inftances to verify the obfervation I had occafion to make before§ concerning the unfair conduct of the deiftical writers, and the ftrange liberties they take in mifreprefenting the fenfe of the Chriftian writers whom they quote.

---

\* Locke's Works, vol. ii. p. 575—579. 4th edit.

† See above, p. 20, & feq.

‡ Chubb's pofthumous Works, vol. i. p. 218, 219.

§ See above, let. vii. p. 90. note.

It

It may not be improper here to take fome notice of the attempt made againft the authority of the facred writings in the late Lord Bolingbroke's *Letters on the Study and Ufe of Hiftory*. In fome of thefe letters he hath ufed his utmoft efforts to fubvert the credit of the fcripture hiftory; but the method he has made ufe of to this purpofe feems not to be well chofen, nor confiftent with itfelf. A principal reafon which his Lordfhip produces to invalidate the credit and authority of the Old Teftament hiftory is, that the Greeks were not acquainted with it; and that their accounts, particularly with regard to the Affyrian empire, do not agree with the accounts given of it in Scripture. And yet he himfelf has taken great pains to fhew, that the ancient Greeks were fabulous writers, and that their accounts of ancient times, either with regard to other nations, or their own, are not to be depended on: and accordingly he hath let us know, that if they had perfectly agreed with the accounts given in the Jewifh Scriptures, he would have had very little regard to them, and would not have looked upon this to be any argument of their truth. Many learned writers have produced teftimonies from heathen authors, tending to ftrengthen fome remarkable paffages in the fcripture hiftory. This his Lordfhip finds great fault with, and chargeth it as a moft partial and abfurd conduct to admit the teftimony of the heathen writers, if they happen at any time to agree with the fcripture accounts, and to reject their teftimony when againft them. But if the matter be fairly weighed, there is nothing in this but what is very reafonable: for, confidering the ftrong prejudices of the heathens againft the Jews, whofe whole religion and policy were fo oppofite to theirs, it is evident that no great ftrefs can be laid upon what they fay againft them, and their hiftory; and yet if any thing be found in their writings, which tendeth to confirm the facts recorded in the Jewifh facred books, it is juft to take advantage of this; fince it is plain this could not be owing to a favourable prepoffeffion towards the Jews, or their hiftories, but to the force of truth, or to fome traditions which they looked upon as authentic. For though the teftimonies of enemies are not much to be regarded, when they are to the prejudice of thofe for whom they have a declared averfion, yet the teftimony of enemies in favour of thofe to whom they are known to be enemies, has been always looked upon to be of great weight,

In

In order to invalidate the fcripture hiftory, his Lordfhip has thought fit to repeat what had been often mentioned by the writers on that fide: That the Jewifh facred books were loft in the Babylonifh captivity; that there have been fuch corruptions and alterations in the copies, that there can be no dependence upon them; that there is no proof of the Gofpels having been written in the apoftolic age; that they were not diftinguifhed from the fpurious gofpels; that there had been formerly evidence againft Chriftianity, but that it was deftroyed; that the Chriftian clergy, through whofe hands the Scriptures have been tranfmitted to us, were guilty of numberlefs frauds and corruptions; and that the many differences among Chriftians about the fenfe of Scripture fhew, that it is abfolutely uncertain; and that there is now no certain ftandard of Chriftianity at all. Thefe and other objections, which his Lordfhip hath difplayed with no fmall oftentation, I fhall not here take any particular notice of, having confidered and obviated them in the *Reflections on Lord Bolingbroke's Letters on the Study and Ufe of Hiftory, efpecially as far as they relate to Chriftianity and the Holy Scriptures,* publifhed at London, 8vo. 1753 *. About the fame time, the Right Reverend the Lord Bifhop of Clogher publifhed *A Vindication of the Hiftories of the Old and New Teftament, in Anfwer to the Objections of the late Lord Bolingbroke:* in which he hath both detected and expofed feveral miftakes his Lordfhip had fallen into with refpect to other ancient authors whom he cites, and hath vindicated the facred writings againft the attempts made in thofe Letters to invalidate their credit and divine authority.— Thefe, with Mr. Harvey's *Remarks on Lord Bolingbroke's Letters, as far as they relate to the Hiftory of the Old Teftament,* are the only anfwers I have feen to his Lordfhip's *Letters on the Study and Ufe of Hiftory.* But we fhall foon have occafion to return to this noble Lord, who afterwards in his pofthumous works appeared ftill more openly againft the Chriftian caufe, and even againft what have been hitherto accounted fome of the moft important principles of natural religion.

* Thefe Reflections are to be found in the fecond volume of this work, to which the reader is referred.

L E T.

# LETTER XVI.

*Mr. Hume, a fubtile and ingenious Writer, but extremely fceptical and fond of Novelty—He propofes to free Metaphyfics from that Jargon and Obfcurity which has ferved only as a Shelter to Superflition and Error—His Doctrine concerning the Relation of Caufe and Effect examined—He declares, that the Knowledge of this Relation is of the higheft Importance, and that all our Reafons concerning Matter of Fact and Experience, and concerning the Exiftence of any Being, are founded upon it—Yet he fets himfelf to fhew, that there is no real Connexion between Caufe and Effect, and that there can be no certain, nor even probable, Reafoning from the one to the other—Reflections upon the great Abfurdity and pernicious Confequences of this Scheme—The Inconfiftencies this Writer hath fallen into.*

SIR,

I NOW fend you fome obfervations upon Mr. Hume, an ingenious writer, who hath lately appeared againft the Chriftian caufe, and that in a manner which feems to have fomething new in it, and different from what others had written before him, efpecially in what he calls his *Philofophical Effays concerning Human Underftanding.* The fecond edition of this book, with additions and corrections, which is what I have now before me, was publifhed in London, 1750. This gentleman muft be acknowledged to be a fubtile writer, of a very metaphyfical genius, and has a neat and agreeable manner of expreffion. But it is obvious to every judicious reader, that he hath in many inftances carried fcepticifm to an unreafonable height; and feemeth everywhere to affect an air of making new obfervations and difcoveries. His writings feem, for the moft part, to be calculated rather to amufe, or even confound, than to inftruct and enlighten the underftanding; and there are not a few things in them, which ftrike at the foundation of natural, as well as the proofs and evidences of revealed, religion. This appeareth to me to be, in a particular manner, the character of his *Philofophical Effays:*
and

and you will, perhaps, be of the fame opinion, when you have
confidered the remarks I now fend you.

. If we were to form a judgment of thefe Effays, from the account he himfelf is pleafed to give of them, and of his intention
in writing them, our notion of them would be highly to their advantage. Having taken notice of the abftractednefs of metaphyfical fpeculations, he fays, that he has, " in the following Effays,
" endeavoured to throw fome light upon fubjects, from which
" uncertainty has hitherto deterred the wife, and obfcurity the
" ignorant." He propofes " to unite the boundaries of the
" different fpecies of philofophy, by reconciling profound in-
" quiry with ciearnefs, and truth with novelty;" and thinks " it
" will be happy, if, reafoning in this eafy manner, he can un-
" dermine the foundations of an abftrufe philofophy, which
" feems to have ferved hitherto only as a fhelter to fuperftition,
" and a cover to abfurdity and error [*]." He undertakes to " ba-
" nifh all that jargon, which has fo long taken poffeffion of me-
" taphyfical reafonings, and drawn fuch difgrace upon them [+]."
And after having reprefented *all the received fyftems of philofo-*
*phy,* and all *common theories, as extremely defective,* he promifes
to " avoid all jargon and confufion, in treating of fuch fubtile
" and profound fubjects [‡]."

That part of thefe Effays, which I fhall firft take notice of,
and which is indeed of a very uncommon ftrain, and feems to lie
at the foundation of many of thofe extraordinary things which he
afterwards advances, is what he propofes to confider, p. 47, *&*
*feq.;* where he obferves, that " it is a fubject worthy curiofity,
" to inquire what is the nature of that evidence, which affures
" us of any real exiftence and matter of fact, beyond the prefent
" teftimony of our fenfes, or the records of our memory." He
obferves, that " this part of philofophy has been little cultivated
" either by the ancients or moderns:" but though it is difficult,
it may be " ufeful, by deftroying that implicit faith and credulity,
" which is the bane of all reafoning and free inquiry [§]." After
fuch a pompous profeffion, one would be apt to expect fomething extremely deferving of our attention. Let us therefore

---

[*] Hume's Philofophical Effays, p. 18, 19.      [+] Ibid. p. 27, 28.
[‡] Ibid. p. 97, 106, 107.      [§] Ibid. p. 47, 48, 49.

examine

examine into his fcheme, that we may know what it really is; and then our way will be clear to make the neceffary remarks upon it.

He obferves, that " the relation of caufe and effect is necef-" fary to the fubfiftence of our fpecies, and the regulation of our " conduct in every circumftance and occurrence of human life. " Without this, we fhould never have been able to adjuft means " to ends, nor employ our rational powers either to the produc-" ing of good, or avoiding of evil\*." And, accordingly, he exprefsly declares, that " if there be any relation, any object, " which it imports us to know perfectly, it is that of caufe and " effect: on this we found all our reafonings, concerning matter " of fact and experience: and by this alone we retain any affur-" ance concerning objects that are removed from the prefent " teftimony of our memory and fenfes:" and that " the exiftence " of any Being can only be known by arguments from its caufe, " or its effect +." It appeareth then, that by his own acknow-ledgment, it is of the higheft importance to know the relation of caufe and effect. Let us now fee what inftruction he gives us with regard to that relation.

He abfolutely denies, that this relation can poffibly be known *a priori*, and afferts, that it entirely arifes from experience ‡: that it is this only " that teaches us the nature and bounds of " caufe and effect, and enables us to infer the exiftence of one " object from that of another §." But he takes a great deal of pains to fhew, that experience cannot furnifh a reafonable foun-dation for fuch an inference. He had laid it down as a prin-ciple, that all arguments from experience can at beft only be pro-bable: but he will not allow even this in the prefent cafe: he fets himfelf to prove, that " not fo much as any probable ar-" guments can be drawn from caufe to effect, or from effect to " caufe ||:" that " the conjunction of the effect with the caufe " is entirely arbitrary, not only in its firft conception, *a priori*, " but after it is fuggefted by experience \*\*:" that, " indeed, " in fact, we infer the one from the other; but that this is not " by a chain of reafoning; nor is there any medium which may

\* Hume's Philofophical Effays, p. 89, 90.   † Ibid. p. 123. 258.
‡ Ibid. p. 50. 52, 53.   § Ibid. p. 258.
|| Ibid. p. 62, 63.   \*\* Ibid. p. 53, 54.

" enable

" enable the mind to draw such an inference*. The only ground
" of such an inference, is the supposed resemblance between the
" past and future; but that it is impossible any argument from
" experience should prove that resemblance: and yet if there be
" not such a resemblance, all experience becomes useless, and can
" give rise to no inference or conclusion †." He positively af-
serts, that " we know only by experience the frequent conjunc-
" tion of objects, without being ever able to comprehend any
" thing like connexion between them ‡." And he frequently
observes, that the connexion is only in our own thoughts or
conceptions, not in the things themselves; and resolves the conjunction between cause and effect, and the inference drawn from
the one to the other, wholly into custom; that it is a " customary
" connexion in the thought or imagination betwixt one object,
" and its usual attendant §;" that custom, he always calls *a habit* ‖;
and represents it as owing to a repetition of acts; at other times,
he ascribes it to an *instinct*, or *mechanical tendency*, and represents it as a necessary *act of the mind*, and *infallible in its
operations* **: yet afterwards, speaking of the same custom or
instinct, he says, that, like *other instincts, it may be fallacious
and deceitful* ††.

The great argument he produces, and upon which he lays the
greatest stress, to shew that we can have no certainty in our con-
clusions concerning the relation of cause and effect, nor reason
from one to the other, is, that we have no idea of that connexion which unites the effect to the cause, or of the force, power,
or energy, in the cause, which produces the effect; nor consequently, any medium whereby we can infer the one from the
other. He sets himself particularly to shew, that neither external objects give us the idea of power, nor reflections on the
operations of our own minds ‡‡.

If what our author offers on this head had been only to display
the subtilty of his metaphysical genius, and shew how little we
are able distinctly to explain the manner even of those things of
which we have the greatest certainty, we should have allowed him

---

\* Hume's Philosophical Essays, p. 60, 61.　　† Ibid. p. 65, 66.
‡ Ibid. p. 115.　　§ Ibid. p. 123.
‖ Ibid. p. 73, 74. 91. 120.　　** Ibid. 73. 91.
†† Ibid. p. 251.　　‡‡ Ibid. p. 105, 106.

to amufe himfelf, and his readers, with a little philofophical play. But what he here advances, concerning caufe and effect, power and connexion, he makes the foundation of conclufions relating to matters of great importance,

> —————————*Hæ nugæ feria ducunt*
> *In mala*—————————

By endeavouring to deftroy all reafoning from caufes to effects, or from effects to caufes, and not allowing that we can fo much as probably infer the one from the other, by arguing either *a priori*, or from experience, he fubverts, as far as in him lies, the very foundation of thofe reafonings, that are drawn from the effects which we behold in the frame of the univerfe, to the exiftence of one fupreme, intelligent, all-powerful caufe; and accordingly we fhall find that he himfelf afterwards applies this principle to this very purpofe. Another ufe that he makes of this doctrine concerning caufe and effect is, what we would not have expected from it, to confound all difference between phyfical and moral caufes; and to fhew that the latter have the fame kind of cafuality with the former. This is the purport of his eighth effay, which is concerning *liberty* and *neceffity*\*: though if he argued confiftently, he muft deny that there is any fuch thing in nature as *neceffity*, or *neceffary connexion;* or that there is either phyfical or moral caufe at all.

You will fcarce expect, that I fhould enter upon a laborious confutation of fo whimfical a fcheme, though propofed to the world with great pomp, and reprefented by the author himfelf as of *vaft importance.* I fhall content myfelf with making fome general obfervations upon it.

And firft, whereas this writer frequently, throughout thefe effays, lays a mighty ftrefs upon experience, as the great guide of human life, and the only foundation of all other knowledge, efpecially with refpect to matter of fact, and the exiftence of objects, he here plainly endeavours to fhew, that there can be no argument from experience at all; nor can any reafonable conclufion be drawn from it: for he will not allow, that argument can be drawn or inference made from experience, but what is founded on the

---

\* Hume's Philofophical Effays, p. 129, & feq.

fuppofed

supposed relation or connexion betwixt cause and effect. If therefore there be no relation or connexion betwixt cause and effect at all, in the nature of things, which it is the whole design of his reasoning on this subject to shew, then all certainty of experience, all proof from it, entirely fail; all experience, as he himself expresses it, *becomes useless, and can give rise to no inference or conclusion*\*.

Secondly, Another remark I would make upon Mr. Hume's way of arguing is, that it proceeds upon a wrong foundation, and which is contrary to truth and reason, *viz.* that we cannot have any reasonable certainty of the truth of a thing, or that it really is, when we cannot distinctly explain the manner of it, or how it is. The sum of his argumentation, as I have already hinted with relation to cause and effect, is, that we cannot be certain of any such thing as power or energy, because we cannot conceive or explain precisely wherein it consists, or how it operates. But this is a very fallacious way of reasoning. Though we cannot metaphysically explain the manner in which the cause operateth upon the effect, yet we may, in many cases, be sure that there is a connexion between them; and that where there are certain effects produced, there are powers correspondent or adequate to the production of those effects. The mind, in such cases, when it sees an effect produced, is led, by a quick and undoubted process of reasoning, to acknowledge that there must be a cause which hath a power of producing it; or else we must say, that it is produced without any cause at all, or that nothing in nature hath any power of producing it; which is the greatest of all absurdities. He urgeth, that " it must be allowed, that when we know a power, " we know that very circumstance in the cause, by which it is " enabled to produce the effect." And then he asks, " Do we " pretend to be acquainted with the nature of the human soul and " the nature of an idea, or the aptitude of the one to produce the " other\*?" But certainly we may know, that there is something in the cause which produceth the effect, though we cannot distinctly explain what that circumstance in the cause is, by which it is enabled to produce it. We must not deny, that there is in the mind a power of raising up ideas, and recalling them, and fixing the attention upon them, becaufe we cannot explain how this is done. The argument Mr. Hume offers to prove, that we can have no affurance of the reality of force or power, *viz.* becaufe we cannot diftinctly conceive or explain how it ope-rateth, would equally prove, that we cannot be fure that we have any ideas at all, becaufe we cannot well explain the nature of an idea, or how it is formed in the mind. He himfelf, on another oc-cafion, obferves againft Malebranche, and the modern Cartefians, who deny all power and activity in fecond caufes, and afcribe all to God; that " we are indeed ignorant of the manner in which " bodies operate upon one another; and fo we are of the manner " or force by which the mind, even the fupreme mind, operates, " either on itfelf or on body. Were our ignorance therefore a " fufficient reafon for rejecting any thing, we fhould be led into " that principle of refufing all energy to the Supreme Being, as " much as to the groffeft matter*." He here feems to cenfure it as a wrong way of arguing, to deny that a thing is, becaufe we cannot diftinctly conceive the manner how it is; or to make our ignorance of any thing a fufficient reafon for rejecting it: and yet it is manifeft, that his own reafoning againft power or cauf-ality, force or energy, depends upon this principle; and indeed, by comparing the feveral parts of his fcheme, there is too much reafon to apprehend, that he had it in view to deny all force and energy, and all power whatfoever, in the fupreme as well as in fecondary caufes; or at leaft to reprefent it as very uncerta n. I think this gentleman would have done better to have faid, as a late ingenious author of his own country, " We have no adequate " idea of power; we fee evidently that there muft be fuch a thing " in nature; but we cannot conceive how it acts, nor what con- " nects the producing caufe with the produced effect." Cheva-lier Ramfay's principles of natural and revealed religion, vol. i. p. 109.

Thirdly, A third remark is, that many of our author's argu-ings on this fubject are contrary to the moft evident dictates of common fenfe. Such is that, where he afferts, that not fo much as a probable argument can be drawn, in any cafe, from experi-ence, concerning the connexion betwixt caufe and effect; or

* Hume's Philofophical Effays, p. 117, 118.

from

from whence we may conclude, that from a fimilar caufe we may
expect fimilar effects\*. Thus, *e. g.* according to his way of
reafoning, it cannot fo much as probably be concluded from experience, that if a quantity of dry gunpowder be laid in any place,
and fire be applied to it, it will caufe an explofion; or that if
it hath fuch an effect to-day, a like quantity of powder, the fame
way circumftanced, will produce the fame effect to-morrow.
No probable reafon can be brought to fhew, that that which has
had the effect in thoufands of inftances in time paft, will, though
all circumftances appear perfectly fimilar, have the fame effect in
time future.　He grants, indeed, that, in fuch cafes, the mind is
determined to draw the inference; yet he afferts, that the underftanding has no part in the operation.　But furely, when, from
obfervation and experience, we come to know and judge of the
ordinary courfe of nature, the underftanding may juftly draw
a probable argument or conclufion, that from fuch and fuch
caufes, fo circumftanced, fuch effects will follow.　This inference is perfectly rational.　And it is a ftrange way of talking,
that, even from a number of uniform experiments, we cannot
fo much as probably infer a connexion between the caufe and
the effect, the fenfible qualities and the fecret powers.　The reafon he gives, is, that " if there be any fufpicion, that the courfe
" of nature may change, and that the paft may be no rule for
" the future, experience can give rife to no inference or con-
" clufion †."　But is the probability of a thing deftroyed, according to any way of reafoning allowed hitherto, becaufe it is
barely poffible it may happen otherwife, though there are ten
thoufand to one againft it?　Mr. Hume elfewhere, when arguing
againft miracles, lays it down as a principle, that there is a conftant uniformity in the courfe of nature, never to be violated;
but here, in order to fhew, that no probable reafon can be brought
from experience, concerning the connexion of caufe and effect,
he fuppofes, that there may be a fufpicion that the courfe of nature may change.　Thus this gentleman knows how to affume
and alter principles, as beft fuits his own prefent convenience.
Reafon leadeth us to conclude, that the courfe of nature is the
appointment and conftitution of that moft wife and powerful

---

\* Hume's Philofophical Effays, p. 61, 62, 63.　　　† Ibid. p. 65, 66.

Being, who made that world, and settled that law and order which
he judged fittest and properest; and then reason leadeth us also
to conclude, that, except in very extraordinary cases, the same
order will continue; and extraordinary cases do not hinder the
probability of the ordinary course. So that reason affords a proper medium for a probable conclusion concerning what effects
are to be expected. He affirms, indeed, that all inferences of
this kind are only the effects of custom or habit, not of reasoning *.
But why is custom or habit here mentioned in opposition to reason, or as exclusive of it? May they not both concur? It is evident that they often go together, and mutually strengthen one
another. Custom alone, without reason, is often not to be depended on: but in this case reason gives its suffrage; and, in all
arguings in experimental philosophy, reason argues from similar
causes to similar effects. It is by reason we draw those inferences, and the inferences are rational. It must not be said, that
in this case there is no reasoning at all; but that the reasoning is
often so obvious, that it carries conviction by the very constitution of the human mind, which naturally acquiesceth in it as
satisfactory. It seems evident, that the great Author of our being
hath formed our minds, so as to reason in this manner; and he
would not have done this, if it had not been both of great use in
human life to make such inferences, and if there were not a real
foundation for it in the nature of things. This writer himself
owns, that " none but a fool or a madman will ever pretend to
" dispute the authority of experience, or to reject that great guide
" of human life: but he thinks it may be allowed a philosopher
" to have so much curiosity as to examine the principle of human
" nature, which gives this weighty authority to experience †."
But I cannot help thinking, that if we were to judge of philosophy by the specimen this gentleman hath given of it in this instance, many would be apt to conclude, that there is a great difference, and even opposition, between philosophy and common
sense; that what is so obvious and apparent to the common sense
and reason of mankind, that he is a fool and a madman, who
doubts of it, yet in philosophy is not so much as probable.

Another instance, in which our author's scheme is not very

---

* Hume's Philosophical Essays, p 73. 74. & passim.    † Ibid. p. 65. 66.

reconcileable

reconcileable to the common fentiments of mankind, is, that he
fays, that "though we learn, by experience, the frequent *con-*
"*junction* of objects, yet we are unable to comprehend any thing
"like *connexion* between them; and that there appears not in
"all nature any thing like *connexion*, conceivable by us; all
"events are entirely loofe and feparate; one event follows ano-
"ther; but we never obferve any tie betwixt them; they feem
"conjoined, but never connected\*." But it is evident, that
in many cafes we have a diftinct idea of conjunction or contiguity,
as in a heap of fand; and of connexion, as betwixt caufe and
effect; and the connexion in this cafe is not merely in our
thoughts, as this gentleman is pleafed to reprefent it; but this
very connexion in our thoughts is founded on a connexion which
we perceive in the things themfelves. They are not connected
as caufe and effect, becaufe we think them fo; but we perceive
them to be connected, becaufe we find they are fo: nor is this
owing merely to a cuftom or habit in our minds, but there is in
nature a real foundation for it.

Fourthly, Another remark which occurs to me, upon confidering Mr. Hume's fcheme, is, that he hath fallen into feveral inconfiftencies and contradictions: and, indeed, it is not to be
wondered at, that a man who argueth againft common fenfe,
however fubtile and ingenious he may otherwife be, fhould alfo
be inconfiftent with himfelf. I have already taken notice of the
paffages in which he reprefenteth experience as uncertain, and
that not fo much as a probable argument can be drawn from it;
and yet in his fixth effay, which is concerning *probability*, he
fhews that experience may not only furnifh probable conclufions, but what he calls *proofs;* which he explains to be fuch arguments from experience, as leave no room for doubt or oppofi-
tion†. And he frequently fpeaks of experience in very high
terms, as a certain guide. Again, in feveral paffages above referred to, he exprefsly declares, that in making experimental
conclufions, there is no place for *reafoning;* that the inference
in this cafe is entirely owing to cuftom, and the underftanding has
no part in it: and yet he elfewhere owns, that there is great fcope
of *reafoning* in inferences of this kind from obfervation and ex-

\* Hume's Philofophical Effays, p. 120.　　† Ibid. p. 93.

perience;

perience; and that not only men greatly furpafs the inferior animals in this way of reafoning, but that one man very much ex-
cels another\*. And he declares, that " all our *reafonings* are
" founded on a fpecies of analogy; where the caufes are entirely
" fimilar, the analogy is perfect; and the inference drawn from
" it is regarded as certain and conclufive †;" though he had faid,
that " it is impoffible that any arguments from experience can
" prove fuch a refemblance ‡." Another inconfiftency, which
may be obferved in Mr. Hume's reafoning on this fubject, is,
that though he reprefents the connexion betwixt caufe and effect to be only a connexion in our thoughts, not in the things
themfelves §, yet he afferts, that " there is a kind of pre-efta-
" blifhed harmony between the courfe of nature, and the fuccef-
" fion of our ideas; and though the powers and forces, by which
" the former is governed, be wholly unknown to us, yet our
" thoughts and conceptions have ftill, we find, gone on in the
" fame train with other works of nature ‖:" where he feems to
fuppofe, that there is a real connexion in the nature of things,
to which the connexion in our minds correfpondeth. The general ftrain of his arguing in feveral of his effays, feems to be
defigned to prove, if it proves any thing, that we cannot be fure
that there is any fuch thing as caufe or caufal connexion in the
univerfe: yet he fays, " it is univerfally allowed that nothing
" exifts without a caufe of its exiftence; and that chance is a
" negative word, and means not any real power which has any
" where a being in nature \*\*." Here he falls into the common
way of fpeaking, that every thing which exifteth muft have a
caufe of its exiftence; otherwife we muft acknowledge the operation of chance. And he obferves, that " there is no fuch thing
" as chance in the world ††." Caufes therefore muft be acknowledged, though we cannot explain the manner of their caufality.
And he himfelf, in reckoning up the principles of the connexion
of our ideas, diftinctly mentions *refemblance, contiguity,* and
*caufation;* and this laft he makes to be the moft common and
ufeful of all ‡‡: and yet, in the courfe of his reafoning, he really

---

\* Hume's Philofophical Effays, p. 170, 171.　　† Ibid. p. 165.
‡ Ibid. p. 65.　　　　　　　　　　　　　　§ Ibid. p. 123. 126.
‖ Ibid. p. 90.　　　　　　　　　　　　　\*\* Ibid. p. 151.
†† Ibid. p. 93.　　　　　　　　　　　　‡‡ Ibid. p. 32. 84.

leaves no place for *caufation*, diftinct from *fimilarity or refemblance*, and *contiguity*. It may be mentioned, as another inftance of his inconfiftency, that he frequently makes *power* and *necefary connexion* the fame thing; and argues, that if there be any connexion between caufe and effect at all, it muft be a neceffary one; for that cannot be called a caufe, that is not neceffarily connected with the effect \*: and yet, in his Effay on *liberty* and *neceffity*, when fpeaking of the influence of motives upon the mind, he faith, that, " as this influence is *ufually* conjoined with " the action, it muft be efteemed a caufe, and be looked upon as " an inftance of the neceffity which we would eftablifh †:" where he plainly fuppofeth, that it is not effential to the notion of a caufe, that it is infallibly and always connected with the effect; but that it is fufficient, if it be ufually joined with it. And to the fame purpofe, he faith, that " all caufes are not conjoined to " their ufual effects, with like conftancy and uniformity‡." Indeed, his whole Effay on Liberty and Neceffity, though feemingly built upon the fcheme he had advanced in his foregoing Effays, with relation to caufe and effect, is really not reconcileable to it. In all his reafonings in thefe Effays, concerning caufe and effect, he had argued, that there is no fuch thing as *neceffary connexion*, or indeed any connexion at all, betwixt caufe and effect: and upon this fcheme, it is idle to talk of a neceffity either in phyfical or moral caufes: And yet in his Effay on Liberty and Neceffity, he plainly argues upon the fuppofition of a real connexion; though he will only call it a conjunction betwixt caufe and effect: And he all along fuppofeth the influence of caufes, and the power of motives; and that a neceffity muft be acknowledged in moral as well as phyfical caufes. He would have us to begin the queftion concerning Liberty and Neceffity, not " by examining the faculties of the foul, but by examining " the operations of body, and of brute unintelligent matter §:" And with regard to this, he obferves, that " it is univerfally " allowed, that matter, in all its operations, is actuated by a " neceffary force; and that every effect is fo precifely determined " by the nature and energy of its caufe, that no other effect, in

---

\* Hume's Philofophical Effays, p. 93. 103. 151.   † Ibid. p. 154.
‡ Ibid. p. 138.   § Ibid. p. 147.

" fuch

" fuch particular circumſtances, could poſſibly have reſulted
" from the operation of its cauſe\*:" and he expreſsly aſſerteth,
that " the conjunction betwixt motives and voluntary actions, is
" as regular and uniform as that betwixt the cauſe and effect, in
" any part of nature†." Thus we ſee, that he can acknowledge
cauſe and effect, and the connexion betwixt them, when he has
a mind to take advantage of this, for overthrowing the liberty of
human actions. And he concludes the Eſſay, with taking notice
of the objection which might be raiſed againſt what he had advanced, *viz.* that " if voluntary actions be ſubjected to the ſame
" laws of neceſſity with the operations of matter, there is a con-
" tinued chain of neceſſary cauſes, pre-ordained and pre-deter-
" mined, reaching from the original cauſe of all, to every ſingle
" volition of every human creature. While we act, we are at
" the ſame time acted upon. There is no contingency any-
" where in the univerſe, no indifferency, no liberty." This objection he putteth very ſtrongly‡; and yet I cannot ſee, that,
according to the hypotheſis he had advanced in the foregoing
Eſſays, there can be any juſt foundation for it: for if there be
only a mere conjunction of events, but no cauſal influence, it
cannot be ſaid, that, whilſt we act, we are acted upon. On the
contrary, nothing is acted upon, nor is there any power, force, or
energy in nature. All events are looſe, ſeparate, and uncon-
nected, and only follow one another, without connexion; and
therefore there can be no continued chain of neceſſary cauſes at
all. This would be the proper anſwer, according to the principles he had laid down, if he had thought thoſe principles would
bear. But he hath not thought fit to make uſe of it; but, in contradiction to his own ſcheme, ſeems here to admit a chain of
neceſſary cauſes, phyſical and moral, in order to load providence;
and plainly repreſents the objection as unanſwerable§.

Thus I have conſidered, pretty largely, our author's extraordinary ſcheme; and the obſervations that have been made may
help us to judge of this gentleman's character as a writer, whether it deſerveth all the admiration and applauſe, which he himſelf, as well as others, have been willing to beſtow upon it. We

* Hume's Philoſophical Eſſays. p. 131, 132.    † Ibid. p. 141.
‡ Ibid. p. 157, 158.    § Ibid. p. 162.

may fee, by what hath been obferved, how far he hath anfwered what he had prepared the reader to expect, *clearnefs* and *precifion*, in his way of treating thefe *curious and fublime fubjects*. He had particularly propofed, with regard to power, force, and energy, " to fix, if poffible, the precife meaning of thefe terms ; " and thereby remove part of that obfcurity, which is fo much " complained of in this fpecies of philofophy\*."

What Mr. Hume hath offered, concerning caufe and effect, puts me in mind of a remarkable paffage in Lord Bolingbroke's pofthumous works, which I fhall mention on this occafion. " Whatever knowledge," faith his Lordfhip, " we acquire of ap-" parent caufes, we can acquire none of real caufality, or that " power, that virtue, whatever it be, by which one being acts on " another, and becomes a caufe. We may call this by different " names, according to the different effects of it ; but to know it " in its firft principles, to know the nature of it, would be to " know as God himfelf knows ; and therefore this will be always " unknown to us, in caufes that feem to be moft under our in-" fpection, as well as in others that are the moft remote from it." And he reprefents thofe " philofophers as ridiculous, who, when " they have difcovered a real actual caufe, in its effects, by the " phænomena, reject it, becaufe they cannot conceive its caufa-" lity, nor affign a fufficient reafon why and how it is †." This may feem to bear hard upon Mr. Hume : but what is more to be wondered at, he hath in effect paffed a cenfure upon himfelf. He indeed gives a high encomium on fceptical philofophy, in the beginning of his fixth Effay : that " every paffion is morti-" fied by it, but the love of truth ; and that paffion never is, nor " can be carried to too high a degree. It is furprifing therefore, " that this philofophy, which, in almoft every inftance, muft be " harmlefs and innocent, fhould be the fubject of fo much " groundlefs reproach and obloquy ‡." But afterwards, in his twelfth Effay, which is of the academical or fceptical philofophy, he gives no advantageous notion of fcepticifm. He fays, that " the grand fcope of all the inquiries and difputes of the fceptics is, to deftroy reafon by ratiocination and argument §."

---

\* Hume's Philofophical Effays, p. 101, 102.
† Lord Bolingbroke's Works, vol. iii. p. 541.
‡ Hume's Philofophical Effays, p. 70.     § Ibid. p. 245.

And,

And, fpeaking of the fceptical objections againft the relation of caufe and effect, he faith, that " while the fceptic infifts upon " thefe topics, he feems, for the time at leaft, to deftroy all af- " furance and conviction:" and then he adds, that " thefe argu- " ments might be difplayed at a greater length, if any durable " good or benefit to fociety could ever be expected to refult from " them. For," faith he, " here is the chief, and moft confound- " ing objection to exceffive fcepticifm, that no durable good can " ever be expected from it, while it remains in its full force and " vigour *." And he had faid, that " nature will always maintain " her rights, and prevail in the end, over any abftract reafon- " ing whatfoever †:" and if fo, I think we may juftly conclude, that any abftract reafoning which is contrary to the plain voice of nature ought to be rejected, as falfe and trifling, and of no real ufe or fervice to mankind.

But it were well, if the worft thing that could be faid of our author's exceffive fcepticifm were, that it is trifling and ufelefs. It will foon appear, that, as he hath managed it, it is of a perni- cious tendency: but you will probably be of opinion, that enough hath been faid of this gentleman, and his oddities, for the pre- fent.                                        I am, &c.

* Hume's Philofophical Effays, p. 251.        † Ibid. p. 71.

# LETTER XVII.

*Observations on Mr. Hume's Essay concerning a particular Pro-*
*vidence and a future State—His Attempt to shew, that we can-*
*not justly argue from the Course of Nature to a particular in-*
*telligent Cause, because the Subject lies entirely beyond the Reach*
*of human Experience, and because God is a singular Cause, and*
*the Universe a singular Effect; and therefore we cannot argue*
*by a Comparison with any other Cause, or any other Effect—*
*His Argument examined, whereby he pretends to prove, that,*
*since we know God only by the Effects in the Works of Nature,*
*we can judge of his Proceedings no farther than we can now*
*see of them, and therefore cannot infer any Rewards or Pu-*
*nishments beyond what are already known by Experience or Ob-*
*servation—The Usefulness of believing future Retributions ac-*
*knowledged by Mr. Hume, and that the contrary Doctrine is*
*inconsistent with good Policy.*

SIR,

IT appears from what was observed in my former letter, that
few writers have carried scepticism in philosophy to a greater
height than Mr. Hume. I now proceed to consider those things
in his writings that seem to be more directly and immediately designed against religion. Some part of what he calls his *Philoso-*
*phical Essays concerning Human Understanding*, manifestly tends
to subvert the very foundations of natural religion, or its most
important principles. Another part of them is particularly levelled against the proofs and evidences of the Christian revelation.

The former is what I shall first consider, and shall therefore
examine the eleventh of those essays, the title of which is, *con-*
*cerning a particular providence and a future state.* Mr. Hume
introduces what he offers in this essay as sceptical paradoxes advanced by a friend, and pretends by no means to approve of them.
He proposes some objections as from himself, to his friend's way
of arguing, but takes care to do it in such a manner, as to give
his friend a superiority in the argument: and some of the worst
parts of his essay are directly proposed in his own person. The
                                                              essay

effay may be confidered as confifting of two parts. The one feems to be defigned againft the exiftence of God, or of one fupreme intelligent caufe of the univerfe: the other, which appears to be the main intention of the effay, is particularly levelled againft the doctrine of a future ftate of rewards and punifhments.

I fhall begin with the former, becaufe it comes firft in order to be confidered, though it is not particularly mentioned till towards the conclufion of the effay. He obferves, in the perfon of his Epicurean friend, that " while we argue from the courfe of " nature, and infer a particular intelligent caufe, which at firft " beftowed and ftill preferves order in the univerfe, we embrace " a principle which is both uncertain and ufelefs." The reafon he gives why it is uncertain is, " becaufe the fubject lies entire- " ly beyond the reach of human experience[*]." This is a fpecimen of the ufe our author would make of the principles he had laid down in the preceding effays. He had reprefented experience as the only foundation of our knowledge with refpect to matter of fact, and the exiftence of objects: that it is by experience alone that we know the relation of caufe and effect: and he had alfo afferted, that not fo much as a probable argument can be drawn from experience to lay a foundation for our reafoning from caufe to effect, or from effect to caufe. I fhall not add any thing here to what was offered in my former letter to fhew the abfurdity, the confufion, and inconfiftency of thefe principles. I fhall only obferve, that this very writer, who had reprefented all arguments drawn from experience, with relation to caufe and effect, as abfolutely uncertain, yet makes it an objection againft the argument from the courfe of nature to an intelligent caufe, that *the fubject lies entirely beyond the reach of human experience.* What the meaning of this is, it is not eafy to apprehend. It will be readily allowed, that we do not know by experience the whole courfe of nature; yet enough of it falls within the reach even of human obfervation and experience, to lay a reafonable foundation for inferring from it a fupreme intelligent caufe. In that part of the univerfe which cometh under our notice and obfervation, we may behold fuch illuftrious characters of wifdom, power, and goodnefs, as determine us, by the

---

[*] Hume's Philofophical Effays, p. 224.

moft

moſt natural way of reaſoning in the world, to acknowledge a moſt wiſe, and powerful, and benign Author and Cauſe of the univerſe. The inference is not beyond the reach of our faculties, but is one of the moſt obvious that offereth to the human mind. But perhaps what the author intends by obſerving, that *this ſubject lies entirely beyond the reach of human experience*, is this: That notwithſtanding the admirable marks of wiſdom and deſign which we behold in the courſe of nature and order of things, we cannot argue from thence to prove a wiſe and intelligent Cauſe of the univerſe, or that there was any wiſdom employed in the formation of it, becauſe neither we, nor any of the human race, were preſent at the making of it, or ſaw how it was made. This muſt be owned to be a very extraordinary way of reaſoning, and I believe you will eaſily excuſe me if I do not attempt a confutation of it.

Mr. Hume, after having argued thus in the perſon of his Epicurean friend, comes in the concluſion of this eſſay to propoſe another argument as from himſelf. " I much doubt," ſaith he, " whether it be poſſible for a cauſe to be known only by its ef-" fect, or to be of ſo ſingular and particular a nature as to have " no parallel, and no ſimilarity with any other cauſe or object " that has ever fallen under our obſervation. It is only when " two ſpecies of objects are found to be conſtantly conjoined, " that we can infer the one from the other: and were an effect " preſented which was entirely ſingular, and could not be com-" prehended under any known ſpecies, I do not ſee that we " could form any conjecture or inference at all concerning its " cauſe. If experience, and obſervation, and analogy, be in-" deed the only guides we can reaſonably follow in inferences " of this nature, both the effect and cauſe muſt bear a ſimilarity " and reſemblance to other effects and cauſes which we know, " and which we have found in many inſtances to be conjoined " with each other\*." Mr. Hume leaves it to his friend's reflec-tions to *proſecute the conſequences of this principle*, which he had hinted before, might lead *into reaſonings of too nice and delicate a nature* to be inſiſted on. The argument, as he hath managed it, is indeed ſufficiently obſcure and perplexed; but

\* Hume's Philoſophical Eſſays, p. 232, 233.

the

the general intention of it feems to be this; that all our arguings from caufe to effect, or from effect to caufe, proceed upon analogy, or the comparing fimilar caufes with fimilar effects. Where therefore there is fuppofed to be a fingular caufe, to which there is no parallel (though he much doubts whether there can be a caufe of fo fingular a nature), and a fingular effect, there can be no arguing from the one to the other; becaufe in that cafe we cannot argue by a comparifon with any other caufe, or any other effect. Except therefore we can find another world to compare this with, and an intelligent caufe of that world, we cannot argue from the effects in this prefent world to an intelligent caufe: *i. e.* we cannot be fure there is one God, except we can prove there is one other God at leaft; or that this world was formed and produced by a wife intelligent caufe, unlefs we know of another world like this, which was alfo formed by a wife intelligent caufe, and perhaps not then neither: for he feems to infift upon it, that there fhould be *many inftances* of fuch caufes and effects being *conjoined with each other*, in order to lay a proper foundation for *obfervation, experience, and analogy, the only guides we can reafonably follow in inferences of this nature.* He immediately after obferves, that " according to the " antagonifts of Epicurus, the univerfe, an effect quite fingular " and unparalleled, is always fuppofed to be the proof of a deity, " a caufe no lefs fingular and unparalleled." If by calling the univerfe a fingular and unparalleled effect, he intends to fignify that no other univerfe has come under our obfervation, it is very true: but it by no means follows, that we cannot argue from the evident marks of wifdom and defign which we may obferve in this univerfe that we do know, becaufe we do not know any thing of any other univerfe. This grand univerfal fyftem, and even that fmall part of it that we are more particularly acquainted with, comprehendeth fuch an amazing variety of phænomena, all which exhibit the moft incontestable proofs of admirable wifdom, power, and diffufive goodnefs, that one would think it fcarce poffible for a reafonable mind to refift the evidence. But fuch is this fubtile metaphyfical gentleman's way of arguing in a matter of the higheft confequence, the abfurdity of which is obvious to any man of plain underftanding. It is of a piece with what he had advanced before, that there is no fuch thing as caufe or effect

at all, nor can any probable inference be drawn from the one
to the other; than which, as hath been already shewn, nothing
can be more inconsistent with common sense, and the reason of
all mankind.

The other thing observable in this essay, and which seems to
be the principal intention of it, relateth to the proof of a providence and a future state. He introduces his friend as putting
himself in the place of Epicurus, and making an harangue to the
people of Athens, to prove that the principles of his philosophy
were as innocent and salutary as those of any other philosopher.
The course of his reasoning or declamation is this: that " the
" chief or sole argument brought by philosophers for a Divine
" Existence is derived from the order of nature; where there ap-
" pear such marks of intelligence and design, that they think it
" extravagant to assign for its cause, either chance, or the blind
" unguided force of matter: That this is an argument drawn from
" effects to causes: and that when we infer any particular cause
" from an effect, we must proportion the one to the other, and
" can never be allowed to ascribe to the cause any qualities, but
" what are exactly sufficient to produce the effect: and if we
" ascribe to it farther qualities, or affirm it capable of producing
" any other effect, we only indulge the licence of conjecture
" without reason or authority *:" That therefore " allowing God
" to be the author of the existence or order of the universe, it
" follows, that he possesses that precise degree of power, intelli-
" gence, and benevolence, which appears in his workmanship,
" but nothing farther can ever be proved †. Those therefore are
" vain reasoners, and reverse the order of nature, who, instead of
" regarding this present life, and the present scene of things, as
" the sole object of their contemplation, render it a passage to
" something farther. The Divinity may indeed possibly possess
" attributes which we have never seen exerted, and may be go-
" verned by principles of action, which we cannot discover to be
" satisfied: but we can never have reason to infer any attributes,
" or any principles of action in him, but so far as we know them
" to be exerted or satisfied." He asks, " Are there any marks of
" distributive justice in the world?" And if it be said, that " the

---

* Hume's Philosophical Essays, p. 215.          † Ibid. p. 220.

" justice

"justice of God exerts itself in part, but not in its full extent,"
he answers, " that we have no reason to give it any particular
" extent, but only so far as we see it at present exert itself\* :"
That " indeed when we find that any work has proceeded from
" the skill and industry of man, who is a being whom we know
" by experience, and whose nature we are acquainted with, we
" can draw a hundred inferences concerning what may be ex-
" pected from him, and these inferences will all be founded on
" experience and observation.   But since the Deity is known to
" us only by his productions, and as a single being in the uni-
" verse, not comprehended under any species or genus, from
" whose experienced attributes or qualities we can by analogy
" infer any attribute or quality in him, we can only infer such
" attributes or perfections, and such a degree of those attributes,
" as is precisely adapted to the effect we examine: but farther
" attributes or farther degrees of those attributes, we can never
" be authorized to infer or suppose by any rules of just reason-
" ing."   He adds, that " the great source of our mistakes on
" this subject is this: we tacitly consider ourselves as in the place
" of the Supreme Being, and conclude, that he will on every
" occasion observe the same conduct, which we ourselves in his
" situation would have embraced as reasonable and eligible:
" whereas it must evidently appear contrary to all rules of ana-
" logy to reason from the intentions and projects of men to those
" of a Being so different, and so much superior — so remote and
" incomprehensible, who bears less analogy to any other being
" in the universe, than the sun to a waxen taper."   He concludes therefore, " that no new fact can ever be inferred from
" the religious hypothesis:  no reward or punishment expected or
" dreaded beyond what is already known by practice and obser-
" vation †."   This is a faithful extract of the argument in this
essay, drawn together as closely as I could, without the repetitions with which it aboundeth.

I shall now make a few remarks upon it.

The whole of his reasoning depends upon this maxim, that
when once we have traced an effect up to its cause, we can never
ascribe any thing to the cause but what is precisely proportioned

---

\* Hume's Philosophical Essays, p. 203.        † Ibid. p. 230, 231.

to the effect, and what we ourselves difcern to be fo: nor can
we infer any thing farther concerning the caufe, than what the
effect, or the prefent appearance of it, necessarily leads to.  He
had to the fame purpofe obferved in a former effay, that " it is
" allowed by all philofophers, that the effect is the meafure of the
" power*."  But this is far from being univerfally true: for we
in many inftances clearly perceive, that a caufe can produce an
effect which it doth not actually produce, or a greater effect than
it hath actually produced.  This gentleman's whole reafoning
proceeds upon confounding neceffary and free caufes; and indeed he feems not willing to allow any diftinction between
them, or that there are any other but neceffary and material
caufes†.  A neceffary caufe acts up to the utmoft of its power,
and therefore the effect muft be exactly proportioned to it.  But
the cafe is manifeftly different as to free and voluntary caufes.
They may have a power of producing effects, which they do not
actually produce: and as they act from difcernment and choice,
we may, in many cafes, reafonably afcribe to them farther views
than what we difcern or difcover in their prefent courfe of action.
This author himfelf owns, that this may be reafonably done
with refpect to man, whom we know by experience, and whofe
nature and conduct we are acquainted with; but denies that the
fame way of arguing will hold with refpect to the Deity.  But
furely, when once we come from the confideration of his works
to the knowledge of a felf-exiftent and abfolutely perfect Being,
we may, from the nature of that felf-exiftent and abfolutely perfect caufe, reafonably conclude, that he is able to produce certain effects beyond what actually come under our prefent notice
and obfervation, and indeed that he can do whatfoever doth not
imply a contradiction.  This univerfe is a vaft, a glorious, and
amazing fyftem, comprehending an infinite variety of parts: and
it is but a fmall part of it that comes under our own more immediate notice.  But we know enough to be convinced, that it
demonftrateth a wifdom as well as power beyond all imagination
great and wonderful: and we may juftly conclude the fame concerning thofe parts of the univerfe that we are not acquainted
with.  And for any man to fay, that we cannot reafonably afcribe

---

* Hume's Philofophical Effays, p. 125.    † Ibid. p. 131, 132. 141. 151.

any degree of wifdom or power to God, but what is exactly proportioned to that part of the univerfal frame which comes under
our own particular obfervation, is a very ftrange way of arguing!
The proofs of the wifdom and power of God, as appearing in
our part of the fyftem, are fo ftriking, that it is hard to conceive
how any man that is not under the influence of the moft obftinate
prejudice, can refufe to fubmit to their force: and yet there are
many phænomena, the reafons and ends of which we are not at
prefent able to affign.  The proper conduct in fuch a cafe is,
to believe there are moft wife reafons for thefe things, though
we do not now difcern thofe reafons, and to argue from the uncontefted characters of wifdom in things that we do know, that
this moft wife and powerful agent, the author of nature, hath
alfo acted with admirable wifdom in thofe things, the defigns
and ends of which we do not know.  It would be wrong therefore to confine the meafures of his wifdom precifely to what
appeareth to our narrow apprehenfions, in that part of his works
which falleth under our immediate infpection.  This was the
great fault of the Epicureans, and other atheiftical philofophers, who, judging by their own narrow views, urged feveral things as proofs of the want of wifdom and contrivance,
which, upon a fuller knowledge of the works of nature, furnifh
farther convincing proofs of the wifdom of the great Former of
all things.

In like manner, with refpect to his goodnefs, there are numberlefs things in this prefent conftitution, which lead us to regard him as a moft benign and benevolent Being.  And therefore it is highly reafonable, that when we meet with any phænomena, which we cannot reconcile with our ideas of the divine
goodnefs, we fhould conclude, that it is only for want of having
the whole of things before us, and confidering them in their
connexion and harmony, that they appear to us with a diforderly
afpect.  And it is very juft in fuch a cafe to make ufe of any
reafonable hypothefis, which tendeth to fet the goodnefs of God
in a fair and confiftent light.

The fame way of reafoning holds with regard to the juftice and
righteoufnefs of God as the great Governor of the world.  We
may reafonably conclude, from the intimate fenfe we have of the
excellency of fuch a character, and the great evil and deformity

of

of injuſtice and unrighteouſneſs, which ſenſe is implanted in us by the author of our being, and from the natural rewards of virtue, and puniſhment of vice, even in the preſent conſtitution of things, that he is a lover of righteouſneſs and virtue, and an enemy to vice and wickedneſs. Our author himſelf makes his Epicurean friend acknowledge, that in the preſent order of things, virtue is attended with more peace of mind, and with many other advantages above vice\*: and yet it cannot be denied, that there are many inſtances obvious to common obſervation, in which vice ſeemeth to flouriſh and proſper, and virtue to be expoſed to great evils and calamities. What is to be concluded from this? Is it that, becauſe the juſtice of God here ſheweth itſelf only *in part*, and not *in its full extent* (to uſe our author's expreſſion), therefore righteouſneſs in God is imperfect in its degree, and that he doth not poſſeſs it in the full extent of that perfection, nor will ever exert it any farther than we ſee him exert it in this preſent ſtate? This were an unreaſonable concluſion, concerning a being of ſuch admirable perfection, whoſe righteouſneſs as well as wiſdom muſt be ſuppoſed to be infinitely ſuperior to ours. It is natural therefore to think, that this preſent life is only a part of the divine ſcheme, which ſhall be completed in a future ſtate.

But he urgeth, that the great ſource of our miſtakes on this ſubject is, that " we tacitly conſider ourſelves as in the place of " the Supreme Being, and conclude that he will on every oc- " caſion obſerve the ſame conduct, which we ourſelves in his " ſituation would have embraced as reaſonable and eligible. " Whereas it muſt evidently appear contrary to all rules of ana- " logy, to reaſon from the intentions and purpoſes of men to thoſe " of a Being ſo different and ſo much ſuperior, ſo remote and " incomprehenſible†." But though it were the higheſt abſurdity to pretend to tie down the infinite incomprehenſible Being to our ſcanty model and meaſures of acting, and to aſſume that he will *on every occaſion* (for ſo our author is pleaſed to put the caſe) obſerve the ſame conduct that we ſhould judge eligible; ſince there may be innumerable things concerning which we are unable to form any proper judgment, for want of having the ſame comprehenſive view of things that he hath; yet on the other hand,

* Hume's Philoſophical Eſſays, p. 221. † Ibid. p. 230.

there

there are some cases so manifest, that we may safely pronounce
concerning them, as worthy or unworthy of the divine perfections.    And as our own natures are the work of God, we may
reasonably argue from the traces of excellencies in ourselves to
the infinitely superior perfections in the great Author of the universe, still taking care to remove all those limitations and defects
with which those qualities are attended in us.    This is what Mr.
Hume himself elsewhere allows in his *Essay on the Origin of our
Ideas.*   " The idea of God," saith he, " as meaning an infinitely
" intelligent, wise, and good Being, arises from reflecting on the
" operations of our own minds, and augmenting those qualities
" of goodness and wisdom without bound or limit."   See his
*Philosophical Essays,* p. 24, 25.    Since therefore we cannot
possibly help regarding goodness and benevolence, justice and
righteousness, as necessary ingredients in a worthy and excellent
character, and as among the noblest excellencies of an intellectual
being, we are unavoidably led to conclude, that they are to be
found in the highest possible degree of eminency in the absolutely
perfect Being, the Author and Governor of the world.   These are
not mere arbitrary suppositions, but are evidently founded in
nature and reason :   and though in many particular instances we,
through the narrowness of our views, cannot be proper judges
of the grounds and reasons of the divine administration, yet in
general we have reason to conclude, that if there be such a thing
as goodness and righteousness in God, or any perfection in him
correspondent to what is called goodness and righteousness in us,
he will order it so, that in the final issue of things, a remarkable
difference shall be made between the righteous and the wicked :
that at one time or other, and taking in the whole of existence,
virtue, though now for a time it may be greatly afflicted and op-
pressed, shall meet with its due reward ;  and vice and wickedness,
though now it may seem to prosper and triumph, shall receive
its proper punishment.    Since therefore, by the observation of
all ages, it hath often happened, that in the present course of human affairs, good and excellent persons have been unhappy, and
exposed to many evils and sufferings, and bad and vicious men have
been in very prosperous circumstances, and have had a large
affluence of all worldly enjoyments, even to the ends of their
lives, and that, as this gentleman himself elsewhere expresseth it,

                                                   " such

" fuch is the confufion and diforder of human affairs, that no
" perfect œconomy or regular diftribution of happiness or mifery
" is in this life ever to be expected\*;" it feems reafonable to
conclude, that there fhall be a future ftate of exiftence, in which
thefe apparent irregularities fhall be fet right, and there fhall be
a more perfect diftribution of rewards and punifhments to men
according to their moral conduct.   There is nothing in this way
of arguing but what is conformable to the foundeft principles of
reafon, and to the natural feelings of the human heart.   But
though a future ftate of retributions in general be probable, yet
as many doubts might ftill be apt to arife in our minds concerning it, an exprefs revelation from God, affuring us of it in his
name, and more diftinctly pointing out the nature and certainty
of thofe retributions, would be of the moft fignal advantage.

I fhall have occafion to refume this fubject, when I come to
confider what Lord Bolingbroke hath more largely offered in relation to it.   At prefent it is proper to obferve, that though Mr.
Hume feems to allow his Epicurean friend's reafoning to be
juft, yet he owns, that " in fact men do not reafon after that
" manner;" and that " they draw many confequences from the
" belief of a divine exiftence, and fuppofe that the Deity will in-
" flict punifhments on vice, and beftow rewards on virtue, be-
" yond what appears in the ordinary courfe of nature.   Whe-
" ther this reafoning of theirs," adds he, " be juft or not, is no
" matter: its influence on their life and conduct muft ftill be the
" fame.   And thofe who attempt to difabufe them of fuch pre-
" judices, may, for aught I know, be good reafoners, but I can-
" not allow them to be good citizens and politicians: fince they
" free men from one reftraint upon their paffions; and make the
" infringement of the laws of equity and fociety in one refpect
" more eafy and fecure†."   I think it follows from this by his
own account, that he did not act a wife or good part, the part of
a friend to the public or to mankind, in publifhing this Effay,
the manifeft defign of which is to perfuade men, that there is
no juft foundation in reafon for expecting a future ftate of rewards and punifhments at all.   Nor is the conceffion he here

---

\* Hume's Moral and Political Effays, p. 241, 245.
† ———— Philofophical Effays, p. 231.

makes very favourable to what he addeth in the next page, concerning the univerfal liberty to be allowed by the ftate to all kinds of philofophy. According to his own way of reprefenting it, Epicurus muft have been caft, if he had pleaded his caufe before the people; and the principal defign of this Effay, which feems to be to fhew not only the reafonablenefs, but harmlefsnefs, of that philofophy, is loft: for if the fpreading of thofe principles and reafonings is contrary to the rules of good policy, and the character of good citizens; if they have a tendency to free men from a ftrong *reftraint upon their paffions*, and to make the *infringement of the laws of equity and fociety more eafy and fecure;* then fuch principles and reafonings, according to his way of reprefenting the matter, ought in good policy to be reftrained, as having a bad influence on the community.

There is one paffage more in this Effay which may deferve fome notice. It is in page 230, where he obferves, that " God dif-
" covers himfelf by fome faint traces or outlines, beyond which
" we have no authority to afcribe to him any attribute or per-
" fection. What we imagine to be a fuperior perfection may
" really be a defect. Or, were it ever fo much a perfection, the
" afcribing it to the Supreme Being, where it appears not to
" have been really exerted to the full in his works, favours more
" of flattery and panegyric, than of juft reafoning and found phi-
" lofophy." The courfe of his arguing feems to be this: That it would favour of *flattery*, not of *found reafoning*, to afcribe any attribute or perfection to God, which *appears not to have been exerted to the full in his works.* And he had obferved before, that " it is impoffible for us to know any thing of the caufe,
" but what we have antecedently, not inferred, but *difcovered to
" the full* in the effect*." It is plain therefore, that according to him we ought not to afcribe any perfection to God, but what is not merely *inferred,* but *difcovered to the full* in his works. It is alfo manifeft, that according to him there is no attribute or perfection of the Deity exerted or difcovered to the full in his works; for he had faid juft before, that he *difcovers himfelf only by fome faint traces or outlines.* The natural conclufion from thefe premifes taken together is plainly this: that it would be

flattery and prefumption in us to afcribe any attribute or perfection to God at all. And now I leave it to you to judge of the
obligations the world is under to this writer. In one part of this
Effay, he makes an attempt to fubvert the proof of the exiftence
of God, or a fupreme intelligent caufe of the univerfe: and here
he infinuates, that it would be wrong to afcribe any perfection
or attribute to him at all. And the main defign of the whole
Effay is to fhew, that no argument can be drawn from any of his
perfections, to make it probable, that there fhall be rewards and
punifhments in a future ftate, though he acknowledgeth that it
is of great advantage to mankind to believe them.

You will not wonder after this, that this gentleman, who has
endeavoured to fhake the foundations of natural religion, fhould
ufe his utmoft efforts to fubvert the evidences of the Chriftian
revelation. What he hath offered this way will be the fubject
of fome future letters.

## LETTER   XVIII.

*An Examination of Mr. Hume's* Essay on Miracles—*A Summary
of the first Part of that Essay: which is designed to shew, that
Miracles are incapable of being proved by any Testimony or
Evidence whatsoever—His main Principle examined, that Experience is our only Guide in reasoning concerning Matters of
Fact: and that Miracles being contrary to the established Laws
of Nature, there is an uniform Experience against the Existence
of any Miracle—It is shewn, that no Argument can be drawn
from Experience, to prove that Miracles are impossible, or that
they have not been actually wrought—Miracles not above the
Power of God, nor unworthy of his Wisdom—Valuable Ends
may be assigned for Miracles—They are capable of being proved
by proper Testimony—This applied to the Resurrection of
Christ—And it is shewn, that the Evidence set before us in Scripture is every way sufficient to satisfy us of the Truth of it, supposing that Evidence to have been really given as there represented.*

SIR,

I NOW proceed to consider Mr. Hume's celebrated *Essay on
Miracles*, which is the tenth of his *Philosophical Essays*, and
has been mightily admired and extolled, as a masterly and unanswerable piece.   I think no impartial man will say so, that has
read the ingenious and judicious answer made to it by the Reverend Mr. Adams, now Rector of Shrewsbury.   It is intitled,
*An Essay in Answer to Mr. Hume's Essay on Miracles, by Wil-
liam Adams, M. A.*   That which I have by me is the second
edition, with additions, London, 1754.   Besides this, I have seen
a short but excellent discourse, by the Reverend Dr. Rutherforth,
intitled, *The Credibility of Miracles defended against the Author of the Philosophical Essays*—" In a discourse delivered at
" the primary visitation of the Right Reverend Thomas Lord
" Bishop of Ely.—Cambridge, 1751."   These in my opinion are
sufficient.   But since you desire that I would also take a particular

ticular notice of Mr. Hume's Effay, I fhall obey your commands, and enter on a diftinct confideration of this boafted performance.

Mr. Hume introduceth his *Effay on Miracles* in a very pompous manner, as might be expected from one who fets up in his Philofophical Effays, for teaching men better methods of reafoning than any philofopher had done before him. He had taken care at every turn to let his leaders know how much they are obliged to him for throwing new light on the moft *curious* and *fublime effects*, with regard to which the moft celebrated philofophers had been *extremely defective* in their refearches. And now he begins his *Effay on Miracles* with declaring, that " he " flatters himfelf that he has difcovered an argument, which, if " juft, will, with the wife and learned, be an everlafting check " to all kinds of fuperftitious delufion; and confequently, will " be ufeful as long as the world endures: for fo long," he prefumes, " will the account of miracles and prodigies be found in " all profane hiftory *."

This Effay confifteth of two parts. The firft, which reacheth from p. 173 to p. 186, is defigned to fhew, that no evidence which can be given, however feemingly full and ftrong, can be a fufficient ground for believing the truth and exiftence of miracles: or, in other words, that miracles are in the nature of things incapable of being proved by any evidence or teftimony whatfoever. The fecond part is intended to fhew, that fuppofing a miracle capable of being proved by full and fufficient evidence or teftimony, yet in fact there never was a *miraculous event in any hiftory* eftablifhed upon fuch evidence. The firft is what he feems principally to rely upon: and indeed, if this can be proved, it will make any particular inquiry into the teftimony produced for miracles, needlefs.

The method he makes ufe of in the firft part of his Effay, to fhew, that no evidence or teftimony that can be given is a fufficient ground for a reafonable affent to the truth and exiftence of miracles, is this: He lays it down as an undoubted principle, that experience is our only guide in reafoning concerning matters of fact, and at the fame time infinuates, that this guide is far

* Hume's Philofophical Effays, p. 174.

from

from being infallible, and is apt to lead us into errors and mistakes.   He obferves, that the validity and credibility of human teftimony is wholly founded upon experience: That in judging how far a teftimony is to be depended upon, we balance the oppofite circumftances, which may create any doubt or uncertainty: That the evidence arifing from teftimony may be deftroyed, either by the contrariety and oppofition of the teftimony, or by the confideration of the nature of the facts themfelves: That when the facts partake of the *marvellous* and *extraordinary*, there are two oppofite experiences with regard to them; and that which is the moft credible is to be preferred, though ftill with a diminution of its credibility in proportion to the force of the other which is oppofed to it: That this holdeth ftill more ftrongly in the cafe of miracles, which are fuppofed to be contrary to the laws of nature; for experience being our only guide, and an uniform experience having eftablifhed thofe laws, there muft be an uniform experience againft the exiftence of any miracle: and an uniform experience amounts to a full and entire proof.   To fuppofe therefore any teftimony to be a proof of a miracle, is to fuppofe one full proof for a miracle, oppofed to another full proof in the nature of the thing againft it, in which cafe thofe proofs deftroy one another.   Finally, that we are not to believe any teftimony concerning a miracle, except the falfehood of that teftimony fhould be more miraculous than the miracle itfelf which it is defigned to eftablifh.   He alfo gives a hint, that as it is impoffible for us to know the attributes or actions of God otherwife than from the experience which we have of his productions, we cannot be fure that he can effect miracles, which are contrary to all our experience, and the eftablifhed courfe of nature: and therefore miracles are. impoffible to be proved by any evidence.

Having given this general idea of this firft part of Mr. Hume's Effay on Miracles, I fhall now proceed to a more particular examination of it.

It is manifeft that the main principle, which lieth at the foundation of his whole fcheme, is this: that experience is our only " guide in reafoning concerning matters of fact\*."   You will

* Hume's Philofophical Effays, p. 174.

have

have obferved, from what hath been remarked in my former letters, that this author brings up the word *experience* upon all occafions.   It is, as he hath managed it, a kind of cant term, propofed in a loofe indeterminate way, fo that it is not eafy to
form a clear idea of it, or of what this writer precifely intends by
it.   He had declared, that it is only by experience that we come
to know the exiftence of objects: that it is only by experience
that we know the relation between caufe and effect: and at the
fame time had endeavoured to fhew, that experience cannot furnifh fo much as even a probable argument concerning any connexion betwixt caufe and effect, or by which we can draw any
conclufion from the one to the other.   He had afterwards applied the fame term, experience, to fhew that no argument can
be brought to prove the exiftence of one fupreme intelligent
caufe of the univerfe, becaufe this is *a fubject that lies entirely
beyond the reach of human experience;* and that we can have no
proof of a future ftate of retributions, becaufe we know no more
concerning providence than what we learn from experience in
this prefent ftate.   And now he comes to try the force of this
formidable word againft the exiftence of miracles, and to raife
an argument againft them from experience.

But that we may not lofe ourfelves in the ambiguity of the
term as he employs it, let us diftinctly examine what fenfe it
bears as applied to the prefent queftion.   In judging of the truth
of the maxim he hath laid down, *viz.* that experience is our
only guide in reafoning concerning matters of fact, it is to be
confidered, that the queftion we are now upon properly relates
not to future *events*, as the author feems fometimes to put it*,
but to paft matter of fact.   What are we therefore to underftand
by that experience, which he makes to be our only guide in
reafoning concerning them?   Is it our own particular perfonal
experience, or is it the experience of others, as well as our own?
And if of others, is it the experience of fome others only, or of all
mankind?   If it be underftood thus, that every man's own perfonal obfervation and experience is to be his only guide in reafoning concerning matters of fact; fo that no man is to believe
any thing with relation to any facts whatfoever, but what is
agreeable to what he hath himfelf obferved or known in the courfe

* Hume's Philofophical Effays, p. 175.

of his own particular experience; this would be very abfurd, and
would reduce each man's knowledge of facts into a very narrow
compafs; it would deftroy the ufe and credit of hiftory, and of
a great part of experimental philofophy, and bring us into a ftate
of general ignorance and barbarifm.   Or, is the word *experience*
to be taken in a larger and more extenfive fenfe, as comprehending not merely any particular man's experience, but that of
others too?  In this cafe we have no way of knowing experience,
but by teftimony.   And here the queftion recurs; is it to be
underftood of the experience of all mankind, or of fome perfons
only?  If the experience referred to be the experience or obfervation of fome perfons only, or of a part of mankind, how can this
be depended on as a certain guide?  For why fhould their experience be the guide, exclufively of that of others?  and how do we
know, but that many facts may be agreeable to the experience
of others, which are not to theirs?  But if the experience referred
to be the experience of all mankind in general, that muft take in
the experience both of all men of the prefent age, and of thofe in
paft times and ages, it muft be acknowledged, that this rule
and criterion is not eafily applicable: for will any man fay,
that we are to believe no facts but what are agreeable to the experience of mankind in all ages?  Are we, in order to this, to take
in whatfoever any man or men in any age or country have had
experience of?  and to judge by this how far it is reafonable to
believe any paft fact or facts of which we ourfelves have not had
fenfible evidence?  Even on this view of the cafe, it might probably take in many facts of a very extraordinary nature, and which
have happened out of the common courfe of things; of which
there have been inftances in the experience and obfervation of
different nations and ages.   And at this rate experience will not
be inconfiftent with the belief even of miracles themfelves, of
which there have been feveral inftances recorded in the hiftory
of mankind.

   But farther, in reafoning from experience, either our own or
that of others, concerning matters of fact, it is to be confidered,
what it is that we propofe to judge or determine by experience
in relation to them.   Is it whether thefe facts are poffible, or
whether they are probable, or whether they have been actually
done?   As to the poffibility of facts, experience indeed, or the

*obfervation*

obfervation of fimilar events known to ourfelves or others, may
affure us that facts or events are poffible, but not that the contrary is impoffible. Concerning this, experience cannot decide
any thing at all. We cannot conclude any event to be impoffible, merely becaufe we have had no experience of the like, or
becaufe it is contrary to our own obfervation and experience, or
to the experience of others: for, as this gentleman obferves in
another part of his Effays, " the contrary of every matter of fact
" is ftill poffible; becaufe it can never imply a contradiction*."
And again he fays, fpeaking of matters of fact, " there are no
" demonftrative arguments in the cafe, fince it implies no con-
" tradiction, that the courfe of nature may change†." No argument therefore can be brought to demonftrate any thing or
fact to be impoffible, merely becaufe it is contrary to the courfe
of our own obfervation and experience, and that of mankind,
provided it doth not imply a contradiction, or provided there be
a power capable of effecting it. Another thing to be confidered,
with regard to facts, is, whether they are probable: And here
experience, or the obfervation of fimilar events, made by ourfelves or others, may be of great ufe to affift us in forming a
judgment concerning the probability of paft facts, or in forming
conjectures concerning future ones. But if the queftion be,
Whether an event has actually happened, or a fact has been
done; concerning this, experience, taken from an obfervation of
fimilar events, or the ordinary courfe of caufes and effects, cannot give us any affurance or certainty to proceed upon. We
cannot certainly conclude, that any fact or event has been done,
merely becaufe we or others have had experience or obfervation
of a fact or event of a like nature: nor, on the other hand, can
we conclude, that fuch a certain event hath not happened, or
that fuch a fact hath not been actually done, becaufe we have not
had experience of a like action or event being done, or have had
experience of the contrary being done. The rule, therefore,
which he lays down of judging which fide is fupported by the
greater number of experiments, and of balancing the oppofite
experiments, and deducting the leffer number from the greater,
in order to know the exact force of the fuperior evidence‡, is

*  Hume's Philofophical Effays, p. 48.　†  Ibid. p. 62:　‡  Ibid. p. 176.

*very*

very uncertain and fallacious, if employed in judging whether matters of fact have been really done: for the fact referred to, and the evidence attending it, may be so circumstanced, that though it be a fact of a singular nature, and to which many instances of a different kind may be opposed, we may yet have such an assurance of its having been actually done, as may reasonably produce a sufficient conviction in the mind. The proper way of judging whether a fact or event, of which we ourselves have not had sensible evidence, hath been actually done, is by competent testimony. And this in common language is distinguished from experience, though this writer artfully confounds them.

This therefore is what we are next to consider, *viz.* the force of human testimony, and how far it is to be depended upon.

And with regard to the validity of the evidence arising from human testimony, he observes, that " there is no species of rea-" soning more common, more useful, and even necessary to hu-" man life, than that derived from the testimony of men, and " the reports of eye-witnesses and spectators." The whole certainty or assurance arising from testimony he resolveth into what he calls *past experience*. That " it is derived from no other prin-" ciple than our observation of the veracity of human testimony, " and of the usual conformity of facts to the report of witnesses." And he mentions, as grounds of the belief of human testimony, that " men have commonly an inclination to truth, and a senti-" ment of probity; that they are sensible to shame when detected ".in a falsehood; and that these are qualities discovered by ex-" perience to be inherent in human nature *." But he might have put the case much more strongly, by observing, that human testimony, by the acknowledgment of all mankind, may be so circumstanced, as to produce an infallible assurance, or an evidence so strong, that, as our author expresseth it in another case, none *but a fool or a madman* would doubt of it. It is a little too loose to say in general, that it is *founded only on past experience*. It hath its foundation in the very nature of things, in the constitution of the world and of mankind, and in the appointment of the Author of our being, who it is manifest hath formed and designed us to be in numberless instances determined by this evidence,

* Hume's Philosophical Essays, p. 176, 177.

which

which often comes with fuch force, that we cannot refufe our
affent to it without the greateft abfurdity, and putting a manifeft
conftraint upon our nature\*.　Mr. Hume himfelf, in his Effay
on Liberty and Neceffity, hath run a parallel between moral and
phyfical evidence, and hath endeavoured to fhew that the one is
as much to be depended on as the other.　He exprefsly faith,
that " when we confider how aptly natural and moral evidence
" link together, and form only one chain of argument, we fhall
" make no fcruple to allow, that they are of the fame nature, and
" derived from the fame principles †."

It will be eafily granted, what our author here obferves, that
" there are a number of circumftances to be taken into confider-
" ation in all judgments of this kind: and that we muft balance
" the oppofite circumftances that create any doubt or uncertainty;
" and when we difcover a fuperiority on any fide, we incline to
" it, but ftill with a diminution of affurance in proportion to the
" force of its antagonift ‡."　Among the particulars which may
diminifh or deftroy the force of any argument drawn from human teftimony, he mentions the contrariety of the evidence, contradictions of witneffes, their fufpicious character, &c.: and then
proceeds to take notice of " what may be drawn from the nature
" of the fact attefted, fuppofing it to partake of the extraordinary
" and the marvellous."　He argueth, that " in that cafe the evi-
" dence refulting from the teftimony receives a diminution greater
" or lefs in proportion as the fact is more or lefs unufual.　When
" the fact attefted is fuch a one as has feldom fallen under our
" obfervation, here is a conteft of two oppofite experiences, of
" which the one deftroys the other as far as its force goes; and
" the fuperior can only operate upon the mind by the force which
" remains."　This is a plaufible, but a very fallacious way of
reafoning.　A thing may be very unufual, and yet, if confirmed
by proper teftimony, its being unufual may not diminifh its
credit, or produce in the mind of a thinking perfon a doubt or
fufpicion concerning it.　Indeed vulgar minds, who judge of
every thing by their own narrow notions, and by what they
themfelves have feen, are often apt to reject and difbelieve a

---

\* See concerning this, Ditton on the Refurrection, part. 2.
† Hume's Philofophical Effays, p. 144.　　‡ Ibid. p. 177.

thing,

thing, that is not conformable to their own particular cuftoms or experience.    But wifer men and thofe of more enlarged minds judge otherwife; and, provided a thing comes to them fufficiently atteſted and confirmed by good evidence, make its being unufual no objeſtion at all to its credibility.    Many uncommon faſts, and unufual phænomena of nature, are believed by the moſt fagacious philofophers, and received as true without hefitation, upon the teſtimony of perfons who were worthy of credit, without following the author's rules, or making their own want of experience or obfervation an objeſtion againſt thofe accounts. And upon this dependeth no fmall part of our knowledge.    Mr. Adams hath very well illuſtrated this by feveral inſtances, and hath juſtly obferved, " that the moſt uniform experience is fometimes outweighed by a fingle teſtimony; becaufe experience in this cafe is only a negative evidence, and the flighteſt pofitive teſtimony is for the moſt part an overbalance to the ſtrongeſt negative evidence that can be produced\*."

Our author here very improperly talks of a *conteſt between two oppofite experiences,* the one of which deſtroys the other.    For when I believe a thing unufual, I do not believe a thing oppofite to mine own experience, but different from it, or a thing of which I have had no experience; though if it were a thing contrary to my own experience, provided it were confirmed by fufficient teſtimony, this is not a valid argument againſt its truth, nor a fufficient reafon for difbelieving it.    This gentleman himfelf hath mentioned a remarkable inſtance of this kind in the Indian prince, who refufed to believe the *firſt relations concerning the effects of froſt.*    This inſtance, though he laboureth the point here, and in an additional note at the end of his book, is not at all favourable to his fcheme.    He acknowledgeth, that in this cafe of freezing, the event follows *contrary to the rules of analogy, and is* SUCH AS A RATIONAL INDIAN *would not look for.*    The conſtant experience in thofe countries, according to which the waters are always fluid, and never in a ſtate of hardnefs and folidity, is againſt freezing.    This, according to his way of reafoning, might be regarded as a *proof* drawn from conſtant experience, and the uniform courfe of nature, as far as they

---

\* Adams's Eſſay in anfwer to Hume on Miracles, p. 19, 20.

knew

knew it. Here then is an inftance, in which it is reafonable for men to believe upon good evidence an event no way conformable to their experience, and contrary to the rule of analogy, which he yet feems to make the only rule by which we are to judge of the credibility and truth of facts.

From the confideration of facts that are unufual, he proceeds to thofe that are miraculous, which is what he hath principally in view; and with regard to thefe, he endeavoureth to fhew, that no teftimony at all is to be admitted. " Let us fuppofe," faith he, " that the fact which they affirm, inftead of being only mar-
" vellous, is really miraculous; and fuppofe alfo that the tefti-
" mony, confidered apart, and in itfelf, amounts to an entire
" proof; in that cafe there is proof againft proof, of which the
" ftrongeft muft prevail, but ftill with a diminution of its force
" in proportion to that of its antagonift\*." It may be proper to remark here, that this writer had in a former Effay defined a proof to be *fuch an argument drawn from experience, as leaves no room for doubt or oppofition*†. Admitting this definition, it is improper and abfurd for him to talk of *proof againft proof:* for fince a proof, according to his own account of it, leaves no room for doubt or oppofition; where there is a proper proof of a fact, there cannot be a proper proof at the fame time againft it: for one truth cannot contradict another truth. No doubt his intention is to fignify, that there can be no proof given of a miracle at all, and that the proof is only on the other fide; for he there adds, " A miracle is a violation of the laws of nature; and as a
" firm and unalterable experience hath eftablifhed thofe laws"
[he fhould have faid, hath difcovered to us that thefe are the eftablifhed laws, *i. e.* that this is the ordinary courfe of nature] " the
" proof againft a miracle, from the very nature of the fact, is as
" entire as any argument from experience can poffibly be ima-
" gined." He repeats this again afterward, and obferves, that
" there muft be an uniform experience againft every miraculous
" event, otherwife the event would not merit the appellation;
" and as an uniform experience amounts to a proof, there is
" here a direct and full proof from the nature of the fact, againft
" the exiftence of any miracle‡." He feems to have a very

---

\* Hume's Philofophical Effays, p. 108.　　† Ibid. p. 93.　　‡ Ibid. p. 181.

high opinion of the force of this way of reasoning, and therefore takes care to put his reader again in mind of it in the latter part of his Essay. " 'Tis experience alone," saith he, " which gives " authority to human testimony; and 'tis the same experience " that assures us of the laws of nature. When therefore these " two kinds of experience are contrary, we have nothing to do, " but to substract the one from the other — And this substrac- " tion with regard to all popular religions amounts to an entire " annihilation\*." And it is chiefly upon this that he foundeth the arrogant censure, which, with an unparalleled assurance, he passeth upon all that believe the Christian religion, *viz.* that " whosoever is moved by faith to assent to it, is conscious of a " continued miracle in his own person, which subverts all the " principles of his understanding, and gives him a determination " to believe whatever is most contrary to custom and experi- " ence." It is thus that he concludes his Essay, as if he had for ever silenced all the advocates for Christianity, and they must henceforth either renounce their faith, or submit to pass with men of his superior understanding for persons miraculously stu- pid, and utterly lost to all reason and common sense.

Let us therefore examine what there is in this argument that can support such a peculiar strain of confidence; and I believe it will appear, that never was there weaker reasoning set off with so much pomp and parade.

There is one general observation that may be sufficiently ob- vious to any man, who brings with him common sense and at- tention, and which is alone sufficient to shew the fallacy of this boasted argument; and it is this: That the proof arising from experience, on which he layeth so mighty a stress, amounteth to no more than this, that we learn from it what is conformable to the ordinary course and order of things, but we cannot learn or pronounce from experience that it is impossible things or events should happen in any particular instance contrary to that course. We cannot therefore pronounce such an event, though it be con- trary to the usual course of things, to be impossible; in which case no testimony whatsoever could prove it. And if it be pos- sible, there is place for testimony. And this testimony may be

---

* Hume's Philosophical Essays, p. 202, 203.

fo ftrong and fo circumftanced, as to make it reafonable for us to believe it. And if we have fufficient evidence to convince us that fuch an event hath actually happened, however extraordinary or miraculous, no argument drawn from experience can prove that it hath not happened. I would obferve by the way, that when this gentleman talks of an *uniform experience*, and *a firm and unalterable experience*, againft the exiftence of all miracles, if he means by it fuch an univerfal experience of all mankind as hath never been counteracted in any fingle inftance, this is plainly fuppofing the very thing in queftion, and which he hath no right to fuppofe, becaufe, by his own acknowledgment, mankind have believed in all ages, that miracles have been really wrought. By uniform experience, therefore, in this argument muft be underftood, the general or ordinary experience of mankind in the ufual courfe of things. And it is fo far from being true, as he confidently affirms, that fuch an uniform experience amounts to a *full* and direct *proof*, from the nature of the fact, againft the exiftence of any miracle, that it is no proof againft it at all. Let us judge of this by his own definition of a miracle. " A miracle," faith he, " may be accurately defined, a tranfgref- " fion of a law of nature by a particular volition of the Deity, or " by the interpofal of fome invifible agent." Now our uniform experience affordeth a full and direct proof, that fuch or fuch an event is agreeable to the eftablifhed laws of nature, or to the ufual courfe of things; but it yieldeth no proof at all, that there cannot in any particular inftance happen any event contrary to that ufual courfe of things, or to what we have hitherto experienced; or that fuch an event may not be brought about by a particular volition of the Deity, as our author expreffeth it, for valuable ends worthy of his wifdom and goodnefs.

He cannot therefore make his argument properly bear, except he can prove that miracles are abfolutely impoffible. And this is what he fometimes feems willing to attempt. Thus, fpeaking of fome miracles pretended to have been fully attefted, he afks, " What have we to oppofe to fuch a cloud of witneffes, but " the abfolute impoffibility, or miraculous nature of the event *?" where he feems to make the *miraculous nature* of an event, and

* Hume's Philofophical Effays, p. 195.

Y 2

the *absolute impossibility* of it, to be the same thing. And he
elsewhere makes an attempt to prove, that we have no reason to
think, that God himself can effect a miracle. He urges, that
" though the Being, to whom the miracle is ascribed, be in this
" case Almighty, it does not, upon that account, become a whit
" more probable: since it is impossible for us to know the attri-
" butes or acts of such a Being, otherwise than from the ex-
" perience we have of his productions in the usual course of
" nature\*." But when once we conclude, from the effects in
the works of nature, that he is Almighty, as this gentleman seems
here to grant, we may, from his being Almighty, reasonably
infer, that he can do many things which we do not know that
he hath actually done, and can produce many effects which he
hath not actually produced: for an Almighty Being can do any
thing that doth not imply a contradiction: and it can never be
proved, that a miracle, or an event contrary to the usual course of
nature, implieth a contradiction. This writer himself expressly
acknowledgeth, in a passage I cited before, that " it implies
" no contradiction, that the course of nature may change†:"
and he repeats it again afterwards, that " the course of nature
" may change‡." And as to the extraordinariness of any fact,
he saith, that " even in the most familiar events, the energy of
" the cause is as unintelligible, as in the most extraordinary and
" unusual §." What we call the course of nature is the appointment of God, and the continuance of it dependeth upon his
power and will: it is no more difficult to him to act contrary to
it in any particular instance, than to act according to it. The
one is in itself as easy to Almighty Power as the other. The true
question then is concerning the divine will, whether it can be
supposed that God, having established the course of nature, will
ever permit or order a deviation from that regular course, which
his own wisdom hath established: and with regard to this, it
will be readily granted, that it is highly proper and wisely appointed, that in the ordinary state of things, what are commonly
called the laws of nature should be maintained, and that things
should generally go on in a fixed stated course and order; with-

---

\* Hume's Philosophical Essays, p. 95.　† Ibid. p. 62.
‡ Ibid. p. 66.　§ Ibid. p. 114.

out which there could be no regular study or knowledge of nature, no use or advantage of experience, either for the acquisition of science, or the conduct of life. But though it is manifestly proper, that these laws, or this course of things, should generally take place, it would be an inexcusable presumption to affirm, that God, having established these laws and this course of nature in the beginning, hath bound himself never to act otherwise than according to those laws. There may be very good reasons, worthy of his great wisdom, for his acting sometimes contrary to the usual order of things. Nor can it in that case be justly pretended, that this would be contrary to the immutability of God, which is Spinosa's great argument against miracles: for those very variations, which appear so extraordinary to us, are comprehended within the general plan of his providence, and make a part of his original design. The same infinite wisdom, which appointed or established those natural laws, did also appoint the deviations from them, or that they should be over-ruled on some particular occasions; which occasions were also perfectly foreseen from the beginning by his all-comprehending mind. If things were always to go on without the least variation in the stated course, men might be apt to overlook or question a most wise governing providence, and to ascribe things (as some have done) to a fixed immutable fate or blind necessity, which they call nature. It may therefore be becoming the wisdom of God to appoint, that there should be, on particular occasions, deviations from the usual established course of things. Such extraordinary operations and appearances may tend to awaken in mankind a sense of a Supreme Disposer and Governor of the world, who is a most wise and free as well as powerful Agent, and hath an absolute dominion over nature; and may also answer important ends and purposes of moral government, for displaying God's justice and mercy, but especially for giving attestation to the divine mission of persons, whom he seeth fit to send on extraordinary errands, for instructing and reforming mankind, and for bringing discoveries of the highest importance to direct men to true religion and happiness.

It appeareth then, that no argument can be brought from experience to prove, either that miracles are impossible to the power of God, or that they can never be agreeable to his will; and

therefore

therefore it is far from yielding a direct and full proof against the
exiſtence of miracles.   It may illuſtrate this to conſider ſome of
the inſtances he himſelf mentions.   " Lead cannot of itſelf re-
" main ſuſpended in the air: Fire conſumes wood, and is ex-
" tinguiſhed by water."   Our uniform experience proves, that
this is the uſual and ordinary courſe of things,  and agreeable to
the known laws of nature: it proves, that lead cannot naturally
and ordinarily, or by its own force, be ſuſpended in the air; but
it affordeth  no proof at all,  that it cannot be thus ſuſpended in
a particular inſtance  by the will of God,  or by a ſupernatural
force or power.   In like manner our experience proves, that fire
conſumes wood, in the natural courſe of things; but it yieldeth
no proof, that, in a particular inſtance, the force of fire may not
be ſuſpended or overruled, and the wood preſerved from being
conſumed by the interpoſal of an inviſible agent.   Another inſtance he mentions is, that " it is a miracle that a dead man ſhould
" come to life: becauſe that has never been obſerved in any age
" or country *;"  but its never having been obſerved, if that had
been the caſe, would have furniſhed no proof at all that a dead
man cannot be raiſed to life by the power and will of God, when
a moſt valuable and important end is to be anſwered by it.   And
if we have good evidence to convince us,  that a man had been
really dead, and that that man was afterwards really reſtored to life,
(and this is a matter of fact of which our ſenſes can judge, as
well as of any other fact whatſoever) no argument can be drawn
from experience to prove that it could not be ſo.   Our experience
would indeed afford a proof, that no merely natural human power
could effect it; or that it is a thing really miraculous, and contrary to the uſual courſe of nature: but it would not amount to a
full and direct proof, nor indeed to any proof at all, that it could
not be effected by the divine power.

And now we may judge of the propriety of the inference he
draws from the argument, as he had managed it.   " The plain
" conſequence is," ſaith he, " and it is a general maxim worthy
" of our attention, that no teſtimony is ſufficient to eſtabliſh a
" miracle, unleſs the teſtimony be of ſuch a kind, that its falſe-
" hood would be more miraculous than the fact which it endea-

---

* Hume's Philoſophical Eſſays, p. 181.

" vours

" vours to eftablifh: and even in that cafe, there is a mutual
" deftruction of arguments, and the fuperiority only gives us an
" affurance fuitable to that degree of force, which remains after
" deducting the inferior. When any one tells me, that he faw
" a dead man reftored to life, I immediately confult with myfelf
" whether it be more probable, that this perfon fhould ever de-
" ceive or be deceived, or that the fact he relates fhould really
" have happened: I weigh the one miracle againft the other, and,
" according to the fuperiority which I difcover, I pronounce my
" decifion, and always reject the greater miracle*."

You cannot but obferve here, this writer's jingle upon the
word *miracle*. As he had talked of proof againft proof, fo he
here talks as if in the cafe he is fuppofing there were miracle
againft miracle; or as if the queftion were concerning two extraordinary miraculous facts, the one of which is oppofed to the
other. But whereas in that cafe one fhould think the greater
miracle ought to take place againft the leffer, this gentleman,
with whom miracle and abfurdity is the fame thing, declares that
he always *rejects the greater miracle.* But to quit this poor
jingle, it is allowed, that the raifing a dead man to life muft, if
ever it happened, have been a very fignal miracle; *i. e.* as he de-
fines it, a violation of the law of nature by a particular volition
of the Deity. The queftion therefore is, whether any evidence
is given which may be depended on, to affure us, that however
ftrange or extraordinary this event may be, yet it hath actually
happened. That the thing itfelf is poffible to the Deity, however it be contrary to the ufual courfe of nature, cannot be reafonably contefted: becaufe it cannot be proved to involve a contradiction, or any thing beyond the reach of Almighty Power.
For it would be to the laft degree abfurd to fay, that he who formed
this ftupendous fyftem, or who contrived and fabricated the wonderful frame of the human body, and originally gave it a principle of life, could not raife a dead man to life. It would be a
contradiction, that the fame man fhould be living and dead at
the fame time, but not that he who was dead fhould afterwards be
reftored to life: and therefore if it be the will of God, and his
wifdom and goodnefs feeth it proper for anfwering any very im-

---

* Hume's Philofophical Effays, p. 182.

portant

portant purpofes, he is able to effect it.   But then, whether he
hath actually effected it, is another queſtion : and here it will be
readily owned, that in a cafe of fo extraordinary a nature, the evidence or teſtimony upon which we receive it, ought to be very
ſtrong and cogent.

Mr. Hume is pleafed here to put the cafe in a very loofe and
general way.   " When any one tells me," faith he, " that he faw
" a dead man reſtored to life, I immediately confider with myſelf,
" whether it be more probable that this perfon ſhould either de-
" ceive or be deceived, or that the fact he relates ſhould really
" have happened."  He puts it, as if there was nothing to depend
upon but the teſtimony of a fingle perfon, without any affignable
reafon for fuch an extraordinary event; and when thus propofed, naked of all circumſtances, no wonder that it hath an odd
appearance !   But that we may bring the queſtion to a fair iffue,
let us apply to it what our author without doubt had principally
in his view, the refurrection of our Lord Jefus Chriſt.   Taking
the cafe therefore according to the reprefentation given of it in the
holy Scriptures, let us examine whether, fuppofing all thofe circumſtances to concur which are there exhibited, they do not
amount to a full and fatisfactory evidence, fufficient to lay a juſt
foundation for a reafonable affent to it.   Let us then fuppofe,
that in a feries of writings publiſhed by different perfons in different ages, and all of them inconteſtably written long before
the event happened, a glorious and wonderful perfon was foretold, and defcribed by the moſt extraordinay characters, who
ſhould be fent from heaven to teach and inſtruct mankind, to
guide them in the way of falvation, and to introduce an excellent difpenfation of truth and righteoufnefs : That not only the
nation and family from which he was to fpring, the place of his
birth, and time of his appearing, was diſtinctly pointed out, but
it was foretold that he ſhould endure the moſt grievous fufferings
and death, and that afterwards he ſhould be exalted to a divine dominion and glory, and that the Gentiles ſhould be enlightened
by his doctrine, and receive his law : That accordingly, at the
time which had been fignified in thefe predictions, that admirable
Perfon appeared : That he taught a moſt pure and heavenly doctrine, prefcribed the moſt holy and excellent laws, and brought
the moſt perfect fcheme of religion which had ever been publiſhed

lifhed to the world; and at the fame time exhibited in his own facred life and practice an example of the moft confummate holinefs and goodnefs: That in proof of his divine miffion he performed the moft wonderful works, manifeftly tranfcending the utmoft efforts of all human power or fkill, and this in a vaft number of inftances, and in the moft open and public manner, for a courfe of years together: That he moft clearly and exprefsly foretold, that he was to undergo the moft grievous fufferings, and a cruel and ignominious death, and fhould afterwards rife again from the dead on the third day: And to this he appealed as the moft convincing proof of his divine miffion: That accordingly he fuffered the death of the crofs, in the face of a vaft multitude of fpectators; and notwithftanding the chief men of the Jewifh nation, by whofe inftigation he was crucified, took the moft prudent and effectual precautions to prevent an impofition in this matter, he rofe again from the dead at the time appointed, with circumftances of great glory, in a manner which ftruck terror into the guards who were fet to watch the fepulchre: That afterwards he fhewed himfelf alive to many of thofe who were moft intimately acquainted with him, and who, far from difcovering a too forward credulity, could not be brought to believe it, till they found themfelves conftrained to do fo by the teftimony of all their fenfes: That as a farther proof of his refurrection and exaltation, they who witneffed it were themfelves enabled to perform the moft wonderful miracles in his name, and by power derived from him, and were endued with the moft extraordinary gifts and powers, that they might fpread his religion through the world, amidft the greateft oppofitions and difcouragements: That accordingly this religion, though propagated by the feemingly meaneft and moft unlikely inftruments, and not only deftitute of all worldly advantages, but directly oppofite to the prevailing fuperftitions, prejudices, and vices both of Jews and Gentiles, and though it expofed its publifhers and followers to all manner of reproaches, perfecutions, and fufferings, yet in that very age made the moft furprifing progrefs; in confequence of which the religion of Jefus was eftablifhed in a confiderable part of the world, and fo continueth unto this day.

　Such is the view of the evidence of the refurrection of Jefus; and, taking it altogether, it forms fuch a concatenation of proofs, as is every way fuitable to the importance of the fact, and which was never equalled in any other cafe. To fuppofe all this evidence to have been given in atteftation to a falfehood, involveth in it the moft palpable abfurdities. It is to fuppofe, either that God would employ his own prefcience and power to give teftimony to an impoftor, by a feries of the moft illuftrious prophecies and numerous uncontrolled miracles; or, that good beings, fuperior to man, would extraordinarily interpofe for the fame purpofe, to countenance and derive credit to a perfon falfely pretending to be fent from God, and feigning to act in his name; or, that evil fpirits would ufe all their arts and their power to atteft and confirm a religion, the manifeft tendency of which was to deftroy idolatry, fuperftition, and vice, wherever it was fincerely believed and embraced, and to recover mankind to holinefs and happinefs; which is a contradiction to their very nature and character: It is to fuppofe, that a number of perfons would combine in attefting falfehoods, in favour of a perfon who they knew had deceived them, and of a religion contrary to their moft inveterate and favourite prejudices, and by which they had a profpect of gaining nothing but mifery, reproach, fufferings, and death; which is abfolutely contrary to all the principles and paffions of the human nature: It is to fuppofe, that perfons of the greateft fimplicity and plainnefs would act the part of the vileft impoftors; or, that men who were fo bad, fo falfe, and impious, as to be capable of carrying on a feries of the moft folemn impofitions in the name of God himfelf, would, at the hazard of all that is dear to men, and in manifeft oppofition to all their worldly interefts, endeavour to bring over the nations to embrace a holy and felf-denying inftitution; or, that they were enthufiafts, who were carried away by the heat of their own diftempered brains to imagine, that for a feries of years together the moft extraordinary facts were done before their eyes, though no fuch things were done at all, and that they were themfelves enabled actually to perform the moft wonderful works in the moft open and public manner, though they performed no fuch works: It is to fuppofe, that fuch mad enthufiafts, who were alfo mean and contemptible in their condition, and for the moft part ignorant and illiterate, were not only capable of forming the nobleft fcheme of religion which was ever publifhed to mankind, but were able to overcome all the learn-

ing,

ing, wealth, power, eloquence of the world, all the bigotry and superstition of the nations, all the influence and artifices of the priests, all the power and authority of the magistrates: That they did this by only alledging, that they had a commission in the name of a person who had been crucified, whom they affirmed, but without giving any proof of it, to have been risen from the dead, and to be exalted as the Saviour and Lord of mankind: All this is such a complication of absurdities, as cannot be admitted but upon principles that are absolutely abhorrent to the common sense and reason of men. It were easy to enlarge farther on this subject; but this may suffice at present, especially considering that Mr. Adams hath urged many things to this purpose with great clearness and force, in his answer to Mr. Hume's Essay, p. 31—36 And what is there to oppose to all this? Nothing but the single difficulty of restoring a dead man to life, which is indeed a very extraordinary and miraculous event, but is not above the power of God to effect, and, supposing a good and valid reason can be assigned for it worthy of the divine wisdom and goodness, involveth in it no absurdity at all. And such a reason it certainly was, to give an illustrious attestation to the divine mission of the holy Jesus, and to the divine original of the most excellent dispensation of religion that was ever published among men. To talk, as this author does, of the diminution of the evidence in proportion to the difficulty of the case, is trifling: for the evidence is here supposed to be fully proportioned to the difficulty and importance of the case; since there is both a power assigned every way able to effect it, and a valuable end, which makes it reasonable to think it was becoming the divine wisdom and goodness to interpose for effecting it.

You will perhaps think this may be sufficient with regard to the first part of Mr. Hume's *Essay on Miracles.* In my next I shall endeavour to make it appear, that we have the highest reason to think, that the evidence, which hath been argued to be sufficient if given, was really and actually given: and shall answer the several considerations he hath offered to shew, that supposing miracles capable of being proved by evidence or testimony, yet no evidence was ever actually given for miracles, which can be reasonably depended upon.

# LETTER XIX.

*Reflections on the second Part of Mr. Hume's* Essay on Miracles, *which is designed to shew, that in fact there never was a
miraculous Event established upon such Evidence as can be
depended on—What he offers, concerning the necessary Conditions and Qualifications of Witnesses in the Case of Miracles,
considered—It is shewn, that the Witnesses to the Miracles in
Proof of Christianity had all the Conditions and Qualifications
that can be required to render any Testimony good and valid—
Concerning the Proneness of Mankind in all Ages to believe
Wonders, especially in Matters of Religion—This no Reason
for rejecting all Miracles without farther Examination—The
Miracles wrought in Proof of Christianity not done in an ignorant and barbarous Age—His Pretence, that different Miracles wrought in favour of different Religions destroy one
another, and shew that none of them are true—The Absurdity
of this Way of Reasoning shewn—Instances produced by him
of Miracles well attested, and which yet ought to be rejected as
false and incredible—A particular Examination of what he
hath offered concerning the Miracles attributed to the Abbé de
Paris, and which he pretends much surpass those of our Saviour in Credit and Authority.*

SIR,

I NOW proceed to consider the second part of Mr. Hume's
*Essay on Miracles.* The first was designed to shew, that miracles are incapable of being proved by any evidence whatsoever,
and that no evidence or testimony that could be given, let us
suppose it ever so full and strong, would be a sufficient ground
for believing the truth and existence of miracles. And now in
his second part he proceeds to shew, that supposing a miracle
capable of being proved by full and sufficient evidence or testimony, yet in fact there never was a *miraculous event* in any history established upon such evidence as can reasonably be depended
upon. To this purpose he offereth several considerations. The
first is designed to prove, that no witnesses have ever been pro-

duced

duced for any miracle, which have all the neceſſary conditions and qualifications, to render their teſtimony credible. The ſecond conſideration is drawn from the proneneſs there has been in mankind in all ages to believe wonders; and the more for their being abſurd and incredible; eſpecially in matters of religion; and that therefore in this caſe all men of ſenſe ſhould rejeƈt them without farther examination. His third obſervation is, that they are always found to abound moſt among ignorant and barbarous nations. His fourth obſervation is drawn from the oppoſite miracles wrought in different religions, which deſtroy one another; ſo that there is no miracle wrought, but what is oppoſed by an infinite number of others. He then goes on to give an account of ſome miraculous faƈts which ſeem to be well atteſted, and yet are to be rejeƈted as falſe and incredible. This is the ſubſtance of this part of his Eſſay, which he concludes with an inſolent boaſt, as if he thought he had ſo clearly demonſtrated what he undertook, that no man who had not his *underſtanding* miraculouſly ſubverted could oppoſe it. But I apprehend it will appear, upon a diſtinƈt examination of what he hath offered, that there is little ground for ſuch confident boaſting.

The principal conſideration is that which he hath mentioned in the firſt place, drawn from the want of competent teſtimony to aſcertain the truth of miraculous faƈts. He affirms, " that " there is not to be found in all hiſtory any miracle atteſted by " a ſufficient number of men, of ſuch unqueſtionable good ſenſe, " education, and learning, as to ſecure us againſt all deluſion in " themſelves; of ſuch undoubted integrity, as to place them be- " yond all ſuſpicion of any deſign to deceive others; of ſuch " credit and reputation in the eyes of mankind, as to have a great " deal to loſe in caſe of being deteƈted in any falſehood; and " at the ſame time atteſting faƈts performed in ſuch a public man- " ner and in ſo celebrated a part of the world, as to render the " deteƈtion unavoidable: all which circumſtances are requiſite " to give us a full aſſurance in the teſtimony of men *."

Here he ſuppoſes, that where theſe circumſtances concur, we may have *full aſſurance in the teſtimony of men* concerning the

---

* Hume's Philoſophical Eſſays, p. 183.

faƈts

facts they relate, however extraordinary and unufual. Let us therefore examine the conditions and qualifications he infifts upon, as neceffary to render a teftimony good and valid, and apply them to the teftimony of the witneffes of Chriftianity, and the extraordinary miraculous facts whereby it was confirmed, efpecially that of our Saviour's refurrection.

The firft thing he infifteth upon is, {that the miracle fhould be *attefted by a fufficient number of men.* He hath not told us what number of witneffes he takes to be fufficient in fuch a cafe. In fome cafes very few may be fufficient: yea, a fingle evidence may be fo circumftanced as to produce a fufficient affurance and conviction in the mind, even concerning a fact of an extraordinary nature: though where there is a concurrence of many good witneffes, it is undoubtedly an advantage, and tendeth to give farther force to the evidence. And as to this, Chriftianity hath all the advantages, that can reafonably be defired. All the apoftles were the authorized witneffes of the principal facts by which Chriftianity is attefted: fo were the feventy difciples, and the hundred-and-twenty, mentioned Acts ii. 15. 21, 22. who had been with Jefus from the commencement of his perfonal miniftry to his afcenfion into heaven: to which might be added many others who had feen his illuftrious miracles, as well as heard his excellent inftructions. The accounts of thefe things were publifhed in that very age, and the facts were reprefented as having been done, and the difcourfes as having been delivered, in the prefence of multitudes; fo that in effect they appealed to thoufands in Judea, Jerufalem, and Galilee. It is true, that as to the refurrection of Chrift, this was not a fact done before all the people; but there was a number of witneffes to it, fufficient to atteft any fact. Chrift fhewed himfelf alive after his paffion to feveral perfons at different times; whofe teftimony give mutual fupport and force to one another. He fhewed himfelf alfo to all the apoftles in a body, to feveral other difciples, and at laft to five hundred at once. To which it may be added, that all the extraordinary facts and wonderful works wrought by the apoftles and firft publifhers of Chriftianity, many of which were of a very public nature, and done in the view of multitudes, came in aid of their teftimony.

As

As to the qualifications of the witnesses, the first thing he requireth is, that " they should be of such unquestioned good sense, " education, and learning, as to secure us against all delusion in " themselves." The reason why this gentleman here mentioneth *learning* and *education*, as necessary qualifications in witnesses, is evident. It is undoubtedly with a view to exclude the apostles, who, except St. Paul, appear not to have been persons of education and learning. But no court of judicature, in inquiring into facts, looks upon it to be necessary that the persons giving testimony to the truth of those facts should be persons who had a learned education: it is sufficient, if they appear to be persons of sound sense and honest characters, and that the facts were such as they had an opportunity of being well acquainted with. And thus it was with regard to the first witnesses of Christianity. They were not indeed persons eminent for their learning, knowledge, and experience in the world: if they had been so, this might probably have been regarded as a suspicious circumstance, as if they had themselves laid the scheme, and it was the effect of their own art and contrivance. But they were persons of plain sense, and sound understanding, and perfectly acquainted with the facts they relate. This sufficiently appeareth from their writings, and the accounts they have left us. Their narrations are plain and consistent, delivered in a simple unaffected stile, without any pomp of words, or ostentation of eloquence or literature on the one hand, and on the other without any of the rants of enthusiasm. All is calm, cool, and sedate, the argument of a composed spirit. There is nothing that betrayeth an over-heated imagination: nor do they ever fly out into passionate exclamations, even where the subject might seem to warrant it. The facts they relate were of such a nature, and so circumstanced, that they could not themselves be deceived in them, supposing they had their senses, or be made to believe they were done before their eyes when they were not done. This must be acknowledged as to the facts done during Christ's personal ministry. For they were constantly with him in his going out and coming in, and had an opportunity of observing those facts in all their circumstances for a course of years together; and therefore could be as perfectly assured of them, as any man can be of any facts whatsoever, which he himself hears and sees. And as to his resurrection, they were not

forward

forward rafhly to give credit to it by an enthufiaftic heat: they examined it fcrupuloufly, and would not receive it, till compelled by irrefiftible evidence, and by the teftimony of all their fenfes.

The next thing he infifteth upon is, that " the witneffes fhould " be of fuch undoubted integrity, as to place them beyond all " fufpicion of any defign to deceive others." Apply this to the witneffes of the miraculous facts whereby Chriftianity was attefted, and it will appear, that never were there perfons who were more remote from all reafonable fufpicion of fraud, or a defign to impofe falfehoods upon mankind. They appeared by their whole temper and conduct to be perfons of great probity and unaffected fimplicity, ftrangers to artful cunning, and the refinements of human policy. It mightily ftrengthens this when it is confidered, that, as the cafe was circumftanced, they could have no temptation to endeavour to impofe thefe things upon the world if they had not been true, but had the ftrongeft inducements to the contrary. They could have no profpect of ferving their worldly intereft, or anfwering the ends of ambition, by preaching up a religion, contrary to all the prevailing paffions and prejudices of Jews and Gentiles, a principal article of which was falvation through a crucified Jefus. They could fcarce have had a reafonable expectation of gaining fo much as a fingle profelyte, to fo abfurd and foolifh a fcheme, as it muft have been, fuppofing they had known that all was falfe, and that Jefus had never rifen at all. How could it have been expected in fuch a cafe, that they fhould be able to perfuade the Jews to receive for their Meffiah, one that had been put to an ignominious death by the heads of their nation, as an impoftor and deceiver? or, that they fhould perfuade the Gentiles to acknowledge and worfhip a crucified Jew for their Lord, in preference to their long-adored deities, and to abandon all their darling fuperftitions for a ftrict and felf-denying difcipline? The only thing that can be pretended as a poffible inducement to them, to endeavour to impofe upon mankind, is what this writer afterwards mentions. " What greater " temptation," faith he, " than to appear a miffionary, a prophet, " and ambaffador from heaven? Who would not encounter many " dangers and difficulties, to attain fo fublime a character? or, " if perfuaded of it himfelf, would fcruple a pious fraud in prof-
" pect

" pest of so holy an end * ?"   But there is no room for such a
suspicion in the case we are now considering.   If they had pretended a revelation in favour of a Messiah, suited to the Jewish
carnal notions and prejudices, who was to erect a mighty worldly
dominion, arrayed with all the pomp of secular glory and grandeur,
they might have expected honour and applause in being looked
upon as his ministers.  But what honour could they propose, from
being regarded as the disciples and apostles of one that had been
condemned, and put to a shameful death by public authority?
To set up as his ambassadors, and pretend to be inspired by his
spirit, and to be commissioned by him to go through the world,
preaching up Jesus Christ, and him crucified; this was in all
appearance the readiest way they could take to expose themselves
to general scorn, derision, and reproach: and they must have been
absolutely out of their senses, to have expected, that any veneration should be paid to them under this character, supposing they
had no other proof to bring of their crucified master's being risen,
and exalted in glory as the universal Lord and Saviour, but their
own word.   Thus it appears, that they could have no inducements or temptations, according to all the principles or motives
that usually work upon the human mind, to attempt to impose
this scheme of religion, and the facts by which it was supported,
if they had known them to be false: and if they had been false,
they must have known them to be so.   But this is not all.   They
had the strongest possible inducements to the contrary.   The
scheme of religion they preached, and which these facts were designed to attest, was directly opposite to their own most rooted
prejudices.   On the supposition of Christ's not having risen,
they must have been sensible that he had deceived them; that the
promises and predictions with which he had amused them were
false; and that consequently they could have no hopes from him,
either in this world or in the next.   At the same time they could
not but foresee, that by pretending he was risen from the dead,
and setting him up for the Messiah after he had been crucified,
they should incur the indignation of the body of their own nation,
and the hatred and contempt of those in chief authority among
them.   They could not possibly expect any thing but what they

* Hume's Philosophical Essays, p. 200.

met with, perfecutions, reproaches, fhame, and fufferings, both from Jews and Gentiles. Their expofing themfelves to thefe things may be accounted for, if they were perfuaded that what they witneffed was really true, though even in that cafe it required great virtue and conftancy, and divine fupports. But that they fhould, in manifeft oppofition to their own religious prejudices and worldly interefts, without the leaft profpect of any thing to be gained by it here or hereafter, perfift to the very death in attefting a faifehood, known by themfelves to be fo; and that they fhould, for the fake of one who they knew had deceived them, expofe themfelves to the greateft evils and fufferings, to which all men have naturally the ftrongeft averfion, is a fuppofition that cannot be admitted with the leaft appearance of reafon, as being abfolutely fubverfive of all the principles and paffions of human nature. Our author ought to acknowledge the force of this reafoning, fince he taketh pains throughout his whole Effay on Liberty and Neceffity, to fhew, that we may in many cafes argue as furely and ftrongly from the power and influence of motives on the human mind, as from the influence of phyfical caufes; and that there is as great a certainty, and as neceffary a connexion in what are called moral caufes as in phyfical. This author undoubtedly in that effay carrieth it too far, when, in order to fubvert human liberty, he would have it thought, that in all cafes the power of motives worketh with as neceffary a force upon the mind, as any phyfical caufe doth upon the effect. But that in many particular cafes things may be fo circumftanced with regard to moral caufes, as to afford a certainty equal to what arifes from phyfical, cannot reafonably be denied. And fuch is the cafe here put. And he exprefsly declareth, that " we " cannot make ufe of a more convincing argument than to prove, " that the actions afcribed to any perfon are contrary to the courfe " of nature, and that no human motives in fuch circumftances " could ever induce them to fuch a conduct *."

This writer further requireth, that " the witneffes fhould be " of fuch credit and reputation in the eyes of mankind as to have " a great deal to lofe in cafe of being detected in any falfehood." If the meaning be, that they muft be perfons diftinguifhed by

---

* Hume's Philofophical Effays, p. 135.

their

their rank and fituation in the world, and of great reputation for
knowledge, and for the eminency of their ftation and figure in
life; this in the cafe here referred to would, inftead of ftrengthening, have greatly weakened the force of their teftimony. It might
have been faid, with fome fhew of plaufibility, that fuch perfons,
by their knowledge and abilities, their reputation and intereft,
might have it in their power to countenance and propagate an
impofture among the people, and give it fome credit in the
world. If the facts recorded in the gofpel, the miracles and
refurrection of Jefus Chrift, had been patronized and attefted
by the chief priefts and rulers of the Jewifh nation, it would undoubtedly have been pretended, that they had political defigns in
view, and that, confidering their authority and influence, they
might more eafily impofe thofe things upon the multitude. On
this view of things, the evidence for thofe important facts would
have been far lefs convincing than now it is. And therefore
the Divine wifdom hath ordered it far better, in appointing that
the firft witneffes of the gofpel were not the worldly *wife, mighty*,
or *noble*, but perfons of mean condition, and yet of honeft characters, without power, authority, or intereft. And whereas
this writer urgeth, that the witneffes ought to be of *fuch reputation as to have a great deal to lofe in cafe of being detected in
a falfehood*, it ought to be confidered, that a man of true probity, though in a low condition, may be as unwilling to be brand-
ed as a cheat and an impoftor, and as defirous to preferve his
good name, which may be almoft all he has to value himfelf upon,
as perfons of greater figure and eminence in the world, who may
more eafily find means to fupport themfelves, and to evade detection and punifhment. The apoftles indeed rejoiced that they
were counted *worthy to fuffer fhame for the name of Chrift*, Acts
v. 41. But this was not owing to their being infenfible to fhame,
but to the teftimony of a good confcience, and to the full perfuafion they had of Chrift's divine miffion, and the divinity of
the religion they preached in his name. This particularly was
the principle upon which St. Paul acted, who was a man of reputation among the Jews, and would never have made a facrifice of this, and of all his worldly interefts and expectations, to
join himfelf to a defpifed perfecuted party, and againft whom he
himfelf had conceived the ftrongeft prejudices, if he had not

Z 2

been

been brought over, by an evidence which he was not able to
refift, to the acknowledgment of the Chriftian faith, and of the
extraordinary facts on which it was eftablifhed.

The laft thing he infifteth upon is, that the facts attefted by
the witneffes fhould be " performed in fuch a public manner,
" and in fo celebrated a part of the world, as to render the detec-
" tion unavoidable." This may be applied with the greateft propriety to the extraordinary and miraculous facts by which Chriftianity was attefted. Juftly doth St. Paul appeal to King Agrippa,
in the admirable apology he made before him and the Roman
Governor, Feftus, and which was delivered before a numerous
and auguft affembly of Jews and Romans, that *none of thefe
things were hidden from him: for*, faith he, *this thing was not
done in a corner*, Acts xxvi. 26. Chrift's whole perfonal miniftry, and the wonderful works he wrought, were tranfacted
not in a private and fecret, but in the moft open and public manner poffible, in places of the greateft concourfe, and before
multitudes of people affembled from all parts. The fame may
be faid of many of the miracles wrought by the apoftles in the
name and by the power of a rifen Jefus: and particularly never
was there any event of a more public nature than the extraordinary effufion of the Holy Ghoft on the day of Pentecoft. The
firft publifhers of Chriftianity preached the religion of Jefus, and
performed miracles in confirmation of it, not merely in fmall
villages, or obfcure parts of the country, but in populous cities,
in thofe parts of the world that were moft celebrated for the liberal arts, learning and politenefs. They publifhed their religion, and the wonderful facts by which it was fupported, throughout the Leffer Afia, Greece, Italy; in the cities of Jerufalem,
Antioch, Ephefus, Corinth, Theffalonica, Philippi, Athens, and
Rome itfelf. If therefore their pretences had been falfe, they
could fcarce have poffibly efcaped a detection: efpecially confidering that they were every-where under the eye of watchful
adverfaries, unbelieving Jews as well as heathens, who would
not have failed to detect and expofe the impofture, if there had
been any. As to what the author afterward allegeth, that " in
" the infancy of new religions the wife and learned commonly
" efteem the matter too inconfiderable to deferve their attention
" and regard; and when afterwards they would willingly de-
" tect

" teft the cheat, in order to undeceive the deluded multitude,
" the feafon is now gone, and the records and witnelfes, who
" might clear up the matter, are perilhed beyond recovery*;"
this pretence hath no place in the cafe we are now confidering with regard to Chriftianity. That religion met with the
greateft oppofition even in its infancy. Perfons of principal
authority in the nation where it firft arofe, bent their attention, and employed their power, to fupprefs it. And in all places
where it was afterwards propagated, there were unbelieving
Jews, who ufed their utmoft efforts to ftir up the heathens againft
it, who of themfelves were ftrongly inclined by their own prejudices to oppofe it : and this at the very time when, if the facts
had been falfe, it would have been the eafieft thing in the world
to have detected the falfehood; which in that cafe muft have been
known to thoufands: fince many of the facts appealed to were
of a very public nature.

Thus I have confidered the conditions and qualifications he
infifteth upon, as neceffary to give us a *full affurance in the teftimony of men* with regard to miracles; and have fhewn, that all
the conditions that can be reafonably defired, concur, with the
higheft degree of evidence, in the teftimony given by the apoftles
and firft witneffes of Chriftianity, to the extraordinary facts
whereby its divine authority was eftablifhed. Their teftimony
had fome advantages which no other teftimony ever had. St.
Luke obferves, that *with great power gave the apoftles witnefs
of the refurrection of the Lord Jefus,* Acts iv. 33. The teftimony they gave was accompanied with a Divine power. The
force of their teftimony did not depend merely on their own
veracity, but may be faid to have been confirmed by the atteftation of God himfelf. It is with the utmoft propriety therefore,
that the facred writer of the Epiftle to the Hebrews reprefenteth
God, as *bearing them witnefs, both with figns and wonders, and
with divers miracles and gifts of the Holy Ghoft, according to his
own will,* Heb. ii. 4. And it is inconteftably true in fact, that
fo ftrong and convincing was the evidence, that great numbers
both of Jews and Gentiles were brought over in that very age
to the faith of a crucified and rifen Saviour. Nor was this the

---

* Hume's Philofophical Effays, p. 202.

effect

effect of a too forward credulity, since it was in direct opposition
to their prejudices, passions, and worldly interests. The principles and inducements which usually lead men to form wrong
and partial judgments, lay wholly on the other side, and, instead
of being favourable to Christianity, tended rather to determine
men to disbelieve and reject it. So that it may be justly said,
that the propagation of that scheme of religion which is held forth
in the gospel had something in it so wonderful, taking in all the
circumstances of the case, that it affordeth a manifest and most
convincing proof of the truth of the extraordinary facts upon
which it was founded.

I now proceed to make some observations upon the other considerations this gentleman offers in this second part of his essay;
and which indeed can at best pass for no more than presumptions;
and only shew, that the testimony given to miracles is not rashly
to be admitted, and that great care and caution is necessary in
judging of them, which will be easily allowed.

The second consideration, and upon which he seems to lay a
great stress, is this: that " we may observe in human nature a
" principle, which, if strictly examined, will be found to dimi-
" nish extremely the assurance we might have from human tes-
" timony in any kind of prodigy." He says, " that though for
" the most part we readily reject any fact that is unusual and in-
" credible in an ordinary degree, yet when any thing is affirmed
" utterly absurd and miraculous, the mind rather more readily
" admits such a fact, upon account of that very circumstance,
" which ought to destroy all its authority. The passion of *sur-
" prise* and *wonder* arising from miracles, being an agreeable
" emotion, gives a sensible tendency towards the belief of those
" events from which it is derived ------ But if the spirit of religion
" join itself to the love of wonder, there is an end of common
" sense; and human testimony in these circumstances loses all
" pretensions to authority\*." And again he observes, that
" should a miracle be ascribed to any new system of religion,
" men in all ages have been so much imposed on by the ridicu-
" lous stories of this kind, that this very circumstance will be
" a full proof of a cheat, and sufficient with all men of sense,

---

\* Hume's Philosophical Essays, 184, 185.

" not

" not only to make them reject the fact, but even reject it with-
" out farther examination." And he repeats it again, that it
" should make us form a general refolution never to lend any
" attention to it, with whatever fpecious pretext it may be
" covered *." He here undertaketh to anfwer for all *men of
fenfe*, that they will reject all miracles produced in proof of religion without farther examination; becaufe men in all ages have
been much impofed on by ridiculous ftories of this kind.   But
this certainly is the language, not of reafon and good fenfe,
which will difpofe a man fairly to examine, but of the moft obftinate prepoffeffion and prejudice.   No kinds of hiftorical facts,
whether of an ordinary or extraordinary nature, can be mentioned,
in which men have not been frequently impofed upon.   But this
is no juft reafon for rejecting fuch facts at once without examination: and the man that would do fo, inftead of proving his
fuperior good fenfe, would only render himfelf ridiculous.   That
there have been many falfe miracles will be readily acknowledged; but this doth not prove that there never have been any true
ones.   It ought indeed to make us very cautious, and to examine miracles carefully before we receive them; but it is no reafon at all, or a very abfurd one, for rejecting them all at once
without examination and inquiry.   Thus to reject them can only
be juftified upon this principle, that it is not poffible there fhould
be a true miracle wrought in favour of any fyftem of religion.
But by what medium will he undertake to prove this? He feems
exprefsly to admit, that in other cafes, " there may poffibly be
" miracles, or violations of the ufual courfe of nature, of fuch
" a kind as to admit of proof from human teftimony *." This
conceffion is not very confiftent with what he had laboured in
the firft part of his effay to fhew, with regard to all miracles in
general, *viz.* that they are incapable of being proved by any
teftimony.   But now, provided miracles be not produced in
proof of religion, he feems willing to allow, that they may *poffibly admit of proof from human teftimony.* The only cafe therefore in which they are never to be believed, is when they are
pretended to be wrought in favour of religion.   But in this he
feems to have both the reafon of the thing, and the general fenfe

---

* Hume's Philofophical Effays, p. 204, 205.          Ibid. p. 203.

of

of mankind, againſt him. It is certainly more reaſonable to believe a miracle, when a valuable end can be aſſigned for it, than
to believe it when we cannot diſcern any important end to be
anſwered by it at all. And one of the moſt valuable ends for
which a miracle can be ſuppoſed to be wrought ſeems to be this,
to give an atteſtation to the divine miſſion of perſons ſent to inſtruct mankind in religious truths of great importance, and to
lead them in the way of ſalvation. Our author ſeems ſometimes
to lay a mighty ſtreſs on the general opinion and common *ſentiments* of mankind\*." And there are few notions, which, by his
own acknowledgment, have more generally obtained in all nations and ages, than this, that there have been miracles actually
wrought on ſome occaſions, eſpecially in matters of religion,
and that they are to be regarded as proofs of a divine interpoſition. This is a principle which ſeems to be conformable to the
natural ſenſe of the human mind.

The obſervation he makes concerning the *agreeable emotion*
produced by the *paſſion of wonder and ſurprize,* and the ſtrong
propenſity *there is in mankind to the extraordinary and the marvellous,* proves nothing againſt this principle. The paſſion of
wonder and ſurprize was certainly not given us in vain, but for
very wiſe purpoſes; and it may be preſumed, that this paſſion, as
well as others, may be rightly exerciſed upon proper objects.
But I cannot agree with this gentleman, that men are naturally
diſpoſed and inclined to believe a thing the rather for its being
*utterly abſurd and miraculous,* eſpecially in matters of religion.
They may indeed, and often do, believe abſurdities; but they
never believe a thing merely becauſe it is abſurd, but becauſe,
taking all conſiderations together, they do not look upon it to be
abſurd. It may be obſerved by the way, that this writer here
makes *abſurd* and *miraculous* to be terms of the ſame ſignification,
whereas they are very different ideas. A miracle, when ſuppoſed to be wrought by a power adequate to the effect, and for
excellent ends, is indeed wonderful, but has no abſurdity in it at
all. It is true, there have often been very abſurd things recommended to popular belief under the notion of miracles; and ſuch
pretended miracles have been received without much examina-

---

\* Hume's Eſſays, moral and political, p. 307.

tion,

tion, when wrought in favour of the eſtabliſhed ſuperſtition. But
even real miracles are received with difficulty, when they are
wrought in oppoſition to it; and where the influence of the
prieſthood, the prejudices of the vulgar, and the authority of the
magiſtrate, are on the one ſide; which was the caſe of Chriſtianity
at its firſt appearance. Conſidering the nature of that religion,
how contrary it was to the prevailing notions and prejudices
both of Jews and Gentiles, the ſtrictneſs of the morals it preſcribed, the ſcheme of ſalvation through a crucified Saviour
which it propoſed, the meanneſs of the inſtruments by which it
was propagated, and the numberleſs difficulties it had to encounter with; the miracles wrought in atteſtation of it could not have
met with a favourable reception in the world, if there had not been
the moſt convincing evidence of their being really wrought. The
ſtrangeneſs of the facts, inſtead of producing belief, would rather have turned to its diſadvantage, and could ſcarce have failed
being detected in ſuch circumſtances, if they had been falſe.

His third obſervation is, that it " forms a very ſtrong preſump-
" tion againſt all ſupernatural relations, that they are always found
" chiefly to abound among ignorant and barbarous nations; or
" if a civilized people have ever given admiſſion to any of
" them, they have received them from ignorant and barbarous
" anceſtors\*." But no preſumption can be drawn from this to
the prejudice of Chriſtianity, which did not make its appearance
in an ignorant and barbarous age, but at a time when the world
was greatly civilized, and in nations where arts and learning had
made a very great progreſs. And it muſt be conſidered, that it
had not only their inveterate prejudices, their darling paſſions,
and inclinations, but their pretended miracles to encounter with;
extraordinary facts received from their anceſtors, who *tranſmitted them,* as he expreſſeth it, *with that inviolable ſanction and
authority, which always attends ancient and received opinions.*
How ſtrong and cogent therefore muſt the force of the evidence
in behalf of the Chriſtian religion, and the extraordinary miraculous facts deſigned to ſupport it, have been, which, in the hands
of ſuch mean inſtruments, could make ſo great a progreſs in a

---

\* Hume's Philoſophical Eſſays, p. 186, 187.

civilized

civilized and enlightened age, and prove too hard for the religion of the empire; which, besides its being interwoven with the
civil establishment, had the prescription of many ages to plead,
and was supported by pretended miracles, prodigies, and oracles!
Mr. Hume is pleased to take notice on this occasion of the management of that cunning impostor, Alexander*. But though,
the better to carry on the cheat, he had laid the scene among the
barbarous Paphlagonians, who were reckoned among the most
stupid and ignorant of the human race; and not only put in
practice all the arts of imposture (though it doth not appear, that
he pretended to work miracles among the people, or put the
proof of his authority upon them), but had procured a powerful
interest among the great to support him, he and his impostures
soon sunk into oblivion, and so undoubtedly would Christianity
too have done, if its extraordinary facts had no better foundation
in truth and fact than his pretensions had.

" I may add," saith he, " as a fourth reason which diminishes
" the authority of prodigies, that there is no testimony for any,
" even those which have not been expressly detected, that is not
" opposed by an infinite number of witnesses; so that not only
" the miracle destroys the credit of the testimony, but even the
" testimony destroys itself." He goes on to observe, that " in
" matters of religion, whatever is different is contrary: that it is
" impossible that all these different religions should be established
" on a solid foundation: that every miracle pretended to have
" been wrought in any of these religions, as it is designed to
" establish that particular system, has the same force to over-
" throw every other system; and consequently to destroy the
" credit of those miracles on which that system was established.
" So that all the prodigies of different religions are to be regard-
" ed as contrary facts, and the evidences of these prodigies as
" opposite to one another†." This writer is here pleased to confound *prodigies* and *miracles*, which ought to be distinguished.
Many things that have passed under the notion of prodigies,
are very far from being miracles, in the strict and proper sense
in which we are now considering them: and if we speak of

* Hume's Philosophical Essays, p. 188, 189.    † Ibid. p. 190, 191.

miracles

miracles properly fo called, the fuppofition he here goes upon,
*viz.* that all religions have been founded upon miracles, and
have put the proof of their authority upon them, is manifeftly
falfe.     It is well known, that Mahomet did not pretend to
eftablifh his religion by miracles; nor indeed can it be proved,
that any fyftems of religion had any tolerable pretenfion of being
originally founded upon miracles, but the Jewifh and the Chriftian;
and thefe, though in fome refpects *different*, are not *contrary*, but
mutually fupport each other; the former being introductive and
preparatory to the latter.     But if his fuppofition fhould be admitted, that all religions in the world have been founded upon
the credit of miracles, it is hard to comprehend, the force of his
reafoning.     By what logic doth it follow, that becaufe miracles
have been believed by mankind in all ages and nations to have
been wrought in proof of religion, therefore miracles were never
really wrought at all in proof of religion, nor are they ever to be
believed in any fingle inftance?  With the fame force it may be
argued, that becaufe there have been and are many oppofite
fchemes of religion in the world, therefore their being oppofite
to one another proves that they are all falfe, and that there is no
fuch thing as true religion in the world at all.     But let us fuppofe
ever fo great a number of falfehoods oppofed to truth, that oppofition of falfehood to truth doth not make truth to be lefs true,
or deftroy the certainty and evidence of it.     Suppofing the religions to be oppofite, and that miracles are faid to be wrought
in atteftation of thofe oppofite religions, it may indeed be fairly
concluded that they cannot be all true, but not that none of them
is fo.     Our author himfelf feems to be apprehenfive, that this
might be looked upon as a fallacious way of reafoning.     " This
" argument," fays he, " may appear very fubtile and refined; but
" is not in reality different from the reafoning of a judge, who
" fuppofes, that the credit of two witneffes, maintaining a crime
" againft any one, is deftroyed by the teftimony of two others,
" who affirm him to have been two hundred leagues diftant at
" the fame inftant when the crime is faid to have been commit-
" ted *.  This gentleman has here given us a moft extraordinary
fpecimen how well qualified he would be to determine caufes if

---

* Hume's Philofophical Effays, p. 192.

he

he fat in a court of judicature. If there came feveral witneffes before him, and their teftimony was oppofite to one another, he would without farther examination rejeçt them all at once, and make their oppofition to one another to be alone a proof that they were all falfe, and none of them to be depended upon. But it hath been hitherto thought reafonable, when teftimonies are oppofite, to weigh and compare thofe teftimonies, in order to form a proper judgment concerning them. In cafe of *alibi's*, which is the cafe the author here puts, the teftimonies do not always deftroy one another. A juft and impartial judge will not immediately rejeçt the teftimonies on both fides without examination, becaufe they contradiçt one another, which is the method our author feems here to recommend as reafonable, but will carefully compare them, that he may find out on which fide the truth lies, and which of the teftimonies is moft to be credited, and will give his judgment accordingly. This certainly is the courfe which right reafon prefcribeth in all cafes, where there is an oppofition of teftimony, and which it is to be prefumed this gentleman himfelf would recommend in every cafe, but where the caufe of religion is concerned. For here, notwithstanding all his pretenfions to freedom of thinking, his prejudices are fo ftrong, that he is for proceeding by different weights and meafures from what he and all mankind would judge reafonable in every other inftance. He hath fhewed himfelf fo little qualified to judge impartially in matters of this nature, that I believe *men of fenfe*, to ufe his own phrafe, will lay very little ftrefs on any judgment he fhall think fit to pronounce in this caufe.

The only part of Mr. Hume's *Effay on Miracles* which now remaineth to be confidered, is that which relates to fome particular accounts of miraculous façts, which he would have us believe are as well or better attefted, than thofe recorded in the Gofpels, and yet are to be rejeçted as falfe and incredible. The firft inftance he mentioneth is that of the Emperor Vefpafian's curing a blind and a lame man at Alexandria, and which he affirms is one of the beft attefted miracles in all profane hiftory. This has been urged by almoft every deiftical writer who hath treated of miracles; and how little it is to the purpofe in the prefent controverfy hath been often fhewn. Not to repeat what Mr. Adams hath well urged concerning it, it may be fufficient to obferve,

that

that it appeareth from the accounts given us by the hiſtorians who
mention it *, that the deſign of theſe miracles was to give weight
to the authority of Veſpaſian, newly made Emperor by the great
men and the army, and to make it be believed that his elevation to
the imperial throne was approved by the gods. I believe every
reaſonable man will be of opinion, that in any caſe of this kind
there is great ground to ſuſpect artifice and management. And
who would be ſo preſumptuous as to make too narrow a ſcru-
tiny into the truth of miracles, in which the intereſts of the great,
and the authority of a mighty Emperor, were ſo nearly concerned? And if, as this writer obſerves from Tacitus, ſome who
were preſent continued to relate theſe facts, even after Veſpaſian
and his family were no longer in poſſeſſion of the empire; it doth
not appear, that the perſons referred to were ſuch as had been in
the ſecret of the management, which probably lay in few hands;
or if they were, it is not to be wondered at that they ſhould afterwards be unwilling to own the part they had in this affair; eſpecially ſince no methods were made uſe of to oblige them to diſ-
cover the fraud.

The next inſtance he produceth is the miracle pretended to
have been wrought at Saragoſſa, and mentioned by Cardinal De
Retz, who, by Mr. Hume's own account, did not believe it.
But certainly a man muſt have his head very oddly turned, to attempt to draw a parallel between the miracles of our Saviour
and his apoſtles, and miracles pretended to have been wrought
in a country where the inquiſition is eſtabliſhed, where the influence and intereſts of the prieſts, the ſuperſtitions and prejudices of the people, and the authority of the civil magiſtrate, are
all combined to ſupport the credit of thoſe miracles, and where
it would be extremely dangerous to make a ſtrict inquiry into the
truth of them; and even the expreſſing the leaſt doubt concerning them might expoſe a man to the moſt terrible of all evils
and ſufferings.

But that which Mr. Hume ſeems to lay the greateſt ſtreſs upon,
and on which he enlarges for ſome pages together, is, the miracles reported to have been wrought at the tomb of the Abbé de
Paris. Having obſerved, that in the *Recueil des Miracles de*

---

* Tacit. Hiſt. lib. 4. verſus finem.     Sueton. in Veſpaſ. cap. 8.

*l'Abbé*

*l'Abbé de Paris*, there is a parallel run between the miracles of
our Saviour and those of the Abbé, he pronounces, that " if the
" inspired writers were to be considered merely as human testi-
" mony, the French author is very moderate in his comparison,
" since he might with some appearance of reason pretend, that
" the Jansenist miracles much surpass the others in credit and
" authority *."

This has been of late a favourite topic with the deists. Great
triumphs have been raised upon it, as if it were alone sufficient
to destroy the credit of the miraculous facts recorded in the New
Testament. I shall therefore make some observations upon it,
though in doing so I shall be obliged to take notice of several
things which Mr. Adams hath already observed, in his judicious
reflections upon this subject, in his answer to Mr. Hume's *Essay
on Miracles*, from page 65 to page 78.

The account Mr. Hume pretends to give of this whole affair
is very unfair and disingenuous, and is absolutely unworthy of
any man that makes pretensions to a free and impartial inquiry.
He positively asserts, that the miraculous facts were so strongly
proved, that the Molinists or Jesuits were never able distinctly to
refute or detect them; and that they could not deny the truth of
the facts, but ascribed them to witchcraft and the devil. Yet
certain it is, that the Jesuits or Molinists did deny many of the
facts to be true as the Jansenists related them; that they asserted
them to be false, and plainly proved several of them to be so.
Particularly the Archbishop of Sens distinctly insisted upon
twenty-two of those pretended miraculous facts, all which he
charged as owing to falsehood and imposture.

He farther observes, that twenty-two of the Curés or Rectors
of Paris pressed the Archbishop of Paris to examine those miracles, and asserted them to be known to the whole world. But
he knew, or might have known, that some of those very miracles which those gentlemen desired might be particularly inquired
into, and which they represented as undeniably true and certain,
were afterwards examined, and the perjury of the principal
witnesses plainly detected †. And the Archbishop, who, he tells

* Hume's Philosophical Essays, p. 196.
† See Mr. des Voeux's Critique Generale, p. 242, 243.

us,

us, wifely forbore an inquiry, caufed a public judicial inqueft to be made, as Mr. Adams obferves, and in an ordonnance of November 8, 1735, publifhed the moft convincing proofs, that the miracles fo ftrongly vouched by the Curés, were forged and counterfeited[*].

Mr. Hume is pleafed to obferve, that "the Molinift party "tried to difcredit thofe miracles in one inftance, that of Made-"moifelle le Franc, but were not able to do it:" where he fpeaks, as if this were the fingle inftance in which they tried to difcredit thofe miracles, which is far from being true. This indeed was taken particular notice of, becaufe it was the firft hiftory of a miraculous faft which the Janfenifts thought fit to publifh, with a pompous differtation prefixed. It was cried up as of fuch unqueftionable truth, that it could not be denied without doubting of the moft certain facts: and yet the ftory was proved to be falfe in the moft material circumftances, by forty witneffes judicially examined upon oath. It was plainly proved, that fhe was confiderably better of her maladies before fhe went to the tomb at all: that fhe was no ftronger when fhe returned from the tomb than fhe was when fhe went to it: and that fhe ftill ftood in need of remedies afterwards. Mr. Hume indeed takes upon him to declare, that the proceedings were the moft irregular in the world, particularly in citing but a few of the Janfenift witneffes, whom they tampered with: and then he adds, "befides they were foon overwhelmed with a cloud of new wit-"neffes, an hundred and twenty in number, who gave oath "for the miracles." He doth not fay, they all gave oath for this particular miracle, but for the miracles: and indeed moft of thofe teftimonies were very little to the purpofe, and feemed to be defigned rather for parade and fhow than for proof; and nothing turned more to the difadvantage of the Janfenifts, and their endeavouring ftill to maintain the credit of this miracle, after the falfehood of it had been fo evidently detected: the more witneffes they endeavoured to produce for this, the more they rendered themfelves fufpected in all the reft. They alleged fome want of formality in the proceedings, but were never able to difprove the principal circumftances of the facts alleged on the

[*] Adams's Effay, p. 71.

other

other fide, and which were absolutely inconsistent with the truth
and reality of the miracle *.

Mr. Hume refers his reader to the *Recueil des Miracles de*
*l'Abbé Paris*, in three volumes: but especially to the famous
book of Mr. de Montgeron, a counsellor or judge of the parlia-
ment of Paris, and which was dedicated to the French King.
But if he had read on both fides, or had thought fit to lay the
matter fairly before his reader, he might have informed him, that
thefe books have been folidly anfwered by Mr. Des Voeux, a
very ingenious and judicious author, who had himself been bred
up among the Janfenifts, and was at Paris part of the time that
this fcene was carrying on. See his *Lettres fur les Miracles*,
publifhed in 1735, and his *Critique Générale du Livre de Mr. de*
*Montgeron*, in 1741. See alfo what relates to this fubject in the
19th and 20th tomes of the *Bibliotheque Raifonnée*.

There never was perhaps a book written with a greater air of
affurance and confidence, than that of Mr. de Montgeron. He
intitles it, *The Truth of the Miracles wrought by the Intercession*
*of M. de Paris and other Appellants, demonfrated againf M.*
*the Archbifhop of Sens.* It was natural therefore to expect, that
he would have attempted to juftify all thofe miracles which that
prelate had attacked. But of twenty-two which are diftinctly
infifted upon by the Archbifhop, there are feventeen which Mr.
de Montgeron does not meddle with. He hath paffed by thofe
of them againf which the ftrongeft charges of falfehood and impofture lay. Five of the miracles attacked by the Archbifhop, he
takes pains to juftify; to which he has added four more, which
that prelate had not diftinctly confidered. Mr. Des Voeux,
who has examined this work of Mr. de Montgeron with great
care and judgment, hath plainly fhewn, that there are every-where
to be difcovered in it marks of the ftrongeft prepoffeffion †.
Carried away by the power of his prejudices, and by his affection
to the Janfenift caufe, to which he was greatly attached, he has
in feveral inftances difguifed and mifreprefented facts in a man-

---

* This whole matter is fet in a clear light in Mr. Des Voeux's Differtation fur les Miracles, &c. p. 46. 49. and in his Critique Générale, p. 204.
231, 232.

† The character of Mr. de Montgeron is well reprefented by Mr. Adams,
in his Anfwer to Hume, p. 71. 75.

ner

ner which cannot be excufed or vindicated. The laſt-mentioned
author has charged him with faults, not merely of inadvertency,
but with direct falfifications defigned to impofe upon the public.
See the fixth letter of his *Critique Générale*, page 208, *et feq.*
Mr. Hume has taken care not to give his reader the leaſt hint of
any thing of this nature.

The remarks which have been now made may help us to judge
of Mr. Hume's conduct in his management of this fubject.

I fhall now proceed to make fome obfervations upon the remarkable differences there are between the miracles recorded in
the gofpels, and thofe afcribed to the Abbé de Paris; by confidering which it will appear, that no argument can be juſtly drawn
from the latter to difcredit the former, or to invalidate the proofs
produced for them.

I. One obfervation of no fmall weight is this: at the time when
the miracles of the Abbé de Paris firſt appeared, there was a
ſtrong and numerous party in France, and which was under the
conduct of very able and learned men, who were ſtrongly prepoffeffed in favour of that caufe which thofe miracles feemed
to be intended to fupport: and it might naturally be expected,
that thefe would ufe all their intereſt and influence for maintaining and fpreading the credit of them among the people. And
fo it actually happened. The firſt rumours of thefe miracles
were eagerly laid hold on; and they were cried up as real and
certain miracles, and as giving a clear decifion of Heaven on the
fide of the appellants, even before there was any regular proof fo
much as pretended to be given for them *. To which it may be
added, that the beginning of this whole affair was at a very promifing conjuncture, *viz.* when the Cardinal de Noailles was archbiſhop of Paris; who, whatever may be faid of his capacity and
integrity, which Mr. Hume highly extols, was well known to
be greatly inclined to favour the caufe of the appellants. It was
therefore a fituation of things very favourable to the credit of
thofe miracles, that they firſt appeared under his adminiſtration,
and were tried before his officials; and though the fucceeding
archbiſhop was no friend to the Janfeniſts, yet when once the
credit of thofe miracles was in fome meafure eſtabliſhed, and

---

\* See Critique Generale, let. vi.

they had got the popular vogue on their fide, the affair was more eafily carried on. But at the firft appearance of Chriftianity, the circumftances of things were entirely different. There were indeed parties among the Jews, the moft powerful of which were the Pharifees and Sadducees, befides the priefts and rulers of the Jews, and the Sanhedrim, or great council of the nation: but not one of thefe afforded the leaft countenance to the firft witneffes and publifhers of the Chriftian religion. Our Lord, far from addicting himfelf to any party, freely declared againft what was amifs in every one of them: he oppofed the diftinguifh-ing tenets of the Sadducees; the traditions, fuperftitions, and hypocrify of the Pharifees, and the prejudices of the vulgar. Chriftianity proceeded upon a principle directly contrary to that, in which all parties among the Jews were agreed, *viz.* upon the doctrine of a fpiritual kingdom, and a fuffering Meffiah: and accordingly all the different fects and parties, all the powers civil and ecclefiaftical, united their interefts and endeavours to oppofe and fupprefs it. Whatever fufpicion therefore might be enter-tained with regard to the miracles faid to have been wrought at the tomb of the Abbé de Paris, which had a ftrong party from the beginning prepared to receive and fupport them, no fuch fufpicion can reafonably be admitted as to the truth and reality of the extraordinary facts whereby Chriftianity was attefted, which, as the cafe was circumftanced, could fcarce poffibly have made their way in the manner they did, or have efcaped detection, if they had not been true.

II. Another confideration, which fhews a remarkable differ-ence between the miracles recorded to have been wrought by our Saviour and his apoftles, and thofe afcribed to the Abbé de Paris, is this: That the former carry plain characters of a divine inter-pofition, and a fupernatural power; and the latter, even taking their own account of them, do not appear to be evidently miracu-lous, as they may be accounted for without fuppofing any thing properly fupernatural in the cafe. Our Lord Jefus Chrift not only healed all manner of difeafes, but he raifed the dead: he commanded the winds and the feas, and they obeyed him: he fearched the hearts, and knew the thoughts of men: he gave many exprefs and circumftantial predictions of future contingencies, both relating to his own fufferings and death, and to his confequent

resurrection

refurrection and exaltation, and relating to the calamities that fhould come upon the Jews, the deftruction of Jerufalem and the temple, and the wonderful propagation and eftablifhment of his church and kingdom in the world, which it was impoffible for any man, judging by the rules of human probability, to forefee: he not only performed the moft wonderful works himfelf, but he imparted the fame miraculous power to his difciples, and poured forth upon them the extraordinary gifts of the Holy Ghoft, as he had promifed and foretold; gifts of the moft admirable nature, which were never paralleled before or fince, and which were peculiarly fitted for fpreading and propagating the Chriftian religion.   With regard to thefe, and other things which might be mentioned, no man has ever pretended to draw a comparifon between the miracles afcribed to the Abbé de Paris and thofe of our Saviour: and accordingly one of the moft zealous and able advocates for the former, M. Le Gros, exprefsly acknowledgeth, that there is *an infinite difference between them*, and declares, that he *will never forget that difference*.   The only inftance in which a parallel is pretended to be drawn, is with regard to miraculous cures, which, alone confidered, are the moft uncertain and equivocal of all miracles.   Difeafes have often been furprifingly cured, without any thing that can be properly called miraculous in the cafe.   Wonderful has been the effect of medicines adminiftered in certain circumftances: and fome maladies, after having long refifted all the art and power of remedies, have gone off of themfelves by the force of nature, or by fome furprifing and unexpected turn, in a manner that cannot be diftinctly explained.   Yet it may be obferved, that there were feveral circumftances attending the miraculous cures wrought by our Saviour and his apoftles, which plainly fhewed them to be divine. The cures were wrought in an inftant, by a commanding word. The blind, the lame, thofe that laboured under the moft obftinate and inveterate difeafes, found themfelves immediately reftored at once with an Almighty facility.   If there had been only a few inftances of this kind, it might poffibly have been attributed to fome odd accident, or hidden caufe, which could not be accounted for: but the inftances of fuch complete and inftantaneous cures wrought by our Saviour were very numerous.   They extended to all manner of difeafes, and to all perfons without ex-

ception

 caption who applied to him: yea, he cured some that did not apply to him, who did not know him, or who were his enemies, and had no expectation of a cure, in which cases it could not be pretended that imagination had any share.   In all these respects, there was a remarkable difference between the miraculous cures wrought by our Saviour, and those pretended to have been wrought at the tomb of the Abbé de Paris.   Several of their most boasted cures, and which were pretended to have been sudden and perfected at once, appear from their own accounts to have been carried on by slow degrees, and therefore might have been brought about in a natural way.   Some of these cures were days, weeks, and even months, before they were perfected.   One nine days devotion followed another, and they were suffered to languish, and continue praying and supplicating for a considerable time together; and if the cure happened, and the distemper came to a crisis during the course of their long attendance, and whilst they were continuing their devotions, this passed for a miraculous cure, though it might well be done without any miracle at all: especially as several of those persons continued to be taking remedies, even whilst they were attending at the tomb.   It is manifest from the relations published by themselves, that with regard to several of those who were pretended to be miraculously cured, their maladies had already begun to abate, and they had found considerable ease and relief in a natural way before they came to the tomb at all: and some of them seem by the force of their imagination to have believed themselves cured, when they were not so, or to have taken a temporary relief for an absolute cure. Several of the cures, the accounts of which were published with great pomp, could not with any propriety be said to have been perfected at all; since the persons said to have been cured still continued infirm, and had returns of their former disorders.   This can scarce be supposed, if the cures had been really miraculous, and owing to an extraordinary exertion of the power of God, who would not have left his own work imperfect.   See all these things fully proved by many instances, in M. des Voeux's *Lettres sur les Miracles;* particularly in the fifth of these letters.

To all which it may be added, that of the vast numbers who came to the tomb to be cured, and who had recourse to the Abbé's intercession, there were but few en whom the cures were

wrought,

wrought, in comparifon of thofe who found no benefit at all,
though they applied to him with the utmoft devotion, and continued to do fo for a long time together: and indeed, confidering
how many there were that applied for help and cure, and how
much they were prepoffeffed with the notions countenanced in the
Romifh church, of the power of departed faints, of the prevalency
of their interceffion, and the efficacy of their relics, and to what
a height their imagination was raifed by their prejudices in favour
of the appellants, by the high opinion they had of the Abbé's
extraordinary fanctity, by the rumours of miracles daily fpread
and propagated, and by the vaft crowds which attended at the
tomb, it would have been really a wonder, if, amongft the multitudes that came for cure, there had not been feveral who found
themfelves greatly relieved.   The advocates for the miracles
mightily extol the extraordinary faith and confidence the fick
perfons had in the interceffion of the bleffed Deacon, as they call
him: and the force of their imagination, when carried to fo extraordinary a pitch, might in fome particular cafes produce great
effects.   Many wonderful inftances to this purpofe have been
obferved and recorded by the ableft phyficians, by which it appears what a mighty influence imagination, accompanied with
ftrong paffions, hath often had upon human bodies, efpecially in
the cure of difeafes: it hath often done more in a fhort time this
way, than a long courfe of medicines have been able to accomplifh.
It is not therefore to be much wondered at, that as the cafe was
circumftanced, amidft fuch a multitude of perfons, fome furprizing cures were wrought: but it could not be expected that
the effect would be conftant and uniform.   If it anfwered in fome
inftances, it would fail in many more: and accordingly fo it was
with regard to thefe pretended miraculous cures.   And if this
had been the cafe in the extraordinary cures wrought by our Saviour, there would have been ground of fufpicion, that what
fome have alleged might poffibly have been true, that his miracles owed their force, not to any fupernatural energy, but to
the power of imagination.   But taking thefe miracles as they
are recorded in the gofpels, it is manifeft, that there can be no
juft ground for fuch a pretence.   They exhibit evident proofs
of a divine interpofition, which cannot be faid of thofe reported
to have been wrought at the Abbé's tomb.   M. de Montgeron,

in his book dedicated to the King, publifhed an account of eight or ninecures; and it is to be fuppofed, that he fixed upon thofe which he thought had the appearance of being moft fignally miraculous: and yet the very firft of thofe miracles, *viz.* that affirmed to have been wrought upon Don Alphonfo de Palacio, appeareth plainly, by taking the whole of the relation as M. Montgeron himfelf hath given it, to have had nothing in it properly miraculous, as Mr. Adams hath clearly fhewn *. And with regard both to that and the other miracles fo pompoufly difplayed by M. de Montgeron, M. Des Voeux has very ingenioufly and judicioufly, after a diftinct examination of each of them, made it appear, that they might have been wrought without fuppofing any miraculous or fupernatural interpofition at all. See the laft letter of his *Critique Générale.*

III. Another confideration, which fhews the great difference there is between the miracles wrought at the firft eftablifhment of Chriftianity, and thofe faid to have been wrought at the tomb of the Abbé de Paris, and that no argument can reafonably be brought from the latter to the prejudice of the former, is taken from the many fufpicious circumftances attending the latter, from which the former were entirely free. Chrift's miracles were wrought, in a grave and decent, in a great but fimple manner, becoming one fent of God, without any abfurd or ridiculous ceremonies, or fuperftitious obfervances. But the miracles of the Abbé de Paris were attended with circumftances that had all the marks of fuperftition, and which feemed defigned and fitted to ftrike the imagination. The earth of his tomb was often made ufe of, or the waters of the well of his houfe. The nine days devotion was conftantly ufed, and frequently repeated again and again by the fame perfons; a ceremony derived originally from the pagans, and which hath been condemned as fuperftitious by fome eminent divines of the Romifh church †. Another circumftance to be obferved, with relation to Chrift's miracles, is, that, as hath been already hinted, they were not only perfected at once, but the perfons found themfelves healed and reftored without trouble or difficulty. But in the cafe of the

* Adams's Effay, in Anfwer to Hume, p. 76, 77.
† Lettres fur les Miracles, p. 258, 259. 336, 337.

cures affirmed to have been wrought at the Abbé's tomb, it appeareth from their own accounts, not only that they were gradual and flow, but that the perfons on whom thefe cures were wrought, frequently fuffered the moft grievous and exceffive pains and torments, and which they themfelves reprefent to have been greater than ever they had felt before, or were able to exprefs; and thefe pains often continued for feveral days together in the utmoft extremity*. To which may be added, the violent agitations and convulfions, which became fo ufual on thefe occafions, that they came at length to be regarded as fymptoms of the miraculous cures; though they could not be properly regarded in this view, fince many of thofe who had thofe convulfions found no relief in their maladies, and even grew worfe than before. They were frequently attended with ftrange contortions, fometimes frightful, fometimes ridiculous, and fometimes inconfiftent with the rules of modefty and decency†. And accordingly they have been condemned by fome of the moft eminent Janfenift divines. In 1735 there was publifhed at Paris a remarkable piece, intitled, *Confultation fur les Convulfions*, figned by thirty appellant doctors, men of great reputation among the Janfenifts for learning, judgment, and probity; the greater part of whom had at firft entertained favourable thoughts of thofe convulfions; and fome of them had publicly declared them to be the work of God. But now they pronounced them to be unworthy of God, of his infinite majefty, wifdom, and goodnefs: They declared that it was a folly, a fanaticifm, a fcandal, and in one word, a blafphemy againft God, to attribute to him thefe

---

* Lettres fur les Miracles, p. 339, & feq.

† Some of thefe that were feized with thefe convulfions, or pretended to be fo, were guilty of the moft extravagant follies. They pretended to prophecy, and uttered feveral predictions, which the event foon proved to be falfe. One of them went fo far as to foretel, that the church-yard of St. Medard, which had been fhut up by the King's order, fhould be opened, and that M. de Paris fhould appear in the church, in the prefence of great numbers of people, on the firft of May following. See this and other remarkable things relating to thefe convulfions, in M. Vernet's Traité de la Verité de la Religion Chretienne, fect. 7. chap. 22, 23. And there cannot be a greater proof of the power of M. de Montgeron's prejudices, than that in the laft edition of his book, in three volumes 4to. he has particularly applied himfelf to fupport and juftify thefe convulfions.

operations; and did not scruple to intimate, that they rendered the miraculous cures, to which they were pretended to be annexed, suspected. These doctors, who were called the *Consultants*, condemned all the convulsions in general. Others of the Jansenist divines, whom M. de Montgeron has distinguished by the title of the *Antisecourists*, and whom he acknowledges to be among the most zealous appellants, and to be persons of great merit and eminence, though they did not condemn all the convulsions; yet passed a very severe censure upon those of them which that gentleman looks upon to be the most extraordinary and miraculous of all. And with regard to these convulsions in general, it may be observed, that, by the acknowledgment of the most skilful physicians, nervous affections have frequently produced strange symptoms; that they are often of a catching contagious nature; and easily communicated; and that they may be counterfeited by art. Many of those that were seized by M. Herault, the Lieutenant of Police, acknowledged to him that they had counterfeited convulsions: in consequence of which there was an 'ordonnance' published by the King, January 27, 1732, for searching out and apprehending those impostors. And yet Mr. Hume has thought proper to represent it, as if M. Herault, though he had full power to seize and examine the *witnesses* and *subjects* of these miracles, *could never reach any thing satisfactory against them.*

These must be owned to be circumstances, which administer just grounds of suspicion, and which make a wide difference between the miracles pretended to have been wrought at the tomb of the Abbé de Paris, and those that were performed by our Saviour, and by the apostles in his name.

IV. The next observation I shall make is this: that several of the miracles ascribed to the Abbé, and which were pretended to be proved by many witnesses, were afterwards clearly convicted of falsehood and imposture; which brings a great discredit upon all the rest: whereas nothing of this kind can be alleged against the miracles by which Christianity was attested. The affair of Anne le Franc, of which some account was given above, shews, as M. Des Voeux justly observes, how little dependence is to be had upon informations in this cause directed by Jansenists. But this is not the only instance of this kind. They had published, that

that La Dalmaix had been miraculously cured by the Abbe's intercession; and this was proved by a letter pretended to have
been written by herself. And yet this pretended miraculous
cure was afterwards denied by the person herself, by her mother, and all her sisters: and by a sentence of a court of judicature of May 17, 1737, a person was declared to be convicted of
having forged that, and some other letters, under the name of
Dalmaix*. The Sieur le Doux openly retracted the relation of
a miracle said to have been wrought upon himself. M. Des
Vœux gives several other instances of false miracles, published
by the Jansenists, and afterwards acknowledged to be so†. Jean
Nivet was represented, by decisive informations, as cured of his
deafness, and yet it is certain that he was deaf after, as well as
before. The record of the informations made by Mr. Thomas-
sin is full of contradictions, which discover the falsehood and
perjury of the principal actress, and of the only witness of the
miracle, as the Archbishop of Sens has well proved: though
many of these proofs are passed over in silence by M. le Gros,
who undertook to answer him‡. Some of the witnesses and
persons concerned withdrew, to escape the search that was made
for them, and to shun the examination and inquiry, which the
king had ordered; and others, who had attested that they were
cured by the intercession of the Abbé de Paris, afterwards retracted it. The certificates themselves, on which so great a stress
is laid, tend in many instances to increase the suspicion against
those facts, which they were designed to confirm. The very
number of those certificates, many of which are nothing at all to
the purpose, and serve only for shew, are plain proofs of art and
design. The manner of drawing up those certificates, and the
relations of the miracles, and the style and form of expression,
shew, that the persons in whose names they are drawn had the
assistance of persons of a capacity much superior to their own.
Long pieces, in a correct style, and in perfect good order, were
published under the name of mean and illiterate persons. M. le
Gros owns, that the relation of Genevieve Colin was reformed

* Vernet, ubi supra, cap. xxi.
† Lettres sur les Miracles, p. 171, et seq. Critique Generale, p. 204,
&c. 233, 234.
‡ Lettres sur les Miracles, p. 242, 243.

as to the ftyle, by a perfon whom fhe defired to do it. Thus they had it in their power, under pretence of reforming, to alter it, and got the. fimple perfon to fign the whole. Five witneffes in the cafe of Anne le Franc depofe, that their certificates left with the notary were altered, falfified, and embellifhed with divers circumftances. Many of the relations which were at firft publifhed, and were not thought full enough, were afterwards fuppreffed, and do not appear in M. de Montgeron's collection; and others more ample were fubftituted in their ftead, and embellifhed with many ftriking circumftances, which were omitted in the firft relation. Many of the witneffes in their depofitions carry it farther than, according to their own account, they could have any certain knowledge: Some of them appear to have been furprized into their teftimonies by falfe or imperfect reprefentations; and artifices were employed to procure certificates from phyficians, without bringing the cafe fully before them, or fuffering them fairly to examine it.

To all which it may be added, that there is great reafon to fufpect, that many poor people feigned maladies, and pretended to be cured, on purpofe to procure the gifts and benefactions of others; which many of them did to good advantage. It is well known, and has been often proved, that in the Romifh church there have been inftances of perfons, who made a trade of feigning maladies, and pretending to be miraculoufly cured. Such a one was Catharine de Prés, who was afterwards convicted by her own confeffion; of which Father Le Brun hath given a particular account, *Hift. Crit. des Prat. Superftit.* liv. ii. cap. 4. who hath alfo detected feveral other falfe miracles which had been believed by numbers of that church. And may we not reafonably fufpect the fame of many poor people who came to the tomb of the Abbé de Paris? See all thefe things fhewn in M. Des Vœux's *Lettres fur les Miracles*, Letter V, VI. and efpecially in Letters VII. and VIII. of his *Critique Générale*, where he particularly examineth every one of the miracles produced by M. de Montgeron. It is his obfervation, that the more carefully we confider thofe relations, and compare them with the pieces that are defigned to juftify them, the more plainly the falfehoods of them appeareth. And accordingly he hath found out not merely a fingle contradiction, but numerous contradictions,

in the relations of the feveral miracles, compared with the certificates, and the pieces produced in juftification of them.   And
therefore he afks with good reafon, what becomes of demonftrations built on fuch relations and fuch certificates?   He very
properly obferves, that the falfity even of a fmall number of
facts, which are pretended to be proved by certificates, that were
collected by thofe who took pains to verify the miracles, are fufficient to difcredit all others founded on fuch certificates.

If the fame things could have been juftly objected againft the
miracles recorded in the New Teftament, Chriftianity, confidering the other difadvantages it laboured under, could never have
been eftablifhed.   But the cafe with regard to thefe miracles was
very different.   They were not indeed proved by certificates,
which may be procured by art and management.   The firft publifhers of the Chriftian religion did not go about to collect evidences and teftimonies; nor was there any need of their doing
fo in facts that were publicly known, and the reality of which
their enemies themfelves were not able to deny.   They acted
with greater fimplicity, and with an open confidence of truth.
Their narrations are plain and artlefs; nor do they take pains to
prepoffefs or influence the reader, either by artful infinuations,
or too *violent affertions;* which our author mentions as a fufpicious circumftance.   Never were any of their enemies able to
convict them of falfehood.   Far from ever denying the facts they
had witneffed, or withdrawing for fear of having thofe facts inquired into, as feveral did in the other cafe, they openly avowed
thofe facts before the public tribunals, and before perfons of the
higheft authority: they never varied in their teftimony, but per-
fifted in it with an unfainting conftancy, and fealed it with their
blood.   And it gives no fmall weight to their teftimony, that
they witneffed for facts, which were defigned to confirm a fcheme
of religion contrary to their own moft rooted prejudices.   Nor
can it be alleged, that they were themfelves divided about the
reality and divinity of the miracles wrought by Chrift and his
apoftles, much lefs that they rejected and condemned many of
them as foolifh, fcandalous, and injurious to the Divine Majefty;
which was the cenfure paffed upon fome of the extraordinary
facts relating to the Abbé de Paris, by the moft eminent Janfenift divines.

Finally,

"Finally, the laſt obſervation I ſhall make is this: that the miracles of our Saviour and his apoſtles appear to have been wrought
for an end worthy of the divine wiſdom and goodneſs. The declared deſign of them was to give an atteſtation to the divine
miſſion of the moſt excellent perſon that ever appeared in the
world, and to confirm the beſt ſcheme of religion that was ever
publiſhed, the moſt manifeſtly conducive to the glory of God,
and to the ſalvation of mankind. Here was an end worthy of
God, and for which it was fit for him to interpoſe in the moſt
extraordinary manner. Accordingly this religion, thus atteſted
and confirmed, was eſtabliſhed in the world, and ſoon triumphed
over all oppoſition. All the power of the adverſary, civil or ſa-
cerdotal, could not put a ſtop to its progreſs, or to the wonderful works done in confirmation of it. The effects which followed, conſidering the amazing difficulties it had to ſtruggle with,
and the ſeeming weakneſs and meanneſs of the inſtruments made
uſe of to propagate it, proved the reality of thoſe miracles, and
that the whole was carried on by a divine power. But if we
turn our views on the other hand to the miracles pretended to
have been wrought at the tomb of the Abbé de Paris, it doth not
appear that they anſwered any valuable end. There has indeed
been an end found out for them, *viz.* to give a teſtimony from
heaven to the cauſe of the appellants. But we may juſtly conclude from the wiſdom of God, that in that caſe it would have
been ſo ordered, as to make it evident that this was the intention of them, and that he would have taken care that no oppoſition from men ſhould prevail, to defeat the deſign for which he
interpoſed in ſo extraordinary a manner. But this was far from
being the caſe. Mr. Hume indeed tells us, that " no Janſeniſt
" was ever at a loſs to account for the ceſſation of the miracles,
" when the church-yard was ſhut up by the king's edict. 'Twas
" the touch of the tomb which operated thoſe extraordinary ef-
" fects, and when no one could approach the tomb, no effect
" could be expected\*." But ſuppoſing that the deſign of thoſe
extraordinary divine interpoſitions was to give a teſtimony from
heaven to the cauſe of the appellants, it is abſurd to imagine,
that it would have been in the power of an earthly prince, by

\* Hume's Philoſophical Eſſays, p. 209.

ſhutting

shutting up the tomb, to put a stop to the course of the miraculous operations, and to render the design of God of none effect *. It strengthens this, when it is farther considered, that the whole affair of these pretended miracles turned in the issue rather to the disadvantage of the cause it was designed to confirm. It hath been already observed, that some of the most eminent among the appellant doctors, and who were most zealously attached to that cause, were greatly scandalized at several of those miracles, and especially at the extraordinary convulsions which generally attended them. The censures they passed upon them gave occasion to bitter contentions, and mutual severe reproaches and recusations. Some of the Jansenist writers themselves complain, that whereas before there was an entire and perfect union and harmony among them, as if they had been all of one heart and soul, there have been since that time cruel divisions and animosities, so that those who were friends before became irreconcileable enemies †. And can it be imagined, that God would execute his designs in so imperfect a manner? that he would exert his own divine power to give testimony to that cause, and yet do it in such a way as to weaken that cause instead of supporting it, to raise prejudices against it in the minds of enemies, instead of gaining them, and to divide and offend the friends of it, instead of confirming and uniting them? Upon the whole, with regard to the attestations given to Christianity, all was wise, consistent, worthy of God, and suited to the end for which it was designed. But the other is a broken, incoherent scheme, which cannot be reconciled to itself, nor made to consist with the wisdom and harmony of the divine proceedings. The former therefore is highly credible, though the latter is not so.

The several considerations which have been mentioned do each of them singly, much more all of them together, shew such signal differences between the miracles recorded in the gospels and those ascribed to the Abbé de Paris, that it must argue a peculiar

---

* M. de Montgeron indeed will not allow that the miraculous operations ceased at the shutting up of the tomb; but by the miraculous operations he principally understands the convulsions, which continued still to be carried on; but which many of the principal Jansenists were far from looking upon as tokens of a divine interposition.

† Crit. Gener. lettre v. p. 159, & seq.

degree of confidence to pretend to run a parallel between the one
and the other, much more to affirm, as Mr. Hume has done,
that the latter *much furpaſs* the former in *credit and authority.*
This only ſhews how gladly theſe gentlemen would lay hold on
any pretence to invalidate the evidences of Chriſtianity. Thus,
Mr. Chubb, in a difcourfe he publiſhed on miracles, in which
he pretends impartially to repreſent the reaſonings on both ſides,
produced with great pomp a pretended miracle wrought in the
Cevennes in 1703, and repreſented it as of equal credit with
thoſe of the goſpel. M. le Moyne, in his anſwer to him, hath
evinced the falſehood of that ſtory in a manner that admits of no
reply *: and yet it is not improbable, that ſome future deiſt may
ſee fit ſome time or other to revive that ſtory, and oppoſe it to
the miracles recorded in the New Teſtament.

Mr. Hume concludes his Eſſay with applauding his own performance, and is the better pleaſed with the *way of reaſoning* he
has made uſe of, as he thinks, " it may ſerve to confound thoſe
" dangerous friends, or diſguiſed enemies to the Chriſtian reli-
" gion, who have undertaken to defend it by the principles of
" human reaſon. Our moſt holy religion," ſaith he, " is founded
" on faith, not on reaſon †: and it is a ſure method of expoſing
　　　　　　　　　　　　　　　　　　　　　　　　　　　　　　" it,

* Le Monye on Miracles, p. 422, &c.

† This author, who takes care to make the principles of his philoſophy
ſubſervient to his deſigns againſt religion, in the fifth of his Philoſophical
Eſſays, where he undertakes to treat of the nature of belief, gives ſuch an
account of it as ſeems to exclude reaſon from any ſhare in it at all. He
makes the difference between *faith* and *fiction* to confiſt wholly in ſome ſentiment of feeling, which is annexed to the former, not to the latter : That the
ſentiment of belief is nothing but the conception of an object more lively
and forcible, more intenſe and ſteady than what attends the mere fiction of
the imagination: and that this manner of conception ariſes from the cufto-
mary conjunction of the object with ſomething preſent to the memory or
ſenſes. See his Philoſophical Eſſays, p. 80—84. This gentleman is here,
as in many other places, ſufficiently obſcure, nor is it eaſy to form a diſtinct
notion of what he intends. But his deſign ſeems to be to exclude reaſon or
the underſtanding from having any thing to do with belief, as if reaſon never
had any influence in producing, directing, or regulating it; which is to open
a wide door to enthuſiaſm. But this is contrary to what we may all obſerve, and frequently experience. We in ſeveral caſes clearly perceive, that
we have reaſon to regard ſome things as fictitious, and others as true and
real. And the reaſons which ſhew the difference between a fiction and a
　　　　　　　　　　　　　　　　　　　　　　　　　　　　　　　　reality

" it, to put it to fuch a trial, as it is by no means fitted to endure."
And he calls thofe, who undertake to defend religion by reafon,
*pretended Chriftians\**.　Such a mean and ungenerous fneer is
below animadverfion: all that can be gathered from it is, that
thefe gentlemen are very uneafy'at the attempts which have been
made to defend Chriftianity in a way of reafon and argument.
They, it feems, are mightily concerned for *the prefervation* of
our holy faith, and in their great friendfhip for that caufe would
give it up as indefenfible.　And if the beft way of befriending the
Chriftian religion be to endeavour to fubvert the evidences by
which it is eftablifhed, our author hath taken effectual care to convince the world of his friendly intentions towards it.　As to the
brief hints he hath given towards the end of his Effay againft the
Mofaic hiftory, and the miracles recorded there, I fhall not here
take any notice of them, both becaufe Mr. Adams hath clearly
and fuccinctly obviated them, in his anfwer to that Effay, p. 88
—94, and becaufe I fhall have occafion to refume this fubject,
when I come to make obfervations on Lord Bolingbroke's *Pofthumous Works*, who hath with great virulence and bitternefs
ufed his utmoft efforts to expofe the Mofaic writings.

reality fhew, that we ought in reafon to believe the one and not the other:
and fo reafon may go before the fentiment of belief, and lay a juft foundation for it, and be inftrumental to produce it.　And in this cafe the belief
may be faid to be ftrictly rational.

\* Hume's Philofophical Effays, p. 164, 165.

## L E T T E R  XX.

*Additional Observations relating to Mr. Hume—A Transcript*
*of an ingenious Paper, containing an Examination of Mr.*
*Hume's Arguments in his Essay on Miracles—Observations*
*upon it—The Evidence of Matters of Fact may be so circum-*
*stanced as to produce a full Assurance—Mr. Hume artfully*
*confounds the Evidence of past Facts with the Probability of*
*the future—We may be certain of a Matter of Fact after it*
*hath happened, though it might before-hand seem very impro-*
*bable that it would happen—Where full Evidence is given of*
*a Fact, there must not always be a Deduction made on the*
*Account of its being unusual and extraordinary—There is*
*strong and positive Evidence of the Miracles wrought in Attes-*
*tation of Christianity, and no Evidence against them—The*
*miraculous Nature of the Facts no Proof that the Facts were*
*not done—A Summary of Mr. Hume's Argument against the*
*Evidence of Miracles—The Weakness of it shewn—Considering*
*the vast Importance of Religion to our Happiness, the bare*
*Possibility of its being true should be sufficient to engage our*
*Compliance.*

SIR,

THE four preceding letters comprehend all the observations
that were made upon Mr. Hume in the second volume of
the *View of the Deistical Writers*, 8vo. edit. But soon after that
volume was published, I received a letter from a gentleman of
sense and learning, which particularly relates to that part of it
which was designed in answer to Mr. Hume. He was pleased
to say it gave him *uncommon satisfaction*, and at the same time
sent me a paper which he seemed to be very well pleased with,
that had been drawn up by a young gentleman, then lately dead.
It was designed as a confutation of Mr. Hume upon his own
principles, which he thought had not been sufficiently attended
to in the answers that had been made to that writer; and he allowed me, if I should be of opinion that any thing in it might be
serviceable to a farther confutation of Mr. Hume, to make use
of

of his fentiments either by way of note or appendix, as I fhould
judge moft convenient.    I returned an anfwer, in a letter which
I fhall here infert, as it contains fome reflections that may be
of advantage in relation to the controverfy with Mr. Hume: but
firft it will be proper to lay before the reader the paper itfelf here
referred to, which is concifely drawn, and runs thus:

# AN EXAMINATION OF Mr. HUME's ARGUMENTS

### IN HIS

## ESSAY ON MIRACLES.

THE objects of human underftanding may be diftinguifhed
either into propofitions afferting the relation between general
ideas, or matters of fact.

In the former kind, we can arrive at certainty, by means of a
faculty in our fouls, which perceives this relation either inftantly
or intimately, which is called Intuition, or elfe by intermediate
ideas, which is called Demonftration.

But we can only form a judgment of the latter by experience.
No reafoning *a priori* will difcover to us, that water will fuffo-
cate, or the fire confume us, or that the loadftone will attract fteel;
and therefore no judgment can be made concerning the truth or
falfehood of matters of fact, but what is conftantly regulated by
cuftom and experience, and can therefore never go higher than
probability.

When we have frequently obferved a particular event to happen in certain circumftances, the mind naturally makes an induction, that it will happen again in the fame circumftances.
When this obfervation has been long, conftant, and uninterrupted, there our belief that it will happen again approaches infinitely
near to certainty.    Thus no man has the leaft doubt of the fun's
rifing to-morrow, or that the tide will ebb and flow at its accuf-
tomed periods: but where our obfervations are broke in upon by
frequent interruptions and exceptions to the contrary, then we
expect fuch an event with the leaft degree of affurance: and in
all intermediate cafes, our expectations are always in proportion
to the conftancy and regularity of the experience.

This method of reafoning is not connected by any medium or
chain of fteps, but is plainly to be obferved in all animate beings,

brutes as well as men\*.    And it would be as abfurd to afk a
reafon, why we expect to happen again, that which has regularly
come to pafs a great many times before, as it is to inquire, why
the mind perceives a relation between certain ideas.

They are both diftinct faculties of the foul: and as it has been
authorized by fome writers of diftinction, to give the denomination of fenfe to the internal as well as external perceptions, the one
may be called the *fpeculative*, and the other the *probable fenfe*.

From this laft-mentioned principle Mr. Hume has deduced an
argument to fhew, that there is great improbability againft the
belief of any miraculous fact, how well foever attefted: and
as religion may feem to be greatly affected by this conclufion
(fuppofing it to be true), before we come directly to confider
the argument, it may not be amifs to inquire how far religion,
as a practical inftitution, may be concerned therein.

And for this purpofe it is to be obferved, that probable evidence for the truth or falfehood of any matter of fact differs effentially from demonftration, in that the former admits of degrees, in the greateft variety, from the higheft moral certainty
down to the loweft prefumption; which the latter does not.

Let it alfo be further obferved, that probable evidence is in
its nature but an imperfect kind of information, the higheft degree of which can never reach abfolute certainty, or full proof:
and yet to mankind, with regard to their practice, it is in many
cafes the very guide of their lives.

Moft of our actions are determined by the higheft degrees of
probability; as for inftance, what we do in confequence of the
fun's rifing to-morrow; of the feafons regularly fucceeding
one another; and that certain kinds of meat and drink will nou-
rifh.    Others are determined by leffer degrees.    Thus rhubarb
does not always purge; nor is opium a foporific to every perfon
that takes it; and yet for all that they are of conftant ufe for
thefe purpofes in medicine.    In all cafes of moment, when to
act or forbear may be attended with confiderable damage, no
wife man makes the leaft fcruple of doing what he apprehends

---

\* May not the long fought after diftinction between brutes and men confift in this: That whereas the human underftanding comprehends both
claffes, the brutal fagacity is confined only to matters of fact?

may be of advantage to him, even though the thing was doubtful, and one fide of the queſtion as fupportable as the other: but in matters of the utmoſt confequence, a prudent man will think himſelf obliged to take notice even of the loweſt probability, and will act accordingly.   A great many inſtances might be given in the common purſuits of life, where a man would be confidered as out of his ſenfes, who would not act, and with great diligence and application too, not only upon an over-chance, but even where the probability might be greatly againſt his fuccefs.

Suppoſe a criminal under ſentence of death were promiſed a pardon, if he threw twelve with a pair of dice at one throw; here the probability is thirty-fix to one againſt him, and yet he would be looked upon as mad if he did not try.   Nothing in ſuch a cafe would hinder a man from trying, but the abſolute impoſſibility of the event.

Let us now apply this method of reaſoning to the practice of religion.   And ſuppoſing the arguments againſt miracles were far more probable than the evidence for them, yet the vaſt importance of religion to our happinefs in every reſpect would ſtill be very ſufficient to recommend it to the practice of every prudent man; and the bare poſſibility that it might prove true, were there nothing elſe to ſupport it, would engage his aſſent and compliance; or elſe he muſt be ſuppoſed to act differently in this reſpect to what he generally does in all the other concerns of his life.   So that whether Mr. Hume's reaſonings be true or falſe, religion has ſtill ſufficient evidence to influence the practice of every wife and confiderate man.

This being premiſed, let us now proceed to confider Mr. Hume's arguments.   His reaſoning may be briefly expreſſed in this manner: We have had a long, univerſal, and uninterrupted experience, that no events have happened contrary to the courſe of nature, from conſtant and unvaried obſervations: we have therefore a full proof, that the uniform courſe has not been broke in upon, nor will be, by any particular exceptions.   But the obſervation of truth depending upon, and conſtantly following human teſtimony, is by no means univerſal and uninterrupted, and therefore it does not amount to a full proof, that it either has, or will follow it in any particular inſtance.   And therefore the proof ariſing from any human teſtimony can never equal the proof that is deduced againſt a miracle from the very nature of the faſt.

This I take to be a full and fair ſtate of this gentleman's reaſoning.

But the anſwer is very plain : if by human teſtimony, he would mean the evidence of any one ſingle man indifferently taken, then indeed his ſecond propoſition would be true; but then the concluſion will by no means follow from it: but if by human teſtimony he would underſtand the evidence of any collection of men, then the ſecond propoſition is falſe, and conſequently the concluſion muſt be ſo too.

That twelve honeſt perſons ſhould combine to aſſert a falſehood, at the hazard of their lives, without any view to private intereſt, and with the certain proſpect of loſing every thing that is and ought to be dear to mankind in this world, is, according to his own way of reaſoning, as great a miracle, to all intents and purpoſes, as any interruption in the common courſe of nature; becauſe no hiſtory has ever mentioned any ſuch thing, nor has any man in any age ever had experience of ſuch a faſt.

But here it may be objected, that though it be allowed to be as great a miracle for twelve honeſt men to atteſt a falſehood, contrary to their plain intereſt in every reſpect, as that any alteration ſhould happen in the common courſe of nature, yet theſe evidences being equal, they only deſtroy one another, and ſtill leave the mind in ſuſpence.

This objection draws all its force from Mr. Hume's aſſertion, that an uniform and uninterrupted experience amounts to a full proof, which when examined will not be found true; and indeed I wonder that a writer of his accuracy ſhould venture on ſuch an expreſſion, ſince it is confeſſed on all hands, that all our reaſonings concerning matters of faſt ever fall ſhort of certainty, or full proof.

And beſides, the very ſame objection which he makes againſt the veracity of human teſtimony, to weaken its authenticity, may be retorted with equal force againſt his unvaried certainty of the courſe of nature; for doubtleſs the number of approved hiſtories we have relating to miracles, will as much leſſen the probability of what he calls a full proof on his ſide of the queſtion, as all the forgeries and falſehoods that are brought to diſcredit

credit human teſtimony, will weaken it on the other. But the
beſt way to be aſſured of the falſehood of this objection is to examine it by what we find in our own minds; for that muſt not
be admitted as an univerſal principle, which is not true in every
particular inſtance.

According to Mr. Hume, we have a full proof of any fact atteſted by twelve honeſt diſintereſted perſons. But would not the
probability be increaſed, and our belief of ſuch a fact be the
ſtronger, if the number of witneſſes were doubled? I own, my
mind immediately aſſents to it. But if this be true, it will then
evidently follow, that the proof againſt a miracle, ariſing from
the nature of the fact, may, and has been exceeded by contrary
human teſtimony.

Suppoſe, as before, that the teſtimony of twelve perſons is juſt
equal to it, and we have the evidence of twenty for any particular miracle recorded in the Goſpel ; then ſubſtracting the weaker
evidence from the ſtronger, we ſhall have the poſitive evidence
of eight perſons, for the truth of a common matter of fact.

Q. E. D.

The anſwer I returned to the letter in which this paper was
incloſed was in ſubſtance as follows :

SIR,

I am very much obliged to you for the kind manner in
which you have expreſſed yourſelf with regard to me: and it
is a pleaſure to me to find, that my reply to Mr. Hume is approved
by a gentleman of ſo much good ſenſe, and of ſuch eminency in
his profeſſion, as I am well informed you are accounted to be.

I agree with you, that Mr. Hume is an elegant and ſubtile writer, and one of the moſt dangerous enemies to Chriſtianity that
has appeared among us. He has a very ſpecious way of managing an argument. But his ſubtilty ſeems to have qualified him
not ſo much for clearing an obſcure cauſe, as for puzzling a
clear one. Many things in his *Philoſophical Eſſays* have a very
plauſible appearance, as well as an uncommon turn, which he vi-
ſibly affects; but, upon a cloſe examination of them, I think one
may venture to pronounce, that few authors can be mentioned
who have fallen into greater abſurdities and inconſiſtencies. And
it were to be wiſhed there was not a ſufficient ground for the ſe-

vere cenfure you pafs upon him, when you fay, that, " with all " his art, he has plainly difcovered a bad heart, by throwing out " fome bitter fneers againft the Chriftian revelation, which are " abfolutely inconfiftent with a ferious belief, or indeed with any " regard for it, though in fome parts of his writings he affects a " different way of fpeaking."

You obferve, that " we feem to be greatly deficient in the lo- " gic of probability, a point which Mr. Hume had ftudied with " great accuracy." And I readily own, that there is a great ap- pearance of accuracy in what Mr. Hume hath advanced concern- ing the grounds and degrees of probability, and the different de- grees of affent due to it. But though what he hath offered this way feems plaufible in general, he hath been far from being fair or exact in his application of it.

The paper you have fent inclofed to me, and which you tell me was drawn up by the young gentleman you mention, contains a fketch of an attempt to fhew how Mr. Hume might be confut- ed on his own principles, and is executed in fuch a manner, that one cannot but regret, that a gentleman of fo promifing a ge- nius, and who might have proved fignally ufeful, was fnatched away by a fever about the twentieth year of his age. You allow me to make what ufe of it I judge proper, and feem to expect that I fhould tell you my fentiments of it with the utmoft franknefs and candour. And this obligeth me to acquaint you, that though I look upon the confutation of Mr. Hume in the way this gen- tleman hath managed it to be fubtile and ingenious, yet in fome things it doth not feem to me to be quite fo clear and fatisfac- tory, as were to be wifhed in a matter of fo great confequence. He has, I think, from a defire of confuting Mr. Hume upon his own principles, been led to make too large conceffions to that gentleman, and hath proceeded upon fome of his principles as true and valid, which I think may be juftly contefted.

Mr. Hume frequently intimates, that there neither is nor can be any certainty in the evidence given concerning matters of fact, or in human teftimony, which can be fecurely depended on ; and that at beft, it can be only probable. And the ingeni- ous author of the paper, having obferved, after Mr. Hume, that we can form no judgment concerning the truth or falfehood of mat- ter of fact, but what is conftantly regulated by cuftom or experience,

rience, adds, that " it can never go higher than probability."
And again he faith, that " probable evidence is in its nature but
" an imperfect kind of information ; the higheft degree of which
" cannot reach abfolute certainty or full proof :" where he feems
not to allow, that the evidence concerning matters of fact can ever
arrive at fuch a certainty as to make up a *full proof*. And he repeats it again, that " it is confeffed on all hands, that all our rea-
" fonings concerning matters of fact ever fall fhort of certainty or
" full proof." And yet if we allow Mr. Hume's definition of a
full proof, that it is *fuch an argument from experience as leaves
no room for doubt or oppofition*, the evidence for a matter of fact
may be fo circumftanced as to amount to a full proof, and even
to a certainty ; for I can fee no reafon for confining certainty to
the evidence we have by intuition or by demonftration. In treating of certainty as diftinguifhed from probability, a twofold certainty may very properly be allowed. The one is, the certainty
by intuition or by demonftration. The other is, a certainty
relating to matter of fact. This is indeed of a different kind from
the former : but I think it may no lefs juftly be called certainty,
when it fo fully fatisfieth the mind, as to leave not the leaft room
for doubt concerning it, and produceth a full affurance. And
that this is often the cafe with relation to matters of fact cannot
reafonably be denied. The words *fure* and *certain* are frequently applied in common language to things of this kind, and, for
aught I can fee, very properly. And in the beft and exacteft
writers it is often defcribed under the term of *moral certainty*,
an expreffion which this gentleman himfelf makes ufe of[*]. And
it is a great miftake to imagine, that the word *moral* in that cafe

---

[*] The ingenious gentleman feems to grant what may be fufficient, when
he faith, that probability " in fome cafes approaches infinitely near to certainty." If it be allowed, that matter of fact may be fo certain, that the mind
may be fully affured of it, and fo as to leave no room for a reafonable doubt,
this is all that is really neceffary in the prefent controverfy. And this is
what Mr. Hume himfelf feems fometimes to allow. But at other times he
gives fuch an account of human teftimony as tends to render it in all cafes uncertain. And the defign of his reprefenting it as never rifing higher than
probability, feems to be to convey an idea of uncertainty and doubt as infeparably attending all human teftimony. And to guard againft the wrong ufe
that may be made of this, is the defign of what I have here obferved.

is always ufed as a term of diminution, as if it were not to be
entirely depended upon.   It is only defigned to fhew that this
certainty is of a different kind, and proceedeth upon different
grounds, from that which arifeth from demonftration ; but yet
it may produce as ftrong an affurance in the mind, and which
may undoubtedly be depended upon.   That there was a war carried on in England in the laft century between King and Parlia-
ment, I only know by human teftimony.   But will any man fay,
that for that reafon I cannot be fure of it ?  Many cafes might be
mentioned with regard to matters of faft which we know by human teftimony, the evidence of which is fo ftrong and convincing, that we can no more reafonably doubt of it, than of the
truth of any propofition which comes to us demonftrated by the
ftricteft reafoning.   Mr. Hume himfelf feems fenfible, that it
would be wrong to fay, that every thing which is not matter of
demonftration comes only under the notion of probability.   And
therefore though he frequently feems to clafs all matters of faft
under the head of probabilities, yet in the beginning of his Effay
on Probability, he feems to find fault with Mr. Locke for di-
viding all arguments into *demonftrative* and *probable*, and obferves, that to conform our language more to common ufe, we
fhould divide arguments into *demonftrations*, *proofs*, and *probabilities:* where he feems to place what he calls *proofs*, which
he explains to be fuch arguments from experience as leave no
room for doubt or oppofition, in a higher clafs than probabilities.
And Mr. Locke himfelf, though he feems to confine certainty
to demonftration, yet allows concerning fome probabilities arifing
from human teftimony, that " they rife fo near to certainty, that
" they govern our thoughts as abfolutely, and influence our ac-
" tions as fully, as the moft evident demonftration ; and in what
" concerns us, we make little or no difference between them and
" certain knowledge.   Our belief thus grounded rifes to affur-
" ance *."   And in that cafe I think probability is too low a
word, and not fufficiently expreffive, or properly applicable to
things of this kind.   For according to Mr. Locke's account of it,
and the common ufage of the word, that is faid to be probable

* Effay on Human Underftanding, book iv. chap. xv. fect. 6.

which

which is *likely to be true*, and of which we have *no certainty*, but only *some inducements*, as Mr. Locke fpeaks, to believe and receive them as true.

Another thing obfervable in Mr. Hume's reafoning on this fubject is, that in treating of probability or the evidence of facts, which he foundeth wholly upon experience, he confoundeth the evidence of paft facts with that of the future: and the young gentleman himfelf feems not fufficiently to diftinguifh them. The inftances he produceth to fhew, that the judgments which the mind forms concerning the probability of events *will always be in proportion to the conftancy and regularity of the experience*, all relate to the probability of future events from the experience of the paft.   But the queftion about the probability of any future fact hath properly nothing to do in the prefent controverfy between Mr. Hume and his adverfaries, which relateth wholly to the evidence of paft facts; and it is only an inftance of this writer's art, that, by confounding thefe different queftions, he may perplex the debate, and throw duft in the eyes of his readers.  It will be granted, that with relation to future facts or events, the utmoft evidence we can attain to from paft obfervation or experience is a high degree of probability; but with relation to paft matters of fact, we may in many cafes arrive at a certainty, or what Mr. Hume calls a full proof: yea it often happens, that the evidence of paft facts may be fo circumftanced, that we may be certain that fuch an event really came to pafs, though, if the queftion had been put before the event, the probability from paft experience would have been greatly againft it. Nothing therefore can be more weak and fallacious than Mr. Hume's reafoning, when from this principle of forming conclufions concerning future events from paft experience, he endeavours to deduce an argument againft the belief of any miraculous fact, how well foever attefted.   For though, if the queftion were concerning a future miracle in any particular inftance, if we fhould judge merely from paft experience, the probability might feem to lie againft it; yet if the queftion be concerning a paft miraculous fact, there may be fuch proof of it, as may not leave room for a reafonable doubt that the miracle was real'y done, though before it was done it might feem highly improbable that it would be done.

Another

Another fallacy Mr. Hume is guilty of, is his suppofing that in all cafes where the fact, in itfelf confidered, is unufual, and out of the way of common experience, whatever be the evidence given for it, there muft ftill be a deduction made, and the affent given to it is always weakened in proportion to the unufualnefs of the fact. Now this doth not always hold. A fact of an extra-ordinary nature may come to us confirmed by an evidence fo ftrong, as to produce a full and undoubted affurance of its hav-ing been done: and in fuch a cafe there is no deduction to be made; nor is the affent we give to the truth of the fact at all weakened on the account of its being unufual and extraordinary. Thus, *e. g.* that a great king fhould be openly put to death by his own fubjects, upon a pretended formal trial before a court of judicature, is very unufual, and before it came to pafs would have appeared highly improbable; but after it happened, there is fuch evidence of the fact as to produce a full affurance that it was really done: and the man who fhould go about ferioufly to make a doubt of it, and make a formal deduction from the credit of the evidence, on the account of the ftrangenefs of the fact, and fhould pretend that we muft believe it with an affent only proportioned to the evidence which remaineth after that deduc-tion, would, under pretence of extraordinary accuracy, only ren-der himfelf ridiculous. It will indeed be readily owned, that more and greater evidence may be juftly required with regard to a thing that is unufual and out of the common courfe, than is required for a common fact; but when there is evidence given fufficient to fatisfy the mind, its being unufual and extraordi-nary ought not to be urged as a reafon for not giving a full cre-dit to it, or for pretending that the teftimony concerning it is not to be depended upon. For the evidence for a fact out of the courfe of common obfervation and experience may be fo cir-cumftanced, as to leave no room for the leaft reafonable doubt; and the affent to it may be as ftrong and firm as to any the moft common and ordinary event: nor is any thing in that cafe to be deducted from the credit of the evidence, under pretence of the fact's being unufual or even miraculous.

You will allow me on this occafion to take notice of a paffage in your letter, in which, after having obferved that Mr. Hume had ftudied the point about probability, and treated upon it with

great

great accuracy, you give it as your opinion, that " the beſt way
" of anſwering him would be in the way himſelf has chalked out,
" by comparing the degrees of probability in the evidence on
" both ſides, and deducting the inferior." Here you ſeem to
ſuppoſe, that there is evidence on both ſides in the caſe of miracles, and that, upon balancing the evidence, that which hath the
higher degrees of probability ought to be preferred, at the ſame
time making a deduction from it in proportion to the weight of
the contrary evidence. But the ſuppoſition you here proceed
upon appears to me to be a wrong one, *viz.* that in the caſe in
queſtion there is evidence on both ſides, and conſequently an oppoſition of evidence, *i. e.* evidence againſt the miracles wrought
in proof of Chriſtianity, as well as evidence for them. There
is indeed poſitive ſtrong evidence on one ſide, to ſhew that thoſe
facts were really done: an evidence drawn from teſtimony ſo
circumſtantiated, that it hath all the qualifications which could
be reaſonably deſired to render it full and ſatisfactory\*. But
what evidence is there on the other ſide? No counter-evidence
or teſtimony to ſhew the falſehood of this is pretended by Mr.
Hume to be produced; nor are there any circumſtances mentioned, attending the evidence itſelf, which may juſtly tend
to render it ſuſpicious. Nothing is oppoſed to it but the miraculous nature of the facts, or their being contrary to the uſual
courſe of nature; and this cannot properly be ſaid to be any evidence to prove that the facts were not done, or that the teſtimony given to them was falſe. Nor needs there any deduction
to be made in the aſſent we give to ſuch a full and ſufficient teſtimony as is here ſuppoſed, on that account: becauſe, as the caſe
was circumſtanced, it was proper that thoſe facts ſhould be beyond and out of the common courſe of nature and experience:
and it was agreeable to the wiſdom of God, and to the excellent ends for which thoſe facts were deſigned, that they ſhould
be ſo: ſince otherwiſe they would not have anſwered the intention, which was to give a divine atteſtation to an important revelation of the higheſt uſe and benefit to mankind.

It is an obſervation of the ingenious author of the paper you
ſent me, " That twelve honeſt perſons ſhould combine to aſſeit

\* See this fully ſhewn in anſwer to Mr. Hume, p. 280, & ſeq.

" a falſe-

" a falfehood, at the hazard of their lives, without any view to
" private intereft, and with the certain profpect of lofing every
" thing that is and ought to be dear to mankind in this world,
" is, according to Mr. Hume's own way of reafoning, as great
" a miracle, to all intents and purpofes, as any interruption in
" the common courfe of nature." But then he obferves, that
the thing thefe witneffes are fuppofed to atteft being alfo a miracle, contrary to the ufual courfe of nature, it may be objected,
that thefe evidences being equal, they only deftroy one another,
and ftill leave the mind in fufpenfe. The anfwer he gives to
this does not feem to me to be fufficiently clear. He firft obferves, that " this objection draws all its force from Mr. Hume's
" affertion, that an uniform and uninterrupted experience is a
" full proof, which when examined will not be found true, be-
" caufe it is confeffed on all hands, that all our reafonings con-
" cerning matters of fact ever fail fhort of certainty, or full
" proof." But befides that this doth not always hold, fince it has
been fhewn, that our reafonings concerning matters of fact may
in fome cafes amount to fuch a certainty as may be juftly called
a full proof, it may ftill be urged, that an uniform uninterrupted
experience, though not ftrictly a full proof, yet is fuch a proof
againft a miracle as is able to counterbalance the evidence for it:
in which cafe the objection ftill holds, and the mind is kept in
fufpenfe. And the gentleman himfelf feems afterwards to grant,
that a fact's being contrary to the ufual courfe of nature affordeth fuch a proof againft it from the nature of the thing, as is fufficient to counterpoife the evidence of twelve fuch witneffes as
are fuppofed, though he thinks it would not do fo, if the number of witneffes were doubled; and that this fhews that the proof
againft a miracle arifing from the nature of the fact may be exceeded by contrary human teftimony, which is what Mr. Hume
denies. And he argues, that if we fuppofe the teftimony of
twelve perfons for a miracle to be juft equal to the evidence
arifing from the nature of the thing againft it, and that we have
the evidence of twenty for any particular miracle recorded in
the Gofpel, then fubftracting the weaker evidence from the
ftronger, we fhall have a furplus of the pofitive teftimony of
eight perfons, without any thing to oppofe it.

I am perfuaded, that the defign of the ingenious gentleman, in
putting

putting the cafe after this manner, was to fignify it as his real opinion, that the teftimony of twelve fuch witneffes as are here fuppofed, in proof of a miracle's having been really wrought, did not more than countervail the argument againft it arifing from the ftrangenefs of the fact: but he had a mind to put the cafe as ftrongly as he could in favour of Mr. Hume, and yet to fhew, that there might ftill be an excefs of proof, according to his own account, on the fide of miracles; which deftroys his main hypothefis, that the evidence for a miracle can never exceed the evidence againft it. It appears to me however, that this is making too large a conceffion, and that it is not the propereft way of putting the cafe. It proceedeth upon the fuppofition, which hath been already fhewn to be a wrong one, that a thing's being miraculous, or contrary to the ufual courfe of nature, is alone in all circumftances a proper *proof* or *evidence* againft the truth of the fact; whereas the cafe may be fo circumftanced, that the miraculoufnefs of the fact is in reality no *proof* or *evidence* againft it at all. It will indeed be acknowledged, as was before hinted, that greater evidence is required with regard to a fact which is miraculous, than for any fact in the common and ordinary courfe. But when fuch evidence is given, to prove that a miraculous fact was really done, as is fuitable to the importance of the fact, and which cannot be rejected without admitting fuppofitions which are manifeftly abfurd; in fuch a cafe, a thing's being miraculous is no juft reafon for not giving a full affent to the teftimony concerning it. For its being miraculous, in the cafe that hath been put, hath nothing in it abfurd or incredible; whereas that twelve men of found minds and honeft characters fhould combine to atteft a falfehood, in oppofition to all their worldly interefts and prejudices, and to every principle that can be fuppofed to influence human nature, without any affignable caufe for fuch a conduct (which has been fhewn to be the cafe with regard to the witneffes for Chriftianity), is abfolutely abfurd, nor can in any way be accounted for. As to the pretence, that in this cafe there is a miracle on both fides, and that the one is to be oppofed to the other, and deftroys its evidence; this fophifm, which has impofed upon many, and in which the chief ftrength of Mr. Hume's effay lies, deriveth its whole force from an abufe of the word miracle, and a confounding, as this writer

hath

hath artfully done, a miracle and an abfurdity, as if it were the fame thing. That twelve men fhould, in the circumftances fuppofed, combine to atteft a falfehood, at the hazard of their lives and of every thing dear to men, cannot properly be called a miracle, according to any definition that can be reafonably given of a miracle, or even according to Mr. Hume's own definition of a miracle, that " it is a tranfgreffion of a law of nature by a " particular volition of the Deity, or by the interpofal of fome " invifible agent:" but is a manifeft abfurdity. But in the cafe of an extraordinary event, contrary to the ufual courfe of natural caufes, and wrought for a very valuable purpofe, and by a power adequate to the effect, there is indeed a proper miracle, but no abfurdity at all. It is true, that its being unufual and out of the ordinary courfe of obfervation and experience, is a good reafon for not believing it without a ftrong and convincing evidence, a much ftronger evidence than would be neceffary in common and ordinary facts. But when there is an evidence of its having actually been done, which hath all the requifites that can be juftly demanded in fuch a cafe, and at the fame time fufficient reafons are affigned, worthy of the divine wifdom and goodnefs, to fhew that it was proper to be done, its being unufual and extraordinary is no proof at all that it hath not been done, nor can in any propriety of language be called an *evidence* againft it; and therefore no fubftraction is to be made from the credit given to fuch a fuppofed full and fufficient evidence merely on this account. Perhaps my meaning will be better underftood, by applying it to a particular inftance: and I choofe to mention that which is the principal miracle in proof of Chriftianity, our Lord's refurrection. The fact itfelf was evidently miraculous, and required a divine power to accomplifh it. It was therefore neceffary, in order to lay a juft foundation for believing it, that there fhould be fuch an evidence given as was proportioned to the importance and extraordinarinefs of the fact. And that the evidence which was given of it was really fuch an evidence, appears, I think, plainly from what I have elfewhere obferved concerning it *. But if we fhould put the cafe thus: that not only was the fact extraordinary in itfelf, and out of the

---

* See above, p. 275, & feq.

common courfe of nature, but the evidence given of it was in-
fufficient, and not to be depended upon, and had circumftances
attending it which brought it under a juft fufpicion: or, if contrary evidence was produced to invalidate it; *e. g.* if the foldiers
that watched the fepulchre, inftead of pretending that the body of
Jefus was ftolen away whilft they were afleep, which was no
evidence at all, and was a plain acknowledgment that they knew
nothing at all of the matter, had declared that the difciples come
with a powerful band of armed men, and overpowered the guard,
and carried away the body: or, if any of the Jews had averred,
that they were prefent and awake when the foldiers flept, and
that they faw the difciples carry away the body: or, if any of the
difciples to whom Jefus appeared, and who profeffed to have
feen and converfed with him after his refurrection, had afterwards declared, that they were among the difciples at thofe times
when he was pretended to have appeared, and that they faw no
fuch appearances, nor heard any fuch converfations as were pretended. On this fuppofition, it might be properly faid that there
was evidence given on both fides, *viz.* for and againft Chrift's
refurrection, and confequently that there was a real oppofition
of evidence; in which cafe it would be neceffary carefully to
examine the evidences, and compare them one with another, in
order to judge which of them deferved the greater credit, and
how far one of them weakened or impaired the force of the other.
But as the cafe was circumftanced, fince there was a very ftrong
pofitive evidence given, that Chrift really rofe from the dead,
and fhewed himfelf alive after his refurrection by many infallible
proofs, and no contrary evidence produced againft it, nor any
thing alleged to render the evidence that was given of it juftly
fufpected; and fince there are alfo very good reafons affigned,
worthy of the divine wifdom and goodnefs, which rendered it
highly proper that Chrift fhould be raifed from the dead: on this
view of the cafe, the extraordinarinefs of the fact, alone confidered, cannot properly be called an *evidence* againft the truth of it,
nor be juftly urged as a reafon for not yielding a full affent to
the evidence concerning it: for it was neceffary to the ends propofed by the divine wifdom, that the fact fhould be of an extraordinary and miraculous nature; and if it had not been fo, it
would not have anfwered thofe ends. I think therefore it may

juſtly be affirmed, that, taking the caſe in all its circumſtances, conſidering the great ſtrength and force of the evidence that is given for the faɛt, and the many concurring proofs and atteſtations by which it was confirmed, together with the excellent and important ends for which it was deſigned, there is as juſt ground to believe that Chriſt roſe again from the dead, as that he was crucified; though the latter be a faɛt not out of the ordinary courſe of nature, and the former was evidently ſo. And here it may not be improper to mention a remarkable obſervation of Mr. Locke. He had, in giving an account of the grounds of probability, ſuppoſed one ground of it to be the conformity of a thing with *our own knowledge, obſervation, and experience* : and after taking notice of ſeveral things to this purpoſe, he obſerves, that " though common experience and the ordinary courſe of " things have juſtly a mighty influence on the minds of men, to " make them give or refuſe credit to any thing propoſed to their " belief, yet there is one caſe wherein the ſtrangeneſs of the faɛt " leſſens not the aſſent to a fair teſtimony given of it : for where " ſuch ſupernatural events are ſuitable to ends aimed at by him " who has the power to change the courſe of nature; there un- " der ſuch circumſtances they may be fitter to procure belief, by " how much the more they are beyond or contrary to common " obſervation. This is the proper caſe of miracles, which, well " atteſted, do not only find credit themſelves, but give it alſo to " other truths which need ſuch a confirmation*.

Thus this great maſter of reaſon is ſo far from thinking with Mr. Hume, that a thing's being miraculous, or beyond the common courſe of obſervation and experience, abſolutely deſtroys all evidence of teſtimony that can be given concerning the truth of the faɛt, that in his opinion it doth not ſo much as leſſen the aſſent given to it upon a fair teſtimony; provided the ſupernatural faɛts thus atteſted were ſuitable to the ends of the divine wiſdom and goodneſs, *i. e.* wrought in atteſtation to a revelation of the higheſt importance, and of the moſt excellent tendency; and that in that caſe the more evidently miraculous the faɛt is, the fitter it is to anſwer the end propoſed by it.

The ingenious author of the paper you ſent me has very pro-

* Locke's Eſſay on Human Underſtanding, book iv. chap. xvi. ſec. 13.

perly fummed up Mr. Hume's argument againſt the evidence of miracles, thus: We have had a long, univerſal, and uninterrupted experience, that no events have happened contrary to the courſe of nature, from conſtant and unvaried obſervations. We have therefore a full proof, that this uniform courſe has not been broken in upon, nor will be, by any particular exceptions.

But the obfervation of truth depending upon, and conſtantly following human teſtimony, is by no means univerſal and uninterrupted: and therefore it does not amount to a full proof, that it either has or will follow in any particular inſtance.

And therefore the proof ariſing from any human teſtimony, can never equal the proof that is deduced againſt a miracle from the very nature of the fact.

This he takes to be a full and fair ſtate of Mr. Hume's reaſoning: and it appears to me to be ſo. And he ſays, " The aufwer is " plain. If by human teſtimony he would mean of any one " ſingle man indifferently taken, then his ſecond propoſition " would be true; but then the concluſion would by no means " follow from it: but if by human teſtimony he would underſtand " the evidence of any collection of men, then the ſecond propo- " ſition is falſe, and confequently the concluſion is ſo too."

This anſwer relateth only to the ſecond propoſition *. But it might have been ſaid, that neither of the propoſitions are to be depended upon, and that they are utterly inſufficient to ſuppor. the concluſion he would draw from them. For as to the firſt propoſition, it aſſumes the very point in queſtion: it affirms, that no events have ever happened contrary to the courſe of nature; and that this we know by a long, univerſal, and uninterrupted experience. If this be meant univerſal and uninterrupted experience of all mankind in all ages, which alone can be of any

---

* Though the ingenious gentleman hath not directly and formally anſwered the firſt propoſition, yet he has plainly ſhewn that he doth not admit it, when he ſaith, that " the very ſame objection Mr. Hume makes againſt " the veracity of human teſtimony, to weaken its authenticity, may be retort- " ed with equal force againſt his unvaried certainty of the courſe of nature. " And that doubtleſs the many approved hiſtorics we have relating to mira- " cles, will as much leſſen the probability of what he calls a full proof on his " ſide of the queſtion, as all the forgeries and falſhoods that are brought to " diſcredit human teſtimony will weaken it on the other."

force in the prefent argument, how doth it appear that we know by univerfal and uninterrupted experience, that no fuch events have ever happened? Are there not feveral events of this kind recorded by credible teftimonies to have happened? The whole argument then is upon a wrong foundation. It proceedeth upon an univerfal and uninterrupted experience, not broken in upon in any inftance. And there is good teftimony to prove, that it hath been broken in upon in feveral inftances. And if it hath been broken in upon in any inftances, no argument can be brought from experience to prove that it hath not, or may not be broken in upon; and fo the whole reafoning falls. If it be alledged, that thefe teftimonies, or indeed any teftimonies at all, ought not to be admitted in this cafe, the queftion returns, For what reafon ought they not to be admitted? If the reafon be, as it muft be according to Mr. Hume, becaufe there is an univerfal un-interrupted experience againft them, this is to take it for granted, that no fuch events have ever happened: for if there have been any inftances of fuch events, the experience is not univerfal and uninterrupted. So that we fee what the boafted argument againft miracles from uniform experience comes to. It in effect comes to this, that no fuch events have ever happened, becaufe no fuch events have ever happened.

As to the fecond propofition, though if we fpeak of human teftimony in general, it will be eafily allowed, that it is not to be abfolutely and univerfally depended upon; yet, as hath been already hinted, it may in particular inftances be fo circumftanced, as to yield a fatisfying affurance, or what may not impro-perly be called a full proof. Even the teftimony of a particular perfon may in fome cafes be fo circumftanced, as to leave no room for reafonable fufpicion or doubt. But efpecially if we fpeak of what this gentleman calls *a collection of men*, this may in fome cafes be fo ftrong, as to produce a full and entire con-viction, however improbable the attefted fact might otherwife appear to be. And therefore if we meet with any teftimonies relating to particular events of an extraordinary nature, they are not immediately to be rejected, under pretence of their being contrary to paft experience; but we muft carefully examine the evidence brought for them, whether it be of fuch a kind as to make it reafonable for us to believe them: and that the evidence

brought

brought for the miraculous facts recorded in the gospel are of this kind hath been often clearly shewn.

The only farther reflection I shall make on this gentleman's paper is, that it contains good and proper observations concerning our being determined in matters of practice by probabilities: That in all cases of moment, where to act or forbear may be attended with confiderable damage, no wife man makes the least fcruple of doing what he apprehends may be of advantage to him, even though the thing were doubtful: but in matters of the utmost confequence, a prudent man will think himfelf obliged to take notice of the lowest probability, and will act accordingly. This he applies to the practice of religion, and obferves, that confidering the vaft importance of religion to our happinefs in every refpect, — the bare poffibility that it might prove true, were there nothing elfe to fupport it, would engage his affent and compliance: or elfe he muft be fuppofed to act differently in this refpect to what he generally does in all the other concerns of his life.

This obfervation is not entirely new, but it is handfomely illuftrated by this gentleman, and feems very proper to fhew, that thofe who neglect and defpife religion, do in this, notwithftanding their boafted pretences, act contrary to the plain dictates of reafon and good fenfe. But we need not have recourfe to this fuppofition. The evidence on the fide of religion is vaftly fuperior. And if this be the cafe, no words can fufficiently exprefs the folly and unreafonablenefs of their conduct, who take up with flight prejudices and prefumptions in oppofition to it; and by choofing *darknefs rather than light*, and rejecting *the great falvation* offered in the Gofpel, run the utmoft hazard of expofing themfelves to a heavy condemnation and punifhment.

Thus I have taken the liberty you allowed me of giving my thoughts upon the paper you fent me. I cannot but look upon the young gentleman's attempt to be a laudable and ingenious one, though there are fome things in his way of managing the argument, which feem not to have been thoroughly confidered, and which, I am fatisfied, he would have altered, if he had lived to take an accurate review of the fubject.

This, with a few additions fince made to it, is the fubftance of the anfwer I returned to the worthy gentleman who had written to me,

me, and which I have here inferted, becaufe there are fome things
in it that may tend to the farther illuftration of what I had offered in my remarks on Mr. Hume's *Effay on Miracles*.    My next
will contain fome additional obfervations relating to the Abbé de
Paris, and the miracles attributed to him; together with reflections on fome paffages in Mr. Hume's *Enquiry concerning the
Principles of Morals*, which feem to be intended to expofe Chriftianity.

*Some Reflections on the extraordinary Sanctity ascribed to the*
*Abbé de Paris—He carried Superstition to a strange Excess,*
*and by his extraordinary Austerities voluntarily hastened his*
*own Death—His Character and Course of Life, of a different*
*kind from that rational and solid Piety and Virtue which is*
*recommended in the Gospel—Observations on some Passages in*
Mr. Hume's Enquiry concerning the Principles of Morals—
*He reckons Self-denial, Mortification, and Humility among the*
*Monkish Virtues, and represents them as not only useless, but*
*as having a bad Influence on the Temper and Conduct—The*
*Nature of Self-denial explained, and its great Usefulness and*
*Excellence shewn—What is to be understood by the Mortifica-*
*tion required in the Gospel—This also is a reasonable and ne-*
*cessary Part of our Duty—Virtue, according to Mr. Hume, hath*
*nothing to do with Sufferance—But by the Acknowledgment of*
*the wisest Moralists, one important Office of it is to support and*
*bear us up under Adversity—The Nature of Humility explain-*
*ed—It is an excellent and amiable Virtue.*

SIR,

THE miracles of the Abbé de Paris have made so great a noise
in the world, and so much advantage hath been taken of
them by the enemies of Christianity, and particularly by Mr.
Hume, that I thought it necessary to consider them pretty largely
above in the nineteenth Letter. Some things have occurred
since, which have some relation to that matter, and which I shall
here take notice of.

In that Letter, p. 352, mention is made of the high opinion
the people had conceived of the Abbé's extraordinary sanctity, as
what tended very much to raise their expectations of miracles to
be wrought at his tomb, and by his intercession. If we inquire
whence this opinion of his extraordinary sanctity arose, and upon
what it was founded, we shall find it to have been principally
owing to the excessive austerities in which he exercised himself
for several years; of which therefore, and of some remarkable

things

things in his life and his character, it may not be improper to give some account. The particulars I shall mention are set forth at large by the learned Mr. Mosheim, in a differtation on the miracles of the Abbé de Paris, and which I did not meet with till after the publication of the second volume of the *View of the Deistical Writers.* It is intitled, *Inquifitio in veritatem miraculorum Francifci de Paris fæculi noftri thaumaturgi* \*. What he there tells us concerning Monf. de Paris is faithfully taken from thofe who hold him in the higheft admiration, the Janfeniftical writers. And from their accounts it fufficiently appears, that his whole life, and efpecially the latter part of it, was one continued fcene of the moft abfurd fuperftition, and which he carried to an excefs that may be thought to border upon madnefs.

He was the eldeft fon of an ancient, rich, and honourable family, and therefore born to an opulent fortune: though his father, when he faw his turn of mind, very prudently left him but a part of it, and that in the hands and under the care of his younger brother. But though he ftill had an ample provifion made for him, he voluntarily deprived himfelf of all the conveniencies, and even the neceffaries, of life. He chofe one obfcure hole or cottage after another to live in, and often mixed with beggars, whom he refembled fo much in his cuftoms, fordid and tattered garb, and whole manner of his life, that he was fometimes taken for one, and was never better pleafed, than when this expofed him in the ftreets and ways to derifion and contempt. Poverty was what he fo much affected, that though he applied to his brother for what his father had left him, yet that he might not have the appearance of being rich, he chofe not to take it as what was legally due to him, but to fupplicate for it in the humbleft terms, as for an alms freely beftowed upon a miferable object that had nothing of his own. And yet afterwards in his laft will, he difpofed of it as his own to various ufes as he thought fit, efpecially for the benefit of thofe who had been fufferers for the Janfenift caufe. For feveral of the laft years of his life, he feemed to make it his bufinefs to contrive ways to weaken or harrafs, and torment his body, and thereby haften his own death.

* Vide Jo. Laur. Mofhemii Differtationum ad Hiftoriam Ecclefiafticam pertinentium volumen fecundum.

Whilft

Whilst he gave away his income to the poor, he himself voluntarily endured all the evils and hardships which attended the extremity of want and poverty. Mean and wretched was his garb; black bread, water, and herbs, but without oil, salt, or vinegar, or any thing to give them favour, was his only sustenance, and that but once a day. He lay upon the ground, and was worn away with continual watching. After his death were found, his hair shirt, an iron crofs, a girdle, stomacher, and bracelets of the same metal, all bestuck with sharp points. These were the instruments of penitence, with which he was wont to chastife himself, the plain marks of which he bore on his body. By such a courfe he brought himself not only into great weaknefs of body, but into diforders of mind: and this, which was the natural effect of his manner of living, he attributed to the influence of the devil, whom God had in just judgment permitted to punish him for his fins. And in inquiring into the caufes of the divine difpleafure, he fixed upon this, that he had still too great a love for human learning and knowledge, and therefore from thenceforth did all he could to divest himfelf of it, and would have fold his well-furnished library, if he had not been prevented by fome of his friends, whofe interest it was to preferve it. For two years together he refufed to come to the holy fupper, under pretence that it was not lawful for him to come, God having required him to abstain from it; and it was with great difficulty that he was brought to it at last, by the threatenings and even reproaches of his confeffor. Finally, that no kind of mifery might be wanting to him, he chofe for his companion, to dwell with him in his cottage, a man that was looked upon to be crazy, and who treated him in the most injurious manner. He did all he could to hide himfelf from his friends, in one forry cottage after another; and about a month before his death, fixed himfelf in a little lodge in the corner of a garden, expofed to the fun and wind. When by fuch feverities he had brought himfelf into an univerfal bad habit of body, and it was vifible to his friends, that if he continued in that courfe he could not long fupport under it, a phyfician was called in, who only defired him to remove to a more commodious habitation, to allow himfelf more fleep, and a better diet, and efpecially to take nourifhing broths for reftoring his enfeebled conftitution. But all the per-

C c 4                                    fuafions

suasions of his physician, confessor, and of his friends, and the tears of an only brother, could not prevail with him to follow an advice so reasonable and practicable; though he was assured, that, if he used that method, there was great hope of his recovery, and that his life could not be preserved without it. And when at last, to satisfy their importunity, he seemed so far to comply, as to be willing to take some broth, it was only an appearance of complying, for he took care to give such orders to the person who was to prepare it for him, that it really yielded little or no nourishment. Thus it was manifest, that he had determined to hasten, as much as in him lay, his own death. And accordingly he told his confessor, that this life had nothing in it to make it worth a Christian's care to preserve it. His friends acknowledge, that his death was the effect " of the almost incre- " dible austerities that he exercised during the last four years of " his life." His great admirer the Abbé de Asfeld testifies, that he heard him declare it as his purpose to yield himself a slow sacrifice to divine justice.

This his extraordinary course of austerities, together with the zeal he expressed to the very last for the Jansenist cause, which he shewed also by the dispositions he made in his will, as well as by his appealing, as with his dying breath, to a future general council against the constitution *Unigenitus*, procured him so extraordinary a reputation, that he has passed for one of the greatest saints that ever appeared in the Christian church. No sooner was he dead, but an innumerable multitude of people ran to his corpse, some of whom kissed his feet, others cut off part of his hair as a remedy against all manner of evil; others brought books or bits of cloth to touch his body, as believing it filled with a divine virtue. Thus were they prepared to believe and expect the most wonderful things.

Whosoever impartially considers the several things that have been mentioned, and which are amply verified in the places referred to in the margin*, will not think the learned Mosheim in the wrong, when he pronounceth, that it cannot in consistency with reason be supposed, that God should extraordinarily interpose by his own divine power, to do honour to the bones and

* See Mosheim, ut supra, from p. 364. to p. 395.

ashes

afhes of a man weak and fuperftitious to a degree of folly, and who was knowingly and wilfully acceffory to his own death. In vain do his admirers, as he himfelf had done, extol his thus def-troying himfelf as an offering up himfelf a voluntary facrifice to divine juftice. If a man fhould under the fame pretence difpatch himfelf at once with a piftol or poniard, would this be thought a proper juftification of his conduct? And yet I fee not why the pretence might not as well hold in the one cafe as in the other; fince it makes no great difference, whether the death was fwifter or flower, provided it was brought on with a deliberate intention and defign.

How different is this from the beautiful and noble idea of piety and virtue which the Gofpel furnifheth us with, and from the perfect pattern of moral excellence which is fet us by our bleffed Saviour himfelf in his own holy life and practice! That the great apoftle St. Paul was far from encouraging fuch aufte-rities as tended to hurt and deftroy the bodily health, fufficiently appears from the advice he gave to Timothy, *Drink no longer water, but ufe a little wine, for thy ftomach's fake, and thine of-ten infirmities*—1 Tim. v. 23. He condemneth thofe that, under pretence of extraordinary purity, were for obferving the *ordi-nances* and *traditions* of men, *Touch not, tafte not, handle not;* and brands their practice under the name of *will-worfhip*, a *vo-luntary humility*, and *neglecting*, or, as the word might he ren-dered, *not fparing the body*, Col. ii. 20, 21, 22, 23. That which in the cafe of Abbé de Paris is cried up by his admirers as a car-rying religion to the higheft degree of perfection, *viz.* his ab-ftaining from flefh, and confining himfelf to herbs, is reprefented by the apoftle Paul as a fign of weaknefs in the faith—Rom. xiv. 2.

It hath always appeared to me to be the glory of the Chriftian religion, as prefcribed in the New Teftament, that the piety it teacheth us is folid and rational, remote from all fuperftitious extremes, worthy of a God of infinite wifdom and goodnefs to require, and becoming the true dignity of the reafonable nature. It comprehendeth not only immediate acts of devotion towards God, but a diligent performance of all relative duties, and the faithful difcharge of the various offices incumbent upon us in the civil and focial life. It requireth us indeed to bear with a noble

fortitude

fortitude the greateſt evils, when we are regularly called to ſuf-
fer for the cauſe of God, but not raſhly to expoſe ourſelves to
thoſe evils, or to bring them upon ourſelves.

The wiſe and beneficent author of nature hath ſtored the whole
world about us with a variety of benefits: and can it be thought
to be agreeable to his will, that, inſtead of taſting his goodneſs in
the bleſſings he vouchſafeth us, we ſhould make a merit of never
allowing ourſelves to enjoy them?   How much more rational is
it to receive thoſe bleſſings with thankfulneſs, and enjoy them
with temperance, according to that of St. Paul—*Every creature
of God is good, and nothing to be refuſed, if it be received with
thankſgiving: for it is ſanctified by the word of God and prayer,*
1 Tim. iv. 4, 5.   Can it be pleaſing to our merciful heavenly
Father, that we ſhould not merely humble and chaſten ourſelves
on ſpecial occaſions, but make it our conſtant buſineſs to torment ourſelves, and to impair and deſtroy the bodies he hath
given us, and thereby unfit ourſelves for the proper offices of
life?   Is it reaſonable to imagine, that under the mild diſpenſation of the Goſpel, which breathes an ingenuous cheerful ſpirit,
and raiſeth us to the noble liberty of the children of God, the
beſt way of recommending ourſelves to his favour ſhould be to
deny ourſelves all the comforts he affordeth us, and to paſs our
lives in perpetual ſadneſs and abſtinence?   Could it be ſaid in
that caſe, that *godlineſs is profitable unto all things, having promiſe of the life that now is, and of that which is to come?* 1 Tim.
iv. 8.   It is true, that mortification and ſelf-denial are important goſpel duties, but how different from the extremes of ſuperſtitious rigour will appear, when I come to vindicate the evangelical morality againſt the objections of Mr. Hume.   It was not
till Chriſtians began to degenerate from that lovely form of rational, ſolid piety and virtue, of which Chriſt himſelf exhibited
the moſt perfect example, that they laid ſo mighty a ſtreſs on
thoſe ſevere and rigorous auſterities, which neither our Saviour
nor his apoſtles had commanded.   And in this reſpect ſome of
thoſe who were anciently deemed heretical ſects carried it to a
greater degree of ſtrictneſs than the orthodox themſelves.   And
many zealots there have been in falſe religions, and particularly
ſome of the heathen devotees in the Eaſt Indies, who in ſevere
penances, and rigid auſterities, and in voluntary torments inflicted

flicted on their own bodies, have far exceeded the Abbé de Paris himself.

I think no farther obfervations need be made with regard to Mr. Hume's *Effay on Miracles*, which is directly levelled againft Chriftianity. But any one that is acquainted with his writings muft be fenfible, that he often takes occafion to throw out infinuations againft religion, which he ufually reprefents either under the notion of fuperftition or enthufiafm. Even the morals of the gofpel have not efcaped his cenfure, though their excellence is fuch as to have forced acknowledgments from fome of thofe who have been ftrongly prejudiced againft it.

There is a paffage to this purpofe in his *Inquiry concerning the Principles of Morals*, which deferves particular notice. In that Inquiry, as in all his other works, he affumes the merit of making new difcoveries, and placing things in a better light than any man had done before him; and wonders that a theory fo *fimple and obvious* as that which he hath advanced; *could have efcaped the moft elaborate fcrutiny and examination\**. I will not deny that there are in that Inquiry fome good and curious obfervations; but I can fee little that can be properly called new in his theory of morals, except his extending the notion of virtue (and it is concerning the principles of morals, and therefore concerning moral virtue, that his Inquiry proceeds) fo as to comprehend under it every agreeable quality and accomplifhment, fuch as *wit, ingenuity, eloquence, quicknefs of conception, facility of expreffion, delicacy of tafte* in the finer arts, *politenefs* †,

---

\* Enquiry concerning the Principles of Morals, p. 172.

† It has been hinted to me by a worthy friend, that fome have thought I did wrong in not allowing *politenefs* to be ranked among the moral virtues. And therefore to prevent miftakes, I now obferve, that if by politenefs be meant a kind, obliging behaviour, expreffive of humanity and benevolence, and flowing from it, it may be juftly reckoned among the virtues : and in this fenfe a plain countryman, who is good-natured and obliging in his deportment to the utmoft of his power, may be faid to be truly a polite man. But this feems not to be the ufual acceptation of the word in our language. By *politenefs* is commonly underftood a being well verfed in the forms of what is ufually called *good breeding*, and a genteel behaviour. And taken in that fenfe, however agreeable and ornamental it may be, I apprehend it is not properly a moral virtue ; nor is the want of it a vice. And I believe it will fcarce be denied, that a man may be really a good and worthy perfon, and yet not be what the world calls a polite well-bred man.

*cleanlinefs,*

*cleanliness*, and even *force of body**. I cannot fee what valuable
end it can anfwer in a treatife of morals to extend the notion of
virtue fo far.  It is of high importance to mankind rightly to diftinguifh things that are morally good and excellent from thofe
which are not fo; and therefore great care fhould be taken, that
both our ideas of thefe things, and the expreffions defigned to
fignify them, fhould be kept diftinct.  Wit, eloquence, and what
we call natural parts, as well as acquired learning, politenefs,
cleanlinefs, and even ftrength of body, are no doubt real advantages, and when under a proper direction, and rightly applied,
are both ornamental and ufeful, and are therefore not to be neglected, but, as far as we are able, to be cultivated and improved.
This will be eafily acknowledged: and if this be all Mr. Hume
intends, it is far from being a new difcovery.  But thefe things
make properly no part of moral virtue; nor can a man be faid to
be good and virtuous on the account of his being poffeffed of
thofe qualities.  He may have wit, eloquence, a polite behaviour,
a fine tafte in the arts, great bodily ftrength and refolution, and
yet be really a bad man.  And when thefe things are feparated
from good difpofitions of the heart, from probity, benevolence,
fidelity, integrity, gratitude, inftead of rendering a man ufeful
to the community, they qualify him for doing a great deal of
mifchief.  Thefe qualities therefore fhould be carefully diftinguifhed from thofe which conftitute a good moral character, and
which ought to be principally recommended to the efteem and
approbation of mankind, as having in themfelves a real invariable
worth and excellence, and as deriving a merit and value to every
other quality.  Nor is it proper, in a treatife of morals, which
pretends to any degree of accuracy, to confound them all together under one common appellation of virtue.

And as Mr. Hume enlargeth his notion of virtue, fo as to take
in feveral things that do not feem properly to belong to the moral
difpofitions and qualities, fo he excludeth from that character
fome things which are recommended in the gofpel as of importance to the moral temper and conduct, particularly humility
and felf-denial.  He obferves, that " celibacy, fafting, penance,

---

* See the 6th, 7th, and 8th fections of the Inquiry concerning the Principles of Morals, particularly p. 127, 128. 131. 135. 137. 162. 165.

" mortification,

" mortification, felf-denial, humility, folitude, and the whole
" train of monkifh virtues, are every-where rejeſted by men of
" fenfe, becaufe they ferve no manner of purpofe: they neither
" advance a man's fortune in the world, nor render him a more
" valuable member of fociety, neither qualify him for the enter-
" tainment of company, nor increafe his power of felf-enjoy-
" ment——On the contrary, they crofs all thefe defirable ends,
" ſtupify the underſtanding, and harden the heart, obfcure the
" fancy, and four the temper\*." Our author is here pleafed
to clafs *humility, mortification,* and *felf-denial,* which are evidently required in the gofpel, with *penances, celibacy,* and what
he calls the monkifh virtues; and pronounceth concerning all
alike, that they are rejeſted by all *men of fenfe,* and not only ferve
no manner of purpofe, but have a bad influence in ſtupifying
the underſtanding, hardening the heart, and fouring the temper.
This is no doubt to caſt a flur upon the gofpel fcheme of morality. And on the other hand he cries up his own theory of
morals, as reprefenting *Virtue in all her engaging charms.* That
" nothing appears but gentlenefs, humanity, beneficence, affa-
" bility, nay even at proper intervals, play, frolic, and gaiety.
" She talks not of ufelefs auſterities and rigours, fufferance and
" felf-denial, &c. †." A fcheme of morals which-includeth *play,*
*frolic,* and *gaiety,* and has nothing to do with *felf-denial, mor-*
*tification,* and *fufferance,* will no doubt be very agreeable to
many in this gay and frolicfome age. But let us examine more
diſtinſtly what ground there is for our author's cenfures, as far
as the Chriſtian morals are concerned.

To begin with that which he feemeth to have a particular averfion to, *felf-denial.* This is certainly what our Saviour exprefsly
requireth of thofe who would approve themfelves his faithful
difciples. He infiſteth upon it, as an effential condition of their
difciplefhip, that they fhould deny themfelves—Mat. xvi. 24.
Mark viii. 34. And if we do not fuffer ourfelves to be frightened by the mere found of words, but confider what is really intended, this is one of the moſt ufeful leffons of morality, and a
neceffary ingredient in a truly excellent and virtuous charaſter.
One thing intended in this felf-denial is the reſtraining and go-

\* Inquiry concerning the Principles of Morals, p. 174:  † Ibid. p. 188.

verning

verning our appetites and paffions, and keeping them within
proper bounds, and in a due fubjection to the higher powers of
reafon and confcience: and this is certainly an important part of
felf-government and difcipline, and is undoubtedly a noble at-
tainment, and which argueth a true greatnefs of foul. And
however difficult or difagreeable it may at firft be to the animal
part of our natures, it is really neceffary to our happinefs, and
layeth the beft foundation for a folid tranquillity and fatisfaction
of mind. Again, if we take felf-denial for a readinefs to deny
our private intereft and advantage for valuable and excellent
ends, for the honour of God, or the public good, for promoting
the happinefs of others, or our own eternal falvation, and for
ferving the caufe of truth and righteoufnefs in the world ; in
this view nothing can be more noble and praife-worthy. And
indeed whoever confiders that an inordinate felfifhnefs, and ad-
dictednefs to a narrow flefhly intereft, and the gratification of the
carnal appetites and paffions, is the fource of the chief diforders
of human life, will be apt to look upon felf-denial to be of great
confequence to morals. Without fome degree of felf-denial,
nothing truly great, noble, or generous is to be atchieved or attained. He that cannot bear to deny himfelf upon proper occafions,
will never be of any great ufe either to himfelf or to others, nor
can make any progrefs in the moft virtuous and excellent endowments, or even in agreeable qualities, and true politenefs.
This writer himfelf, fpeaking of *the love of fame*, which, he tells
us, rules in all generous minds, obferves, that as this prevaileth,
*the animal conveniences fink gradually in their value*\*. And
elfewhere, in the perfon of the Stoic philofopher, he faith, that
" we muft often make fuch important facrifices, as thofe of life
" and fortune, to virtue:" And that " the man of virtue looks
" down with contempt on all the allurements of pleafure, and all
" the menaces of danger—toils, dangers, and death itfelf carry
" their charms, when we brave them for the public good†." And
even after having told us, that virtue talks not of fufferance and
felf-denial, he adds, that " virtue never willingly parts with any
" pleafure, but in hope of ample compenfation in fome other

---

\* Inquiry concerning the Principles of Morals, p. 188.
† See the 19th of his Moral and Political Effays, p. 213.

" period

" period of their lives. The fole trouble fhe demands is of a juft
" calculation, and a fteady preference of the greater happinefs \*."
Here he allows, that virtue may reafonably part with prefent
pleafure, in hope of an ample compenfation in fome other period
of our lives, when upon a juft calculation it contributes to our
greater happinefs. But then he feems to confine the hope of the
compenfation which virtue is to look for, to fome future period
of this prefent life, which, confidering the fhortnefs and uncertainty of it, is little to be depended on, and may perhaps be
thought not a fufficient foundation for a man's denying himfelf
prefent pleafures and advantages. But the gofpel propofeth a
much more noble and powerful confideration, *viz.* the fecuring
a future everlafting happinefs; and fuppofing the certainty of
this, of which we have the fulleft affurance given us, nothing
can be more agreeable to all the rules of reafon and juft calculation, than to part with prefent pleafure, or to undergo prefent
hardfhips, to obtain it.

What hath been offered with regard to the important duty of
felf-denial may help us to form a juft notion of *mortification*,
which is nearly connected with it, and which our author alfo find-
eth great fault with. The chief thing intended by it is the fub-
duing our flefhly appetites, and our vicious and irregular inclinations and defires. To this purpofe it is required of us, that we
*mortify the deeds of the body,* Rom. viii. 13. that we *mortify our
members that are on the earth, fornication, uncleannefs, inordinate
affection, evil concupifcence, and covetoufnefs, which is idolatry,*
Col. iii. 5.; and that we *crucify the flefh, with the affections and
lufts,* Gal. v. 24. Mortification taken in this view is a noble act
of virtue, and abfolutely neceffary to maintain the dominion of
the fpirit over the flefh, the fuperiority of reafon over the inferi-
or appetites. Where thefe prevail, they tend to *ftupify the underftanding, and harden the heart,* and hinder a man from being
a *valuable member of fociety,* which is what Mr. Hume moft un-
juftly chargeth upon that mortification and felf-denial which is
required in the gofpel. Mortification is properly oppofed to
that indulging and pampering the flefh, which tendeth to nou-
rifh and ftrengthen thofe appetites and lufts, which it is the part

---

\* Inquiry concerning the Principles of Morals, p. 188.

of a wife and virtuous man to correct and subdue. Even fasting upon proper seasons and occasions, however ridiculed by Mr. Hume and others, may answer a very valuable end, and make a useful part of self-discipline. It may tend both to the health of the body, and to keep the mind more clean and vigorous, as well as, when accompanied with prayer, promote a true spirit of devotion. But in this as in every thing else, the Christian religion, considered in its original purity as laid down in the New Testament, preserveth a most wise moderation, and is far from carrying things to extremes, as superstition hath often done. It doth not any-where insist upon excessive, or what our author calls useless rigours and austerities. And so far is that mortification which the Gospel prescribeth, and which is nothing more than the keeping the body under a just discipline, and in a due subjection to the law of the mind, from being inconsistent with the true pleasure and satisfaction of life, that it layeth the most solid foundation for it. Mr. Hume himself takes notice of the "*supreme joy* which is to be found in the victories over vice, " when men are taught to govern their passions, to reform their " vices, and subdue their worst enemies, which inhabit within " their own bosoms *."

Not only does this gentleman find fault with self-denial and mortification, but with *sufferance.* Virtue, according to his representation of it, *talks not of sufferance and self-denial.* And yet certain it is, that among the best moralists of all ages it has been accounted one of the principal offices of virtue, to support us with a steady fortitude under all the evils that befal us in this present state, and enable us patiently and even cheerfully to bear them. A virtue that cannot suffer adversity, nor bear us up under it with dignity, and in a proper manner, is of little value in a world where we are exposed to such a variety of troubles and sorrows. And in this the Gospel morality is infinitely superior to that of the most admired pagan philosophers. Mr. Hume has reckoned among virtues " an undisturbed philosophi- " cal tranquillity, superior to pain, sorrow, anxiety, and each " assault of adverse fortune †." But what is this philosophical

* Moral and Political Essays, p. 213.
† Inquiry concerning the Principles of Morals, p. 152.

tranquillity

tranquillity, fo much boafted of, relying only upon itfelf, compared with that which arifeth from the confolations fet before us in the gofpel, from the affurances of divine affiftances and fupports, from the love of God and fenfe of his favour, from the lively animating hopes of glory, and the eternal rewards which fhall crown our patience, and perfevering continuance in well-doing?

The laft thing I fhall take notice of, as reprefented under a difadvantageous character by Mr. Hume, though highly commended and infifted on by our Saviour, is *humility:* and this rightly underftood is one of the moft amiable virtues, and greateft ornaments of the human nature.   Our author is pleafed to talk of a *certain degree of pride and felf-valuation,* the want of which is *a vice,* and the oppofite to which is *meannefs* \*.   But to call a proper generofity of mind, which is above a mean or bafe thing, *pride,* is an abufe of words, which ought not to be admitted, if we would fpeak with exactnefs, in an inquiry concerning morals. It is to give the name of an odious vice to a very worthy difpofition of foul.   The gofpel humility is a very different thing from meannefs.   It is very confiftent with fuch a juft felf-valuation, as raifeth us above every thing falfe, mean, bafe, and impure, and keepeth us from doing any thing unbecoming the dignity of the reafonable nature, and the glorious character and privileges we are invefted with as Chriftians.   True humility doth not abfolutely exclude all fenfe of our own good qualities and attainments; but it tempers the fenfe we have of them with a juft conviction of our abfolute dependance upon God for every good thing we are poffeffed of, and of our manifold fins, infirmities, and defects.   It is oppofed to a vain-glorious boafting and felf-fufficiency, and to fuch a high conceit of our abilities and merits, as puffeth us up with a prefumptuous confidence in ourfelves, and contempt of others, and which is indeed one of the greateft hinderances to our progrefs in the moft excellent and worthy attainments.   It manifefteth itfelf towards God, by an entire unreferved fubjection and refignation to his authority and will, by proper acknowledgments of our own unworthinefs before him, and a fenfe of our continual dependance upon him, and conftant

---

\* Inquiry concerning the Principles of Morals, p. 146, 147.

need of his gracious affiftance. And it expreffeth itfelf towards men, by caufing us to yield a due fubmiffion to our fuperiors, and to be affable and condefcending to our inferiors, courteous and obliging towards our equals, in honour preferring one ano-ther, as St. Paul expreffeth it, and ready to bear with each other's weakneffes and abfurdities. In a word, it diffufeth its kindly influence through the whole of our deportment, and all the offices of life. Nothing is fo hateful as pride and arrogance. And true humility is fo amiable, fo engaging, fo neceffary to render a perfon agreeable, that no man can hope to pleafe, who hath not at leaft the appearance of it. Our author himfelf ob-ferves, that " among well-bred people, a mutual deference is " affected, contempt of others difguifed *:" and that " as we are " naturally proud and felfifh, and apt to affume the preference " above others, a polite man is taught to behave with deference " towards thofe he converfes with, and to yield the fuperiority " to them in all the common occurrences of fociety†." So that, according to him, a fhew of humility and preferring others to ourfelves, is a neceffary part of good behaviour; and yet he is pleafed to reckon humility among thofe things that neither ren-der a man a more valuable member of fociety, nor qualify him for the entertainment of company, but on the contrary crofs thefe defirable purpofes, and harden the heart, and four the temper.

But enough of Mr. Hume; who, if we may judge of him by his writings, will fcarce be charged with the fault of having car-ried humility to an excefs. A pity it is that he hath not made a better ufe of his abilities and talents, which might have laid a juft foundation for acquiring the praife he feems fo fond of, as well as rendered him really ufeful to the world, if he had been as in-duftrious to employ them in ferving and promoting the excellent caufe of religion, as he hath unhappily been in endeavouring to weaken and expofe it !

* Inquiry concerning the Principles of Morals, p. 161, 162.
† Moral and political Effays, p. 184, 185.

# POSTSCRIPT.

A FTER great part of this work was finifhed, and fent to the
prefs, I met with a book, which I have read with great
pleafure, intitled, *The Criterion; or, Miracles examined, with
a View to expofe the Pretenfions of Pagans and Papifts; to compare the miraculous Powers recorded in the New Teftament,
with thofe faid to fubfift in latter Times; and to fhew the great
and material Difference between them in point of Evidence: from
whence it will appear, that the former muft be true, and the
latter may be falfe.* The fubject is evidently both curious and
important, and is treated by the author, who, I hear, is the Rev.
Mr. Douglafs, in a judicious and mafterly way. It was publifhed at London in 1754, and therefore before the publication of
the fecond volume of the *View of the Deiftical Writers.* And
if I had then feen it, I fhould certainly have thought myfelf
obliged to take particular notice of it. The worthy author has
made judicious obfervations upon Mr. Hume's *Effay on Miracles,* efpecially that part of it which relateth to the miracles afcribed to the Abbé de Paris, which he has infifted on for an
hundred pages together. And it is no fmall fatisfaction to me,
that there is a perfect harmony between what this learned author
has written on this fubject, and what I have publifhed in the preceding part of this work, though neither of us knew of the
other's work. He fhews, as I have endeavoured to do, that
fraud and impofture were plainly detected in feveral inftances:
and that where the facts were true, natural caufes fufficient to
produce the effect may be affigned, without fuppofing any thing
miraculous in the cafe. This he has particularly fhewn, with
regard to each of the miracles infifted on by Mr. de Montgeron,
which he accounts for much in the fame way that Mr. des Voeux
hath more largely done, though he had not feen that gentleman's
valuable writings, to which I have frequently referred for a fuller
account of thofe things, which I could do little more than hint

at. The reader will find in Mr. Douglafs's work a full proof of the wonderful force of the imagination, and the mighty influence that ftrong impreffions made upon the mind, and vehement paffions raifed there, may have in producing furprizing changes on the body, and particularly in removing difeafes: of which he hath produced feveral well-attefted inftances, no lefs extraordinary than thofe attributed to the Abbé de Paris, and which yet cannot reafonably be pretended to be properly miraculous.

As I have thought myfelf obliged to take notice of that part of this gentleman's book, which hath fo near a connection with the work in which I have been engaged; fo it is but juft to obferve, that it is alfo, with regard to every other part of it, a learned and accurate performance.

What he propofes to fhew is, that the evidence for the gofpel facts is as extraordinary as the facts themfelves; and that no juft fufpicion of fraud or falfehood appeareth in the accounts; while every thing is the reverfe, with regard to the evidence brought for the pagan or popifh miracles.

He obferves, that the extraordinary facts afcribed to a miraculous interpofition among the Pagans of old, or the Chriftians of latter times, are all reducible to thefe two claffes. The accounts are either fuch as, from the circumftances thereof, appear to be falfe; or, the facts are fuch as, by the nature thereof, they do not appear to be miraculous. As to the firft, the general rules he lays down, by which we may try the pretended miracles amongft Pagans and Papifts, and which may fet forth the grounds on which we fuppofe them to be falfe, are thefe three : That either they were not publifhed to the world till long after the time when they were faid to be performed : Or, they were not publifhed in the places where it is pretended the facts were wrought, but were propagated only at a great diftance from the fcene of action: Or, they were fuffered to pafs without due examination, becaufe they coincided with the favourite opinions and prejudices of thofe to whom they were reported; or, becaufe the accounts were encouraged and fupported by thofe who alone had the power of detecting the fraud, and could prevent any examination, which might tend to undeceive the world. Thefe obfervations he applies to the pagan and popifh miracles ; fome of the moft remarkable of which he diftinctly mentions, and fhews, that there

are

are none of them that do not labour under one or other of these defects.

After confidering thofe pretended miracles, which, from the circumftances of the accounts given of them, appear to be falfe, he next proceedeth to thofe works, which, though they may be true, and afcribed by ignorance, art, or credulity, to fupernatural caufes, yet are really natural, and may be accounted for, without fuppofing any miraculous interpofition ; and here he enters on a large and particular difcuffion of the miracles attributed to the Abbé de Paris, and of fome other miracles that have been much boafted of in the Romifh church.

Having fully examined and expofed the pagan and popifh miracles, he next proceeds to fhew, that the objections made againft them, and which adminifter juft grounds of fufpicion, cannot be urged againft the gofpel miracles. And here he diftinctly fhews, Firft, that the facts were fuch that, from the nature of them, they muft needs be miraculous, and cannot be accounted for in a natural way, or by any power of imagination, or ftrong impreffions made upon the mind ; and, Secondly, that thofe facts are fuch as, from the circumftances of them, they cannot be falfe. And to this purpofe, he makes it appear, that they were publifhed and appealed to at the time when they were performed, and were coeval with the preaching of Chriftianity, which was manifeftly founded upon them. They were alfo publifhed and attefted at the places where the fcene of them was laid, and on the fpot on which they were wrought: and the circumftances, under which they were firft publifhed, give us an affurance, that they underwent a ftrict examination, and confequently that they could not have efcaped detection, had they been impoftures.

Mr. Douglafs thinks it not fufficient barely to prove, that the teftimony for the gofpel-miracles is ftronger than that which fupporteth any other pretended miracles ; he further fhews, by a variety of confiderations, that it is the ftrongeft that can be fuppofed, or that from the nature of the thing could be had. And then he proceeds to obferve, that, befides the unexceptionable proof from teftimony, the credibility of the gofpel-miracles is confirmed to us, by collateral evidences of the moft ftriking nature, and which no fpurious miracles can boaft of: Such as, the great change that was thereby introduced into the ftate of religion:

the

the proofs that God was with the firſt publiſhers of Chriſtianity, in other inſtances beſides thoſe of miracles, particularly in aſſiſting them ſupernaturally in the knowledge of the ſcheme of religion which they taught, and of which they were not capable of being the authors or inventors, and enabling them to give clear predictions of future events.    And particularly he inſiſteth upon that moſt expreſs and circumſtantial prediction of the deſtruction of the city and temple of Jeruſalem, and the diſperſion of the Jewiſh nation, as a demonſtration that Jeſus acted under a ſupernatural influence.    The laſt thing he urgeth as a collateral evidence is, that the miracles recorded in Scripture were performed by thoſe who aſſumed the character of prophets, or teachers ſent from God, and their miracles were intended as credentials to eſtabliſh their claim, to add authority to the meſſages they delivered, and the laws they taught — A character which, he ſhews, both the pagan and popiſh miracles are entirely deſtitute of.

This is a brief account of the plan of Mr. Douglaſs's work, which fully anſwereth the title : and it is with great pleaſure I take this opportunity to acknowledge the merit of the learned author, and the ſervice he hath done to the Chriſtian and Proteſtant cauſe.

I am, Sir, &c.

# LETTER XXII.

*Lord Bolingbroke's Posthumous Works an insolent Attempt upon*
*Religion, natural and revealed—Not written according to the*
*Laws of Method—His fair Professions, and the advantageous*
*Account he gives of his own Design—He exalteth himself above*
*all that have written before him, Ancients and Moderns:*
*blames the Free-thinkers for taking unbecoming Liberties; yet*
*writes himself without any Regard to the Rules of Decency—*
*His outrageous Invectives against the Holy Scriptures, parti-*
*cularly the Writings of Moses and St. Paul—The severe Cen-*
*sures he passeth on the most celebrated Heathen Philosphers—*
*But, above all, the virulent and contemptuous Reproaches he*
*casteth upon Christian Philosophers and Divines—A general*
*Account of his Scheme, and the main Principles to which it is*
*reducible.*

SIR,

THE account you gave me of the late pompous edition of the
works of the late Lord Viscount Bolingbroke in five large
volumes 4to. made me very desirous to see them. But it was
some time after the publication of them, before I had an opportunity of gratifying my curiosity. I have now read them with
some care and attention.

The works he had published in his own life-time, and which
are republished in this edition, had created a high opinion of the
genius and abilities of the author. In them he had treated chiefly
concerning matters of a political nature; and it were greatly to
be wished for his own reputation, and for the benefit of mankind,
that he had confined himself to subjects of that kind, in that part
of his works which he designed to be published after his decease.
These his posthumous works make by far the greater part of this
collection. His *Letters on the Study and Use of History*, which
were published before the rest, had prepared the world not to
look for any thing from him, that was friendly to Christianity or
the holy Scriptures. But I am apt to think, that the extreme
insolence, the virulence and contempt with which in his other

posthumous

posthumous works he hath treated those things that have been hitherto accounted most sacred among Christians, and the open attacks he hath made upon some important principles of natural religion itself, have exceeded whatever was expected or imagined. There is ground to apprehend, that the quality and reputation of the author, his high pretensions to reason and freedom of thought, his great command of words, and the positive and dictatorial air he every-where assumes, may be apt to impose upon many readers, and may do mischief in an age too well prepared already for receiving such impressions. Upon these considerations, you have been pleased to think, that a distinct examination of this writer might help to furnish a very proper supplement to the view which hath been taken of the deistical writers of the last and present century. I was, I must confess, not very fond of the employment: for what pleasure could be proposed in raking into such a heap of materials, which are thrown together without much order, and among which one is sure to meet with many things shocking to any man that has a just veneration for our holy religion, and who hath its honour and interests really at heart?

Before I enter on a distinct consideration of what Lord Bolingbroke hath offered both against natural and revealed religion, I shall make some general observations on his spirit and design, and his manner of treating the subjects he has undertaken, which may help us to form a judgment of his character as a writer, and how far he is to be depended upon.

The manner of writing his Lordship hath generally chosen is by way of essay. He has been far from confining himself to the laws of method; and perhaps thought it beneath so great a genius to stoop to common rules. But there is certainly a medium between being too stiff and pedantic, and too loose and negligent. He is sensible that he has not been very methodical, and seems to please himself in it. He declares, that " he does not observe " in these Essays, any more than he used to do in conversation, " a just proportion in the members of his discourse* :" and that he has thrown his reflections upon paper as they " occurred to " his thoughts, and as the frequent interruptions to which he

---

* Bolingbroke's Works, vol. iii. p. 460.

" was

" was expofed would give him leave*." He condefcends to
make a kind of apology for this way of writing, when he fays,
" I will endeavour not to be tedious; and this endeavour will
" fucceed the better perhaps by declining any over-ftrict obfer-
" vation of method†." But I am apt to think he would have
been lefs tedious, and more enlightening to his reader, if he had
been more obfervant of the rules of method. He might then
have avoided many of thofe repetitions and digreffions, which fo
frequently recur in thefe Effays, and which, notwithftanding all
the advantages of his ftyle, and the vivacity of his imagination,
often prove, if I may judge of others by myfelf, very difagreeable and irkfome to the reader.

As to his defign in thefe writings, if we are to take his own
word for it, very great advantage might be expected from them
to mankind. He believes " few men have confulted others, both
" the living and the dead, with lefs precipitation, and in a great-
" er fpirit of docility, than he has done : He diftrufted himfelf,
" not his teachers, men of the greateft name, ancient and modern.
" But he found at laft, that it was fafer to truft himfelf than
" them, and to proceed by the light of his own underftanding, than
" to wander after thofe *ignes fatui* of philofophy ‡." He is fenfible that " it is the modeft, not the prefumptuous inquirer, who
" makes a real and fafe progrefs in the difcovery of divine truth §:
and that " candour and knowledge are qualifications which
" fhould always go together, and are infeparable from the love of
" truth, and promote one another in the difcovery of it ∥." He
contents himfelf to be " governed by the dictates of nature, and
" is therefore in no danger of becoming atheiftical, fuperftitious,
" or fceptical **."

In his introduction to his Effays, in a letter to Mr. Pope, he
gives a moft pompous account of his intentions, and evidently
raifeth himfelf above the greateft men, ancient and modern. He
" reprefents metaphyfical divines and philofophers, as having be-
" wildered themfelves, and a great part of mankind, in fuch inex-
" tricable labyrinths of hypothetical reafonings, that few can find

---

* Bolingbroke's Works, vol. iii. p. 556.　　† Ibid. p. 312.
‡ Ibid. p. 320.　　§ Ibid. p. 344.
∥ Ibid. p. 492.　　** Ibid. vol. v. p. 492.
　　　　　　　　　　　　　　　　" their

" their way back, and none can find it forward into the road of
" truth\*." He declares that " natural theology, and natural re-
" ligion, have been corrupted to such a degree, that it is grown,
" and was long since, as neceffary to plead the caufe of God
" againft the divine as againft the atheift; to affert his exiftence
" againft the latter, to defend his attributes againft the former,
" and to juftify his providence againft both †." That " truth and
" falfehood, knowledge and ignorance, revelations of the Creator,
" inventions of the creature, dictates of reafon, fallies of enthu-
" fiafm, have been blended fo long together in fyftems of theology,
" that it may be thought dangerous to feparate them ‡." And
he feems to think this was a tafk referved for him. He propofes
" to diftinguifh genuine and pure theifm from the prophane mix-
" tures of human imagination; and to go to the root of that er-
" ror which encourages our curiofity, fuftains our pride, forti-
" fies our prejudices, and gives pretence to delufion; to difcover
" the true nature of human knowledge, how far it extends, how
" far it is real, and where and how it begins to be fantaftical §;"
" that the gaudy vifions of error being difpelled, men may be ac-
" cuftomed to the fimplicity of truth." For this he expects to
be " treated with fcorn and contempt by the whole theological
" and metaphyfical tribe, and railed at as an infidel ‖." But " lay-
" ing afide all the immenfe volumes of fathers and councils,
" fchoolmen, cafuifts, and controverfial writers, he is determin-
" ed to feek for genuine Chriftianity with that fimplicity of fpirit
" with which it is taught in the gofpel by Chrift himfelf\*\*."
The guides he propofes to follow are, " the works and the word
" of God ††." And he declares, that " for himfelf he thought it
" much better not to write at all, than to write under any reftraint
" from delivering the whole truth of things as it appeared to
" him ‡‡."

But though he thus profeffes an impartial love of truth, and to
deliver his fentiments with freedom, yet he feems refolved, where
he happens to differ from the received opinion, not to fhew a decent regard to the eftablifhed religion of his country. He praifeth

---

\* Bolingbroke's Works, vol. iii. p. 327.      † Ibid. p. 327, 328.
‡ Ibid. p. 331.                                  § Ibid. p. 328.
‖ Ibid. p. 330.                                  \*\* Ibid p. 339.
†† Ibid. p. 347.                                 ‡‡ Ibid. vol. iv. p. 54.

Scævola and Varro, who, he fays, " both thought that things " evidently falfe might deferve an outward refpect, when they " are interwoven with a fyftem of government. This outward " refpect every good fubject will fhew them in fuch a cafe. He " will not propagate thofe errors, but he will be cautious how he " propagates even truth in oppofition to them *." He blames not only that arbitrary *tyrannical fpirit* that puts *on the mafk of religious zeal,* but that *prefumptuous factious fpirit* that has appeared *under the mafk of liberty;* and which, if it fhould prevail, *would deftroy at once the general influence of religion, by fhaking the foundations of it which education had laid.* But he thinks, " there is a middle way between thefe extremes, in which a rea- " fonable man and a good citizen may direct his fteps †." It is to be prefumed therefore, that he would have it thought that this is the way he himfelf hath taken. He mentions with approbation the maxims of the Soufys, a fect of philofophers in Perfia: one of which is: " If you find no reafon to doubt concerning the opi- " nions of your fathers, keep to them, they will be fufficient for " you. If you find any reafon to doubt concerning them, feek " the truth quietly, but take care not to difturb the minds of " other men." He profeffeth to proceed by thefe rules, and blameth fome who are called Free-thinkers for imagining, that as " every man has a right to think and judge for himfelf, he has " therefore a right of fpeaking according to the full freedom of " his thoughts. The freedom belongs to him as a rational crea- " ture: He lies under the reftraint as a member of fociety ‡."

But notwithftanding thefe fair profeffions, perhaps there fcarce ever was an author who had lefs regard to the rules of decency in writing than Lord Bolingbroke. The holy Scriptures are received with great veneration among Chriftians; and the religion there taught is the religion publicly profeffed and eftablifhed in thefe nations; and therefore, according to his own rule, ought to be treated with a proper refpect. And yet on many occafions he throws out the moft outrageous abufe againft thofe facred writings, and the authors of them. He compares the hiftory of the Pentateuch to the romances Don Quixote was fo fond of;

---

* Bolingbroke's Works, vol. iii. p. 331. † Ibid. p. 332.
‡ Ibid. p. 333; 334.

and pronounces that they who receive them as authentic are not much lefs mad than he *. That " it is no lefs than blafphemy to " affert the Jewifh Scriptures to have been divinely infpired;" and he reprefents thofe that attempt to juftify them as having " ill hearts as well as heads, and as worfe than atheifts, though " they may pafs for faints†." He chargeth thofe with impiety, " who would impofe on us, as the word of God, a book which " contains fcarce any thing that is not repugnant to the wifdom, " power, and other attributes of a Supreme All-perfect Being‡." And he roundly pronounceth, that " there are grofs defects and " palpable falfehoods in almoft every page of the Scriptures, and " the whole tenor of them is fuch, as no man, who acknowledges " a Supreme All-perfect Being, can believe to be his word§." This is a brief fpecimen of his invectives againft the facred writings of the Old Teftament, and which he repeateth on many occafions. He affecteth indeed to fpeak with feeming refpect of Chriftianity, yet he has not only endeavoured to invalidate the evidences that are brought to fupport it, but he paffeth the feve-reft cenfures upon doctrines which he himfelf reprefenteth as original and effential doctrines of the Chriftian religion. He makes the moft injurious reprefentation of the doctrine of our redemption by the blood of Chrift, and chargeth it as repugnant to all our ideas of order, of juftice, of goodnefs, and even of theifm‖. And after a moft virulent invective againft the Jewifh notion of God, as partial, cruel, arbitrary, and unjuft, he afferts, that the character imputed to him by the Chriftian doctrine of re-demption, and future punifhments, is as bad or worfe**. Great is the contempt and reproach he hath poured forth upon St. Paul, who was the penman of a confiderable part of the New Tefta-ment, and whofe name and writings have been always defervedly had in great veneration in the Chriftian church. He chargeth him with diffimulation and falfehood, and even with madnefs††. He afferts that his gofpel was different from that of Chrift, and contradictory to it‡‡; that he writes confufedly, obfcurely, and

---

* Bolingbroke's Works, vol iii. p. 280.    † Ibid. p. 299. 306.
‡ Ibid. p. 308.    § Ibid. p. 298.
‖ Ibid. vol. iv. p. 318. vol. v. p. 291. 532.    ** Ibid. p. 532, 533.
†† Ibid. vol. iv. p. 172. 306.    ‡‡ Ibid. p. 313. 327, 328.

unintelligibly;

unintelligibly;—and where his gofpel is intelligible, it is often abfurd, profane, and trifling*.

Some of thofe gentlemen who have fhewn little refpect for the holy Scriptures, have yet fpoke with admiration of many of the fages of antiquity: but Lord Bolingbroke has on all occafions treated the greateft men of all ages with the utmoft contempt and fcorn. It is allowable indeed for fincere and impartial inquirers after truth, to differ from perfons of high reputation for know-ledge and learning, ancient and modern: and fometimes it is the more neceffary to point out their errors, left the authority of great names fhould lead men afide from truth. But whilft we think ourfelves obliged to detect their miftakes, there is a decent regard to be paid them: it would be wrong to treat them in a reproachful and contemptuous manner. Yet this is what our author hath done. If all the paffages were laid together, in which he hath inveighed againft the wifeft and moft learned men of all ages, efpecially the philofophers, metaphyficians, and divines, they would fill no fmall volume. And indeed thefe kind of de-clamatory invectives recur fo often in thefe Effays, as cannot but create great difguft to every reader of tafte. I fhall mention a few paffages out of a multitude that might be produced, and which may ferve as a fample of the reft. He faith of the philo-fophers, that " they feem to acquire knowledge only as a necef-" fary ftep to error, and grow fo fond of the latter, that they " efteem it no longer human, but raife it by an imaginary apo-" theofis up to a divine fcience: That thefe fearchers after truth, " thefe lovers of wifdom, are nothing better than venders of falfe " wares: And the moft irrational of all proceedings pafs for the " utmoft efforts of human reafon†." He reprefents metaphyfi-cal divines and philofophers as having " wandered many thou-" fand years in imaginary light and darknefs‡." He frequently chargeth them with *madnefs*, and fometimes with *blafphemy:* and that they " ftaggered about, and joftled one another in their " dreams§." Speaking of Plato and Ariftotle, he fays, " their " works have been preferved, perhaps more to the detriment than " to the advancement of learning‖." And though he fometimes

---

* Bolingbroke's Works, vol. iii. p. 330, 331. 　　† Ibid. vol. iii. p. 490.
‡ Ibid. vol. iv. p. 8. 　　§ Ibid. vol. iii. p. 553, 554. vol. iv. p. 129. 150.
‖ Ibid. vol. iii. p. 592.

commends

commends Socrates, he pronounces, that he " fubfituted fan-
" taftical ideas inftead of real knowledge, and corrupted fcience
" to the very fource:" That " he loft himfelf in the clouds —
" when he declared, that the two offices of philofophy are, the
" contemplation of God, and the abftracting of the foul from
" corporeal fenfe:" And that he and Plato were mad enough to
think themfelves capable of fuch contemplation and fuch abftrac-
tion*. Befides many occafional paffages fcattered throughout
thefe Effays, there are feveral large fections which contain almoft nothing elfe than invectives againft Plato and his philofophy.
He fays, that philofopher " treated every fubject, whether cor-
" poreal or intellectual, like a bombaft poet, and a mad theolo-
" gian†:" That " he who reads Plato's works like a man in his
" fenfes, will be tempted to think on many occafions that the
" author was not fo:" And that " no man ever dreamed fo wild-
" ly as this author wrote‡." He chargeth him with a " falfe
" fublime in ftyle, and that no writer can fink lower than he
" into a tedious focratical irony, into certain flimfy hypothetical
" reafonings that prove nothing, and into allufions that are mere
" vulgarifms, and that neither explain nor inforce any thing
" that wants to be explained or inforced§." He reprefents all
the commentators and *tranflators* of Plato as *dull* or *mad;* and
calls Ficinus *delirious*, and Dacier *fimple* and a *bigot*, and a
*Platonic madman*‖. The true reafon of the particular diflike
he every-where expreffes againft that philofopher feems to be
what he calls his " rambling fpeculations about the divine and
" fpiritual nature, about immaterial fubftances, about the immor-
" tality of the foul, and about the rewards and punifhments of a
" future ftate**."

As to the Stoics, he declares, " that their theology and morality
" were alike abfurd:" That, in endeavouring to account how it
came that there is evil in the world, and that the beft men have
often the greateft fhare of this evil, " they talked mere nonfenfe,
" figurative, fublime, metaphyfical, but nonfenfe ftill††." The
ancient *theifts* in general he reprefents as having been feduced

* Bolingbroke's Works, vol. iv. p. 113.    † Ibid. p. 129.
‡ Ibid. p. 344. 357.    § Ibid. p. 140, 141. 353, 354.
‖ Ibid. p. 107, 140. 355.    ** Ibid. p. 347, 348.
†† Ibid. vol. v. p. 247. 317.

many

many ways into a confederacy with the atheists, and particularly blames them for pretending to connect moral attributes, such as we conceive them, with the physical attributes of God; which, he affirms, gave great advantage to the objections of the atheists *.

But there is no fort of men against whom he inveighs with greater licence of reproach than the Christian divines and philosophers. He frequently speaks of the ancient fathers with the utmost contempt: That they were superstitious, credulous, lying men;—and that " the greatest of them were unfit to write " or speak on any subject that required closeness of reasoning, " an evangelical candour, and even common ingenuousness †." As to the more modern divines, he takes every occasion of insulting and abusing them. Not only doth he represent them as " declaimers who have little respect for their readers,—as hired " to defend the Christian system,—and as seeking nothing more " than the honour of the gown, by having the last word in every " dispute ‡;" but he says, " they talk a great deal of blasphemy " on the head of internal divine characters of Scripture §." He often repeats it, that *atheists deny God*, but the *divines defame him*, which, he thinks, is the *worse of the two*. He charges them with *madness*, and *worse than madness* ‖: That " they have " recourse to trifling distinctions, and dogmatical affirmations, " the last retrenchments of obstinacy **:" That " of all fools, the " most presumptuous, and at the same time most trifling, are " metaphysical philosophers and divines ††." He charges them, in an address he makes to God, with " owning his existence only " to censure his works, and the dispensations of his provi- " dence ‡‡." And frequently represents them as in *alliance with the atheists*, as *betraying the cause of God* to them, and as doing *their best, in concert with these their allies*, to destroy both the *goodness* and *justice* of God §§. He declares, that " he who fol- " lows them cannot avoid presumption and profaneness, and " must be much upon his guard to avoid blasphemy ‖‖:"  " That

---

* Bolingbroke's Works, vol. v. p. 316.
† Ibid. vol. iii. p. 337, 338. vol. iv. p. 586.
‡ Ibid. p. 290. vol. v. p. 286. 314.          § Ibid. vol. iii. p. 272.
‖ Ibid. vol. iv. p. 273.                        ** Ibid. vol. v. p. 188.
†† Ibid. p. 493.                                ‡‡ Ibid. p. 339.
§§ Ibid. p. 341. 346. 393, &c.                  ‖‖ Ibid. p. 464.

" the

" the preachers of natural and revealed religion have been loudeſt
" in their clamours againſt Providence, and have done nothing
" more than repeat what the atheiſts have ſaid;—and that they
" attempt to prove that the Supreme Being is the tyrant of the
" world he governs \*." And the ſame charge he advanceth
againſt the Chriſtian philoſophers in general.

But beſides theſe general invectives againſt Chriſtian philoſophers and divines, he hath particularly attacked ſome of the moſt
celebrated names in a manner little reconcileable to good manners, and the decency which ought to be obſerved towards perſons of diſtinguiſhed reputation, even when we think them in
the wrong. Speaking of " many reverend perſons, who," he
ſays, " have had their heads turned by a preternatural fermentation
" of the brain, or a philoſophical delirium,"—he obſerves, that
" none has been more ſo than Dr. Cudworth.—He read too
" much to think enough." He repreſents him as having " given
" a nonſenſical paraphraſe of nonſenſe;"—and that " the good
" man paſſed his life in the ſtudy of an unmeaning jargon: and
" as he learned, ſo he taught †." He charges Biſhop Cumberland with " metaphyſical jargon, and theological blaſphemy ‡."
Stillingfleet is ſpoken of with contempt; as alſo Huet, Bochart,
and the Chriſtian antiquaries §. Nor is archbiſhop Tillotſon
treated with greater regard. He talks in a very ſlighting way of
thoſe that have written on the law of nature, particularly Grotius,
Selden, and Puffendorf: That they " puzzle and perplex the
" plaineſt thing in the world, and ſeem to be great writers on
" this ſubject, by much the ſame right as he might be called a
" great traveller, who ſhould go from London to Paris by the
" Cape of Good Hope ‖." There is none of the Chriſtian philoſophers of whom he ſpeaks with ſo much reſpect as Mr. Locke;
yet he repreſents him as having " dreamed that he had a power
" of forming abſtract ideas;" and mentions this as a proof, that
" there is ſuch a thing as a philoſophical delirium \*\*." And he
charges it upon him as a great inconſiſtency, that he ſhould write
a Commentary on St. Paul's Epiſtles, and a Diſcourſe on the

---

\* Bolingbroke's Works, vol. v. p. 484, 485.
† Ibid. vol. iii. p. 353. vol. iv. p. 92. ‡ Ibid. vol. v. p. 82.
§ Ibid. vol. iii. p. 264. vol iv. p. 13. ‖ Ibid. vol. v. p. 68.
\*\* Ibid. vol. ii. p. 441, 442.

Reaſonableneſs

Reafonablenefs of Chriftianity, after he had written an Effay on Human Underftanding\*.

But there is no one perfon whom he treats with fo much rudenefs and infolence as the late eminently learned Dr. Samuel Clarke. He calls him a prefumptuous dogmatift, and reprefents him as having " impioufly advanced, that we know the rule God " governs by as well as he,—and that, like another Eunomius, " he prefumes to know God, his moral nature at leaft, and to " teach others to know him, as well as he knows himfelf †." He chargeth him with a *foolifh and wicked rhodomontade*, " with " pretending to make infallible demonftrations, like the Pope's " decrees, and fending every one to the devil who does not be- " lieve in them ‡: and with a rhapfody of prefumptuous reafon- " ings, of prophane abfurdities, of evafions that feem to anfwer " while they only perplex, and in one word, the moft arbitrary " and leaft reafonable fuppofitions §." He faith, that " the re- " trenchments caft up by him are feeble beyond belief." That " he boafts like a bully, who looks fierce, fpeaks big, and is " little to be feared ||." Not only does he call him an *audacious and vain fophift*\*\*, but he carries it fo far as to fay, that " he " and Wollafton do in effect renounce God, as much as the " rankeft of the atheiftical tribe ††. With regard to the laft mentioned celebrated writer, Mr. Wollafton, befides the fevere reproach caft upon him in the paffage I have juft cited, Lord Bolingbroke elfewhere treats him as " a licentious maker of hypo- " thefes—and a whining philofopher." He reprefents all that he hath faid about the immortality of the foul " as a ftring of " arbitrary fuppofitions;" and that " his difcourfe on that fub- " ject is fuch as would lead one to think, that the philofopher " who held it was a patient of Dr. Monro's not yet perfectly " reftored to his fenfes ‡‡. He acknowledges him indeed to have been a man of *parts and learning*, but charges him with *writing nonfenfe;* that he, and fuch as he, were *learned lunatics;* and he treats his way of arguing about a future ftate, as a *fpecimen of*

---

\* Bolingbroke's Works, vol. iv. p. 166. 295:
† Ibid. vol. iii. p. 52. vol. v. p. 449.
‡ Ibid. p. 252.
§ Ibid. p. 272.
|| Ibid. p. 289. 293.
\*\* Ibid. p. 293.
†† Ibid. p. 484, 485.
‡‡ Ibid. vol. iii. p. 515. 518, vol. v. p. 383.

*that fort of madnefs* which is called a *dementia quoad hoc*\*. The fame cenfure he paffeth on the late Lord Prefident of Scotland, " that he was indeed a man of capacity, good fenfe, and know- " ledge, but was in a *delirium*, and mad, *quoad hoc*, when he wrote " againft Tindal †."

You cannot but have obferved, in reading over feveral of the paffages which have been produced, that it is familiar with Lord Bolingbroke to reprefent thofe as mad and out of their fenfes who happen to differ from him, at leaft as mad with regard to the par- ticular point in difference. I fhall only mention one paffage more to this purpofe out of the many that might be produced. Having compared the reafoners *a priori* to perfons in *Bedlam*, and the fe- veral forts of madmen there, he adds, that " atheifts are one fort " of madmen, many divines and theifts another fort;"—and that " thefe forts of madmen are principally to be found in colleges " and fchools, where different fects have rendered this fort of mad- " nefs, which is occafionally elfewhere, both epidemical and tra- " ditional ‡." If one were to imitate this author's manner of talk- ing, one might be apt to charge him as being feized with a fort of madnefs, when certain fubjects come in his way—metaphyfics; artificial theology; Plato and Platonic philofophy; fpiritual fub- ftance, and incorporeal effence; but, above all, the Chriftian di- vines and clergy. Thefe, when he happens to meet with them, bring one of his fits upon him, and often fet him a-raving for feveral pages together. But I confefs I too much diflike fuch a way of writing to make recriminations of this kind. And yet his lordfhip tells the divines of the *difcretion of their adverfaries,* and would have them *return it with difcretion.* And he repre- fents the *orthodox bullies,* as he calls them, as " affecting to tri- " umph over men, who employ but part of their ftrength, as tiring " them with impertinent paradoxes, and provoking them with un- " juft reflections, and often by the fouleft language §."

I am apt to think, that by this time you are weary of reading over fuch a heap of abufive reflections, fo unbecoming any man of learning and education, much more one fo converfant in the polite world as Lord Bolingbroke has been. The tranfcribing

---

\* Bolingbroke's Works, vol. v. p. 474.          † Ibid. p. 523.
‡ Ibid. p. 369, 370.          § Ibid. vol. iii. p. 272, 273.

them out of his Effays was no very agreeable employment. But
they fo often occur there, and make fo remarkable a part of the
works of this right honourable author, that it was abfolutely
neceffary to take fome notice of them. One thing may be fafely
collected from his writing after this manner, *viz.* that he had
a very high opinion of the fuperiority of his own underftanding,
and a fovereign contempt for all thofe that were in different
fentiments from him, whether philofophers, ancient or modern,
or divines, but efpecially for the latter.

If we examine what foundation there is for thefe high pretenfions, or what new and important difcoveries this writer hath
made in religion or philofophy, which may be of real ufe to mankind, the principal things in his fcheme may be reduced to the
following heads:

1. That there is one Supreme All-perfect Being, the eternal
and original caufe of all things, of almighty power and infinite
wifdom; but that we muft not pretend to afcribe to him any
moral attributes, diftinct from his phyfical, efpecially holinefs,
juftice, and goodnefs: that he has not thefe attributes, according
to the ideas we conceive of them, nor any thing equivalent to
thofe qualities as they are in us; and that to pretend to deduce
moral obligations from thofe attributes, or to talk of imitating
God in his moral attributes, is enthufiafm or blafphemy.

2. That God made the world, and eftablifhed the laws of this
fyftem at the beginning: but that he doth not now concern himfelf in the affairs of men, or that if he doth, his providence only
extendeth to collective bodies, but hath no regard to individuals,
to their actions, or to the events that befal them.

3. That the foul is not a diftinct fubftance from the body:
that the whole man is diffolved at death: and that though it may
be ufeful to mankind to believe the doctrine of future rewards
and punifhments, yet it is a fiction, which hath no real foundation in nature and reafon: and that to pretend to argue for future retributions from the apprehended unequal diftributions of
this prefent ftate, is abfurd and blafphemous, and is to caft the
moft unworthy reflections on divine Providence.

4. That the law of nature is what reafon difcovereth to us concerning our duty as founded in the human fyftem: that it is clear
and obvious to all mankind; but has been obfcured and perverted

by

by ancient philofophers and modern divines: that it has not been fet in a proper light by thofe who have undertaken to treat of it; and therefore he hath reprefented it in its genuine purity and fimplicity: and that the fanctions of that law relate to men not individually, but collectively confidered.

5. That from the clearnefs and fufficiency of the law of nature, it may be concluded, that God hath made no other revelation of his will to mankind: and that there is no need or ufe for any extraordinary fupernatural revelation.

6. That it is profane and blafphemous to afcribe the Jewifh Scriptures to revelation or infpiration from God: that the hiftory contained there is falfe and incredible, and the fcheme of religion taught in thofe writings is abfolutely unworthy of God, and repugnant to his divine perfections.

7. That the New Teftament confifts of two different gofpels, oppofite to one another, that of Chrift and that of St. Paul: that Chriftianity in its genuine fimplicity, as taught by Jefus Chrift, and contained in the evangelical writings, is a benevolent inftitution, and may be regarded as a republication of the law of nature, or rather of the theology of Plato: that the morals it teaches are pure, but no other than the philofophers had taught before, and that fome of its precepts are not agreeable to the natural law; and fome of its original doctrines, particularly thofe relating to the redemption of mankind by the death of Chrift, and to future rewards and punifhments, are abfurd, and inconfiftent with the attributes of God.

Thefe appear to me to be the moft remarkable things in the late Lord Bolingbroke's *Pofthumous Works*, as far as natural and revealed religion's concerned. And the method I propofe to purfue in my obfervations upon them is this:

I fhall firft confider the attempts he hath made to fubvert the main principles that lie at the foundation of all religion, *viz.* thofe relating to the moral attributes of God, a particular providence extending to the individuals of the human race, the immortality of the foul, and a future ftate of retributions. I fhall next examine the account he hath given of the law of nature, and of the duties and fanctions of that law. After which it will be proper to confider what he hath offered concerning divine revelation in general, with a view to fhew that an extraordinary revelation
lation

lation of the will of God to mankind is abfolutely needlefs, and that therefore we may conclude, that God hath never given fuch a revelation at all. I fhall proceed, in the next place, to a particular and diftinct examination of the objections he hath urged againft the truth and divine original of the Mofaic revelation, and the Scriptures of the Old Teftament; and fhall conclude with confidering what more directly relateth to the Chriftian revelation properly fo called, to its proofs and evidences, and to its laws and doctrines, all which he hath endeavoured to expofe.

This I hope may be fufficient to anfwer the defign I have in view, which is to obviate the principal mifchiefs to religion, which Lord Bolingbroke's Works feem fitted to produce. Other things there are in thefe volumes, which might furnifh matter for many reflections, but which I fhall take little or no notice of, as they do not come within the compafs of the plan I propofe.

I am, &c.

# LETTER XXIII.

*Lord Bolingbroke asserts the Existence of God against the Atheists, but rejects the Argument a priori, and that drawn from the general Consent of Mankind—He is for reducing all the divine Attributes to Wisdom and Power, and blames the Divines for distinguishing between the physical and moral Attributes—He asserts, that we cannot ascribe Goodness and Justice to God, according to our Ideas of them, nor argue with any Certainty about them—That it is absurd to deduce moral Obligations from the moral Attributes of God, or to pretend to imitate him in those Attributes—Observations upon his Scheme—It is shewn, that the moral Attributes are necessarily included in the Idea of the absolutely perfect Being—The Author's Objections against ascribing those Attributes to God, or distinguishing them from his physical Attributes, particularly considered— His manifold Inconsistencies and Contradictions.*

SIR,

IN my last a general account was given of the scheme Lord Bolingbroke seems to have had in view in his Posthumous Works, and of the main principles to which it is reducible. I now proceed to a more distinct examination of those principles; and shall begin with that which lieth at the foundation of all religion, the existence and attributes of God. And it must be acknowledged, that his Lordship every-where in the strongest terms asserteth the existence of the one Supreme All-perfect Being, the Great Author of the universe. He represents this as *strictly demonstrable*, and treats the opinion of the atheists as *infinitely absurd;* and that they can *only cavil,* but *cannot reason,* against the existence of the first cause; of which, he thinks, we may be in reason as sure as of our own existence. There are several passages in his works, in which he expresseth himself devoutly with regard to the Supreme Being, and professeth seriously to adore him. And there are some instances of his addressing him with great solemnity, and in a religious manner *.

* See particularly vol. iii. p. 247. 358. vol. v. p. 338, &c.

I need

I need not take any notice of what he hath briefly offered for demonſtrating the exiſtence of a Deity *. He has ſaid nothing on this head, but what has been frequently urged to great advantage by others before him; and particularly by Dr. Clarke, in what his Lordſhip is pleaſed to call his *pretended demonſtration of the being and attributes of God* †.

Our author indeed is for confining the proof to the argument *a poſteriori*, and is for abſolutely rejecting the argument *a priori*, whereas Dr. Clarke inſiſts upon both: and I cannot help thinking that both may be highly uſeful; and that they are then moſt effectual, and come with the greateſt force, when they come in aid of one another.

As Lord Bolingbroke rejects the argument *a priori* for the exiſtence and perfections of God, ſo he ſeems not willing to allow that which is drawn from the general conſent of mankind. He ſays, it will indeed prove, that men generally believed a God, but not that ſuch a Being exiſts; and he repreſents it as *trifling to inſiſt upon it* ‡. And in a letter occaſioned by one of Archbiſhop Tillotſon's ſermons, vol. iii. p. 257, *& ſeq.* he finds fault with that great divine for making uſe of that argument, and diſingenuouſly repreſents it, as if he had reſted the proof of a Deity principally upon it §; which he is far from doing, though it muſt be acknowledged to be a conſideration of great weight. He particularly blames the Archbiſhop for aſcribing this conſent to the nature of the human mind, on which God has impreſſed an innate idea of himſelf; but he owns, that afterwards he ſoftens it by ſaying, that " the human mind is ſo diſpoſed, that men " may diſcover, in the due uſe of its faculties, that there is a " God ||." And he ſpeaks of ſome divines who explain it thus: that the belief of God is founded on a certain natural proportion there is between this great truth and the conceptions of the human mind. But our author thinks, that " ſuch a *natural and in-* " *timate proportion* between the exiſtence of God, and the con- " ceptions of the human mind, may appear chimerical, and per- " haps is ſo **;" and obſerves, that " polytheiſm was more con-

---

* Bolingbroke's Works, vol. iii. p. 353, 354.     † Ibid. p. 52.
‡ Ibid. p. 247.     § Ibid. p. 258. 267.     || Ibid. p. 258.
** Ibid. p. 259, 260.

" formable

" formable to the natural conceptions of the human mind, efpe-
" cially in the moft ancient and ignorant ages, than the belief
" of One firft intelligent Caufe, the fole Creator, Preferver, and
" Governor of all things." Yet he afterwards declares, that
" the idea of an All-wife and All-powerful Being, the firft caufe
" of all things, is fo *proportionable to human reafon,* that it muft
" have been received into the minds of men, as foon as they be-
" gan to contemplate the face of nature, and to exercife their
" reafon in fuch contemplations *." And in his reflections on
M. Maupertuis, who had flighted the argument from the general
confent of mankind, he obferves, that " it is general enough to
" fhew *the proportion which this truth bears to the univerfal*
" *reafon of mankind* †." You cannot but obferve here, that he directly makes ufe of that manner of expreffion which he had before blamed others for ufing.

But it will be proper more diftinctly to inquire into the idea
this writer gives of God, and of the divine perfections. The
only attributes of God which he infifteth upon as neceffary to
be known by us are, his power and wifdom. We rife," fays he,
" from a knowledge of ourfelves, and of the works of God, to
" a knowledge of his exiftence, and his *wifdom* and *power*, which
" we call infinite ‡." He blames thofe who prefume to define
the moral attributes of an All-perfect Being; and thinks " we
" ought to content ourfelves to know that he exifts by the ne-
" ceffity of his nature, and that his *wifdom* and *power* are infi-
" nite §." He declares, that " a felf-exiftent Being, the firft
" Caufe of all things, infinitely *powerful* and infinitely *wife*, is
" the God of natural theology : that as the whole fyftem of the
" univerfe bears witnefs to this truth, fo the whole fyftem of na-
" tural religion refts on it, and requires no broader foundation.
" Thefe fyftems are God's fyftems ‖." We fee here there is no
mention made of the divine goodnefs, as included in the idea we
form of a deity. Natural theology, or natural religion, requires
no broader a foundation than the acknowledging the wifdom and
power of God. And fo it generally is in the account our author gives of God and his attributes; as if *optimus* were not to

* Bolingbroke's Works, vol. iv. p. 195.    † Ibid. p. 256.
‡ Ibid. p. 88.    § Ibid. vol. v. p. 235.    ‖ Ibid. p. 316.

be joined with *maximus* in the deist's creed, or in the idea natural religion teaches us to form of God.    And accordingly he finds fault with what he calls *artificial theology*, for pretending " to connect moral attributes, such as we conceive them, and " such as they are relatively to us, with the physical attributes " of God."    He says, " there is no sufficient foundation for " this proceeding in the phænomena of nature, and that in several " cases they are repugnant."    And he expresly mentions it among the wrong notions of the ancient theists, and which gave advantage to the atheists with regard to the question about the original of evil, that they maintained, that " God is just and " good, and righteous, and holy, as well as powerful and wise." He blames them for saying, that " love was the first principle of " things, and that it determined God to bring forth his creatures " into existence[*];" and that, as Seneca says, *usque ad delicias amamur*.    And elsewhere quoting a passage of Dr. Clarke, in which God is represented as having a *tender and hearty concern for the happiness of man*, he says, " these are strange words to " be applied to the Supreme Being[†]."    And he argueth at great length against those who suppose, that God made man only to be happy.

He frequently censureth the divines for distinguishing between God's physical and moral attributes: and " cannot see one reli- " gious purpose, that this distinction is necessary to answer[‡]. " God's moral attributes," he says, " can only be discerned in " the works of God, and in the conduct of his providence: and " that it is evident, they are not, cannot be so discerned in them, " as to be the object of our imitation[§]."    He represents it as great presumption to pretend to deduce our moral obligations from the moral attributes of God ; and that the absurdity of this cannot be too often exposed[||].    And after having asserted, that we cannot rise from our moral obligations to God's supposed moral attributes, he adds, that " he calls them *supposed*, because " after all that has been supposed to prove a necessary connec- " tion between his physical and moral attributes, we may observe

[†] Bolingbroke's Works, vol. v. p. 316, 317.    [†] Ibid. p. 63.
[‡] Ibid. p. 62.    [§] Ibid. p. 63.
[||] Ibid. p. 87.

" them

" them in his wifdom ;—and that the effects of his wifdom give
" us fometimes ideas of thofe moral qualities, which we acquire
" by reflections on ourfelves, and fometimes not*." He thinks
the divines are to be blamed, " for talking of God's infinite good-
" nefs and juftice, as of his infinite wifdom and power †;"
and obferves, that " every thing fhews the wifdom and power
" of God, conformably to our ideas of wifdom and power, in
" the phyfical world and in the moral: but every thing does not
" fhew in like manner the juftice and goodnefs of God, con-
" formably to our ideas of thofe attributes in either ‡." That
" though the wifdom of God does not appear alike in all the
" phænomena, yet, as far as we can difcover, it appears in the
" greateft and leaft to our aftonifhment, and none of them can be
" ftrained into a repugnancy to it: but the fame cannot be faid
" of the moral attributes which we afcribe to the Supreme Being,
" according to our ideas of them. It cannot be difputed, and
" all fides agree, that many of the phænomena are repugnant to
" our ideas of goodnefs and juftice §." He declares it as his
opinion, that " God's natural attributes abforb the moral ‖;"
and particularly, that " the moral attributes of the Supreme
" Being are abforbed in his wifdom; and that we fhould con-
" fider them only as different modifications of his phyfical attri-
" butes; and muft always talk precarioufly and impertinently,
" when we prefume to apply our ideas of them to the appear-
" ances of things**." And he chargeth the divines " as pro-
" ceeding in all their reafonings about the nature, moral attri-
" butes, and will of God, not only without regard to the phæ-
" nomena, but often in direct contradiction to them ††."

This is not a matter that he treats merely in fome occafional
paffages. The chief defign of feveral of his fragments and effays
in his fifth volume, particularly of the fourth, feventh, fortieth,
forty-firft, and forty-ninth, is to argue againft thofe who affert
the moral attributes of God as diftinguifhed from his phyfical:
or who fay, that thofe moral attributes, his holinefs, goodnefs,
juftice, and truth, are the fame in him, that they are in the ideas

---

* Bolingbroke's Works, vol. v. p. 88.    † Ibid. p. 528.
‡ Ibid. p. 311.    § Ibid. p. 368.
‖ Ibid. p. 313, 314.    ** Ibid. p. 335. 453.
†† Ibid. p. 310.

we form of thofe perfections; which, he fays, cannot be conceived *without manifeft prefumption and blafphemy:* upon this
doctrine he chargeth men's *falfe conceptions and licentious reafonings* about the divine nature and providence. He adds, that
" thefe *falfe conceptions and licentious reafonings* may proceed
" likewife from the *analogical doctrine;* which, though it afcribes
" not to God human notions, yet afcribes to him fomething,
" whatever it be, equivalent to them\*." He affirms, that " good-
" nefs and juftice in God—are fomething tranfcendent, and of
" which we cannot make any true judgment; and that it is im-
" poffible we fhould argue with any certainty about them†."
I fhall only farther obferve, that he brings a charge in this refpect,
not only againft the Chriftian divines, but againft the heathen
philofophers. The reafon he affigns, why they were " unable
" to propagate natural religion, and to reform mankind, is be-
" caufe they proceeded in Dr. Clarke's method, to argue *a priori*
" from the moral attributes of God, his goodnefs, juftice, &c.
" which they affumed to be the fame in him that they are in our
" ideas ‡."

By comparing thefe feveral paffages together, it appears, that,
according to this writer, we are unable to form any idea of the
moral attributes of God: for if we cannot conceive of them according to our ideas, we cannot form any conception of them at
all: that it is wrong to diftinguifh them from his phyfical attributes, or to fay they are connected with thofe attributes: that
there is not only no fuch thing in God as goodnefs or juftice as
we conceive of them, but nothing in him analogous or equivalent
to thofe qualities as they are in us, or which is fitted to produce
correfpondent effects: that therefore it ought not to be faid of
God, that he is juft and good, holy and true, or that he is a
lover of mankind, or is concerned for our happinefs, but only
that he is powerful and wife: that we can only know God's
moral attributes *a pofteriori* from the effects, and that many of
the phænomena in nature are repugnant to thofe attributes,
and inconfiftent with them: fo that it is impoffible for us to argue with any certainty about them. This is the plain intention

* Bolingbroke's Works, vol. v. p. 541.  † Ibid. p. 311. 359, 360.
‡ Ibid. p. 234.

of the paſſages which have been cited, and others might be produced to the ſame purpoſe; though we ſhall find him afterwards
plainly contradicting ſeveral things which here he has advanced.

If we conſider what his reaſon could be for ſetting up an hypotheſis ſo contrary to true theiſm, for which yet he would be
thought to have ſo great a zeal, there are two things which he
appears to have had in view.

1. That we are in no caſe to deduce our moral obligations
from the moral attributes of God, or to propoſe to imitate God in
thoſe attributes. He declares, that " the laws of nature are ab-
" ſurdly founded in the moral attributes of God\*;" *i. e.* it is abſurd to talk of his juſtice, goodneſs, righteouſneſs and truth, as
giving riſe to thoſe laws, or appearing in the conſtitution of
them. And as to the pretence of imitating the Deity in his moral excellencies, this is what he openly and avowedly condemns.
This particularly is the deſign of the fourth of his fragments and
eſſays in his fifth volume. He expreſsly aſſerts, that " God's mo-
" ral attributes cannot be ſo diſcerned by us as to be the objects
" of our imitation†." He pronounces, that " it is abſurd, and
" worſe than abſurd, to aſſert that man can imitate God, except in
" a ſenſe ſo very remote, and ſo improper, that the expreſſions
" ſhould never be uſed, much leſs ſuch a duty recommended‡."
And that " thoſe writers or preachers who exhort us to imitate
" God, muſt mean, not the God whom we ſee in his works, and
" in all that his providence orders; but the God who appears in
" their repreſentations of him, and who is often ſuch a God as no
" pious theiſt can acknowledge §." He declares for himſelf, that
" he dares not uſe *theological familiarity, and talk of imitating*
" *God;* and treats that doctrine as *extravagant, falſe,* and *pro-*
" *phane* ‖." He ſays, that " by aſſuming to imitate God, we give
" the ſtrongeſt proof of the imperfection of our nature, whilſt we
" neglect the real, and aſpire to a mock honour, as pride, ſeduc-
" ed by adulation, is prone to do; and as religious pride, wrought
" up by ſelf-conceit into enthuſiaſm, does above all others \*\*."
And he mentions it as an inſtance of the impertinence of Socrates's doctrine, that " he conjured his auditors in the priſon to make

---

\* Bolingbroke's Works, vol. v. p. 90.　† Ibid. p. 63.　‡ Ibid. p. 62.
§ Ibid. p. 63.　‖ Ibid. p. 44. 65.　\*\* Ibid. p. 67.

" themſelves

" themfelves as like as poffible to their great exemplar, the Su-
" preme Being*." Thus has this dogmatical and prefumptuous
author taken upon him to pafs a fevere and infolent cenfure upon
that which has been the doctrine of the moft excellent philofophers and moralifts, and of one far fuperior to them all, our bleffed Saviour himfelf. See Mat. v. 45. 48. Luke iv. 35, 36.
And he has particularly inftanced in God's caufing his fun to
fhine on the evil and the good, and fending rain on the juft and
unjuft, as a proof that we cannot and ought not to afpire after an
imitation of him † ;" though our Lord fets this goodnefs of providence before us as a noble pattern, to engage us to an extenfive benevolence, and that we fhould be ready to do good even
to our enemies themfelves. There are indeed depths in God's
providential difpenfations, with regard to which we cannot pretend to imitate him, for want of knowing the reafons upon which
he proceeds; but this does not hinder, but that we may and
ought to endeavour to refemble him in his illuftrious moral excellencies, as far as we can difcern them in his works and in the
revelations of his word, which in many inftances we are able to do.

2. Another thing which he hath evidently in view, in denying
that we can have any idea of the moral attributes of God, fo as
to make a true judgment of them, or to argue with any certainty
about them, is to deftroy the argument which is drawn from the
confideration of thefe moral attributes, to fhew the probability
of a future ftate of retributions. For if God be perfectly good
and juft, this leads us to conclude that he will order it fo, that in
the final iffue of things, a remarkable diftinction fhall be made
between the righteous and the wicked; and that virtue fhall
upon the whole be crowned with its due reward, and vice meet
with condign punifhment: and fince this is not uniformly done
in this prefent ftate, it is reafonable to believe that there fhall be
a future ftate of rewards and punifhments. This is a way of
arguing, which, by his own acknowledgment, has been urged
by fome of the beft and wifeft men in all ages. To avoid this
confequence, he will not allow that there is any fuch thing as
juftice and goodnefs in God according to our ideas, or any thing
anfwering to what we call juftice and goodnefs: and that it is

---

* Bolingbroke's Works, vol. iv. p. 117, 118.   † Ibid. vol. v. p. 63.

prefumption in us to determine what thofe attributes require that God fhould do *. And indeed to guard againft this feems to have been a principal point with his lordfhip. It is for this that he denies, that providence extendeth its care to the individuals of the human race: and one of his chief prejudices againft the Chriftian revelation appears to me to be its fetting thefe things in fo ftrong a light.

You eafily perceive, that this part of our author's fcheme is not of a trifling nature. It is not a mere fpeculative error, but which, purfued to its proper confequences, muft have a mighty influence on religion and morals. I fhall therefore examine it diftinctly, and fhall firft offer fome general confiderations concerning God's moral attributes, to fhew that they muft neceffarily be afcribed to the Supreme Being: and then fhall proceed to obviate the principal objections he hath advanced: after which I fhall point to the manifold inconfiftencies and contradictions he hath fallen into in relation to this fubject.

I fhall begin with fome general confiderations concerning God's moral attributes.

And 1. It is effential to the idea of God, that he is the *all-perfect* Being. So our author frequently calls him, and makes it neceffary for us to regard him under that notion †. That is a remarkable declaration which he makes Vol. III. p. 299. " I " know, for I can demonftrate by connecting the cleareft and " moft diftinct of my real ideas, that there is a God, a firft intel- " ligent caufe of all things, whofe infinite wifdom and power " appear evidently in all his works, and to whom therefore I " afcribe moft rationally every other perfection, whether con- " ceivable or not conceivable by me." Here he mentions dif- tinctly, as his manner is, God's *infinite wifdom and power*, and takes no particular notice of his goodnefs; but furely this muft be fuppofed to be included, when he adds, that not only wifdom and power, but *every other perfection conceivable by us*, muft be moft rationally afcribed to God. For is not goodnefs a perfec- tion? And is it not conceivable by us? Yea, is it not the moft amiable of all perfections, and that which gives a luftre and glory to all the reft? Is it poffible to conceive a perfect character

* Bolingbroke's Works, vol. v. p. 453.    † Ibid. vol. iii. p. 253.

without

without it? Almighty power and infinite wifdom, if they could be fuppofed feparated from goodnefs and righteoufnefs, in the great Governor of the world, would create horror and averfion inftead of love and efteem. A God deftitute of juftice and goodnefs would be fuch a God, as he moft wrongfully reprefents the God of Mofes and St. Paul to be, an unjuft, a cruel, a partial, and arbitrary Being\* !

He is fenfible, that in our ideas of perfection, goodnefs and righteoufnefs, or his moral attributes, are neceffarily included: and that confequently according to the rule he had laid down, *viz.* that it is *rational* for us to afcribe to God every perfection, whether *conceivable* or *inconceivable by us*, we ought moft certainly to afcribe to him righteoufnefs, goodnefs, and truth. He endeavours therefore to guard againft this by faying, though in plain contradiction to what he had before advanced:— " Let us not " meafure his perfections by ours. Let us not prefume fo much " as to afcribe our perfections to him, even according to the " higheft conceptions we are able to form of them; though we " reject every imperfection conceivable by us, when it is im- " puted to him †." He obferves, that " the firft and ftrongeft " impreffions that we receive of benevolence, juftice, and other " moral virtues, come from reflections on ourfelves and others ; " from what we feel in ourfelves, and from what we obferve in " other men. Thefe we acknowledge to be, however limited " and imperfect, the excellencies of our own nature, and there- " fore conceiving them without any limitation or perfection, we " afcribe them to the Divine." But he fays, " a very fhort " analyfis of the excellencies of our own nature will be fufficient " to fhew, that they cannot be applied from man to God with- " out profanenefs, nor from God to man without the moft fhame- " ful abfurdity ‡." It will be eafily acknowledged, that we cannot afcribe any of thofe qualities in our nature, which neceffarily connote imperfection, to God in a literal and proper fenfe ; but to fay that we ought not to afcribe thofe, which we cannot but look upon as the nobleft excellencies and perfections of an intelligent Being, and of which we clearly difcern the traces and

* Bolingbroke's Works, vol. v. p. 567.    † Ibid. vol. iii. p. 558.
‡ Ibid. vol. v. p. 88, 89.

refemblances in our own nature, to the infinitely perfect Being,
at the fame time taking care to remove every imperfection with
which they are attended in us and our fellow-creatures, is highly
abfurd, and a manifeft contradiction to the common fenfe of
mankind. It is to fay, that we are to conceive of God as the
infinitely perfect Being, and yet we are not to afcribe to him
thofe excellencies which we cannot poffibly avoid regarding as
neceffarily included in the idea of infinite perfection. Nor is
this, as he is pleafed to reprefent it, a making man the *original*,
and God only a *copy* *; or, as he elfewhere expreffeth it, a fuppofing God to be no more than an *infinite man* †. This argument, if it may be called fo, is only a playing upon words. The
word *man* carries in it the idea of a finite, imperfect, created
being; and therefore to call God an infinite man has a very
odd found. But if the meaning only be, that as man is an intelligent being, fo God is infinite intelligence; and as man has
moral difpofitions, the imperfect feeds and principles of goodnefs, juftice, benevolence, God hath all thefe in the higheft poffible degree of eminency, without any imperfection and defect;
what is there in this unworthy of the fupreme and abfolutely perfect Being? It is true that, as he obferves, *we do not know the
manner of his being* ‡; but as this by his own acknowledgment is
no argument againft afcribing to him wifdom and power, fo
neither is it againft our afcribing to him juftice and goodnefs.
He there afferts, that " we rife from the knowledge of ourfelves,
" and of the other works of God, to a knowledge of his exiftence,
" and of his wifdom and power, which we call infinite." And
may it not equally be faid, that we rife from the confideration of
his works, and the illuftrious difplays of beneficent goodnefs to
be found there, and from the knowledge of the moral fentiments
in our own breafts, and which we cannot but approve, to the
knowledge of his goodnefs, and moral excellencies? And fince,
by the very conftitution of our minds, we cannot help regarding
them as perfections, we are naturally led to afcribe them in the
fupreme degree to the *All-perfect* Being. And to fay, that when
we do fo, we make ourfelves the original, and him only the copy,
is a ftrange mifreprefentation: for in that cafe we rife from the

* Bolingbroke's Works, vol. v. p. 87. † Ibid. p. 310. ‡ Ibid. p. 88.

imperfect

imperfect traces and lineaments of thofe excellencies in our own
fouls, or which we difcern in others, to the fupreme goodnefs and
benevolence, of which all human and created goodnefs is but a
very faint and imperfect copy.   And what can be more reafonable than to conclude, that he muft be infinitely good and juft,
and true, who made us capable of difcerning and feeling the
amiablenefs and excellence of thofe moral difpofitions and qualities, and who hath fpread fuch beauty and order, and fuch a pro-
fufion of bleffings, throughout this vaft fyftem!

Again, the moral attributes of God may be farther argued from
this, that they are really infeparable from infinite wifdom and
intelligence: and fince wifdom could not be perfect without
goodnefs and juftice, thefe moral attributes muft be afcribed to
the Supreme Being as well as wifdom, which our author every-
where afcribes to him.   We may as reafonably fuppofe him
without the one as the other.   As there are innumerable things
which fhew his wifdom, fo there are which demonftrate his goodnefs and benignity.   And if there are feveral appearances which
we find it hard to reconcile to our ideas of goodnefs, fo there are
which feem not to be confiftent with wifdom.   And the anfwer
is the fame in both cafes, that it is owing to our ignorance, and
the narrownefs of our views; and we fhall foon find our author
in effect acknowledging this.   Power and wifdom without
goodnefs and righteoufnefs are fo far from giving us a proper
idea of an All-perfect Being, that it is the idea of a very imperfect one.   This writer himfelf obferves, that " if God be in-
" finitely wife, he always knows and always does that which
" is fitteft to be done: to choofe the beft end, and to proportion
" the means to it, is the very definition of wifdom*."   And accordingly he afferts, that the wifdom of God always determineth
him to do that *which is fitteft upon the whole.*   And this neceffarily fuppofeth an univerfal rectitude of his nature.   It includes
both a perfect unerring knowledge of what is fitteft and beft,
and a difpofition and determination to act accordingly, and to
do what is, all things confidered, beft and fitteft to be done.   And
this is really to acknowledge God's moral attributes: for, as our
author obferves, " that which is fitteft to be done is always juft

" and good \*." So that God's wifdom is neceffarily fuppofed to
be connected with his juftice and goodnefs, as well as they with
his wifdom; and a regard to both is comprehended in choofing
what is fitteft to be done. Wifdom feparated from juftice and
goodnefs would not be true wifdom, which always includes the
worthieft ends and propereft means, but craft, which is not a
real perfection, but the contrary.

This writer fhews that he is fenfible of this, when he afferts,
that God's moral attributes are only " different modifications of
" his wifdom; and are barely names that we give to various ma-
" nifeftations of the infinite wifdom of one fimple uncompounded
" Being." And he blames the divines for fuppofing, " that they
" are in him, what they are in us, diftinct affections, difpofitions,
" and habitudes †." He fays, that " after all that has been faid
" to prove a neceffary connexion between his phyfical and moral
" attributes, we may obferve them in his wifdom ‡." And that
" if they are fo intimately connected with his power and wifdom,
" and fo much the fame in nature, that they cannot be feparated
" in the exercife of them, in this cafe his natural attributes
" abforb the moral §." But what are we to underftand by abforb?
May they not be intimately connected, and yet be of diftinct
confideration? Are not the divine power and wifdom intimately
connected? Can they ever be feparated in the exercife? Is his
power ever a blind power, deftitute of wifdom and intelligence?
Or, is his wifdom an impotent wifdom, deftitute of power?
Yet he owns the ideas of power and wifdom in God to be diftinct, though they are neither of them really diftinguifhed from
his effence. He is indeed pleafed to pafs a cenfure on the divines, for *parcelling out a divine moral nature into various attributes like the human* ‖. And he fometimes feems to find fault
with the diftinguifhing any attributes at all in God. He fays,
that " fince the wifdom of God is as much God as the will of
" God, and the will as the wifdom, it is abfurd to diftinguifh
" them: that it is fomething worfe to reafon about the divine, as
" we do about the human intellect, and to divide and parcel out
" the former upon the plan of the latter. Since the will of God

---

\* Bolingbroke's Works, vol. v. p. 313.          † Ibid. p. 335.
‡ Ibid. p. 88.        § Ibid. p. 313.          ‖ Ibid. p. 453.

" is

" is not like that of man, dark and liable to be feduced, why
" are we led to conclude that a fuperior faculty is neceffary to
" determine it, as the judgment of reafon does, or fhould, deter-
" mine that of man?" Yet he immediately after diftinguifhes
between the *will* and *knowledge* of God, and fuppofes it neceffary to diftinguifh them *to be* (as he expreffes it) a *little more
intelligible**: and elfewhere he talks of the *rule which infinite
wifdom prefcribes to infinite power*†. And all along throughout
his effays he fpeaks of wifdom and power as diftinct attributes of
God. The one therefore does not, to ufe his expreffion, *abforb*
the other, though they are not feparated in the exercife. This
fhews that perfections may be intimately connected without being
abforbed, or, in other words, confounded one with another:
and therefore it is no argument, that there are no fuch diftinct
attributes as juftice, or righteoufnefs and goodnefs, becaufe they
are intimately and infeparably connected with his power and
wifdom. On the contrary, this fuppofes that there are fuch attributes. For it would be abfurd to talk of their being connected
with his wifdom, or of their being to be *abforbed* in his wifdom,
if there were no fuch qualities, or attributes: and fince, as Lord
Bolingbroke himfelf elfewhere acknowledgeth, *we muft fpeak of
God after the manner of men*‡, if we fpeak of thefe qualities at
all, we muft fpeak of them as diftinct attributes.

Let us now confider our author's objections.

1. He urges, that " the moral as well as phyfical attributes of
" God can only be known *a pofteriori*. They muft be difcerned
" in the works of God, and in the conduct of Providence.
" And it is evident they are not, cannot be fo difcerned in them,
" as to be the objects of our imitation§. Every thing fhews
" the power and wifdom of God, conformably to our ideas of
" wifdom and power in the phyfical world and in the moral; but
" every thing does not fhew in like manner the juftice and good-
" nefs of God, conformably to our ideas of thefe attributes in
" either‖. None of the phænomena can be ftrained into a re-
" pugnancy to the divine wifdom; but it cannot be difputed,
" that many of them are repugnant to our ideas of goodnefs and

* Bolingbroke's Works, vol. v. p. 5.     † Ibid. vol. iii. p. 53.
‡ Ibid. vol. v. p. 468.     § Ibid. p. 63.     ‖ Ibid. p. 311.

    " juftice."

" juſtice\*." Some other paſſages to the ſame purpoſe were mentioned above, which I need not here repeat. In oppoſition to this it may be obſerved, that, as was before hinted, the characters of goodneſs and benignity are conſpicuous in the conſtitution of things, as well as of wiſdom and power. And if there are ſeveral particular phænomena not conformable to our ideas of goodneſs and righteouſneſs, there are alſo ſeveral appearances not conformable to our ideas of wiſdom, and the reaſons and deſigns of which do not appear. It is well known, that many are the objections which the atheiſts have made againſt the wiſdom of God, as appearing in the conſtitution both of the natural and moral world. It is his own obſervation, that " we muſt be " prepared to meet with ſeveral appearances which we cannot " explain, nor therefore reconcile to the ideas we endeavour to " form of the divine perfection. If it be true, that infinite wiſ- " dom and power created and govern the univerſe, it cannot but " follow, that ſome of the phænomena may be proportionable, " and that others muſt be diſproportionable to our and to every " other finite underſtanding†." He very properly expoſes the abſurdity of the atheiſts in arguing againſt the exiſtence, attributes, and providence of God, from the difficulties relating to them; and obſerves, that " theſe difficulties do not embarraſs the " theiſt — and inſtead of being ſurpriſed to find them, he would " be ſurpriſed not to find them —— That there muſt be many " phænomena both phyſical and moral, for which he can, and " for which he cannot account — And that there are ſecrets of " the divine nature and œconomy which human reaſon cannot " penetrate ‡." The difficulties therefore relating to the divine goodneſs are no reaſon for not acknowledging that goodneſs, any more than the difficulties relating to the divine wiſdom are a good reaſon againſt acknowledging the wiſdom of God. We may here apply his own way of arguing. " The power of executing," ſays he, " is ſeen in every inſtance; and though we cannot diſcern " the wiſdom of contrivance and direction in every inſtance, yet " we ſee them in ſo many, that it becomes the higheſt abſurdity " not to acknowledge them in all." And he takes notice of the

---

\* Bolingbroke's Works, vol. v. p. 368.    † Ibid. p. 365.
‡ Ibid. vol. iii. p. 186, 187.

folly of atheists in objecting against it, whereby they only shew
their own ignorance.   He adds, that " the wisdom of God is not
" so often discernible by us as the power of God, nor the good-
" ness as the wisdom.   But a multitude of the phænomena being
" conformable *to our ideas of goodness*, we may reason about it as
" we did just now about the divine wisdom\*;" *i. e.* that though
we cannot discern the goodness of God according to our ideas in
every thing, yet we see it in so many, that it would be the highest absurdity not to acknowledge it in all; where he seems to
me plainly to give up the point, and to assert, that we ought to
acknowledge the goodness of God, even according to our ideas
of goodness, as well as his wisdom, to be an attribute belonging
to the Supreme Being: and that this may be justly argued from
his works.

But let us proceed to consider some other of his objections:
He argues against ascribing moral attributes, or the excellencies of our nature to God, because we cannot ascribe to him fortitude and temperance.   He asketh, " How can we deduce forti-
" tude from the attributes of God, or ascribe this virtue to him,
" who can endure no pain, nor be exposed to any danger?   How
" temperance, when it would be the most horrid blasphemy to
" suppose him subject to any human appetites and passions, and
" much more to some so inordinate as to require a particular
" virtue to restrain and govern them?   I might bring many more
" instances of the same kind.   But he who will not be convin-
" ced by these, how absurdly the laws of nature are founded by
" some writers in the moral attributes of God, will be convinced
" by none †."   He seems to have a good opinion of this way of
arguing, for he urges it more than once ‡.   But though fortitude,
as it signifies a bearing up under evils and sufferings, and temperance, as it signifies the restraining and governing the appetites
and passions, cannot be properly ascribed to God, because they
necessarily connote the being liable to evils and imperfections, it
doth not follow, that therefore righteousness and goodness, and
universal benevolence, which imply no such imperfection, and
are the noblest excellencies of an intelligent nature that we can

poffibly conceive, may not be applied to the Supreme and Abfolutely-perfect Being: and as to fortitude and temperance, though
they cannot be properly afcribed to God, no more than piety
and fubmiffion and refignation to the divine will, which are eminent human virtues, yet they are the objects of the divine approbation, and our obligation to them may be juftly argued and
deduced from God's moral attributes, from his holinefs and the
rectitude of his nature, which caufeth him to delight in moral
beauty and order, and to require that his reafonable creatures
fhould act in a manner becoming the excellent faculties he hath
given them; and that they fhould maintain that temper and conduct which tendeth to the true perfection and happinefs of their
natures, which thefe virtues manifeftly do.

He farther objects, that " our ideas of the divine attributes
" muft neceffarily be inadequate, both on account of the infinite
" diftance between the divine and human nature, and on ac-
" count of the numberlefs and to us unknown relations, re-
" fpectively to all which the divine providence acts : which, if
" we did know them, we fhould be unable to compare, and in
" which, therefore, the harmony of the divine perfections would
" not be difcernible by us—That therefore we are very incompe-.
" tent judges of the moral attributes of God, and of what they re-
" quire God fhould do in the government of the world—Nor can
" we make any true judgment, or argue with any certainty about
" them," as he endeavours to prove from the authority of St.
Paul, and Dr. Barrow\*. This only proves what will be eafily
allowed, that we cannot comprehend or fee the whole extent of
the divine proceedings ; and that he may in many cafes have
reafons for his proceedings which we are not acquainted with ;
but does not prove, that there is no fuch thing as goodnefs or
righteoufnefs in God, according to our ideas of them, nor any
thing equivalent to them; or that we can in no cafe argue from
what his goodnefs and righteoufnefs require, nor judge of the
equity of his proceedings. Although the Scriptures often fpeak
of God's ways of providence as above human comprehenfion,
yet they alfo reprefent him as fometimes appealing to men them-

* Bolingbroke's Works, vol. v. p. 359. 362.

felves concerning the equity of his proceedings. Our author indeed reprefents this as an abfurdity, but he does not prove it fo, or fhew that there is any thing in it unworthy of the moft wife and righteous and benevolent Governor of the world. Will it follow, that becaufe there are fome difficult cafes concerning which we cannot judge, that therefore we cannot judge in any cafe at all? We may in fome cafes fafely argue from our ideas of the divine goodnefs and juftice; *e. g.* that he will order it fo, that a remarkable difference fhall be made upon the whole between good and bad men; and that virtue fhall be rewarded, and vice and wickednefs punifhed. Will any man fay, that we cannot fafely conclude from the goodnefs and juftice of the Supreme Being, that he will not fuffer or appoint an innocent creature to be eternally miferable? He obferves, fpeaking of God's knowledge, power and wifdom, that " though we cannot frame " full and adequate ideas of them, it will not follow that we have, " properly fpeaking, no knowledge at all of his attributes, nor of " the manner in which they are exercifed—That our ideas of " divine intelligence and wifdom may be neither fantaftic nor " falfe, and yet God's manner of knowing may be very different " from ours\*." In like manner it may be faid, concerning God's moral attributes, his juftice and goodnefs, that though we cannot frame full and adequate ideas of them, it will not follow that we have, properly fpeaking, no knowledge of them at all, and of the manner in which they are exercifed. Our ideas of them are neither falfe nor fantaftic, though in many inftances they may be exercifed in a way different from our apprehenfion. To this may be applied what he faith againft Archbifhop King, that " though we have not a direct knowledge of the nature of " God by archetypal ideas, yet we are not reduced to know " nothing of him except by analogy. It is a real knowledge, " and may be faid to be direct, if we may be allowed to call any " knowledge by demonftration direct †."

Another argument urged by this writer, to fhew that the divines are in the wrong to talk of God's infinite goodnefs and juftice as of his wifdom and power, is this : that " the latter pre- " ferve their nature without any conceivable bounds, and the

---

\* Bolingbroke's Works, vol. v. p. 524, 525.      † Ibid. p. 539.

" former

" former muſt ceaſe to be what they are, unleſs we conceive
" them bounded.   Their nature implies neceſſarily a limitation
" in the exerciſe of them\*."   In anſwer to this, it may be
obſerved, that God's wiſdom and power, conſidered in themſelves, and as they are in God, are infinite; ſo alſo are his goodneſs and juſtice: but conſidered relatively in the exerciſe of them
as terminated in the creature, the one may be ſaid to be limited as
well as the other; *i. e.* the effects of neither of them are properly
infinite.   Infinite power and wiſdom, as exerciſed on the creature, produce finite and limited effects; ſo doth infinite goodneſs
and juſtice: but ſtill conſidered as qualities and attributes of
the divine eſſence, they are infinite, of an eminent and tranſcend-
ent nature, and would be really in God, though there were no
creature formed.   He did not begin to be good when the creatures began to exiſt, though then the exerciſe of goodneſs, under
the direction of his wiſdom, reſpecting the creatures, began.

His other objections proceed all upon a groſs miſrepreſentation
of the ſentiments of thoſe whom he hath thought fit to oppoſe.
He chargeth Dr. Clarke with aſſerting, that juſtice and goodneſs,
and the reſt of the moral attributes, are in God juſt what they
are in our *imperfect, unſteady, complex ideas;* and that the rule
according to which God exerciſeth thoſe attributes, *viz.* the
nature and reaſon of things, is obvious to the underſtanding of
all intelligent beings†.   This is not true, if underſtood of the
whole nature and reaſon of things in all its vaſt extent; nor has
that learned divine any-where aſſerted that it is ſo.

Again he repreſents the divines as aſſerting, that " the will of
" God is not determined by the harmonious concurrence of all
" his attributes," and that " his goodneſs and juſtice do not act
" in *a concurrence with his wiſdom‡.*"   He charges them with
maintaining, that " goodneſs in God is the only directing and
" governing principle, and not wiſdom: and that wiſdom ought
" to contrive, and power to execute, under this direction."   And
he argues, that " if it were ſo, the happineſs of man ought to be
" proportionable to the goodneſs of God, that is, infinite."   And
in oppoſition to this he aſſerts, that " wiſdom ought to be deemed

---

\* Bolingbroke's Works, vol. v. p. 528.       † Ibid. p. 252.
‡ Ibid. p. 313. 342.

" the

" the directing principle of divine conduct *." Nor will any
divine deny that wifdom is the directing principle. They all
plead for the harmonious concurrence of the divine attributes,
though they are not for confounding thofe attributes. Goodnefs
in God is not to be regarded as a blind inftinct, which neceffarily
acteth at all times, and in every inftance, to the utmoft extent
of its capacity, and to the higheft poffible degree ; but as a moft
wife goodnefs, *i. e.* a goodnefs which is always in conjunction
with, and under the direction of, infinite wifdom. For goodnefs
without diftinction or difcernment could fcarce be accounted a
virtue or a perfection. Such a notion of the divine goodnefs
would be, difhonourable to God, and of ill confequence to the
interefts of religion and virtue in the world. But his goodnefs
is that of a moft holy and underftanding mind, and is always exercifed in fuch a way as feemeth moft fit to his infinite wifdom,
which governeth the outward effects of it, and appointeth when,
where, and how, it fhall be communicated. We are not merely to
fix our views on goodnefs and benevolence, in confidering what
God may do or may not do with regard to the happinefs of his
creatures; but to take in every confideration, that of his wifdom,
his juftice, his holinefs and righteoufnefs, and the majefty of his
government.

He frequently accufes the divines, and even the ancient theifts,
for fuppofing that God made man for this end, to communicate
happinefs to him. But then, that he may more effectually expofe
this notion, he claps in the word *only*, as if they maintained, that
God had no other end in view in creating man, but to make him
happy to the utmoft poffible degree, to give him an *happinefs
without allay*, as he expreffeth it, and to *make him not only mo-
derately, but immoderately happy in the world* †. It is thus that
he thinks fit to reprefent their fenfe: and he fays, " this is an
*hypothefis which the phænomena contradict* ‡. But though it
cannot reafonably be denied, that, according to the beft conceptions we can form, one principal motive in God's making reafonable beings was to communicate happinefs to them, yet I
think we do not know enough of God, nor have a fufficiently

* Bolingbroke's Works, vol. v. p. 341.          † Ibid. p. 345. 392. 421.
‡ Ibid. p. 345.

comprehensive view of things, and of the reasons an infinite mind might have for his proceedings, to pronounce confidently, that he had, and could have, no other reason or motive. It may well be supposed, that in bringing this vast universe and the various orders of beings in it into existence, he had in view the exercise and display of his own glorious perfections, not merely of any one, but of all his perfections, his majesty and greatness, his wisdom, power, holiness, and goodness, in conjunction. This is an end worthy of God, as far as he can be said to propose an end to himself. And when it is said, that he made his reasonable creatures with a design to communicate happiness to them, it must be understood thus: that he had it in view to make them happy, in such a way, in such measures and degrees, in such times, seasons, and proportions, as should seem fit to his infinite wisdom, and should be most worthy of them, and becoming his own glorious perfections. His end in creating them was not absolutely to make every individual of them happy at all events, however they should behave; but conditionally to make them happy in the right use and improvement of their own powers, and in such a way as is consistent with moral agency and government, and becoming his own infinite wisdom, goodness, righteousness, and purity.

It is farther with a view to expose the doctrine of the divines relating to the goodness of God, that he represents it as their general sentiment, that all things were made merely for the sake of man; that this vast universal system was formed for him alone: and he sets himself to shew, as he might easily do, the absurdity of supposing the whole universe to have been made merely for some minute part of it*. This particularly is the subject of the 45th and 46th of his fragments and essays. But it is observable, that he himself, after having abused the divines for supposing that God made man to communicate happiness to him, expressly asserts, that " God has made us happy, and has put it " into our power to make ourselves happier, by a due use of our " reason, which leads us into the practice of moral virtue, and " all the duties of society †." " That we are obliged to our " Creator for a certain rule, and sufficient means of arriving at

---

* Bolingbroke's Works, vol. v. p. 330.      † Ibid. p. 384.

" happiness,

" happinefs, and have none to blame but ourfelves, when we
" fail of it\*."   " That God made us to be happy here.—He
" may make us happier in another fyftem of being.—That there
" is even in this world much more good than evil, and the pre-
" fent ftate of mankind is happy in it †."—" And that the end of
" the human ftate is human happinefs ‡."

You are, I doubt not, by this time prepared for what I propofed to fhew in the laft place, the contradictions and inconfiftencies our author has fallen into in treating of this fubject.   I
fuppofe you to bear in mind the fevere cenfures he hath paffed
upon the divines for pretending to connect the phyfical and moral attributes of God, and for afcribing to him moral attributes,
juftice and goodnefs, according to our ideas.   And now I defire you to compare the paffages already produced with thofe that
follow.

God fhews us our duty, " by which we ftand in the relation
" of fubjects and fervants to a gracious and beneficent Lord and
" Mafter, who gave us laws neither captious nor ambiguous, and
" who commands us nothing which it is not our intereft to per-
" form §.   He here fuppofes it to be a thing evident from the
law of nature, that we ftand in relation to God as our *gracious
and beneficent Lord and Mafter*, who has our intereft and happinefs in view in the very laws he enjoins.   And is not this plainly
to afcribe goodnefs to him, even according to our ideas of goodnefs?   And elfewhere he reprefents it, as if he could not afk
more of a *beneficent Creator* than he has done for us ||.   He fays,
" the theift acknowledges whatever God has done to be juft and
" good in itfelf, though it doth not appear fuch in every in-
" ftance, conformably to his ideas of juftice and goodnefs.   He
" imputes the difference to the defect of his ideas, and not to any
" defect of the divine attributes.—Where he fees them, he owns
" them explicitly: where he does not fee them, he pronounces
" nothing about them.   He is as far from denying them" (*i. e.*
from denying the juftice and goodnefs of God) " as he is from
" denying the wifdom and power of God \*\*."   The moft orthodox divine could hardly exprefs himfelf more fully on this

\* Bolingbroke's Works, vol. v. p. 588.   † Ibid. p. 391, 392.
‡ Ibid. p. 544.   § Ibid. p. 97.   || Ibid. p. 481.   \*\* Ibid. p. 311, 312.

head than Lord Bolingbroke has here done. To the same purpose he introduces a meditation or soliloquy of a sincere and devout theist, in which he represents him as saying, among other
things, " Man enjoys numberless benefits by the fitness of his
" nature to this constitution, unasked, unmerited, freely bestow-
" ed. The *wisdom and goodness* of God are therefore manifest.
" May I enjoy thankfully the benefits bestowed on me by the
" divine liberality: may I receive the evils to which I am ex-
" posed patiently, nay willingly \*."

But what deserves particularly to be remarked is, that whereas
he represents the ascribing goodness and justice to God according to our ideas, to be what gives great advantage to the atheists
with regard to the original of evil ; as if he thought it impossible
to reconcile the evil that is in the world with God's moral attributes, and the supposition of his being good and righteous and
holy, as well as powerful and wise; he has taken great pains to
confute his own arguments. For not a few of his fragments and
essays in his fifth volume are taken up in endeavouring to remove and answer that objection, and to shew that the evil there
is in the present constitution of things in this world, is reconcileable to the justice and goodness of God, even according to
the ideas we form of them †. He undertakes to defend the *goodness* of God against the atheists and divines ‡! And having, as he
pretends, done this, he proceeds to vindicate the *justice* and
*righteousness* of God *against the same confederates* §. Thus the
same author, who had used his utmost efforts to shew, in opposition to the divines, that moral attributes, particularly justice
and goodness, ought not to be ascribed to God according to the
ideas we conceive of them, and that we cannot form any judgment concerning them, takes upon him afterwards to vindicate
those very attributes against the divines, who, he pretends, are
for destroying them. So strangely inconsistent is this writer's
scheme, that on the one hand, with a view to invalidate the argument for a state of future retributions drawn from the moral
attributes of God, he endeavours to take away those attributes,

---

\* Bolingbroke's Works, vol. v. p. 338, 339—See also l. iii. p. 358.
† See vol. v. frag. 43, 44. 48, 49, 50, 51, 52, 53, 54.
‡ Ibid. p. 325.                                     § Ibid. p. 393.

or confound them with the phyfical, and to fhew that there is
no fuch thing as goodnefs or juftice in God according to our
ideas, nor any thing equivalent to them; and that the phænomena are repugnant to thofe attributes: and on the other hand,
with the fame view of weakening or deftroying the argument
for a future ftate from thofe attributes, he fets himfelf to prove,
that the prefent ftate of things is fufficiently conformable to our
ideas of the divine juftice and goodnefs, and that thefe attributes
are fo fully exercifed or difplayed here, that there is no need
for any further manifeftation or difplay of them hereafter.

I fhall only produce one paffage more, and it is a very remarkable one. Towards the conclufion of his laft volume, when he
pretends to draw a line of feparation between natural and artificial theology, he obferves, that by that, *viz.* natural theology,
" we are taught to acknowledge and adore the infinite wifdom
" and power of God, manifefted in every part of his creation,
" and afcribe *goodnefs* and *juftice* to him wherever he intend-
" ed that we fhould fo afcribe them, that is, wherever either
" his works, or the difpenfations of his providence, do as necef-
" farily communicate thefe notions to our minds, as thofe of
" wifdom and power are communicated to us in the whole ex-
" tent of both. Wherever they are not fo communicated,
" we may affume very reafonably, that it is on motives ftrictly
" conformable to all the divine attributes, and therefore to good-
" nefs and juftice, though unknown to us, from whom fo many
" circumftances, with a relation to which the divine providence
" acts, muft be often concealed: or, we may refolve all into
" the wifdom of God, and not prefume to account for them
" morally\*." The laft part of this paffage hath a reference to
his fcheme of refolving all into the divine wifdom. But you
cannot but obferve here, that after his repeated invectives againft
the divines, and againft artificial theology, for afcribing moral
attributes to God, juftice and goodnefs, according to our ideas
of them, he has in effect here acknowledged all that the divines
themfelves teach. They believe that God is always good and
juft, though they do not pretend to account for the exercife of
goodnefs and juftice in every particular inftance: but that enough

---

\* Bolingbroke's Works, vol. v. p. 517.

we know to convince us of both: the notions of which, this writer himfelf here owns to be, in many inftances at leaft, neceffarily communicated to us from his works; and furely then we fhould endeavour to refemble him in thefe his moral perfections, as far as we know them.

Before I conclude this letter, I fhall take fome notice, becaufe I fhall not afterwards have fo proper an opportunity for it, of what he hath obferved concerning eternal ideas in God, and concerning the eternal reafons and fitneffes of things.

He finds great fault with Dr. Cudworth, Dr. Clarke, and others, for talking of ideas in God, as if they fuppofed his manner of knowing to be exactly the fame with ours; which certainly was far from their intention. He pronounces, that " the " doctrine of eternal ideas in the divine mind has been much " abufed by thofe who are in the delirium of metaphyfical theo- " logy. It cannot be underftood in a literal fenfe." And he thinks " fuch a way of talking is profane as well as prefumptuous; " and that it is filly too, and mere cant\*." He has feveral obfervations, which are for the moft part very juft, to fhew, that God's manner of knowing is very different from ours, and that he does not know by the help or intervention of ideas as we do†. I need not take particular notice of thofe obfervations, which contain little in them, that will not be acknowledged by thofe whom he has thought to oppofe. The rafh and improper ufe of the word *ideas*, as applied to God, hath no doubt led to miftakes, and to wrong and unwarrantable ways of expreffion: as any one muft be convinced that knows what contentions there have been in the fchools about the divine ideas, which have given rife to arrogant and foolifh queftions, fcarce confiftent with the veneration that is due to the fupreme incomprehenfible Being. Yet the modeft ufe of that expreffion is not to be too rigidly cenfured. Our author himfelf, who blames it fo much in others, hath on feveral occafions fallen into the fame manner of expreffion himfelf. Thus he obferves, that " it might be determined in the " *divine ideas*, that there fhould be a gradation of life and intellect " throughout the univerfe‡:" and he repeats it again, " that this

* Bolingbroke's Works, vol. iii. p. 356.
† Ibid. p. 355, 356, 357. vol. v. p. 35, 36, 37, 38.       ‡ Ibid. p. 357.
" appeared

" appeared neceffary or fit in the *divine ideas*, that is, to fpeak
" more rationally, to the fupreme divine reafon or intention\*."
Where he ufeth the term *divine ideas* as equivalent to the *divine
reafon and intention*, though he thinks the latter more proper.
He elfewhere declares, that " the *ideas* of God, if we may afcribe
" *ideas* to him, no more than his ways, are thofe of man†." And
in one of his moft celebrated pieces, publifhed in his own life-
time, he faith, that " God in his *eternal ideas*, for we are able
" to conceive no other manner of knowing, has prefcribed to
" himfelf that rule by which he governs the univerfe he creat-
" ed‡." Here he not only afcribes ideas to God, but *eternal
ideas*, by which God hath prefcribed to himfelf a rule for his governing the world. This rule he there explaineth to be " a fit-
" nefs arifing from the various natures, and more various rela-
" tions of things, in the fyftem which he hath conftituted:"
which fitnefs he there fuppofeth to have been known to God in
his *eternal ideas*. And yet he hath frequently inveighed againft
Dr. Clarke, for fpeaking of the eternal reafons and relations of
things. This particularly is the fubject of the fecond, fifty-
eighth, and fifty-ninth of his fragments and effays in the fifth
volume of his works. He treats that learned divine as if he
maintained, that thefe reafons and fitneffes of things were real
natures, exifting independently of God, and co-eternal with
him: and yet he himfelf, fpeaking of Dr. Cudworth and others,
obferveth, that when they talk of eternal ideas and effences independent on the will of God, " they do not mean by thefe eter-
" nal independent natures, any natures at all, but fuch intelligible
" effences and *rationes* of things, as are objects of the mind §."
And it is his own obfervation, that " God knew from all eternity
" every fyftem that he created in time—the relations things
" fhould bear—and the proportions they fhould have ||:" And
that " to the divine omnifcience the future is like the prefent;"
and therefore he thinks it improper to talk of *prefcience* in God.
He reprefents it as " a great truth, that the whole feries of things
" is at all times actually prefent to the divine mind, fo that we

---

* Bolingbroke's Works, vol. v. p. 365.       † Ibid. p. 344.
‡ See Idea of a Patriot King, in vol iii. of his Works, p. 53.
§ Bolingbroke's Works, vol. v. p. 15.       || Ibid. p. 7.

" may

" may fay properly, that God knows things, becaufe they are
" actual to him\*." According to his own reprefentation therefore it may be juftly faid, that all the fitneffes and relations of
things were from the beginning actually prefent to the divine
mind. And he accordingly declares, that God was *determined* by
his *infinite wifdom* to *proceed with his creatures* in *all the exer-*
*tions* of *his power, according to the fitnefs of things* †: or in
other words, as he elfewhere expreffeth it, God does *not govern*
*by mere arbitrary will,* but always *does that which is fittefl to be*
*done;* and which he from all eternity faw would be fitteft to be
done. And this feems to be all that is really intended by thofe
who fpeak of the eternal reafons and fitneffes of things. Whether
therefore the manner of expreffion be ftrictly proper or not, this
writer had no right to pafs fo fevere a cenfure upon it as he has
done, fince it comes fo near to his own.

   But I believe you will think it is time to quit this fubject,
and pafs on to fome other things in Lord Bolingbroke's works,
which relate to things of no fmall importance, and which will
deferve a particular confideration.

                                   I am yours, &c.

---

\* Bolingbroke's Works, vol. v. p. 457, 458.          † Ibid. p. 435:

## LETTER XXIV.

*The Doctrine of Divine Providence nearly connected with that
of the Existence of God—Lord Bolingbroke's Account of it
considered—He acknowledges a general, but denies a particular
Providence, and asserts, that Providence relates only to collective Bodies, but doth not extend to Individuals—The true
Notion of Providence stated—What we are to understand by
a particular Providence—The Reasonableness of believing it,
and the great Importance of it shewn—The contrary Scheme
is absurd, and inconsistent with itself, and of the worst Consequence to Mankind—The Objections against a particular Providence examined—Concerning occasional Interpositions—They
are not properly miraculous, nor Deviations from the general
Laws of Providence, but Applications of those Laws to particular Cases—To acknowledge such Interpositions is not to suppose the World governed by Miracles, nor to introduce an
universal Theocracy like the Jewish—Angels may be employed
in particular Cases as Ministers of Providence.*

SIR,

THE doctrine of divine providence hath a very near connexion with that of the existence of the Deity, and is no
less necessary to be believed. To acknowledge a God that brought
all things into existence, and yet to deny that he afterwards taketh
care of the creatures he hath made, or that he exerciseth any inspection over them, as a moral governor, or concerneth himself
about their actions, and the events relating to them, is, with regard to all the purposes of religion, the same thing as not to acknowledge a God at all. It is one great excellence of the holy
Scriptures of the Old and New Testament, that they every-where
teach us to have a constant regard to the divine providence, as
presiding over the universal system, and all the orders of beings
in it, and as in a particular manner exercising a continual care
and inspection towards mankind, observing all their actions,
and ordering and disposing the events relating to them with infinite wisdom, righteousness, and goodness. But this doctrine

of providence, which, one fhould think, ought mightily to recommend the Scriptures to every good mind, feems to have been
one principal ground of the prejudices which Lord Bolingbroke
hath conceived againft thofe facred writings.    It is true, that he
frequently affecteth to fhew a zeal for divine providence: he
fets up as an advocate for its proceedings againft the divines,
who, he pretends, join with the atheifts in mifreprefenting and
oppofing it.    But if his fcheme be narrowly examined, it will
appear, that, notwithftanding his fair pretences, he doth not acknowledge a providence in that fenfe in which it is moft ufeful
and neceffary to believe it.

He declares, that " in afferting the juftice of providence, he
" has chofen rather to infift on the moft vifible and undeniable
" courfe of a general providence, than to affume a difpenfation
" of particular providences *."    He obferves, that " the world
" is governed by laws, which the Creator impofed on the phy-
" fical and moral fyftems, when he willed them into exiftence,
" and which muft be in force as long as they laft; and any change
" in which would be a change in the fyftems themfelves.    Thefe
" laws are invariable, but they are general, and from this gene-
" rality what we call contingencies arife †."    " The courfe of
" things rolls on through a vaft variety of contingent events;
" for fuch they are to our apprehenfion; according to the firft
" impreffions of motion that were given it by the firft Mover, and
" under the direction of an univerfal providence ‡."    " As to
" the brute animals, they are left under the direction of inftinct:
" and as to men, God has given his human creatures the materials
" of phyfical and moral happinefs, in the phyfical and moral con-
" ftitution of things.    He has given them faculties and powers,
" neceffary to collect and apply thefe materials, and to carry on
" the work—This the Creator has done for us.    What we fhall
" do for ourfelves, he has left to the freedom of our elections.
" This is the plan of divine wifdom: and we know nothing more
" particular, and indeed nothing more at all, of the difpenfations
" of providence than this §."    This then is all the part he allows
to providence in the moral world, that God has given man rea-

---

* Bolingbroke's Works, vol. v. p. 414;        † Ibid. p. 426.
‡ Ibid. p. 379.        § Ibid. p. 473; 474.

fon, and, as he elfewhere obferves, paffion*, and has left him
to the freedom of his own will, without ever concerning himfelf farther about the individuals of the human race, or exercifing
any infpection over men's moral conduct, in order to the rewarding the good, or punifhing the bad. That this is his intention is manifeft, by comparing this with other paffages. He
exprefsly declares, that " it is plain from the whole courfe of
" God's providence, that he regards his human creatures col-
" lectively, not individually, how worthy foever every one of
" them deems himfelf to be a particular object of the divine
" care †." This, of God's regarding men collectively, not individually, is what he frequently repeats; and it appears to be a
principal point in his fcheme. With the fame view he declares,
that the fanctions of the law of nature relate not to individuals,
but to collective bodies ‡. He finds fault with the notion, which,
he fays, obtained among the heathens, " that God was conftantly
" attentive to the affairs of men §." And he afferts, that " God
" may forefee, or rather fee, all the moft contingent events that
" happen in the courfe of his general providence; but not pro-
" vide for particular cafes, nor determine the exiftence of parti-
" cular men ||." He obferves, that " the divine providence has
" provided means to punifh individuals, by directing men to
" form focieties, and to eftablifh laws, in the execution of which
" civil magiftrates are the vicegerents of providence: and when
" the immorality of individuals becomes that of a whole fociety,
" then the judgments of God follow, and men are punifhed col-
" lectively in the courfe of a general providence." So that he
allows no punifhments by providence for individuals, but thofe
which are executed by the civil magiftrates. And if a man can
efcape punifhment from them, he has nothing to fear from God,
except the whole community be as bad as himfelf: and even
then the punifhment may not happen in that or the next age,
till he fhall be no more.

  Our author indeed fometimes declares, that " he neither affirms
" nor denies particular providences **." And after having obferved, that there is little credit to be given to the reports con-

* Bolingbroke's Works, vol. v. p. 417.  † Ibid. p. 431.
‡ Ibid. p. 90. § Ibid. p. 211. || Ibid. p. 462. ** Ibid. p. 413, 414.

          cerning

cerning particular acts of providence, wrought on particular
occasions, he adds, that " yet he will not presume to deny, that
" there have been any such\*." He makes the same declaration
afterwards towards the end of his book †. But notwithstanding
these professions, it is a point that he hath very much laboured
to destroy, the belief of a particular providence. This is the express design of several of his Fragments and Essays in the fifth
volume of his works; especially of the fifty-fifth, fifty-sixth,
fifty-seventh, sixty-second, and sixty-fourth, of those Essays;
in all which he argues directly, and in some of them largely,
against that doctrine. And after having observed, that *what we
find in the book of nature is undoubtedly the word of God,* he
asserts, that " there we shall find no foundation for the scheme
" of a particular providence ‡." He declares indeed, " that he
" will not be so uncharitable as to say, that divines mean to
" blaspheme [in their doctrine of a particular providence]," yet
that this he will take upon him to say, that he " who follows
" them cannot avoid presumption and profaneness, and must be
" much on his guard against blasphemy §."

That I may observe some order in my reflections upon this
subject, I shall first offer some observations for stating the right
notion of divine providence, and what we are to understand by
a particular providence: and then shall proceed to shew the
absurdity and ill consequences of the author's scheme: and
lastly, consider the arguments he hath urged in support of it,
and the objections he hath made against the doctrine of a particular providence.

By the doctrine of providence I understand the doctrine of an
all-perfect mind, preserving and governing the vast universe in
all its parts, presiding over all the creatures, especially rational
moral agents, inspecting their conduct, and superintending and
ordering the events relating to them, in the best and fittest manner, with infinite wisdom, righteousness, and equity. And such
a providence cannot reasonably be denied by those, who believe
that the world was originally formed by a most wise and powerful
and infinitely perfect Cause and Author: for whatever reasons

---

\* Bolingbroke's Works, vol. **v.** p. 420.　† Ibid. p. 546.
‡ Ibid. p. 471.　§ Ibid. p. 464.

induced

induced him to create the world, which may be juftly fuppofed
to have been for the communication of his goodnefs, and for
the joint exercife and difplay of his glorious attributes and perfections, muft equally difpofe him to take care of it, and govern
it, when made. Accordingly the Epicureans and others who
denied a providence, did alfo deny that the world was made by
God, and attributed the formation of it, not to the wifdom, the
power, and will of an intelligent caufe, but to a wild chance, or
fortuitous concourfe of atoms, or to an equally blind fatal neceffity. And fo far their fcheme, however falfe and abfurd, was
confiftent with itfelf. For they could find no effectual way
to exclude God from the government of the world, which was
what they wanted to get rid of, but by excluding him from the
making of it too. Suppofing one fupreme abfolutely-perfect
Caufe and Author of all things, who made this vaft univerfe, and
all the orders of beings in it, which is what Lord Bolingbroke
not only allows, but exprefsly afferts, it follows by the moft evident confequence, that the fame infinite power, wifdom, and
goodnefs, which gave exiftence to the world and all things in it,
ftill prefideth over the univerfal frame in all its parts. The
beautiful and conftant order which is ftill maintained in the inani-
mate material fyftem, plainly fheweth, that this ftupendous frame
of nature, confifting of fuch an inconceivable variety of parts, is
is under the conftant fuperintendence of a moft wife and powerful prefiding mind, ever prefent to his own work. But the providence of God is efpecially to be confidered as exercifed towards
reafonable creatures, moral agents, which are undoubtedly the
nobleft and moft excellent of his creatures. The material fyftem,
whatever order or beauty appeareth in it, is not itfelf confcious
of that beauty and order. Nor are mere fenfitive beings capable of
making proper reflections upon it, or of admiring, adoring, obeying the great Parent of the univerfe. This is the fole privilege
of rational intelligent beings. If therefore the providence of
God extendeth to any of his creatures at all, we may be fure that
he exercifeth a fpecial care over his reafonable creatures; and
fince he hath given them fuch noble faculties and moral powers,
will govern them in a way fuitable to thofe faculties and powers.
And this certainly is the moft admirable part of the divine adminiftration in the government of the univerfe. For to govern

　　　　　　　　numberlefs

numberlefs myriads of active intelligent beings, in their feveral orders and degrees, each of whom have a will and choice of their own, and a power of determining their own actions; to exercife a conftant fuperintendency over them, and to order the events relating to them, and to difpenfe to them proper retributions, not only according to their outward actions, but the inward dif-pofitions and principles from which thofe actions flow; I fay, thus to govern them, without infringing the liberty which belong-eth to them as moral agents, muft needs argue a wifdom as well as power that exceedeth our comprehenfion. Yet who will un-dertake to prove that this is impoffible, or even difficult, to an infinite, all-comprehending mind? We may reafonably conceive that that immenfe Being, whofe effence poffeffeth every part of this vaft univerfe, is prefent to every individual of the human race. And if that moft wife, holy, and abfolutely-perfect Being, the Great Governor of the world, be always prefent to every in-dividual of the human race, then every individual, and all their particular actions, cafes, and circumftances, muft be under his providential infpection and fuperintendency. And as he know-eth all thefe things when they actually happen, fo he, to whom, by our author's own acknowledgment, future things are as if they were prefent, faw them before they came to pafs. And therefore it was not difficult for him to form fuch a comprehenfive fcheme of things in his infinite mind, as fhould extend to all their particular cafes, and the events relating to them, in a manner perfectly confiftent with the exercife of their reafonable moral powers, and the ufe of their own endeavours.

And now it appears what is to be underftood by the doctrine of a particular providence. It fignifies, that Providence ex-tends its care to the particulars or individuals of the human race, which is what this writer denies: that God exercifeth a continual infpection over them, and knoweth and obferveth both the good and evil actions they perform, and even the moft fecret affections and difpofitions of their hearts: that he obferveth them not merely as an unconcerned fpectator, who is perfectly indifferent about them, but as the fupreme ruler and judge, fo as to govern them with infinite wifdom, in a way confiftent with their moral agency, and to reward or punifh them in the propereft manner, and in the fitteft feafon. And as all their actions, fo the events

which

which befal them, are under his supreme direction and superintendency. Particular events are, in the ordinary course of things, ordered in such a manner, as is subordinate to the general laws of providence relating to the physical and moral world. And what are usually called occasional interpositions, are properly to be considered as applications of general laws to particular cases and occasions. They make a part of the universal plan of providence, and are appointed and provided for in it, as having been perfectly foreseen from the beginning, and originally intended in the government of reasonable beings.

The doctrine of a particular providence taken in this view is of vast consequence, and, if duly considered and believed, could scarce fail to have a happy influence over our whole temper and deportment. How solicitous, how earnestly desirous should this make us to approve ourselves to our supreme governor and judge, and to walk always as in his sight! What an animating consideration is it, when we set about the performance of a good action, to be assured, that God in his holy providence observeth the good deed in every circumstance, and is ready to assist and support us in it, and most certainly will not suffer it to pass unrewarded! On the other hand, what an effectual restraint would it be to wicked actions, if we had this thought strongly impressed upon our minds, that they are all perfectly known in every circumstance to the most wise and righteous governor of the world; and that if he should not at present follow them with immediate punishment, yet the time is coming, when he will call us to a strict account for them! Finally, a firm belief of a particular providence, as most wisely ordering and disposing the events relating to particular persons, is a source of satisfaction and comfort amidst all the uncertainties and fluctuations of this present world. No consideration is so well fitted to produce a cheerful resignation, and an inward solid peace and joy of heart, as this: that all things, all particular cases and circumstances, are under the direction and government of the most perfect wisdom, righteousness, and goodness; and that nothing can befal us without the direction or permission of the supreme disposer.

Nothing therefore could be worse founded than the boasts of the Epicureans, who expected to be applauded as friends and benefactors to mankind, on the account of their endeavours to

deliver

deliver them from the apprehenfions of a providence. This might indeed be fome relief to very bad men, and tend to make them eafy in their fins; but it was an attempt to rob good men of that which is the chief fupport and comfort of their lives, and the moft powerful encouragement to the fteady uniform practice of piety and virtue. Lord Bolingbroke therefore was very ill employed, when he ufed his utmoft efforts to deftroy the doctrine of providence, as extending its care and infpection to individuals; fince without this, the acknowledgment of what he calls a general providence would be of no great advantage, and would be, with regard to all the purpofes of religion, little better than to deny that there is a providence at all.

This leads me to what I propofed to fhew in the next place, *viz.* the abfurdity and the ill confequences of the fcheme his Lordfhip hath advanced.

It is an abfurd and inconfiftent fcheme. He pretends to allow, that God's providence extends to nations and large communities, that it regards men collectively, but not individually. But it is hard to conceive how a proper care could be taken of collective bodies, if the individuals of which they were compofed were abfolutely neglected, and no regard had to them at all. A human government, that would have no regard to the cafes of particular perfons, to do them right or fecure them from wrong, could fcarce be accounted a government. Befides it may be afked what his Lordfhip means by collective bodies. There was a time when men had not yet formed themfelves into political focieties: muft it be faid that they were then not the objects of providence at all? Or, will it be allowed that providence extended its care to them whilft they were only in families? And how could families, either larger or fmaller, be taken care of, if the individuals, of which families confift, were neglected? And when feveral families united together, and formed larger communities, muft it be faid, that providence quitted its care of the families to which it had extended before, and confined its infpection to thofe larger communities? And then it might be enquired, how large muft a community be, in order to its being the proper object of divine providence? Does providence take notice of fingle cities, or fmaller republics, or only of thofe communities which are become fo numerous as to be united into large nations

or

or empires? It may be farther afked, in what fenfe is it to be underftood, that providence extends its care to collective bodies?
All that he underftands by it feems to be this: that "the courfe
"of things has been always the fame; that national virtue and na-
"tional vice have always produced national happinefs or mifery
"in a due proportion, and are by confequence the great fanctions
"of the law of nature*." The appointing this general conftitution then feems to be all the concern that he allows to divine providence with regard to large communities or collective bodies:
and the only fanctions he allows of the law of nature (as I fhall
have occafion more diftinctly to fhew, when I come to confider
the account he gives of that law) are the public happinefs or miferies of large focieties or nations; and thefe are often fome
ages in operating. It frequently happens, that nations and large
communities continue for a confiderable time in great outward
profperity, when there is little national virtue remaining. And
our author himfelf acknowledges, that the motives drawn from
the effects of virtue and vice on collective bodies, are "fuch as
"particular perfons will be apt to think do not concern them,
"becaufe they confider themfelves as individuals, and catch at
"pleafure rather than happinefs †." And as nations are made up
of families and fmaller focieties, if thefe be not well conftituted,
as they cannot be where there is no fenfe of religion, no fear of
God, or regard to a providence as extending to individuals, there
cannot be much national order or virtue.

Lord Bolingbroke would, in my opinion, have been more
confiftent with himfelf, if he had abfolutely denied that providence hath any regard to mankind at all, than to pretend that it
extends to collective bodies, but not to individuals: for the
fame arguments, which prove a providence as extending to mankind in general, do alfo, if rightly confidered, prove that it is
exercifed towards particular perfons, and extendeth to particular
cafes and circumftances. This writer fets himfelf, as hath been
already obferved, with great appearance of zeal, to vindicate the
goodnefs and juftice of divine providence in its difpenfations
towards mankind, in oppofition both to atheifts and divines.
But how the juftice and goodnefs of providence towards mankind

---

* Bolingbroke's Works, vol. v. p. 472.     † Ibid. vol. iv. p. 228.

can be vindicated, if no regard be had to individuals, it is hard to
fee.  He himfelf obferves, that " juftice requires that punifh-
" ments fhould be meafured out in various degrees and meafures,
" according to the various circumftances of particular cafes, and
" in proportion to them #."  And again he repeats it, " that
" juftice requires that rewards and punifhments fhould be mea-
" fured out in every particular cafe, in proportion to the merit
" and demerit of each individual †."  How then can he pretend
to vindicate the juftice of providence in this prefent ftate, when
he makes it effential to juftice that regard fhould be had to the
cafe of individuals, and yet affirms that providence doth not confider men individually at all, but only colleEtively?

And as his fcheme is abfurd and inconfiftent with itfelf, fo it
is attended with the moft pernicious confequences, which ought
to create a horror of it in every well-difpofed mind.  If providence hath no regard to individuals, there can be no fenfe of the
divine favour for good aEtions, no fear of the divine difpleafure
for evil ones; and, as will appear to be his Lordfhip's fentiment,
no future account to be apprehended.  Thus every man is left
to do what is right in his own eyes, without the dread of a fupreme Governor and Judge.  It is true, God hath eftablifhed
general laws at the beginning, but he concerneth himfelf no farther.  And our author will not allow that in thefe general laws,
or the plan originally formed in the divine mind, God had any
regard unto, or made any provifion for, particular perfons, actions, or events.  Good men therefore have no refource in their
calamities; no ground to apply to God for fupport under them;
no expeEtation of affiftance from him, or from any other being
aEting under his direEtion, as the minifters and inftruments of his
providence: they are deprived of the comforts arifing from a
confcioufnefs of his fpecial approbation and complacency, and
from the profpeEts of reward from him here or hereafter.  Thus
*hope* is excluded, which, as his Lordfhip obferves, " above all
" things foftens the evils of this life, and is that cordial drop
" which fweetens every bitter potion, even the laft ‡."  On
the other hand, wicked men have nothing to fear from God for
their evil aEtions.  He fays indeed, in a paffage cited above, that

* Bolingbroke's Works, vol. v. p. 494.     † Ibid. p. 495.     ‡ Ibid. p. 379.

" providence

" providence has provided means to punish individuals, by direct-
" ing men to form societies, and to establish laws, in the execu-
" tion of which civil magistrates are the vicegerents of provi-
" dence:" but I do not see with what propriety upon his scheme
civil magistrates can be said to be the vicegerents of providence;
for if providence doth not confider men individually at all, how
can magistrates, in punishing individuals, be regarded as the
vicegerents of providence? Or if providence constituted them
its vicegerents, and there were no fanctions at all proposed for
particular persons but those of the civil laws, it would follow,
that men may be as wicked as they will, and give as great a loose
as they please to their appetites and passions, provided they can
manage so as to escape punishment from human judicatories,
which a man may do, and yet be a very bad man. Human magistrates are often themselves corrupt. Solomon's observation is
certainly just: *I have seen the place of judgment, that wickedness
was there, and the place of righteousness, that iniquity was there,*
Eccl. iii. 16. Very unjust things are often done under colour
of forms of law. Or, suppose the laws good, and the magistrates
just and upright, no human laws can reward or punish inward
good or bad affections, intentions, and dispositions of the heart.
If therefore there were no regard to a supreme Governor or
Judge, to the divine approbation or displeasure, as extending to
individuals, or to a future account, there is great reason to think,
that mankind in general would be far more wicked and dissolute
than they are. It is his Lordship's observation, that, " amidst
" the contingencies of human affairs, the odds will always be on
" the side of appetite — which reason cannot quite subdue in the
" strongest minds, and by which she is perpetually subdued in
" the weakest \*.'" And accordingly the ablest politicians have
thought the aids of religion, which especially includes a regard
to providence as extending to individuals, absolutely necessary
for strengthening the bands of civil government.

I shall now consider the arguments Lord Bolingbroke hath
offered in support of his scheme, and the objections he hath advanced against the doctrine of a particular providence.

He frequently intimates, that the doctrine of a particular pro-

---

\* Bolingbroke's Works, vol. v. p. 479.

vidence is needlefs; " fince the ordinary courfe of things, pre-
" ferved and conducted by a general providence, is fufficient to
" confirm what the law of nature and reafon teaches us *." But
it appears from what hath been already obferved, that the doctrine of a general providence, as he underftands it, *i. e.* a providence that has no regard to individuals at all, to their actions, or
to the events that befal them, is far from being fufficient to the
purpofes of religion and virtue, or of human focieties: that it
neither furnifheth proper comfort and fupports for the encouragement of good men, nor is fufficient to ftrike terror into bad
men, and to be a reftraint to vice and wickednefs. It hath alfo
been fhewn, that the notion of a general providence, as excluding all regard to individuals, and to their actions and concern-
ments, cannot be fupported, nor made to confift with reafon or
with itfelf. And whereas it is reprefented as a degrading the
divine Majefty, to fuppofe him to concern himfelf about what
relates to fuch inconfiderable beings, as are the individuals of the
human race: this objection, though varnifhed over with a pretence of confulting God's honour, doth at the bottom argue
mean and unworthy notions of him. It is in effect a judging of
God by our own imperfections. Our views are narrow and
limited, and cannot take in many things at once, nor attend to
fmaller matters without neglecting things of greater confequence:
but it is otherwife with a Being of infinite perfection, who is
intimately prefent to every part of this vaft univerfe, and knoweth and taketh care of all things at once, with the fame eafe as if
he had only one fingle thing to attend to. He is capable of exercifing a moft wife providential care towards all his creatures in
a way fuited to their feveral natures, conditions, and circumftances: nor can the multiplicity of things occafion the leaft confufion or perplexity in his all-comprehending mind.

The arguments which he urgeth againft a particular providence, in the fifty-feventh of his Fragments and Effays, for feveral pages together †, proceed upon a continued mifreprefentation of the fenfe of thofe whom he has thought fit to oppofe.
He there chargeth the divines as maintaining, that God ought by
particular providences to interpofe in every fingle inftance, for

* Bolingbroke's Works, vol. v. p. 404.     † Ibid. p. 424, & feq.

giving an immediate reward to every good action, and for punifhing every evil one, even in this prefent ftate. He fuppofes
them alfo to hold, that fome men are neceffarily determined to
good actions by divine influences communicated to them, and
others for want of thofe influences unavoidably determined to
evil; and then he argues, that on fuch a fuppofition there would
be no room for free choice, nor confequently for virtue or vice,
merit or demerit, nor therefore juftice or injuftice *. He urgeth
further, that if good men were conftantly and remarkably diftinguifhed by a particular providence, it would be apt to produce
prefumption in them, to deftroy or prevent their benevolence,
and confequently their goodnefs; and to harden the wicked†:
and that even on that fuppofition, the providence of God could
not be vindicated in the opinion of mankind, or of divines themfelves, fince ftill it would not be agreed who were good men.
The Mahometans, Chriftians, and different fects of the latter,
would infift upon it, that goodnefs includes a belief of their diftinguifhing tenets, and an attachment to their feveral fyftems of
religion. " One would pafs for a good man at Rome, another
" at Geneva," &c. ‡. But he feems not to have confidered, that
upon the fuppofition he puts, there could be no place for this
objection: fince if every good man and good action was to be
immediately and remarkably diftinguifhed by a particular interpofition of divine providence, and every bad man and evil action
to be immediately punifhed, there would be no room left for men's
paffing different judgments concerning the goodnefs or badnefs
of perfons or actions; for on that fuppofition, there would be a
vifible determination of heaven in favour of every good man and
good action; fo that no man could doubt, upon feeing any perfon
thus remarkably favoured and diftinguifhed, that he was really
good, whatever denomination he might pafs under. But the
truth is, no divine ever advanced fuch an hypothefis as he here
argueth againft. By the doctrine of a particular providence,
they do not mean a conftant particular interpofition of divine
providence for rewarding every good man and virtuous action,
and punifhing every bad man and every wicked action, in an un-

* Bolingbroke's Works, vol. v. p. 425, 426.　† Ibid. p. 428, 429:
‡ Ibid. p. 431, 432. ·

mediate

mediate and visible manner here on earth: on the contrary, they universally maintain, that this present state is a state of trial and discipline; and that it would be no way agreeable to the nature of such a state to have all good men and good actions immediately and remarkably rewarded, and all wicked men immediately punished: that the temporary sufferings of good men, and the prosperity of the wicked, are permitted for very wise ends, and may be reasonably and consistently accounted for, on the supposition that this present life is a state of trial; though they could not well be accounted for, if this were designed to be a state of final retributions, or to be the only state of existence allotted us.

The greatest part of what he offers against a particular providence in the sixty-second of his Fragments and Essays, relates to *occasional* interpositions, which he pretends would be miracles if they were real. "Such," he says, "they would be strictly, "whether they were contrary to the established course of nature "or not; for the miracle consists in the extraordinary interposi-"tion, as much as in the nature of the thing brought to pass: "That the miracle would be as real in the one case as in the "other; and the reality might be made evident enough by the "occasion, by the circumstance, by the repetition of it on similar "occasions, and in similar circumstances; and, above all, by "this circumstance, that the assumed particular providence was "a direct answer to particular prayers and acts of devotion of-"fered up to procure it †." Here he takes upon him to give a new and arbitrary definition of a miracle. Though a thing hath nothing in it contrary to the established course of nature, yet it is to be regarded as a miracle, if there be supposed to be any special agency of the divine providence in it, suited to particular occasions and circumstances; and, above all, if it be supposed to come in answer to prayer. But if the occasional interpositions he refers to be perfectly agreeable to the general laws of nature and of providence, and be only special applications of general laws to particular occasions, I do not see how they can be properly said to be miraculous at all; or how their being supposed to come in answer to prayer can make them so.

But he urgeth farther, that "if providence were directed ac-

"cording

" cording to the particular defires, and even wants, of perfons
" equally well qualified and intitled to the divine favour, the
" whole order of nature, phyfical and moral, would be fubverted,
" the affairs of mankind would fall into the utmoft confufion—
" and if this fcheme were true, the world would be governed by
" miracles, till miracles loft their name*."

But all this proceeds upon a great miftake of the point in
queftion. None of the divines that hold a particular providence,
*i. e.* a providence which extendeth its care to particular perfons
or individuals of the human race, maintain or fuppofe, that God
muft interpofe to fatisfy all the different defires and prayers of
men, many of which, as he obferves, are repugnant to one another.
If the prayers be of the right kind, fuch as reafon and religion
prefcribe, they muft be always offered up with this condition or
limitation, which the Scripture exprefsly directs us to, *viz.* that
we muft defire the things we pray for, fo far and no farther than
they are agreeable to the divine will, and to what it feemeth fit
to God in his infinite wifdom to appoint. Suppofing therefore
a good man doth not obtain the particular bleffing he prays for,
he may reft fatisfied in this, that it is what the divine wifdom
doth not fee fit to grant; and he only defired it under that condition. Or if he receives that particular good thing he prayed
for, and regards it as an anfwer to his prayer, ftill there is nothing
miraculous in the cafe. There is nothing done in contravention
to the ufual courfe of things which the divine wifdom hath eftablifhed. It may juftly be fuppofed to be a law of the moral
world, that it is proper for us, in teftimony of our dependence
upon God, and in acknowledgment of his providence, to apply
to him by prayer for the bleffings we ftand in need of: and that
prayer fo qualified as God requireth, proceeding from an honeft
and upright heart, and from good affections and intentions, and
accompanied with the ufe of proper endeavours on our parts, is
among the means appointed by divine wifdom for obtaining the
moft valuable benefits, efpecially thofe of a fpiritual nature. And
the bleffings thus communicated may be juftly faid to be communicated, not in a miraculous way, but in a way that is perfectly agreeable to the general laws of providence, and the order

* Bolingbroke's Works, vol. v. p. 460.

which the divine wisdom hath appointed. Any one that considers this will easily see how little what our author has here offered is to the purpose; and yet he goes on to declaim after his manner, that particular providence puts a force on the mechanical laws of nature, and on the freedom of the will, in a multitude of instances; and that those who maintain this doctrine suppose, that the laws of gravitation must be sometimes suspended, sometimes precipitated, in compliance with men's desires, and the tottering edifice must be kept miraculously from falling[*].

Among the extraordinary interpositions of divine providence, he reckons " the metaphysical or physical influence of spirits, " suggestions, silent communications, injections of ideas. These " things," he declares, " he cannot comprehend; and he com- " pares them to the altering or suspending the course of the sun, " or revolutions of the earth, in the physical system. And that " all such interpositions in the intellectual system, as should give " thoughts and new dispositions to the minds of men, cannot be " conceived without altering in every such instance the natural " progression of the human understanding, and that freedom of " the will which every man is conscious that he has[†]." Our author has here let us know what he thinks of all revelations, inspirations, or communications from God the Supreme Spirit, or from subordinate created spirits, to the human mind; that he regards them as inconsistent with the *laws of the intellectual system,* and the *natural progression of the human understanding,* or essential *freedom of the will.* But whence could he know enough of the laws of the intellectual system, to be able to pronounce that this is inconsistent with those laws? That one man may suggest or communicate thoughts and ideas to another by words and language, and that there is nothing in this contrary to the nature and order of the understanding, or freedom of the will, is universally acknowledged: and why then should it be thought inconsistent with these, for God himself, or spiritual beings superior to man, to communicate thoughts or ideas to the human mind? The most natural way of working upon men as reasonable creatures, and of influencing their actions in a way agreeable to the just order of their faculties, is by suggesting proper

* Bolingbroke's Works, vol. v. p. 460.　　† Ibid. p. 414, 415.

thoughts

thoughts or ideas to their minds, and our not being able particularly to explain how this is done, is no juft objection againft it. This writer himfelf elfewhere, fpeaking of *that extraordinary action of God upon the mind which the word Infpiration is now ufed to denote,* exprefsly acknowledges, that " it is no more in-" comprehenfible than the ordinary action of mind on body, or " body on mind\*." And indeed it cannot without the higheft abfurdity be denied, that God can work upon the fpirits of men by an immediate influence, and yet in fuch a way as is perfectly agreeable to their rational natures, and which may not put any conftraint upon the freedom of their wills. And many cafes may be fuppofed, in which his doing fo may anfwer valuable ends. It may alfo be eafily conceived, that he can make impreffions upon men's minds by various other means, which he may make ufe of in his wife and fovereign providence to this purpofe, without at all infringing the order of things in the natural or moral world.

He farther argues, that to fuppofe a providence extending to individuals, and particular occafional interpofitions, " is to fup-" pofe that there are as many providences as there are men :" or, as he elfewhere expreffeth it, that " common providence " would break into a multitude of particular providences for " the fupply of wants, and grant of petitions †." But there is no real foundation for this pretence. There is one univerfal providence, which may be confidered as extending to particular perfons and cafes, all of which are perfectly known to God, and (as was before hinted) occafion no confufion or diftraction in his infinite mind. Our author indeed declares, that " they " who have attempted to fhew that God may act by particular " and occafional interpofitions, confiftently with the preferva-" tion of the general order, appear to him quite unintelligible ‡." If it were fo, our not being able diftinctly to fhew how particular occafional interpofitions may confift with the doctrine of a general providence, would be no argument at all againft it : fince, as he himfelf obferves upon another occafion, " It is impertinent " to deny the exiftence of any phænomenon, merely becaufe we

---

\* Bolingbroke's Works, vol. iii. p. 468.     † Ibid. p. 420.
‡ Ibid. p. 414.

" cannot account for it \*." And yet we may eafily conceive in general, that they are perfectly reconcileable, fince, as hath been already hinted, thefe occafional interpofitions are ufually no more than the applications of the general laws of providence to particular cafes and circumftances. That there may be, or that there have been, fuch interpofitions, he does not pretend abfolutely to deny : but, he fays, that " we have no foundation for them in " our own experience, or in any hiftory except that of the bible †." And yet foon after obferves, that " every religion boafts of many " inftances, wherein the divine providence has been thus ex- " ercifed ‡." And certain it is, that this hath been the general fentiment of mankind. Befides the ordinary courfe of things, which is to be regarded as under the conftant care and direction of a fovereign providence, there have been events of a remarkable and uncommon nature, though not properly miraculous, of which there are accounts in the moft authentic hiftories, and in which men have been apt to acknowledge a fpecial interpofition of divine providence. The moft important events have been brought about by the feemingly fmalleft and moft unlikely means. Things have been often ftrangely conducted through many intricate turns to produce events contrary to all human expectation. Actions have been over-ruled to effects and iffues quite oppofite to the intentions of the actors. The moft artful fchemes of human policy have been ftrangely baffled and difappointed. Surprifing changes have been wrought upon the fpirits of men, and reftraints laid upon their paffions, in a manner that can fcarce be accounted for, and upon which great events have depended. Such things have naturally led mankind to acknowledge a divine hand, and a providence, over-ruling human affairs. I am fenfible many of thofe who honour themfelves with the title of free-thinkers will be apt to afcribe this to fuperftition or enthufiafm. But what right have they to pronounce againft the general fentiments of mankind, and which feem to have arifen from the obfervation of events which argue the over-ruling interpofition of a fuperior invifible agency ?

He obferves with a fneer, that " there is many an old woman

---

\* Bolingbroke's Works, vol. iii. p. 468.        † Ibid. vol. v. p. 414.
‡ Ibid. p. 413.

" who

" who is ready to relate, with much fpiritual pride, the particular
" providences that attended her and hers *." As to the charge
of fpiritual pride, it is no more than he hath advanced againft all
that believe a particular providence, interefting itfelf in the affairs of men; the belief of which he imputeth to *high notions of
human importance.* That he himfelf had high notions of his
own fagacity cannot be doubted; but the fentiments he is pleafed
to afcribe to the old woman, feem to me to be more reafonable,
and would, if generally entertained, have a much better influence
on mankind than his own. Is it not much better, and more
agreeable to reafon and nature, for dependent creatures to regard
the benefits they receive, and the good events which befall them,
as owing to the interpofition of a moft wife and benign providence, and to acknowledge with thankfulnefs the condefcending
care and goodnefs of God, in fuch inftances; than to pafs them
over with a regardlefs eye, from an apprehenfion that God doth
not concern himfelf with the affairs of men; that he is utterly
unmindful of individuals, and taketh no notice of their aftions, or
of the events that relate to them? And this is the goodly fcheme
which this author hath taken fo much pains to eftablifh.

But he urgeth, that it is of no ufe to acknowledge particular
interpofitions of divine providence, fince they cannot be diftinguifhed from events that happen in the courfe of God's general
providence. " The effects," faith he, " that are affumed of par-
" ticular providences, are either falfe, or undiftinguifhable from
" thofe of a general providence, and become particular by no-
" thing more than the application which vain fuperftition or
" pious fraud makes of them †." And he obferves, that this
holds with refpeft to the cafe not only of particular perfons, but
of collective bodies. " Their circumftances are fo nearly alike,
" and they return fo often to be equally objects of thefe fuppofed
" providences, that no man will dare to determine where thefe
" providences have been, or fhould have been employed, and
" where not ‡." It appears then, that though he fometimes
feems to acknowledge the care of divine providence as extending to collective bodies, though not to individuals, yet in reality

---

* Bolingbroke's Works, vol. v. p. 418.　† Ib. p. 420. See alfo p. 450.
‡ Ibid. p. 460.

　　he

he does not admit that providence interpofes with regard to the
one more than the other; or that in either cafe we can juftly
afcribe any of the events that befall men, whether individually
or collectively confidered, to divine providence; fince we cannot difcern or diftinguifh in what events providence has been
employed, and in what not. But the truth is, we need not be
put to the difficulty of thus diftinguifhing, if we believe that providence is really concerned in them all. It over-ruleth both the
affairs and events relating to nations and to particular perfons,
difpofing and governing them in the fitteft matter, according to
what feemeth moft fit to his infinite wifdom, to which all circumftances are perfectly known. And even where the events
feem contrary, profperous to one nation or particular perfon,
adverfe to another, providence is to be regarded in both. For we
can never err in judging that all events whatfoever are under
the wife direction and fuperintendency of a fovereign providence,
though, when we undertake to affign the particular reafons of
God's providential difpenfations, we may eafily be miftaken.

Our author farther objecteth againft the doctrine of a particular providence, that it fuppofes all mankind to be under an univerfal theocracy like the Jewifh; and he obferves, that even in
that cafe it would not have the effect to engage men to virtue,
or deter them from vice and wickednefs, any more than it did
the Jews *. But he here confoundeth things that are of diftinct
confideration. The heathens, and all mankind in all ages, have
been under the care and fuperintendency of divine providence,
and even of a particular providence, in the fenfe in which we
are now confidering it; *i. e.* a providence, which extendeth to
the individuals of the human race, infpecting their actions, and
difpofing and governing the events relating to them. But they
were not under the Jewifh theocracy, which was a peculiar conftitution, eftablifhed for very wife purpofes, the reafons and ends
of which I fhall afterwards have occafion more particularly to
confider. At prefent I fhall only obferve, that though under
that conftitution we may juftly fuppofe there were extraordinary
interpofitions in a way of mercy and judgment, both national,
and relating to particular perfons, more frequently than there

* Bolingbroke's Works, vol. v. p. 430.

would

would have been under another conflitution; yet the defign of
it was not, as our author fuppofes, that providence fhould interpofe for giving a prefent immediate reward to every good man,
and every good action, and for immediately punifhing every bad
one.   We find frequent pathetical complaints even under that
difpenfation, of the calamities and fufferings of good men, and
the profperity of the wicked.   This gave occafion to the 37th
and 73d Pfalms.   See alfo Plafm xvii. 14. Jer. xii. 1, 2.   The
proper ultimate reward of good men, and punifhment of the
wicked, was ftill referved for a future ftate of retributions, which,
though not exprefsly mentioned in their law, was believed and
expected; as appeareth from what Solomon hath faid concerning it, Ecclef. iii. 16, 17. xii. 14.

I fhall conclude this letter with taking notice of an obfervation
of our author, which is defigned to take off the force of an argument that Mr. Wollafton had offered.   " It will be of little fer-
" vice," faith he, " to the fcheme of particular providences, to
" fay, like Wollafton, that there may be incorporeal, or at leaft
" invifible beings, of intellect and powers fuperior to man, and
" capable of mighty things: and that thefe beings may be the
" minifters of God, and the authors of thofe providences."   He
pretends, that there is no proof that there are fuch beings; and
ridicules the doctrine of Genii or Dæmons, as having been
" owing to ancient aftrologers, and the knaves or madmen that
" profeffed theurgic magic."   And he argues, that " if thefe
" angels act by the immediate command of God, it is in oppofi-
" tion to his general providence, and to fupply the defects of
" it; and that it is to give up the government over mankind to
" thofe beings*."   But it is with an ill grace that this writer
feems here to queftion the exiftence of angels, when yet he frequently intimates, that there are many orders of beings much
fuperior to man, and that man is of the loweft order of intellectual beings.   He reprefents it as a thing highly probable, that
" there is a gradation from man, through various forms of fenfe,
" intelligence, and reafon, up to beings unknown to us, whofe
" rank in the intellectual world is even above our conception †."
And that " there may be as much difference between fome other

* Bolingbroke's Works, vol. v. p. 463, 464.   † Ibid. p. 329, 350:

" creatures

" creatures of God and man, as there is between man and an
" oyſter\*." And if it be allowed, that there are created intelli-
gences much ſuperior to man, where is the abſurdity of ſuppoſing
that they are employed by divine wiſdom as the inſtruments and
agents of providence in its adminiſtrations towards the human
race? Higher orders of creatures may, in the original plan of
providence, be deſigned to aſſiſt, and exerciſe ſome ſuperintendency over the lower. It may reaſonably be conceived, that
this may contribute to promote the beauty and order of the univerſe, and to connect the different orders of beings, and to carry
on a proper intercourſe between them. It is certain, that the
exiſtence, and the interpoſition of ſuch beings on ſpecial occaſions, have been generally believed by mankind in all ages.
And it is clearly determined in the revelation contained in the
holy Scripture: ſo that it may be now aſſumed not merely as a
reaſonable hypotheſis, but as a truth that can be depended upon.
Nor does the making uſe of angels as agents or inſtruments in
the adminiſtrations of providence argue any *defect* of providence,
as he is pleaſed to inſinuate, which ſtill overſees and directs the
whole. For when God makes uſe of inſtruments in the courſe
of his providence, it is not becauſe, like human governors, he
is unable to do it immediately by himſelf, and cannot be per-
ſonally preſent: for he is ſtill preſent to every part of the creation; and all things are under his direction and ſuperintendency.
But he is pleaſed to make uſe of ſome of his creatures as inſtruments in conferring benefits, or inflicting chaſtiſements upon
others, for the better carrying on the order and œconomy of his
kingdom, and for many wiſe ends which we cannot pretend at
preſent diſtinctly to aſſign.

In my next I ſhall conſider what Lord Bolingbroke hath offered concerning the immortality of the ſoul, and a future ſtate
of retributions, which will let us farther into the true intention
of his ſcheme.      I am, &c.

---

\* Bolingbroke's Works, vol. iv. p. 177.

www.ingramcontent.com/pod-product-compliance
Lightning Source LLC
Chambersburg PA
CBHW052330110726
47901CB00005B/1186